THE BRIDES OF SKYE

THE COMPLETE SERIES

JAYNE CASTEL

JAYNE CASTEL

All characters and situations in this publication are fictitious, and any resemblance to living persons is purely coincidental.

The Brides of Skye: The Complete Series, by Jayne Castel

Copyright © 2019 by Jayne Castel. All rights reserved. No part of this publication may be reproduced, stored in a retrieval system, or transmitted in any form or by any means—electronic, mechanical, recording, or otherwise—without the prior written permission of the author.

Published by Winter Mist Press

Edited by Tim Burton

Cover photography courtesy of www.shutterstock.com
Scotch thistle vector image courtesy of Wikipedia Commons.
Map of Isle of Skye by Jayne Castel

The Beast's Bride
Excerpt from the poem, 'Ae Fond Kiss' by Robert Burns.

The Rogue's Bride
The Wild Mountain Thyme poem, courtesy of
www.rampantscotland.com/songs/blsongs_thyme.htm

Visit Jayne's website: www.jaynecastel.com

Historical Romances by Jayne Castel

DARK AGES BRITAIN

The Kingdom of the East Angles series
Dark Under the Cover of Night (Book One)
Nightfall till Daybreak (Book Two)
The Deepening Night (Book Three)
The Kingdom of the East Angles: The Complete Series

The Kingdom of Mercia series
The Breaking Dawn (Book One)
Darkest before Dawn (Book Two)
Dawn of Wolves (Book Three)
The Kingdom of Mercia: The Complete Series

The Kingdom of Northumbria series
The Whispering Wind (Book One)
Wind Song (Book Two)
Lord of the North Wind (Book Three)
The Kingdom of Northumbria: The Complete Series

DARK AGES SCOTLAND

The Warrior Brothers of Skye series
Blood Feud (Book One)
Barbarian Slave (Book Two)
Battle Eagle (Book Three)
The Warrior Brothers of Skye: The Complete Series

The Pict Wars series
Warrior's Heart (Book One)
Warrior's Secret (Book Two)
Warrior's Wrath (Book Three)
The Pict Wars: The Complete Series

Novellas
Winter's Promise

MEDIEVAL SCOTLAND

The Brides of Skye series
The Beast's Bride (Book One)
The Outlaw's Bride (Book Two)
The Rogue's Bride (Book Three)

The Brides of Skye: The Complete Series

The Sisters of Kilbride series
Unforgotten (Book One)
Awoken (Book Two)
Fallen (Book Three)
Claimed (Epilogue novella)

The Immortal Highland Centurions series
Maximus (Book One)
Cassian (Book Two)
Draco (Book Three)
The Laird's Return (Epilogue festive novella)

Stolen Highland Hearts series
Highlander Deceived (Book One)
Highlander Entangled (Book Two)
Highlander Forbidden (Book Three)
Highlander Pledged (Book Four)

Guardians of Alba series
Nessa's Seduction (Book One)
Fyfa's Sacrifice (Book Two)
Breanna's Surrender (Book Three)

Epic Fantasy Romances by Jayne Castel

Light and Darkness series
Ruled by Shadows (Book One)
The Lost Swallow (Book Two)
Path of the Dark (Book Three)
Light and Darkness: The Complete Series

THE BRIDES OF SKYE: THE COMPLETE SERIES

***

For Tim, who has gotten very fond of these journeys to Scotland!

***

Contents

THE BEAST'S BRIDE 9

THE OUTLAW'S BRIDE 203

THE ROGUE'S BRIDE 377

ABOUT THE AUTHOR 561

THE BEAST'S BRIDE

BOOK ONE
THE BRIDES OF SKYE

JAYNE CASTEL

JAYNE CASTEL

The beauty who refuses to be wed. The beast who loves her in vain. A twist of fate that brings them together.

Rhona MacLeod is the beautiful, willful daughter of a clan-chief on the Isle of Skye. Desperate to remain free and bow to no man, she refuses all the suitors who ask for her hand.

Taran MacKinnon is one of Clan-chief MacLeod's most trusted warriors. He carries a secret passion for his chief's middle daughter. However, Rhona has never been able to see beyond his scars and forbidding appearance that have earned him the name 'The Beast of Dunvegan'.

Frustrated by Rhona's defiance, her father makes a decision that will force his daughter to take a husband—games that will bring warriors from all over the island, and from the mainland, to compete. Rhona must wed the victor. Finally, Taran has a chance to prove himself. If he wins the games, he can have the woman he wants—but can he win her heart?

Map

"Beauty is not in the face; beauty is a light in the heart."
Kahlil Gibran

Chapter One

The Beauty and the Beast

Dunvegan Castle, Isle of Skye, Scotland

Early summer, 1346 AD

"YE WILL NOT wed me then?"

"I'm glad to see yer ears aren't full of porridge, Dughall MacLean. Aye, ye heard me right."

The young man—broad and muscular with a shock of peat-brown hair—glared at Lady Rhona MacLeod. Dughall folded his thick arms across his chest, staring her down.

Rhona lifted her chin and held his gaze steadily.

"So ye think ye are too good for the likes of me?" A storm gathered in his eyes as he spoke.

Despite her brave front, nervousness fluttered up from the pit of Rhona's belly. They stood alone in the gardens that lay south of the castle's curtain wall. Rhona was unarmed, and her father's men waited some distance away at the entrance to the gardens. She didn't have her sisters at her side either; their presence always made her bolder.

At her back, Rhona could feel the weight of Dunvegan Castle silently watching over them. The dove-grey fortress rose sheer from perpendicular edges of rock to the north, its massive battlements stark against the windswept sky.

In contrast to the barren moorland and craggy peaks that surrounded it, the garden was a small, sheltered spot. It was a softer world, although Rhona now regretted agreeing to take a walk with Dughall there. It was too private; a canopy of green and beds of herbs and flowers surrounded the pair.

Rhona forced herself not to shrink back from her angry suitor. Instead, she watched him, waiting for his temper to cool.

Dughall took a threatening step toward her, closing the distance between them. "A rare, fiery beauty, ye are, Rhona," he growled, "but I would tame ye."

Annoyance flared within Rhona at his presumption, making her forget her fear. "And that's why we wouldn't be suited," she countered, her tone sharpening. "Ye should find yerself a biddable wife."

He moved closer still. "Ye'd be biddable." He lowered his voice. "Once I were through with ye."

Rhona clenched her jaw. "Don't threaten me."

His face twisted—Dughall's pleasantly handsome features turning ugly in an instant. Rhona shifted back from him, but he grasped her arm. "Ye need to learn yer place. Ye are a spoilt, haughty bitch, but I still want ye. And one day ... I'll have ye."

Heart thumping, Rhona attempted to wrench her arm free. However, he held her in an iron grip. "Unhand me," she snarled, fear turning her savage.

He grinned, his dark blue eyes narrowing. "Or what?"

Rhona hissed out a breath. "Let me go."

"Beg ... and I might."

"What are ye doing, Dughall?"

A man's voice—low and powerful—interrupted them. Rhona twisted her head to see a huge warrior, with a fur mantle about his broad shoulders, striding toward them.

Relief flooded through Rhona at the sight of Taran MacKinnon. Yet even so, the warrior's formidable appearance struck her. He was a terrifying sight. Taran wore a heavy mail shirt under his mantle. His dark-blond hair was cropped short, a severe style that did nothing to soften his presence, and a rough stubble covered his strong jaw. He wore a grim expression, yet it was not that which drew Rhona's eye but the scars marring his face.

They were impossible to ignore.

One cut vertically from his forehead, missing his eye and scoring his right cheek. The other slashed sideways across his left cheek. The scars were disfiguring, and despite that Taran had served her father for a few years now, Rhona found it difficult not to stare. The cold look in his ice-blue eyes, the hard set of his mouth, warned that he was not a man to be messed with.

Her father kept this warrior at his side for a reason.

Dughall snorted, his gaze tracking Taran's arrival. But his grip on Rhona's arm released, and he moved away from her.

"The Beast of Dunvegan nears," he sneered. "Yer father's faithful hound."

"Aye." Rhona stepped back, instinctively moving toward Taran. His presence made her feel braver. "And he has a vicious bite, as ye well know."

"Lady Rhona." Taran stopped next to her, his grey-blue gaze searching for any sign of injury. "Are ye hurt?"

Rhona shook her head. "I was just explaining to Dughall that I would rather wed a stinking goat than him. He didn't take the news well."

"Bitch!" Dughall advanced, his hands fisting.

In an instant Taran had drawn the heavy sword that hung at his hip and stepped before Rhona, shielding her with his body.

"Be wise, Dughall," he warned softly, "Leave now, before I spill yer blood."

A tense silence fell. Dughall's face screwed up, and he spat on the ground at Taran's feet. "The Devil take ye both."

The man stalked from the garden, between rows of rosemary and lavender. Only when he disappeared from sight did Rhona loose the breath she'd been holding.

To her annoyance, she found that her pulse was racing. As much as it galled her to admit it, Dughall had scared her.

Feeling the weight of Taran's gaze, she inclined her head. "What?"

"Have a care, Lady Rhona," he replied, resheathing his sword. "Some men don't take kindly to being spurned."

Rhona frowned. "I don't need ye to preach to me, Taran." She huffed out a breath. "Although I'm glad ye arrived when ye did."

"I heard raised voices. I sensed trouble brewing."

Rhona sighed and pushed a heavy lock of auburn hair from her face. Now that the tension had released, her legs felt oddly weak. The sensation annoyed her. She was the daughter of a warrior. She'd been taught to fight, and yet when Dughall had seized her arm, she'd been unable to free herself. That angered her. She didn't think of herself as feeble like other women, and yet she'd been helpless.

"I'm out of practice," she muttered. "Why did we stop our fighting lessons?"

"Ye stopped them." Did she imagine it, or was there a trace of mirth in his voice? "Ye said ye were too occupied by other matters."

"Well, I'm not anymore," she replied, meeting his gaze squarely. "We shall resume them tomorrow at noon."

"Aye—as ye wish."

"Good." Rhona gathered her skirts and moved past him before flashing Taran a smile. "Next time I spurn a man, I want to be ready to geld him if he touches me."

Taran MacKinnon watched the second daughter of Malcolm MacLeod walk away from him, heading out of the garden and back toward the castle.

Now that her gaze was averted, his own devoured her.

She wore a kirtle of green plaid with a straw-colored leine underneath. The garment was fitted, highlighting her statuesque form and lush curves, and the dip of her waist. She walked with a determined stride, her long, curling dark-red hair tumbling down her back.

Taran's breathing hitched as he watched her—the fire-haired woman he'd wanted for a while now.

Only, she didn't return the sentiment. To Rhona, he was merely her father's warrior. *Scar-face*—The Beast of Dunvegan.

The name Dughall had thrown at him didn't bother Taran, he'd heard it enough times over the years for the insult to lose its sting. But he didn't want Rhona to look at him that way.

A bee buzzed by, on its lazy path to the bed of roses behind him. Taran inhaled the sweet scent of the flowers and closed his eyes for a moment.

Being near Rhona MacLeod was agony. She'd ensnared him, dug her thorns deep into his flesh. Standing close to her for a few moments had been both pleasure and pain.

He heaved in a deep breath, opened his eyes, and followed Rhona out of the garden. Sparring with her tomorrow would be sweet torture.

He could hardly wait.

Chapter Two

A Man's World

"YE WILL HAVE to choose a husband sooner or later, lass. Don't make me choose one for ye."

Malcolm, clan-chief of the MacLeods, glared at his daughter before spearing a leg of roast fowl with a knife. Next to him, his wife, Una, cast her husband a reproachful look. She'd been trying to get him to eat less of late. He was a big, bearded man with a wild mane of greying auburn hair. At fifty winters the clan-chief's girth was increasing with each year; over the past few months, gout had pained him terribly.

"Aye, Da," Rhona replied, favoring him with a contrite smile, "but let it not be Dughall MacLean. The man's a brute."

She was merely trying to appease him. Rhona had no intention of wedding anyone. She'd seen nothing of marriage in her twenty winters to make her want to shackle herself to a man. Her mother had died many years earlier, yet Rhona remembered how oppressed she'd been, how Malcolm MacLeod's word was law in all things. Her father treated his second wife no differently, although Una didn't seem as cowed as her mother had been.

Beside Rhona her elder sister, Caitrin, shifted uncomfortably on the wooden bench, a hand straying to her swollen belly. Next to Caitrin, the youngest of the three sisters, Adaira, bowed her head. Her silky brown hair fell across one cheek, her mouth twitching as she fought a smile.

"Most men are brutes," Caitrin murmured, censure in her sea-blue eyes. "I wish ye well finding one that isn't."

Rhona's gaze narrowed. "Those are fine words coming from a wedded woman with a bairn on the way."

Caitrin's gaze held hers a moment before dropping to the trencher of pottage before her. Rhona continued to watch Caitrin, her own frown deepening. Her sister would never have said such a thing if her husband, Baltair, had been present.

Fortunately for them all, he was away hunting, and Caitrin—who was heavy with bairn—had come to live in Dunvegan until after the birth. Once the child was born, she would return home to the MacDonald's broch, Duntulm, which lay upon the northern coast of the isle.

Caitrin's situation was just another reason why Rhona had no intention of choosing a husband.

Her sister had changed since wedding Baltair MacDonald two years earlier. It was as if a light had gone out within her; she seemed so distant these days.

"What kind of man would sway ye then, sister?" Adaira asked, observing Rhona over the rim of a cup of wine, her hazel eyes mischievous. "Must he be handsome, strong, or kind?"

At the head of the table, their father snorted. "Spare me the witless chatter of women."

This comment drew a snort of laughter from his son, Iain. Like his daughters, Iain was born of his first wife, who had died when Rhona was eight. He'd just reached his sixteenth summer and had recently developed a sneering attitude toward his elder sisters.

Rhona cast her brother and father a withering look before her attention shifted to her stepmother. Una was a beauty with clear skin, sharp blue eyes, and raven hair. She'd once been the wife of the chieftain of the Frasers of Skye. Ever since she'd left her first husband for Malcolm MacLeod, there had been a rift between the two clans. Una was now favoring her husband with a simpering smile, as if he had not just insulted her sex.

Rhona gritted her teeth. She hated that it was a man's world, and that women like Una would play down their own cleverness to flatter their husbands' egos.

I'll not wed.

Picking up her cup of sloe wine, Rhona took a sip. They sat at a long table in the Great Hall. The chieftain's table took pride of place at one end, next to a hearth set into the wall. Even now, in summer, a log burned—for inside the thick walls of Dunvegan Keep the air was always cool and damp.

Above them rose a ceiling of wooden rafters, like the ribcage of a great beast, blackened with smoke. This was the grandest space in the keep, but this evening Rhona felt constrained by it.

Caitrin with her sad eyes, and Adaira with her headful of girlish fancies.
Una with her smug smile.
Iain with his smirk.
Rhona's father with his insistence that his daughters be bred like sows.
I should have been born a man.

Rhona's gaze shifted across the hall then, gliding over the tables where kin and her father's warriors ate their supper. The rumble of voices was like the sound of the surf on a shingle shore. Her gaze alighted on Taran, seated at the far end of one of the tables. Even at meal times, he was still clad in his mail shirt—ready to serve her father at a moment's notice.

He might have been scarred and ugly, but she envied him.

No one insisted *he* wed or bore sons. Taran MacKinnon was free to live as he pleased.

"Show me how to free myself from a man's grip."

"What, like Dughall had ye in yesterday?"

"Aye—I need to know how to break a hold."

Taran raised an eyebrow. "I thought ye wanted to practice at swordplay?"

Rhona shook her head, favoring him with a slow smile. "Not today. We've done that for years. I want to be able to fight without a sword or a dagger in my hand."

The pair of them stood in the training yard—a small area wedged in between the stables and the armory. Stained and pitted grey walls reared up around them, and a blue sky full of racing clouds stretched overhead. There was no one else about, Rhona had made sure of it, choosing the time when most folk would be eating their noon meal.

Like Taran, Rhona was dressed in a mail shirt today over a léine—a loose tunic that reached the knee. She had swapped her kirtle for a pair of braies and long boots, while her long hair was pulled back in a thick braid.

Taran found the sight distracting.

"Aye ... very well," he replied after a pause. Truthfully, he wasn't that keen to give her such a lesson. MacLeod wouldn't be pleased to learn that his daughter was being taught to brawl.

On the other hand, he rarely had the opportunity to be in such proximity to Rhona, or to touch her.

He approached the young woman, stopping before her so that they stood only two feet apart. "Grab me then ... like Dughall did with ye."

Rhona nodded, her lovely features tensing with concentration. She had a proud face, with high cheekbones and a slight cleft in her chin. However, it was her storm-grey eyes that caught his attention: large and limpid with long lashes.

Rhona reached out with her right hand, her fingers fastening around his left forearm. Taran inwardly cursed the leather bracer that prevented their skin from coming into contact.

"He held me like this," she explained, "and then he yanked me against him." Taran felt a tug at his arm, but he did not budge.

She frowned, huffing out a breath. "Clearly, I'm not as strong as him."

Taran smiled. "Strength will only get ye so far—agility and flexibility are just as important."

He watched her frown ease. "Really?"

"Aye ... yer mistake yesterday was to give him time. The first rule is to act quickly."

Her mouth curved, an expression that made him grow still. "So, what should I have done?"

He raised a foot, nudging her in the shin with his toe. "Kick first." He then raised the hand she held, turning the palm toward him. "Then do this ... as if ye are trying to read yer palm. See how it makes yer wrist twist and exposes the underside of yer hand?"

Rhona nodded, her gaze shifting to where she still gripped his forearm.

"Now reach under and around the arm that's caught and catch yer attacker's hand ... like this."

His fingers hooked over the heel of her hand, and the warmth and smoothness of her skin made his breathing catch. Forcing himself to concentrate, Taran stepped back from her, rotating his body in an arc while twisting her wrist.

Rhona lurched sideways, stumbling as she nearly lost her footing.

He favored her with a tight smile, trying to ignore the feel of her hand in his. "There ... easy."

Rhona gave an unladylike snort before righting herself and releasing him. "For ye, maybe ... ye are three times my size."

"I told ye before—size makes no matter. If ye move fast and loose like that, ye can bring any man down."

Her eyes lit up, her full lips stretching into a wicked smile. "Can *I* try?"

Taran nodded. "Ready?"

"Aye ... grab me."

Her words, said with earnest ignorance, made his pulse quicken. How often had he dreamed of doing just that?

Taran stepped forward, catching hold of her arm and holding tight. He thought he might have to remind Rhona of the moves—yet before he knew it, she kicked him hard in the shin. She then twisted, raised her palm, and took hold of the meat of the hand that held her. An instant later she pivoted like a dancer.

Taran, caught off guard by her swiftness, pitched forward and fell to his knees.

Male laughter rang out across the training yard, and Taran glanced up to see his friend Gordon leaning up against the armory door, observing them. The warrior's swarthy face was creased in amusement, his dark eyes twinkling.

"I never thought I'd see the day Taran MacKinnon would be brought to his knees by a maid."

Rhona glanced up and grinned. "Did ye see that, Gordon?"

"Aye ... impressive, Lady Rhona."

Taran rose to his feet. "Just teaching Lady Rhona some tricks, should any of her suitors take liberties."

The mirth left Gordon's face. "A fine idea, although I'd not let MacLeod know about this."

Or of the many sword-fighting lessons I've given her over the years, Taran thought grimly. MacLeod would skin him alive if he ever found out. It would have been worth it though, for Taran had cherished every moment he'd spent with Rhona.

"Don't worry," Rhona replied with an airy wave. "I never tell him … and I hope the pair of ye won't either."

She turned to Taran then, those luminous eyes fixing upon him in a way that made his chest constrict.

Lord, how he wanted her. And yet he knew it was hopeless. She would never see him differently.

"Teach me more," she said, her mouth curving. "I want to learn it all."

Chapter Three

Too Far

"HOLD STILL, LADY Rhona ... I've nearly finished."

Rhona loosed an irritated breath, waiting while her hand-maid completed the final touches to her hair. She hated sitting still, especially when she felt agitated.

"There, milady." Liosa stepped back, admiring the cascade of curls and braids she'd painstakingly created. "All done."

The hand-maid, whom she and Adaira shared, looked so pleased with herself that Rhona forced herself to smile. "Thank ye, Liosa," she murmured. "That will be all ... Adaira can help me with everything else."

"Aye, milady." Liosa bounced in a curtsey, still smiling, and bustled off.

Rhona waited until the hand-maid had left the chamber, the heavy door thudding shut, before she sighed and glanced down at the silver-grey kirtle she'd chosen for today. She'd hoped the color would appear drab on her. But from the dreamy way Adaira was gazing at her, she guessed the gown had the opposite effect.

The sisters stood in the small bower they shared: a square stone room with a hearth at one end and a tiny window that looked north over the sparkling waters of Loch Dunvegan. They'd once shared this bower with Caitrin too before she'd wed—the three of them tucked up together in the large bed, keeping each other awake at night with stories and teasing.

"Ye look breathtaking," Adaira breathed. Her sister's heart-shaped face was solemn. "I wish I was tall like ye. It must feel liberating to be able to meet a man's eye."

Rhona huffed. "Aye, although not all of them like it."

"What do ye mean?"

"Most men like to be able to look down upon a woman ... makes them feel powerful."

Adaira's brow furrowed. "I'm sure they aren't all the beasts ye make them out to be."

Rhona favored Adaira with an arch look. "And ye'd have the experience to know?"

Adaira lifted her chin, flicking her walnut-colored hair off her face. "I'll have suitors of my own soon enough."

"And for yer sake, I hope they're young and bonny … not like the man who's been invited to eat with us today." It was impossible for Rhona to keep the sourness out of her voice. As if to punish his daughter for her stubbornness, Clan-chief MacLeod had invited the recently widowed Aonghus Budge from Islay, an isle that lay to the south of their own. Over twenty-five years her senior, Chieftain Budge was the last man in the world she wished to wed.

A gentle knock sounded on their door, and a moment later it opened to reveal Caitrin.

Their elder sister's face was pale, and she had dark circles under her eyes. Her belly—huge now—thrust out before her. She wore a loose, tent-like kirtle that accentuated just how big her stomach had grown over the last few weeks. Rhona was no midwife, yet she guessed her sister's time was near.

"Are ye ready?" Caitrin asked with a wan smile. "Da awaits."

Rhona's nostrils flared. No, she wasn't ready—and she never would be. Yet Caitrin didn't deserve the sharp edge of her tongue. Neither did Adaira. The pair of them weren't to blame for today, so Rhona merely nodded.

The aroma of roast goose and the less savory smell of cabbage, turnip, and onion pottage greeted Rhona as she led the way into the Great Hall, her sisters following close behind her. Servants carried out baskets of bread and wheels of cheese to the table; while others circled with ewers, pouring wine, ale, and mead. A lad sat next to one of the huge hearths that dominated either end of the hall and played a small harp. The happy tune didn't match Rhona's mood.

Usually, she looked forward to feasts such as these—roast goose was one of her favorite meats—but not today. Her stomach had closed. She had no appetite.

The rumble of conversation stopped when Rhona appeared. She made her way down the hall and along the aisle between the rows of tables, head held high. No one here would know how she dreaded this feast.

Her father watched her approach, as did the man seated to his right: Aonghus Budge.

The chieftain of the Budges of Islay rose to his feet, his thick lips curving into a smile. "Lady Rhona, ye have grown into a lovely lass."

Rhona forced a smile in return and curtsied. "Good day, Chieftain Budge."

She took her seat at the table, thankfully across from her suitor rather than next to him.

"Aye, Rhona's the image of my mother as a lass," Malcolm MacLeod boomed, reaching for a cup of wine. "She has the same red hair and wild temperament. It takes a rare man to tame such a woman … yet my father did."

Rhona inhaled sharply and dropped her gaze to the empty platter before her. She hated it when her father spoke of her in such terms.

"A strong-willed girl like Rhona needs an equally strong man." Her stepmother, Una, spoke up. "A soft-hearted, weak husband would ruin her."

"Ye need not worry there," Aonghus Budge assured the clan-chief's wife, his attention still fixed upon Rhona. "I know how to handle a woman."

Rhona ground her teeth. *Aye—and I've seen how ye do.*

She remembered the soft blonde woman he'd once been wedded to. They'd visited Dunvegan around five summers earlier for Lammas—a feast that took place late in the summer, which heralded the harvest. Rhona recalled seeing the poor woman voice an opinion during the meal, she couldn't remember what about, and the way Aonghus had backhanded his wife across the face in reply.

Rhona glanced up, her gaze traveling to her suitor. He watched her under heavy lids, his florid face flushing further under her scrutiny. Like her father, he'd been strong and muscular as a younger man, yet at forty-three winters he was now growing fat. A flaccid, high-colored face ran into a short, thick neck. The ring-encrusted hand that grasped his cup of ale was blunt and coarse with grime-edged fingernails.

Rhona's bile rose. She would never let him near her. She'd sink a knife into her breast first. If her father thought to soften her attitude, this wasn't the way to go about it. More than ever she felt determined to avoid the trap that had brought many a woman misery.

The feast began, and Rhona picked at her meal. Her body had drawn taut like a bowstring as she waited for the arrow to fly. Sooner or later her suitor would bring up the subject of marriage.

Aonghus had just begun his third cup of ale when he did. "Lady Rhona ... ye will have heard that I was widowed this past winter?"

Rhona looked up, her gaze meeting his. "Aye ... and how did yer wife die?"

A shadow moved in the depths of Aonghus Budge's blue eyes. The question was impertinent, for she already knew the answer—all of Skye did. However, she continued to hold his gaze. *Good.* The sooner he realized she would make him a poor wife the better.

"She took a fall," he said after a long pause. "Down the tower stairs ... and broke her neck. God rest her soul."

Rhona pursed her lips. *Poor woman.* What hell she must have endured as this man's wife.

"As I was saying." Aonghus started again, undeterred. "I am widowed ... and in need of a wife. I'm looking for a strong, hardy woman to bear me plenty of sons. I think ye will suit me well."

Rhona clenched her jaw so hard it hurt. Her fingers tightened around the cup of wine before her. How she wished to throw it in his face. "No ... I won't suit ye at all."

Silence fell at the chieftain's table.

Everyone went still, even the servants who had been moving from feaster to feaster, refilling cups, halted their passage. Either side of Rhona, Caitrin and Adaira paled. Caitrin dropped her gaze to the table, while Adaira's eyes grew huge and frightened.

"Excuse me?" Aonghus broke the hush, his gravelly voice now harsh. "What did ye say?"

An angry breath rushed out of Rhona, a red haze obscuring her vision. Enough. She was tired of this mummery. She'd not be trapped or forced to wed this man. She'd hid her true feelings long enough.

"Ye heard me," she growled. Her heart started to race then. She was bold, yet knew when she'd taken things too far.

"Rhona." Una's voice lashed across the table. "How dare ye speak to our guest so. Apologize. Now."

Rhona ignored her stepmother. The woman didn't have—nor would she ever have—any authority over her.

Instead, Rhona held Aonghus Budges's eye—aware that next to him, her father had turned the color of liver. "I will not wed ye, Aonghus Budge—not now, not ever."

"Ye have gone too far this time, wench. Ye insulted our guest and shamed me in front of my hall ... my kin."

Rhona stood before her father, inside his solar. They were alone. He'd summoned her there directly after the feast had ended. A large room with south-facing windows, the solar had a great hearth in one corner with a stag's head mounted above it. Thick furs covered the floor, and richly detailed tapestries depicting hunting scenes hung from the pitted stone walls.

Meeting Malcolm's eye, Rhona tensed. He hadn't raised a hand to her since childhood, yet she feared he might now. His legs were braced, his bulky body hunched, and his hands were fisted by his sides. His face still had a dangerously high color.

"Da ... I—"

"Silence!" He advanced on Rhona, towering over her. Even growing old and fat, he was still an imposing man who dominated any space he occupied. Sometimes Rhona forgot just how tall her father was. But she didn't now.

"I've spoiled ye ... indulged ye," he choked out the words, "and this is how ye repay me. Ye made a fool of me today, Rhona, and I'll not have it."

"But I—"

"Still yer tongue." He grabbed Rhona by the shoulders, pinning her to the spot. "I will not hear another word."

Rhona swallowed and heeded him. Her father was not a man to tangle horns with.

"Aonghus Budge will not have ye now," he growled. "Ye have offended his pride and put my relationship with him at risk."

The news caused a wave of relief to crash over Rhona. She would weather her father's displeasure if it meant she would be free of Chieftain Budge. However, she was careful not to let joy show on her face. Her father would not thank her—not in his current mood

"Aye, ye have spurned yet another suitor," Malcolm continued, "but this will be the last time ye do."

Rhona stared at him, a chill replacing the relief of moments earlier. What did he mean by that?

Malcolm MacLeod pushed his face close to hers. His breath stank of wine, and his grey eyes had turned flinty. "At Mid-Summer this year I will hold games outside this keep," he continued. "Men from all over this isle, and beyond, will be called upon for yer hand." He paused here, perhaps noting his daughter's suddenly strained expression, the horror on her face. Grim victory lit in his eyes as he finished. "Ye shall wed the winner."

Chapter Four

What News of My Wife?

"MY LIFE IS over." The words burst out of Rhona, brittle and choked. She stared out the window at the wind-swept hills to the south, beyond the gardens.

"Nonsense," came Caitrin's gentle reply. Her gaze was shadowed as she observed Rhona. "Yer life is just beginning. Ye don't know who will win yer hand. He might be a man ye could grow to love."

The two sisters sat opposite each other in what had once been their mother's solar. It was an airy chamber decorated with plaid cushions and bouquets of dried heather. Heavy floral tapestries covered the damp stone walls. Rhona had a basket of wool at her feet that she was supposed to be spinning, while Caitrin worked upon a tiny tunic for the coming bairn.

Rhona tore her eyes from the view and cast her sister a withering look. "Ye sound like Adaira," she replied, not bothering to dilute her scorn. "I don't want to be trapped, dominated ... treated like a dog."

Caitrin heaved in a deep breath and leaned back in her chair, wincing slightly as she adjusted her position. Her face appeared strained; the babe did not sit easily in her belly and often seemed to cause her discomfort. "Ye will have to become a wife one day, Rhona," she pointed out after a pause. "There's no use continuing to fight it."

Rhona's mouth thinned. She didn't want to argue with her sister, but she completely disagreed with her. Why should she wed? Men could choose, so why not her?

She favored Caitrin with a narrow look. "Are ye pleased ye wed?"

Her sister tensed, and for a moment, Rhona regretted her bitter words. She knew Caitrin wasn't happy. Often she would see the melancholy in her sister's eyes, that faraway look when she thought no one was looking. She'd wed Baltair, the chief of the MacDonalds of Duntulm, two years earlier—and had rarely smiled since.

"Happy enough," Caitrin replied, her voice dull. She glanced away then. "I chose Baltair ... no one forced me to wed him."

Rhona watched her. Curiosity rose within her. There was a weight of things unsaid in her sister's expression, her soft voice. Rhona realized then that Caitrin had never really confided in her.

"Do ye suffer?" she asked, forgetting her own misery for a moment. "Is Baltair cruel to ye?"

She watched her sister's tension increase. Her lovely face tightened, and her gaze shuttered. "He's my *husband*," she replied, her voice barely above a whisper. "I'm luckier than a lot of women."

Rhona frowned. "That's no answer, Caitrin."

Her sister's blue eyes flashed in a rare show of irritation. "What do ye want me to say?" she challenged. "That he beats me nightly, that he belittles me at every chance? Would that please ye?"

Rhona stared back at her. "No," she replied, her voice subdued. "Of course not."

"Then don't pry ... ye might not like what ye hear."

Caitrin's face twisted suddenly. With a gasp, she dropped her embroidery onto her lap and clutched at her lower belly. A moment later she hissed a curse—one that Rhona had only ever heard her father's men use in the training yard. Certainly not the sort of thing her beautiful sister would utter.

"Caitrin ... what's wrong?" Rhona kicked her basket of wool aside and knelt before her sister, grasping her ice-cold hands.

Caitrin glanced up, face strained, eyes wide. "The bairn ... I think it's time."

Heart pounding, Rhona launched herself to her feet. "Adaira!" she bellowed, knowing that their sister was resting in the bower next door. "Fetch the midwife!"

The birth was a difficult one. Caitrin struggled for the rest of the day and the entire night that followed. Her grunts and cries filtered down through all levels of the keep, and when the midwife told her she should bear the pain more stoically, Caitrin screamed obscenities at her.

Although Rhona wasn't the type of lass to be shocked by cursing, hearing such words uttered by her sister made her wince. It worried her too, for Caitrin seemed in such agony. Sweat poured down her red cheeks. Her eyes were wide and desperate.

During the long night that followed, Rhona and Adaira didn't leave Caitrin's side. Eventually, Adaira succumbed to fatigue, slumping in the narrow wooden chair beside her sister's bed. However, Rhona remained awake. Her eyes burned, her shoulders ached, and yet she stayed at Caitrin's side, gripping her hand tightly when the next onslaught of birthing pains attacked her.

As dawn approached, the gaps between them shortened. Caitrin was almost delirious with pain, her breathing coming in gasps.

"Breathe deeply, Lady Caitrin," the midwife admonished her. "S-l-o-w-l-y."

Caitrin cast her a malevolent look, although she did not curse at her this time. She had long since lost the strength to abuse the poor woman. She was too tired.

"Just a short while longer." Rhona urged as Caitrin's fingers clenched around hers. Her sister squeezed so tightly that Rhona heard the bones in her hands creak. But she didn't cry out. Caitrin needed her to be strong.

"I can't," Caitrin choked out the words, tears streaming down her face. "I'm so tired. I can't take—" Her voice choked off as another wave of pain assailed her.

"Ye will," Rhona replied, fear turning her voice fierce. "Ye must."

Their gazes met and held. At that moment Rhona forgot about her own unhappy situation, about the games that loomed in just a couple of weeks. At that moment, she would have happily agreed to wed the odious Aonghus Budge if it would have kept her sister safe.

"Come, Caitrin," Rhona said, her tone pleading now. "Don't think of the pain, don't think about how tired ye are ... just think of the bairn inside ye. It must be born. Once this is over the pain will stop."

Caitrin's fingers clenched around hers. "Stay with me, Rhona," she gasped. Her face was flushed, her mouth tight with pain. "Don't leave me."

"I'll never leave ye," Rhona replied. Her vision blurred, and her chest ached from the love she felt for her sister. "I'm right here at yer side, and I always will be."

A tiny wailing babe was born as the first ribbons of violet and gold decorated the eastern sky. The lusty sound of his cries filled the birthing chamber. His small, red face was scrunched up and angry.

Caitrin sobbed with relief and sank back on the pillows.

"Ye did it." Adaira was weeping as she clutched her sister's hand. "He's so beautiful, Cate. Ye are so clever."

Beautiful. To Rhona, the babe looked anything but. Covered in blood and birthing fluid, he wasn't a comely sight. However, Caitrin did not appear to mind. Her face was a picture of joy as the midwife wrapped the bairn in a soft woolen shawl and handed him to her.

"What will ye name him?" Adaira asked, scrubbing at the tears that still trickled down her cheeks.

"I don't know," Caitrin murmured. "Baltair wanted him named after his father ... Eoghan."

"And where is yer husband?" Rhona huffed, casting a look at the midwife who had sent for him as soon as she'd realized Caitrin was going into labor. The woman, whose face now sagged with exhaustion, returned her look. "He was hunting some distance away, Lady Rhona. He's probably riding here as we speak."

"He shouldn't be away from her … not when his wife is heavy with child," Rhona pointed out.

She looked away from the midwife, to where Caitrin held the babe in her arms, gazing down at its face with a look of adoration. Caitrin didn't appear to care that Baltair wasn't here.

She hadn't asked after him once during the long labor.

Rhona stepped out into the bailey and stretched her tired back. She really should go to bed, and yet after such a fraught night, she found she'd now reached the point where she was over-tired. She was also ravenously hungry and would soon go down to the kitchens and get cook to fix her something. She'd missed supper the night before and breakfast too.

A blustery bright morning greeted her. The air was sultry, although clouds scudded across the pale blue sky and the wind blew dust devils across the courtyard. Rhona yawned and pushed her hair out of her eyes. The sun felt warm on her skin, and she turned her face up to it.

The bailey was a hive of industry this morning. Men were shoeing horses in the far corner, the tang of hot iron filtering across the yard, while others unloaded barrels off a cart that had just trundled into the keep. A servant was bringing up a pail of water from the well near the Sea-gate.

Meanwhile, two warriors sparred with wooden swords to the left of the steps leading into the keep. Rhona found her gaze drawn to them.

It was Taran and his friend Gordon. Stripped to the waist, the two men moved around each other, attacking and parrying. Curious, Rhona's gaze settled upon Taran's torso. She'd never seen him shirtless before and was surprised to see that his chest and back weren't scarred like his face.

In fact, the opposite was true.

Gordon had a lithe, strong body, but Taran's was broad, sculpted, and quite beautiful. Rhona watched, fascinated. The muscles in his back clenched and flexed as he moved. Although he was a big man, there wasn't an ounce of fat on him either; his bulk was all muscle.

Realizing she was staring, Rhona tore her gaze away. Fatigue had turned her witless this morning.

"Good morning, Lady Rhona," Taran called out. He'd seen her and stepped back from Gordon. He now regarded her with that calm, direct look she'd come to know well. "How are Lady Caitrin and the bairn faring?"

Rhona favored him with a tired smile. She appreciated him asking after Caitrin. "They're both well, thank ye … although my sister is drained."

A frown creased Taran's brow. He opened his mouth to reply but paused as the thunder of hooves interrupted him. Rhona glanced away to the Sea-gate, where a man upon a lathered horse had just ridden in. She drew in a sharp breath, her gaze narrowing.

Baltair MacDonald had finally arrived.

Drawing the beast up short, he leaped off its back and threw the reins to a lad who'd emerged from the stables.

Without a word of thanks, he then turned on his heel and strode toward the keep.

Nearby, Taran and Gordon didn't resume their sword practice. Instead, they tracked the newcomer's progress across the courtyard.

Rhona also watched him approach. Baltair MacDonald was a handsome man, it couldn't be denied. Tall with long dark hair that flowed over his broad shoulders, he had chiseled features and peat-brown eyes.

Yet the man held an arrogance that grated upon Rhona. He'd always treated her and Adaira as if they were inconsequential. Baltair's attention alighted briefly upon her now, his expression coldly dismissive when he stopped before her. "What news of my wife?"

Rhona regarded him, unsmiling. "She has given ye a son," she replied coolly. "The babe was born but a short while ago."

Something flickered across Baltair MacDonald's face, although it was difficult to ascertain exactly what. Perhaps she had glimpsed joy in those dark eyes. It was so fleeting she might have mistaken it.

Not bothering to thank Rhona for the news, Baltair mounted the steps, brushing past her. "Where is she?"

"In the tower chamber."

She glanced over her shoulder, watching his retreating back, and wondered—not for the first time—why her sister had ever wed such a man.

Chapter Five

Interrupted by the Shrew

"HOW IS YER sister this morning?"

Rhona glanced up from where she was spreading butter on a slice of bannock. Her gaze met her father's. "Much better ... she ate a good supper last night, and her color is much improved."

Malcolm MacLeod nodded, his face relaxing a little, although beside him Una sniffed. "Caitrin is too delicate to bear many children," she said with an expression that Rhona found patronizing. "She takes after her mother."

Rhona tensed at this. She hated it when Una mentioned her mother. Martha MacLeod had died many years ago, yet Una held a strange jealousy toward the chieftain's first wife.

It seemed that Malcolm shared his daughter's view, for he cast Una an irritated look. "Martha bore four bairns without problems," he reminded his wife. "It was not childbirth that ended her ... but a fever."

Una's full mouth pursed at this, and Rhona waited for an acerbic reply. However, none came.

Malcolm reached for his fourth wedge of bannock—a large flat cake made with oatmeal and cooked upon an iron griddle. He then slathered it thickly with butter and heather honey.

"So I hear yer fiery Rhona is to be wed?" An amused male voice interrupted.

Baltair MacDonald sat farther down the table, his hands clasping a cup of fresh goat's milk.

Rhona cast him a swift, dark look, but he merely smirked. From the look on his face, he'd brought the subject up to cause trouble.

"Aye," Malcolm replied with his mouth full. He broke off a piece of bannock and fed it to the wolfhound that sat expectantly at his feet. "I've sent word out—and men from all over the isle, and beyond, have answered."

Rhona's belly cramped at this news, and she swallowed her mouthful of food without enjoyment.

"Even the Frasers?" Baltair asked, a smirk still upon his handsome face. "Surely not?"

MacLeod's face grew thunderous, while Una pursed her lips and cast Baltair a censorious look. Rhona watched a muscle bunch in her father's cheek. Even the mention of the name 'Fraser' was enough to put him in a sour mood. Of late, the Fraser chieftain had been mischief-making: hunting in MacLeod lands, denying travelers passage through his territory, and even refusing to trade with his neighbors.

"No, not them," Malcolm MacLeod growled. "If just one Fraser dares venture here for the games, I'll have him stoned out of Dunvegan."

"I wonder how many warriors will come," Una spoke up, her voice overly bright as she sought to change the subject. "Many have already left to fight at the king's side for the glory of Scotland. There may be few left who are free to travel here to win Rhona's hand."

Malcolm favored his wife with an irritated look. However, her words had managed to distract him from thoughts of his arch-enemy. "The glory of Scotland, indeed," he rumbled. "It's time we took back what is ours. The English think we've gone soft, but we'll show those arrogant bastards."

Baltair snorted in agreement at this, and MacLeod turned his attention to the MacDonald chieftain. "Have ye heard from yer brother? He fights for King David now, does he not?"

"Aye," Baltair grunted. "With the English sailing south to fight the French, he believes our time grows near. David will strike within the next few months."

Malcolm nodded, his brow furrowing. "The timing for the games isn't ideal," he admitted. "But my Rhona's a bonny lass ... I'm sure a good number will turn up on the day. Besides, we only need one winner."

"It was a clever idea," Baltair replied. "If the lass won't choose a husband, take matters into yer own hands." He still wasn't looking Rhona's way, as if she was beneath his notice.

Rhona inhaled deeply, her anger rising. Was it any wonder she wished to remain unwed? There were far too many men upon the isle like Baltair MacDonald—men who believed a woman was of no use at all, except for cooking, sewing, and swiving.

"Rhona may find a good husband this way," Una replied with a cool smile. "Better than she deserves."

"Rhona deserves a man as strong and brave as her," Adaira piped up from where she sat next to Rhona. "At least this way, they get to fight for her hand."

Rhona cast her sister a quelling glance, but Adaira was not looking at her. Instead, she was glaring at Una, her face uncharacteristically fierce. A rush of affection flowed through Rhona.

Her sister looked particularly lovely when riled. Her hazel eyes had almost darkened to green, and her mouth had set in determination.

Una huffed in response although she made no reply.

"And what of ye, Adaira?" Baltair asked. "Surely ye too want to wed?"

Rhona watched the way her brother-in-law gazed at Adaira and felt her hackles rise. Whereas he made a point of ignoring Rhona, he stared boldly at Adaira this morning. His voice, usually rough, was as smooth as cream.

"I will," Adaira replied, suddenly going all meek and flustered under his gaze. She looked down at her half-eaten bannock. "Once Rhona has found a husband."

"The sooner the better," Malcolm cut in, brushing crumbs off his broad chest. "All this talk of suitors and handfastings makes me weary. Sons are far less trouble."

No one at the table replied to that, although Rhona saw her brother, Iain's, chest puff up at the compliment. She also noted that Baltair still watched Adaira, a wolfish gleam in his eyes.

"Have ye heard? Caitrin wasn't the only one to give birth in the keep yesterday," Adaira hurried after Rhona as they left the Great Hall. "Milish has had a litter of pups!"

Despite her now waspish mood, Rhona found herself smiling. "Has she?" Milish was a wolfhound bitch—a matriarch that ruled the pack of dogs her father kept.

"Taran has Milish and the pups in one of the stables," Adaira replied with a grin. "I'll take ye to them."

"Go on then." Rhona's smile widened. "Lead the way."

The young women left the keep and descended the steps into the bailey. Adaira called out cheerfully to servants and guards as she passed by, and they acknowledged her in turn with smiles and waves. It didn't surprise Rhona how popular her sister was—for she had a warm smile and kind word for most folk. However, her sister's open, trusting nature sometimes worried Rhona.

As it had earlier.

The look Baltair had given her sister was alarming; Rhona wondered if she should warn Adaira about him.

Warn her of what?

A bold stare wasn't forbidden—and it seemed that Rhona was the only one at the table who had noticed or cared. Adaira would tell her she was being a goose. Maybe it was best to keep her observations to herself.

They found Milish with her litter in a straw-lined stable. The bitch wore a serene expression as six small bodies wriggled against her teats, their eyes screwed shut.

Rhona knelt down next to the hound, stroking her grizzled muzzle. "Haven't ye done well, lass?"

"Aren't they beautiful?" Adaira's eyes gleamed with tears as she gently picked up one of the pups and cradled it against her breast. "So tiny and defenseless."

"Not for long they won't be." A male voice intruded. Rhona glanced up to see Taran looming in the stable doorway. "Soon they'll be yipping, fighting, and causing no end of trouble. Enjoy the peace while it lasts."

Rhona smiled. She knew Taran's grumblings were just a ruse—for it was he who was in charge of her father's hounds. She'd seen the bond he shared with them.

"Can I have one, Taran?" Adaira asked, turning to him. She still clutched the puppy. It was a fat-bellied creature with tufted grey fur.

The Beast of Dunvegan gave a rare smile. It softened those disfiguring scars and made him appear younger. Rhona realized then that she had no idea how old Taran was. She had thought him at least thirty, yet now realized he was younger than that.

"Ye will need to ask yer father, Lady Adaira," he replied, leaning against the door frame and folding his arms across his chest. "But if he agrees then, aye—ye may have one."

Adaira beamed at him. She then turned and carefully placed the wriggly puppy back with its mother. "I shall ask him now. Then I'll go and tell Caitrin about the puppies."

"Tell Caitrin, I'll be up soon to see her," Rhona said as her sister made for the door, cheeks flushed with excitement.

"Aye," Adaira sang, sliding past Taran and out into the sunlight. "See ye shortly."

Alone with Taran in the stables, Rhona sighed. "Adaira will love ye forever now."

He chuckled, a deep warm sound. "And she didn't before, Lady Rhona?"

Rhona gave him an arch look and rose to her feet, brushing straw off her kirtle. "Adaira thinks well of most folk ... as ye know. Sometimes it worries me."

His expression turned serious, and the Taran she was used to returned. "Why ... has something happened?"

Rhona shook her head, suddenly wishing she'd held her tongue. Taran was as loyal as the hounds he tended. Any threat to Rhona or her sisters and he became fierce.

"No ... it's just that ... sooner or later she'll be wed," Rhona replied. She looked away, her gaze dropping to the feeding puppies. Suddenly, she felt uncomfortable confiding in Taran. "I know she's a woman now, but there's something childlike about Adaira ... I won't be able to protect her anymore."

"Of course ye will."

She glanced up, meeting his gaze.

"Ye have heard about the games?"

He nodded. "Ye are displeased?"

Rhona snorted, not caring that the sound was unladylike. "I'm livid ... but Da doesn't care. I'm just a problem he wants dealt with."

The warrior's face tensed, and she thought for a moment he would reply. However, silence stretched between them, and he broke her gaze. There wasn't really anything he could say, she supposed. Taran was her father's man—and he would never speak against him.

"I'd better go," she said briskly. "Caitrin will be waiting for me."

Taran nodded and stepped back to let her pass. "Good day, Lady Rhona."

Rhona moved past him before stopping. She turned back, her gaze snaring his. "Don't think this is going to turn me into some feeble, sniveling wench," she told him firmly. "I still want to continue our training."

His mouth curved, making his scars alter shape. "Of course, Lady Rhona ... when is our next meeting?"

Rhona smiled back. "Tomorrow at dawn."

Rhona left the stables and stalked back into the keep, taking the stairwell steps two at a time.

She wasn't sure why, but Taran MacKinnon sometimes made her feel uncomfortable. He was a man who said little, yet she often found herself wondering what he really thought. Over the years he'd become a friend of sorts, and yet she knew little about the man beneath the scars and the chainmail.

Was there more to him than the warrior, the loyal servant?

She shook her head, dismissing the thought. What did she care? He was Taran—a man who lived to serve her family, a man who indulged her whims far too often.

It was a steep climb up to her sister's lodgings. Caitrin had given birth in the tower chamber—a large room with a view west over the glittering loch—and she would remain there for another day or two. The birth had weakened her, and she had lost a lot of blood.

As she climbed, Rhona heard a babe's lusty wail. Little Eoghan had a powerful set of lungs.

She had almost reached the landing when she heard voices: a man's low pitch, followed by a woman's soft, pleading tone.

"A bonny creature, ye are. Let's have a look at ye."

"Please ... I need to go."

"Not just yet. What's the hurry?"

"My sister is waiting. I can't—"

"Hush that sweet mouth. I have a better use for it."

Clenching her jaw, Rhona rushed up the last set of steps and launched herself onto the landing. Her gaze swept right, focusing on where Adaira cowered against the wall. Baltair MacDonald had bailed her up, using his arms to bracket her as he leaned in for a kiss.

"What's this?" Rhona hissed. She advanced on them, fists clenched at her sides.

Adaira gave a gasp of relief, ducked under Baltair's arm, and rushed to Rhona. Her face, which had been so alive with joy earlier as she'd held the puppy, now held a traumatized expression. Her eyes glittered with tears.

Baltair straightened up. His look of surprise faded, and he grinned.

"Interrupted by the shrew—how vexing."

"What were ye doing?" Rhona choked out, so angry she could barely get the words out. "Vile dog ... with yer wife and bairn just yards away!"

He arched a dark eyebrow. "Adaira and I were having a private conversation. Ye should mind yer manners, lass—and yer own business."

"This *is* my business. Ye are a guest in this keep. How dare ye corner my sister!"

"Rhona." Adaira plucked at her sleeve, her voice tight with fear. "Maybe we should—"

"Caitrin will know of this," Rhona snarled, cutting Adaira off. "As will our father."

Baltair turned to face her squarely, folding his arms across his chest. He didn't look remotely cowed by the threat. The opposite in fact. "Go on then," he challenged, favoring her with a cold smile. "I dare ye."

Chapter Six

Truth and Deception

RHONA SAT DOWN next to her sister and forced a smile. "Ye look so much better this morning. It's good to see some color in yer cheeks."

Caitrin, propped up against a nest of pillows, smiled back. "I do feel better ... although I'm so tired." She glanced down at the babe, swaddled in linen, who slept in her arms. Rhona followed her gaze to the small head covered in soft black hair before clenching her jaw.

Will he grow up to be like his father?

Caitrin looked up, her gaze meeting Rhona's. Her soft smile faded. "Is something wrong? Ye are flushed." She glanced toward the closed door. "I heard raised voices earlier ... were ye arguing with someone?"

Rhona inhaled deeply. This was her chance. She had only to say a few words, and Caitrin would know about Baltair.

What would have happened if I hadn't interrupted him?

The man was a foul letch, preying on Adaira just yards from where his wife and child lay. He deserved to be revealed. The whole keep should know what he was—and yet when Caitrin's soft gaze rested upon her once more, Rhona found the words stuck in her throat.

Caitrin had just endured a difficult birth. Even recovering she appeared frail, exhausted.

The news would destroy her.

Rhona would feel vindicated as she told her sister, spurred on by the memory of Baltair's sneering face as he challenged her. But her victory would be short-lived. She didn't want to make Caitrin suffer.

Rhona slowly loosed the breath she'd been holding. "I was just talking to Baltair and Adaira," she replied, forcing herself not to look away as she spoke. "He wanted ye to come downstairs to the Great Hall for the noon meal, but we both insisted against it. Ye are too weak."

Caitrin sighed, leaning back against the pillows. "Thank ye, Rhona ... men can be insensitive sometimes."

Rhona bit the inside of her cheek to stop herself from replying. Baltair was far worse than that. Although she would spare Caitrin for the moment, she couldn't keep silent about this.

Someone had to know.

She would tell her father.

Malcolm MacLeod frowned at his daughter, his mouth pursing.

Rhona stood before him, as self-confident and haughty as ever. She'd been subdued for a day or two after he'd told her about the games, yet it seemed she'd rallied—especially in defense of her sister.

"Mind yer tongue, lass," he grumbled. "It's not wise to lay such accusations at a chieftain."

Rhona's jaw tensed, her grey eyes growing hard. "Just because he leads the MacDonalds of Duntulm, it doesn't make him beyond reproach. He cornered Adaira, and would have kissed her if I hadn't interrupted."

Malcolm huffed out a breath and put the quill he was holding back into the ink-pot. He was trying to write a letter—one that required a lot of concentration—and wasn't in the mood for this conversation.

"He was probably just being playful ... sometimes men do that, lass."

Rhona's face went taut, her mouth thinning. "He wasn't being playful, Da. What if he gets Adaira alone? What if he—"

"Enough," Malcolm grumbled. For the love of God. What had he ever done to deserve such a difficult daughter? He couldn't wait till she was wedded—a husband would calm her down. "Ye go too far," he continued. "Baltair has not committed any crime against yer sister. Perhaps she encouraged him? Adaira can be a flirt."

"She didn't welcome his attention," Rhona growled back. Her cheeks had gone red, and her hands were fisted at her sides.

"Ye don't know that."

"I saw her face. She was terrified of him."

Malcolm let out a gusty sigh and scratched his beard. "I'm sorry, lass, but this tale must remain between us. I can't risk bad blood with the MacDonalds, not with the Frasers sharpening their swords at our backs." His mood darkened as he spoke these words. Bile stung the back of his throat as the bannocks he'd eaten earlier repeated on him.

His daughter's gaze narrowed. "What have they done now?"

MacLeod glowered at her. "Morgan Fraser is fast becoming a thorn in my arse," he growled. "I've just received a letter from him, which I'm trying to respond to." He gestured to the sheet of parchment before him. "The piece of dung dares challenge me for lands. He's now claiming that Hamra Rinner Vale belongs to him."

His daughter's expression didn't change. She continued to watch him with that bullish look he'd come to know well over the years. "And does it?"

"No!" Spittle flew from his mouth as he boomed out the answer. "The greedy bastard knows we hunt deer on that land. They belong to me, and I'll not give them up."

Malcolm reached for a cup of milk he'd had a servant bring up. Hopefully, it would do the trick and soothe his acid stomach. "We may soon have to face off against the Frasers," he said once he'd taken a gulp, wiping his mouth with the back of his hand. "I'll not start a feud with Baltair MacDonald over something so trivial."

His daughter glared back at him, fury radiating out from her. However, he didn't care that she was angry. He'd been far too lenient with her over the years.

"This incident makes it clear to me that once ye are wed I will need to find Adaira a husband before winter arrives," he informed Rhona. "The lass dances about Dunvegan as flightily as a brownie. She'll ruin herself before long if things continue."

"I told ye before, father," Rhona ground the words out, her voice hoarse with barely suppressed temper. "Adaira was not to blame. Baltair cornered her."

Malcolm reached for his quill once more. He'd had enough of her prattle. "Keep silent about this," he warned her. "If I hear whispers of this story, I shall have ye whipped."

"But, Da—"

"Leave me now, Rhona." He waved her away. "I've a letter to write."

A grey dawn broke over Dunvegan Castle, bringing with it a misty rain. Dressed in plaid braies and a léine belted at the waist, Rhona exited the keep and walked toward the training yard.

Despite the morning's gloom, it wasn't cold. The misty rain kissed her skin, and the air smelt alive and fresh as only dawn air could. Rhona loved this time of day, the early dawn in that short time before the castle awoke. However, this morning she wasn't in the mood to enjoy it.

Her father's dismissive attitude the day before still stung. His complete lack of concern for Adaira's wellbeing enraged Rhona. All he cared about was keeping the peace with the MacDonalds. He hadn't even been able to listen to her properly, his thoughts focused instead on his petty feud with the Frasers.

Unhappiness warred with anger this morning though. She was used to her father's stubbornness. However, being dismissed by him only days after he'd made such a heavy-handed decision about her future, made Rhona feel as if he didn't care for her at all.

He just wanted her wedded and out of the way.

A man stepped out of the dawn's mist ahead—a tall, broad-shouldered figure that she'd know anywhere.

"Good morning, Lady Rhona," Taran greeted her.

"Morning," Rhona answered, her voice as lackluster as her spirits.

Taran's scarred visage tensed as he drew near. "Is something wrong?"

She shook her head. "I slept badly, that's all."

He raised an eyebrow. "We can practice another time if ye are not feeling up to it?"

"I'm well," she snapped, rolling up the sleeves of her léine. Truthfully, she needed something to distract her from her thoughts. The games were just ten days away now—the date loomed before her like an execution.

"Last time ye showed me how to break a man's hold if he grabbed my arm," she said walking past him into the training yard. "This time I want ye to show me what to do if a man catches me from behind."

"Very well," he replied, following her into the yard. "As ye wish."

Rhona stopped in the center of the yard and waited. A moment later she heard the scuff of Taran's boots as he stepped up behind her. Then his arms went around her, clasping her tight.

The contact made Rhona stifle a gasp of shock. She'd never been in such close physical contact with a man. It was a strange, unnerving sensation.

"Can ye break free?" Taran asked. His voice was gruff. He was so close that she felt his breath feather against her ear.

Rhona tried to move but found herself locked, as if in an iron cage. "No."

"If a man grabs ye like this, the first thing ye want to do is try to head-butt him in the face. Now ... throw yerself back against me and try to break my nose with the back of yer head."

Rhona smiled. "Really?"

"Aye ... try it."

Rhona arched against him and threw her head back. However, Taran shifted his head to one side to avoid the blow. "Good," he grunted. "At this point, I might try to lift ye off yer feet. There are two things ye can do to prevent this. The first is to drop as if yer legs can no longer support ye. This will turn ye into a dead weight and make it harder for me to shift ye. Or ye can hook yer foot back behind my ankle and use it to anchor yerself. Try that."

Rhona did as bid, stretching her leg back and entwining it with Taran's. However, his legs were strong, big, and muscular. It was like trying to wrap her ankle around a tree trunk.

"That's right," he replied. "Now, if I try to lift ye, I won't be able to." Taran attempted to pull her off the ground, but Rhona didn't budge. "This will give ye another chance to head-butt me ... or rip off one of my ears if ye get yer arm free."

"What the Devil are ye two up to?"

Malcolm MacLeod's deep voice boomed across the deserted yard, causing both Rhona and Taran to freeze.

Rhona glanced left to see her father bearing down on them. Even the fact he was limping slightly from his gout didn't make him any less intimidating. Two of his wolfhounds skulked at his heels, following their master into the yard.

"Da." Heat rose to Rhona's cheeks. All the times over the years she'd trained with Taran and her father had never known. He wasn't an early riser, especially of late, and Taran had sworn the servants and other warriors to secrecy. Rhona tensed—had someone betrayed them? "Ye are up early?" She tried to ignore the fact her father's eyes were bulging and his bearded face had turned the color of liver.

"I'm taking the dogs out for a hunt," he snarled, stopping before them. "What are ye doing with my daughter, MacKinnon?"

Taran let go of Rhona and stepped away from her. Rhona glanced over at him to find his face unreadable. His gaze was direct as it met her father's. "Lady Rhona bid me teach her the art of hand-to-hand combat and self-defense, Chief," he replied.

"It looked like ye were embracing her to me."

"I was showing her how to get free of a hold."

The clan-chief's attention shifted from Taran, spearing Rhona with a look she knew well. "How long has this been going on?"

Rhona swallowed but held his gaze. "A while."

"I didn't give ye permission to train my daughter, MacKinnon," her father's gaze returned to Taran. "How dare ye go behind my back."

"It's not his fault," Rhona interjected. She didn't want Taran blamed for this—let her father's wrath fall on her. He could be vicious with his warriors if they displeased him; he'd be gentler with her. "I bid him do it ... made him swear to tell no one."

Malcolm MacLeod stepped close, and even though she could almost meet his eye, Rhona dropped her gaze. Dread rose within her. Would he beat her for this? She'd defied him deliberately, and she understood his anger.

"There will be no more training," MacLeod said, his voice a low, threatening growl. "Is that clear?"

Rhona nodded, desperation constricting her throat. Her one small freedom—gone.

"I didn't hear ye?" Her father bellowed in her face.

"Chief, I—" Taran began.

MacLeod cut him off. "Not another word from ye."

"Aye, Da," Rhona replied, her gaze still fixed upon the straw-flecked ground between them. "It's clear."

Chapter Seven

Caged

TARAN CLIMBED THE guard tower's circular staircase, returning to his quarters. Unlike many of the young warriors who served MacLeod, Taran didn't sleep in the barracks that took up the lower floor. Instead, his position as one of the chieftain's personal guard had earned him a chamber of his own.

Taran was grateful for that, for, after the scene in the training yard, he was in no mood for company. Reaching the third-floor landing, he strode into his chamber and shoved the door shut behind him. The noise reverberated in the stone tower.

Standing inside his private chamber—a space he'd only just vacated a short while earlier—Taran felt caged. The chamber was small, with damp stone walls and a tiny hearth at one corner, which was unlit this morning, for it was high summer. Clothing hung from hooks on the wall, and a narrow pallet lay under a tiny shuttered window.

Taran raked a hand through his short hair and ground out a low curse.

That was it—the end of his contact with Lady Rhona. He wasn't going to fool himself. He'd receive more than a tongue-lashing when MacLeod returned from taking his dogs out. However, he'd take whatever punishment came.

It had been worth it to be able to spend time with Rhona over the years. Their practice sessions had been irregular at best, yet he'd lived for them. Most of the practice had been with wooden swords, although the past two sessions—when he'd taught her how to defend herself using her hands—would remain forever in his memory.

The close contact with Rhona had been sweet torture. The feel of her body in his arms earlier had made it difficult for him to form a coherent thought. She was oblivious to the effect she had on him, oblivious to the fact he was a man at all. He should hate her for that, but he didn't. He'd never stop wanting her.

Now all of that would end.

Taran inhaled deeply. A boulder sat on his chest; he couldn't breathe. He crossed to the window and yanked open the wooden shutters.

Leaning up against the stone window ledge, Taran glared out at the misty morning. He couldn't believe that the chief had been up so early. Of late, as his gout worsened, he'd become less mobile.

Not this morning though.

Life was about to change, and not for the better. Lady Rhona was about to be taken from him.

Taran gritted his teeth and swung away from the window. *Dolt ... she wasn't yers in the first place.*

He'd been shocked to hear of the games MacLeod was going to hold. The thought of men competing for her hand made Taran feel sick. He'd always known the day of her wedding would come, but he'd imagined Lady Rhona would be allowed to choose her husband, and that it would be a man she loved. That would have made it easier to bear. He'd be miserable all the same, but he'd know that she, at least, was happy.

But the expression on her face the first time he'd seen her after the announcement—Rhona had looked as if she awaited her beheading. Her expression after the confrontation with her father in the training yard had been the same. He'd seen the despair in those storm-grey eyes, the simmering fury she dared not unleash—not in front of her father.

The walls closed in further. If he stayed here, trapped by his own thoughts, he'd go mad. Taran left his chamber, descended the steps, and departed the guard tower, crossing the mist-wreathed bailey. In the Great Hall beyond, there were still a handful of men breaking their fast, Taran's friend Gordon among them.

"There ye are." Gordon flashed him a smile as he sat down. "Ye are just in time. Connel has just finished the last of the bannocks and will scoff the rest of the bread too if ye are not quick."

The warrior in question, a heavy-set young man with a shock of straw-colored hair and a florid face, shot Gordon a dark look. Yet he couldn't answer, for his mouth was full.

Taran nodded and reached for the last chunk of bread. Truthfully, he had little appetite this morning, yet he'd only draw attention to himself if he didn't eat.

"Is something amiss?" Taran glanced up to find Gordon watching him, a shrewd look on his face. "Ye look like ye woke up to find a dog turd in yer boots."

Beside him, Connel Buchanan snorted before reaching for a mug of milk. "Happened to me once," he admitted with a grimace. "One of my father's hounds."

Gordon grinned, his gaze never leaving Taran. "We were just talking about the games," he informed him. "Connel here has thrown in his name."

Taran raised an eyebrow. "Really?"

Connel gave him a disgruntled look. "Why the shock? I've as good a chance as any man."

Gordon smirked. "I'm surprised MacLeod let ye take part. Ye are barely able to grow a beard."

Connel scowled back. "I'm old enough to take a wife." His gaze narrowed as it swept from Gordon to Taran. "Why don't ye two compete for the fair Lady Rhona?"

"My heart is already spoken for, lad," Gordon replied. "Greer won't look kindly upon me competing for the hand of another."

Gordon's reply didn't come as a surprise to Taran. Greer was the comely daughter of Dunvegan's cook. Gordon had pursued the lass tirelessly over the past year and was close to succeeding in winning her over.

Connel's gaze fixed upon Taran. "What about ye, 'Scar-face'?"

Taran didn't appreciate the younger man's tone or the sneer that went with it. But he didn't rise to the bait. He'd been belittled so often about his looks over the years that he didn't take offense. He'd have flattened the nose of nearly every man in this keep if he had. He merely fixed Connel with a cold look. "I think not."

"Why not?" Connel pressed. His gaze was challenging although the sneer faded.

Taran drew in a deep breath. "These games go against Lady Rhona's wishes," he replied. "I'll not be part of them."

Rhona stood on the steps to the bailey and watched Baltair MacDonald prepare to leave Dunvegan. A few feet away Caitrin settled herself upon a nest of cushions on a cart, babe in arms. Lady MacDonald's face pinched as she tried to get comfortable; even so, it would be a bumpy journey to the MacDonald stronghold of Duntulm in the north.

Approaching the wagon, Rhona cast Baltair a dark look. Caitrin wasn't ready to travel—she'd only given birth three days earlier. She'd lost a lot of blood and was still weak. Yet her brother-in-law was impatient to return home.

Baltair wore a sour expression this morning as he tightened his horse's girth. Observing him, Rhona wondered if her father had spoken to Baltair after all. Perhaps that was the cause of his hasty departure. Whatever the reason, it was selfish and careless of him to take Caitrin away from Dunvegan so soon.

An invisible vise gripped Rhona around her chest as she reached out and took Caitrin's hand. Her sister's fingers were thin and cold, but as always, when she looked into Caitrin's sea-blue eyes, Rhona found it difficult to read her mood. She'd previously been so open, so free with her thoughts and feelings. These days her lovely face was a mask.

Anxiety curled in the pit of Rhona's belly. Once Caitrin returned to Duntulm, she would be alone again with Baltair MacDonald.

"Please send word when ye reach Duntulm," Rhona urged, her voice low. "Let me know that ye have arrived safely and that ye are well."

Caitrin favored her with a soft smile before nodding. "I'll write ye a letter after we arrive."

Rhona swallowed an avalanche of things she longed to say. She wanted to urge Caitrin to be honest with her. She wanted to reveal Baltair's true nature publicly, right now. Here, with her father and his retainers looking on.

Malcolm had come out with Una to see his daughter off. Surely, he'd show pity if he saw Caitrin distressed, in fear for her safety. He couldn't be so hard-hearted?

But Rhona knew the truth of it in the depths of her heart. Baltair was Caitrin's lawful husband; she was no longer a MacLeod. She belonged body and soul to another man.

Rhona released her sister's hand and let her own fall to her side. She then curled her fingers into a fist, her nails cutting into her palms. Panic assailed her as she imagined herself in Caitrin's place, forced to obey a man like Baltair MacDonald.

I don't want that. I'll not be owned by a man.

"Travel well, sister." Adaira had appeared at Rhona's shoulder. She reached out and clasped Caitrin's hands with hers. "Come back to see us soon."

"I will," Caitrin assured her. "As soon as I'm strong enough and Eoghan has grown a little, I'll visit."

This comment earned Caitrin a warning glance from her husband. Holding Baltair's gaze, Caitrin's features tightened. She then looked down to where her son nestled in her arms. "I'll come as soon as I'm able," she promised softly.

With a sinking heart, Rhona wondered when she'd actually see her sister again.

"Come, wife." Baltair's voice lashed across the courtyard. "Enough prattling with yer sisters. We've got a full day's journey ahead of us."

Linking her arm through her younger sister's, Rhona guided Adaira back to the foot of the steps, where their father, step-mother, and a few retainers waited. There, they watched Baltair kick his stallion into a brisk trot, leading the way out through the Sea-gate and down the narrow causeway that wound down to the shore.

As the cart bearing Caitrin disappeared from view, Adaira gave Rhona's arm a gentle squeeze.

Rhona reached for her sister's hand and wordlessly squeezed back. She didn't trust herself to speak right now, didn't trust herself not to say things her father would punish her for. He and Una were within earshot.

Heaving a deep breath, Rhona sought to control her urge to rage. Instead, she stared at the point where Caitrin had disappeared.

Caged. She felt trapped by the stone walls of this keep, by the wishes of her overbearing father.

She could now count the days till the games on both hands. Day by day, the cage was growing smaller, the walls closing in.

She couldn't go through with this—could not passively wait for her fate. She wouldn't end up like Caitrin.

Chapter Eight

A Ready Excuse

RHONA KNEW SHE had to act quickly. With the games looming, she had to flee Dunvegan and the Isle of Skye, if she was to have any chance of escaping an unwanted marriage.

She pondered her decision for a full day after Caitrin's departure. Alone in the gardens behind the keep, she circled the beds of roses and the long avenues of lavender and rosemary, oblivious to her surroundings as she planned.

Her mother wasn't from this isle. Martha MacLeod had hailed from the mainland, from Argyle. Rhona's mother had spoken often of her home, of Gylen Castle, where her brother, Rhona's uncle, still lived now. She'd loved Gylen and had wanted to return there, one last time. Cruelly, death had come for her too swiftly.

Rhona would go there.

Her uncle still ruled Gylen, and she had a number of cousins there too. Some of them had visited over the years, and she remembered them as warm, kind folk. Rhona would find a way across the water and head south into Argyle, where she'd throw herself at their sympathies. She could instead find herself a nunnery on the mainland and take the veil, but that plan didn't appeal much. Rhona knew she didn't have the right temperament to become a nun. She was too impatient, too willful. However, if her uncle didn't welcome her, she'd have to resort to that.

The idea didn't thrill her, but at least it would be *her* choice.

The destination decided, Rhona then set about plotting how she would reach it. She would go out on a ride or a hunt and at the first opportunity slip away. Then she would ride south, to the southern village of Kyleakin, the point nearest the mainland. She had coin, a small bag of silver pennies that she had squirreled away over the years. Her father and kin had given her pennies on birthdays or at Yuletide, and whereas Caitrin and Adaira spent theirs on pretty shawls and kirtles at market, Rhona had saved hers.

It was almost as if she'd known this day would come.

She should have enough to buy passage across the water from Kyleakin to the mainland, and for a horse to carry her south after that. The only other things she needed were time, opportunity—and courage.

The thought of fleeing didn't scare her. But the realization that she would have to leave everything she knew and loved, including her sisters, made Rhona feel sick.

Who would protect Adaira with her gone? Caitrin was beyond her help, but Adaira still needed her.

And yet, the truth of it was that she would soon likely be unable to help her younger sister anyway. If she stayed and the games took place, who knew what man would win her hand? She'd heard that many warriors were coming from the mainland. It was highly likely she wouldn't even stay at Dunvegan.

"These are delicious." Rhona took a bite of twice-baked oat-cake and chewed it with gusto before favoring Greer with a smile. "I don't suppose ye could spare some?"

Greer glanced up from where she was rolling out pastry. "Of course, milady. Do ye need anything else?"

Rhona nodded. "Adaira and I are visiting Dunvegan market this morning. We thought to spread out a blanket by the loch's edge and have our noon meal there."

Greer smiled, revealing a deep dimple on one cheek. "I'll fix ye a basket then."

Comely, with thick brown hair she always wore in a long braid down her back, Greer was Rhona's age. Despite their differing rank, the two young women had always shared an easy rapport. Of late, Rhona had seen Greer spending time with Gordon MacPherson, Taran's friend. They'd danced together at Beltane, and Rhona had felt a pang of envy for the lass—not because she wanted Gordon, but because the cook's daughter was free to choose her own future.

"Hurry up then, lass." Greer's mother, Fiona—Dunvegan's cook—clicked her tongue and cast her daughter an impatient look. "Don't keep Lady Rhona waiting."

Greer dusted her hands off on her apron. "What would ye like?"

"Nothing fancy," Rhona replied, feigning casualness. She needed food that would keep well enough for her journey, but which wouldn't raise anyone's suspicions. It was two days since Caitrin's departure; Rhona couldn't risk waiting any longer. "Oat-cakes, a wedge of hard cheese, and some apples will do nicely … and a skin of water." Rhona tensed then as Greer reached for a large wicker basket. "We're riding to the market … so a cloth bag will be easier to carry."

The young woman nodded, no sign of suspicion on her face. Rhona was so nervous this morning that she worried others could sense it. Fortunately, unlike Adaira, she was adept at not letting her feelings show on her face for the whole world to see. Even so, involving Greer and Fiona in her plans put her on edge.

Da won't punish them, she assured herself as she watched Greer disappear into the larder to fetch the cheese and apples. *They have no idea what I'm up to.*

What am I doing? Rhona's heart pounded as she let herself into her father's solar. *How will I explain myself if I'm caught in here?*

Rhona didn't have a ready excuse, just a desperation to leave this isle—and to do that, she needed maps of Skye and the mainland.

The morning sun filtered in through the window, illuminating the dust motes that floated down from the ceiling. Servants had been in here and opened the shutters to air the chamber. It was a mild morning, yet they had laid the hearth. Even at the height of summer, this keep remained damp and cold.

Moving to her father's desk, Rhona's gaze searched the piles of parchment and the stacks of books that covered it.

She remembered then that Malcolm MacLeod kept his maps in a clay vase. Turning from the desk, she spied it sitting upon a shelf next to the MacLeod drinking horn. Rhona's heart sank when she saw that the vase was packed with scrolls; she didn't have time to sort through them all.

Fortunately, the map of Skye was the first she picked out. She quickly unscrolled it, her gaze sliding over the familiar lobster-shaped outline of the isle. The map showed the road south from Dunvegan and the various routes she could take to reach Kyleakin. Breathing quickly now, her ears straining for the sound of her father's heavy tread, Rhona rolled up the map and started rifling through the vase for one of the mainland.

Malcolm MacLeod was slow in the mornings. He rose late these days and tended to linger over his bannocks. However, his unexpected appearance at dawn in the training yard warned her not to grow complacent where her father was concerned. He was growing old and fat, but he had a mind like a whetted blade. The man missed little.

It took some searching, but at last, she found a small scroll that showed the western seaboard of the mainland, and Argyle. There, perched on the coast, was Gylen Castle.

Stuffing both scrolls up the sleeve of her kirtle, Rhona strode to the door of the solar and slowly opened it, peering out into the corridor beyond.

All clear.

Stepping out, she glanced left and right before hurrying toward the steps that led to the bower she shared with Adaira. She'd hidden a satchel under the bed with the provisions she'd gotten earlier from the kitchens. The satchel also contained her slingshot. Her father, who had taken her hunting with him when she was a child, had taught her how to use it, although these days she was likely a bit rusty. Hopefully, she'd be able to forage and hunt along the way.

Rhona had nearly reached the stairs when a tall, broad-shouldered figure stepped out of the shadows.

Swallowing a cry of fright, Rhona stopped. "Taran," she gasped, "ye gave me a fright."

"Apologies, Lady Rhona." Taran regarded her a long moment before his brow furrowed. "Ye are flushed. Is something amiss?"

Rhona shook her head and favored him with a bright smile. She'd forgotten that her father's right hand often patrolled the hallways of the keep. "I'm perfectly well, thank ye. I've just come back from a walk in the bailey."

His frown deepened. "But ye have come from the wrong direction," he pointed out.

Braving his ice-blue stare, she raised her chin. At times like these, she forgot that Taran MacKinnon had defied her father in order to train her. 'MacLeod's Hound' indeed. The suspicion in his gaze made her already fast pulse accelerate. "I visited the library too," she informed him, "… not that I need to explain myself to ye."

She was being rude, yet she couldn't let him question her further. She had to get away from Taran before he noted how she clutched the hem of her sleeve in her palm. He would know then that she'd stolen something.

Without another word, she brushed past him and hurried, stiff-backed, up the stairs. Taran let her go, although she felt the weight of his gaze between her shoulder blades until she disappeared from sight.

Chapter Nine

A Visit to Market

RHONA SWUNG UP onto the saddle and readied herself to move out.

Adjusting her skirts, she glanced down at the outfit she'd chosen for today. Preparing for departure had been tricky. It was difficult to bring anything extra with her without raising suspicion. She'd dressed carefully in a brown kirtle that was hard-wearing and good for travel. Underneath her skirts, she wore woolen leggings, essential for the long ride ahead—otherwise, the saddle would chafe her.

Nervousness thrummed through Rhona this morning. She'd hardly been able to sleep over the previous two nights as she planned her escape meticulously, going over each stage of it again and again.

Dunvegan's monthly market couldn't have come at a better time.

Rhona hadn't wanted to involve Adaira in her escape, but in the end, she realized her sister would provide the perfect cover for her. If she rode out on a hunt, her father's men would have to accompany her. It would make it much harder to slip away. Adaira, who would suspect nothing until it was too late, would be easier to fool.

Her sister had needed little convincing to attend the market. Usually, she went on her own as Rhona preferred not to spend her pennies on frivolities. But today, she was delighted to have a companion.

Adaira led her pony, a shaggy bay gelding named Bramble, out of the stables, before she glanced at Rhona. "Why are ye bringing a cloak for?" she asked, her attention shifting to the mantle that was bundled up behind the saddle. "It's a warm morning."

"Ye never know what the weather has in store on this isle," Rhona quipped with a smile. "It may get cold later."

Adaira shrugged. "It's not like ye to care about such things." Her sister then turned back to her pony, tightening its girth.

Rhona let out a slow breath, glad her sister had let the matter drop. She'd hidden the carefully wrapped parcel of food inside the cloak. It was the only way she could carry her supplies without raising suspicion. Like Adaira, she carried a leather satchel across her front. But unlike her sister's satchel, which would be empty save the last of her pennies, Rhona's contained her purse of pennies, her slingshot, and the maps she'd taken from her father's solar.

Finally, Adaira mounted her pony, and they were off. In contrast to Adaira's stocky mount, Rhona rode a fiery chestnut mare, Lasair. The horse's name meant 'Flame', in honor of her mistress's temperament. The stable master had questioned Rhona's choice when she'd picked the mare out three years earlier, but Lasair had proved to be her equal when it came to independence and spirit.

She hadn't taken Lasair out for a few days, and the mare was full of unspent energy this morning, jogging her way out of the Sea-gate and down the winding causeway. Rhona felt the solid weight of the curtain wall rising above her as Lasair pranced and snorted, yet she didn't look back. This was supposed to be an ordinary morning's outing, and she had to behave normally.

Even so, it was hard to contain her excitement and nervousness.

A warm wind gusted in from the south and wispy clouds scattered across a hard blue sky. Adaira was right; it was a lovely morning—too warm for a cloak. It was high summer now, and the slow journey toward the harvest had begun.

The village of Dunvegan sat a short ride from the castle, on the southern edge of the loch, and every month it held a merchant's market. Traders from all corners of the isle converged there just before each full moon, bringing cloth, jewelry, ornaments, pottery, and toiletries to sell.

The road to Dunvegan village was narrow and rutted, hugging the edge of the glittering lock. Sun-browned hills rose either side, bare of vegetation save for the flush of green around the castle. Brambles grew at the road's edge, where berries had just started to form. The warm air was heavy with the brine scent of the loch and the aroma of heather. Rhona breathed the familiar smells in deeply and attempted to settle the fluttering moths in her belly. She was so nervous now that she could feel the steady tattoo of her heart against her breast bone. Her palms, which gripped the reins, were slippery with sweat.

The waiting was torture. She'd be relieved when she was finally on her way—galloping south to freedom.

"I'm glad the sun's out," Adaira sighed. "Last month it rained so heavily they all had to pack up early."

Rhona glanced sideways at her sister. Adaira's long brown hair was loose this morning, and it blew around her face. She wore a wide, excited smile, her hazel eyes scanning the road ahead.

Rhona's chest constricted. How she would miss her sister's smile.

Bramble plodded faithfully. The pony was the quietest of Malcolm MacLeod's stable. Their father had gifted him to Adaira on her thirteenth birthday, and she'd fallen in love with him on sight. Adaira was a keen rider and took Bramble out most days. She often grew restless in winter when bad weather prevented their rides.

Rhona's mare tossed her head, impatient for a run. She then gave a playful buck.

"Lasair's full of herself today," Adaira commented. "Did they give her oats for supper last night?"

"She's just telling me off for not taking her out more often," Rhona replied, urging the mare forward. The truth was that Lasair sensed her rider was on edge this morning. She knew Rhona wanted to flee.

Adaira grinned at that, and the pressure in Rhona's chest increased.

How would her sister fare without her? Would she be angry, feel abandoned?

"Adaira," she said quietly. "Ye must be wary of men ... please promise me ye will."

Adaira's smile slipped. "Stop fussing ... not all men are like Baltair MacDonald."

"Some are worse."

"Stop it, Rhona. Ye are just trying to scare me. None of the warriors in the keep would dare behave in such a way."

Rhona inhaled deeply. Sometimes, her sister's innocence truly worried her. "Many of them watch ye," she replied. "I've seen them in the Great Hall. They know it'll be yer turn to wed soon. Men like Dughall MacLean will approach ye."

Adaira shuddered. "I don't like him."

Relief flowed through Rhona. Finally, some sense. "Aye, and ye are right not to."

Adaira's brow furrowed. "Why? What has he done?"

Rhona met her eye. "A couple of weeks ago he was taking a walk with me in the garden and proposed. When I rejected him, he grew angry and grabbed hold of me."

Adaira gasped.

"Taran stepped in," Rhona continued. "If he hadn't things might have gotten ... difficult."

Adaira's expression softened in relief before her eyes then clouded. "I just want to wed for love," she said quietly. "Why is Da so keen to sell us off like fattened sows?"

"An unwed daughter is a burden," Rhona replied, bitterness lacing her voice. "We are useful only in marriage, for we can unite families or gain land for our clan."

Adaira pondered this a moment before she answered. "Caitrin is unhappy," she said softly.

"Aye." Rhona turned her gaze to the road ahead so Adaira wouldn't see her own despair. "And if we're not careful, we'll suffer the same fate."

Silence fell between them then, the mood turning somber.

Rhona's vision misted. This was potentially the last time she'd ever see her sister. She didn't want Adaira's memory of her to be tainted with sadness. Grief sat like a heavy stone in her belly as the full realization of the situation sank in. Unless Adaira one day visited her upon the mainland, they'd be estranged forever.

Rhona swallowed. *Stop it*, she chastised herself. *Don't think on it ... if ye do, ye won't go.*

A short while later, the sisters rode into Dunvegan village. A sprawl of low-slung stone houses with thatched roofs, the village spread out along the loch side. Softly curved hills stretched south of the village, while Loch Dunvegan stretched north. The prevailing winds on this side of the isle meant that there was little in the way of trees and shrubbery here. Rhona would have little cover as she rode south. She was grateful Lasair was full of energy this morning—she'd need it.

The Stag's Head Inn lay at the heart of the village, with a view out across the loch. Behind it stretched a wide space where the merchants and traders had set up their stalls. Excited voices reached the sisters as they drew up in front of the inn. A large crowd filled the market square. The sight pleased Rhona; it would make slipping away all the easier.

They stabled their horses at the inn. After a morning exploring the market, the plan was that they would enjoy a meal at The Stag's Head before riding home. A meal at the inn was a ritual that Caitrin had once shared with them. The Stag's Head was famed for its mutton stew and oat dumplings.

However, Rhona would not be dining at the inn today.

She followed Adaira as she virtually skipped her way out of the stables and into the market. Her sister squealed in delight as the scent of rose and lavender wafted over them. "The soap man is here!"

Despite her tension and distracted thoughts, Rhona found herself smiling. Usually, they made do with coarse blocks of lye at home. Yet occasionally a soap merchant crossed from the mainland, bearing heavenly scented, colored blocks, as well as perfumed oils and lotions.

Adaira was now heading straight for him.

Rhona followed her to the stall, where Adaira set about sniffing each tablet of soap she picked up. In the end, they were too tempting.

"Good morning Lady Adaira ... Lady Rhona." The soap merchant beamed at them. All the vendors here knew MacLeod's daughters on sight; it was impossible for them to be anonymous in this crowd. The clan-chief's daughters were well-loved in the village. Folk didn't hide their delight to see them.

"Good morn, Artair," Adaira greeted the man with a bright smile. "Where are yer wife and daughter today?"

"Visiting my wife's sister," he replied, his broad face flushing with pleasure. "She's having her third bairn."

Rhona found herself smiling, listening as Adaira started chatting to the merchant. She was entirely too familiar with him; Una would have reprimanded her for it. And yet that was what made Adaira so special. Her warmth, her ability to treat everyone—from the high to the low—with genuine attention.

"I'm getting the milk and honey tablet for myself," Adaira announced. She then pointed to the dusky-pink block to her left. "Go on ... get yerself some rose soap."

Rhona sighed. "I don't need any scented soap at present."

"Who said anything about ye 'needing' it?" Adaira favored her with a wry look. "Every woman needs a sweet-smelling soap ... isn't that right, Artair?"

"Aye, Lady Adaira," he replied, giving her an indulgent smile. "The rose soap is our best seller."

Rhona huffed. She could see she was outnumbered here. She handed over the penny, took the soap, and slipped the scented block into her satchel. It would be something to remember her sister by.

Grief slammed into her anew.

Don't think about it.

"Good day, Artair," Adaira sang out. She cast another smile in the soap merchant's direction. The man was still beaming at her like a moon-calf.

Oblivious to her sister's turmoil, Adaira linked her arm through Rhona's. "Come, let's take a look at those silks!"

The young women wove their way through the sea of men and women who, like them, browsed the market. The sun warmed their backs, and the aroma of baking bannocks filled the air. An elderly woman was cooking the flat cakes over a griddle and selling them to the hungry crowd. Her name was Eva. No one knew just how old she was, although judging from the web of wrinkles that creased the crone's face, she was easily the oldest person Rhona had ever seen.

"Lady Rhona," the crone called out with a toothless smile. "How about one of Skye's finest oat-cakes?"

Rhona smiled back, before shaking her head. "Maybe later, Eva. I must save my appetite for a bowl of stew at the inn."

Continuing through the crowd, Rhona took in her surroundings. She noted the details she'd often taken for granted: the rosy cheeks of the women, the warm burr of men's voices, and the smiles of the folk who greeted them.

The vise crushed Rhona's ribcage now as the full realization of what she was about to do sank in.

She would leave all of this behind.

The sisters reached the cloth merchant's stall, where a pyramid of brightly colored bolts of fabric rose up before them. Adaira fell upon them, gaze gleaming.

"This green silk is beautiful," Adaira gasped. Rhona tore her gaze away from the milling crowd to see that her sister was holding a bolt of glimmering fabric up to the light. "Look, Rhona ... we could use this for yer wedding gown."

Cold washed over Rhona, obliterating the sadness she was feeling at leaving this place, these people.

Wedding gown.

Just two words, and yet they struck dread into her heart. She had to get away from here before it was too late.

Chapter Ten

Racing South

"ADAIRA ... I NEED the privy," Rhona whispered into her sister's ear. "I should have gone before we left the castle. I'll return to the inn and be back soon."

Adaira glanced up, from where she was admiring a delicate woolen shawl, her gaze distracted. "Of course. I'll still be here ... come find me."

Rhona nodded, forcing a smile. "Don't spend all yer pennies."

Adaira laughed. "I'll try not to. Go on then ... off ye go."

Rhona turned and wove her way back through the milling crowd toward The Stag's Head Inn. Her eyes stung, but she drew in a steadying breath, forcing back the welling tears. It was an effort not to look back, not to take one last look at her sister. Yet she forced herself not to. If Adaira caught her gazing at her, all teary-eyed, she'd know something was amiss.

I could take her with me. The thought niggled at her, not for the first time over the past days, but Rhona dismissed it. What she was doing was dangerous. She'd risk her own neck, and her own reputation, but she wouldn't put Adaira through it. Not only that, but she wasn't sure Adaira would go with her meekly either. Her sister wasn't desperate like Rhona was—not yet anyway.

She continued her path through the crowd. It was difficult not to hurry when every fiber of her being now urged her to run. She needed to be many leagues from here by nightfall.

Rhona focused her thoughts on what lay ahead, not what she was leaving behind. She knew that if she dwelled upon Adaira any longer, she would falter. She needed to remind herself why she was doing this.

The games loomed upon the horizon like an approaching storm. She would not suffer being wed to a man she didn't want. She wouldn't suffer being wed at all.

Rhona set her jaw and marched into the stables behind the inn. Today was the start of a new life, one where she'd carve her own destiny.

Her mare whickered as Rhona approached the stall. Murmuring gently to Lasair, she saddled her before leading her through the yard and out the front to the loch side, avoiding the busy market and her sister.

Beyond she heard the chatter of voices, as the market got busier still. Adaira wouldn't miss her for a while yet, not while a sea of colorful fabrics and baubles tempted her.

Upon the loch shore, Rhona sprang up onto Lasair's back and urged the mare into a brisk trot. They skirted the southern edge of the loch, leaving the village behind, and then Rhona guided her left. They crossed the road before Lasair broke into a bouncy canter.

The first of a series of rolling hills that stretched south rose before her, and the wind fanned her cheeks. A smile split Rhona's face. She crouched low over the saddle and gave the mare her head.

"Foolish wench!" Malcolm MacLeod roared, spittle flying. "Surely ye must have seen which way she went?"

"No, Da." Tears streamed down Adaira's face. She stood before the chieftain in his solar, trembling in the face of his rage. "I'm sorry, but I didn't ... the market was busy and I—"

"Silence!" MacLeod shifted his gaze past his daughter's shaking form, to where Taran stood silently by the door. "Why weren't ye with them, MacKinnon?"

Taran stiffened at the accusation. "The lasses always go to the Dunvegan market without an escort, Chief," he growled back. "Ye agreed to that years ago."

It was a rare day that Taran challenged MacLeod, yet he wasn't about to let himself be blamed for this. The news that Rhona had disappeared felt like a punch to the gut. Taran's hands clenched by his sides. There wasn't any point in laying blame.

MacLeod glared at him, his bearded face thunderous. "Ride after Rhona," he snarled.

"What if someone has taken her?" Adaira gasped, daring to interrupt her father. "She might not have run away. She might be hurt."

Taran's belly clenched at these words, although they had little effect on MacLeod. He continued to hold Taran's gaze. "Then, I'll have the culprit dragged back here and gelded," he growled. "Track her down, MacKinnon, and bring her home."

Taran nodded. "Shall I gather men to ride with me?"

MacLeod shook his head. "There's no time ... and I don't want anyone else to know she's missing. News of this mustn't leave this chamber ... not with the games so close." He shifted a gimlet stare to his daughter. "If anyone asks, Rhona has a fever and is in her bed-chamber. Is that clear?"

Adaira nodded, her tear-streaked face pale and strained.

MacLeod looked at Taran once more. "Find her," he rumbled, "and don't return here until ye do."

Taran gave a brusque nod, turned on his heel, and marched from the solar. Descending the stairwell to the ground level of the keep, he strode out into the bailey and headed for the stables. There, he swiftly saddled Tussock, his rangy bay gelding. The stables were busy this morning, with men, dogs, and horses everywhere. But Taran spoke to no one as he prepared to ride out, his gaze firmly fixed upon his task.

"Where are ye off to?" Connel Buchanan, who'd just returned from a deer hunt bellowed to Taran when he led his horse out into the yard.

"Out on an errand for MacLeod," Taran called back. He took care to keep his tone nonchalant, with the bored edge the other men were used to hearing from him.

Connel's eyes gleamed with curiosity at this. "Why's that?"

Taran ignored him. Connel was as nosy as he was loud; he'd be the last man Taran would confide in. MacLeod had been clear: no one was to know of Rhona's disappearance.

He left the keep at a slow trot, making his way down the narrow winding path from the Sea-gate to the rutted road below. It was only when he was a good distance from the castle that he urged Tussock into a canter. It wouldn't do to be seen racing away from Dunvegan at a flat gallop—it would only set tongues wagging.

Reaching the nearby village, where the market was now finishing up for the day, Taran drew his gelding up and let his gaze sweep from west to east. Adaira had not seen what direction her sister had left in, so it was up to him to track her down.

Firstly he rode into the village, where he discreetly asked some of the folk he encountered if they had seen MacLeod's fire-haired daughter this afternoon. None had. He then went to The Stag's Head. The inn-keeper hadn't seen her, but one of the stable lads had.

"I saw Lady Rhona lead her horse out of here mid-morning," the lad admitted, putting down the pitch-fork he'd been using to muck out one of the stalls. "I didn't see which way she went though."

Taran frowned as he considered the possibilities.

Clearly, Rhona hadn't been abducted. So where had she gone?

Rhona could have gone to Duntulm, but that would be foolish, for her sister couldn't shelter her, and Baltair MacDonald would merely send her home. To his knowledge, Rhona had no other connections upon the isle. Yet, he knew she had kin on the mainland. Lady Martha had hailed from Argyle.

If he'd been Rhona, he'd ride south to Kyleakin and find passage across the water.

It was a bold move, but Rhona wasn't like other maids. She was a strong rider, and with his tuition over the years could handle herself with a knife, sword, and her hands. She was also stout-hearted and not easily daunted. Even so, it wasn't a safe journey for a woman alone. Desperation had made her reckless, foolish.

Taran thanked the lad and swung up onto Tussock's back. Leaving the inn, he urged the horse into a canter, skirted the village, and headed up the first rise south. He'd have to ride hard to catch Rhona up, for she traveled upon a leggy chestnut mare that could outrun most of the horses in MacLeod's stable. Still, what Tussock lacked in speed, he made up for in endurance.

If he kept up an even pace, he'd catch Rhona before she reached the coast.

Lasair raced south, her hooves flying over the dry grass and heather strewn over the ground. The mare had a thirst for adventure and was enjoying being out in open country, galloping free and unchecked.

As the day wore on, the landscape around Rhona changed. Mountains rose against the eastern horizon, bare-backed ridges with thick forest nestled between them where deer roamed. To the south thrust a wall of carven grey peaks: the Black Cuillins. Sloping charcoal sides ran down to the dry hills below, the mountain range's sharp outline etched against the sky. Rhona skirted the base of the mountains, riding southeast now. To the south of these mighty mountains lay the Lochans of the Fair Folk, a collection of pools said to be blessed by the Fae. She'd visited the spot twice, once for a gathering of the MacLeod kin, and the second time for her father's handfasting to Una. They had been wed next to one of the waterfalls.

Rhona would have liked to visit the lochans again, but it would mean a detour, and she had no time for that. Instead, she pressed on southeast, stopping twice briefly during the afternoon to rest and water Lasair.

By the time the light started to fade, Rhona's belly felt hollow with hunger. She'd been so nervous that morning, she'd been unable to stomach more than a mouthful of bannock. The anxiety had fled now she was on her way, and she was ravenous.

Yet she didn't stop. She didn't dare. She needed to get as much distance between her and Dunvegan as possible before nightfall.

Dusk settled, stretching rosy fingers across the western sky. The shadow of the Black Cuillins now behind her, Rhona pressed on. She slowed Lasair to a gentle trot and moved through the gloaming until a cloak of darkness settled over the world, making it impossible to travel any farther.

At that point, she drew Lasair to a halt and made camp for the night. Securing the mare on a long tether to a boulder so that the horse could graze, Rhona settled herself on the ground on the opposite side of the boulder. She leaned against the rock, still warmed from the sun, and unwrapped her precious parcel of food. She was hungry enough to devour the lot, yet she stopped herself after two oat-cakes and an apple. She needed to be careful, although she'd hopefully be able to buy more food at Kyleakin.

Finishing her light supper, Rhona brushed crumbs off her kirtle and gazed up at the night sky where, one by one, the stars were twinkling into existence like tiny jewels against the inky void beyond. She was lucky, for the night was a mild one. She didn't even need to wrap herself up in her cloak, so instead, she bundled it up and used it as a pillow.

Rhona yawned loudly, letting tiredness settle upon her like a warm blanket. For the first time since leaving Dunvegan, she allowed herself to dwell on what she'd left behind. She imagined Adaira's stricken face when she realized what Rhona had done, and their father's rage. She actually shuddered at the thought. Rhona was afraid of her father. He didn't suffer disobedience in his hounds, his men, or his women.

Rhona only hoped that Adaira had escaped his wrath.

She slept lightly that night, dozing only as the hours stretched by. It was an isolated area, far from any villages or farms, and so she passed the night undisturbed. However, as soon as the first blush of the approaching dawn light illuminated the sky, Rhona was up once more. She would not lose the advantage she had gained the day before.

Rhona had left Lasair saddled overnight, with her girth loosened so she'd be comfortable. As such it took only a few moments preparation and the pair of them were cantering south once more into a misty dawn. As she rode, Rhona was surprised to find a smile creeping over her face. She wasn't out of danger yet, and still felt upset at leaving Adaira, but the sense of freedom she felt this morning made her feel as if she'd just been reborn.

This is who I truly am, she thought. *Who I was born to be.*

Chapter Eleven

The Way of the World

ALTHOUGH RHONA PUSHED Lasair as hard as she dared, they didn't manage to reach Kyleakin by the end of the day. They were close, she knew it, but the coastal village was still out of sight as the last of the sun drained from the sky, casting the world into darkness once more.

Letting out a sharp huff of annoyance, Rhona drew the mare to a halt in a wooded valley. After riding south of the Black Cuillins, her journey had taken her sharply southeast, through the mountainous landscape that had slowed her journey somewhat. Huge peaks had risen overhead, making Rhona feel impossibly small. It was a wild, lonely part of the isle, and Rhona had passed no one on her travels—something she was grateful for.

At a certain point on her journey, she spied the peaked roof of a great building in the distance: Kilbride Abbey, Skye's only convent. Rhona had drawn Lasair up a moment, her gaze narrowing as she viewed the stone bulk rising against the western sky. She must be in the heart of MacKinnon territory now if she could see the abbey.

Could she save herself a trip to the mainland and find sanctuary there?

Rhona's mouth twisted. No—the life of a nun wasn't for her. Besides, her father would merely travel to Kilbride and drag her home by the hair.

The only way she'd escape her fate was to leave this isle for good.

Rhona had urged Lasair on once more, turning the mare inland. She'd consulted her father's map of Skye numerous times on the journey and decided that this was a faster route than riding south and skirting the coast. Even so, the hilly terrain slowed Lasair down.

As dusk approached, they left the most rugged land behind them, riding across craggy heather moor interspersed by valleys where hazel, birch, and hawthorn grew in untidy clumps.

There was a burn at the bottom of this valley, where Rhona stopped for the night. Clear water trickled across peaty soil. Rhona knelt at its banks and splashed water on her face before filling her water bladder and drinking deeply. The light had almost drained from the sky now; it was a deep purple against the silhouette of the birch trees surrounding her. The twitter of roosting birds serenaded her, and the silver glow of the waxing moon had appeared in the sky.

Rhona loosed a tired breath. The distance she'd traveled today hadn't seemed great when she looked at her map. She'd been so sure she'd reach Kyleakin by nightfall.

Tonight, she unsaddled Lasair properly and rubbed her down with a twist of grass, for the horse had worked hard over the past two days. Lasair huffed a breath into her hair when she'd done, and Rhona favored her with a weary smile. "Just a wee bit longer, lass ... ye have done well."

Rhona lowered herself onto the ground, a few yards away from where she'd tethered her horse, under the sheltering boughs of a birch. Her backside and thighs ached tonight as she was unused to spending so long in the saddle. This evening a little of the shine had gone out of her adventure. Even so, she had no regrets about leaving; she was just anxious to reach the coast, before her father's men caught up with her.

He would have sent a party to find her and drag her back to Dunvegan—and she knew it was always easier being the hunter rather than the quarry. Some of her father's men were skilled hunters and trackers. She just hoped they didn't travel at night, or she'd never make it to the coast.

Rhona frowned, irritated by the worries that plagued her. Of course they didn't travel at night. They weren't wolves or owls. Just like her, they would need to rest their horses.

Even so, she was on edge this evening. To distract herself from her thoughts, she opened her package of food. Only two oat-cakes and a small wedge of cheese remained. She'd eaten more than she'd planned on the journey and had hoped to be having supper in a tavern in Kyleakin tonight.

Rhona sighed. After a day out riding in the fresh air, she was starving. She didn't want to finish her remaining food, but she knew she would need to. She'd just have to resupply as soon as she reached the coast in the morning, or try her luck with the slingshot if she got desperate.

Leaning back against the rough trunk of the birch, she started to nibble on an oat-cake.

It was then she felt the hair on the back of her arms prickle.

Rhona swallowed her mouthful of food and put the oat-cake down, her heart fluttering against her ribs. She glanced around her, squinting to make out the details of her surroundings in the gloaming. Beside her, Lasair snorted, suddenly restless.

Rhona's pulse quickened further.

Although she couldn't see anyone, her instincts—and her horse—warned her that someone was nearby, watching her from the shadows.

Slowly, Rhona reached into her satchel and withdrew a knife. It had a long sharp blade, a knife that cook used for boning fowl. Rhona had taken it from the kitchens when Greer and Fiona's attention had been elsewhere. She gripped the bone hilt tightly and held the knife close to her waist as she rose to a squat and surveyed her surroundings.

"I know ye are there." Her voice sounded surprisingly fearless, even though her heart now hammered. "Stop lurking in the shadows, and step out where I can see ye."

A long silence followed, and then a few yards away the shadows shifted, and a tall, broad shape stepped out from behind a birch.

Rhona's breathing caught. She knew him.

Even in the half-light, with only his silhouette visible, she recognized Taran MacKinnon's bulk. Few men in Dunvegan had such broad shoulders or walked with such predatory stealth.

"Taran," she choked out his name, rising to her feet. Relief washed over her that it was him and not Dughall MacLean who stalked her. Even so, he was not a welcome sight. "Ye nearly made my heart stop."

"Apologies, Lady Rhona." His voice, gravelly and low, filled the dusk hush. "I didn't mean to scare ye."

Rhona frowned, peering at him. "And where are the others?"

"I'm alone. Yer father sent me to bring ye home."

Alone. The news surprised Rhona as much as it pleased her. "I'm not going back to Dunvegan," she replied firmly. "Tell Da ye couldn't find me."

He loosed a gentle sigh. "I can't do that."

"Why not? Just tell him I traveled too swiftly and crossed to the mainland before ye could catch me."

"He told me not to return until I bring ye with me."

Rhona tensed, her fingers flexing upon the knife's hilt. "I'm never going back there. Turn around and leave. Pretend ye never saw me."

She couldn't see his face, but she saw movement and realized he was shaking his head. "I can't do that."

He advanced toward her then, long strides that ate up the distance between them.

"Stop!" She darted to the side, keeping the knife low and close as he'd once shown her. "Get back from me."

Her heart, which had momentarily settled, now beat a frantic tattoo against her ribs. Panic rose within her, and she decided to take a different approach with him. Taran had always been good to her, indulged her even. Maybe she could sway him.

"Don't return to Dunvegan then," she said, her voice low as she backed slowly away from him. "Cross to the mainland with me. I'm sure my uncle would welcome a warrior like ye at his keep."

"I follow yer father," Taran replied. His tone was flat, completely devoid of emotion. "I'll not betray him. He bid me bring ye home, and I will."

"Get away from me, *Beast*," Rhona snarled. Fear pulsed through her now, not of Taran but of having her freedom torn from her when she'd only just tasted it.

She watched him halt, his body stiffening at the insult. Rhona stilled too. She'd heard others name him such at Dunvegan, but she had never called him 'Beast' before. In other circumstances, she'd have felt sorry for it. Yet not now, not when he stood between her and a new life.

She took another, quick, step back from him then, desperate to widen the distance between them. A heartbeat later, her foot caught on a root, and she stumbled. With a cry, Rhona fell backward.

He was on her in an instant.

She never knew such a big man could move so fast.

Rhona tried to fight him off, pushing back against the heavy body that slammed into her, but he was too strong, too fast. Desperate, she drove her knee up, aiming for his cods. During their training, Taran had told her numerous times to strike a man there if attacked. But she couldn't lift her knee as he now leaned his weight over her body, crushing her into the dirt. His hands fastened like iron shackles around her wrists, pinning them to the ground.

"Bastard!" She spat the insult at him. "Let me go!"

"Do ye promise to behave yerself if I do?" His voice was low, and—did she imagine it—tinged with wry amusement.

Fury surged within Rhona, but she swallowed it. "I promise ... just get off me. Ye are crushing my ribs."

He moved then, rolling off Rhona and rising to his feet with a speed that unnerved her. She'd forgotten that Taran MacKinnon could move with frightening swiftness. She should have remembered that, for she'd sparred with him often enough over the years.

A heartbeat later, Taran reached down, took Rhona by the arm, and pulled her to her feet. She was not a frail or tiny woman, and yet he lifted her as if she weighed nothing.

The moment Rhona was on her feet she reacted. As he'd taught her, just days earlier, she twisted, shoved herself against him, and threw her head back. She wanted to head-butt him, break his nose. But, once again, Taran thwarted her.

He grabbed hold of her wrists and yanked them behind her, pressing them into the small of her back.

"That was a half-arsed attempt, Lady Rhona. I hope if someone really intends to do ye harm, ye would do better than that." He then started fastening a cord around her wrists. "Ye have to be ready to hurt yer attacker," he chided. "That move wouldn't have fought off even old Niall, the rat-catcher."

Rhona let forth a string of gutter curses—words she'd personally never uttered to anyone before. None were insults befitting a high-born young lady. "Ye have no right to tie me up like a hog," she gasped at the end of the rant.

"Ye made me a promise," Taran replied, completely unruffled by her venom, "and ye broke it. I'll not trust yer word again."

Rhona fell silent, shocked that a warrior who had indulged her, even gone against her father's wishes in order to train her, was so unyielding now. She realized then that he wouldn't be moved. No amount of yelling, cursing, or threatening would change his mind.

I'm going home.

Tears welled in Rhona's eyes. She couldn't bear it. He was taking her back to Dunvegan.

"Ye don't understand, Taran." She choked out the words, letting her despair show. "I want to choose my own husband. Who knows what man will win the games? I could end up wedded to a brute."

"I'm sorry for ye, Lady Rhona." Taran took her by the arm and guided her back to the tree where she'd been sheltering before his arrival. There he gently pushed her down into a sitting position. "But ye cannot run away like this. It won't change anything. Ye will only make MacLeod angry."

Rhona's mouth twisted. "And what would ye have me do instead?"

Taran didn't answer that. Instead, he moved over to a nearby tree and settled down. Although she couldn't see his face, Rhona could just make out the gleam of his eyes as he watched her.

Silence stretched between them for a while, broken only by the hoot of a distant owl, before Taran spoke again. "It's not an easy fate," he began quietly, "to be a clan-chief's daughter. Did ye ever consider taking the veil? You could go to Kilbride?"

Rhona huffed. "How long do ye think I'd last before the abbess cast me out? A day?"

Taran answered with a soft snort. "A week ... at least."

Chapter Twelve
Nothing Good

AS SOON AS the first rays of sun spilled over the edge of the mountains to the east, Taran packed up camp, and they made for home.

In daylight, Taran MacKinnon's face was as inscrutable as his voice had been in darkness. If anything, the long night had given Taran a hard edge. He was taciturn as he prepared the horses, his scarred face cold. He said little to Rhona, other than issue instructions, and she answered him with sullen grunts. Rhona hadn't slept overnight. She couldn't—not when she'd just had her freedom stolen from her. Instead, her thoughts circled incessantly as she dwelt on her fate.

Taran set off northwest upon his stocky bay gelding, Tussock, leading Lasair on a tether. Rhona's hands were bound before her as she rode. A cloak of despair settled over her; they were headed back the way she'd come.

All that risk, all that urgency. For nothing.

A warm, overcast day greeted them, with no refreshing breeze to fan their faces as they rode. The horses sweated, their long tails switching at the clouds of midges that plagued them. The mugginess grew as the morning drew out, and by the time they stopped at noon, sweat drenched Rhona's back. The midges had tormented her all morning, and with her hands bound she hadn't been able to swat them away from her face. She felt as if she'd breathed them in, as if they'd burrowed up her nostrils and into her hair.

As they traveled, a large red mountain rose to the northwest, its outline hazy, for the landmark was still some way off. That was Beinn na Caillich, or 'The Hill of the Hag' as many knew it. Dread twisted in Rhona's belly at the sight of the mountain. They'd traveled farther than she'd realized this morning. This time tomorrow she'd be back in Dunvegan.

At noon they stopped for a short spell. Taran tried to feed her some bread and cheese, for Rhona couldn't feed herself with her hands tied. However, she refused the food. She'd been hungry after her frugal supper the night before, but her belly had closed today. The sight of food made her feel ill. Dread robbed her of appetite.

Taran didn't force the issue or comment. Instead, he rose to his feet, brushed crumbs off his braies, and fixed a cool gaze upon Rhona. "Come, lass ... it's time to move on."

Rhona scowled at him, not bothering to move. She felt as if she'd only just sat down. She was weary, body and soul.

"Lady Rhona." Taran hunkered down before her. "I know this isn't pleasant for ye ... if I could change things I would."

She met his eye. "I thought we were friends, Taran," she replied softly. "Why would ye do this to me?"

His gaze guttered, a shadow moving in its depths. "This isn't my decision."

Rhona clenched her jaw. She was growing tired of the excuse he kept repeating whenever she challenged him. "Now I know why folk call ye 'MacLeod's Hound'," she growled out. "Ye are as loyal as a dog. Ye have no will of yer own."

He drew back from her at that, a shield raising between them. Taran then rose to his feet, pulling Rhona with him. "Ye waste yer breath insulting me, Lady Rhona," he rumbled. "I've been called far worse than that over the years."

Rhona and Taran spent the rest of the day traveling in silence.

The afternoon pressed on, as humid and smothering as the morning had been. Clouds of midges plagued them the whole way. Rhona blinked and sneezed from the insects.

Taran drew up for the day at the foot of the Black Cuillins, just a few furlongs from where Rhona had camped on her journey south. He brought down a grouse with his slingshot and roasted it over a small fire while, around them, the light slowly faded. Night fell very late this time of year, and the twilights seemed endless. Mercifully, as the air cooled, the midges disappeared. Even so, Rhona's skin itched at the memory of them. How she wished to bathe in a cool creek or loch and wash away the sweat and dirt of the day.

Seated by the fire, her wrists still bound, Rhona watched Taran turn the grouse on a spit. She inhaled the aroma of wafting gamey meat mixed with the pungent scent of burning peat. Her belly growled, aching with hunger. Despite that her insides felt knotted at the thought of returning to Dunvegan, she had to admit that she was hungry.

Hearing the rumbling of her belly, Taran glanced up. "It's almost ready."

Rhona looked away, avoiding his gaze. Self-pity enveloped her. She wasn't one to let despair beat her. But this evening she could see nothing but a bleak future before her.

When the grouse was ready, Taran pulled the steaming meat off the bones and placed a large portion of it on an oiled cloth. He then put it on the ground beside Rhona and untied her wrists.

Her belly betrayed her, growling loudly once more. She wasn't used to missing meals, even if this was the first time all day she'd felt hungry.

Rhona started to pick at her grouse, while Taran returned to his side of the fire and began his supper. As she ate, Rhona found her gaze kept returning to Taran.

The glow of the fire pit between them highlighted the disfiguring scars on the warrior's face. They were old, yet deep—scars that had left thick silver ridges after the healing. His face was grim as he ate. As always, he wore that heavy mail shirt—he hadn't even shed it during the worst of the day's heat. The firelight glinted off the silver rings, illuminating the harsh planes of his face. Unlike a lot of her father's men, he cut his hair very short. It was a style that only added to the austerity of his look.

Glancing up from his meal, Taran's gaze snared hers. "Do I hold a fascination for ye, Lady Rhona?"

Rhona swallowed a mouthful of grouse, heat flaring in her cheeks at being caught staring.

Silence stretched between them before she finally answered. "I'm sorry, Taran," she began hesitantly. Her cheeks warmed further; apologizing didn't come easy to Rhona MacLeod. "About what I said earlier ... I know ye swore an oath when ye arrived at Dunvegan. Ye are bound to my father."

Taran's expression softened a little. "Aye, but that doesn't mean I'm happy about all of this. I hate to see ye suffer."

Rhona inclined her head. "Why did ye come after me alone?"

He pulled a face. "Yer father's orders. He doesn't want anyone to know ye tried to run off."

Rhona huffed a rueful laugh. "He won't be able to hide it."

"He bid Adaira tell everyone ye were taken ill in yer chamber and were not to be disturbed," he replied. "I'm sure there will be tongues wagging upon our return, but since some of the warriors have already arrived to prepare for the games, he wants to keep this quiet."

Taran's words made fear knot itself in the pit of Rhona's belly. Her father would be wrathful; she needed to ready herself for it.

Her supper suddenly felt oily in her belly, and she swallowed the bile that now stung her throat. Across the fire, Taran's grey-blue gaze remained upon her, steady and direct. He too knew what awaited her in Dunvegan.

The rain pattered down, stippling the surface of the loch, when they reached Dunvegan at last. The summer shower had freshened the air and brought out all the smells: the salt of the loch, the sweetness of grass, and the rich scent of warm earth. Thunder rumbled in the distance as slate-grey clouds rolled in from the west.

Lasair side-stepped, snorting nervously at the sound of the approaching storm. Rhona reached forward and soothed her with a stroke to the neck. Shortly before arriving at Dunvegan village, Taran removed the restraints from her wrists. It would look suspicious if he brought her home a captive.

Following the loch-side road north, the two riders didn't speak. Rhona spared a glance in Taran's direction, noting the sternness of his expression as he stared straight ahead. It was the look of a determined man, one who'd almost completed the task his chief had given him.

They rode up the steep causeway, passing through the Sea-gate and into the bailey. Folk turned to watch them, and Rhona stiffened. It seemed her disappearance wasn't the well-kept secret her father had hoped. It would make his mood all the sourer upon their reunion.

Inside the courtyard, they drew more stares. Unfortunately, Dughall MacLean was one of the warriors to spot them first. He'd been shoeing a horse but straightened up when the two riders clattered into the yard.

"What's this?" he said with a smirk, his gaze raking over Rhona. "Not laid-up with the grippe, after all, are ye?"

"Leave it, MacLean," Taran rumbled, drawing up his horse and swinging down from the saddle.

Dughall's smirk faded, although his eyes remained sharp. "Led ye on a merry dance, did she?"

Despite that Rhona braced herself for the blow, the impact of her father's palm hitting her across the face nearly knocked her off her feet.

"Disobedient, headstrong bitch," Malcolm MacLeod snarled, drawing his arm back once more. "Ye have defied me for the last time."

The second blow threw Rhona back against the wall. Her skull cracked against stone, and her vision swam. Sagging against the cold stone, Rhona raised a hand to her face. Her fingers came away bloody, and she realized her bottom lip was bleeding; one of her father's rings had cut her.

"I gave ye everything, but ye appreciated nothing. Ye humiliate me ... ye shame yerself." His voice was choked, and glancing up, Rhona saw he was standing motionless facing her, his big fists clenching and unclenching. Fear arrowed through her, making it difficult to breathe.

He looked as if he wanted to kill her.

"I'm sorry, Da," she whispered. And she was. Suddenly, all the fight had gone out of her. His rage was a terrible thing to behold, and she only wished to hide from it.

MacLeod glared at her, his eyes narrow, glittering slits. His face had turned the color of raw meat, and a nerve ticked in his cheek.

"Not sorry enough," he growled. "I'm done with ye." He turned his head toward the closed door to the solar. "MacKinnon!"

The door flew open, and Taran strode inside. He abruptly halted, his face pale and taut. He stared at where Rhona leaned against the wall, still cradling her injured mouth. Their gazes met, and she saw his ice-blue eyes turn flinty.

"Take this wench up to the tower room and lock her in. She'll not leave it till the day of the games—is that clear?"

Taran hesitated, a muscle bunching in his jaw. Then he nodded.

"Get on with it then," the clan-chief growled. "I've nothing more to say to her."

Tears welled in Rhona's eyes at the venom in her father's voice. His loathing of her was worse than his rage. She'd have preferred his fists to this cruel dismissal.

"Da ... I—"

"Take her away, MacKinnon. Before I lose what's left of my self-control."

Malcolm MacLeod turned away then and crossed to the window. The shutters were open, although rain was driving inside, wetting the stone sill. Taran stepped close to Rhona, his fingers closing around her upper arm.

"Come," he murmured.

Rhona let Taran lead her out of the solar. Her legs were shaking so much she barely made it. In the hall outside, she wrenched free of his restraining hand and flattened herself against the wall. Her vision swam, and a sob rose up within her. However, she kept it sealed inside, her hand pressing against her injured mouth.

"Lady Rhona," Taran rasped her name. He stepped close, his gaze clouded with worry. "Are ye hurt?"

When she didn't answer, he reached up, his fingers encircling her wrist. Then he gently pulled her hand from her mouth. "Ye are bleeding."

"Aye." The word gusted out of her. The cut to her lip was nothing compared to the rent inside her. "He hates me now, Taran ... I saw it in his eyes."

"No, lass," Taran replied softly. "Ye are his flesh and blood. When his anger cools, he'll remember that."

Rhona shook her head. "No, he won't. I know that look in his eye. It's the same one he gets when he speaks of Morgan Fraser. Ye should have let me leave Skye, Taran. Nothing good can come of this now."

Chapter Thirteen

Locked Away

TARAN SLAMMED HIS fist into the stable wall. Wood splintered, and the horse in the nearby stall snorted. The beast then kicked out with a shod hoof at the partition between them.

Rage pulsed inside Taran as he stood there, ignoring the pain in his clenched knuckles. He'd drawn blood, but he didn't care. He punched the wall again, his fist breaking through into the layer of mud and straw that formed the exterior wall to the stables.

This was a mess, and it was his doing.

The rage twisted into self-loathing. Rhona was right. He was MacLeod's dog. He deserved every bit of her derision and more. The despair, the fear, he'd seen in her eyes when he'd entered the solar still haunted him. She'd said nothing on the journey up to the tower room, and she'd turned her back on him when he'd left, locking the heavy door behind him. He'd stayed in the hall beyond though, for a long while after, unable to leave her. Only when he'd caught the sounds of muffled sobs had he turned and fled to the stables, to vent his rage.

"There ye are." A voice intruded, and Taran turned to find Gordon standing a few feet behind him. His friend's brow was furrowed.

"What?" he rasped, wishing Gordon would leave. He was in no mood for company right now.

Gordon's gaze flicked from Taran to the hole in the wall behind him. "So, it's true then ... Lady Rhona ran off?"

"Aye," Taran growled. "MacLeod bid me fetch her, and so I did."

"She's been punished?"

Taran nodded. "Locked in the tower room until the games."

Gordon heaved a sigh and moved into the stall where Taran stood. "I feared it would come to this. The lass has always been too wild."

Taran raked a hand through his hair, his gaze fixing upon the beams above him as he attempted to master his temper. "Aye, yet it seems a harsh price to pay. She begged me to let her go, Gordon ... but I didn't."

Gordon snorted. "And just as well. MacLeod would flay ye alive."

At that moment Taran didn't care. "I'm a coward."

He lowered his gaze to find Gordon standing before him, frowning. "We both know ye are not. Ye are loyal to the chief."

"Aye, and I was always proud of it … but not anymore."

Gordon inclined his head, his expression sharpening. "If I didn't know better, I'd think ye in love with Lady Rhona."

The dark look Taran gave him in answer made Gordon draw back. A moment later he laughed. "My mistake." He reached forward, clasping Taran by the shoulder. "Come on. Let's get a cup of ale and a hot meal in the Great Hall … ye look like ye need both."

"I'm not hungry."

"Ye will be when ye see what Fiona's prepared for today's nooning meal: venison pie."

Taran couldn't have cared less, yet Gordon's earlier comment about him being in love with Rhona had made him wary. The last thing he wanted was folk thinking that. He couldn't bear their smirks, their whispered comments.

The Beast of Dunvegan is in love.

Gordon wouldn't mock him, but he was one of the few Taran trusted. He needed to regain control. He needed to put the shield back in place and get a leash on his temper. It wouldn't serve him now.

Taran followed Gordon out of the stall, massaging his stinging knuckles as he went. Leaving the stables, the two men crossed the rain-lashed yard. Thunder crashed overhead, and dark purple and black clouds loomed. Shaking off the rain from their clothing, the warriors left the storm behind and entered the cavernous space of the Great Hall. Owing to the weather, folk had come early to the nooning meal. The tables were nearly full, and the toothsome aroma of pie filled the air. At the far end, upon the raised dais, MacLeod and his kin had taken their seats at the chieftain's table.

Rhona was, unsurprisingly, absent. Confined to the tower room, she would no longer join the rest of the keep for meals here.

Gordon and Taran took their seats at the end of one of the long scrubbed wooden tables. It wasn't the place Taran would have chosen to sit, especially not in his current mood, for Connel and Dughall sat opposite. He didn't like the way they both smirked at him.

A servant placed two large pies before Taran and Gordon, while another slammed down frothing tankards of ale. Gordon dug in to his meal, ripping through the buttery pastry shell to the dark meat stew underneath. However, the sight of the food made Taran's belly clench. He was too wound up to be hungry. Instead, he took a long draft of ale.

Around him, men fell upon their pies, the clatter of spoons and the thud of tankards blending with the rumble of their voices. Taran forced himself to start eating, aware that not to do so would raise eyebrows. But each mouthful tasted like ash.

"Why the scowl, Scar-face?" Connel's voice drew Taran out of his brooding. He glanced up to find the straw-haired youth grinning at him. "I hear ye are a hero. Tracked Lady Rhona down and dragged her home. Well done."

Taran didn't answer. Instead, he lifted his tankard to his lips and took a large gulp.

"Aye ... although I find it odd he sent ye out on yer own," Dughall spoke up. The warrior had finished his pie and was watching Taran with a hooded gaze. "How can we be sure the lady's virtue is intact?"

Connel cast Dughall a wry look. "Fear not ... ye can count on The Beast's honor. He'd cut off his own rod rather than sully a highborn woman with it."

Taran clenched his jaw. He then helped himself to another tankard of ale from a passing servant. Once again, he remained silent. Connel and Dughall were baiting him. They wanted to anger him.

Next to him, Gordon gave a snort of derision. "At least he's got a rod," he said to Connel. "That slug in *yer* braies can't be named such."

Gordon's comment caused barks of laughter to erupt around them. But Connel didn't look amused. He favored Gordon with a sour look and was about to respond when Dughall interrupted him.

"I hope ye are right, Buchanan." Dughall's gaze didn't leave Taran as he spoke, the threatening edge to his voice hard to miss. "When I win her hand at the games, I want my lady wife to be a virgin when I take her."

Connel snorted. "Ye are competing against me so I wouldn't be so full of yerself."

Dughall's lip curled, and he gave Connel a look that told him exactly what he thought of that assertion. His attention then returned to Taran. "Fifty warriors have pledged to compete at the games," he said. "Lady Rhona is a prize it seems."

Taran glared back at him before he finally answered. "Aye, she is."

"I can't believe ye ran away. Ye could have taken me with ye!"

Rhona turned from the window to meet her sister's angry glare. She'd been waiting for this confrontation, although with less dread than the one with her father.

"It's just as well that I didn't," she replied. Her cut lip stung as she spoke. "Since ye would be in trouble now too."

Adaira scowled, a rare expression for such a sweet-tempered lass. Her hazel eyes sparkled with unshed tears. "I was so worried." Her voice wobbled slightly. "I thought someone had carried ye off ... had done ye harm."

Rhona stared back at her. She hadn't thought Adaira would come to that conclusion. Her throat constricted, and she swallowed. "I'm sorry. I didn't want to leave without saying anything, but I had to."

Adaira scrubbed at the tears that had escaped and were now cascading down her cheeks. "Da is in a terrible rage."

Rhona suppressed a shudder. "I know."

Adaira's gaze dropped to her sister's swollen lip. "He hit ye?"

Rhona nodded before turning away. She didn't want to talk about it.

The shutters to the tower room were open, revealing a cool afternoon. The sky was still grey, but the storm had spent itself before moving east. The air that drifted in was fresh and clean.

Rhona took the scene in numbly. None of this seemed real. Two days ago she'd been free, riding with the wind in her face toward a future of her own making. Now she was to be confined to this chamber till the games. She could already feel the walls closing in on her.

The soft pad of slippered feet warned her of Adaira's approach. A moment later she felt an arm loop around her waist. Adaira hugged her tight, the strength of her embrace warning Rhona of the emotions her sister held on a tight leash.

"The world is so unfair," her sister whispered. The broken sound of her voice made Rhona's vision blur. "I can't stand to see ye unhappy."

Rhona's mouth twisted at the irony of it. She could stand anything except seeing either of her sisters hurt. The bond between them had always been strong, enough to weather anything—even this.

"Whatever happens, don't let them break ye," Adaira continued, her voice turning vehement. "It's bad enough that Caitrin is like a ghost these days. I don't want to lose ye too. If ye had succeeded in running away, we never would have seen each other again. Was freedom worth that much?"

A tear trickled down Rhona's face. Reaching up, she knuckled it away. She knew Adaira didn't understand why she'd had to flee. "It ripped a hole in my heart," she answered softly, "but aye, it would have been worth it."

Silence stretched between them. The sisters stayed where they were, Adaira clinging to Rhona like a barnacle. Rhona let her, for her sister's embrace brought her comfort.

"What will ye do now?" Adaira asked finally.

"I don't know ... nothing it seems."

"Ye could try to sneak away again ... take me with ye this time. There's that passageway in the dungeon we discovered years ago. We could leave that way."

Rhona shook her head. She'd already considered the hidden passage as a means of escape and dismissed it in favor of taking a horse south to Kyleakin. Rhona, Caitrin, and Adaira had stumbled upon the passageway one summer while exploring the dungeon. Folk at Dunvegan had long talked about the existence of a hidden passageway somewhere in the keep. Once they discovered it, the sisters made a pact to keep its location secret.

Tears flowed, hot and silent, down Rhona's cheeks. "Da will post guards outside my door at night. Even if we got past them, they'd run us down like deer. We wouldn't get far."

"But I want to help."

Rhona took Adaira's hand and squeezed. She didn't deserve such a sweet-natured sister. She'd acted selfishly, and yet Adaira still loved her, still wanted to help her. "Ye are helping," Rhona replied softly. "More than ye realize."

Chapter Fourteen

The Day of the Games

THE DAY OF the games dawned warm and sunny. The weather didn't care if Rhona was miserable, that she'd dreaded each sunset that brought her closer to her fate. The time had sped by—and Rhona awoke to honeyed sunlight filtering through the shutters into her chamber.

A short while later, Liosa brought a platter of food up to her. The handmaid found Rhona swathed in a thick robe, perched on the sill of the open window, knees pulled up under her chin.

"Morning." Liosa favored her with a smile and carried the tray over to the table that sat in the center of the chamber. "Lady Adaira didn't think ye would be hungry, but Fiona insisted."

Rhona's gaze glanced off the fresh bannock, butter, and honey, and the mug of milk that accompanied it. Her belly lurched. "Adaira's right," she replied. "I can't eat."

Rhona remained seated on the window sill while Liosa padded about the room, readying the clothes Rhona would wear for today. They'd already picked out her outfit: an emerald-green kirtle over a dove-grey léine. The kirtle, edged with gold thread, had a low rounded neck and long bell-like sleeves. It was the costliest item of clothing that Rhona owned, and had she not felt so miserable, she'd have enjoyed wearing it.

As it was, she felt like hurling it from the window.

Rhona dressed in silence, while Liosa said little—unusual, for the handmaid was usually full of observations in the morning. Neither of them spoke as Rhona fastened the laces of her kirtle down the front of her bodice.

Outside, the excited chatter of women in the bailey below filtered up. The folk of Dunvegan had been looking forward to this day for weeks; everyone loved games, for it broke up the routine of everyday life and gave servants a break from their chores.

"I've never seen the keep so busy," Liosa said finally. "Men from as far away as Caithness and Lothian have come to compete."

Rhona drew in a deep breath at this news. "How long will the games last?" she asked. In her misery, she hadn't considered the details of what her father was planning.

"Two days. It'll start with a day and a half of strength tests, and then the finalists will wrestle each other for yer hand."

Rhona inhaled once more, trying to ignore the anxiety that twisted inside her belly like a trapped eel. She smoothed her sweaty palms upon the silky material of her kirtle and squared her shoulders. She'd be damned if she'd let anyone see her despair.

"Come on then," she said, turning to Liosa and meeting her eye. "Let's get this over with."

A summer's breeze laced with the scent of crushed grass feathered against Rhona's cheeks. She sat upon the stands before the competition field and waited for the first of the strength games: the tossing of the caber.

Erected out of slabs of pine, the stands rose three tiers high. Much preparation had gone into this day. The MacLeod plaid—a crosshatch of yellow, black, and grey, threaded with red—fluttered from the ring that encircled the competition field.

Excited spectators chattered around Rhona, while crowds of village folk gathered around the perimeter of the field. She sat in-between her father and Adaira, hands folded upon her lap. Since leaving the tower room, no one besides Adaira had spoken to her. Caitrin hadn't come to the games, as her infant son had a fever, although Baltair was here. He sat farther along the bench, laughing over something with the man seated next to him.

Baltair had not greeted Rhona, or even acknowledged her—not something that bothered Rhona. But it stung that her father ignored her. Even Una stared right through her.

It was all part of her punishment. Rhona's fingernails bit into her palms. How she wished she was far from here.

Men, clad only in plaid braies, their naked chests gleaming in the morning sun, walked out onto the field. Rhona's throat closed at the sight of them.

So many ... at least fifty.

Most of the faces she didn't recognize, however, some she did. A blond, grinning young warrior called Connel, and Dughall MacLean. Of course—she'd known he'd compete.

The latter stood at the front of the group, dark blue eyes riveted upon the stands—upon her. Rhona ignored him. *Let him stare,* she thought. *If he wins the games, I'll scratch his eyes out on our wedding night.*

But Connel and Dughall weren't the only faces she recognized in the crowd. Rhona's breathing stilled when she saw a big, broad-shouldered figure with short dark-blond hair and a scarred face standing at the back of the group.

Taran MacKinnon.

Confusion swept over Rhona, muddling her thoughts for a few moments. Connel and Dughall she understood, for both of them had made their interest in her clear.

But Taran?

Betrayal followed swiftly on the heels of confusion. She'd been furious with Taran for dragging her back to Dunvegan, yet she'd believed he'd had some sympathy for her plight. What was he doing competing for her hand?

Rhona clenched her jaw till it ached. She glared at Taran, willing him to meet her gaze, yet he did not. Instead, his ice-blue stare seemed unfocused, as if he was deep in thought.

Beside her, Malcolm MacLeod rose to his feet. The chatter in the stands quietened, and the crowd of warriors waiting below shifted their gazes to the clan-chief.

"Welcome." Her father's voice carried across the field. "For some of ye, Dunvegan is yer home, while for others ye have traveled far to reach us. I greet ye all and thank ye for doing us this honor."

A few of the warriors below cheered at this, while others beamed up at MacLeod. Malcolm then turned to where Rhona sat silently next to him. "Daughter, stand up."

Rhona complied, hands still clasped before her. Dozens of hungry male gazes raked over her. She felt as if they were stripping her clothing from her. Rhona raised her chin, barely suffering the indignity.

"Aye." Her father's voice held a smug note as he continued. "Lady Rhona MacLeod is a fiery beauty. She'll make one of ye a fine bride and bear ye plenty of sons ... but ye will have to fight for her. The motto of this family is 'Hold Fast'. The MacLeods face down our enemies without fear, and we charge toward our destinies. I encourage all of ye to do the same."

A cheer went up, and when it died away, all gazes fixed upon Malcolm MacLeod, awaiting his next words. Tension rose around them, and Rhona saw the excitement in the contestants' eyes, their eager smiles. The sight just made Rhona feel ill.

Her father's command, when it came, fell like an executioner's axe, splitting the silence. "Let the games begin."

The morning was torture. Rhona sat there, silent and tense, watching as one-by-one, the warriors competed at tossing the caber. They heaved a long log off the ground and balanced it vertically, staggering forward before tossing it. The log spun, turning end over end before striking the earth with a dull thud.

Three men succeeded in tossing it farther than the others. Two of them were warriors from the mainland, both sons of clan-chiefs, while the third was Taran MacKinnon.

Rhona watched him toss the caber into the air. She'd seen Taran shirtless before and remembered his sculpted torso.

She wasn't the only one to notice. Two women seated beneath Rhona started to whisper and giggle.

"He may be an ugly brute, but he's got the body of a god," one of them tittered.

"Aye," her companion replied with a smirk. "I'd wager the rest of him is just as big and strong."

Rhona's face flushed at their bawdy language. She glowered down at the women, hating their smugness. It wasn't their fate that was to be decided here.

The Braemar Stone and hammer throw contests came next. Dughall did well in the former. Rhona watched him take his position. He took the large, heavy stone in his hand, and cradled it in the crook of his neck. Dughall's body tensed, his gaze focused on the strip of grass before him. A moment later he tossed the stone from standing, hurling it away from him. A cheer went up in the stands. He'd bested all the warriors who'd gone before him.

Rhona didn't join them.

Grinning, Dughall glanced up into the stands, his attention focusing on Rhona.

"Dughall MacLean looks confident today," Una murmured to her husband.

"Aye," Malcolm grunted, unimpressed. "He's cocky, but let's see if he lasts the distance."

"I can't believe Taran is competing," Adaira whispered to Rhona, her gaze wide as she watched the warrior stride up to take his turn at hurling the Braemar Stone. "I didn't think he was interested in taking a wife."

Rhona frowned, although she had to admit her sister was right. In all the years Taran had served her father, he'd been a lone wolf. Unlike some of the other warriors, who flirted with the servants inside the keep and stole glances at MacLeod's three daughters, he'd seemed oblivious to women.

Of course, that was ridiculous. He was an adult man; he would have needs like any other.

"I don't know what his game is," Rhona muttered, wincing as another bout of cheering rocked the stands—Taran had thrown well. "I can't believe he'd betray me like this."

Adaira turned to her, eyes as big as moons, as something occurred to her. "Do ye think he's in love with ye?"

"What?" Rhona almost snarled the question. Sometimes her sister could be as silly as a goose.

Unfazed, Adaira continued. "Don't look so shocked. It makes sense. Maybe that's why he's never taken a wife."

"Nonsense," Rhona snapped, turning her attention back to the competition. "It makes no sense at all."

By the time the first day of the games was over, Rhona had a terrible headache. Her mother had suffered from such pains, but until today Rhona had not. Her temples pulsed with red-hot agony, and the gilded late afternoon light hurt her eyes as she climbed onto the wagon that would take her back to Dunvegan Keep.

The pain made it difficult to concentrate, to focus. It felt as if an iron band had fastened around her skull and was slowly tightening. The intensity of the pain made Rhona feel giddy and nauseated.

For the first time since returning to Dunvegan, she longed for her cool, dark tower room, where she could shut out the daylight and the world.

The spectators moved on, their voices drifting through the warm air as they returned to their homes, their chores, and preparation for supper. Meanwhile, the contestants filed back to the keep, ready for an evening of drinking, feasting, and entertainment. Rhona had heard that a bard had come with the men from Lothian and would entertain the revelers.

Rhona was relieved she wasn't invited.

Instead, she fled up the steps to her tower room, her head throbbing with every step. Adaira joined her for a spell, and Liosa brought up a tray of supper, before Rhona sent them both away.

"I'll see ye first thing tomorrow morning," she assured her sister, who looked at her with a worried frown and hurt in her eyes. "For now I just need to sleep."

After Adaira and Liosa had gone, Rhona splashed cool water on her face, closed the shutters tight, and stretched out upon her bed. Agony constricted her skull with each breath, and she closed her eyes.

The noise from the rest of the keep, although muffled by thick stone, still reached her: the raucous laughter of men and the shrill, excited voices of women.

Everyone had enjoyed the first day of the games. All except Rhona.

With a groan, she turned over and pressed her aching forehead into the cool pillow. She only wished the pain would carry her away, pull her into oblivion, so that she would not have to suffer another day of this humiliation.

Chapter Fifteen

Decide My Fate

"READY FOR THIS, *Scar-face*?"

Connel Buchanan challenged Taran across the training ring. Two days outside under the hot sun hadn't agreed with Connel's pale skin. His grinning face was pink and shiny, his straw-colored hair tied back at the nape of his neck.

"Aye, I'm ready," Taran replied, not returning the grin. It was getting late in the day and he, like all the others who'd won the strength tests and progressed to the wrestling, was starting to tire. Connel was too, Taran noted. The redness in his cheeks wasn't just due to the sun, and sweat beaded his heavy brow.

The watching crowd had swelled as the day progressed, spectators now jostling around the edge of the wrestling ring. Taran hadn't looked up at the stands for most of the day. Yet he knew Rhona would be there, pale-faced and hollow-eyed next to her father.

"Wrestlers—take yer positions," Aonghus Budge called out from where he stood, legs akimbo at the edge of the ring. Although recently widowed, the clan-chief of the Budges of Islay was too unfit and portly to compete in the games. He'd brought a couple of warriors with him, but neither had gotten further than the strength contests the day before. As such, MacLeod had chosen Budge to oversee the wrestling matches.

Connel and Taran readied themselves. They gripped each other around the waist and the back. Taran rested his chin on Connel's shoulder and readied himself for the bout, gripping his opponent firmly. Connel did the same.

"Hold!" Aonghus's voice boomed across the ring.

The two men slammed into each other with brute force. The aim was simple: Taran had to either get Connel to break his hold or touch the ground with any part of his body save his feet. The best of five bouts won.

Connel was a stocky, heavily-built young man; a physique that had advantaged him during the strength games. However, he wasn't as strong as Taran. His bare feet scrabbled on the grass, his toes digging in, as Taran drove him back.

The contest didn't last long. Connel went down on one knee during the first bout, lost his hold in the second, and collapsed on one side in the third. Chieftain Budge grabbed Taran by the hand and pulled their arms aloft. "The winner!"

Cheers thundered across the field.

Breathing heavily, Taran went over to the ringside, where Gordon waited. His friend passed him a mug of ale. "Here ... ye look like ye could do with this. Although Connel needs it more by the looks of things."

Taran glanced over at where Connel stormed out of the ring, with face like thunder, and huffed out a breath. "Sore loser."

He lifted the mug to his lips and took a deep draft. The surrounding cheering died away, a murmur of anticipation taking its place. The whole day had been leading up to this moment.

The last two competitors left standing. The deciding wrestling match.

Taran's opponent stood on the far side of the ring, watching him.

Dughall MacLean was staring him down, challenging him to meet his glare, but Taran ignored the warrior for the moment.

Let him wait.

"Dughall's good," Gordon advised Taran. "He'll try to take ye down with his feet. Make sure ye are ready for him."

Taran nodded. "Aye ... I've been watching him wrestle," he replied. "I know his tricks."

He glanced north then, for the first time looking to the stands. This was to be the final contest of the games, the one that decided everything. He'd been avoiding looking in Rhona's direction, but he needed to now.

Seated between her father and Adaira, Rhona wore a low-necked green kirtle over a grey léine, clothing that hugged her statuesque form. Her long dark-red hair was loose, spilling over her shoulders, framing a face that had never been more beautiful. Even pale and tense, her full lips compressed, she captivated him.

Her grey eyes met his gaze and held for a long-drawn-out moment. Her skin tightened over her high cheekbones. He didn't need to exchange words with Rhona to know she was furious.

She looked at Taran as if she wanted to grab a pike and gut him.

He didn't blame her, but he didn't regret this either.

He'd been unable to sleep for the first two nights after their arrival back in Dunvegan. He'd wrestled with his conscience, his duty, and his desire—and in the end, his desire had won.

All his life he'd stood aside and let others claim what they wanted. For once he'd make a stand for himself. If he lost to Dughall MacLean, he would be bitter, but at least he would know he'd tried.

Either way, Rhona would hate him. But at least with him, she'd never be mistreated.

"Wrestlers," Aonghus Budge boomed once more, impatience in his voice. "Take yer positions."

Taran tore his gaze from Rhona and passed the empty mug back to Gordon. The warrior met his eye and winked. "I'd wish ye luck, but I know ye have no need of it ... ye never have. Ye have always won out of sheer force of will, and this time will be no different."

Taran's mouth curved into a wry smile. He appreciated Gordon's confidence in him. They'd soon find out if it was warranted.

Rhona twisted her fingers together until the joints hurt.

She was living a dark and terrible dream. Two men—both of whom she knew and neither of whom she wanted—were about to compete for her hand.

Taran MacKinnon and Dughall MacLean.

Either way, she was doomed.

Bile rose, stinging the back of Rhona's throat. Fate was cruel indeed. It was punishing her for her headstrong ways. Of all the warriors who'd competed here over the past days, it had come down to these two.

Hysteria bubbled up within her as she watched the two men grapple with each other, taking up positions.

"Hold!" Aonghus Budge barked.

The warriors slammed together, circling, their bare toes digging into the trampled grass as each tried to over-power the other. The roar of the surrounding crowd was so loud that it broke like thunder over the stand.

Rhona stopped breathing. She watched Dughall hook his left leg around Taran's right. The two men danced right and then left, crablike, and then Taran toppled sideways.

The crowd bayed, and Aonghus Budge grinned. He took hold of Dughall's hand and held it aloft. "The first bout goes to ... Dughall MacLean!"

Rhona swallowed. She felt as if she was going to be sick. Dughall couldn't win this. Fate could not be so cruel.

"This is yer fault, lass." Rhona glanced right to find her father studying her. Malcolm MacLeod's face was unreadable, his gaze shuttered. "Ye had the choice of many men ... but now ye really will end up with one ye don't want."

Rhona stared back at him. Part of her wanted to plead with him, wanted to break down in tears and beg him to stop these games. Yet she knew it would gain her nothing. All she had left was her pride; she wouldn't destroy the only thing that was keeping her rooted to her seat.

Her father blinked and then turned his face away, focusing on the match below.

"Hold!"

Taran and Dughall grappled once more. This bout was fast, edged in violence. The two men spun around each other, clinging in a death-grip. Dughall's leg struck out once more, but Taran danced out of his way. Taran was the bigger and heavier built man of the two, yet Rhona had seen that agility and flexibility almost counted more in a sport like this.

Her chest began to ache as Dughall brought Taran down once more, with a flip that sent his opponent crashing down onto his back.

Rhona muttered a curse under her breath, tore her gaze from the wrestling, and stared down at her hands. This really was happening.

"Do ye want Taran to win?" Adaira asked, her voice barely audible over the roar of the excited crowd. "Ye would prefer him over Dughall?"

Rhona's gaze snapped to where her sister watched her. Adaira's pretty face was pale, her eyes seeming unnaturally big this afternoon.

"I don't want either of them to win," she choked out the words.

"But ye just cursed."

"That's because soon the games will be over … the next bout will decide my fate."

Rhona swung her attention back to the wrestling as the third bout commenced. She hadn't told her sister the truth. She had no desire to be Taran's wife, but she'd choose him over Dughall. Taran was no comely young warrior, but she'd spent enough time in his company to know he wasn't cruel. He wasn't a bully like Dughall.

Sweat glistened off Taran's bare back as the wrestling resumed. His scarred face screwed up in concentration as he fought for dominance. The expression made him look even more frightening than usual. In contrast, a grimace twisted Dughall's handsome face, turning him ugly. He twisted and shoved against his opponent.

Dughall's leg struck out, just as Taran's foot kicked forward and hooked behind Dughall's calf.

Letting out a roar, Dughall lost his balance and lunged sideways.

Cheering erupted as he slammed into the ground.

Wiping the sweat off his forehead with the back of his arm, Taran straightened up. A heartbeat later, Chieftain Budge grabbed his hand and yanked it aloft. "The third bout goes to Taran MacKinnon!"

Rhona watched Dughall spit on the ground and snarl something at Taran. It was too far away for her to make out the words, yet the insult seemed to have little effect on Taran. He merely gave Dughall a cold look while he shrugged out the muscles in his shoulders and waited for Budge to call them forward once more.

The fourth bout seemed to go on for an age. The warriors grappled, their grunts rising into the charged air. Dughall tried to hook his leg around Taran's numerous times, but at each attempt his opponent blocked him.

The bout ended when Taran spun them both around and kicked out at Dughall's ankle. The latter jumped back, lost his balance, and went down on one knee.

Two to two—the contestants were now on equal footing.

"God's bones," Adaira muttered next to Rhona. "I can't bear it."

Rhona clenched her jaw, grinding her teeth. The tension had turned her into a wreck. Sweat coursed down her back and between her breasts, and her heart pounded as if it had been her down there wrestling.

"The final and deciding bout." Aonghus Budge strode into the center of the ring, hands aloft. His ruddy face glowed as his gaze swept the crowd. "Who will win the hand of the lovely Lady Rhona? Contestants ... step forward."

Dughall and Taran did as bid. They stepped up either side of Budge, each taking the chieftain's opposite hand as he raised their arms high. Aonghus grinned at them, his attention shifting from Taran to Dughall. "Make this one count, lads." His voice rang out across the field. "Which one of ye will be lucky enough to tame that wild mare?"

This comment brought laughter and sniggers from the stands and the gathered crowd below. Rhona sucked in an angry breath, noting that although Dughall had grinned at the comment, Taran did not.

The warriors took their positions.

"Hold!"

And so it began.

The cheering was deafening. Around Rhona folk clambered to their feet, bellowing insults or encouragement. In order to see what was going on below, she was forced to stand up. However, her legs nearly gave way under her when she did so. Adaira grabbed her, looping her arm through Rhona's.

"Courage, sister," she murmured. "It's almost over."

Around and around they went, first one way, and then the other. Fast as an eel, Dughall struck, again and again, trying to hook his leg around one of Taran's huge calves. And after half a dozen tries, he managed.

Only this time it didn't end as it usually did.

Taran used his strength to his advantage, heaving Dughall against him. It was a parody of a lover's embrace—and would have looked foolish if there hadn't been so much at stake. They tottered forward a few paces, Dughall struggling and snarling in Taran's arms, and then backward.

A heartbeat later, Taran twisted around and launched the full weight of his body forward, unbalancing them both. Limbs still tangled, the two contestants crashed to the ground like two mighty trees, Dughall crushed beneath Taran.

Chapter Sixteen

Behold

TARAN ROSE TO his feet. He barely noticed the roaring and cheering crowd. Dughall still lay sprawled on the ground, chest heaving. The fall had winded him.

"We have a winner!" Aonghus was suddenly at Taran's side, gripping his hand and holding it high. Did he imagine it, or was there a vindictive gleam in the man's eyes? "Taran MacKinnon has won the Dunvegan Games, and in doing so he has won the hand of Rhona, daughter of Malcolm MacLeod."

The cheering continued, crashing across the arena like waves upon a shingle beach. Dughall rolled onto his side, his gaze seizing Taran's. "Ye fought dirty, Beast."

Taran favored the warrior with a dismissive look. "Aye, but then so did ye."

He looked away from Dughall, ignoring the hate on the man's face, and shifted his attention to the stands. The crowd was in a frenzy; folk applauded and whistled.

Yet amongst it all, Rhona remained as still as a statue carved from granite.

Taran's chest constricted. Her skin was ashen. He hadn't expected to see joy on her face at his victory, in fact, he hadn't let himself think about victory at all. He'd never thought he'd even get this far. Some of the warriors he'd competed against over the past two days had been formidable. And yet here he was.

And there Rhona was, looking as if her life was about to end.

Gordon appeared at his side then and slapped him on the shoulder. His friend was smiling. "Well done. He was a slippery bastard, but I knew ye would get the better of him."

Taran huffed. Exhaustion dragged down at him. His body ached. "Did ye? I wasn't so sure for a while there."

Their gazes held, and Gordon's smile wavered. "Are ye sure this is what ye want?" he asked, his voice almost drowned out by the cheering.

It was Taran's turn to smile, although the expression wasn't a humorous one. "It's too late for regrets," he replied. "I wouldn't have competed if I hadn't wanted to wed Lady Rhona."

Gordon watched him, understanding lighting in his eyes. "Ye kept that secret hidden well," he murmured. "Ye had me convinced of the contrary when I dared suggest ye loved her."

Taran waved him away, breaking eye contact. He didn't want to talk about his feelings for Rhona, or why he'd never confided in Gordon. Truthfully, he was beginning to wonder if he was the world's biggest fool. He'd just won the hand of a woman who would most likely hate him.

Eventually, the surrounding crowd quietened and a tense hush settled over the hillside. A cool breeze fanned in from the loch, feathering across Taran's heated skin as he watched the clan-chief of the MacLeods rise to his feet.

"Come forward, Taran MacKinnon." Malcolm MacLeod's voice boomed down from the stands. There was a harsh edge to it, and Taran realized that despite the chief's calm demeanor, MacLeod was angry.

At him—for winning his daughter's hand.

Taran left Gordon's side and did as his chieftain bid. He walked forward to the edge of the arena, his gaze meeting MacLeod's.

"Congratulations." There was no warmth there. Taran had served MacLeod since his sixteenth winter. His loyalty to the chief was unquestionable. Hence the name 'MacLeod's Hound' that those who'd been jealous of his status at Dunvegan Castle had given him. However, Taran had the sense that all of that was about to change. He'd stepped out of line, reached too far above himself. The clan-chief hadn't stopped him from competing—perhaps believing Taran would never reach the finals—but looking at the man's face now, Taran knew the truth of it.

MacLeod would never trust him again.

"Ye have won my daughter's hand," Malcolm MacLeod continued before inclining his head. "Stand up, Rhona ... so yer intended can look upon ye properly."

Beside MacLeod, Rhona obeyed. Her eyes glittered, and her jaw clenched. Even from yards away, Taran could see the tension quivering in her body. She looked like a deer set to flee.

"Behold the victor." Malcolm MacLeod's lip curled as he spoke. "A fine warrior, indeed. The Beast of Dunvegan has won his beauty."

This comment brought whispers, giggles, and smirks from the watching crowd.

Taran grew still. Never had MacLeod used that name with him. It was a taunt he expected from the likes of Dughall or Connel—not his chief. Malcolm's use of it now only made his resentment of Taran plainer.

Rhona's throat bobbed as she swallowed. But she didn't speak—nor was she expected to.

MacLeod's slate-grey eyes, so like his daughter's, speared Taran. "A warrior who has demonstrated such prowess, such skill, should receive his reward sooner rather than later." His voice dropped to a drawl. "Since we have so many visitors here, we shall not disappoint them ... the pair of ye shall be wed at sundown this evening, and Dunvegan will celebrate yer union with a great feast."

These words brought gasps from the surrounding crowd. Behind Taran, he heard Dughall spit a curse.

Rhona's eyes flew open wide, and she took a step toward MacLeod. She murmured something to her father, her expression panicked.

"Nonsense, lass," MacLeod cut his daughter off, his voice ringing across the stands. "Ye have plenty of fine clothes—choose one of them. Leave the rest of the preparations to the servants." His gaze shifted back to Taran. "Go bathe and make yerself presentable MacKinnon ... for yer bride awaits."

Rhona picked her way down the spiral stone stairwell. In her left hand she held her skirts aloft, while with her right, she steadied her passage. She'd barely eaten all day and was starting to feel light-headed.

"Rhona ..." Adaira's concerned voice sounded behind her. "Are ye well?"

"No," Rhona snapped. She'd never been further from well in her life. It felt as if all of this were happening to someone else, as if she watched from afar.

Adaira didn't reply. Rhona's tone had obviously warned her off.

Silently, the two sisters descended the tower and made their way along a vaulted hallway to the Great Hall. The twang of a harp and the rumble of excited voices reached them as they approached.

Rhona's stomach lurched, and her step faltered. She halted, frozen like a mouse under the glare of a swooping owl.

Adaira stopped next to her. "Rhona?"

Smoothing her sweating palms on the silken material of her kirtle, Rhona sucked in a deep breath, and then another. She'd never fainted—she wasn't that kind of woman. Yet at that moment, her limbs trembled under her, and her body felt as if it might crumble. She realized then that she was afraid, deathly afraid.

She dared not look at Adaira, for the pity she knew she'd see in her sister's eyes would be her undoing. Instead, she stared forward at where those open doors yawned like some dark maw before her.

"I'm not sure I can do this," she whispered.

A cool, slender hand touched hers. Adaira's fingers closed around hers, reassuringly strong and steady. "I wish I could spirit ye away from here," she murmured. "I understand now why ye fled."

Rhona squeezed her sister's hand back. "Ye are not still angry with me ... for leaving ye here?" It was good to focus on something else, something other than what lay before her.

"No ... not anymore." A beat of silence passed, before Adaira continued, her voice hardening. "Da shouldn't have forced ye into this."

Rhona shut her eyes and struggled to master her emotions. She needed to remain in control, put on a mask for all those curious stares that would stab her the moment she stepped into the Great Hall. She wouldn't put on a show for them. They'd had enough entertainment for one day.

"No," she said softly. "It's not right, but I can't change it now. I tried to run and failed ... there's nowhere to go now but forward. I must face this." And with that, Rhona inhaled deeply and released her sister's hand.

Opening her eyes, she walked the final few yards to the Great Hall.

Taran was the first to notice his bride-to-be enter the hall. Dressed in flowing pale blue, her thick red mane—threaded with white daisies—piled up on her head, Rhona looked like a queen as she glided toward him.

Head held high, she glanced neither right nor left. However, she wasn't looking at him either; her gaze seemed fixed upon the wall behind him where axes, swords, and shields hung upon rough stone.

The crowd had parted to admit her, all gazes riveted upon Malcolm MacLeod's second daughter—the one who had refused to wed.

The one who was about to marry the ugliest man in the keep.

Taran saw their smirks and heard their sniggers, the whispered words between the ladies' hands as their gazes darted from Rhona to Taran. He knew what they were saying, what amused them so.

Clenching his jaw, Taran shifted his attention back to Rhona. He didn't care what they said about him—he'd developed a tough hide over the years—but he did care that Rhona was now the subject of ridicule. By winning the games, he'd humiliated her.

But it was too late to be sorry for it now.

The priest stood behind him, and MacLeod and his wife watched from the side of the dais that Rhona now approached.

Even if he'd wanted to, Taran couldn't stop this.

Rhona forced herself to stop staring at the great shield, which had once belonged to her grandfather, upon the wall. With great reluctance, she lowered her gaze and let it rest upon Taran.

She'd never seen him dressed this way.

Taran wore braies of plaid, bearing the green and red cross-hatching of his clan, the MacKinnons. Supple boots of dark leather covered his lower legs. Across his broad shoulders and muscular torso, he wore a crisp white léine. His rugged jaw was freshly shaven, his short dark-blond hair still slightly damp from bathing.

Rhona stiffened as she studied him. His ice-blue eyes were steady as he watched her approach; nothing on his scarred, forbidding face gave his thoughts away.

Why are ye doing this?

She wanted to rage at him, yet her anger would have to wait till later.

The priest, a slight young man with thinning dark hair and sharp blue eyes, stepped forward. Rhona stopped next to Taran before the dais, and both of them faced the priest. "Please join hands."

Rhona swallowed before reaching out with her left hand. A heartbeat later, Taran took it, his big hand enveloping hers. His touch though was gentle, his skin warm and dry. He didn't seem to be nervous, not like her.

The priest stepped down to meet them. In his hands, he held a length of MacLeod plaid: yellow, black, and grey, threaded with red.

Slowly, he bound it around their joined hands, and then he began to speak. The man had a quiet, yet powerful voice that carried over the hushed crowd. "Behold the bride and groom … who will be joined today in the sight of God in holy matrimony."

The priest continued, reciting the words Rhona had heard many times, for she'd attended a number of handfastings over the years. But Rhona barely listened today.

She could hear little over the thundering of her own heart.

Chapter Seventeen

The Bedding Ceremony

"TO THE BRIDE and groom!"

Malcolm MacLeod stood at the head of the chieftain's table, drinking horn aloft. His gaze scanned the room as if he dared anyone to contradict him.

None would.

Seated next to her new husband, Rhona watched her father. Handfastings were supposed to be joyous occasions, yet there was no happiness on MacLeod's face this evening. His eyes gleamed, and his bearded jaw was tight.

"To the bride and groom." Voices echoed high into the rafters of the Great Hall, and although Rhona dared not look at the faces of those surrounding her, she could hear mockery there. All of them had expected her to wed the son of another clan-chief, not MacLeod's Hound.

Rhona kept her gaze fastened upon the large, empty wooden platter before her. She would share the coming feast with Taran off it. The aroma of roast venison and mutton wafted through the hall. She wasn't sure how she was going to manage a mouthful without gagging.

Her father sank his bulk back down into the carven chair at the head of the table, and the rest of the hall followed suit. Conversation erupted as guests fell upon the feast.

Rhona swallowed as she watched Taran carve slices of venison and mutton, help himself to turnips mashed with butter and milk, and spoon a good helping of braised onions onto their platter. He then reached for a basket of bread studded with walnuts and held it out to her.

For the first time since the ceremony, Rhona raised her gaze to look at him. And in the midst of the feasters, the pair stared at each other for a heartbeat. It was a silent, guarded look. Taran's face was serious, although his eyes were shadowed. As she watched him, her husband's throat bobbed, before he wet his lips.

He *was* nervous. The realization came as a surprise. The man had appeared hewn from stone until now.

"Bread?" he asked when the silence between them drew taut.

Rhona nodded. She had not smiled once since entering this hall. The way she felt right now, she wondered if she'd ever feel light of heart again. Unspeaking, she took a bread roll and turned her gaze from him.

"Bramble wine for the bride?" A servant appeared at Rhona's elbow.

"Aye." Rhona grabbed the heavy goblet before her and held it aloft. She usually preferred ale to wine and drank sparingly. Tonight was different. Maybe some wine would take the edge off her misery, would make the rest of this ordeal easier to bear.

The servant filled her goblet, and Taran's, before moving on.

Ignoring the man beside her, even if she was acutely aware of his presence, Rhona lifted the goblet to her lips and took a large gulp, welcoming the warmth of the wine as it slid down her throat.

Please Lord make this night pass swiftly, she silently prayed.

However, as the sound of laughter and the lilt of a harp echoed off the stone walls, she realized that this was about to be the longest evening of her life.

"Rhona."

Taran's voice roused Rhona from her thoughts. Taking another sip—of her third goblet of wine—she reluctantly shifted her gaze to him. She found Taran watching her steadily.

"Ye can call me 'wife' now, ye know?" she challenged him. The words slurred in her mouth, warning her that the wine had gone straight to her head. She'd hardly touched the platter of food before her. It was still piled high with food, for Taran appeared to have little appetite either.

His mouth quirked. "I'll need time to get used to that."

She eyed him coldly. Around them, the hall thundered with raucous voices and laughter. It was so loud now that it drowned out the music. Still, the harpist played on at the end of the dais, where the chieftain's table sat.

No one could hear the conversation between the newlyweds, although—across the table—Rhona could sense Adaira watching her. The poor girl was seated in-between Aonghus Budge and Baltair MacDonald. Although Baltair ignored Adaira, Chieftain Budge hadn't. If Rhona hadn't felt so sorry for herself, she would have pitied Adaira this evening. Her sister had worn a hunted expression ever since taking her seat for the feast.

"I'm sorry." Taran's voice was gruff, as if he'd had to tear the words from his throat. "I know this isn't what ye want."

"Then why did ye go through with it?"

Taran didn't answer, although he continued to hold her gaze.

Rhona stared back. The wine had made her bold. She didn't usually stare like this, nor so brazenly hold a man's eye. Cressets burned on the wall behind them, illuminating the lines of Taran's face. He often looked as if he needed a shave, his rugged jaw shadowed, but he'd scraped the stubble off for his handfasting. His smooth jaw drew the eye to the two long scars that marred his face. The one that slashed vertically, from his brow and down his left cheek, was the scar that stood out the most.

She wondered how he'd gotten that awful wound and still kept his eye.

Rhona took another sip of wine, her gaze never wavering from him. "How did ye get those scars?"

The moment the question was out of her mouth, Rhona wanted to call it back. There were some things you just didn't ask someone, no matter how much wine you'd imbibed. Taran's gaze guttered, and he drew back from her as if she'd just spat at him. "It doesn't matter," he replied, his voice terse.

Then he turned his attention from her and reached for his own goblet of wine. Raising it to his lips, he took a long draft. His face had drained of color.

Rhona turned her attention back to her untouched meal. She wanted to apologize, and yet the words stuck in her craw. Why should she? He was the one who'd trapped her. She wanted to break his nose, and yet something inside her twisted at the sight of his ashen face.

"It's time for the bedding ceremony!"

The words Rhona had been dreading all evening reached her through the din of laughter and singing. The feast had long since ended, and the tables had been pushed back so that the revelers could dance.

Rhona and Taran hadn't joined them. Instead, they'd sat in stony silence while the rest of the hall celebrated. Eventually, red-faced and bleary-eyed, Malcolm MacLeod had lurched to his feet and held his drinking horn aloft to make his announcement.

Ice washed over Rhona, despite that the air was close and warm inside the hall. She kept her gaze fixed forward, not daring to look Taran's way. She didn't want to see his reaction.

"Come on then!" Aonghus Budge, even redder in the face than MacLeod, raised his goblet. "Get them up to bed."

Ribald laughter echoed around the hall, and some of the men shouted out coarse comments. Then, a group broke away from the dancing and moved toward the dais.

Rhona dropped her gaze to her hands. Her heart was pounding so hard she thought it might leap from her chest. She glimpsed movement from the corner of her eye and saw that Taran had risen to his feet.

"Don't look so worried, MacKinnon," one of the warriors jeered. "We'll be gentle with ye."

"Aye ... we'll carry yer pretty bride to bed," added another.

Taran let out a soft growl in return. "I don't need yer help. I'll carry her upstairs myself."

This comment brought forth hoots.

"Go on then," someone shouted out from the crowd.

"Rhona," Taran said gently. "Stand up."

Face flushing, Rhona rose to her feet. Her face glowed like a lump of peat. The humiliation wasn't to be borne. She didn't look toward her father or her sister. Instead, she turned to Taran. "Don't touch me," she growled.

Laughter rocked the hall. Taran's face tensed. Then he took a step toward her so that they were nearly touching. "Sorry, lass," he murmured, "but this has to happen."

A heartbeat later, he scooped her up into his arms and stepped away from the table. For a moment, Rhona was too stunned to react. But when the shock passed, she began to struggle. "Let me down."

Taran's arms fastened around her, pinning her against him. He skirted the table and stepped down from the dais. The crowd parted to let him through.

"That's the way to handle her, lad," Chieftain Budge called out. The laughter that followed this comment made a red haze of fury settle over Rhona. It pulsed inside her.

"Bastard," she addressed Taran through gritted teeth. "Put me down."

"I wouldn't," one of the men laughed. "A woman that skittish will run off."

"Make sure ye bed her, MacKinnon," Malcolm MacLeod called out from the dais behind them. "I'll have the sheets checked in the morning—and if they're clean, I'll have both of ye whipped."

Cheers reverberated around the room, and Rhona stopped struggling. Horrified by her father's callous words, she huddled against Taran's broad chest.

She couldn't believe her father had just said that.

Taran ignored them all, MacLeod included, and strode through the midst of the crowd. A group of men followed, heckling them, up to the tower room, where the servants had prepared the chamber for the newlyweds.

The priest was waiting for them. He stood next to the big bed that had been sprinkled with sprays of heather and rose petals.

Rhona knew why he was here—to bless the bed and witness the arrival of the couple. The crowd of drunken warriors, Connel Buchanan among them, jostled into the chamber behind Taran and Rhona.

The priest appeared unfazed by the escort. Instead, he turned to the bed and, dipping a hand into the pot he carried, sprinkled holy water over the coverlet. "Let us bless this bed, Lord so that this couple may remain firm in yer peace and persevere in yer will. May they have a strong union and be blessed with children, and finally arrive at the kingdom of heaven through Christ Our Lord ... amen."

As soon as the priest stepped back from the bed, Connel pushed his way forward. There was a glint in his eye that Rhona didn't like; the young man was well into his cups and wore a mean, bitter expression. "Into bed with ye then. I'll help the bride off with her clothes."

Taran lowered Rhona to the ground and turned, moving so that he barred Connel's way. "Get out."

The words fell heavily in the chamber.

"Ye heard the man," the priest said, as he headed toward the door. "Let the newlyweds have some privacy."

"I don't think so." Connel folded his arms across his chest and stared Taran down. "I think we'll stay and watch."

Taran aped the gesture, his feet shifting into a fighting stance. Rhona couldn't see his face but could feel his rising anger.

"I won't ask ye again," Taran growled. "Leave us."

"Make me," Connel sneered back.

Taran lunged with the same speed he had on the evening he'd caught Rhona. It shocked her now, as it had then, that a big man could move that fast.

A heavy fist slammed into Connel's nose, and the warrior sprawled back into the crowd of men standing behind him. He would have collapsed onto the ground if the other warriors hadn't caught him.

Blood streamed from Connel's nose. He cursed, sagging against the men who held him.

Taran flexed the hand he'd just punched Connel with. His gaze swept the group before him. "Get out ... and take him with ye."

There were a few dark looks, curses, and muttered threats, yet no one else challenged Taran. Instead, they kept hold of Connel, who was frantically trying to stem the flow of blood from his nose, and left the chamber.

Taran followed them before he threw the heavy oaken door shut in their wake. The boom of the thudding door shook the room. Not taking any chances that the bedding party might return, Taran turned the iron key.

He and Rhona were now locked inside.

Chapter Eighteen

I Won't Lie With Ye

"I WON'T LIE with ye." Rhona faced Taran as he turned from locking the door. "Ye will have to force yerself on me."

Taran didn't reply. He merely favored her with a weary look and crossed the room to the sideboard, where the servants had left a ewer of spiced bramble wine and two goblets for them. Wordlessly, Taran poured them both a drink.

Watching him, Rhona could see the tension in his shoulders, the grimness of his jaw. It dawned on her then that he'd been dreading this moment as much as she had.

"I'm not going to rape ye, Rhona," he said, his voice low. There was a note of fatigue to his tone that hadn't been there earlier. He carried the goblets across to Rhona and handed her one.

She took it without a word of thanks, her fingers clenching around the stem. "So, what happens now then?"

His gaze met hers. "I don't know."

Rhona moved away from him, shifting over to the window. Liosa hadn't closed the shutters, for it was a warm evening. A sultry breeze whispered into the chamber, feathering across Rhona's face. She lowered herself onto the padded window seat and took a sip of wine.

Spiced with pepper and cinnamon, costly ingredients that she only usually tasted at Yuletide, the rich red wine was delicious. She really shouldn't drink anymore, for her senses had already been numbed by the wine at the feast. However, the nerves that danced in her belly needed settling. She was trapped in this room with her husband—a man who was supposed to bed her or they'd both be whipped in the morning.

Silence stretched out between them. Eventually, it was Taran who broke it. "I wish it didn't have to be this way. I didn't think yer father would make us wed so soon. I thought ye would be given time ... to warm to me."

Rhona turned to him, scowling. "I used to trust ye, Taran. I'll never do so again."

Taran actually flinched at that, his gaze shadowing. His throat bobbed. "And I hope ye will grow to trust me again."

She shook her head, her mouth twisting. "I hate ye."

Silence fell between them once more, and then he loosed a deep sigh. Crossing to the hearth, which sat unlit on this mild night, he leaned against the mantelpiece, still cradling his untouched goblet of wine. "I've made a mess of things."

"Aye, ye have." Rhona looked away from him, staring out into the dark night. There was no moon out tonight; the sky was pitch-black. She could hear the faint noise of the revelers, who were still dancing, drinking, and singing in the Great Hall below.

The sound made the center of her chest ache as if a heavy hand pressed down upon her breast bone. Her eyes burned, and she blinked, pushing back the tears that threatened. She wouldn't cry. Not here, not now.

Never had she felt so alone.

"It was my father," Taran said. His voice was barely above a whisper, yet in the silent tower room, she heard the words clearly.

"Excuse me?" She tore her gaze from the night and forced herself to look at him.

He met her eye. "Ye asked how I got the scars. It was my father."

Rhona went still for a moment, taking in the two dark slashes disfiguring his face. Then, she drew in a deep, shaky breath. "I shouldn't have asked ye that," she said, the words clumsy. "It was cruel."

"Ye are my wife." His voice was flat, emotionless. "Ye should know about my past." A beat of silence passed between them before he continued. "It happened a long while ago. Da was mad ... a man torn between periods of morose moods and murderous temper. He terrorized my mother and thrashed me daily. Everyone knew what was happening, but none stopped it ... not until the day he beat my mother to death. I tried to prevent him, and he slashed my face with a boning knife." Taran reached up, tracking the vertical scar with his fingertip. "He would have killed me too if our neighbors hadn't finally intervened."

Rhona stared, a sickly feeling welling inside her. "What happened after that?"

Taran's severe face turned even grimmer. "The MacKinnon clan-chief executed him ... took his head off with an axe."

Rhona swallowed. She had no answer for that. Any response would sound glib.

She watched Taran in silence, really looked at him. For the first time ever, she saw beyond his role. To her, he'd only ever been her father's loyal warrior: the man who trained her in secret and the guard who shadowed her father. She'd never given a thought to his past, to his family.

"Do ye have any siblings?" she finally asked, her voice subdued.

He shook his head. "I had a younger sister ... but she died when she was three. Da's madness grew worse from that date."

Despite the warm evening, a shiver went through Rhona. She looked away from him, her gaze focusing on the darkness beyond the room.

He was right, this situation was a mess—and yet it wasn't just of his making, but hers too. She'd been too proud, too arrogant. She'd virtually goaded her father into hosting these games.

"Do ye remember the warrior from Atholl who visited us last winter?" she finally asked.

"Aye," he replied quietly. "The chieftain's son."

Rhona stared out into the night. "He was handsome and kind ... and I was rude to him."

Taran huffed out a breath. "I remember that."

Rhona tensed. "I humiliated him in front of the Great Hall, spurned him when he asked me to dance." She broke off here, wincing at the memory. "He left before dawn the following morning ... Da didn't speak to me for days afterward."

Taran didn't reply.

Rhona heaved in a deep breath and turned from the window. "Why would ye wish to wed such a shrew?"

He held her gaze, the moment drawing out between them. When he finally answered, his voice held a rasp. "Do ye really have no idea?"

Rhona shook her head in answer. She remembered what Adaira had said to her during the games then, and her body went cold.

Taran pushed himself off the mantelpiece and moved toward her. Rhona stared at him, frozen in place.

"I never wanted to feel this way," he continued. "But from the first time ye spoke to me—just after yer sixteenth winter—looked me in the eye, and asked me to teach ye how to wield a sword, I was lost."

Rhona clasped her fingers together, squeezing hard. "I had no idea..."

He came to a halt, around three feet from where she sat. His mouth twisted. "I'm good at hiding how I feel ... it's how I've survived." He raked a hand through his hair, a gesture she'd never seen him do before. "I never intended to tell ye. Loving ye from afar was safe, easy. I'd resigned myself to the fact ye would wed someone else."

Loving ye from afar. The words made Rhona's breathing still.

"What changed?" She folded her arms across her chest, a protective gesture that created a barrier between them. "Ye didn't have to enter the games."

"Madness of a kind seized me," he admitted with a bitter smile. "I couldn't bear the thought of the likes of Dughall having ye. I told myself that if ye wedded me, ye would be protected at least. I might be foul to look upon, but I'd never raise a hand to ye. I'd never treat ye ill."

Rhona's chest squeezed hard. "Ye aren't *foul* to look upon."

His face twisted. "There's a good reason why folk call me 'The Beast of Dunvegan'."

"And they shouldn't." The words tumbled out of her. "It's not true."

"The fact remains, I'm no woman's choice of husband."

Rhona didn't deny it; she couldn't bring herself to lie to him. She'd never been the type to flatter or soften things. Even so, for the first time, she felt the loneliness and pain of this man's life. Scarred, shunned, isolated—no wonder he so loyally served her father. He had nothing else.

She glanced away, blinking rapidly. Tears threatened once more, and yet they weren't for her own predicament this time. The wine was turning her weepy.

"I lied before," she said softly. "I don't hate ye … I just feel trapped. Da has just managed to achieve what he's always wanted—to lock me away."

A hush settled over the chamber, and they both let it draw out. Rhona was aware of Taran's nearness, his gaze upon her. Yet neither of them felt the need to speak for the moment. After the conversation that had just passed between them, Rhona was reeling. She wondered if he felt the same.

"So, what are we going to do about tonight?" she asked finally, addressing the problem that loomed over them like a great shadow.

"Yer father wasn't lying earlier," he replied. "He's angry with us both. Ye for defying him … me for daring to compete for ye. He'd happily wield the switch himself."

Rhona drew herself up, turning back to Taran. "He wouldn't beat me."

Taran raised an eyebrow. "He raised a hand to ye after ye escaped," he reminded her. "Do ye wish to test him?"

Rhona's pulse quickened. She wanted to deny it, yet she remembered how he'd struck her after her failed escape. She saw too the truth of the situation on Taran's face. She could bear the pain of being whipped, but the humiliation of it—for her father usually administered his floggings in front of an audience—would be difficult to recover from. She'd never be able to hold her head high inside this keep again.

And yet the thought of consummating this marriage, with this big, intimidating man before her, terrified her.

Rhona raised her goblet to her lips and took a large gulp of wine. She couldn't do it.

"Ye look terrified," Taran observed, his voice rueful. "Am I really such an ogre?"

Rhona gave a nervous laugh and took another sip of wine. "No, but I'm a maid … and this situation is …"

"Difficult."

She snorted. "Ye are the master of understatement tonight."

His mouth curved into a rare smile. "What if we made a game of it?"

Rhona stilled, gaze narrowing. "What?"

His smile faded, and his ice-blue eyes grew intense. "If we are to lie together tonight, we need to take things slowly, to ease into it."

Silence fell between them. Rhona's heart started to hammer. She didn't like the direction this conversation was leading them in. She was entering never-explored territory.

After a few moments, Taran continued. "Let us play a game of riddles. Ye ask me one. If I answer it incorrectly, I must take off an item of clothing."

Rhona inhaled sharply. "And what if ye get it right?"

"Then *ye* must remove a garment of my choosing."

Rhona's mouth had gone dry, her breathing shallow. "I don't like the sound of this game."

He raised an eyebrow. "Do ye have a better one in mind?"

"Knucklebones."

He snorted. "I'd beat ye."

"I wouldn't be so sure … I'm a fiend at knucklebones."

"Let's play riddles … a game that requires us to think," he replied. "Knucklebones is boring."

The directness of his gaze made Rhona's body grow warm, and her stomach dipped and pitched as if she perched upon a high swing. Such a game was too intimate, too risky—and yet an unexpected thrill of excitement went through her.

She raised her chin to meet his gaze. Drawing her shoulders back, Rhona inhaled deeply. "Very well. Who goes first?"

Chapter Nineteen

Riddles

SHE DIDN'T LIKE this game. It moved too quickly.

They'd only been playing it a short while and already they were both down to their last items of clothing. Rhona wore nothing but her long léine. Taran on the other hand was naked save for his braies.

The lamplight played across the muscular lines of his bare chest. Rhona remembered what those ladies in the stands had said about his body during the games, and felt heat rise, flowering across her chest and up her neck. They'd been crude, but they'd both been right—Taran MacKinnon's naked body was magnificent to gaze upon.

"I don't like riddles," she protested as she took off the necklace she'd worn for the handfasting. Gold and amber, it had once belonged to her mother. Her hands were trembling slightly, and it took her an age to unclasp the necklace. "It isn't fair anyway—men have more items of clothing to take off."

"No, we don't."

"But ye were always going to win."

Taran favored her with a small smile, although his gaze remained serious. "Or could it be that yer riddles are too easy?"

She glowered at him. "Or yers too hard?" She'd actually asked him the hardest riddles she could come up with, and yet he seemed to know them all.

"Come on," he replied. "It's yer turn."

Rhona huffed a breath and sat down upon the window seat. The warm night air tickled the naked backs of her arms. She felt exposed sitting here, wearing only her léine. The material was thin and clung to her form; she was thankful that Taran didn't let his gaze stray from her face as he waited for her riddle.

"All right then," she grumbled. "How about this one? What is the sister of the sun, though made for the night? The fire causes her tears to fall, and when she is near dying they cut off her head."

Taran frowned at that, scratching his chin as he pondered it. He sat upon a stool opposite her. Rhona watched him, holding her breath as she waited for him to come up with the answer. Taran seemed stumped.

"It's a candle?" he asked finally.

Rhona's heart leaped. *God's nails ... I've lost.* "Aye," she croaked. "That's right."

Silence drew out between them as she summoned the nerve to rise to her feet. They both knew what she had to do; there was no need for Taran to command it. "What happens," she croaked as she reached for the hem of her shift, "when we're both naked."

His gaze grew limpid, even as it never left her face. "We go to bed."

The promise in those words made her knees wobble beneath her. She truly was in the midst of a situation beyond her control, swept along by a tide she had long stopped fighting. The wine had taken the edge off, but even so, she was scared.

Holding her breath, Rhona grabbed her shift's hem and pulled it up over her head in one swift movement. There was no point in drawing out the embarrassment. Best to get it over with.

A heartbeat later, she stood there, naked before him.

Taran's gaze did leave her face then. It swept down over the length of her body and then up so that he met her gaze once more. She watched his lips part, his pupils dilate. Rhona's legs trembled underneath her in response.

He gave her a long look. "I suppose this means it's my turn."

Panic rose in Rhona's chest. She wanted him to remain clothed; the longer this game went on, the longer she'd have to avoid the inevitable. She reached for her goblet of wine but found it empty. *Satan's cods.* She needed more wine if she was to endure this.

"Are ye ready?" he asked.

Rhona swallowed before wetting her lips. She had no more clothing to remove, and if she answered one more of his riddles correctly, he'd be completely naked. Men didn't wear anything under their braies.

Reluctantly, she nodded.

"Truly no one is outstanding without me, nor fortunate," he began. "I embrace all those whose hearts ask for me. He who goes without me goes about in the company of death, and he who bears me will remain lucky forever. But I stand lower than earth and higher than heaven."

Inhaling deeply, Rhona paused. Curse him, but she knew the answer to this one. However, she needed to pretend otherwise. "Happiness?" she asked after a moment.

His brow furrowed. "The answer was 'humility' ... but I think ye knew that."

Rhona tensed. "No, I didn't."

He cocked his head. "No cheating."

"I'm not!" Rhona glared back at him. She fought the urge to cover herself up, to cross her arms over her bared breasts.

"Ready for another riddle then?" His voice had a husky edge to it now.

Rhona inhaled deeply, steadying herself. "Go on."

"I have one, and ye have one," he began slowly. "So do the woods, fields, streams and seas, fish, beasts, crops, and everything else in this revolving world."

Rhona drew in a measured breath. "That's a tricky one," she admitted after a moment. Good—she didn't know this riddle; she could answer honestly. Rhona plucked the first idea that swam into her thoughts. "Is it 'a shadow'?"

A beat of silence passed before Taran smiled. "Aye, that's right."

Rhona's breathing hitched. *God's bones ... no.*

Wordlessly, Taran rose to his feet and began to unlace his braies. Rhona watched him, her pulse skittering, her breathing suddenly ragged. She regretted ever agreeing to this wretched game. This was going too far. The chamber suddenly felt tiny, airless.

Taran's braies dropped to the stone floor, and he stepped out of them.

Rhona kept her gaze resolutely fixed upon his face. She wouldn't look down; she didn't want to see his rod. She wanted to bolt from this room and run howling into the night, naked or not. And yet she did nothing of the kind. She remained frozen to the spot as Taran approached her.

In just three paces he was standing before her, so close there was barely any space between them. She inhaled the warm male scent of his skin, aware of the heat that emanated from his body. She was a tall woman, but she felt small next to him.

"Rhona." He said her name in a caress, and despite herself, she shivered. Rhona averted her gaze, fixing it upon his shoulder. She couldn't bear to look him in the eye; it was too intense, too intimate. A moment later he lifted a hand and trailed his fingertips down her jawline to the slight cleft in her chin. "Ye are the loveliest sight I've ever looked upon. A man could die from wanting ye."

She sucked in a breath at these words, at the simmering need in them. She wasn't ready for this, didn't know how to respond or what to do, and yet a strange heat flared in her lower body at his words. There was a raw edge to him, to his words, that ensnared her.

His hand tracked lower, his fingertips tracing the column of her neck down to her collar bone, before trailing a lazy path between her breasts. His touch swept over the curve of her left breast, the backs of his hand grazing her nipple.

Rhona's breathing caught.

Taran moved then, dipping his head and lowering himself before her. He took her breast into his mouth.

Rhona gasped. Her hands went to his shoulders with the intention of pushing him away, but as he began to suckle, drawing her in, her fingers dug into his flesh and held on.

She didn't shove him from her. Instead, she held on for dear life as ripples of pleasure arched out from the tip of her left breast. A moment later he released her nipple and shifted to its twin. He was gentle at first, and then the pressure increased.

Rhona stifled a groan and swayed on her feet. She felt as if her legs might give way under her at any moment. His mouth was working magic on her; she had no idea she could feel this way. The way he suckled her made another sensation rise within her, an aching hunger. She didn't understand it, and the feeling scared her. What could she possibly be hungry for?

Taran tore his mouth from her breast and straightened up. He gazed down at her, his expression fierce. "It's time ... are ye ready?"

Rhona nodded, trying to quell the trembling in her limbs. "What must I do?"

"Lie down on the bed."

The command sent a tremor through her. She edged around him, moving toward the bed in tentative steps.

Fear and an odd excitement pulsed within her. How was it possible to be afraid, and yet yearn for something? It felt as if she had strayed into a strange dream. What was she doing alone in this chamber, stark naked, with Taran MacKinnon?

We are man and wife, she reminded herself, *and this is our wedding night.*

Keeping her gaze upon his face, she lay down upon the coverlet, amongst the sprays of heather and rose petals. The sweet, woody scent enveloped her.

Taran towered above Rhona, and for a long moment, he merely observed her, his gaze drinking her in.

Rhona attempted to steady her breathing. Her body flushed as his gaze slid down the length of her, branding her. Her skin tingled, and her breasts ached.

Without meaning to, she let her own gaze shift from his face, down the hard, muscular planes of his chest, to his groin.

She stifled a gasp. He was fully aroused and very big. The hard column of his erection reared up against his belly. Rhona swallowed. Dampness flooded between her thighs at the sight of it, even as her pulse started to thunder.

Caitrin had told her that her first time with Baltair had been traumatic. Would Taran hurt her?

Chapter Twenty
Nothing to Prove

TARAN LOWERED HIMSELF onto the bed, and she felt it give under his weight. On his knees, he moved between her thighs, parting them.

Mortification flooded through Rhona. He had spread her thighs wide, exposing her to him. There was nowhere to hide. No one had ever looked upon her there. She watched him gaze down at her, saw the flush that suddenly stained his cheekbones. His chest was now rising and falling fast; she felt the tremble in his body.

Looming over her, Taran placed the head of his shaft against the entrance to her womb and began to gently rub himself against her. Rhona gasped at the sensation, at the slick heat of their flesh meeting.

A throb began deep in her belly.

He continued to move against her, shifting his hips in slow, sinuous circles.

Groaning, Rhona threw back her head against the coverlet and rode the waves of pleasure. Unbidden, her thighs parted wider, and she hooked one leg around his hips, drawing him against her. She was no longer afraid. She now ached to have him inside her. She didn't care if it hurt; she felt as if she could die from wanting.

"Rhona," he gasped her name. "I want to take this slow ... I don't want to hurt ye."

She whimpered in response and met his gaze. She wasn't sure how much more of this she could take before she started begging.

They stared at each other for a long moment, and then Taran breathed a curse. Reaching down, he grasped her hips, lifting her up to meet him. And then, slowly, he slid into her.

It didn't hurt at first, just a full sensation as she stretched to accommodate him. But then, a sharp, stinging pain caught her by surprise. Rhona gasped, her body growing taut. Her eyes widened, and she grasped hold of Taran's wrists, stilling him.

He gazed down at her. "That's it, lass," he murmured. "The worst is over ... it shouldn't hurt anymore."

And with that, he lowered himself further. Rhona felt the full length of him penetrate her. A wonderful aching sensation filled her womb.

"Oh," she gasped, releasing his wrists.

"That's right," he rasped. There was an edge to his voice as if he was barely clinging onto control. "Give yerself to it."

Rhona obeyed him. She closed her eyes and let her head roll back once more. Caitrin hadn't told her that it could feel like this, no one had.

However, her eyes snapped open, her head lifting, when Taran started to move inside her. Pleasure coiled deep within her womb, tightening, building. The intensity of it frightened her. "Taran," she gasped. "I can't ..."

Taran murmured her name, hushing her. He took hold of her left knee, for her right leg was still wrapped around his hips, and lifted it high. He then drove into her. He took her in slow thrusts, his gaze never leaving hers.

Rhona heard a woman's cry echo through the chamber—it must have been her own, although she had never before made such a sound. It was a wild, keening cry. Her body trembled, need thrumming through her. And yet there was more, so much more, she could sense it as the aching pleasure deep within coiled tighter still.

She was reaching toward it, brushing the edge of it, when Taran's body arched above her.

She stared up at him, fascinated, watching him go rigid. The sinews on his neck stood out as he threw his head back and choked back a cry. Even now, even at this moment, the man still fought for control.

Then she felt the heat of him release inside her, and Taran's body shuddered.

Rhona awoke slowly, blinking in the warmth of the sun that filtered in through the open window.

She had slept deeply, her limbs loose and rested. However, her mouth and throat felt parched, and her head ached.

Too much wine.

Stifling a groan, Rhona pushed herself up onto one elbow. Her gaze settled upon the naked man who lay sprawled upon the bed next to her. For a moment, she just let her eyes feast upon him.

How had she ever thought Taran MacKinnon ugly?

His face, relaxed in sleep, was much softer than when he was awake. Even the scars seemed less evident. His mouth, which often appeared a hard slash, was sensual this morning, his usually furrowed brow smooth. She realized then how much of the cares of the world he carried with him.

Her gaze slid down to his body, and memories of the night before flooded back. Heat crept up Rhona's neck as she remembered what they'd done, how she'd arched under him and cried out. He'd taken her once more before exhaustion pulled them both down into its clutches. That coupling had been even better than the first. He'd brought her to the brink, and then taken her over the edge with him.

Rhona's cheeks flushed hot as she recalled how she'd gasped his name, had pleaded with him for more. She ran a hand over her face, stifling a groan of mortification. How would she ever look him in the eye again?

Taran stirred, his eyes flickering open. "Morning," he rasped. "Lord ... my mouth feels like a piece of leather."

"Too much wine will do that to ye," she replied huskily. "I'll get us some water." Rhona slid off the bed, pulled on a robe, and padded over to the sideboard, where a ewer of water and two cups sat. Filling them, she returned to the bed.

Taran had pulled up the sheet to cover his naked loins when she handed him the cup. Rhona's chest constricted; she didn't know whether to be disappointed or relieved by his modesty.

She perched on the edge of the bed and drank the water. An awkward silence fell between them. Eventually, Taran broke it. "Are ye well, Rhona?"

She glanced up, meeting his gaze. "Aye."

"Last night ... I ... we ..." His voice trailed off. The look on his face was so pained she almost pitied him.

"Don't worry," she replied. "Ye didn't force me, Taran. I lay with ye willingly." The relief in his gaze made her smile. "What? Did ye think I'd rage at ye?"

His mouth curved. "I didn't think that far ahead. I got carried away last night."

Rhona took another sip of water and observed him over the rim of her cup. It was odd how shy she was of him this morning. It made her realize that although they were wed, and had lain together as man and wife, they weren't comfortable around each other. Until yesterday their ranks had imposed a certain type of relationship upon them, a distance.

Taran drained his cup before running a hand down his face. "What time is it?"

Rhona glanced toward the window, at where the sun pooled upon the flagstone floor. Outside, she could hear goats bleating and the laughter of children. "Almost noon, I'd say."

He stiffened, gaze widening. "I've never slept so late."

She favored him with an arch look. "Since it's the morning after our wedding, I think my father will forgive ye."

Unfortunately, the mention of Malcolm MacLeod had an instant effect on them both, like a cloud blocking the sun. Taran scowled, and Rhona's mood soured.

Her father might end up overlooking her past defiance now that she was a wife, but she would never forgive him for humiliating her. Nor would she ever forget his parting words as Taran had carried her from the Great Hall.

I'll have the sheets checked in the morning—and if they're clean, I'll have both of ye whipped.

Rhona frowned, her gaze shifting to the crumpled coverlet. There was a small dark stain upon it. Her fingers tightened around the cup. "Ye are not the 'Beast of Dunvegan', Taran," she said, her voice low and fierce. "My father is."

She felt the bed shift. A moment later Taran was sitting next to her, his thigh pressing against hers. He was so close she could see the blond stubble on his jaw. His nearness unnerved her. Rhona gripped her cup tightly, staring down at it. She felt so strange this morning, full of conflicting emotions.

It was as if she'd been asleep her whole life and had just awoken. Everything seemed different.

Taran hooked a finger under her chin, raising it gently so that their gazes met. The tenderness in his grey-blue eyes made her breath catch.

"I never would have wished for any of this, Rhona," he said softly, "and yet I can't bring myself to regret it. If I die tomorrow, I'll go to my cairn a happy man."

She managed a half-smile. "Ye speak hastily … I don't think I'll make a good wife. Ye may regret this yet."

His mouth quirked. He let go of her chin and brought his hand up, stroking her cheek. "Can we start again?" he asked.

"What do ye mean?" His touch made her breathing quicken. She was aware of how close he was sitting, the heat of his naked body.

"Would ye let me woo ye?"

Rhona inclined her head, pushing aside the need that was curling like wood smoke in her belly. She would have smiled if his face hadn't been so serious. "But we're already wed?"

"Aye, but not in the best circumstances. I want a chance to prove myself to ye."

Their gazes held. The earnestness in his eyes made Rhona's throat constrict. It was a strange sensation, one she had never felt before. Did she deserve a man like this? She hadn't treated Taran well at all, and yet it was him who wanted to be worthy of her.

She reached up and cupped her hand over his, pressing it against her cheek. "Ye can woo me if ye like," she murmured, "although ye have nothing to prove."

Chapter Twenty-one

Friendly Advice

RHONA FOUND ADAIRA in the gardens behind the castle. Her sister was collecting flowers, placing them carefully in the wicker basket she carried slung over one arm. It was a humid afternoon, with not even a sea breeze to cool the air. As such, Adaira wore a light linen kirtle. Her thick brown hair was piled up on her head, although tendrils had escaped, curling at the nape.

Adaira didn't see her sister approach. Instead, she swiped at a fly that dove at her face, before muttering a curse as she caught her thumb on a rose thorn.

"I hope I didn't teach ye that word," Rhona teased. "Una would faint to hear it."

Adaira swiveled around, a smile stretching across her face. "I was wondering when ye would surface."

Rhona gave a soft laugh. "Too much wine, I'm afraid."

She saw concern shadow her sister's eyes and held up a placating hand. "Worry not, I am well. The marriage is consummated. Da has no cause to flog us."

Her sister's shoulders relaxed at this news. "I've been so worried."

Rhona smiled. She appreciated her sister's concern; it felt as if she was the only one in the keep who actually cared about her welfare. "Continue with yer collecting," she said, stepping close and peering into Adaira's basket. "We can talk while ye work."

"I was going to make rosewater," Adaira said, moving along the avenue of roses. "Would ye like some?"

"Aye, ye know I love the scent of roses."

Adaira stopped and carefully snipped off three pink roses from a bush. She then cast Rhona a veiled look. "So … what was it like?"

"What?" Rhona replied, pretending she didn't know what Adaira was asking. She knew only too well, for she herself had been filled with curiosity after Caitrin had wed.

"The bedding," Adaira said, a groove forming between her eyebrows. "Is it as awful as Caitrin said?"

Rhona paused, wondering how best to answer her sister. Her experience last night had been a revelation. "I thought it would be an ordeal," she admitted quietly. "I was terrified."

Adaira's blue eyes grew wide, and she straightened up, her slender body growing tense. "So, Caitrin was right?"

Rhona shook her head. "She would have spoken the truth about her own experience ... but mine was different." She broke off here, suddenly embarrassed. "Taran wasn't what I expected."

She didn't think her sister's hazel eyes could get any bigger, but they did then. "Did ye *enjoy* it?"

Rhona cleared her throat before managing a nod.

Adaira's cheeks flushed. "So ... are ye in love with him?"

"What?" Rhona gave a laugh. Adaira could be such a goose. Her head was full of silly ideas. "How could I be?"

Her sister looked crestfallen. "I just thought ... after last night ..."

"Just one night? Love takes time."

Adaira nodded. She then moved on to the next rose bush and started snipping. "It's all backward, isn't it?" she said after a pause. "Ye are supposed to fall in love *before* ye wed."

"Aye," Rhona agreed. "But there are many unions where there is never any love. I'm grateful Taran won the games and not Dughall MacLean."

Adaira shuddered. "That man makes my skin crawl ... although not as much as Baltair MacDonald does."

Rhona frowned. "Has he been bothering ye again?"

"Not since ye interrupted us," Adaira replied. "I think ye offended his pride. He makes a point of looking through me these days ... and I'm grateful for it."

"And I'm relieved ... I wish our sister wasn't wed to the brute."

Adaira glanced up, her gaze shadowed. "She's so unhappy, Rhona. I don't want to wish anyone dead, but I sometimes find myself hoping he chokes on a fishbone. That way Caitrin could come back and live with us."

Rhona sighed. She too had fantasized about Baltair MacDonald meeting his end, although her imaginings had been a lot bloodier than her gentle sister's. "Maybe he will," she replied, before favoring Adaira with a wicked smile. "Or someone will poison his wine."

Gordon was shoeing a horse when Taran found him.

The warrior plunged the glowing iron horseshoe into a pail of cold water after shaping it, and steam billowed. A few feet away the waiting horse snorted and stamped its unshod foot.

Sensing someone's approach, Gordon glanced up. "Good afternoon," he greeted Taran with a grin. "Ye look a bit worse for wear."

Taran grimaced. "Aye, a handfasting will do that to a man."

Gordon straightened up and wiped his sweaty forehead with the back of his arm. "I've never attended a celebration like it." Gordon eyed him, his expression speculative. "The bride didn't scratch yer eyes out, I see?"

Taran's mouth curved. His friend's curiosity was palpable. "No, she didn't."

Gordon put aside the horseshoe, his work forgotten. "And are ye preparing yerselves for a whipping?"

"There'll be no need for that."

Gordon inclined his head before giving a low whistle, his mouth twitching. "Ye rogue. I didn't think she'd let ye anywhere near her."

Taran huffed. "I'll try not to take offense at that."

Gordon scratched his stubbled jaw. "So, all is well between ye?"

"For the moment," Taran replied. He paused here, considering the question he'd sought his friend out to ask. He wasn't sure how to present it, so he decided to be blunt. "Gordon ... how did ye manage to woo Greer?"

Gordon raised an eyebrow. "Who says I've succeeded?"

"Ye are set to wed her at Samhuinn. The girl adores ye."

The warrior cleared his throat and glanced away. Taran's candor had thrown Gordon off guard; he actually looked embarrassed. "I'm not sure what I did to deserve her," he said finally. "Why do ye wish to know?"

"I must woo Rhona."

"But ye are already wed to her."

"It matters not. I want my wife to love me."

Gordon's gaze widened. "Of course," he murmured. "I'd forgotten that ye have been long carrying a torch for her."

"Aye." Taran dragged in a deep breath. The night before seemed like a dream, but everything had moved so fast. He wanted to take things back to how they should have been. "Do ye have any advice?"

A wolfish smile spread across Gordon's face. "Aye, throw the lass down on the bed every night and plow her till she begs for mercy. She'll soon not be able to live without ye."

Taran raised an eyebrow. "Is that it?"

"Aye." Gordon puffed out his chest. "It works for me."

Taran snorted, casting his friend a rueful look. He was still no wiser about how to approach his wife, to win her heart. "Remind me not to ask ye for advice in future."

Supper in the Great Hall was a tense affair that evening. Taran and Rhona joined the chief, his wife, Adaira, and Aonghus Budge at the long table upon the dais. Many of the warriors who had attended the games had left for home, emptying out the keep. Baltair MacDonald had departed for Duntulm as well.

The Great Hall seemed silent after the revelry of the night before.

Rhona broke a piece of crust off the hare pie and chewed it slowly. Beside her, Taran ate with a similar lack of enthusiasm. The mood at the table had robbed them both of appetite.

Malcolm MacLeod sat hunched over his meal. He devoured it with grim determination as if his supper were a foe to be vanquished. He had not spoken a word to either his daughter or his son-in-law since they'd joined him at the table. Beside Malcolm, Una nibbled at her meal, a pinched expression upon her pretty face.

Aonghus Budge broke the weighty silence. He leered across the table at Taran and raised his goblet to him. "Good to hear yer new wife did her bidding last night."

Taran didn't answer. Rhona felt him grow still next to her; the thigh that rested against hers under the table tensed.

Oblivious, Chieftain Budge blundered on. "Although with a face like that, I suppose ye have always had to force yerself on women, eh laddie?"

Una tittered, and Malcolm gave a snort that might have been a laugh.

Rhona inhaled sharply, noting that Taran's fingers had clenched around the bone hilt of the knife he'd been using to cut himself a wedge of cheese.

"He's not the husband I'd have chosen for her, Budge," MacLeod growled. He looked up from his pie, his iron-grey gaze baleful as it swiveled to Taran. "But in the end, Rhona got what she deserved."

"They're well suited then," Aonghus Budge replied.

Rhona raised her goblet to her lips and took a measured sip of wine. After the previous night's overindulgence, she was wary of drinking too much. Across the table, she met Adaira's eye. Her sister wore a pained expression.

Chieftain Budge helped himself to another wedge of pie before he glanced at Adaira. Like the night before, she'd been seated next to him. "I see ye are very different to yer willful sister, Lady Adaira. Mild-mannered and biddable."

Adaira raised her gaze and gave him a startled look. She opened her mouth to reply, but her father cut her off. "Aye, she's a good lass ... a credit to her sire. A daughter who has always known her place."

Rhona watched her sister's slender jaw tense. Irritation flared in her hazel eyes. "I admire my sister," Adaira said, her voice so low it was barely above a whisper. However, it carried down the table. "I wish I had her spirit."

Rhona cast Adaira a grateful smile.

But her sister's comment hadn't pleased their father. "Save yer admiration for those who warrant it," Malcolm replied with a scowl.

Chapter Twenty-two

True Secrets

"I CAN'T BEAR it." Rhona finished unbraiding her hair and turned away from the window. Outside the long twilight was drawing out. The sky to the west had turned dusky, promising another warm day to come. It had been the hottest summer Rhona could ever remember. "How long will he continue to insult us?"

"For as long as it suits him," Taran replied. Like her, he was readying himself for bed. He had just unlaced his heavy mail shirt and was shrugging it off. "Best to ignore it. He'll get bored eventually."

Rhona met his eye. "I wish we could go away from here."

Taran's gaze clouded. "And I wish I had a broch we could live in … unfortunately though, my father was the youngest of five brothers."

"But we could go to live amongst yer kin at Dunan?"

Taran huffed. "I left my birthplace for a reason. The MacKinnon clan-chief makes yer father look like a lamb."

Rhona heaved a sigh. "So, we're trapped here then." She stepped behind the screen in the corner of the chamber and began to undress. Despite the intimacy they'd already shared, she felt shy around her husband. She wasn't used to sharing her space with a man; all her life she'd only ever slept in the same chamber as her sisters. The newness of it put her on edge.

Disrobing, she donned a long linen léine. She emerged from behind the screen to find Taran had stripped down to plaid hose and a sleeveless tunic. He then climbed into bed.

Rhona hesitated. "Do ye not sleep naked?"

The look he gave her was almost pained. "Aye … usually."

"So why don't ye undress?"

His gaze met hers across the chamber. Excitement fluttered under Rhona's ribcage. The day had seemed long, and although all of this was new to her, she'd found herself looking forward to seeing Taran naked again.

His throat bobbed. "I bedded ye last night because it was necessary," he replied quietly, "to save us both a beating. But things are different now. I told ye this morning I wanted to woo ye … and so I shall."

Rhona swallowed. "Didn't ye enjoy it?"

His face tightened. "Aye, very much." His voice had a rasp to it now. "I just want us to get to know each other properly before I bed ye again."

Rhona inclined her head, her gaze narrowing. She had never heard of the like: what husband acted this way?

Taran moved over and patted the mattress next to him. "Come to bed, Rhona. Let us talk."

Body tense, she padded over to the bed and climbed in next to him. "What about?" She knew he was just trying to be kind, respectful. Yet a part of her was disappointed. Last night he'd given her a taste of something she now found herself hungry for.

They lay down next to each other, shoulders touching. "Tell me a secret," he said after a moment, "something no one else but ye knows."

Rhona glanced over at his profile. "Something I haven't even told my sisters?"

He met her eye, smiling. "Aye … a true secret."

Rhona heaved in a deep breath and thought hard. There were a number of things she'd kept to herself over the years. She wasn't sure which secret to share.

"I saw one of the Fair Folk once," she said finally.

He rolled over onto his side toward her, propping himself up on an elbow. "Ye did?"

She wondered if he believed her. The Fair Folk, or the Aos Sí as they were also known, were a part of this isle's folklore. Fairy mounds and stone circles littered the island's green hills. Folk were wary of them.

"I was around eight," Rhona replied. "And out exploring the shore with my sisters. We were collecting shells before the twin fairy mounds north of the keep."

Taran nodded. "I know the place."

"We had lingered too late, and dusk came upon us," Rhona continued. "We were just about to turn for home when I saw a woman standing before the mounds. She was clad in flowing white, her hair long and dark. She had the face of an angel. I've never seen anyone so beautiful."

"Did yer sisters see her too?"

Rhona shook her head. "They'd already turned back." She paused as the memory of that strange day returned to her. The scent of brine from the loch, the mist that curled like crone's hair around the woman's skirts. "We looked at each other, and then she smiled. It was a lovely expression, full of gentleness and warmth … and then she beckoned to me."

"She wanted ye to follow her?"

Rhona glanced back at him and saw that his brow had furrowed. "Aye ... and I would have too if Da's voice hadn't reached me. He'd come out looking for us, ye see. He bellowed my name and broke the spell. I glanced over my shoulder at where my sisters were running toward him, and when I looked back the woman was gone."

"Ye had a narrow escape," Taran said gently. "She would have taken ye."

Rhona nodded. "I knew it too afterward ... that's why I never said anything to my sisters, or to Da." She swiveled around to face him properly. "Yer turn. Tell me a secret."

Taran met her eye. "I'm afraid of rats."

Rhona drew back, incredulous. "Is that it?"

"I'm terrified of the bastards, Rhona. Just the sight of one sends me into a cold sweat."

She favored him with an arch look. "Ye are teasing."

He shook his head. "I wish I was."

She huffed. Taran MacKinnon was the biggest and fiercest of her father's warriors. She couldn't imagine him afraid of anything. Certainly not rodents. "No one likes rats," she said after a moment, "but what do ye find so repellent about them?"

"Their long naked tails," he said with a twist of his face that wasn't feigned. "Their scrabbling feet, beady eyes, and twitching noses. When I was a bairn, Ma used to check my bed every night to make sure there weren't any rats hiding under the sheets ... until Da stopped her. He said she was coddling me too much."

"And no one knows of this fear?"

His gaze seared hers. "Only ye." The way he said the words made Rhona's pulse quicken. She knew so little about her husband.

All that was about to change.

"Keep yer elbows bent and close to yer body," Taran commanded, "and keep yer sword raised at all times."

Rhona snorted, circling him, the hilt of her wooden practice sword gripped tight in both hands. "I know all this."

"Ye are rusty, lass," Taran replied, brow furrowing. "It bears repeating."

Rhona raised an eyebrow. The pair of them faced each other in the practice yard. Now that they were wed, her father could no longer forbid Taran from training her. Three days had passed since their handfasting, and Rhona was eager to restart her lessons with Taran. Dressed in leggings, a loose léine belted at the waist, high boots, and with the wind tugging at her braided hair, she felt ridiculously happy this morning.

Taran attacked unexpectedly, with a speed she'd come to anticipate. The blade of his practice-sword cut through the cool morning air.

Rhona stepped back and brought her blade up to block the attack. She then twisted free and danced sideways, grinning. "Ye are fast, husband ... but not fast enough."

"And ye are full of yerself, wife," he growled back, his gaze twinkling. "Too much so."

He attacked again.

Rhona parried this time, pushing his sword out of the way with her own, before she attacked him.

A smile split Taran's face. He was enjoying this—as much as she was.

Clack. Clack. Clack.

The ring of their colliding blades echoed out over the yard. Rhona was vaguely aware of a crowd gathering around the edge. Greer, the cook's daughter was among them. Like many in the keep, Greer would have heard the rumor that Rhona had long trained in secret; she could feel the curiosity in Greer's stare now as she watched her.

However, Rhona didn't take her eyes off Taran.

When he attacked her again, she counter cut him—stepping back and then swinging her blade around to strike his arm. The wooden blade struck Taran's forearm. He let out a hiss and shifted back, out of reach.

Grinning, Rhona went after him. She stabbed her blade toward his torso, going for his belly.

Taran stepped to the side, his blade sweeping around. Too late, Rhona realized she'd left her flank exposed. An instant later the wooden blade slammed against her ribs.

Rhona lurched to the side, going down on her knees as the breath gusted out of her.

"Only stab when yer opponent is incredibly vulnerable," Taran warned her. "Ye just left yerself wide open to an attack."

Rhona gritted her teeth and climbed to her feet. "I knew that."

Taran huffed. "As I said ... ye are rusty."

"She's a woman," a belligerent voice intruded. "She doesn't know what she's doing."

Rubbing her aching ribs, Rhona glanced over her shoulder at where Dughall MacLean stood at the edge of the practice yard. Connel Buchanan stood next to him. The smirks on both their faces made her hackles rise.

"My wife handles a blade as well as ye, MacLean," Taran replied. His tone was mild, although when she glanced back at him, Rhona saw a warning in his eyes.

Dughall snorted. "Maybe ye should lend her to me awhile then ... let me see for myself." His lip curled. "And then after I've bested her, I've got another sword she can attend."

This comment made Connel snigger, although none of the surrounding crowd appeared to share the young man's mirth.

Taran's gaze narrowed. Tension suddenly crackled in the air.

One look at Dughall's face told Rhona that he nursed a great bitterness toward her husband. A muscle ticked in his cheek, and his large hands fisted by his sides.

Taran cast aside his wooden practice sword and approached Dughall in long strides. Rhona tensed. This was what Dughall wanted. He was deliberately goading Taran, hoping he'd make him lose his temper.

However, Taran MacKinnon wasn't easily drawn into a fight. He'd spent his life weathering taunts and insults. Instead, he pushed his face close to Dughall's, and the two men eye-balled each other for a long moment.

When Taran spoke, his voice was deathly cold. "Never."

Chapter Twenty-three

Lammas Morn

"ARE YE SURE about this, Taran?" Rhona cast a wary glance up at the sky as she followed her husband down to the loch's edge. "It looks like it might rain."

Taran cast her a look over his shoulder and smiled. "Just a few clouds … nothing to worry about."

Rhona pursed her lips. "If ye say so."

Reaching the pebbly edge of Loch Dunvegan, Rhona's gaze alighted upon the small boat awaiting them. She cast Taran a questioning look. "Is this yer surprise?"

Taran smiled once more, an expression that made Rhona's breathing hitch. He looked like a different man when his gaze softened with humor and a smile stretched across his face. It made him look younger. "Aye, the first of them."

Excitement danced in her belly as she gazed at him. Three weeks had passed since their handfasting. But still, Taran hadn't touched her. He'd not even tried to kiss her.

She ached for him to do both.

Rhona adjusted the woolen shawl around her shoulders. A cool breeze breathed in off the loch. The summer was waning, and today was the feast of Lammas, celebrating the first wheat harvest of the year.

Adaira had gone off to visit the bustling Lammas market taking place in Dunvegan village this morning. Local women would decorate the altar of Dunvegan kirk with sheaves of corn, flowers, and breads made from the first reaping of wheat, barley, oats, and rye. Later on, folk would feast on breads, cakes, and ale in the village market square.

Rhona stepped into the boat and settled herself down, adjusting her skirts around her while Taran pushed the craft out onto the water. Climbing in, he then began to row the boat away from the shore.

Despite the dubious sky, Rhona found herself enjoying the outing. She twisted, her gaze taking in the majesty of Dunvegan Castle behind her. Surrounded by green, its great curtain wall and battlements rose high above the loch.

"I've never seen the keep from this angle before," she murmured. "It's beautiful."

"Aye," Taran replied, a smile in his voice. "I thought ye would like it."

Rhona turned back to him, and their gazes met. "I do, thank ye."

Taran looked away first, glancing over his shoulder. He rowed the boat out into the midst of the long loch.

Despite that they'd grown easy in each other's company of late, there was an odd tension this morning. She sensed that he was nervous, that he wished to impress her.

"This isn't another attempt to woo me, is it?" she asked finally, favoring him with a gentle smile. The last weeks had been a succession of romantic gestures. Just yesterday he'd brought her a red rose from the gardens. He'd actually blushed when he handed it to her.

Taran's mouth quirked. "Can't a man take his lovely wife out for a boat ride on Lammas morn?"

Rhona's smile widened although she said nothing. She did appreciate the effort he'd made over the past weeks, but it really wasn't necessary. Heat rose in her cheeks when she thought of what she really wanted: the pair of them naked in bed, leisurely exploring each other's bodies.

Swallowing, Rhona shifted her attention from her husband's broad shoulders to the dark rippling water. Despite that it was late summer, the loch would be breathtakingly cold; it never warmed, not even during the hottest weather.

When they reached the center of the lake, Taran stopped rowing. The boat drifted gently, and Rhona found her gaze drawn back to his.

"I'd like to sing ye a song," he murmured. "Would ye like that?"

Rhona inclined her head. "Ye can sing, Taran?"

He gave her an embarrassed look. "Well enough."

"Then I'd love to hear it."

Taran nodded, his throat bobbing. He glanced away, drew in a slow breath, and then began to sing. He had a gentle tenor, a low, lilting voice that made the fine hair on the back of Rhona's arms prickle.

Breathless, she listened as the words filtered out across the loch.

> "Ae fond kiss, and then we sever;
> Ae fareweel, alas, for ever!
> Deep in heart-wrung tears I'll pledge thee,
> Warring sighs and groans I'll wage thee!
> Who shall say that Fortune grieves him
> While the star of hope she leaves him?
> Me, nae cheerfu' twinkle lights me,
> Dark despair around benights me."

When Taran's voice died away, Rhona drew in a soft breath. "That was beautiful ... but so sad."

"Ma taught me it years ago," Taran replied with a lopsided smile. "It was her favorite song. It wasn't supposed to depress ye though."

"It didn't ... do ye know any others?" Truly, she could listen to his voice all day.

He favored her with an apologetic look. "Only drinking songs ... none of them fit for a lady's ears."

Rhona laughed then, tilting her face up to the sky. The wet splash of raindrops on her cheeks made her gasp. She noted then that the rain clouds she'd spotted earlier were now directly overhead.

She met Taran's gaze once more and gave him a rueful look. "I told ye."

The words were barely out when the drizzle increased to a light patter.

"It's just a summer shower," Taran replied with a shrug.

As if to prove him wrong, the heavens then opened.

Great icy sheets of water washed over Dunvegan Loch, stippling the surface of the water and completely soaking Taran and Rhona.

Muttering a curse, Rhona crouched under the onslaught. Rain sluiced down her face, blinding her. It soaked her clothing and trickled between her breasts.

She glowered at Taran. He sat, water streaming off him. His short blond hair was plastered to his skull, although his eyes glinted. Unlike Rhona, the squall didn't seem to bother him.

"A summer shower?" she growled.

"Worry not, lass," he replied, his mouth curving. "It will pass soon enough."

Rhona reached down and wrung out her sodden skirts.

Taran had been right, the storm had ended as quickly as it had begun—only, it was so heavy Rhona felt as if she'd been doused by buckets of icy water. Back on shore, she realized she was soaked right through to her léine. She removed her woolen shawl and wrung that out too, amazed by the volume of water it yielded.

"Apologies, Rhona." Taran stepped up next to her after pulling the boat onto the shore. "That didn't go as I'd hoped."

Rhona huffed. "Ye should know ye can't trust the weather."

Her gaze left his face then, traveling down his body.

Unlike most days Taran didn't wear his heavy mail shirt this morning, only a loose léine which was now plastered to his body. Rhona stared at his chest, at where his flat nipples were visible through the thin cloth. Her fingers itched to reach for him.

Catching herself, Rhona jerked her gaze away. She had to stop staring at him like some lusty tavern wench.

"Ye said the boat ride was the first of yer surprises," she said, trying to ignore the fact that she suddenly felt breathless. "What's the next one?"

He stepped forward and reached up, brushing a wet curl of hair off her cheek. "Ye aren't annoyed with me then?"

The feel of his fingers against Rhona's skin made hunger curl deep within her. Taran seemed oblivious to the effect even his merest touch had on her.

"Of course not," she husked. "Ye can't control the weather."

He reached for her hand, his fingers entwining through hers. "Come on then, follow me."

Taran led Rhona to the edge of a copse of trees that looked over the water.

He loosed a relieved breath when he spied the wicker basket he'd left there earlier. Tucked under the boughs of a sheltering willow, the basket had escaped the worst of the rain. The blanket he'd left folded up on top was only slightly damp.

Retrieving the basket, he set it down by the water's edge and spread out the blanket for them to sit upon.

Rhona sat down, arranging her wet skirts around her. The sight was distracting, for she'd lifted the hem of her léine and kirtle, revealing pale, shapely ankles and calves. The rain had wet the fabric through, and her clothing clung to her midriff and full breasts in a way that made it difficult for him to keep his gaze averted.

He needed this to go better than the boat ride had. He was starting to feel somewhat of a failure when it came to wooing a woman. He wondered if Rhona thought him a fool.

"A cup of ale for ye, Rhona?" he asked, withdrawing a clay stoppered bottle from the basket.

A warm smile spread across her face. "Aye, what's this, Taran?"

Watching her, Taran found it hard to breathe. How he longed to reach for her, to pull her into his arms. And yet he didn't. Instead, he returned her smile. "I thought I'd have our own Lammas feast prepared. Greer packed the basket for me. There's Lammas bread, butter, boiled eggs, and some oat-cakes sweetened with honey."

"Sounds delicious." Rhona reached into the basket and withdrew the loaf of Lammas bread, a plaited braid made with the first of this harvest's wheat. "It's still warm," she exclaimed.

Taran poured them a cup of ale each while Rhona broke off two pieces of bread and spread on some butter. She then peeled them both an egg each.

"This was a bonny idea," she murmured, holding her cup up to him. "The keep is so busy these days … it's good to spend some time alone together."

Her words warmed him, far more than his first draft of ale did. "The morning isn't a complete disaster then?"

She grinned at him, turning her face up to where the sun now shone its friendly face down upon them, drying their clothing. "No … ye have redeemed yerself."

They ate in silence. Taran enjoyed Rhona's easy company. She wasn't a woman who felt the need to fill a pause with chatter. Instead, they ate and drank, and listened to the soft lap of the water on the shore. Occasionally, Taran caught the faint burst of laughter or voices from Dunvegan village. Even though they were some distance away, the sound carried across the water.

Once they'd finished their meal, Taran poured the last drops of drink into their cups, and they sat, shoulder to shoulder, upon the blanket lingering over their ale.

"I like it here," Rhona murmured. Her voice was slightly drowsy. "I could stay upon this blanket for the rest of the day."

"Then we shall," he replied. Tentatively, he looped an arm around her shoulders, drawing her against him. He ached to do more, and yet he didn't.

Taran had counted each day of the three long weeks that had passed since their handfasting. Every night in that bed with Rhona sleeping within reaching distance had been torture. And yet this was his own doing; he saw from her eyes that she wanted him. Over the past weeks, they'd gotten to know each other, had deepened the easy relationship that had already existed between them into something far stronger.

Taran knew it was time for him to take their relationship forward.

And yet now that he'd reached the crossroads, he found he couldn't.

Chapter Twenty-four

Hold-Fast

RHONA WATCHED HER husband dress, admiring the way the muscles in his back and shoulders rippled as he reached for his léine.

She stifled a sigh. She'd enjoyed Lammas the day before, and the effort Taran had made for her. Only, she'd expected him to at least kiss her—and he hadn't.

Taran pulled on his tunic and turned to her. Their gazes met, and Rhona felt that familiar pull. A knot of excitement pooled in the pit of her belly. She didn't notice his scars at all these days; instead, his eyes mesmerized her, as did his lips. She often caught herself staring at his mouth, imagining what he'd be like to kiss.

She was staring now, but she didn't care. Her body felt restless, her breasts uncomfortably sensitive. Initially, Rhona had been flattered by his insistence on wooing her, but these days his reticence was beginning to frustrate her.

"Will ye join us for the hunt today?" Taran asked with a smile as he fastened his belt. "Yer father's got a hankering for roast boar."

"Aye," Rhona replied, her mood lifting. It had been a while since she'd been out on a hunt. Lasair loved a good run. A hunt would help vent Rhona's frustration.

Taran reached for his mail shirt. "Well, ye had better get dressed then. We ride out within the hour."

Rhona threw back the covers and leaped out of bed. "Why didn't ye say something earlier?"

He favored her with a playful smile, his gaze twinkling. "I didn't think ye would be keen."

A short while later, Rhona was seated upon her chestnut mare, nibbling at a piece of bannock while Taran tightened Tussock's girth beside her. The gelding snorted and pawed at the ground, eager to be off.

A sea of horses, men, and dogs surrounded them. The rumble of male voices and the excited yipping of the hounds filled the misty morning air. Rhona smiled, her senses sharpening. It had been too long since she'd ridden out on a hunt.

They left Dunvegan in a clatter of hooves and barking dogs. Fog, as thick as clotted cream, drifted in off the loch, turning the morning cool. It would burn off soon enough, but for the moment Rhona was relieved she'd donned her woolen cloak before setting out.

Leaving the keep behind, they rode east over bare hills. The shadow of great mountains rose ahead, marching closer as they left the shroud of coastal fog behind. Rhona rode at Taran's side and found herself stealing glances at him. She'd gotten used to having him close to her over the last weeks, and yet at the same time she was growing ever tenser in his company.

What does he want from me?

Taran glanced her way, spearing her with his ice-blue gaze. "What is it, love?"

Pleasure feathered down Rhona's neck at the low timbre of his voice. *Love*. Did he really mean it?

"Nothing," she murmured, tearing her gaze from his and fixing it in the direction of travel. "I'm just enjoying riding out with ye … that's all."

She felt his gaze remain on her, the intensity of it causing heat to flush across her chest. Did he have any idea of the effect his proximity had on her?

"And I, with ye," he replied, with a teasing smile. "I'm glad we've been able to make a new start, Rhona."

Her gaze snapped back to him. They'd done that, but she wanted more. She had no idea how to voice her feelings.

The hunting party continued east and entered a valley between two mountains. A dark pine forest carpeted the ground of the steep vale. Rhona inhaled the scent of pine resin and enjoyed the cool kiss of the woodland air on her skin. This valley was one of her father's favorite hunting grounds for deer and boar.

It didn't take them long to flush out a boar—a small female that the dogs cornered without much trouble. The warriors then closed in bearing boar spears, weakening the animal, before Dughall MacLean finished it off with a stab to the heart.

Congratulating themselves on their easy kill, the men hoisted the carcass onto the back of a horse and continued on their way.

They had ridden deep into the valley, the trees rising high overhead, when a dark shape hurtled out of the forest before them.

It was a large male boar with a wiry black coat and long gleaming tusks. The beast ran at the dogs squealing with rage, while warriors stabbed at it, slowing its path.

Connel Buchanan and Gordon MacPherson were among them. Grinning, Connel circled the boar and drove his spear into its side. Rhona drew up Lasair, her gaze riveted on the scene up ahead. Boar were dangerous, clever, and stout-hearted. Even surrounded, as this one was, it wouldn't surrender without a fight.

The men and dogs tightened the net. One of the hounds went down, howling, as a sharp tusk found its mark. Yet, the boar was starting to tire. Grunting, it staggered around the clearing, blood running down its flanks.

With a whoop, Connel leaped down from his horse to make the final kill.

"Careful Buchanan," Malcolm MacLeod roared. "This boar's a wily one."

"Hold-fast, chief!" Connel shouted back. Shouts of encouragement went up around him. 'Hold-fast' was MacLeod's rallying cry, one he'd used ever since he'd killed a rampaging bull years earlier. He'd been a much younger man then, when, armed only with a dirk, he'd slain the beast and broken off one of its horns as a trophy. It was now the clan-chief's favorite drinking horn.

Connel hoisted his spear high. The boar spear had a crosspiece on the shaft, which would halt the beast. Otherwise, the boar was capable, even when speared, of charging the hunter and killing him.

Lasair snorted, tossing her head nervously and backing up. The scent of blood, violence, and the boar's odor, unnerved the mare. Rhona didn't blame her; a boar hunt was violent and not for the faint of heart.

Although she'd never liked Connel Buchanan much, she had to admit he showed courage facing off against the enraged quarry. She glanced right at Taran; he'd drawn Tussock up next to her, his gaze fixed upon the snorting, grunting boar. She was glad he'd stayed at her side.

"Finish it, Buchanan," Dughall MacLean shouted. "Stick it in the throat."

Connel ignored the warrior. Instead, he danced around the boar, toying with it.

Rhona's brow furrowed.

"What's the fool doing?" Taran muttered from next to her.

She was wondering the same thing.

Connel struck the boar in the hindquarters. With a squeal, it turned and lumbered toward him. Still grinning, the warrior leaped aside and stabbed it in the flank.

"Just end this, Buchanan," MacLeod called out. "Stop showing off."

But Connel didn't heed the chief. He continued to dance around the maddened boar, sticking it and prodding it until the creature huffed and wheezed.

"Stop him," Rhona muttered. She enjoyed a good hunt, but she didn't like to see senseless cruelty. The boar was in pain and confused. She wished her father would step in.

Tussock shifted, as Taran urged him forward. "Connel." His voice lashed across the glade. "Finish it." Yet the warrior didn't heed him either.

Connel danced around the boar once more, sticking it again in the flank. With a shriek of rage, the creature turned on him. Heedless of pain, of the spear now stuck in its side, it lunged. The warrior staggered back, his grin slipping—and tripped.

In an instant, the boar was on him. It gored him repeatedly, in a frenzy of fury and pain. Connel Buchanan's screams echoed through the trees.

Moments later, Gordon brought it down with a spear to the back of the head.

Taran leaped down from Tussock and rushed to Gordon's side. Dughall joined them, and together, the three men heaved the dead boar off Connel.

"Rhona!" Taran called out. "We need yer help."

Swinging down from Lasair's back, she went to them. Rhona was no healer, yet she was the only woman in the party—the only one who had been taught to tend wounds.

She knelt at Connel's side, bile rising in her throat.

One glance and she knew it was bad. The léine and plaid braies Connel wore were now crimson; the tusk had sliced through leather and linen like a knife through curd. Blood pumped out of wounds to his stomach, groin, and upper thigh.

Rhona swallowed. The tusks had pierced an artery. Connel was bleeding out over the ground.

With trembling hands, she ripped the hem from her léine and started to bind it around the wound to Connel's thigh. It was hopeless, but she had to do something.

Face pale, blue eyes wide, the young man stared up at her. He wore a startled expression as if he couldn't believe this was happening to him.

A twig snapped behind them, and Rhona glanced over her shoulder to see that her father had dismounted and now stood behind them. His bearded face was thunderous as he stared down at Connel.

"Chief," the warrior rasped, staring up at him. "Ye were right ... he was a wily bastard."

"Aye, lad," MacLeod replied, his expression softening. "He was." His gaze shifted down to the young man's injuries.

Rhona tore her gaze from her father and looked back, at where her hands pressed into the wound she'd just bound. Red stained her hands. She couldn't staunch the bleeding.

"Close yer eyes, lad," the chief rumbled, his voice softer than Rhona had heard it in a long while. He knelt at the warrior's side, taking hold of Connel's hand. The sight made Rhona's throat constrict. Her father could be fierce, brutal even, yet he inspired loyalty in the men who followed him for a reason. "Rest now."

The man did as bid, his eyelids flickering. His face was the color of milk. Long moments passed, and around them, the forest glade went silent. The men bowed their heads as Connel Buchanan died.

Rhona splashed water on her face and inhaled the scent of rose. The perfume soothed her, dulling the sharp edges of the day she'd just passed.

A senseless, reckless death.

It was difficult to mourn the passing of a callow youth she'd never liked, yet the violence of Connel Buchanan's demise would haunt her dreams in the days to come. Rhona shook her head to clear the memory of the blood and gore. She picked up a square of linen, drying her face.

She emerged from behind the screen to find her husband already abed.

Taran lay on his back staring up at the ceiling, his hands clasped behind his head. A deep groove cut between his eyebrows, giving him a fierce look.

"Ye are angry," she observed, approaching the bed.

"Aye," he ground out. He didn't look her way but continued to stare up at the rafters. "The dolt had his whole life before him."

Rhona gusted out a sigh and sat down upon the bed. "Ma used to say that reckless young men are always the first to die."

He inclined his head to her then, a humorless smile curving his mouth. "She was right."

Rhona met his gaze. "But ye are not reckless, are ye Taran MacKinnon ... quite the opposite I'd say."

He huffed. "What's that supposed to mean?"

"Exactly what I said. Ye are a brave man ... but a thinking one." She frowned then as the memory of how Connel had baited that boar needled her. "Ye would never treat an animal that way either."

His mouth thinned. "Had he lived, I'd have broken his nose for that."

Rhona loosed a sigh. She pulled back the covers and slid into bed. Tiredness pulled down at her, and she sank willingly into the softness. She was aware of the heat of Taran's body just a couple of feet from hers. After what they'd both witnessed, she longed to reach for him, yet she suddenly felt shy.

She wasn't sure of him anymore. Here she was, right next to him, but he merely watched her with that intense look that made her breathing quicken, her pulse race. He could pull her into his arms, could kiss her—yet he did nothing. Did he prefer this arrangement—sleeping in the same bed but never touching?

Perhaps he did.

A long moment passed, and then Taran reached out a hand, stroking her gently on the cheek. "Goodnight, m'eudail," he murmured. *My darling.*

"Goodnight," Rhona whispered back, aching for his hand to linger.

However, he withdrew it and rolled away from her, leaving Rhona with nothing but a view of his broad back.

Chapter Twenty-five

Prove My Worth

"I TAKE THE Vale of Hamra Rinner as my own. From this day forth the land belongs to clan Fraser. Any MacLeod who sets foot upon it will be trespassing. His life will be forfeit."

Malcolm MacLeod slammed his fist down on the table. The noise echoed through the Great Hall. "Thieving, bloody bastards." His bellow shook the rafters. "I'll slay them all … every last stinking Fraser!"

Taran, who'd been spreading honey onto a wedge of bannock, froze. It was just after dawn, and he and Rhona had risen early to join the chief and his wife as they broke their fast. A week had passed since that fateful boar hunt. Aonghus Budge was visiting Dunvegan yet again, and MacLeod had planned to take him hawking this morning. Taran would ride out with them.

"My love." Una put down a cup of milk she'd been sipping, her gaze widening. "Calm yerself."

"Villain!" Malcolm ignored his wife and heaved his bulk up from the table, scattering bannocks as he did so. In his right hand, he gripped a sheet of parchment. "Morgan Fraser has gone too far!"

At the sound of her former husband's name, the chieftain's wife paled. Watching her, Taran wondered if she'd ever loved the Fraser chieftain. She'd needed little persuasion to run off with Malcolm MacLeod. The union mustn't have been a happy one.

"How dare Fraser take the Vale of Hamra Rinner as his own."

Aonghus Budge swallowed a mouthful of food, his watery blue eyes hardening. "Aye, those are yer lands, MacLeod."

"We've hunted stags in that valley for generations," Malcolm snarled. "I'll not have a Fraser tell me we can't."

A rumble of outrage followed this announcement, rippling over the Great Hall like thunder. Taran glanced over at Rhona to find her staring at her father, brow furrowed.

"Ye can't let him get away with it, Da." Iain MacLeod spoke up. The lad's sharp-featured face was taut, his grey eyes flinty.

"I don't intend to, laddie," Malcolm MacLeod growled back. He drew himself up to his full height. Even corpulent and red-faced, he was still a formidable man to look upon. "Finally, the MacLeods and Frasers will meet in battle. We shall stain that valley crimson with Fraser blood." His gaze swept to Iain. "Ride to Duntulm," he barked. "Tell Baltair MacDonald to ride to us with as many warriors as he can spare."

Aonghus Budge rose quickly to his feet, hands clenched by his sides. "The Budges of Islay are with ye too, Malcolm."

MacLeod nodded to his friend. "Thank ye, Aonghus," he rasped. His hand crushed the parchment. "I'll answer Fraser now. We shall meet those dogs in battle at noon, two days from now."

Next to Taran, Rhona leaned forward. "Da ... I will join ye. I can fight."

"No." The word was out of Taran's mouth before he could stop it.

The table went still. Rhona inclined her head toward him, her eyes narrowed. "Excuse me?"

"If my daughter wants to fight, she can," MacLeod replied, favoring Taran with a sneer. "Ye went behind my back to teach her how to wield a sword after all."

Taran stiffened. He didn't like the goading tone to Malcolm's voice, the challenge he'd just laid down. Ignoring the chief, he met Rhona's gaze. "It's too dangerous," he said. "Ye have never seen combat, Rhona."

His wife drew herself up, jaw tightening. "I can handle myself."

He admired her courage, he really did. Yet her confidence was misplaced. She could wield a sword, but she'd lived a sheltered existence within the walls of this keep. How would she react when a battle-crazed warrior rushed her with his sword drawn? She'd handled Connel's death well, but she had no idea what war was like, and her father knew it.

"The answer's still no," he replied, his tone hardening. "I'll not put ye at risk."

Rhona's lips parted as she prepared to answer. But her father's snort forestalled her.

"Far be it for me to stand between a man and his wife," he drawled. He favored Rhona with a smirk. "Ye will have to obey MacKinnon now, daughter."

"Why did ye bother teaching me how to fight?"

Rhona faced Taran, hands on hips. She'd followed him outside into the stables, waiting till they were alone. He turned, his face adopting a forbidding expression she knew well; it was the Taran MacKinnon who served her father, the man who wore his scars like a shield.

"Because ye commanded me to," he replied.

Rhona scowled. "Ye could have refused me. Ye could have gone to my father."

He folded his brawny arms across his broad chest. "Ye know why I didn't."

Anger rose within Rhona in a hot tide. She felt humiliated, patronized. She'd hated how her father, brother, and Aonghus Budge had all smirked at her in the Great Hall. Taran should have supported her, instead, he'd cut her down in front of them all. "So, ye think I'm not capable of fighting in battle, is that it?"

He huffed out an exasperated breath. "I'm just trying to protect ye."

"I don't need yer protection," she shot back, furious now. "I'm a warrior's daughter. I asked ye to train me so that I could fight alongside my menfolk one day. Da will let me … why won't ye?"

Taran's ice-blue gaze hardened. "He agreed merely to have his revenge upon me."

"What? That's ridiculous."

He took a step toward her. "Is it? He's furious I won yer hand. He didn't want ye wed to the likes of me … to the 'Beast of Dunvegan'. He'll see both of us punished for it."

Rhona glared at him. She wanted to deny his words, insult him for them, yet in her gut she knew he spoke the truth. The look on her father's face inside the Great Hall had been clear. He had no respect for her, but if she wanted to ride into battle with him and his men, he'd allow it. Especially if it hurt Taran.

Shoulders rounding, she let the anger drain out of her. Hurt replaced it. Her gaze dropped to the straw-strewn floor as she struggled to control her emotions. "I'm not useless," she whispered. "I'm not a decorative ornament born to wear pretty gowns, press flowers, and embroider cushions. I wish I'd been born a man … ye would all respect me then."

Silence fell between them. She heard the scuff of Taran's boots as he moved closer to her. A heartbeat later, a strong finger gently hooked under her chin and lifted it.

Their gazes met, and Rhona was relieved to see that the shield he'd raised earlier had lowered. "I'm glad ye were born a woman," he murmured, smiling. "And a fierce one at that."

"What does it matter how fierce I am?" she replied. She heard the bitterness in her voice but didn't care. "I'll never get a chance to prove my worth."

"Ye don't need to," he replied, his gaze soft. "Not to me."

"Do ye really want to fight?"

Adaira glanced up from where she was playing with the puppy on the floor of the women's solar. The pup had grown considerably in the past few weeks and had taken to nipping Adaira's hands with its new, needle-like teeth. Adaira bore red welts over her hands and forearms, yet she didn't appear to mind.

Rhona huffed a breath, lowering the embroidery she'd been trying to focus on. "Aye."

Adaira watched her, fascinated. "I wish more women were bold like ye." A grin spread across her face. "Then we'd rule over men rather than them over us."

Rhona snorted. "That's fanciful thinking. Ye saw Da and Taran this morning … I don't decide my fate. They do."

The pup gave a mock growl and started pulling at the hem of Adaira's kirtle. Rhona arched her eyebrow. "Best ye don't let Una see him do that … she'll have Dùnglas skinned."

Adaira gave a gasp, scooping the wriggling pup up into her arms. "Nasty Una … we'll not let her touch ye!" She cuddled him against her breast, her attention returning to Rhona once more.

Rhona glanced back down at her embroidery. She didn't like it when Adaira favored her with one of her 'searching' gazes. It was all too easy to forget that Adaira saw far more than she let on.

"Is all well between ye and Taran?" Adaira asked after a pause.

Rhona's needle slipped, stabbing her in the finger. She loosed a curse and lifted her injured hand to her mouth. "What kind of question is that?"

Adaira's hazel eyes narrowed as she set Dùnglas down on the ground once more. The pup pounced on a ball of wool Adaira had given him to play with. However, this time the young woman didn't shift her gaze to her puppy. Instead, she continued to watch Rhona. "A direct one," she replied, her mouth curving. "And clearly a question ye don't want to answer."

"I don't know why ye would ask it," Rhona replied. She heard the sour note in her voice and suppressed a wince.

Adaira inclined her head. "Ye both looked happy after the handfasting … but of late something has changed. When I see ye together, there's … a distance."

Rhona swallowed the lump that had risen, unbidden, in her throat. Aye, Adaira was too perceptive by half. She hoped no one else had noticed the tension between her and Taran. That was the problem with living in a keep the size of Dunvegan. There were too many curious eyes upon her, too many flapping ears and gossiping tongues. Her relationship with Taran was under constant scrutiny.

"He's a good man," she murmured finally, dropping her gaze from her sister's. "Better than I deserve."

Adaira snorted at the comment but didn't answer, waiting for Rhona to continue.

Staring down at where a drop of blood had beaded once more on her finger, Rhona inhaled sharply. "I'm so confused, Adaira ... I don't know what to do." She glanced up and met her sister's eye. "On the night of our handfasting, Taran admitted that he'd been in love with me for years. That's why he'd defied Da and let me train with him ... of course, I'd been oblivious."

Adaira frowned but again held her tongue.

"I never saw him as a man until that night," Rhona continued. Her chest constricted as she spoke, yet she forced herself to press on. Perhaps sharing her feelings with her sister would help. "We lay together that night ... but he's not touched me since."

The furrow on her sister's brow deepened. "Really? Why not?"

"He says he wants to 'woo' me, for us to be in love before he beds me again." Heat flushed Rhona's cheeks. She couldn't believe she was actually voicing this to her younger sister. "But I'm beginning to think it's an excuse ... that he doesn't *want* me."

Silence fell in the solar, the hush broken only by the yips and grunt of the wolfhound pup as it rolled around the floor, the ball of wool clamped between its paws.

"I don't think that's the case," Adaira said eventually. Her voice was soft, pensive. "I've seen the way he looks at ye." She gave a sigh. "I'd love for a man to gaze at me like that."

Rhona huffed, reaching for her embroidery once more. She wished she hadn't said anything. Adaira was a maid and still believed that love was like the ballads Una sometimes sang in the evenings. Her head was full of silly notions. It didn't matter if Taran bestowed melting looks upon her. These days he treated her like a sister—and it was slowly breaking Rhona's heart.

Chapter Twenty-six

Things Unsaid

MACDONALD WARRIORS THUNDERED into the keep. Pennants of the clan's plaid—green and blue threaded with white and red—snapped and billowed. A hot wind blew in from the south, sending dust devils spinning across the bailey.

Rhona viewed the MacDonalds' arrival from the window of Adaira's bower.

The sisters had been working at their looms together when the horn announcing visitors echoed across the keep. Putting down the tapestry beater—a wooden comb that she used to push down the woven threads—Rhona had crossed to the window. A heartbeat later, Adaira appeared at her side. They craned their necks, watching the sea of horses and men clad in plaid, leather, and chainmail fill the bailey. At the end of the column, a wagon rumbled in. A woman with hair the color of summer wheat, a babe in her arms, perched on the back.

"Caitrin!" Adaira squealed. "He's brought her with him."

Despite her low mood this morning, a smile stretched across Rhona's face. Her sister's arrival was welcome news indeed; so much had happened since she'd last seen Caitrin. She needed to talk to her.

The MacLeods, MacDonalds, and Budges would leave at first light the following morning. Rhona had barely seen Taran over the past day, for he'd been taken up with getting men armed, horses shod, and weapons sharpened before their departure.

The twists and turns of fate came at her so swiftly these days she could barely catch her breath. First this marriage, and now her husband was about to ride off to battle.

What if he falls?

Rhona's chest had twisted at the thought. She was angry with him for not letting her fight, and hurt that he didn't wish to lie with her, but the thought of losing him was like a dirk to her breast.

"He's grown so!" Adaira bent over the babe, tickling him under the chin. Her features tensed then. "He looks so much like his Da."

"That's not surprising, is it?" Caitrin's voice had a reproachful edge to it.

"Aye, but it's not the wee lad's fault," Rhona chimed in. "Some things can't be helped."

Eoghan MacDonald gurgled, his chubby hands reaching up to Adaira. He had a thick head of dark hair already, just like Baltair.

Rhona met Caitrin's eye. Her sister's lovely face was tired and drawn, although the dark smudges under her eyes had gone. She looked thin under the voluminous kirtle and léine, her collarbone more prominent than Rhona remembered.

"Are ye well, Caitrin?" she asked gently.

Her sister nodded. "I'm much stronger now, thank ye."

There was a formality to Caitrin's voice, an edge that warned Rhona from pressing further. The three sisters sat in the women's solar. The windows overlooking the hills to the east were open. The hot breeze breathed in, fanning their faces.

It was then that she realized Caitrin was studying her intently.

Rhona stiffened. "What?"

Her sister's mouth quirked. "Ye seem different ... I can't put my finger on exactly what."

"This heat has made me crabby," Rhona replied with a shrug.

Caitrin gave a soft laugh. "No, it's not that."

"It's obvious, isn't it?" Adaira spoke up. "She's a wedded woman now."

Caitrin smiled, although her blue eyes remained shadowed. "Of course. Taran MacKinnon ... I was surprised when Baltair told me."

Rhona cast Adaira a look of censure. Her younger sister had a wicked smile on her face as if she wished to say more. She'd kick her in the shin if she did.

The mood turned awkward. Rhona sensed Caitrin's curiosity. She knew her sister wanted to ask her about her wedding night, wanted to know if Taran treated her well. But to ask such questions would shine a light upon her own marriage. Caitrin didn't want to talk of Baltair—that much was clear. Once they were alone, Rhona had hoped to have a private word with Caitrin, but now she wasn't sure her sister would welcome such a conversation.

"Taran's not as frightening as everyone thinks," Adaira continued. She then gave a soft sigh. "The opposite in fact. Ye should have seen Rhona's face the day after the handfasting ... she looked like the cat that got the cream."

"Adaira," Rhona growled. "Enough."

"What?" Adaira favored her with a look of mock innocence. "It's the truth."

"Don't be a goose," Rhona snapped, rising to her feet. She couldn't believe Adaira was bringing this up, especially after their conversation the day before. Her sister hadn't understood a thing.

Adaira drew back, her features tightening. "I'm not a fool," she said quietly. "Don't treat me like one."

Rhona and Adaira stared at each other. Caitrin cleared her throat, breaking the tension. "Come ... let's not argue. I'm so happy to see ye both. Ye have no idea how lonely it gets in Duntulm."

Rhona tore her gaze from Adaira and forced a smile. "I'm glad ye are here," she said. "Wee Eoghan too."

As if recognizing his own name, the babe gave a squeal.

"Da said ye would get me a sword."

Taran glanced up from where he was sharpening a blade upon a whetstone, to see Iain MacLeod standing in the doorway to the armory. Even at sixteen winters, the lad carried his father's authority. Auburn-haired, with those penetrating MacLeod grey eyes, Iain wasn't someone Taran had ever warmed to.

The young man's aggressive tone, his pugnacious expression, didn't improve Taran's opinion of him this afternoon.

"Aye," he replied, rising to his feet and gesturing to the wall of swords behind him. "Did ye have a blade in mind?"

"I want a Claidheamh-mor ... like Da's."

Taran resisted the urge to raise an eyebrow. "Yer father has twice yer girth and strength," he pointed out. "Why not try a lighter long-sword?"

Iain's mouth twisted. "I didn't ask for yer opinion, *Beast*. Get me what I asked for."

Taran gave the lad a long, hard look before turning to the armory. There, he pulled a sword off the wall. It was a heavy weapon that had to be wielded with both hands, two inches broad with a double edge and a long, deadly blade. Taran's own sword was of the same make. Only, he was double the weight and strength of Iain MacLeod.

Taran handed the blade to the clan-chief's son, hilt first. The lad took it without a word of thanks. "Is it sharp?"

"Aye."

"Good ... ye will hear from me if it isn't."

Iain turned on his heel, intending to stride out of the armory, and ran into Gordon, who'd just entered the building. The lad bounced off the warrior's broad chest before snarling at him. "Watch where ye are going."

Gordon dipped his head and stepped aside. "Apologies, lad. I'll watch my step in future."

Throwing Gordon a black look, Iain stalked off, clutching the Claidheamh-mor in both hands.

"Jumped up pup," Gordon murmured watching him go. "I can't believe MacLeod's letting him fight."

Taran shrugged. "He thinks it's time the lad was blooded."

Gordon snorted. "God help us all then." He glanced over at Taran, his brow furrowing. "I hear Lady Rhona wants to join us tomorrow?"

"Aye," Taran growled, picking up the sword he was halfway through sharpening. "She's vexed with me for stopping her."

Gordon huffed a laugh. "I've seen her fight ... she's good."

Taran cast his friend a hard look. "The answer's still 'no'."

"More mutton, Rhona?" Taran held out a platter to his wife. Despite that he was hungry enough today to finish the lot, he'd left the last slice of meat for her.

Rhona's storm-grey gaze met his. "No, thank ye," she replied softly. "Ye have it."

Taran forced back a frown. Rhona hadn't been herself over the last few days. At first, he'd thought it was the shock of seeing Connel Buchanan gored by that boar, and then he'd put it down to anger at not being allowed to fight alongside him.

Yet it wasn't anger he saw in her eyes now, but something softer. She looked ... sad.

Taran stiffened, lowering the platter before him. What reason did she have to be unhappy? A chill feathered down his spine. Was she regretting their union?

Taran took a bite of mutton. Moments earlier he'd been enjoying the rich flavor of the meat, yet now it tasted like ash. In the weeks since their handfasting, he'd done everything to make her happy, to make her warm to him as a man.

And now that he saw melancholy in his wife's eyes, something deep within his chest twisted.

She wed the ugliest man upon this Isle, a cruel voice whispered in his head. *Why wouldn't she be regretting it?*

"I hear Rhona wants to join us tomorrow." Baltair MacDonald's voice intruded. Taran glanced up from his meal to see the clan-chief favoring him with an oily smile. "Why don't ye let her fight with us?" Beside Baltair, Caitrin stiffened. She cast her husband a warning look, but he ignored her. "Rumor has it that ye trained her in secret for years," Baltair continued, his smile widening. "Or maybe that was merely a ruse ... perhaps it wasn't a Claidheamh-mor ye were teaching her to wield."

This comment made Aonghus Budge choke on his mutton. Spluttering, the chief reached for a cup of mead. His pale blue eyes shone with amusement. However, at the head of the table, Malcolm MacLeod didn't look entertained.

"MacDonald," he growled a low warning.

Undaunted, Baltair shrugged, his attention still fixed upon Taran. "Maybe she can't fight at all."

Taran heard Rhona's sharp intake of breath next to him, felt the tension rippling from her. He knew that Baltair resented Rhona. She'd told him about the incident with Adaira. Taran wagered that, ever since, Baltair had been waiting for his revenge. He was trying to goad her into saying something that would humiliate her.

Taran wasn't going to let that happen. "My wife wields a sword as well as ye, Baltair," he replied. "I'm just doing what a husband does ... protecting her."

The MacDonald chieftain's mouth twisted. It wasn't the answer he'd expected or wanted. Taran held his gaze in an open challenge. Baltair would insult Rhona again at his peril.

Chapter Twenty-seven

Only a Coward

RHONA WAS SITTING at the window, staring out at the dusky sky, when Taran entered their chamber. It was shortly after supper, a tense meal during which she'd thought her husband and Baltair MacDonald might come to blows.

"Would ye take a walk with me?"

Rhona turned from the window and put down the embroidery she'd barely touched, to see Taran leaning against the doorframe. In his mail shirt and braies, stubble covering his chin, he looked rough—dangerous.

Belly fluttering, Rhona swallowed. Just the sight of him, the impact of their gazes meeting, made her wits scatter. She didn't seem to have the same effect on him though. Taran's expression was unreadable as he watched her.

"What … now?" she asked, nervousness rising within her.

His mouth curved. "Aye … it's a beautiful evening out, and tomorrow I leave for battle. I'd like to take a stroll in the gardens with my wife."

Wife. The way he said it made the fluttering in Rhona's belly increase tenfold. A walk would give them time together—time for her to broach the issue that loomed over them.

"Very well." She rose to her feet, smoothing her light linen kirtle. "I could do with some fresh air."

They left the tower chamber, traveling single-file down the narrow turret stairs. However, once they reached the wider stairwell below, Taran held out his arm to her. Wordlessly, Rhona took it, linking her arm through his. Together, they left the keep via the Sea-gate and made their way down the causeway. Turning off it, they took a path south to where the gardens lay, a riot of color against the stark outlines of the hills beyond. The dying sun had gilded the garden, and a wall of scent hit Rhona as they walked into it.

She inhaled deeply and tried to quell the churning of her belly. She'd forgotten how flowers released their scent in the evening.

"The garden is at its best this time of day," Taran said, echoing her own thoughts. "Yet few bother to visit it now."

"Ye are right," Rhona replied. "Thank ye for suggesting it."

He placed a hand over hers, squeezing gently. "We haven't seen much of each other these past days. I'm sorry for it."

Rhona heaved in a deep breath. "Aye, and tomorrow ye are leaving."

"I shall return."

She cast him a sharp look. "Sure of yerself, aren't ye?"

His mouth twitched. "A warrior has to be."

"But what if ye don't ... what if a Fraser sticks a dirk in yer guts, and I'm left a widow?" Rhona pulled her arm from his and halted, turning to face him. "What then?"

His gaze met hers. "That would be a shame."

Rhona gritted her teeth. Was he trying to vex her? "It would," she muttered, "and an even greater one, for I would have only had one night with my husband before losing him." She placed her hands on her hips, gathering the shreds of her courage. She had to speak now or she never would. "Are ye planning to shun me tonight as well?"

He loosed a sharp breath, his gaze guttering. "Ye talk as if I've treated ye cruelly, Rhona. I'm trying to show ye respect."

"By ignoring me? I'm beginning to think ye regret our handfasting."

He shook his head. "What I regret is the way it all happened. Ye were forced into wedding me. I'm just letting ye get used to being my wife."

Rhona scowled. "There's no time for that. I'm not a delicate flower that has to be handled gently for fear of breaking. Ye are starting to infuriate me, Taran MacKinnon."

His face tensed. "Then, I'm sorry."

Rhona clenched her hands by her sides. If he apologized once more, she swore she'd hit him. "I don't want ye to tell me ye are sorry," she growled. "I want ye to start treating me like yer wife. God's Bones, ye haven't even kissed me yet! What's wrong with ye?"

She regretted the words as soon as they left her mouth. Yet it was too late. She couldn't take them back.

Taran yanked back from her as if she had just struck him.

"Taran," she gasped. "I—"

Her husband took a step away from her, his big body tensing, and turned back toward the entrance to the garden. He might have stridden away from her then, if a man's voice, rough with anger, hadn't intruded.

"Ye will do as ye are told, woman. Is that clear?"

"But we just arrived here ... I don't understand why I have to go back to Duntulm so soon?"

"I don't trust ye in this keep ... not with yer sisters close at hand."

A pause followed, and the fine hair on the back of Rhona's neck prickled. They were listening to Caitrin and Baltair.

"What's wrong with that?" Caitrin's voice was sharp when she answered her husband. "Rhona and Adaira have done me no wrong."

"A blade-tongued shrew and that brainless chatterer. They're a bad influence on ye."

Caitrin's soft laugh echoed through the garden. There was no mirth in the sound, just scorn. "They're my *sisters*, Baltair. I will never forsake them ... not for ye, not for anyone."

A crack followed—the sound of an open palm striking flesh. "Ye will do as ye are told, woman."

Beside Rhona, Taran moved. He left her side and strode into the midst of the gardens. Rhona followed.

They came upon the couple, just as Baltair delivered another slap. Caitrin cried out, staggering back. They stood before a hawthorn hedge. The berries were just beginning to ripen, small red buds bright against the green foliage.

Caitrin glared up at her husband, eyes gleaming. Her left cheek glowed red as she raised a hand to it. Baltair loomed over her. He drew his right arm back to strike her once more. "I've had enough of being crossed by my own wife," he snarled. "I'll teach ye some manners."

"Baltair!" Taran's voice lashed across the garden, causing the two figures near the hedge to freeze. "Lower yer fist!"

The MacDonald clan-chief twisted, his gaze shifting to Taran and then Rhona. Behind him, Caitrin's frightened gaze widened. Baltair ignored Taran, his attention resting upon Rhona.

A cruel smile twisted his face. "Here's the shrew now, accompanied by her gargoyle."

Fury curled within Rhona's belly at his insults. She was sick of them. She carried no weapons, but her hands balled into fists at her sides. However, the words merely seemed to wash over Taran. His stride didn't check as he approached Baltair. He stopped before him, within striking distance.

"What's this?" Baltair met Taran's eye. "Ye shouldn't interfere between a man and his wife, MacKinnon."

"Stand back from Lady Caitrin," Taran ordered. He and Baltair were of a similar height, yet the weight of his presence made it seem as if he loomed over the MacDonald chieftain. Baltair didn't back down though; there was a feral, stubborn glint in his eye. Unease feathered down Rhona's skin when she realized that he was the kind of man who enjoyed altercations with others. He wasn't intimidated in the slightest.

Baltair spat a curse at Taran. An instant later he lashed out at his wife once more.

Taran lunged, grabbing Baltair's wrist in motion. Caitrin cried out and cringed back against the hawthorn. Baltair's fist had stopped barely inches from her face.

Baltair roared and swung around to face the man who'd prevented him from striking his wife. Meanwhile, Taran cast a glance left at where Caitrin huddled. "Go to Rhona," he said.

Not needing to be told twice, Caitrin darted away from them, reaching Rhona's side moments later. Rhona reached out and pulled her sister against her; Caitrin's slender frame was quaking.

His right wrist still gripped by Taran, Baltair swung at him with his free fist. Taran brought his arm up, deflecting the blow easily. He then drove his knee into his opponent's belly. Baltair gasped, stumbled, and fell to his knees, winded.

Taran released him and stepped back, giving the man some space. He cast a glance over his shoulder, his gaze meeting Rhona's for the first time since they'd overheard the argument. His ice-blue eyes were cold. "Take Lady Caitrin away," he said quietly. "She doesn't need to see this."

Rhona hesitated. She didn't want to leave Taran with Baltair. Even winded he was dangerous. She knew he wouldn't leave matters here.

When she didn't move, Taran's face hardened. The scars on his face made him look frightening. "Go!"

Rhona swallowed before nodding. She knew his temper wasn't just directed at Baltair. The words she'd flung at him had cut deep; she'd wounded him.

"Come, Caitrin," she murmured, steering her sister. "Let's go back inside."

Caitrin didn't resist. Together, the two women turned and hurried from the garden without looking back.

Taran waited until the sound of Rhona and Caitrin's feet crunching on pebbles faded. Only then did he speak to Baltair MacDonald.

"Only a coward beats his wife."

Baltair struggled to his feet, still gasping for breath like a winded carthorse. "And only a fool interferes where he's not wanted." His dark-blue gaze met Taran's. "Ye will pay for that, *Beast*."

Baltair lunged again, even faster than earlier. Now that Taran had released him, his right arm swung at his opponent's head. It slammed into Taran's jaw. Taran staggered and bit down on his tongue. Blood filled his mouth, and his temper finally snapped. He reached out, grabbed Baltair by the collar of his léine, and head-butted him hard in the nose.

The MacDonald chieftain went down like a sack of oats. He sprawled back onto a bed of lavender, dislodging the bees that had been buzzing there.

Taran spat out a gob of blood and wiped his mouth with the back of his hand. It took all his self-control not to throw himself on Baltair and beat him senseless. He'd never been quick to anger, but his temper once roused was a dark, wild thing that took a while to settle.

Baltair groaned. His gaze, glassy with pain, met Taran's. Blood flowed out of his nose. His mouth worked as if he might speak, but Taran cut him off.

"Keep yer fists to yerself in future, MacDonald," Taran growled. "If I hear ye have mistreated yer wife again ... I'll come looking for ye."

Caitrin dissolved into floods of tears the moment they were inside the women's solar. Adaira was in there, playing her harp by the window, when her sisters entered. One look at their faces and her fingers halted, cutting off the lilting music that greeted them.

Adaira frowned. "What's wrong?"

Rhona didn't reply. Instead, she led Caitrin over to a chair and let her settle there. Her elder sister covered her face with her hands, her shoulders shaking as she sought to contain her sobs.

After a few moments, Rhona met Adaira's eye. "Baltair," she said quietly. "Taran and I were walking in the gardens when we heard arguing."

Adaira walked across to Caitrin and knelt before her. She reached out and placed her hands on her sister's knees, squeezing. "I knew he was cruel to ye ... even though ye have never said anything. I knew."

Caitrin dropped her hands to look at Adaira. Tears coursed down her face, making the livid marks on her left cheek all the more evident. Rhona drew in a sharp breath at the desolation she saw in her elder sister's blue eyes. Caitrin had always been so strong. At this moment though, she looked broken.

"I hate him," she whispered.

Chapter Twenty-eight

Scars

NIGHT HAD FALLEN in a warm, dark blanket over Dunvegan when Rhona made her way down the steps into the bailey. She had not put on a shawl around her shoulders as the evening was sultry, the air soft against her skin. It was growing late, and the keep slumbered. Caitrin had finally retired for the night; she would share Adaira's chamber with her rather than return to the one she shared with Baltair.

Reaching the bottom of the steps, Rhona's gaze swept the shadowed corners of the yard. There was no sign of her husband here. She'd just come from their chamber; the only other place she could think to look was the stables.

She found him there, alone except for the rows of horses in the stalls. Taran had his back to her as she approached. He was in the tack-room, a partition at the end of the building. Taran was cleaning a saddle, buffing the leather with a soft cloth.

Rhona approached quietly, her tread silent in the slippers she wore. She was around four yards behind him when Taran spoke.

"Ye should be abed asleep, Rhona. It's late."

Rhona halted, surprised that he'd heard her. An awkward moment passed before she spoke. "I know it's late ... that's why I'm here. Are ye not going to join me?"

He shook his head, still not turning his face to look at her. "I'll make a bed for myself here in the stables once I'm done cleaning this."

His voice was low, weary. There was no sign of anger in it, although that just made Rhona feel worse. The words she'd thrown at him had tormented her all evening. Initially, she'd been preoccupied with Caitrin, but once she'd returned to their chamber—and found it empty—she'd been unable to settle. The more time stretched on, the worse she felt.

Heaving in a deep breath, for nerves had suddenly assaulted her, Rhona closed the distance between them and entered the tack-room. The rich scent of oiled leather enveloped her. She stepped up next to her husband so that their shoulders were nearly touching. "I'm sorry, Taran."

He cast her a glance. His gaze was shuttered, his expression impossible to read. "It doesn't matter," he replied. "Just leave things be."

A heartbeat passed. Rhona gnawed at her bottom lip. This was getting painful; she had no idea what to say to him, or how to put things right. But she couldn't walk away knowing she'd hurt him. Each time she opened her mouth, she wondered if she was just making things worse.

"I can't leave it," she said quietly, her voice barely above a whisper. "Taran … I didn't mean what I said back in the gardens."

His gaze snapped back to her. "Yes, ye did."

Rhona's throat closed. "No … I." She broke off here. The coldness of his gaze completely threw her. It wasn't like Rhona to lack confidence, yet at that moment she did. "I was frustrated," she admitted finally. "It was a child's tantrum, and I'm truly sorry for it."

He looked away from her and continued polishing the saddle. However, she noted his shoulders had tensed and his movements were jerky. Rhona moved back from him.

Nothing she said seemed to make any difference. The man before her was a stranger, so different to the husband of the past weeks who had made her laugh, and looked upon her with soft eyes. She should have let things be.

I've ruined everything. Her throat tightened, and tears pricked her eyes.

"I'll leave ye then," she whispered. "Goodnight, Taran."

She'd just started to turn when her husband moved. One moment he was standing at the bench, the saddle before him, and the next he dropped the cloth, took Rhona by the shoulders, and pushed her back against the far wall.

The movement was so sudden that Rhona gasped. His grip on her shoulders was firm, his fingertips digging in. When she raised her chin to meet his gaze, her belly twisted.

His pale-blue gaze glittered. His skin had drawn tight over his features, distorting the two thick scars that slashed across his face. He looked furious.

Taran leaned into her, his mouth twisting. "Take a good look at these scars, Rhona … do ye think any woman would want to kiss a man with a face like mine?"

Shock fluttered through Rhona; she'd never realized he held so much anger inside him.

"Taran," she gasped his name in a plea. She'd never been afraid of him before, but fear coiled within her now. "I don't—"

"*Do* ye?" The question was a growl.

Rhona stared up at him, her gaze never wavering. "I don't understand," she whispered.

His mouth thinned. "Ye demanded to know what was wrong with me, why I've never kissed ye," he growled. "Why don't ye ask yerself if I've ever kissed *anyone*?"

Rhona stilled, realization dawning. She'd thought him experienced; the way he'd pleasured her on their wedding night had made her believe he'd lain with a number of others.

"I thought ye had bedded other women?" she whispered.

He stared down at her. A nerve feathered in his jaw. "Bedded, aye. Kissed, no."

The tension drained out of Rhona's body at these words. It was as if the fog had rolled back, and for the first time, she could see. Suddenly, everything was clear.

"Taran," she breathed. Rhona reached up, her fingertips tracing the deepest of the scars, the one that slashed vertically from his brow to jaw. He flinched under her touch but didn't move away. She traced the length of the scar before running her fingers along the one that slashed across his opposite cheek.

Then, she stood on tiptoe and stretched up to him, placing her lips upon the worst of the two scars.

His hands tightened on her shoulders, and she felt his body tremble against her. "Rhona ... no."

She ignored him. Instead, she trailed her lips along the ridge of flesh. "Yer scars are part of ye," she whispered. "I used to notice them, but after we wed, that changed." She drew back slightly so that their breaths mingled. "Since then, when I look at ye, all I see is the face of the man I love."

Rhona reached up to her shoulder and took one of his hands, drawing it down so that the palm lay flat over the top of her left breast. "Feel my heart," she said huskily. "Feel how it races. I'm telling the truth."

She watched his throat bob. His eyes had changed; they were no longer shadowed. Instead, they now gleamed.

Tenderness rose within Rhona. Taran MacKinnon wore his scars like armor, yet there were deeper ones inside him, ones that time had never healed. She'd ensure they never hurt him again.

She leaned toward him, her mouth pressing against his.

Truthfully, apart from a fumbling attempt by one of her suitors, Rhona had never been kissed. She had no idea what she was doing, but she felt compelled to take the initiative—to prove to him that her words were true.

Rhona moved her lips over his. She felt the rasp of stubble against her cheek, and a frisson of excitement made her stifle a gasp. She liked this. Tentatively, she traced the seam of his lips with the tip of her tongue.

Taran breathed a soft groan. His lips parted under hers, and his hands came up, cupping her face. His tongue slid into her mouth, exploring, tasting.

Rhona moaned and sagged against him. She felt as if she was drowning; Taran filled her senses, her world. The taste of him set her blood alight, and the kiss grew hungry.

When Taran gently bit her lower lip, she whimpered.

Breathing hard, Taran pulled away. His gaze fused with hers, never wavering. Trapped in his arms, Rhona stared up at him. "Kiss me again," she whispered. "Please."

He did, only this kiss was fierce, consuming. Rhona responded, the last of her restraint falling away as his mouth ravaged hers. Her hands slid up his chainmail vest to his neck. She wanted to feel his bare skin, but layers of clothing prevented her.

With a groan, Taran reached down, took hold of her skirts, and pulled them up around her waist. The warm night air brushed against Rhona's naked skin, and excitement pulsed through her. A melting sensation caught fire in the cradle of her hips. She reached down, her fingers fumbling with the laces of his braies.

When she released his shaft from the layers of plaid, her breathing caught. She wrapped her fingers around the thick column. The skin was smooth over the hard heat beneath. Her mouth went dry with need; she'd wanted this ever since their wedding night, had longed to be with him again, to touch him.

Taran gasped her name and kneed her thighs apart. Then his hands slid under her, grasping her buttocks as he lifted her to meet him.

Rhona guided him inside.

The feel of him penetrating her, the stretching, aching pleasure of it made her close her eyes, her head rolling back against the rough stone wall. He was big, but she took him in to the root, her legs wrapping around his hips to draw him in tighter still.

They stayed like that for a long moment, him buried deep inside her, and then Taran leaned into Rhona, trailing kisses up the column of her neck. She trembled under his touch before she offered her mouth to him once more.

He kissed her with languid sensuality this time, his tongue plunging into her mouth, before he started to move his hips to mirror the action.

The slick feel of their bodies moving together, the throbbing, building heat, was too much for Rhona. Her body started to quiver like a bowstring. Pleasure rippled out from her womb, and she cried out against his mouth.

Taran drove into her, deep and hard now, and Rhona clung to him, one hand digging into his scalp as she kissed him with abandon. The pleasure of it was almost too intense, and yet she would not prevent him. If her heart stopped from this, she would die willingly. Another spasm of throbbing, spiraling pleasure caught her, and she cried out, the sound muffled against his mouth.

Rhona clung to Taran, riding the waves that crashed through her. And then, his body grew rigid. Taran tore his mouth from hers, arched back, and let out a roar that shook the room to its foundations.

Taran lay on his side, staring down at the naked body of his wife spread out beside him. A single lantern burned on the mantelpiece on the opposite side of the chamber. It cast a soft light across the room, kissing every curve of Rhona's long-limbed, lush body.

He could have gazed upon her all night long. If only he didn't have to ride off to battle tomorrow. If only time could stand still.

Rhona's eyes were closed as she dozed. After their coupling in the stables, they'd returned to their tower chamber where Taran had torn off both their clothing, carried her over to the bed, and taken her once more. Their bodies were now slick with sweat in the aftermath. The shutters to the room were open, for the night was still and the air sultry.

Taran's gaze trailed up Rhona's body, taking in the auburn nest of curls between her thighs, the cradle of her hips, the dip of her waist, and the swell of her full, pink-tipped breasts. But when his gaze reached her face, it stayed there. Her dark-red hair fanned out across the pillow; she'd never looked so beautiful to him. Her lips, bee-stung from their kisses, were slightly parted, her cheeks flushed.

Gently, he reached out and traced her bottom lip with his fingertip.

She'd had no idea how much he'd wanted to kiss her, or how he'd worried she'd recoil in disgust. He'd barely been able to admit his fears to himself, yet with each passing day since their handfasting, they had grown.

But all his fears had been for nothing.

Rhona had given him her heart.

Feeling his caress, Rhona's eyelashes fluttered. She awoke, regarding him sleepily through half-closed lids. "Haven't ye slept?" she murmured.

"I dozed for a bit," he replied, "but then I realized I'd prefer to watch ye sleep."

Her mouth curved at this admission. "I hope I don't snore."

He huffed. "No ... but ye know I do."

Rhona held his gaze, her eyes darkening as she reached up and stroked his cheek with the back of her hand. "This has been the best night of my life," she murmured.

He captured her hand and brought it to his lips, kissing her knuckles. "And mine," he admitted quietly. "This feels like a dream. I fear that any moment I'll wake and ye will be another man's wife."

"Ye are not dreaming," she replied, her eyes shining. Her hand trailed down his chest to his belly. "This is real." Her fingers trailed lower still to where his shaft had already grown hard for her. She stroked him, her expression turning wicked. "Shall we see exactly how real?"

He groaned at her touch, closing his eyes and losing himself in the sensation. Then he sank down next to her and rolled over onto his back. A heartbeat later, he pulled her astride him.

Rhona laughed. "What are ye doing?"

"Just making sure ye are real, lass."

He lowered Rhona down onto him, and her laughter choked off. He opened his eyes to see her perched above him. His breathing caught at her loveliness: her breasts thrust forward, her auburn hair spilled over her shoulders.

He took hold of her hips and moved her against him, watching as she groaned and threw back her head, exposing a creamy length of neck.

Taran MacKinnon smiled. Aye, this was no dream. Rhona was his.

Chapter Twenty-nine

The Beast's Bride

"DO YE STILL wish to join us in battle?"

The question was unexpected. Rhona had been dozing against Taran's chest, her body languid in the aftermath of their lovemaking, when he spoke.

Propping herself up on an elbow, Rhona favored him with a level gaze. "Aye … I do."

A shadow moved in those ice-blue eyes before he heaved a deep sigh. "My instinct is to keep ye here, safe within the walls of this keep … but if to fight is what ye truly want, I'll not stop ye."

Rhona inclined her head. A strange blend of excitement and fear knotted under her ribcage. "Ye were dead against letting me ride with ye—what changed yer mind?"

He huffed a breath. "One of the things I've always loved about ye is yer wildness. Few women show an interest in learning how to fight. I've trained many men, and yer skills equal theirs. I'll not keep ye locked away for fear that ye will come to harm."

Rhona smiled. Reaching up, she caressed his cheek with her fingertips. "Thank ye, Taran. I'll not take any foolish risks, I promise."

His mouth thinned. "Ye had better not." He caught her hand and brought it to his lips, kissing her palm. "Today won't be pretty, lass. This confrontation between the MacLeods and the Frasers has been a long time coming. This battle isn't about land. It's about wounded pride. Morgan Fraser has wanted his reckoning against yer father for years. He'll never forgive him for taking Una."

Rhona nodded. She understood that. Her father had made a fool of his rival, and Morgan Fraser had been nursing his wounded pride for years. "I'll watch yer back today, my love," she promised softly.

His mouth quirked. "And I yers."

"This is madness." Caitrin put her hands on her hips and raked her gaze over Rhona, taking in the mail shirt, braies, and high leather boots she wore. "I can't believe Taran is letting ye fight."

"Well, he is," Rhona replied. She held out a pair of leather bracers to her sister. "Stop looking so disapproving and fasten these for me. I can't do it on my own."

Caitrin pursed her lips and took the bracers. She then cast a look at where Adaira stood behind them, her wriggling puppy in her arms. Their sister wore a composed expression, although her hazel eyes gleamed.

"Don't tell me ye agree with this?" Caitrin huffed. "Both of ye have lost yer wits."

"Rhona is as fierce as any man," Adaira replied.

Caitrin's jaw firmed. Her left cheek bore a red, swollen welt after the blows her husband had dealt the day before. But Rhona was pleased to see that her sister didn't look cowed or beaten this morning. Instead, she had a stubborn look in her eyes that Rhona welcomed.

"Ye might be able to wield a sword, but battle is something else entirely," Caitrin said, her voice tight. "I've heard that brave men have been known to lose their wits when the violence and death get too much."

Rhona's belly clenched at these words. "I've heard all the tales too," she replied, holding her sister's gaze firmly. "I'm not expecting an afternoon stroll."

She held out her wrist, and Caitrin stepped forward, fastening the bracer. She laced the leather arm guard with deft precision, and Rhona realized that it was likely a task she had done for her husband many times. Once Caitrin had finished lacing the bracers, she stepped back, her gaze shuttered.

"Will ye see Baltair before we leave?" Rhona asked.

Caitrin drew in a deep breath, tension visible in her slender shoulders. After a long moment, she shook her head.

"Do ye really hate him?" Adaira asked softly. Dùnglas had stopped squirming in her arms and was now licking her chin. She ignored the pup.

"Aye," Caitrin murmured. Her gaze glittered as she looked down, staring at the flagstone floor before her. "Every morning I wake and wish I'd never wed him."

"But Baltair was yer choice," Adaira reminded her. "Ye looked so happy the day of yer handfasting."

Caitrin's gaze snapped up, snaring hers. "Aye, and I've rarely smiled since. I made a terrible mistake." She paused here, a nerve flickering in her cheek. "His younger brother wanted to wed me, but I chose Baltair instead. A shallow, vain girl … I chose the more handsome of the two brothers, the heir to the MacDonald lands." Caitrin's voice choked off. "And I have paid the price."

Rhona stared at Caitrin, shocked by her admission. She remembered the younger of the two MacDonald brothers: Alasdair. Sharp featured and lanky with a shock of raven hair that kept falling over one eye, he'd visited Dunvegan a number of times before Caitrin's union to Baltair. He'd been like a puppy around her sister, attentive and eager to please. However, Rhona didn't realize that he'd also been her sister's suitor.

Rhona cleared her throat. "Did Alasdair actually propose?"

Caitrin nodded, looking away.

Silence fell in the solar. It struck Rhona that the three of them really didn't know each other as well as she'd thought. They'd always been close over the years, but it seemed they held much back from each other.

"I always wondered why Alasdair left the isle so suddenly," Adaira mused aloud.

"He went to fight for the king against the English," Caitrin replied, her tone sharpening. "He didn't leave because of me."

Adaira gave her a pained look. It was clear that was what Caitrin wanted to believe. Neither of her sisters was going to contradict her.

Rhona tightened Lasair's girth and stiffened. She could feel the weight of someone's stare. It was stabbing her between the shoulder blades.

Casting a glance over her shoulder, her gaze met Dughall MacLean's. It was not yet dawn. Torches illuminated the bailey as the MacLeods, MacDonalds, and Budges prepared to ride out. Dughall sat astride a heavy grey stallion a few yards away. The warrior's face was cast partly in shadow. He watched her under hooded lids, his face stony. "What's this?" he growled. "The Beast's Bride dresses like a man this morning?"

"Aye, and she fights like one too ... so mind yerself," a male voice quipped. Rhona's gaze shifted to where Gordon MacPherson was leading his horse out of the stables. He cast Rhona a conspirator's look and winked.

Rhona glanced back to Dughall to see he was scowling. "MacKinnon clearly wants to be made a fool of," he growled. "Or maybe he'd like to see his pretty wife gutted on the battlefield."

The threat in Dughall's voice made Rhona tense. She was just about to spit out a cutting reply when Taran stepped up beside her. His face was hard as he met Dughall's gaze. "Mind yer manners, MacLean."

Dughall's face twisted. He then stretched out his neck and spat onto the cobbled yard between them. "Mind yer wife today, MacKinnon ... I'd hate to see her come to any harm."

"That's enough, Dughall," the rumble of the clan-chief's voice broke across the yard like thunder. "Threaten my daughter again, and ye will spend the rest of yer days in my dungeon."

Dughall paled, his jaw bunching. However, he did as bid. Malcolm MacLeod strode toward them, his bulk clad in chainmail, iron, and leather. Iain followed a few feet behind, his own armor clanking as he walked.

Surprised that her father had actually interceded on her behalf, for he barely even talked to her these days, Rhona met Malcolm's eye. Their gazes held for a long moment, and then her father smiled. Actually, it was more like a grimace, although his eyes held more warmth than she'd seen in a long while.

He stopped before her. "I never thought I'd see a daughter of mine ride into battle." His tone was rueful, but unlike the morning he'd caught Taran and Rhona training, there was no anger in it.

Rhona raised her chin. "I *can* fight, Da."

His gaze slid to the sword she carried at her hip. It wasn't a Claidheamh-mor—for that was a man's blade. Instead, Taran had given her a lighter longsword. She also carried a dirk at her waist. "I don't doubt it," he murmured. He reached forward and clasped a large hand over her shoulder, squeezing tightly. His gaze seared hers. "I'm proud to have ye fight with me today."

He released her shoulder and stepped back then, shattering the moment. Rhona swallowed the lump that rose in her throat. Never had her father spoken such words to her. The unexpectedness of it completely threw her.

Malcolm MacLeod moved away and started barking orders at his men. Iain followed him, although not before casting his elder sister a look full of jealous spite. Their father had praised a daughter while his first-born son stood forgotten in his shadow—Iain would never forgive her for that.

Rhona found that she didn't care.

They rode out of Dunvegan as the first glow of dawn warmed the eastern sky. It was a grey morning, and a chill wind blew in from the north, whipping up the surface of the loch and ruffling their horses' manes. The column of riders snaked out of the keep, bits jangling and shod hooves beating out a tattoo that shook the earth.

The MacLeods led the way, followed by the MacDonalds, and then the Budges. Rhona hadn't seen Baltair MacDonald since the previous evening and was grateful to be spared his baleful glare. Taran had told her what had happened after she led Caitrin away; the MacDonald chieftain would be nursing more than a broken nose this morning.

Nonetheless, Rhona found herself wondering if he'd been upset that his wife had not come out to see him off. Did he care for her sister at all?

"Why the fierce look, Rhona? We've yet to meet the Frasers."

Rhona glanced left to find Taran watching her. He'd reined in his bay gelding, Tussock, up next to her mare. They rode so close that their thighs almost touched.

"I wasn't thinking about them," she admitted with a wry smile, "but of Caitrin. I wish she wasn't wedded to that serpent."

Taran's brow furrowed, and he nodded. Silence stretched between them for a few moments before he answered. "It's hard to see someone ye love suffer," he said quietly. "I watched my mother grow from a laughing, beautiful woman to a frightened mouse ... but I was just a bairn and couldn't do a thing about it."

Rhona studied his face. She couldn't even imagine how it must have been, to see his mother slain in front of him. "Ye must have hated yer father," she murmured.

Taran's gaze guttered, his features tightening. "No ... I adored him," he replied. "That's what made it all the harder."

Chapter Thirty

Blooded

THE VALE OF Hamra Rinner lay in the cleft between two craggy peaks. A dark forest of pine and fir covered the lower slopes of the mountains, framing a wide meadow, where a burn wended its way over a bed of grey stones.

It was a lonely spot, far from the nearest village. The Fraser stronghold at Talasgair lay much farther south, upon the isle's western coast. Despite that this was MacLeod territory, the vale had always been the favorite hunting spot of both clans.

The MacLeod war party drew to a halt at the far northern end of the valley, tethering their horses amongst the trees. They would engage the enemy on foot, for it was cumbersome for the warriors wielding two-handed Claidheamh-mor blades to fight on horseback.

It had just gone noon; they'd ridden hard to reach the vale by the appointed hour. Would they find the enemy waiting for them?

Rhona followed the others out into the valley. The sun still hadn't shown its face. She glanced up at the pale sky and spied an eagle circling overhead. She'd never traveled to Hamra Rinner before. The resinous scent of pine filled the air. Up ahead, a stag bounded across the vale before disappearing into the trees carpeting the eastern slopes of the meadow.

"Remember all I taught ye," Taran said as they walked side-by-side. "Go for the throat, the belly, and the groin. Get in close so a man with a long reach can't use it to his advantage."

Rhona nodded, her stomach twisting as the reality of what was coming finally hit her. She was going to have to kill.

Part of her wondered if she was capable of it. What if she let everyone, herself included, down?

But she had no time to voice her worries, for it was then that she caught a flash of color to the south: the distinctive red, blue, and green of the Fraser plaid. Their pennants snapped in the wind.

Malcolm MacLeod raised his hand, signaling for them to halt. "There's that bastard," he growled. "Here to take what's mine."

"He won't, Da," Iain interjected. "We'll slaughter them all."

"That's the spirit, lad." Malcolm MacLeod tore his gaze from the fluttering pennants and glanced over at his son. His gaze narrowed. "Be careful with that sword today ... it's too big for ye."

Rhona watched her brother's cheeks flush. "I'm fine," he muttered.

Beside Rhona, Taran shifted. "I tried to warn him."

Gordon snorted. "Hope he impales himself on it." His comment was murmured, but Rhona heard it nonetheless. It didn't surprise or offend her; Iain might have been her brother, but he was growing into an unpleasant young man.

To the south, the Fraser war band approached. At first, Rhona could only see their banners, and then she caught sight of the men: rows of warriors clad in chainmail. Some wore helms that gleamed despite the dull day, while others went bareheaded.

When the two bands were a furlong apart, a tall, helmeted figure stepped out from the Fraser ranks.

Morgan Fraser strode out toward them, a cloak of plaid bearing the Fraser colors rippling from his broad shoulders. Rhona studied him with interest; he was the same height as her father but much leaner. Despite the heavy armor he wore, the man stalked rather than walked.

Malcolm MacLeod left the ranks of his men and lumbered forward. Unlike the Fraser chief, he wore no helmet. Rhona knew he found them cumbersome and complained that they limited his vision.

The two men stopped around five yards apart.

"MacLeod," Morgan Fraser's voice was a deep boom in the now silent vale. "We meet at last."

In response, Malcolm MacLeod spat on the ground between them. "Aye, Fraser. Ye have got what ye wanted all along."

"I knew I'd rile ye if I took yer land."

"Well, ye did."

"What's wrong? Don't ye like it when someone takes from ye something ye treasure?" The bitterness in the Fraser chief's tone cut the air.

MacLeod threw back his head and laughed, the noise rumbling like an approaching storm. "The lady chose the better man ... ye can't blame her for that."

"That *lady* was my wife, MacLeod."

Rhona heaved in a deep breath and spared a glance in Taran's direction. He was watching the exchange, his brow furrowed. Only blood would appease Morgan Fraser's wounded pride.

Malcolm MacLeod shrugged. "There's little point in talking then, is there?"

"No." The Fraser chieftain stepped back. "Get ready to taste steel."

The battle began with a swiftness that shocked Rhona.

A hunting horn shattered the stillness, its lonely wail echoing off the surrounding peaks. One moment the two bands had been standing, waiting for their chieftains to return to their ranks, the next they drew their weapons and ran screaming at each other.

Despite his girth and advancing years, her father was out front. He swung his Claidheamh-mor above his head bellowing. "Hold fast, MacLeods. Hold fast!"

Rhona's heart started pounding, and her skin prickled. This was it. She drew her sword and leaped forward. Half the band were already racing ahead, Taran among them. She risked being left behind.

The crunch of armored bodies, shields, and weapons colliding shook the earth as the first ranks met. Shouts, grunts, and cries rent the air.

Rhona tried her best to keep Taran in her line of sight, yet it was hard, for he plowed on ahead. She watched him raise his sword and engage the first Fraser warrior who came at him.

An instant later Rhona tore her gaze from her husband. A huge warrior bore down on her, Claidheamh-mor swinging.

Get in close.

Taran's advice rang in her ears. Gripping her longsword tightly with both hands, Rhona dove for him. During their years of swordplay practice, Taran had constantly told her that her biggest advantage was her speed and agility. There was no point trying to best a man of this size and strength. Instead, she went in low.

Her blade bit into the warrior's unprotected legs.

He roared and staggered. Rhona ducked away, narrowly missing the swipe of his sword. Before he had time to recover, she came at him again. She thrust her blade into his armpit, and he went down howling. Bile rose in her throat. Her belly roiled. Rhona swallowed, forcing down the nausea.

There was no time to react. She had to keep moving.

Rhona had heard many tales about battle, some terrifying. One thing she remembered, from the stories her father's men had swapped as they feasted in the Great Hall, was that a strange madness often took hold in the heat of battle. In such times a warrior lost all fear of death. Instead, the need to kill ignited like fire in a warrior's blood.

Rhona wished such a fury would take hold of her.

There was no such euphoria. Just a terrible bone-jarring effort. She was tall and strong, and yet the men who came at her were much bigger and stronger. It took every technique that Taran had taught her to fight them off—and it was even harder to kill them.

Her stomach twisted into a tight ball, while her hands—clutching the hilt of her sword—ached, as did her shoulders and arms. Sweat coursed down her back and between her breasts.

Her own viciousness sickened her. It was survival. The only way she bested the men who lunged at her, swords slashing, was to get in first, to stab them in places where armor and chainmail did not cover.

Throat. Belly. Groin.

Their screams, the stench of blood and worse, wormed their way under her skin, deep into her bones.

At some point, as the battle progressed, she became aware that it was shifting in the MacLeod's favor. There seemed fewer of the enemy to fend off now. She had long lost sight of her father and brother as they'd rushed to the front. The dead and dying lay scattered around her.

Half a dozen yards ahead she saw Taran, battling a huge man. She moved toward Taran, skirting around a Fraser warrior who lay groaning in a pool of spreading blood.

However, before she neared him, Dughall MacLean appeared. Blood splattered the warrior from head to foot and savagery twisted his face. Rhona had once thought him handsome, but she didn't now.

Rhona's step slowed. She expected Dughall to plow past her and into the fray once more. Only he didn't.

Instead, he ran at Taran and clubbed him across the back of the head with his fist.

"No!" Rhona's scream echoed across the vale, swallowed in the thunder of battle.

Taran, who'd just delivered a mortal wound to his opponent, dropped to his knees, his sword falling from nerveless fingers.

Dughall pulled a blade from his belt and raised it to deliver a strike to Taran's unprotected neck.

But he never brought the dirk down.

Dropping her sword and shield, Rhona flew at him. One hand fastened around Dughall's thick wrist, while the other grabbed a handful of hair near his brow-line and yanked, hard.

Dughall reared back, letting go of Taran. He and Rhona toppled backward onto the ground. He would have landed on top of her if Rhona hadn't twisted at the last instant. Still, the impact jarred her shoulder and hip.

Recovering swiftly from her attack, Dughall MacLean turned. When his gaze seized upon Rhona, and he realized who'd attacked him, a wild grin split his face.

Panic jolted through Rhona. There was madness in his eyes. He'd kill her, and then he'd finish off Taran. This was his revenge on them both for slighting him.

But to Rhona's shock, he tossed the dirk aside. "MacLeod bitch," he panted. "Ye have had this coming."

And with that, he lunged for her, his big hands fastening around Rhona's throat.

She reacted instantly the moment his fingers crushed her windpipe, driving her knee up into his cods.

Dughall let out a strangled cry and released her.

Rhona twisted out from under his heavy body and clawed herself away from him. However, he recovered from the blow to the groin faster than she'd anticipated. He landed upon her, flattening Rhona, face-down, to the ground. Air gusted out of her lungs. Winded, she scrabbled against the damp earth and tried to escape from under him.

But Dughall had pinned her fast to the earth; she wasn't going anywhere. His hands fastened around her neck, his fingers clamping down like iron claws over her throat.

Chapter Thirty-one

Shadows

TERROR REARED UP within Rhona. She would die here, throttled by her former suitor. She wanted to use one of the tricks Taran had taught her, but it was impossible, for Dughall's heavy body crushed her into the ground. She kicked and dug her toes into the earth, trying to push up against him, but it was no good. Her legs were useless.

A pressure grew in Rhona's chest, and her ears started to ring. Twisting her head to the side, choking as his grip tightened, she caught sight of the dirk Dughall had tossed aside.

It lay within arm's reach.

Her hands had been clawing at his fingers, trying to pry them free from her throat. Now, she flung a hand out to the dagger. Her fingers grasped the bone hilt.

She drove the dagger back, feeling it bite deep into flesh.

Dughall's roar deafened her, but at that moment the iron band around her windpipe released.

Rhona drew in gulps of air. Her lungs burned. She couldn't seem to breathe properly. That was because Dughall was still sitting on her back, crushing her against the earth.

And then, suddenly he wasn't. The weight upon her chest lifted.

Still choking, Rhona rolled over.

Taran stood over them. His face was ashen, his eyes shadowed with pain. The short blade he held dripped with blood.

Dughall MacLean lay on the ground between them, thrashing as death came for him. His hands grasped around his ruined throat.

The hilt of the dirk Rhona had used against him protruded from his right thigh.

A sob rose in Rhona's chest as she struggled to her feet. Too close. Moments more and Dughall would have choked her. Rhona's legs trembled. A sob rose in her throat.

She tottered forward and collapsed into the cage of Taran's arms.

Crows circled over the Vale of Hamra Rinner, dark silhouettes against a dull sky.

The dead lay scattered across the meadow, their blood soaking into the peaty earth. Chainmail glinted in the watery afternoon light. The MacLeods had won the battle. The Frasers had retreated, hauling their injured with them.

"I stuck that bastard," Malcolm MacLeod announced. He limped toward where Rhona and Taran stood at the edge of the battlefield. Around them, MacLeod, MacDonald, and Budge warriors combed the meadow for survivors and spoils of war. "May Morgan Fraser's wounds fester before death takes him." To emphasize his point, the MacLeod chieftain spat on the ground.

"Da split him open from hip to knee," Iain announced. He followed behind Malcolm, his once shiny armor splattered with blood and gore. Rhona was impressed to see that her brother had proven his worth in the battle. He'd lost his sword though and had finished the fight with a dirk. "He won't survive such a wound."

"Good," Malcolm grunted. His gaze met Rhona's then. "I heard about MacLean ... treacherous dog."

Rhona swallowed. Her throat still ached in the aftermath. Dughall's fingers would leave livid bruises on her neck. Her father's gaze then shifted to Taran. The two men looked at each other for a heartbeat, and then Malcolm MacLeod nodded.

Rhona watched her father limp away before she glanced up at her husband. "I'm afraid that's the closest ye will get to a 'thank ye'."

He favored her with a weary smile. "Fortunately, I don't need his thanks."

"Taran ..." A warrior approached them. He was a young man, his blue eyes hollowed with fatigue. "Gordon MacPherson's been injured. He's asking for ye."

Taran's face blanched. "Where is he?"

"On the other side of the vale. Follow me."

The warrior led the way across the corpse-strewn field. Although Rhona was loath to walk amongst the dead, she doggedly followed her husband. She was fond of Gordon and would see him too.

They had nearly reached the halfway point when Rhona spied the body of Baltair MacDonald. She halted, catching hold of Taran's hand. "Look."

Taran turned, his gaze following hers.

The MacDonald clan-chief lay on his side, curled up around the blade that still protruded from his abdomen. The Fraser warrior he'd fought lay next to him, his throat slit. Baltair had managed to bring him down before dying.

Her brother-in-law's face looked different in death. He was a handsome man, even with the broken nose Taran had given him, although in life his character had harshened his features. They appeared softer now.

"I'd say I was sorry to see him dead," Taran murmured, "but I'll not lie. The world's a happier place without Baltair MacDonald in it."

Rhona squeezed Taran's hand in wordless agreement.

They continued across the battlefield.

Gordon lay propped up against a log on the far side of the valley. Ashen-faced, he still managed to greet Taran with a smile. However, the expression was tight with pain. Rhona drew in a sharp breath when she saw the deep slash down his right thigh. She could see a glint of white—the cut had gone to the bone.

They needed to get him to a healer.

Taran hunkered down before him. Rhona saw the worry in his eyes, although when he spoke, his voice didn't betray it. "Getting yourself into trouble again I see, MacPherson."

Gordon huffed. "One of those Frasers got under my guard," he rasped. "Didn't even see him coming."

Rhona knelt down next to Taran, her gaze shifting to where blood still ran from the gash upon Gordon's thigh. "I need to bind that for ye," she muttered. Rhona pulled up the edge of her mail shirt and grabbed hold of the hem of the léine she wore underneath, ripping a strip free. She was making a habit of this of late.

Gordon's gaze widened. "Lady Rhona ... don't worry yourself over me."

Rhona cast him a quelling look before she shifted closer and started winding the length of linen about his thigh. "I'm not," she replied. "I'm ensuring ye don't bleed to death before we get ye back to Dunvegan."

Gordon's throat bobbed. He shifted his attention back to Taran. "If I don't make it, will ye give Greer a message from me?"

Taran's brow furrowed. "No need for that ... we'll be back home tomorrow. Ye can tell her yerself."

"We've got a live one!"

The shout, a few yards away, made Rhona glance up from her work. A cluster of warriors were forming around a figure that lay prone upon the battlefield.

"It's Morgan Fraser's eldest!"

Malcolm MacLeod lumbered across to join them. He was limping heavily, having strained something during the battle, but his face was set in determination. "Let me have a look at him."

The MacLeod chieftain elbowed his way through the gathering crowd and peered down at the unconscious man. Rhona was too far away to make out the young man's features, yet she caught sight of a shock of red hair—a brighter shade than her own.

"Aye, that's Lachlann Fraser, all right," Malcolm MacLeod growled. "I haven't seen him since he was a lad, but he's got his father's looks."

"What will ye do with him, Da?" Iain had pushed his way in and was now standing next to his father. The young man withdrew the dirk from his belt, his expression turning feral. "Do ye want me to slit his throat?"

Malcolm MacLeod cast his son a cool look. "Ye are a bloodthirsty pup, aren't ye?"

The comment brought a few smiles from the surrounding men. Iain's cheeks flushed, his mouth thinning. Ignoring his son, the clan-chief turned his focus back to the unconscious warrior at his feet. "What's wrong with him?"

"Took a blow to the back of the head by the looks of it," one of the warriors replied. "Knocked him out cold."

A slow smile spread across MacLeod's face. It wasn't a pleasant expression, but one filled with cunning and malice. Rhona's breathing grew shallow at the sight of it; her father was not yet done with punishing Morgan Fraser.

"Pick him up and put him in the wagon with our injured," Malcolm ordered. "We're taking Lachlann Fraser back to Dunvegan, where he will rot in my dungeon for the rest of his short life."

Rhona exhaled sharply. She didn't envy the man his fate; the dungeon in the bowels of the keep, carved out of dark rock, was a sunless, fetid place.

She'd never heard of anyone who'd survived it.

Rhona sat before the hearth, shivering.

They'd made camp for the night around fifty furlongs north of the Vale of Hamra Rinner. A mist curled in, wreathing like smoke across the craggy hills and in-between the tightly-packed tents. Autumn was approaching; the air had a bite to it. But it was not the temperature that made Rhona tremble.

Ever since the battle she'd been on edge. Now, as the day drew to a close and she was able to rest, her limbs wouldn't stop shaking.

"Here." Taran appeared at her side with a steaming cup in his hands. "Some hot spiced wine will settle yer nerves."

Rhona cast him a rueful look. "Does it look like they need settling?"

"Aye ... I've seen more color on the face of a corpse."

Rhona took the cup, her chilled fingers wrapping around its warmth. The rich scent of hot bramble wine filled her nostrils, and she felt a little of the day's tension ebb out of her. She took a gulp of wine, letting its heat burn down her throat, and released a shuddering breath. "That's better," she murmured.

"Did I make a mistake letting ye join us?" Taran asked quietly.

She glanced back at her husband to see him watching her. A deep groove had formed between his eyebrows, and his gaze was shadowed. She could feel his worry for her.

Rhona shook her head. "It was my choice."

Silence fell between them for a few moments before Taran spoke once more. "Many men would have quailed at today's slaughter. But not ye. I watched ye fight. Ye did yer father proud ... ye did yerself proud."

Rhona held his gaze. "And what about ye, Taran," she murmured. "Were ye proud of me?"

He reached up, his palm cupping her cheek as he gazed into her eyes. "I was terrified the whole way through that battle," he admitted. "The thought of losing ye is like a blade to my guts. I'd never have forgiven myself. I'm not sure I want ye fighting alongside me again."

Rhona drew in a trembling breath. She could feel the tension in the hand that cupped her cheek, see it in the lines of his face. He expected her to argue with him, to insist on riding out with her father from now on.

"I'm not sure I want to see another battle," she admitted, her voice barely above a whisper. "One was enough. All that death sickened me ... even Dughall's."

Taran loosed a breath. "Thank the Lord." He moved closer to her, his fingers tracing the lines of her face. "Yer eyes look so haunted tonight. So empty."

Rhona swallowed. "Chase the shadows away, Taran," she said softly. "Please."

His gaze widened for an instant, and then he nodded. Gently, he took her cup of wine and set it aside. Then, he rose to his feet, pulling her with him.

Taran picked her up as if she weighed nothing and turned, carrying her away from the smoldering hearth. Their tent sat just a few yards behind them. Taran ducked into it, and they entered a warm, welcoming space lit by a small brazier in the center. A deerskin lay upon the floor; it would be their bed for tonight.

Taran lowered Rhona so she stood before him, and his mouth claimed hers for a deep, hungry kiss. Rhona groaned, her lips parting as she surrendered to him. Her arms went up, interlocking around his neck.

Their clothing came off—blood-encrusted mail shirts, braies, léines, and boots—until they both stood naked. Rhona entwined herself around Taran, gasping when his hands slid over her body, claiming every inch of her as his own. She pressed herself hard against him, desperate for his strength, his warmth. His love.

Chapter Thirty-two

How Things Change

CAITRIN DIDN'T WEEP when Rhona told her Baltair was dead.

She showed no reaction at all.

Rhona hadn't expected tears, but this carven figure before her, devoid of emotion, of life, made concern flutter up within her. "Caitrin," she said gently, taking a step closer to where her sister stood. "Did ye hear me?"

Caitrin held Eoghan in her arms; the babe had gone still, his blue eyes huge, almost as if he understood what Rhona had just said. Caitrin swallowed before she gave a curt nod.

Across the chamber, Adaira shifted. She had followed Rhona into the solar upon her return to Dunvegan. Unlike the other women, Caitrin hadn't come out to welcome the returning warriors.

"So, the Frasers were defeated?" Caitrin asked finally; the faint rasp to her voice was the only sign of the emotion she was keeping in check.

"Aye," Rhona replied. "Morgan Fraser was badly wounded … it's likely he'll die."

"Who was that man they dragged down into the dungeon?" Adaira asked. Her blue eyes were full of curiosity. "He has hair like flame."

"Lachlann Fraser, the chief's eldest son," Rhona answered.

Adaira pulled a face. "I almost pity him. The pits down there are foul."

Rhona shrugged before turning her attention back to Caitrin. Her elder sister had not moved. Her gaze seemed unfocused, as if she was lost in her thoughts. "Caitrin?"

Her sister blinked. "How did he die?"

"A blade to the belly." It would have been an agonizing death, but there was no need to tell Caitrin that. "They have brought his body back and laid it out in the chapel."

Caitrin's features tensed. "I will go to him later."

Rhona nodded, relieved that she had come to life. Still, her sister's lack of emotion, her detachment, concerned her. Caitrin carried too much within; even with her sisters, she couldn't seem to share what lay within her heart.

"Da wants us all to join him in the Great Hall tonight," Rhona said after a pause. "There will be a feast to honor our victory ... and our dead."

Caitrin's mouth pursed. "Tell him I'm not well enough to attend."

Rhona shook her head. "I'm sorry ... but he's insisting. He says he wants *all three* of us to join him."

Caitrin looked away, her jaw clenching. "I tire of having men tell me what to do," she growled. "All my life I've had to mind them. I look forward to returning to Duntulm, to being left in peace."

Rhona didn't reply. She understood Caitrin's frustration, for she'd endured much of late at her father's hands. And yet, because of him, she was now wed to Taran. Warmth flowed through Rhona at the thought of her husband. Last night he'd made slow, tender love to her; she'd wept in his arms afterward.

She knew too that her sister would find no peace at Duntulm. The MacDonalds of Duntulm were now without a chieftain; sooner or later Caitrin would be subject to the orders of another man. Rhona tensed at the thought.

Caitrin had suffered enough. Couldn't they just leave her in peace?

Taran watched the healer apply a poultice to Gordon's thigh. His friend bore the treatment stoically, although his face had gone grey, and sweat beaded his forehead and top lip. Greer stood beside Gordon, her fingers grasping his. Her eyes glistened.

"Well," Gordon grunted as the healer drew back and reached for a strip of linen to bind the wound. "Will I keep my leg?"

"It's a deep wound," the man replied. Old and bent, with a thick mane of white hair, the healer's bright gaze fixed upon Gordon. "Even if it doesn't fester, ye will bear a limp for the rest of yer days."

Gordon's face tightened at this news.

"*Will* it fester?" Taran asked.

The healer glanced at him. "It's too early to tell ... for now the flesh is healthy. I will return tomorrow to tend the wound."

Taran watched the healer bind Gordon's thigh. Then the elderly man collected up his basket of healing herbs, powders, and tinctures, and bid them all good day. Gordon was one of many warriors he'd have to see today.

When the man had gone, Gordon loosed a long breath, leaning back against the mountain of pillows that Greer had propped him up against. "Great ... I'm going to be a cripple."

Taran's mouth twisted. "A limp hardly makes a man useless."

"MacLeod won't see it that way. Such a warrior isn't much good on the battlefield."

"That doesn't matter to me," Greer spoke up, her voice husky. "Stop complaining Gordon MacPherson. Ye are alive, aren't ye?"

Gordon's gaze met his betrothed's, and the pair of them watched each other for a long moment. Taran suddenly felt as if he was intruding.

"I thought I was done for after the battle," Gordon replied, his gaze never wavering from hers. "All I cared about was not seeing ye again, not being able to tell ye how much I love ye, bonny Greer."

Greer's cheeks flushed. Taran was surprised by his friend's admission. Gordon wasn't a man for emotional talk.

Taran cleared his throat. "I'll leave ye both then."

Gordon nodded, yet his attention never strayed from Greer. Likewise, she stared back at him. The atmosphere in the small chamber inside the guardhouse grew charged.

Taran departed with a smile on his face.

Caitrin MacDonald entered Dunvegan's chapel. Inhaling the scent of incense and the fatty odor of tallow, she let the door thud shut behind her, finding herself within a cool, shadowy space.

Caitrin drew in a deep breath and reached up to the small crucifix she wore about her neck. Kirks and chapels gave her a sense of peace, a calm in a world where she felt controlled by the will of others. There were no booming voices of men here. There was no one to make demands upon her.

She'd left Eoghan with Adaira while she visited her husband. It was a rare moment of solitude.

Moving across the pitted stone floor, Caitrin's gaze shifted to the altar at the far end of the space. Sunlight filtered in through high arched windows on the western wall, dust motes floating down like fireflies. Just beyond the pooling sunlight lay a corpse upon a stone bench.

Baltair.

Caitrin's step slowed. She studied his profile, his dark hair brushed back in a widow's peak. From this distance, he looked as if he were sleeping.

It was hard to believe Baltair MacDonald was actually dead.

Reaching his side, Caitrin stopped. Someone had dressed him in clean clothing, for there were no signs of war upon him. The mortal wound to his belly had been bound and covered. He wore a long mail shirt, plaid braies of MacDonald colors, and a wide leather belt with the clan crest upon it. His hands rested on the pommel of his longsword, which lay upon his chest.

Caitrin's gaze slid up the length of Baltair's body and rested upon his face.

Death had softened it.

She'd once thought him so handsome; just the sight of him before their handfasting had made her knees grow weak. Yet it hadn't taken her long to fear him, for her stomach to knot whenever he walked into a room.

How things change.

Her husband's eyes were closed; he really did look as if he were sleeping. It made Caitrin nervous, and she took a step back from the bench. Even in death, she was afraid of him.

Swallowing the lump in her throat, Caitrin wiped sweaty palms against her kirtle.

Coward.

Her younger sister had just come back from battle, where she'd wielded a sword as well as any man. But here *she* was, scared of a corpse.

Caitrin's hands balled into fists. She was tired of being afraid, sick of jumping at shadows. This man had turned her into a mouse. Once she'd been proud and full of spirit. She'd laughed and flirted with her father's warriors. Smiles had come easily, and when Baltair had asked for her hand, she'd felt smug that such an attractive, charismatic man would want her for a wife.

She barely recognized the woman she'd become.

Steadying her breathing, Caitrin stepped back to the edge of the bench and stared down at her husband.

"Ye no longer have any hold over me," she whispered. Her voice was low, yet it seemed to echo in the empty chapel. "The Devil take ye, Baltair MacDonald."

"To all those who fell defending the MacLeod name and honor." Malcolm MacLeod raised his drinking horn high into the air. Rhona noted the ruddiness of his cheeks; her father was already well into his cups and the night was still young. "Ye will be remembered."

A chorus of 'ayes' went up across the cavernous hall as men and women stood up and raised their cups.

"Yesterday the Frasers discovered that they cross us at their peril," MacLeod continued. "They learned that the MacLeods, MacDonalds, and Budges stick together." The clan-chief's eyes shadowed then. "Brave Baltair MacDonald lost his life in that valley, leaving my daughter a widow. We share her grief, her loss."

Opposite Rhona, Caitrin sat still and silent. Dressed in a charcoal-colored kirtle and veil, as befitted a widow, her sister's gaze was downcast. She didn't acknowledge her father's words. Seated between Caitrin and Aonghus Budge, Adaira cast Caitrin a worried look.

"The MacDonalds of Duntulm must keep strong!" Malcolm MacLeod boomed. He swayed slightly on his feet as he thrust his drinking horn high into the air once more. "I will send word to the mainland, to where Baltair's brother fights for our king. Alasdair will return and take his place as chieftain." These words brought forth a cheer from the MacDonald warriors gathered at a nearby table. But Rhona noticed that Caitrin blanched, her pretty mouth thinning.

Her father was oblivious to her displeasure. Instead, he turned his attention to Aonghus Budge.

"The Budges of Islay have proved their loyalty and quality. Thank ye, Aonghus ... yer friendship is dear to me."

The Budge chieftain acknowledged MacLeod's words with a wide smile. Despite his advancing years and stout figure, Aonghus Budge had fought against the Frasers. He bore minor injuries from the battle: his right arm was in a sling, and he bore a shallow gash to his forehead.

"I seek a way to repay ye," Malcolm droned on. "The Budges and the MacLeods must endure."

Rhona stifled a groan. Drink always made her father loquacious. She wished he'd sit down and let everyone resume eating and drinking. She shared a pained look with Taran beside her. Under the table, he squeezed her hand. Soon enough this feast would be over, and they'd be able to retire to their tower chamber. Excitement fluttered up within Rhona at the thought.

"I have decided that our clans must be united in marriage," Malcolm MacLeod slurred. "I have one daughter not yet wed. Aonghus, I give ye the hand of my youngest, Adaira."

Chapter Thirty-three

A Fine Wife

ADAIRA GASPED, HER face turning ashen. "Da!"

Malcolm MacLeod waved her protest away, his attention still upon the man beside her. Aonghus Budge's grin looked wide enough to split his face.

"A generous gift, Malcolm," Budge replied, "and most appreciated. Adaira is a lovely creature and more biddable than her elder sister. She will make a fine wife."

"Aye." Malcolm MacLeod's brow furrowed at the mention of Rhona's refusal. It hadn't happened that long ago, but to Rhona, it seemed as if a year had passed. She didn't feel like the same person, and yet she would still be loath to wed that toad.

"Ye can't do this, Da." The words were out before Rhona could stop them. Under the table, Taran's fingers tightened around hers. It was a warning, but she didn't heed him. "Adaira can't wed Budge. He's nearly thrice her age!"

Aonghus Budge's grin slipped.

Her father looked her way. His face turned thunderous. "Hold yer tongue, lass."

"Please, Da," Adaira choked out the words. "I don't want this … I can't—"

"Silence!" Spittle flew as their father leaned across the table. Una reached out, plucking at her husband's sleeve to calm him, yet he shoved her hand aside. "I will not have my daughters defy me. Ye will do as ye are bid."

Tears streamed down Adaira's face. Her hazel eyes were wide, desperate. "I won't do it," she gasped. She gripped the edge of the table as if it was her anchor in a stormy sea. "I won't."

"Ye will!" Malcolm MacLeod launched himself forward and threw the contents of his drinking horn in Adaira's face.

The Great Hall of Dunvegan went silent.

Blood-red wine dripped down Adaira's cheeks, staining the pale blue kirtle she wore. Beside her, even Aonghus Budge looked taken aback by MacLeod's outburst. Wine splattered the clan-chief of Islay's cream-colored léine. "I have agreed to the match, Malcolm," he growled finally. "There's no need to lose yer temper."

MacLeod collapsed into his chair. His face was dangerously red now, and he wheezed as if he were out of breath. Una watched him, her face taut with concern. "Malcolm?"

"I'm all right," he mumbled. "Just give me a moment." His gaze remained fixed upon Adaira. She made no move to wipe the wine off her face; instead, she merely stared back at her father, her expression stricken.

The look in her sister's eyes made an iron band fasten around Rhona's chest; it was a look of utter betrayal. Out of the three daughters, their father had always been softest with his youngest. He'd called Adaira his 'fairy maid', his 'wood sprite'. He'd indulged her over the years.

It made his treatment of her now even harder for Adaira to bear.

Across the table, Caitrin met Rhona's eye. Her elder sister's face had gone hard, and her blue eyes bore a flinty look that Rhona had never before seen.

"Ye would do this to Adaira, Da?" Caitrin's voice echoed through the now silent hall. "Wedding her to Budge will kill her."

MacLeod's barrel chest was still heaving, although his eyes narrowed. "So ye have a tongue, after all, lass? I was beginning to think Baltair had cut it out."

A muscle feathered in Caitrin's jaw, but she continued to stare her father down. "Would ye have *yer* fate determined by others?" Her voice was hard and cold. "Would *ye* not fight to choose whom *ye* wed?"

"Women don't get to choose," Malcolm MacLeod snarled back. The glint in his eyes warned them all that his temper was kindling once more. "Ye are fit for breeding and little else." Una cast him a dark look at that, but heedless, the clan-chief plowed on. He reached for a ewer of wine and refilled his drinking horn. "One more word on this subject and I will have all three of ye whipped."

"I loathe him." Adaira choked out the words against her pillow. "He's a beast!"

Rhona sat next to her sister, gently stroking her back while Adaira sobbed upon her bed. She'd said little since following Adaira up here; there weren't any words that could undo their father's decision or lessen the shock.

She was still reeling from it herself.

Guilt pulsed through Rhona. Her belly ached from it.

If I'd agreed to wed Budge, Adaira would have been spared.

Aonghus Budge was a brute, but Rhona was physically tougher than her sister. She'd have endured his cruelty easier. Instead, she'd defied them all and ended up wed to Taran MacKinnon. She should have been miserable now, for that was what her father had wanted, in order to punish her for running away. And yet fate had taken an unexpected twist.

Instead of misery, she'd found love.

But what about her sister?

Rhona heaved in a deep breath. Her sister's shoulders shook from the force of her sobs.

Adaira was gentle and kind, a lass with a giving soul. Rhona had never been that good. Compared to Adaira, she felt selfish and difficult.

"I'm so sorry, Adi," she whispered, using the name their mother had favored Adaira with as a bairn. "If I could undo it, I would."

Rhona glanced across the chamber at where Caitrin sat next to the fireplace. She was nursing Eoghan. Usually, Caitrin wore a serene expression when she was feeding her son, but tonight her expression was harsh. Her gaze smoldered. With a jolt, Rhona realized she'd rarely seen her elder sister so angry. She bristled with it. Baltair's death had unleashed something in her, a fire that had long been smothered. Rhona was glad to see it, although misgiving stirred within her as well.

She knew from bitter experience what happened to women who rebelled.

"Will ye stay on at Dunvegan awhile?" Rhona asked.

Caitrin shook her head. "Baltair must be buried on MacDonald lands. We leave at dawn tomorrow."

With a gasp, Adaira sat up, pushing her walnut brown hair out of her eyes. "No, Caitrin ... ye can't leave. I need ye!"

Caitrin's gaze guttered. "I'm too angry to be of any help to ye. The very sight of Da makes me want to scream. If I stay here, he'll only have ye whipped because of me." Caitrin's gaze shifted to Rhona. "Ye will look after Adaira?"

Rhona swallowed, her throat suddenly tight. "What makes ye think I'll be able to hold my tongue?"

Caitrin's mouth twisted into a rueful smile. "Ye still have fire in yer belly, Rhona—but now happiness has tempered it. I've seen the love and trust between ye and Taran." Her smile faded, and she dropped her gaze to where Eoghan suckled hungrily. "I've no idea what that's like."

Rhona returned to her chamber later that evening with a heavy heart. Taran was there already, waiting for her, although he'd fallen asleep. Still fully clothed, he was stretched out upon the bed, his face gentle in repose.

Shutting the door quietly behind her, Rhona padded over to the bed and gazed down at him. When he was asleep, his scars were less evident; they seemed smoother against his skin, not so disfiguring. When he was angry, those scars made him look terrifying.

The past weeks had taught her that a very different man lay beneath the forbidding exterior that had earned him his reputation as the Beast of Dunvegan. His big heart, his kindness, and his respect for her still awed Rhona.

Her breathing hitched. *What did I do to deserve him?* Guilt writhed in her belly once more as she imagined her sister cringing in bed while Aonghus Budge took her maidenhead.

Rhona felt sick at the thought.

With a heavy sigh, she sat down on the edge of the bed. Feeling the mattress shift, Taran groaned, his eyelids flickering. His gaze settled upon her. When he spoke, his voice was husky with sleep. "How is Adaira?"

"Upset ... terrified."

A shadow passed over his face. Taran propped himself up on an elbow and reached for her hand. Wordlessly, he entwined his fingers through hers and squeezed.

"I feel so useless," Rhona whispered, her vision blurring. She'd managed to keep her upset to herself while with her sisters, but somehow Taran always made her defenses crumble. It was as if he saw right through her shield, to her heart; there was no point in hiding her feelings from him. "It should have been me to wed Budge."

Taran made a sound in the back of his throat. "And ye would never have been mine."

Rhona met his eye. "I can't bear the thought of Adaira going back to Islay with him ... he'll kill her, Taran. Just like he did his last wife."

Taran's gaze narrowed. "He swears her death was an accident."

"And ye believe him?"

A beat of silence passed before Taran shook his head. He watched her, his expression tender, before he released her hand and reached up to push a lock of hair off her cheek.

"Ye are so fiercely protective of yer sisters," he said after a moment. "Why?"

Rhona drew in a shaky breath and scrubbed at a tear that escaped, trickling down her cheek. "Just before my mother died, she called the three of us to her bedside."

The memory of that day crashed over Rhona as she spoke. The sight of her mother, frail with sickness, her once lustrous blonde hair strawlike and spread over the pillows that propped her up in her sickbed. The heartbreaking sadness in those hollowed eyes.

"She told me I had Da's fierce heart ... that she would rely on me to look after my sisters. I remember her final words to us as if she spoke them yesterday: 'Ye will be women one day, in a world ruled by men. And as such ye will have to be doubly strong, sharp, and cunning to survive.'" Rhona broke off there and closed her eyes. "I didn't know what she meant at the time. But I do now."

"Yer loyalty does ye credit," Taran said, brushing away a tear, with his thumb, that trickled down her chin. "It is one of the many things I love about ye … but be careful that it doesn't tear ye up inside." He paused there, and Rhona opened her eyes, meeting his gaze once more. "Ye can't protect yer sisters from the world, any more than ye can hold back the tide or keep death at bay. Things seem bleak for Adaira now, but none of us know what lies in store for her."

"Ye mean Aonghus Budge might die in his sleep before the handfasting and spare her?" Rhona asked, her mouth quirking. There was wisdom in her husband's words, and she knew in her heart that he spoke the truth. Only, it was hard to let go of a lifetime's habit.

"Aye." Taran smiled back. "Don't underestimate yer sister either. Ye have seen the change in Caitrin since Baltair fell. Life molds and shapes us, forges us into who we're meant to be."

Rhona caught his hand and raised it to her mouth, kissing his fingers. "Taran MacKinnon … how did ye get to be so wise?"

He raised a sandy eyebrow. "Are ye mocking me, wife?"

"No … I'm serious. I think I know who ye are … and then ye say something that surprises me. There are depths to ye I never suspected."

He huffed a laugh. "There are to most of us … I just choose to share my thoughts with ye." He sobered then, gazing up at her with a tenderness that made Rhona's breathing constrict. "I didn't have an easy start to life, mo chridhe. It shaped me differently to other men."

My heart.

Rhona's gaze misted once more; her heart ached with love for Taran. His words eased the guilt and worry that stole away her happiness and cast a shadow over the world. He was right. She would always be there for her sisters, but she couldn't control their fate. Even their father, powerful as he was, couldn't foresee all ends. He'd not been able to see that his wayward daughter and the scarred warrior who'd loyally followed him for years were meant for each other. Perhaps his decision to wed Adaira to Aonghus Budge would take a twist none of them expected.

Rhona bent down and kissed Taran, her lips parting his. He groaned against her mouth. When she pulled away, they were both breathless, and the weight that had settled over her shoulders had lifted. "It shaped ye into a wonderful man," she murmured. "I'm blessed to have ye as my husband."

The End.

From the author

I hope you enjoyed the first installment of THE BRIDES OF SKYE.

THE BEAST'S BRIDE was new territory for me, both for its setting (my first Medieval Romance!) and for the 'Beauty and the Beast' theme at the heart of the story. I wanted to put my own personal twist on the theme, which meant going deep into the characters. As always, the story I planned wasn't entirely the one I ended up writing. Taran and Rhona's story took me in directions I didn't expect, and some scenes were gut-wrenching to write. Until now, I'd say that Galan (from BLOOD FEUD) has been my favorite hero ... although now I've written this book, Taran might be in first place!

Of course, you'll be wondering what happens to Adaira and Caitrin now? Fortunately, you won't have to wait long to find out. Books #2 and #3 are both coming soon!

As with all my books, I really enjoyed the historical research that went into this story. The MacLeods are a dominant clan on the Isle of Skye, and they reside at Dunvegan to this day. Malcolm MacLeod was an actual clan-chief, who did steal the wife of the Fraser chieftain, resulting in a bitter feud! History doesn't record Malcolm MacLeod, who apparently did get very fat in his later years, as having any daughters—but since I know that history often forgets such details, I decided to give him Rhona, Adaira, and Caitrin.

The historical backdrop to this novel is real too. In the year of this story, 1346 AD, the Hundred Years War between the English and the French had begun, and King David of Scotland took the opportunity to try and win back Scottish independence. However, things don't work in Scotland's favor. There will be more on the unfolding historical events in Books #2 and #3.

Next up is THE OUTLAW'S BRIDE!

Jayne x

THE
OUTLAW'S BRIDE

BOOK TWO
THE BRIDES OF SKYE

JAYNE
CASTEL

A woman desperate to escape an arranged marriage. A prisoner with nothing to lose. The promise that will change their lives forever.

Adaira MacLeod has just been betrothed to a brutal older man—a chieftain many believe responsible for his last wife's death. Adaira is desperate. She'll do anything to avoid wedding him.

Lachlann Fraser is a chieftain's eldest son and prisoner in the Dunvegan dungeon. Captured after a bloody battle between the MacLeods and Frasers, Lachlann faces a bleak and uncertain future ... until Adaira approaches him to strike a bargain: his life for her freedom.

Lachlann agrees—he has nothing to lose and everything to gain. But some bargains come at a high price.

Map

"Better a broken promise than none at all."
Mark Twain

Chapter One

Betrothed

Dunvegan Castle, Isle of Skye, Scotland

Early autumn, 1346 AD

"SO DELICATE AND fair … I shall enjoy taking yer innocence."

Aonghus Budge's words brought a cold sweat to Adaira MacLeod's skin. He spoke as if they were alone and used a lover's voice. Fear clawed its way up Adaira's throat. She'd barely been able to eat a mouthful of the meal before her anyway. Now, it would be impossible.

"What's wrong?" Chieftain Budge crooned, leaning in closer. "Have yer sisters not told ye what happens between a man and a woman?"

It was shortly after dawn. Adaira sat with her kin and their guest upon the dais in the Great Hall of Dunvegan keep. It was just a day after Adaira's father had announced that Chieftain Budge would wed his youngest daughter.

Adaira was still reeling from the shock of it. She felt utterly betrayed by her father.

The Great Hall was a lofty space dominated by a huge hearth at each end and rows of tables where her father's men now attacked plates of fresh bannocks, spreading them with butter and honey.

The rumble of male voices, interspersed with laughter, echoed through the hall, masking her betrothed's words from the others at the chieftain's table.

Adaira swallowed and reached for a cup of milk, anything to distract her from Budge's love talk. Raising the cup to her lips, she took a tentative sip—a mistake, for her belly now roiled. Across the table, she caught her sister Rhona's eye.

Statuesque, with a mane of thick auburn hair, Rhona sat next to her husband, Taran MacKinnon. They'd only recently wed, but Adaira had never seen Rhona so happy. She swore her sister grew more beautiful with each passing day. Taran, whose scarred face made him forbidding to look upon, had indeed won Rhona's heart.

Rhona put down the wedge of bannock she'd been buttering and fixed Adaira with a look she knew well. Even though Rhona had been unable to discern the words that Aonghus Budge of Islay was murmuring to her, she'd guessed their meaning. There was concern in her sister's eyes.

Adaira had never been good at hiding her feelings. Her father had always said she wore them on her face for the whole world to witness.

"Demure, I see." There was amusement in Budge's voice now. "I like that in a woman ... less cause for me to give ye a beating ... although I'd enjoy that too."

Adaira made the mistake of looking at him then.

The Budge chief was a portly man with florid cheeks and greying brown hair. He was around her father's age—in his mid-forties. There was something about the warrior that had always frightened Adaira, for Aonghus Budge had been a regular visitor to Dunvegan over the years. She wasn't sure if it was the slack expression he often wore or his mean pale-blue eyes that frightened her. His thick lips reminded her of two fat slugs, and he had coarse, blunt-tipped fingers. Her heart quailed at the thought of those hands on her body.

The chieftain grinned, revealing yellowing teeth of which a few were missing. "But with a little fire in yer belly ... that'll make ye fun to bed."

Bile rose in Adaira's throat, burning like vinegar.

She tore her gaze from his and stared down at the uneaten piece of bannock before her. Fear pulsed through her; she was starting to feel light-headed from it.

To distract herself, she glanced right to where her eldest sister, Caitrin, sat. Dressed in a black kirtle, a veil covering her pale-blonde hair, Caitrin was the moon to Rhona's sun. Her beauty was cool and untouchable, even more so this morning for she wore a shuttered expression.

Caitrin was in mourning for her husband, Baltair, the chieftain of the MacDonalds of Duntulm. He'd fallen in battle two days earlier during a confrontation with the Frasers. But despite Caitrin's somber clothing, Adaira knew her sister did not truly mourn Baltair MacDonald. He'd been a cruel, brutal husband. Adaira was relieved her sister was free of him, although she wondered what the future would hold for Caitrin. It wouldn't be long before their father would start looking for another husband for her.

No wonder Caitrin was planning to leave this morning and head north to the MacDonald stronghold of Duntulm. There, she'd be free from her father's scheming for a while at least.

Adaira looked to the head of the table then, to where Malcolm MacLeod himself sat. As usual, her father had the appetite of ten men; a mountain of fresh bannocks sat before him, and he feasted upon them as if he'd not eaten for days. A comely man in his youth, her father's muscular frame now ran to fat. Rhona had inherited his auburn hair and storm-grey eyes—and his fiery temperament.

The MacLeod clan-chief was not a man lightly crossed, as Morgan Fraser had recently discovered. The two clans had feuded for the last few years, ever since the Fraser chief's wife, Una, had run off with Malcolm MacLeod. As always, Una sat silently next to her husband. Dark-haired with sharp blue eyes, Una was a woman who saw much but said little. Adaira had never trusted her.

"There's no point looking to yer father," Budge's voice cut in. "His mind is made up, lass. The stronger ye protest, the more he'll dig his heels in."

Adaira swung her gaze back to her betrothed. "Rhona told me yer wife didn't fall down the tower steps," she gasped out the words before her courage failed. "She said ye pushed her."

Chieftain Budge went still. His pale eyes narrowed, and those thick lips stretched into an unpleasant smile. "Folk love to gossip," he murmured, casting Rhona a dark look. "Ye shouldn't listen to them."

Adaira raised her chin as she'd seen Rhona do countless times when confronting men. The gesture made her feel a little braver. "So ye deny it?"

"My wife was a silly, clumsy woman who should have watched her step," he growled, leaning close once more. "Mind ye take care in the tower when I bring ye home. The steps are slippery and worn with age."

Adaira pushed herself away from the table and rose to her feet. *Enough.* She couldn't stand to be in this man's presence a moment longer.

"Adaira?" Caitrin turned to her, snapping out of the dreamlike state she'd been in since sitting down at the table to break her fast. "What's wrong?"

Everything.

"I feel sick," Adaira replied, forcing her voice not to tremble. "I'm going to my bower."

"Sit down, Adaira!" Malcolm MacLeod's order thundered across the table. "I didn't give ye permission to retire."

Adaira shook her head. "I'm unwell, Da."

"No, ye are not," he boomed, crumbs flying as he spoke with his mouth full. "Ye are drawing attention to yerself. Sit down."

Adaira hesitated. At the long table, many pairs of eyes watched her. Some, like those of Caitrin, Rhona, and Taran were filled with concern. Others, like those of her brother, Iain, and stepmother, Una, were indifferent. However, Aonghus Budge's gaze was victorious. If she obeyed now, he would have won.

Adaira picked up her skirts, turned, and fled.

"Adaira MacLeod!" Her father's roar shook the rafters. "Come back here!"

But Adaira didn't heed him. She sprinted from the Great Hall, her long hair flying behind her like a flag.

Adaira's breathing was coming in sharp sobs when she reached the battlements. A cool breeze, laced with the salt-tang of the sea, feathered across her wet cheeks. It breathed in from the loch below the castle, a welcome and familiar smell that calmed her galloping heart.

She'd pay for her disobedience, but she didn't care. It had been worth it. For a few instants, she'd felt free, her feet flying as she bolted from the Great Hall and up the stairwell beyond.

Adaira gulped in the sea air and approached the battlements, leaning against the cool wall. It was still early in the morning; the sun had not yet warmed the pitted stone. Scrubbing away the tears that still coursed down her cheeks, Adaira raised her face to the sky. An eagle circled overhead in search of prey upon the wind-seared hillsides below. She envied the bird its freedom. Maybe she too could fly.

Reaching out, Adaira gripped the edge of the battlements. She leaned forward, going up on tip-toe.

How easy it would be to launch herself from here. It was a long way down to the bailey courtyard below. She'd never survive the fall.

She'd be free from Aonghus Budge then.

Adaira closed her eyes, her fingers digging into stone. Her heart hammered against her ribs, and her pulse pounded in her ears.

I can't do it.

Adaira lowered her head to the edge of the battlements and heaved a deep sob. She couldn't bear this. Her father was likely to force her to wed Chieftain Budge within the next few days. Like Rhona, who'd been handfasted to Taran on the same day that he'd won her hand in the games, MacLeod would waste no time in ensuring his daughter was shackled.

Adaira sucked in another lungful of air, forcing back the grief that thundered through her like surf upon the shore.

My life is over.

Chapter Two

My Choices are Few

LACHLANN FRASER GLARED up through the darkness. He craned his neck back, his eyes squinting at the tiny slivers of light that filtered in through the grate above. The guards had just thrown him down weevil-infested bread and moldy cheese—his third meal since he'd been in the Dunvegan dungeon.

After three sunless days, the darkness was slowly starting to break him. Lachlann could feel it, chipping away at the corners of his mind, gnawing at his self-control. He wondered how many men had gone mad down here.

The guards hadn't moved away from his cell yet. Coarse laughter filtered down.

"Do ye want some meat to go with yer supper?" A voice echoed from above.

Lachlann didn't reply. He hadn't spoken to the guards since his arrival here; instead, he saved his energy and passed the hours imagining how he'd kill them when he got out.

"Here ... eat up!"

The grating sound of metal echoed through the cell as the guards lifted the grate above once more. Something fell inside, landing with a thud at Lachlann's feet.

A heartbeat later, torchlight flooded into the cell, highlighting the filth-smeared walls and the straw-littered floor. The chunk of bread and cheese that Lachlann had not yet touched lay around him—along with the corpse of a giant rat that the guards had just thrown into his cell.

Lachlann's eyes watered, and he blinked furiously, trying to get used to the light. At the sight of the rat, his stomach clenched.

"What's wrong, lad?" Coarse laughter filtered into the cell. There were two of them up there, chortling at his fate. "It's fresh!"

Another burst of mirth assaulted his ears.

Lachlann sucked in a deep breath. Aye, he'd enjoy killing these two. He'd take the one that laughed all the time first. He'd slit his throat and watch while he choked on his own blood. His friend, the one who tormented him the most, he'd kill more slowly. A wound to his belly perhaps.

A disappointed silence fell before one of the guards gave a snort and tossed something else into the pit. It was a bladder of water, stoppered tight.

Lachlann stifled the urge to grab it, for his mouth felt like dried cracked leather, and his throat was so parched it made it hard to swallow. But he would wait until the guards had gone before he slaked his thirst.

"We've got a proud one here," the mouthy guard observed, a sneering edge to his voice. "Pride will do ye no good here, Fraser. It'll only turn ye mad. In a few days, we'll hear ye howling for yer mother."

Aye, and when I get out of here ye will be howling for yers.

The torchlight receded, the iron grate slammed shut, and Lachlann listened to the heavy thump of receding footsteps.

Inhaling deeply, he leaned forward and scooped up the bladder, bread, and cheese. As he did so, he accidentally brushed against something furry. He yanked his hand back with a shudder. *The rat.*

Lachlann retreated to a corner of the cell and lowered himself down on the floor, his back resting against the cold, damp stone. Summer had ended, the long warm days giving way to the cooler months, but it felt as chill as January down here. Once winter did come, he wouldn't last long.

I'll get free before then.

He'd been promising himself he'd escape from the moment they'd thrown him down here. He repeated the words to himself in a mantra whenever despair welled up within him—as it did now.

He couldn't let himself believe this would be his end.

He was Morgan Fraser's eldest, the heir to a vast tract of lands. Not only that, but he had three ruthless younger brothers who'd be happy to see him gone. He couldn't bear the thought of Lucas inheriting what was rightfully his if he didn't return.

None of them would come for him—none would try to rescue him from the Dunvegan dungeon.

If he was to get free, it would be by his own hand.

Lachlann unstoppered the bladder and took a long, measured gulp. The water was flat, stale, and slightly warm, but it tasted like nectar to his parched throat.

His thoughts shifted then to the reason he was here: the battle that had taken place in the Vale of Hamra Rinner, on the border of their lands. The Frasers and MacLeods had clashed violently. He'd seen Malcolm MacLeod, as fat and gouty as he was, stab his father. MacLeod had managed to get a blade under Morgan Fraser's mail shirt.

A blow to the back of Lachlann's skull had felled him an instant after he'd witnessed MacLeod strike his father down. Now he couldn't be certain if his father was alive or not.

Lachlann took another tentative gulp of water. He had to be careful not to drink it all in one go. God only knew when they'd give him another.

The Fraser defeat at the Vale of Hamra Rinner was a bitter one. If his father had indeed survived, he'd be furious. MacLeod bested him at everything it seemed. He'd stolen Morgan Fraser's wife and had now won back his lands.

But Lachlann knew his father well—he'd never let it go. If the Frasers were known for one thing it was their stubbornness. MacLeod had earned himself an enemy for life, and Morgan Fraser would never let the past lie.

Lachlann lowered the bladder and stoppered it carefully. He then took a bite of cheese. It had a rancid, soapy taste, but it was food. He chewed slowly, forcing himself to think on other things.

The sun setting on the slopes of Preshal More, the mountain just south of Talasgair, and turning it gold. The sound of the wind through the grass on the slopes before his father's stronghold. The salty tang of the sea that filled his lungs as he walked along the wide strand before the Bay of Talasgair.

Home.

I'll see it again, he promised himself as his jaw set in determination. *I won't let this place defeat me.*

"We can't let Adaira wed that man." Rhona MacKinnon looped her arm through her husband's and cast him a fierce look. "He'll kill her."

Taran met her gaze for a moment, his face troubled. They walked down the curving causeway from the castle, heading toward the gardens that lay south of the keep. It was their evening ritual these days, this stroll. However, Rhona couldn't relax this evening, not when Adaira's future was so precarious.

"I like this as little as ye," Taran said after a pause. "But ye know what happens to those who defy yer father."

Rhona drew in a sharp breath at Taran's reminder.

She knew all too well. Rhona had defied her father at every turn for years, and in the end, he'd forced her to wed. Things could have turned out badly indeed for her, but fortune had twisted in her favor.

"This is my doing," she said bitterly. "Da wasn't so inflexible in the past. I've made him this way ... he won't have any daughter stand up to him now."

Taran didn't reply, for they both knew it was the truth.

Aonghus Budge had been meant for Rhona, but she'd spurned him. After the support the chieftain had given the MacLeods of late, her father was determined to strengthen his relationship with the Budges of Islay. He'd not let Adaira stand in his way.

The couple walked in silence then, taking the path that cut south, and entering the gardens. Unlike the heavy confines of the keep, and the thick curtain walls that sometimes felt as if they hemmed Rhona in, the gardens were a place of refuge: a quiet space where she could breathe, where the scent of flowers soothed her.

The scent of the last of the summer roses enveloped Rhona and Taran. They walked amongst the riotous growth of rosemary, sage, and thyme, their boots crunching on the fine pebbles underfoot.

A damp sea breeze wafted across the garden, bringing with it a sharp, briny tang. The air was changing; the softness of summer was gone. But for now, there was warmth enough in the sun for them to venture outdoors without a heavy mantle. Rhona inhaled the sharp crispness of autumn. In just over two months' time, the solstice of Samhuinn would be upon them, and then they would begin the long winter.

Stopping next to a canopy of honey-suckle, Rhona turned to face her husband.

Taran met her eye and grimaced. "Something tells me I'm not going to like what ye are about to say."

Rhona arched an eyebrow. "Ye are right about one thing, Taran," she began, her voice low and determined. "If I confront Da about this, it'll only enrage him. We can't change his mind so we must go around him." Taran's brow furrowed, but Rhona continued doggedly. An idea had been growing in her mind all day; she'd not be thwarted. "We must help her escape Dunvegan."

Adaira hurried into the gardens, one hand clamped over her mouth in an attempt to hold back the sobs that racked her.

Tears streamed down her cheeks, and her vision blurred, yet she knew the path to the gardens so well she could have traveled it blindfolded.

And she knew Rhona and Taran would be there.

She had to see them. They were the only souls in the keep who'd know how she felt.

Adaira entered the heart of the garden through an arch of trailing roses and spied her sister and brother-in-law up ahead. They were standing next to a canopy of honey-suckle—and they appeared to be arguing.

Rhona was talking quickly, waving her hands around for emphasis, while Taran stood before her, arms folded across his broad chest. His expression was thunderous as he barked out sharp replies.

Adaira slowed her pace. Despite her upset, and the panic she could barely contain, she was suddenly wary of intruding.

She was sorry to interrupt them, but she had no one else to turn to.

The crunch of her booted feet on gravel alerted Rhona and Taran to her arrival. They glanced up and stepped away from each other, their expressions almost guilty. Rhona turned her storm-grey eyes—so similar to their father's—toward Adaira. The cross look on her face softened when she saw who interrupted them.

"Adi," she greeted her. "What is it?"

Adaira stopped before them, and her defenses crumbled. She wanted to be brave, but everything had gotten too much. She covered her face with her hands and started to sob.

"I've ... just come from ... Da's solar," she managed in panicked gasps. "The wedding will be ... in three days' time." Adaira drew in a ragged breath and scrubbed at her tears. The upset look on her sister's face, and the concerned expression on Taran's, made it difficult to keep calm. They both understood how grave this was.

"Aonghus Budge will remain here until the handfasting," Adaira continued hoarsely, "and directly after the ceremony he and I will leave for Islay."

Rhona drew in a sharp breath. She then cast an imploring look at her husband. "We must help her."

Taran stared back at his wife, his face taut. Long moments passed before he muttered an oath and raked a hand through his short blond hair. Then he turned his attention to Adaira. "Yer sister has a plan," he said roughly. "I think it's madness, but she won't be swayed."

Adaira went still, her gaze shifting back to Rhona. "Ye do?" she asked hoarsely.

Rhona favored her with a determined look. "Aye. Taran doesn't like it, but I think it's the only way."

Adaira swallowed, straightening her spine. Hope kindled in her breast for the first time since her father had announced her betrothal. "My choices are few right now," she replied. "I'd like to hear it."

Rhona cut a glance to her husband. Taran's face was set in stern lines, his ice-blue eyes hard. Seeing she'd get no support from him on this, Rhona turned her attention fully upon her sister. "We're going to get ye out through that passage in the dungeon."

Adaira's breathing hitched. She watched Taran's expression grow grimmer still. Until today, he likely wouldn't have known of the keep's secret way out. Rhona and Adaira had spoken of the passage recently, for Adaira had suggested her sister use the escape route in the summer, just days before the games when Rhona would be forced to take a husband.

"But won't Da's men catch me?" Adaira asked, her pulse racing. The fragile hope shattered, and fear replaced it. She didn't fancy being hunted.

"Not if someone went with ye," Rhona replied. "A warrior ... someone who knows how to fight, how to survive out in the wild."

Adaira's gaze flicked to Taran. *Surely not?*

"Taran can't go with ye," Rhona said sharply. She'd seen the direction of her sister's gaze. "Da would have him flayed alive for the betrayal."

"Who then?" Adaira whispered, meeting Rhona's eye once more.

Rhona drew in a deep breath, folding her arms across her breasts. "Ye know Da has a new prisoner locked in the dungeon?"

Adaira frowned. "Aye ... Lachlann Fraser." All of Dunvegan knew of the capture of Morgan Fraser's first-born son.

"I plan to free him—his freedom for yers."

This announcement rendered Adaira speechless.

Taran was scowling. He looked at his wife like she'd just lost her wits.

Rhona was the first to break the silence. "I know it's a bold plan, but I've thought it through."

Adaira found her tongue. "And ye believe Lachlann Fraser would help me?"

"Aye, his choices are even fewer than yers. Da will never let him out of that cell. He'll be desperate."

"Ye should never make an alliance with a desperate man," Taran growled. "Ye will never be able to trust him."

Rhona cast her husband a quelling look. "We will make him swear an oath."

"And do ye think it's wise to let our enemies learn of a secret entrance into the keep?"

Rhona tensed, a shadow passing over her face. "We'll make him promise never to reveal it."

Taran snorted. "Ye would take him at his word?"

"We have no choice." Rhona put her hands on her hips and glowered at her husband. "Without our help, he'll never see daylight again. We have to hope that the man has some honor." She turned her attention to Adaira then. "He must escort ye out of Dunvegan and take ye to our kin in Argyle—only then is he free to return home."

Silence fell while Adaira digested her sister's words. She understood Taran's concerns. It was a bold, reckless, and incredibly risky plan. Yet if Lachlann Fraser agreed, it might just work. Adaira knew she'd never make it to Argyle without help.

Still, a heavy weight settled in the pit of her belly at the risk her sister was putting herself, and Taran, at by helping her.

"I can't let ye do this," she whispered, tears welling as despair rose within her once more. "What if Da discovers ye helped me?"

"He won't," Taran replied, his voice rough. Adaira met his gaze and saw his expression had changed. His face was still stern although there was a determined light in his eyes that reminded her of Rhona. "Not if we are clever and careful."

Chapter Three

Just Three Drops

THE CUNNING WOMAN lived on the edge of the village of Dunvegan, in a hovel surrounded by brambles and hawthorn.

Rhona drew up her mare, Lasair, before the gate and swung down from the saddle. Glancing around, she wondered if anyone had seen her leave the keep to ride here, or if any villagers had spotted her along the way. She had a story ready for them if they had: she would say she'd visited the woman for help getting with child. She and Taran hadn't been wed long, but many a wife was anxious for her womb to quicken.

Curling mist wreathed in from the loch this morning. It was Rhona's ally, obscuring her from prying eyes. Even so, she was on edge. Dunvegan was a place where little went unnoticed and unseen. She'd deliberately taken the long way here, skirting the village, yet she still glanced around her, eyes straining as she peered into the mist.

Rhona tied Lasair to the rickety fence and let herself in through the gate. *I can't believe this mad plan is my idea.*

But as mad as it was, she knew she had to do this.

She couldn't stand by and let Adaira wed Budge.

The mist closed in around Rhona now, obscuring the white-washed, thatch-roofed cottages of the village. However, to the north, the keep loomed above the pillowy white blanket. Dunvegan Castle was a dove-grey fortress that appeared carven from the rocks on which it stood. Its curtain wall and craggy battlements stood out against the grey sky. The fortress had once been a prison for Rhona, and it now was for Adaira too.

She would help in any way she could.

Guilt arrowed through her then, for she didn't like to involve Taran in her plans. Her father's retribution would be terrible if he suspected Taran of helping Adaira escape.

Rhona hated putting her husband at risk. Yet she couldn't do this without him—and there was no way he'd allow her to venture into the dungeon and release a prisoner. He'd insisted that part of the plan was to be his responsibility.

A wave of love, so fierce that it made her eyes mist, swept over Rhona. She'd never met a man like Taran MacKinnon: brave and strong, yet with a tenderness and protectiveness that took her breath away.

Rhona made her way up the narrow path to the front door of the hovel, passing a messy garden. As she walked, her eyes picked out a number of plants: woundwort, marigold, boneknit, mint, and chamomile. Herbs were the cunning woman's trade. Locals often requested her help when a healer could not find a cure.

"Afternoon, Lady Rhona." An old woman greeted her at the door. Small and lean, with a weathered face and thick white hair tied back into a severe bun, Bradana Buchanan knew all who lived at Dunvegan—from the high to the low.

"Good day to ye, Bradana," Rhona greeted her with a smile. "I'm in need of one of yer potions. Can I come in?"

The cunning woman nodded and stepped back so that Rhona could enter her hovel. A tidy space scented with the odor of dried herbs, and the more pungent odor of burning peat, greeted her. Surprised, Rhona straightened up. The garden was such a tangle she'd expected the interior of Bradana's home to be in disarray as well. Instead, there wasn't an item out of place. The dirt floor had been swept clean, fragrant bunches of dried herbs hung from the rafters, and a plush fur hanging shielded the hovel's sleeping space from view. A long worktable—where rows of bottles, a pestle and mortar, and earthen jars were neatly stacked—sat against the far wall.

A lump of peat burned in the hearth. Rhona warmed her hands before it; the mist had turned the day cold and damp.

"What sort of potion were ye after, lass?" Bradana asked. The old woman ran a speculative gaze over her. "Surely ye aren't worried that yer womb won't quicken? It's too early for such worries."

Rhona smiled. "Aye, there's plenty of time for that," she replied. "Although if anyone should ask, that's why I visited ye."

Bradana inclined her head, gaze narrowing. "What are ye wanting then?"

Rhona dragged in a breath. "I need a potion to put someone to sleep for a while."

The cunning woman gave a brisk nod. "I can make ye a sleeping draught of valerian root."

Rhona shook her head. "I need something much stronger than that ... a potion that will put someone to sleep quickly and make them slumber a long while." Bradana's face tensed, and Rhona hurriedly added. "Nothing to cause harm."

Bradana observed her for a few long moments, dark-blue eyes gleaming. "May I ask why ye need such a potion, Lady Rhona?"

Rhona chewed at her lower lip. "It's best if ye don't."

The cunning woman gave Rhona a long look. "Lady Rhona," she began quietly after a moment. "My poultices and potions are for the use of good, not ill."

"And this *is* for good," Rhona answered quickly. Panic rose as she realized the cunning woman thought she was planning something villainous. "I wish I could say more, but I'm sworn to secrecy. But please believe me when I say that this potion will save someone's life. I wouldn't ask otherwise."

Bradana Buchanan continued to watch her. It was a probing look that made Rhona feel as if the woman could see right into her soul. Eventually, she huffed out a breath. "I have something," she said. "However, ye must be wary of how ye use it."

Rhona nodded, relieved. "I will, I promise."

The cunning woman crossed to the table and picked up a small clay bottle. "This is a tincture of nightshade," she said, holding up the bottle but not passing it to Rhona. "I keep it for those who have nerve trouble. One drop in a cup of wine will relax ye. Three drops will put someone into a deep, dreamless sleep. And ten drops will kill them."

Bradana handed her the bottle. There was a steely look in her blue eyes, a warning. "Ye never received this from me, Lady Rhona, is that clear?"

Rhona swallowed, before nodding. "Just three drops then."

"Aye ... and no more."

Adaira picked up a sweet bun and took a bite. It stuck in her throat as she swallowed.

Fighting the urge to gag, she turned to the young woman with thick brown hair and hazel eyes who stood at a workbench before her. "How's Gordon faring these days?" Adaira asked.

"Much better, thank ye, milady." Greer twisted her head and flashed Adaira a warm smile. "I appreciate ye asking."

Adaira forced a cheerful smile back. Truthfully, it was difficult to concentrate, hard not to look at the two trays behind Greer, where she was setting out food and drink: cups of apple wine and dishes of mutton stew served with oaten dumplings.

Supper for the men taking their watch in the dungeon tonight.

"I was relieved to hear he'll keep his leg," Adaira continued. She felt bad feigning conversation with Greer, although her concern for Gordon MacPherson was real. The warrior had taken a serious injury to the thigh during the battle against the Frasers.

"So was I," Greer admitted, pushing a lock of hair out of her eyes. "He'll bear a limp for the rest of his days though ... and he won't stop grumbling about it."

"Better a limp than a peg leg," Adaira replied, keeping the smile plastered on her face.

Greer snorted. "Aye, that's what I tell him when his complaining gets too much."

Adaira laughed, although to her ears it sounded like a nervous titter. Until this evening, she'd always felt comfortable in this kitchen. Greer and her mother, Dunvegan's cook, had been good to her over the years. She'd spent a lot of time with them after her mother died. Tonight, Greer's mother, Fiona, was poorly with a bad head. Greer had overseen the day's food preparations.

Swallowing hard, Adaira tried to calm herself. It was hard though as her heart was beating so fast it felt as if it might leap from her chest. She felt sick.

Maybe I should have asked Rhona to do this.

No, her sister had already taken a great risk on her behalf. Adaira needed to complete this task—no one else. She just hoped her nerve wouldn't fail her.

Next door to the kitchen, Adaira could hear the lilt of female voices and laughter. The servants in the scullery were hard at work, washing up after supper had ended in the Great Hall.

Adaira's attention shifted to the haunch of venison that hung from the rafters on the far side of the kitchen. Noting the direction of her gaze, Greer's face turned serious. "It's for the handfasting feast."

It was the reminder Adaira needed. The wedding was looming now. If she messed this up, she'd never escape it. "I imagine ye will be busy with the preparations," she said, her voice suddenly brittle.

"Aye." Greer favored her with a sympathetic look. All of Dunvegan knew she didn't want to wed Aonghus Budge. "I've got a lot of baking to do over the next two days. Hopefully, Ma will feel better tomorrow so she can help."

Taking another bite of bun, Adaira widened her eyes. "I love these, Greer ... ye really are a talented baker."

Greer was, although if Adaira took one more bite, she felt as if she'd throw up.

Greer grinned, her cheeks flushing at the compliment. "Take some away with ye, if ye want, Lady Adaira."

"Can I?" Adaira took a small basket and placed four more buns inside. She cast Greer a hopeful look. "I don't suppose ye have some butter to go with them ... and some of that blackcurrant jelly ye made at mid-summer?"

Greer huffed. "For a wee thing, ye have quite an appetite." She cast a glance behind her at where the trays were waiting. Adaira was interrupting her chores, although she couldn't deny one of MacLeod's daughters. "Very well ... wait here. We've got plenty of butter leftover from today, but I'll have to dig out a pot of jam." She moved toward the pantry, wiping her hands upon her apron. "I'll be back in a moment."

A moment was what Adaira had been waiting for.

As soon as Greer disappeared, she set aside her basket, withdrew the bottle from her sleeve, and approached the two cups of apple wine.

This was a stressful situation. Rhona had told her a tincture of nightshade could be deadly. She needed a steady hand and really didn't want to be rushed. Yet this was the only chance she'd get. Crouching down, so her gaze was level with the cups, she unstoppered the bottle.

To her horror, Adaira saw her hands were shaking.

Calm down. If ye fail in this, it's over.

Carefully, holding her breath to catch a tremor in her wrist, she tilted the bottle.

One, two, three.

In the pantry, she heard Greer mutter a curse as she rummaged through the pots of jam for the elusive blackcurrant. Adaira knew their stores were getting low of that variety—which was why she'd asked for it. However, any moment now, Greer would locate her last jar.

Inhaling sharply, she moved to the second cup. She could feel sweat beading on her upper lip. Her pulse thundered in her ears.

One, two ... three.

It was done.

The Lord preserve her, she hoped she'd got the measurement right.

Adaira stoppered the bottle, rose to her feet, and stepped back sharply. She'd only just hidden the bottle up her sleeve and picked up her basket of buns when Greer burst out of the pantry. The young woman held a small clay pot aloft, her expression victorious. "Here it is—just one left!"

Adaira beamed at her. "Ye are an angel. Blackcurrant is my favorite."

"I know," Greer said with a wink, handing her the pot and a large pat of butter wrapped in linen. "There ye go ... now off with ye. I've got some hungry guards to feed. They'll be wondering where their supper's got to."

Chapter Four

No Place for Ladies

"I'M SORRY, PUP, but I can't take ye with me." The wolfhound puppy, Dùnglas, wriggled in Adaira's arms. He reached up with his front paws, trying to lick her face. Adaira's eyes filled with tears. She'd chosen Dùnglas from a recent litter. His name, which meant 'grey fort', had been her choice too.

She didn't want to leave him behind.

"Go on." She set him down inside the stable and watched as he scampered off to join the other puppies. Their mother lay in the corner of the stall, a long-suffering expression upon her face. The pups were getting to an age where they were becoming mischievous, their needle-sharp teeth nipping at her teats when they fed.

Not wanting to draw out the moment, Adaira turned on her heel. She hastily blinked away tears and hurried from the stables. *No weeping*. She couldn't crumble now, not when she was to make her escape tonight.

Rhona and Taran were risking their necks for her. She had to be brave.

The sun was going down, setting the western sky ablaze. Supper had been a tense affair. Adaira had sat in silence while Aonghus Budge threw her heated glances and whispered more filth. If her father heard any of the comments, he'd made no sign. Instead—his attention tonight had been fixed entirely upon the mutton stew and dumplings before him.

Adaira climbed the stairs that led to the upper levels of the keep. There was no one around; it was still too early for most folk to retire.

In her bower, she found Rhona waiting.

"There ye are!" Her sister hissed, gripping her arm and steering her back through the door into the empty corridor. "Where have ye been?"

"I was putting Dùnglas back down with the other pups," Adaira whispered back. "If he stays in my bower alone overnight, he'll howl."

Rhona's face relaxed. "Good thinking … come on. We need to get ye to our chamber up in the tower. The first of the guards will be taking up his post outside yer room shortly."

"Just wait a moment." Adaira crossed to the bed, where the satchel she'd prepared awaited. The satchel's sides bulged. She'd packed a large water bladder and the four sweet buns, with the butter and blackcurrant jam, all tightly wrapped. Grabbing the satchel, she slung it across her front.

The thump of heavy booted feet ascending the stairs below them, made both women freeze. The guard in question was early.

"Let's go." Rhona's fingertips bit into Adaira's upper arm, but she didn't complain. Instead, she let her sister drag her along the corridor, down a narrower stairwell, and down to the bottom level of the keep. By the time they reached the tower stairs, both of them were out of breath.

The guard would have taken up his position outside her door by now. Their father had recently instructed Adaira to retire directly after supper. The guard would take his place outside her door, assuming she was inside her bower. She would not be disturbed until her hand-maid, Liosa, visited her the following morning.

The sisters did not speak until they were safely ensconced in the tower room.

Shutting the door firmly behind her, Rhona turned to Adaira. Her cheeks were flushed and tense. "Did ye manage it?"

Adaira nodded. "I think so. I had to be careful."

"Ye only added three drops to each cup?"

"Aye ... Greer took some time looking for the food I requested. Even so, she almost caught me."

Rhona loosed a deep breath. "Thank the Lord she didn't. I don't know how ye would have talked yer way out of that." She crossed to the sideboard and picked up a bone-handled dirk and a slingshot. She handed them to Adaira. "Ye need to be able to defend yerself. Do ye remember how to use a slingshot?"

Adaira nodded hesitantly. "I think so," she murmured. She certainly hoped so. She remembered their father showing her how to use a slingshot when they were children. She'd be very rusty, but she was sure she'd regain her skill quickly. Especially if need drove her to it.

Adaira favored Rhona with a sickly smile. "Da watches me like an eagle these days," she murmured. "Do ye think he suspects something?"

Rhona shook her head. "I don't think so. However, those of us left behind must brace ourselves for his rage when he discovers ye gone."

Adaira wrung her hands together, squeezing so hard she heard the bones of her fingers creak. "I don't want ye punished because of me."

With a sigh, Rhona went to her and pulled her into a tight hug. "I won't be. If things go to plan, no one but the cunning woman will know that Taran and I have helped ye." Rhona stepped back, meeting Adaira's eye. "Ye are to meet him in the bailey courtyard, to the right of the front keep steps, later ... once the moon has risen."

Adaira nodded, nervousness coiling in the pit of her belly.

"Taran will take ye to the dungeon and help ye free the prisoner," Rhona continued. She started to pace the chamber, agitated. "The guards should be fast asleep by then."

The coil of nerves in Adaira's belly tightened. She hoped Rhona's sleeping potion would work, although she didn't voice her fear. Heaving a deep breath, Adaira crossed to the open window. It was almost completely dark outside now; the last of the sunset was fading from the sky.

Now we must wait, she thought. The tension was almost unbearable. Waiting was the hardest part.

"Are ye ready, lass?" The low rumble of Taran's voice soothed Adaira's jangled nerves. She'd stepped out into the bailey and waited in the deep shadow of the keep for Taran to join her.

"Aye," she whispered. "Are the guards asleep?"

It was too dark to make out his face although she sensed his expression was grim. "We'll find out soon enough," he murmured. "Follow me."

Adaira fell into step behind Taran and drew her cloak close around her. It was a still night, and the air was damp and cold. She was traveling light, with just the satchel slung around her front. It was heavy with the food and water. The buns would stave off hunger for a short while. She imagined that Lachlann Fraser would appreciate some good food.

It was late. The keep slumbered, and a deep silence had fallen over the fortress. The stillness of the night unnerved Adaira; she'd have preferred the whisper of a wind to take the edge off it.

She followed Taran toward the entrance to the dungeon, marveling at how silent his tread was for a big man. He moved like a shadow, and she was careful to follow suit.

As she walked, Adaira glanced up at the window to the tower chamber, high above her. It was dimly lit, signaling that someone was still awake. Rhona would be up there, awaiting her husband's return.

The sisters' goodbye had been painful. Adaira's chest still ached from the tears she'd seen in Rhona's eyes.

"Promise me, ye will be careful," Rhona had whispered. "Promise me that when ye get free of here, ye will fight to remain so. Don't look over yer shoulder ... don't ever come back."

Adaira had nodded, tears of her own welling.

She couldn't bear the thought of never seeing her sister again, yet she had little other choice. Once she wed Budge, and he took her off to Islay, she'd likely not see Rhona again anyway.

Taran and Adaira entered the dungeon stairwell. Neither of them carried torches, and so they were forced to feel their way downstairs in the dark, using the damp stone wall as a guide.

The glow of light ahead warned Adaira that they were reaching the guard room. Blinking, she followed Taran out into a small space with a low ceiling that had been carved out of the rock. A narrow passage led out of the back: the way to the cells.

Adaira's attention moved to where two guards sat at a table in the corner. The men lay slumped against the wall, mouths gaping. Two trays with empty clay bowls and cups sat before them.

Adaira's breathing hitched. *Are they asleep—or dead?*

Taran pushed back the hood of his cloak and approached the nearest guard. He then snapped his fingers in front of the man's nose. The noise cracked like a whip in the damp air, but the man didn't stir. He reached down and felt for a pulse upon his neck. Taran's breath gusted out. "He's alive." Taran checked the second guard. "And so is this one. They sleep deeply, but they'll live. Ye did well."

Relief swamped Adaira, making her legs go weak. Guilt assailed her then. If her father ever discovered the truth, Rhona's life would be spared, but Taran's wouldn't. He'd swing from a gibbet for this.

She stepped next to Taran, placing a tentative hand on his arm. "I haven't thanked ye properly, Taran," she murmured. "I know ye are doing this for Rhona … ye must love her very much."

Taran turned to her. The guttering light of the torch on the wall illuminated his scarred face. "I couldn't let Rhona do this on her own," he admitted quietly, "but I also can't stand by and see ye wed Aonghus Budge. If I can help in any way … I will."

Adaira swallowed the lump in her throat. "Ye are a good man, Taran MacKinnon. My sister is very lucky."

"Come." Did she imagine it, or did his cheeks color slightly at her praise? Turning from her, he helped himself to a ring of keys hanging on the wall and lifted the torch off its brace. Taran carried the torch over to where another hung at the entrance to the passageway. He lit it and passed it to Adaira. "Let's go find Lachlann Fraser."

Adaira followed Taran down the passageway. A few yards on, they came to another set of stairs that led down even farther underground. Adaira hadn't visited the dungeon in years. It was forever nighttime down here, a smothering darkness that made it difficult to breathe. Not that she wanted to take many deep breaths. The air smelled putrid: mold, stale urine, sweat, and worse. It made her eyes water.

"This isn't a place for ladies," Taran grumbled. "I can't believe ye and yer sisters used to play down here."

Adaira responded with a soft snort. She was wondering the same thing herself.

Moments later, they stepped out onto a wide passage. A row of iron grates lined the stone floor.

Adaira stepped close to Taran. "Do ye know where he is?"

Taran nodded. "The second last one. All the rest are empty at present."

They made their way to the cell in question. Halting before the grate, Taran passed Adaira his torch and crouched down. He selected a key and unlocked the grate before lifting it free.

"Lachlann Fraser." Taran's voice, although low, rang in the stillness. "Are ye awake?"

Chapter Five

Upon Yer Life

A RASPY VOICE broke the silence. "Aye ... what's it to ye?"

The male voice had a harsh edge to it. Adaira's spine stiffened. She hadn't given any thought as to the character of the man imprisoned down here. She hoped Rhona was right, and that he would agree to help her.

"I have someone here who'd like a word with ye," Taran continued. He then inclined his head to Adaira, indicating that it was her turn to speak.

Adaira handed Taran back his torch and moved forward. She then bent her head and peered into the darkness below. Dear Lord, the stench coming from down there was awful. Didn't he have a privy he could use?

"Lachlann Fraser," Adaira began, swallowing bile. "I come bearing an offer. Are ye interested?"

A beat of silence followed before the prisoner spoke once more. This time, his voice was gentler, edged with curiosity. "A lady? What's this?"

"Just answer her, Fraser," Taran growled. "Are ye interested?"

Another pause. "I might be."

Adaira leaned forward, squinting. She couldn't see anything in the gloom. "My freedom for yers," she said quietly, reciting the words she'd practiced with Rhona earlier. "If I set ye free, ye must agree to escort me out of this dungeon to freedom. Ye must protect me with yer life."

A soft, bitter laugh followed. "I agree readily," he drawled. "But I also point out that we stand in the dungeon, with a curtain wall and a portcullis preventing my escape."

"I know a way—a secret way—out of this dungeon," Adaira countered, her voice low, urgent. "If ye will swear upon yer life to protect me, I will show ye it."

Another silence fell, this one heavy. The prisoner was pondering her words.

"And where do ye wish me to take ye?" he asked finally, an edge of wariness to his voice.

"I must leave this isle," she replied. "We shall travel to Kiltaraglen on the eastern coast and find a boat that will take us to the mainland. Ye must escort me to Gylen Castle in Argyle. Once I am safely delivered to my kin there, ye are discharged of any responsibility. Ye are then free to return to yer own kin." Adaira drew in a long, steadying breath. "Do ye still agree?"

Another beat of silence passed before he answered. "Aye."

Relief swamped Adaira. However, when she glanced up and looked at Taran, she saw he was scowling. He wasn't happy about this. "Let's hear ye swear it then," he growled. "Upon yer life, upon everything ye hold dear, ye will protect this woman and see her safely delivered to her destination. Ye shall also promise never to tell a soul how ye escaped this place."

"I swear it." The prisoner's voice was low and steady. "Lady ... I shall take ye wherever ye desire. I will protect ye with my last breath." He paused here. "And I will tell no one how we got out ... although I suggest we stop talking and start moving."

That was good enough for Adaira. She was keen to leave as soon as possible. However, she saw that Taran still hesitated. With a jolt, she realized he didn't trust the prisoner. In truth, she didn't either. But what choice did she have? He'd made an oath, and she would need to trust him to uphold it.

"Come," she murmured. "He's sworn to me; we can't wait any longer."

Taran gave a curt nod, rose to his feet, and took hold of a wooden ladder that was resting against the wall. He lowered it into the cell. "Climb up," he ordered curtly.

Moments later, the scuff of boots on the wooden rungs echoed through the dungeon. And then a tousled head appeared.

Adaira stared at the prisoner, momentarily transfixed. This was her first proper look at him. She'd seen Lachlann Fraser from afar when they'd brought him in unconscious. But then she'd just caught a flash of his bright auburn hair and little else.

He was a few years older than her. Wild red hair framed a handsome, if pale, face. He had eyes the color of moss and beautifully drawn features that were set in a fierce expression. A dark auburn shadow of stubble covered a strong jaw. Adaira stared, mesmerized.

Even stinking and disheveled, he was the most attractive man she'd ever seen.

Likewise, the prisoner stared at her. His expression grew shrewd, those green eyes narrowing as he observed her. Then he drew a slow breath and inclined his head. "Evening, Lady ...?"

"Ye don't need to know her name," Taran growled. "There will be time enough for that later."

Holding his torch aloft, Taran stepped back to allow the prisoner to climb from the cell.

Lachlann Fraser did so. He stretched his long body, his eyes squinting as they adjusted to the torchlight. He was dressed in braies and a loose léine. Both were filthy.

Fraser's gaze settled upon Adaira once more, unsettlingly direct. "Which direction is it then?"

Adaira's breathing quickened under his scrutiny before she tore her attention from the prisoner and focused on Taran.

Her brother-in-law was watching her, concern in his eyes. "Do ye remember the way?"

She nodded her head, although her heart started to hammer against her ribs. It had finally come to this; she was escaping. "Aye," she murmured. "Go back now, and thank ye. I'll never forget this." She was careful not to use Taran's name or to mention her sister's. Once they were far from here, her escort would learn her name and identity. But not yet. Taran was right to be cautious.

Taran nodded and stepped back. Yet he didn't move away just yet. Instead, he turned his attention to Lachlann Fraser. The two men stared at each other for a heartbeat. Taran's face was as hard as hewn granite. "If any harm comes to her ... if ye fail to uphold yer end of the bargain, I'll come looking for ye, Fraser," he growled. "I'll hunt ye down to the ends of the earth. That's a promise."

The ferocity of his words shocked Adaira; she stared at Taran, struck speechless.

Lachlann Fraser sneered. "Don't threaten me, *Scar-face*," he growled.

Tension rippled through the air. Taran's jaw clenched, and he took a step toward Lachlann. Panic trembled inside Adaira as she realized the pair might come to blows.

Without thinking, she stepped in between them, craning her neck to meet Taran's eye. "We're going now," she said, her voice brittle with nerves. She then cast a glance over her shoulder at where Lachlann Fraser wore a murderous expression. "Follow me."

Lachlann couldn't believe it.

He was free. Just like that. He'd been huddled in a corner of the cell, wondering how much longer he'd be able to keep his wits in this endless darkness, when he'd heard a man calling to him from above.

That scar-faced warrior had looked as if he wanted to throw him back down the ladder into the cell and slam the grate shut. And he probably would have, if the choice had been his to make.

But thanks to this young woman leading him down a series of increasingly small passageways, it wasn't.

The girl was quite lovely. She'd been the first thing he'd seen when he'd emerged from the cell. A mane of walnut-colored hair framed a pert face that contained the loveliest pair of hazel eyes he'd ever seen. She was small, her curves hidden by the heavy woolen mantle she wore. Across her front, the young woman carried a bulging satchel. She looked like someone about to set out on a long journey.

And I am to be her escort.

A grim smile spread across Lachlann's face. He'd have gladly made a pact with the devil himself if it meant escape from that putrid cell.

"How did ye manage to get past the guards," he asked casually. "Did yer scar-faced friend kill them?"

"They're drugged," she replied, an edge to her voice. "They shouldn't awaken for a long while."

Drugged. Disappointment flooded through Lachlann. For an instant, he was tempted to leave the lass here and go find those two. He had unfinished business with them both. However, freedom was more important to him right now than petty vengeance. He'd not risk it for the pleasure of killing two lack-wits.

"A hidden passage, eh?" he murmured as they entered another corridor, this one so low they both had to stoop to avoid hitting their heads. "How did ye learn of it?"

"Please save yer questions for later," she replied, her tone sharpening. "I must concentrate now."

Lachlann's smile turned hard. He would indeed, for he had plenty of them. She and her protector had been cagey upon letting him out of the cell, but it was clear to Lachlann that the maid was high-born. She spoke and dressed like a lady. He knew that MacLeod had three daughters. Two were wed apparently, but the youngest was not.

Lachlann's gaze settled upon the girl's slender shoulders. He'd wager that this was Malcolm MacLeod's youngest daughter. He didn't recall her name, but he'd discover it soon enough.

Eventually, the passageway became so low they were virtually crawling through it. It was difficult going, for the girl insisted on carrying the torch with her. Lachlann's back was beginning to ache when they came to a rusted iron grate, much like the ones that covered the cells.

The girl sat back on her heels and looked Lachlann's way for the first time since leaving her companion. She had a shy, hesitant gaze, although he noted the lines of determination on her face. Curiosity gnawed at Lachlann. He wanted to know why this young woman was fleeing in the dead of night and enlisting *his* help to do so.

"This is the way out," she announced. "Can ye open the grate and climb down. I'll hand ye the torch."

Lachlann nodded, grabbing hold of the grate and pulling it upward. It wasn't that heavy and, fortunately, the grate wasn't locked, although the bars were covered with rust—almost entirely corroded in places. Lachlann wagered no one had come this way in a very long while.

A hidden passage under Dunvegan … a secret well worth knowing.

He climbed down, his boots hitting iron rungs, and took the torch the girl handed him. Moments later, she was climbing down the ladder. Halfway down, she paused.

"Wait … I need to close the grate."

He huffed. "Is there any point?"

Her tone was clipped when she replied. "I'd rather leave no evidence of our passing."

Lachlann's mouth quirked. She might appear as meek as a mouse, but the lass had a spine. He shouldn't be surprised, for a coward wouldn't have chosen such a daring escape as this.

Down in the passageway, Lachlann kept hold of the torch. The roles were reversed now. He would lead the way, and she would follow.

Nonetheless, he turned to her. "Straight ahead?"

The lass nodded. "This tunnel is long ... but it eventually comes to a dead-end." She paused here, her brow furrowing. "It's been years since I've been down here, but I remember there was an iron grate in the roof ... and I saw daylight through it."

Lachlann nodded. "Was it locked?"

Her face tensed. "I can't remember."

Lachlann loosed a sigh. "Come on then ... let's hope it isn't."

The tunnel was small and cramped, with wet stone walls and the ever-persistent sound of dripping water. It was an unpleasant space, but nothing compared to the festering cell Lachlann had left behind. He'd happily endure this place if it promised freedom. He longed for fresh air and daylight, things he would never take for granted again.

As the girl had warned, they spent a long while in the tunnel. Shortly after beginning their journey, they ceased to speak. Instead, they shuffled along, bent double, step after step, toward freedom.

By the time they reached the end of it, the torch was starting to die. Lachlann dropped it to the ground and craned his neck to the grate above them. No light of any kind shone through it.

He cut his companion a glance. Her face, lit by the guttering torch on the ground, appeared strained. "I can't see a lock," she murmured, her face tilted up, her gaze narrowed as she peered at their escape route.

"There's only one way to find out," Lachlann replied. Climbing up the ladder, he grabbed hold of the iron bars. It wasn't easy to budge. At first, he suspected the grate really was locked. But then after a moment, he realized that it was merely a bit stuck; it was covered with rotting leaves and what smelt like pine needles. He gave a hard shove, and with a groan of metal, the grate shifted.

They were through.

Lachlann pushed the grate aside and climbed up and out of the tunnel. Rising to his full height for the first time in what felt like hours, Lachlann massaged his aching back. He stood amongst a growth of pines. Moonlight filtered through the trees, and he breathed in the pungent scent of sap.

Freedom had never smelled so good.

"Are ye going to help me out?" An irritated female voice intruded.

Lachlann turned. He'd almost forgotten the woman; they weren't off to a good start.

Reaching down, Lachlann grasped a small, warm hand and pulled the lass up out of the tunnel. The touch of her skin caused a frisson of heat to ripple up his arm. Lachlann caught his breath, his fingers tightening around hers.

The young woman stared at him, her eyes growing wide.

Gently, she pulled back from him, tugging at his hand. Reluctantly, Lachlann let her go.

"I know this place," she observed, shifting her gaze from him. He caught the edge to her voice and knew the touch had affected her as it had him. "These woods lie northeast of the keep. Da and his men often hunt here." She abruptly stopped speaking, realizing she'd unwittingly revealed her identity.

The lass took a step back from him, drawing her mantle close.

"Worry not, Lady MacLeod," Lachlann drawled. "I guessed yer identity the first moment I set eyes on ye. It changes nothing of our agreement. However, I would like to know yer name ... if I may?"

She watched him, her face glowing pale in the moonlight. "Adaira," she said softly.

Lachlann held her gaze. He couldn't believe his luck; this girl was his angel of mercy. What a reprieve—and now he was free, he intended to stay that way.

"Can I ask how ye knew of such a passageway?" he asked. "The dungeon isn't a place for high-born maids."

She swallowed. "My sisters and I discovered it years ago," she replied softly. "We weren't supposed to play in the dungeon. Da would have been furious if he'd known. We used to dare each other, to see who the bravest was ... who could explore the farthest."

Lachlann smiled. "And who discovered the end of the tunnel?"

She looked away. "My sister Rhona."

"Well, Lady Adaira," he murmured. "Argyle is a long way off. I say we travel through the night and rest in daylight. Yer father will be after us come the dawn."

Chapter Six

Aingeal

"I KNEW YE were an angel ... the moment I set eyes upon ye."

The words were muttered between large bites of bun slathered in butter and jam.

Watching Lachlann Fraser devour his second sweet bun, Adaira smiled. "Slow down, or ye will give yerself bellyache."

He nodded but then proceeded to stuff half a bun into his mouth, chewing vigorously. "Ye have no idea how good these are," he managed when he'd swallowed. "I've had nothing but weevil-infested bread and rancid cheese since they threw me down in that hole."

Adaira's smile faded, and she suppressed a shudder at this comment. She looked around her, noting that the sky was growing lighter by the moment. After emerging from the tunnel, they'd fled like hunted deer. Lachlann had led the way east, his long legs covering the ground easily until Adaira had called out to him, begging him to slow his pace. She couldn't run great distances, especially wearing skirts and carrying a heavy satchel and cloak.

Lachlann had relieved her of the satchel, and they'd set off once more, this time at a brisk walk.

Dawn had stolen upon them quickly, arriving with startling swiftness. They now sat on the mossy bank of a creek, taking a much-needed rest. Adaira's lungs still ached from exertion, as did her legs. She'd taken off her heavy cloak and now carried it. Her léine—a long ankle-length tunic she wore under her kirtle—now stuck uncomfortably to her back.

"Ye should eat," Lachlann said as he reached for a third bun. "Or I'll end up finishing all of these."

"I brought them for ye," she replied. "I can eat once we reach the coast. I've got some pennies with me. We'll resupply when we find passage across the water."

Lachlann Fraser raised an eyebrow. "Going hungry on my account ... ye truly are an *aingeal*."

Adaira looked away, her cheeks warming. "Not really," she murmured. "I'm too nervous to eat."

"Well, I'll leave the last bun for ye," he said, his mouth curving. "For when ye get yer appetite back."

Their gazes met briefly, and Adaira returned his smile.

She'd been wary of Lachlann Fraser at first, especially after his confrontation with Taran. Yet he'd behaved honorably so far. He'd carried her satchel and slowed his pace to accommodate her. When he'd taken her hand to help her out of the tunnel, heat had jolted up her arm. The feel of his strong fingers curling around hers, the warmth of his skin, had completely scattered her wits.

She'd been acutely *aware* of him ever since.

Adaira watched Lachlann now as he scanned their surroundings. The good humor faded from his face, and his moss-green gaze narrowed. "We can't stay here much longer. Very soon, someone will notice we are missing."

Adaira nodded, her belly contracting. "My maid usually comes to my bower shortly after dawn. She'll raise the alarm ... if the dungeon guards don't wake up first."

Lachlann ate his third bun, although not with the ferocity of the first two. Around them, the dawn chorus of birdsong echoed through the trees: blackbirds, song thrushes, and warblers. Their chirping took the edge off Adaira's anxiety and soothed her ragged nerves.

"I love the sound of the dawn chorus," she said eventually, "but I can't hear it from my bower. Sometimes I get up early and go to the gardens at dawn just to listen to the birds."

Lachlann's mouth quirked, and Adaira wondered if her comment had amused him. Here they were, running for their lives, and she was admiring birdsong.

Finishing his meal, Lachlann dusted crumbs off his filthy braies. He sat a couple of yards from Adaira, yet she could still smell him. The man was in need of a bath and fresh clothing. However, both would have to wait.

Lachlann then met her eye once more. "Why were ye so desperate to flee Dunvegan?"

Adaira had been expecting the question, but she still tensed when he asked it.

He's my protector now, she reminded herself. *I need to trust him.*

"I'm to wed Aonghus Budge of Islay," she murmured, dropping her gaze.

Lachlann gave a low whistle. "Say no more ... I know all about him."

Adaira's head snapped up. "Aye ... he killed his first wife—and he'd kill me too, I'm sure of it."

Lachlann Fraser's eyes shadowed before he nodded. Remaining silent, he packed away the remaining food, stuffed it into the satchel, and got up. Slinging the satchel across his front, his gaze met Adaira's once more. "In that case, we'd better keep moving."

Adaira winced as she slipped upon a mossy rock and her ankle twisted.

"Can't we rest for a while," she panted. Holding her skirts high, she splashed across the creek bed after Lachlann. Cold water soaked through the soft leather of her boots. Adaira glanced down at them with dismay. The boots were new and made of costly chamois, but they'd be ruined after this journey.

They'd been traveling all morning, without respite. The sun beat down on them; it seemed that summer had returned after days of colder weather. The heat was both a blessing and a curse. It would make sleeping rough easier, but it also made the journey much harder work. Adaira's cheeks glowed like two hot coals.

"No time for that." Lachlann cast a glance over his shoulder. "Yer father will be hunting us now."

Adaira frowned. She knew that—she didn't need reminding of it.

"I know ye are tired," he continued, turning his attention away from her once more. "And as soon as we find a place to hide, we can rest. It's safer traveling at night anyway."

That made sense. They'd been fortunate so far and hadn't seen any other travelers, hunters, or farmers. Yet, as they approached the east coast, that would change.

Adaira plowed on behind him. Her wet boots started to chafe her feet. Lachlann had relieved her of her cumbersome mantle and now carried both that and her satchel. All she had to do was follow—yet she could feel herself flagging.

I'm slowing him down, she thought dully. *If we get caught, it'll be all my fault.*

The realization sent a jolt of panic through her. She couldn't let that happen. Capture was unthinkable. She couldn't let Budge get his hands on her.

And so she struggled on, closing her mind off to the exhaustion that pulled down at her with each step.

How far were they from the coast now? She'd long since lost any sense of direction. Lachlann had assured her they were journeying east, toward the port village of Kiltaraglen.

The village lay directly across the water from the Isle of Raasay. Once they found a boat, they would have to travel south, around the island, before turning east to the mainland.

Kiltaraglen was also the closest port to Dunvegan. Nervousness fluttered under Adaira's ribcage. She hoped Kiltaraglen was a wise choice. Perhaps she should have gone to Duntulm instead—to Caitrin.

Adaira's throat constricted. How she wished to see Caitrin. But such wishes were foolish. Malcolm MacLeod would search for her at Duntulm.

No, Adaira wouldn't involve her sister. She'd already risked Rhona and Taran's necks. Best to stick with the original plan: go to her kin on the mainland. Her mother had spoken often of Gylen Castle, where she'd grown up. It sounded like a welcoming place.

They would take her in; they would protect her.

On and on they trudged as the sun rose high into the sky. And, just when Adaira's step was beginning to falter, when she was considering calling out to Lachlann and begging for him to stop awhile, he did just that.

Breathing hard, Lachlann drew up. Standing at the bottom of a rocky gully, he turned to Adaira. His cheeks were flushed with exertion, and his handsome face was haggard and tired. However, his eyes were sharp.

"I've found a hiding place," he announced, pointing above them. Pines loomed high overhead, and the sides of the ravine rose nearly perpendicular. A few yards above them, upon the eastern side, Adaira spotted a gap. It was wide, although barely high enough for a person to squeeze into, even on their belly.

"We're going to hide in there?" she asked, horrified.

"Aye." Lachlann adjusted the satchel, slinging it and the cloak across his back. Then he began to climb. "Come on, Aingeal. Yer bower awaits."

Peering up at the gap above, Adaira frowned. She wasn't sure she had the strength in her arms to climb, but she'd try. Reluctantly, she followed him up the rocky incline. There were plenty of holds for her fingers and toes. Even so, she'd only gone a couple of yards when she started to falter.

Halting, clinging to the rock like a spider, she glanced up. Lachlann had already reached their destination. He threw the satchel and cloak inside before pulling himself under the ledge on his belly.

"Just a few more feet," he called. He reached down, his hand stretching toward her. "Ye can manage it."

Gritting her teeth, she forced her uncooperative limbs to move. Her legs trembled under her, and the muscles in her upper arms and shoulders burned. Not only that, but her skirts were hampering her movement.

"Grab my hand."

Adaira pushed herself up another foot before lunging toward Lachlann. His hand clasped hers, and her breath gusted out of her. A heartbeat later, he yanked her up the cliff-face and under the ledge where he sprawled.

Adaira found herself face-to-face with him, their bodies pressed close. His heat and nearness overwhelmed her. It was dark in the gap, but she could see the gleam of his eyes.

A moment later, the ripe smell of his unwashed body assaulted her.

"God's bones," she muttered, edging away from him. "Ye stink."

Lachlann gave a soft laugh. "So would ye, if ye had spent a week in yer father's dungeon."

Adaira gritted her teeth. She didn't want to be uncharitable, but the thought of being jammed in this crevice next to a man who was in dire need of a bath revolted her. She wouldn't be able to sleep.

"Worry not," he continued, a sardonic edge to his voice. "As soon as we reach the coast I shall scrub myself with lye and rid myself of these rags."

Silence fell for a few moments before Adaira broke it. "I'm sorry," she murmured, chastised. "It must have been terrible being locked up in the dark, not being able to use a privy or bathe."

Lachlann's mouth quirked. "It wasn't so bad."

"But didn't ye despair?"

"I was too busy trying to think of a way to escape."

Adaira's eyes widened. "Really?"

"Aye," he replied without hesitation. "Two of the guards, in particular, liked to bait me ... I was going to use it to my advantage."

Adaira watched him, impressed. "Ye are resourceful."

"I've always had to be."

"Why's that?"

"I've got three younger brothers chafing at the bit to advance themselves," he said with a wry smile. "Plus, I'm Captain of Talasgair Guard ... and in charge of patrolling the Fraser borders. I always have to think one step ahead."

Adaira propped herself up on one elbow, trying to get comfortable on the hard stone ledge. "Ye will be anxious to return home."

Lachlann didn't reply, and she searched his face, noting that his smile had faded. She wondered if he worried about his father's fate. She'd heard her own father bragging about how no mortal man could recover from the injury he'd dealt Morgan Fraser.

"I'm grateful to ye, Lachlann," she said softly. "I couldn't make it to Argyle without yer help."

He inclined his head. "It was a brave decision," he noted, "to free me and flee from Dunvegan. Most lasses, even faced with the prospect of wedding Aonghous Budge, wouldn't do it."

Adaira loosed a long breath. "As ye saw ... I didn't do it alone." She hesitated, wondering whether to confide in him. What did it matter? They were far from Dunvegan now. He could know the truth. "The man who helped me is named Taran. He's wed to my sister, Rhona. They planned my escape."

Lachlann's dark-auburn eyebrows raised. "That's quite a risk they took."

"I know ... my father can never learn of it."

Lachlann rolled away from her, stretching out onto his back and cupping his hands behind his head. "Well ... no one will hear a word of it from me, Aingeal."

Chapter Seven

Decisions

THEY REACHED THE coast and the village of Kiltaraglen in the middle of the night.

Moonlight frosted the outlines of great mountains and lit their way. Adaira's belly growled as she walked, so loudly that Lachlann eventually turned to her.

"Here." He dug the last bun out of the satchel and held it to her. "Eat this."

Adaira stopped, her gaze dropping to the bun. "Don't ye want it?"

"Aye, but if yer belly growls any louder, it'll alert half the village to our presence."

Adaira favored him with a soft snort. Her stomach wasn't that loud. Even so, she took the bun, sighing with pleasure as her teeth sank into it. Her appetite had returned with a vengeance now. Maybe it was because she'd managed to rest. She hadn't thought she'd sleep during the day, squeezed into that crevice with Lachlann—but she had. She'd fallen into a deep, dreamless sleep, and had only awoken after dark when he'd gently shaken her.

They'd left the creek behind shortly after starting this stretch of the journey, traveling across bare hills. The open landscape made Adaira nervous. Her ears kept straining for the thunder of hoofbeats in the distance. Her father would no doubt send men in this direction, for Kiltaraglen was the nearest port to Dunvegan.

They would need to leave first thing in the morning to stay ahead of him.

Boots crunching on the gravel-strewn road, they crested the brow of a hill, woodland rising up either side. Below them stretched the tiny port of Kiltaraglen.

The village, a collection of thatched roofs lining the edge of the water, slumbered. It was a still, mild night. The water glistened, reflecting the glow of the moon. If Adaira hadn't been so nervous, she'd have found the sight a lovely one.

She'd been to Kiltaraglen once years earlier, for there had been a special market here, and her father had allowed her, Rhona, and Caitrin to visit it. She remembered the village with fondness: the tightly-packed white-washed homes and the long waterfront, where a collection of rickety wooden boats bobbed in the tide.

Adaira swallowed her last mouthful of bun. "There's an inn on the waterfront," she said. "Hopefully it's not too late, and they'll open their doors to us."

Lachlann didn't respond immediately. Instead, his gaze remained on the village below them. He studied it intently. "I don't think it's wise to linger here," he said finally. "We should move on ... tonight."

Adaira tensed. "But surely it's safe to stay here till dawn?"

Lachlann shook his head. "It isn't. The fewer folk who see us the better. Yer father's men will likely arrive here tomorrow, and the inn will be the first place they'll look. The innkeeper will tell them that a couple matching our description lodged there, and then it won't take much digging for them to discover we left by water." Lachlann cast her a fierce, determined look. "It's best we leave no sign of our passing. We should go now."

Adaira drew a shaky breath. This wasn't the news she wanted. Despite that the bun had taken the edge off her hunger, she longed for a decent meal and a bed for the night. She also longed to bathe. At Dunvegan, she'd have added a few drops of lavender oil to the water, for the scent calmed her. She ached for a short reprieve before they set out on the next leg of their journey. Yet she had to admit, his words made sense. She would have to wait till the mainland for a decent meal and a soft mattress.

"But how can we find a boatman to give us passage?" she asked. "No one will be awake at this hour."

A pause followed. Lachlann slowed his pace before drawing to a halt and turning to face her. "We don't have time for that ... we'll have to steal a boat."

Adaira stifled a gasp. "But we're not thieves."

Lachlann's mouth curved into a slow smile, and despite her shock at his pronouncement, Adaira's belly fluttered. Lachlann Fraser's smile was as alluring as it was dangerous. Like the touch of his hand when he'd helped her out of the tunnel, it turned her mind to porridge.

"Now isn't the time for scruples, Aingeal," he replied softly. "Just how desperate are ye to escape Aonghus Budge?"

I can't believe I agreed to this.

Adaira padded along behind Lachlann as they made their way down to the waterfront, hugging the shadows as they went. It seemed an unnecessary precaution, for there appeared to be no one about, but Adaira was glad her protector was being careful. Someone might be lurking nearby. Perhaps the dock was watched at night—or maybe her father's men were here already, looking for her.

Adaira swallowed hard—she hoped not.

They walked down to where a row of small wooden boats bobbed in the water. Unfortunately, the craft were moored right before the inn. The white-washed building, which rose high above all the others in the village, lay in darkness. No light peeked out from behind the closed shutters. Perhaps it was later than Adaira realized. Even the inn-keeper would be abed.

She followed Lachlann down the grassy slope to the water. There, he went to the first boat in the line and hunkered down before the wharf. Working by feel, for the shadows were long here, he started to untie the oiled rope that moored the boat.

"Climb in," he whispered.

Heart hammering, Adaira complied. She lifted her skirts and stepped into the boat. It rocked under her, and she stifled a gasp, lowering herself to the deck. She then shuffled forward and perched upon a plank of wood. Lachlann passed her the satchel and cloak—and then he pushed the boat out into the water.

Adaira clung on to the sides. Her eyes strained in the darkness for any sign of movement around them. Lachlann moved slowly, but even so, every splash, every ripple, seemed obscenely loud.

As he crept out of the shadow of the docks, Adaira caught sight of Lachlann's face illuminated in the moonlight. It was set in grim, determined lines. It seemed Rhona had made the right choice in making him her protector; Morgan Fraser's firstborn was practical, a survivor.

When the water had reached thigh height, Lachlann climbed in and sat himself down opposite Adaira. He picked up the oars and maneuvered the boat around so that he was facing shore. Then he started to row.

The pair of them did not speak. Adaira hardly dared breathe. She kept glancing back over her shoulder at Kiltaraglen, expecting to hear shouts echo out across the water as someone spied them.

Guilt assailed her then. At dawn, a fisherman would wander down to the water to find his boat gone. They were stealing a man's livelihood. How would he feed his family without his boat?

Adaira shoved the thought away. It was too late now to torture herself. She had to put her trust in Lachlann. She realized now that it was too risky to wait till daylight, yet resorting to thievery upset her.

She turned from the village, her gaze traveling east. In daylight, the isle of Raasay rose out of the sound, but tonight she saw only darkness. However, the island would still be there, and they would need to turn south soon.

"Lie down and rest awhile, Adaira." Lachlann broke the silence between them, his voice terse.

Adaira stared back at him, studying the lines of his face. Her heart had settled to its usual rhythm, and now that they were out of danger, she felt weak, wrung out. She was bone-weary.

Still, she resisted. "What about ye?"

He huffed. "Someone's got to row. There is nothing to be gained by both of us having a sleepless night. When dawn breaks, I'll bring the boat ashore so I can rest."

Adaira nodded, stifling a yawn. Despite that she'd slept the day before, she was desperately weary now. Using her cloak as a pillow, she stretched out, curling her torso around the satchel. It wasn't the most comfortable bed she'd ever slept in, but it was wonderful just to lie flat—not to be on her aching feet.

I'll only close my eyes for a short while, she promised herself. *I'll just take a nap.* But the gentle splash of the oars and the subtle roll of the boat had a lulling effect on her. Before she knew it, sleep caught her up in its embrace and carried her away.

Lachlann Fraser stopped rowing and studied the young woman before him. Adaira was curled into a ball, her hands clasped under her cheek. He'd taken to calling her an 'angel', but now she truly looked like one. Her face appeared pale and very young in the hoary light of the moon.

Is she asleep?

It was a breathlessly still night, and even the slightest sound carried. Without the splash of the oars, he heard the steady rise and fall of her breathing.

Yes, she is.

Lachlann's fingers flexed around the oars, and yet he hesitated.

He'd made a pledge to take her to Argyle, but tonight he'd decided that he wouldn't. Gylen Castle was at least three days' travel from here in this tiny rowboat; it would be many days before he saw his home again. In the meantime, Lucas might use Lachlann's absence as an excuse to take his place as chieftain of the Frasers of Talasgair.

Lachlann didn't trust his brother one bit—and he couldn't let him get his hands on the Fraser lands. He had to return home. He didn't have time for this detour.

Once again, his grip on the oars tightened, but he still didn't move.

His conscience was needling him.

Lady Adaira captivated him. She was sheltered—although that was usual with most high-born ladies—and had a beguiling innocence about her. She was also trusting and gentle-hearted.

She'd be upset that he'd broken his promise.

Lachlann loosed a long breath. Adaira would get over it in time. He wouldn't send her back to Dunvegan. He'd arrange for a boat to take her to the mainland from Talasgair, or she could make a new life for herself at the Fraser stronghold if she wished. Either way, her father would never know she remained upon the Isle of Skye.

Adaira would still get what she wanted, to be free of her union with Chieftain Budge.

But right now he needed to think of himself, his own future.

Lachlann turned the boat north and started to row.

Chapter Eight

By Water

ADAIRA AWOKE TO the warmth of the sun bathing her face.

For a moment, she couldn't remember where she was, or why there was a hard plank digging into her back—but then a familiar male voice intruded, and it all came back.

"The aingeal awakes."

Lachlann Fraser.

Adaira pushed herself upright in the boat, rubbed her eyes, and looked around her. They were no longer on the water. The boat sat upon a pebbly beach, beneath sculpted cliffs and a wild sky, where seabirds wheeled overhead. Lachlann was sitting nearby, long legs stretched before him and crossed at the ankle.

"Where are we?" she asked.

"I'm not quite sure. I brought the boat ashore a short while ago."

Adaira massaged a stiff muscle in her shoulder. Her body ached, and her belly was hollow with hunger. She wished now she'd brought more provisions with her. What she would do for a plate of fresh bannocks, slathered with freshly churned butter and heather honey.

Adaira cast Lachlann a shy glance. "So ... how long will we stay here?"

"Long enough for me to bathe and get some rest."

"Bathe?" Adaira tensed. "But ye don't have any soap or a fresh change of clothes."

Lachlann cast her a roguish grin and rose to his feet. As she watched, he pulled off his boots and started to unlace his braies. "Then I'll have to wash both my body and clothing with fresh seawater. It will be bracing, but at least ye won't have to suffer my stench." He finished unlacing his braies and paused. "Ye had best turn around, lest I offend yer innocent eyes."

Adaira sucked in a shocked breath but hurriedly did as bid, shifting around so that her back was to him. Heat suffused her, and she was glad Lachlann couldn't see her burning face. She felt out of her depth, flustered.

Behind her, she heard the sounds of him undressing, then a splash as he entered the water.

A muffled curse followed.

Despite her embarrassment, a smile curved Adaira's mouth. "Is it cold?"

"Freezing," came his choked reply.

Adaira coughed, masking a laugh.

More splashing ensued, and she assumed he was washing his léine and braies. Washed in the saltwater of the loch, the clothing would be stiff and uncomfortable when it dried and would likely chafe his skin. Still, at least he would smell fresher.

While Lachlann bathed, Adaira distracted herself by taking in her surroundings. She wondered where they were exactly. She hadn't realized that the Isle of Raasay or the shores of the mainland had cliffs like these. It reminded her of home.

After a while, Adaira grew bored of staring at the cliffs and the green headland beyond. Eventually, she grew impatient. If Lachlann wanted to rest, he needed to get out of the water and dry his clothing. They'd never get to Argyle at this rate.

When the splashing finally subsided, Adaira let out a long sigh. *Good. Surely he's done now.*

She cast a furtive glance over her shoulder—and froze.

Lachlann was approaching the shore, just a few yards behind her, thigh-deep in water and completely naked. Sensing movement, he stopped, and their gazes met.

Adaira stared, her lips parting in shock.

His body glistened in the morning sun, highlighting each plane of muscle across his chest, shoulders, belly, and thighs. His body was lean and hard. His red hair was much darker when wet, and slicked back from his face.

Without realizing what she was doing, Adaira let her gaze slide from his face, down his chest and flat belly, to the thatch of dark auburn hair at his groin. Heat pooled in her lower belly as she did so.

"There's no point in looking there," he said with a teasing smile. "The freezing water's done its work. I suggest ye take another look later when I've warmed up."

His voice tore Adaira from her reverie. With a choked sound, she whipped her head away from him.

Mother Mary, what was I doing?

"Get dressed," she rasped, mortified.

"I can't yet." The amusement in his voice made Adaira wish a chasm would open up and suck her into it. "My clothing needs to dry first. Hand me yer cloak, will ye?"

Sucking in a deep breath, Adaira did as bid, careful to keep her face averted.

A moment later, he spoke again. "It's safe now ... ye can turn around."

Reluctantly, Adaira twisted, her gaze settling upon him once more. Her cloak was too small, and too short to cover Lachlann properly, but it protected his modesty nonetheless. He'd wrung out his léine and braies and spread them out over two sun-warmed rocks.

Lachlann met her eye, his own gaze gleaming.

Adaira struggled to keep her composure. She was sure her face now glowed red like a lump of burning peat. Clearing her throat, she glanced away. "Shouldn't ye try and get some sleep?"

"Aye ... will ye keep a lookout while I do?"

"Of course," Adaira replied briskly, still refusing to look at him. Instead, she pulled her knees up under her chin and kept her gaze fixed upon the watery horizon.

"Thank ye, Aingeal." The smile in his voice made her embarrassment burn even hotter. "Wake me if anyone approaches."

Adaira gazed up at the castle perched upon the clifftop. "How strange," she mused aloud. "It looks just like Duntulm."

"There are many cliff-top fortresses on this coast," Lachlann replied.

"Really?" Adaira tore her gaze from the high stone walls and the emerald-green hills that surrounded it. "I expected the mainland to look different to our isle. Ma always said it was softer, less dramatic."

"Parts are."

Adaira's attention shifted to Lachlann then. He rowed in long, confident strokes. She took in the way his shoulder muscles bunched and flexed under his still-damp léine. Heat rose within Adaira as remembered what he'd looked like naked.

Shoving the memory aside, she forced herself to focus on the present. "Can't we take the boat ashore at the nearest settlement?" she asked. "I'm faint with hunger."

He gave a curt nod. "Aye ... once we round this headland."

"Ye must be exhausted. Why don't ye let me row for a while?"

Lachlann snorted, meeting her eye. "It'll take us two weeks to reach Gylen Castle if we share the rowing."

Adaira's spine stiffened. "I'm not useless."

"I didn't say ye were. It's just that we'll get there quicker if I row."

Adaira huffed. "Why don't we leave the boat and get horses at the next village?"

"Gylen Castle sits upon an isle just off the coast. If we travel south, and traverse the Sound of Mull, we'll reach it faster."

Adaira frowned. She hadn't realized that.

"How many silver pennies do ye have in yer purse?" Lachlann asked with a smile.

"Three."

"Well, that's enough to keep us fed during the journey. It's just as well we are traveling by boat, because three pennies won't by ye a donkey, let alone two horses."

Adaira fell silent. Lachlann's words reminded her how frivolous she'd been over the years. She wished she'd managed to save more than three silver pennies. Rhona had often teased her about her love for fine fabric, and perfumed oils and soaps. She never missed the monthly market at Dunvegan village, and what coins her father had given her at each Yuletide were spent there.

Frankly, she was surprised she'd managed to save anything at all.

Her fickle ways embarrassed her. She wondered how she must appear to Lachlann Fraser. A silly goose of a girl, with a head full of nonsense.

"Stay with the boat. I'll be back soon."

Lachlann watched disappointment shadow Lady Adaira MacLeod's hazel eyes. "Can't I come with ye?"

Lachlann shook his head. That was the last thing he wanted. They'd landed just below the village of Geary, a small crofting hamlet that sat on the northwestern coast of the isle.

And within MacLeod lands.

Fortunately, Adaira had no idea of their real location.

Traveling this way put Lachlann on edge. Sailing around the coast of MacLeod territory made him nervous. They were close to Dunvegan now, far too close for his liking.

He couldn't risk having Adaira recognized by one of the village folk at Geary. If she spoke to any of them, the game would be up too, for she'd know instantly that they were still upon the Isle of Skye.

"Someone needs to look after the boat," he pointed out. "It's faster if I go alone." He carried one of the silver pennies from Adaira's purse; it would be enough to buy them a decent meal for tonight and enough food for tomorrow morning. He estimated that, at their current speed, they'd reach Talasgair by noon the following day.

Not waiting for her to voice another objection, Lachlann turned and made his way up the shore, toward the narrow path that climbed the hill. He needed to make this journey quickly and draw as little attention to himself as possible. The sooner they were back on the water and rowing away from MacLeod lands, the better.

Adaira was starting to ask too many questions. Although sheltered, the lass was highly perceptive and missed little.

Geary was tiny, little more than a handful of crofters' huts huddled together upon a bleak, windswept hillside. Lachlann knocked on the door of the first hut he encountered, and a woman with two bairns hanging off her skirts answered.

"I don't have much," she said, beckoning him in, "but for a penny, I can fix ye a meal."

Lachlann flashed her a charming smile. "A weary traveler thanks ye."

The woman smiled back, her gaze coy. Lachlann wondered where her husband was; he hoped the man wasn't due back anytime soon. He didn't want any questions.

"I'm a widow," the woman told him as she went to a bench and retrieved a loaf of coarse bread.

Relief suffused Lachlann, although wariness swiftly followed. She had the look of a woman in search of a new husband.

"I'm sorry to hear it," he replied.

"Drowned," she continued, cutting the loaf in half. She then reached for a wheel of cheese. "Left me with these two to raise on my own."

Two grubby faces peered up at Lachlann in the dim light inside the hut.

Lachlann didn't reply. He didn't want to encourage the woman. Instead, he watched as she filled a cloth bag with the bread, cheese, and four boiled eggs. His mouth filled with saliva at the thought of the coming meal. He hadn't eaten anything since those three buns on the morning after their escape from Dunvegan. His belly now burned with hunger.

A penny would have bought him far more in town, but this woman was poor.

He pressed the coin into her palm with a smile and took the cloth bag from her. He then held up the empty water bladder Adaira had given him. "I don't suppose ye have some boiled water I could fill this with?"

"Aye," the woman replied, holding his gaze. She was blonde and curvaceous with a bold stare. "But I've something better than that." She motioned to the barrel behind her. "Apple wine."

Lachlann's smile stretched into a grin. "That'll do nicely."

A short while later, he left the hut, a sack of food and drink in hand.

The woman followed him to the door, her two children still clinging to her like limpets. She batted at them, irritated, but they wouldn't let go. "There's no need to rush off," she called after him. "Dusk will be upon us shortly. Why don't ye stay the night?"

"I thank ye for the kind offer." Lachlann cast her another careless smile, although he didn't slow his stride. "But the tide waits for no man."

Chapter Nine

A Stolen Kiss

"HEAVENS … THIS IS strong wine." Adaira lowered the bladder, eyes smarting, and handed it to Lachlann. "It has a kick like a pony."

Lachlann raised the bladder to his mouth and took a long draft. "I know … it's delicious."

The pair of them sat upon a pebbly beach, in an isolated cove a half hour's journey from where Lachlann had bought supplies. He'd not been away long and had been eager to depart the moment he returned. Adaira had wanted to eat first, but he'd been insistent. He'd pushed the boat into the water, leaped in, and rowed away as if the devil was on his tail.

Adaira didn't understand why they couldn't have found lodgings for the night in the village. Surely it was more comfortable than sleeping out under the stars?

"What was the name of the village … did they tell ye?" Adaira asked. Her words slurred slightly as she spoke. She'd eaten a good supper of bread, cheese, and boiled eggs, but the wine had gone straight to her head.

"I didn't ask."

Adaira studied him. Dusk was settling, and the golden light kissed the proud lines of his face. "Is this yer first trip to the mainland?" she asked.

He shook his head. "Two years ago I visited kin in Inbhir Nis."

Adaira's eyes widened. She longed to visit the large towns on the mainland, including the capital, Dùn Èideann. "What's Inbhir Nis like?"

He met her eye, his mouth quirking in a way that made her pulse quicken. "The town sits on the banks of a great river that leads east out to sea," he replied. "It's a busy port full of fishermen and shipbuilders." He paused here. "There was once a great stone keep overlooking the town, but it's in ruins now … after Robert the Bruce leveled it."

Adaira loosed a sigh. "There are so many places I long to see. Don't ye wonder about the world beyond our borders?"

"Sometimes," Lachlann admitted. She saw the gleam in his eyes and knew that her comment had amused him. Adaira didn't mind though. The wine had relaxed her, and she felt in an expansive, dreamy mood.

"Where would ye visit, if ye could?" she asked.

He shrugged. "I don't know ... France maybe. The Frasers are said to hail from Anjou."

Adaira's gaze widened. "Really?"

"Aye, that's why our motto is in French: 'Je suis prest' ... *I'm ready*."

Adaira inclined her head, smiling. "Ours is 'Hold Fast'."

Lachlann snorted. "I know ... I heard yer father bellow it as he charged us in battle."

"Da says the MacLeods are of Viking stock," Adaira continued, deliberately steering him away from that subject. "Our ancestor was a man called Leod. Da says he was a son of Olaf the Black ... a Norse king who raided this isle."

"That doesn't surprise me," Lachlann replied. "I could well imagine yer father leading a boatload of Norsemen, burning and pillaging as he went."

Adaira didn't reply. She couldn't really contradict him, for she knew first-hand that Malcolm MacLoed was a man to be reckoned with: feared by his enemies and respected by his allies.

They fell silent for a spell. Lachlann offered the bladder of wine to her once more, but Adaira shook her head. She felt light-headed and strange, as if her limbs were floating. The wine had sharpened her senses too. She was keenly aware of the soft evening air caressing her face, and of the attractive man seated just two feet from her.

Not that she needed the wine to be aware of Lachlann Fraser. His nearness was a constant distraction. She could literally feel the heat of his body warming the air between them.

Blinking, Adaira tried to focus on something else. "I wonder where we are." She sank back on her elbows and turned her face up to the sea breeze. "It reminds me so much of home."

"Aye, it's a pretty stretch of coast," he murmured.

Something in his voice made Adaira glance his way. Lachlann sat, propped up on an elbow, watching her. It was a searching look, one that made Adaira's pulse quicken.

Adaira swallowed, her mouth suddenly dry. "Why are ye looking at me like that?"

Lachlann gazed at the young woman before him. The wine had caused the stress of the day to slough away. He'd even forgotten his aching back, shoulders, and arms—from all the rowing he'd done.

"Because ye are bonny," he murmured.

He watched Adaira wet her lips nervously. Yet she continued to hold his gaze.

Innocent, and yet with a certain boldness.

It wasn't a lie; he did find her beautiful. Not in the obvious way some women were—no, Adaira MacLeod's attractiveness lay in something earthier. Her long walnut-colored hair lay in heavy waves around an elfin face. Frank hazel eyes, flecked with green, watched him with guileless interest.

Now that she no longer wore her heavy cloak, he'd noticed that her figure, although girlish, had a delicious lushness at her hips and bust. Her dark-green kirtle was laced over the swell of full, high breasts.

And yet it was her mouth that fascinated him the most: delicate, yet full. Her lips parted slightly as their stare drew out. He saw her bosom rise sharply as she sought to control her breathing.

Lachlann's pulse quickened in response.

"Ye shouldn't say such things," she whispered.

He gave a soft laugh. "Why not?" He shifted closer to her, his hand lifting to where a heavy curl lay across her throat. "I'm merely stating the obvious. Ye are lovely, and I long to kiss ye."

Her breathing hitched then, and before she could protest, Lachlann leaned in and kissed her softly on the mouth. It was a light touch, the merest brushing of the lips, and yet it sent a jolt through his groin that made him catch his breath.

Reaching up, he caressed her cheek with the back of his hand. She trembled, and he leaned in for another kiss. This time he lingered, and when she sighed, her soft lips parting slightly, he slid the tip of his tongue between them and deepened the kiss.

Adaira moaned.

The sound unleashed something within Lachlann, a hunger that he had trouble controlling. She was a maid; this was likely to be the first time she'd ever been kissed. He didn't want to frighten her.

But he couldn't stop. His tongue explored her mouth as they melted into each other.

Lord, she's delicious.

Maybe it was the wine, but he'd never enjoyed a kiss like this. His hands ached to reach down and explore her lithe body, caress those lush breasts. He'd never wanted anything so much. He was grateful that the loose folds of his braies hid his arousal; he didn't want her to panic.

Then his hand grazed the tip of her left breast, and she gasped against his mouth.

Heat surged through Lachlann. He'd only leaned in to steal a kiss, yet the sounds she made nearly made him forget himself.

With a great effort, he pulled back from her.

Breathing hard, they both stared at each other. The sight of her parted lips, her eyes hooded with desire, made him stifle a groan of his own. Suddenly, he ached for Adaira MacLeod—and yet he knew to take things any further would ruin her. He wasn't a man with many scruples, and yet even he couldn't do that.

"Apologies," he rasped. "I forgot myself."

Adaira drew in a shuddering breath. Her heart thumped painfully against her ribs, and her body pulsed with need.

What just happened?

One moment she'd been sitting there, enjoying the warmth of the wine in her belly, a languorousness in her limbs, and the next Lachlann Fraser was kissing her.

And to her shock, she'd hadn't wanted him to stop.

Despite the embarrassing scene earlier that day, Adaira had enjoyed Lachlann's company during the journey. He'd been caring and considerate of her. She'd found it easy to talk to him and had appreciated the way he'd taken charge.

She felt safe with him.

But underlying it all, there had been a growing tension between them, an awareness that made every interaction feel charged—like the air right before a storm.

Lachlann's kiss had been consuming, intoxicating.

But Lachlann Fraser was an outlaw, the son of her father's arch-enemy. They shouldn't be kissing at all.

And yet she couldn't stop watching him. He observed her too, those moss-green eyes deepening to jade. She noted the sharp rise and fall of his chest, the slight flush across his high cheekbones. He dragged a hand through his shaggy dark-red mane—hair that Adaira longed to run her own fingers through.

Mother Mary, what's wrong with me?

Perhaps she should go straight to a nunnery the moment she reached Argyle. If a man's kiss unraveled her so quickly, she'd be easy prey in future.

Adaira swallowed, reached for her cloak, and wrapped it about her. The evening, which had seemed mild earlier, now felt chill. Since leaving Dunvegan, she'd often felt overwhelmed by Lachlann's presence, but now she felt completely lost.

If he hadn't pulled back, she'd have let him ravish her.

Lachlann cleared his throat and moved back so that around two yards of pebbly beach separated them. "It grows late." His voice was more subdued than usual and still carried a hoarse edge to it. "We should both get some sleep."

Lachlann pushed the boat out into the water and climbed in. Then he glanced Adaira's way and caught her watching him. Her look was veiled, and she hurriedly averted her gaze, but he'd seen enough. He'd avoided a number of entanglements over the past few years and knew when a woman had gone soft on him.

Dolt ... ye shouldn't have kissed her.

He'd not cared at the time, for lust raged through his veins, demanding to be sated. But now, in the cool light of morning, he realized he'd unwittingly created a situation for himself.

Suppressing a curse, Lachlann settled himself upon the plank and picked up the oars. However, before he did so, his gaze fell once more upon the young woman seated a couple of feet away. She was deliberately avoiding his eye now. This situation would only get more awkward if he didn't address it.

"Adaira," he said softly. "Look at me a moment."

She turned her face, her gaze meeting his.

"About last night," he began, "let's forget it ever happened." Adaira's hazel eyes widened. For an instant, Lachlann could have sworn he saw hurt flare in their depths. However, he pressed on. "I overstepped the boundaries of our agreement ... I won't touch ye again."

"Very well," she replied softly, although the edge to her voice warned Lachlann that he'd just offended her.

Lachlann loosed a sigh. *Great.* He'd only succeeded in making things more uncomfortable than before. The easy rapport they'd developed during the journey had evaporated. It was just as well they wouldn't be traveling companions for longer than today.

Wisely, he decided to end the conversation there.

Lachlann maneuvered the boat out into deeper water and began to row. His shoulder muscles protested, as did his back, but he clenched his jaw and rowed on. The first thing he'd do upon his return to Talasgair would be to have the servants prepare a hot bath for him. Then he'd soak in it with a tankard of ale at his elbow.

Glancing once more at Adaira, he saw that she was looking away again, her attention focused upon the green headland they were circuiting.

What will happen to her?

The thought was fleeting, yet it irritated Lachlann. Adaira MacLeod's future wasn't his concern. He had more pressing things to worry about—like ensuring Lucas wasn't taking up their father's chair in the Great Hall.

Looking away from her, he concentrated on steering the rowboat past a cluster of rocks and along the last stretch of coast that would lead him home.

"Why are we landing here?"

Adaira's gaze swept the wide bay they'd just entered and shifted to the foaming line of surf rolling into the shingle beach before them. To her right rose a rocky headland. The landscape was distinctive; centuries of wind and rain had carved it into great stone terraces, and behind it reared a huge tawny mountain.

It's so similar to Skye, she mused. *How strange.*

Her attention shifted to the sloping hillside to her left. A hamlet of stone cottages with sod roofs sat at its base, while a fortress perched upon a crag above.

"Lachlann ... where are we?" Adaira glanced back at her escort, however, he wasn't looking her way. After his stinging words earlier that morning, the rest of the journey had passed in silence. Hurt by his obvious regret at kissing her, Adaira had felt foolish. She now resolved to keep him at arm's length, although he seemed to have made the same decision, for he wouldn't meet her eye.

Lachlann jumped out of the boat into the waist-deep surf and began to haul the boat into shore. "We've arrived at our destination," he announced.

Adaira's heart leaped in her chest. She glanced back up at the grim-looking fortress that loomed over the bay. Surely this wasn't Gylen Castle? Her mother had described it as a great stone tower perched on the edge of a rocky coast, surrounded by emerald-green. This place looked too stark to fit such a description. "Are ye sure?"

"Aye." He pulled the boat through the last of the waves and dragged it up onto the beach.

Adaira continued to stare at the broch above her. She could see that part of it lay in ruin. It looked like one of those round towers that the ancient folk of Skye had inhabited, long before the Norsemen arrived upon the shores of her isle. There was one such ruined tower not far from Dunvegan that she and her sisters had once explored.

"It's not what I imagined," she murmured. "I expected Gylen Castle would be ... grander."

Lachlann huffed out a laugh, although there wasn't any humor in it. His mood had suddenly turned strange. "It's grand enough ... although this isn't Gylen Castle or Argyle."

Adaira stiffened. She dragged her gaze from the fortress and focused on Lachlann.

"Where have ye brought me?" Her voice cut through the rumble of the surf and the whine of the wind that whipped her hair in her eyes. "Answer me, Lachlann."

He looked at her then, and the hard look in his eyes made a chill seep into her bones. It was like observing a stranger, and she realized with a sinking sensation in the pit of her belly that, despite spending the last couple of days with him, she didn't know Lachlann Fraser at all.

"This is Talasgair," he said finally. "My father's stronghold."

Chapter Ten

Till My Last Breath

TALASGAIR.

ADAIRA STARED at Lachlann.

For a moment, his words didn't sink in, but when they did, she inhaled sharply, as if someone had just punched her in the belly.

No wonder this coastline looked familiar. While she'd slept during their departure from Kiltaraglen, he'd rowed north.

That had indeed been Duntulm she'd spied on the clifftop.

That was why he'd left her on the shore when he went for supplies. The crofters' village would have been on her father's land; no wonder he'd been on edge and keen to move on quickly.

Betrayal slammed into Adaira with such force that she gasped.

"Ye deceived me!" The words were hoarse; she could barely get them out. "Ye made me a promise, and ye broke it."

Lachlann shrugged. "Deceived is a strong word … let's not get overwrought."

"Overwrought?" The word came out in an outraged whisper.

Adaira wasn't quick to temper like Rhona or her father. All those who loved her described her nature as sweet and carefree. Few things got under her skin. Yet rage coiled in her now as she stared at the man she'd trusted, the man she'd set free.

The man she'd kissed so eagerly.

Her heart thundered in her chest, beating so loudly she was sure he could hear it.

"I'll not stay here," she ground out finally.

With that, she jumped out of the boat and into the surf. The cold water bit at her legs, the waves pulling at her heavy skirts, yet she ignored the discomfort.

Adaira started to push the rowboat back into the bay. "I'll row myself to Argyle."

"Slow down." The thinly-veiled amusement in Lachlann's voice made a red haze settle over Adaira's vision. He'd betrayed her, and now he was laughing at her. "Ye aren't going anywhere, Aingeal."

He placed a hand upon her shoulder then.

Rage exploded within Adaira, a deep, feral thing that lashed out from a place she didn't even know existed.

She whipped around and struck out at him. Her palm hit his face with a loud 'crack'.

"Don't touch me," she snarled, "and don't call me that ever again. I'm not yer 'Aingeal', ye cheating, lying bastard!"

The shock on his face was almost comical.

Adaira flung herself away from him and shoved her weight against the boat, angling it into the surf.

She'd gone two paces when strong arms fastened about her waist and hauled her backward.

"Sorry about this," Lachlann grunted in her ear, "but I meant it. Ye are staying here for the moment. It would be easier to let ye go yer own way, but ye wouldn't be safe on yer own. I owe ye that much."

Adaira spat out a curse, one she'd heard her father make once when his horse stood on his foot, and drove her elbow into Lachlann's chest.

However, he didn't let go of her. He yanked her against him, trapping her under one arm, while with the other he grabbed hold of the boat.

Then he turned and dragged them both to shore.

Adaira was hysterical by the time they reached it. Fury pulsed through her, and she forgot fear, forgot anything except the fact that she'd given this man his freedom, and he'd tricked her, used her.

She clawed at him, kicked and wriggled in his grip like an eel. If he was going to take her prisoner, she'd not make it easy for him.

"Adaira ... stop it!" Lachlann's voice held no amusement now. "Ye will only do yerself harm."

His words didn't calm her; they only enraged her further. She shouted curses at him, wielding them like sharp boning knives.

They stumbled onto the shingle beach, their boots sinking into the fine grey pebbles. The hull of the rowboat crunched onto the shore as Lachlann let go of it. He needed two hands to manage Adaira now as she became frenzied.

Fear snaked through her then, penetrating the rage.

What was he planning to do with her? Would he send her back to Dunvegan—back to Aonghus Budge?

How Adaira wished she'd asked Taran to show her how to defend herself against attackers, as he had with Rhona. How she wished she was a man. And as they tumbled to the ground, and Lachlann held her still, pinning her limbs against the pebbles, she cursed her weak woman's body. Lachlann was much taller and stronger than her.

"Stop it!" Lachlann stared down at her, his green eyes dark with mounting anger. "I mean ye no harm, Adaira. This is only a detour. If ye wish to continue to Argyle, one of my father's men will take ye."

She glared up at him, her teeth bared. She didn't believe him, not after this lie. She never would again.

"I had to return home," he continued. His handsome face was taut and his gaze narrowed. "My father may be dying—or possibly dead already. I can't risk one of my brothers taking my place as chieftain."

Ice washed over Adaira. *Ambition*. He'd broken his promise to her for purely selfish reasons.

Adaira fought the hands that gripped her wrists. However, she couldn't budge them an inch. He was sitting on her thighs. She was trapped.

"Serpent," she hissed. "I trusted ye."

He gave an exasperated snort. "Well, then ye have just learned a harsh life lesson." He stared down at her. "Ye won't trust so easily in future."

The arrogance of his words momentarily rendered Adaira speechless. Her throat constricted, and her chest felt as if it had a boulder sitting upon it. In the past, she might have wept, but she was still too angry. She wished she had her dirk to hand; she'd have stabbed him in the heart with it. Instead, it was in her satchel.

"Come." He let go of her wrists and heaved himself to his feet. He then retrieved her cloak and satchel from the boat. "We're wasting time here."

"No." Adaira rose to her feet and backed away from him. "I'm not going anywhere with ye."

Lachlann's gaze grew hard. "Are ye going to continue to fight me, Adaira?"

"Aye, till my last breath, ye dog!"

He huffed a breath before slinging the satchel across his front and tucking the cloak through it.

"This is yer last chance. Ye either walk up to the fortress with me, or I carry ye up, slung over my shoulder like a sack of oats. Which will it be?"

Adaira spat at him, whirled, and took off down the beach. Seabirds wheeled overhead, their cries sounding like mocking laughter. The soft shingle hampered her gait, slowing her, but she paid it no mind. She had to get away from him. She was in danger here, more so than if she'd stayed at Dunvegan.

She'd gone half a dozen paces when Lachlann caught her.

He grabbed hold of her arm and swung her around. Then, ducking his head to avoid her flailing fists, he picked her up and swung her over his shoulder. "No more chances," he grunted. "If this is how ye wish to arrive at Talasgair, then so be it."

Adaira didn't stop struggling, didn't stop fighting him, the whole way up the hill. Desperation and fear turned her savage. She was aware that they walked past cottages, where cottars and their families worked fields of kale, turnips, and onions. Folk stopped to gawk at them, but Adaira didn't care. Their murmurs and choked-back laughter just served to enrage her further.

It was a long walk, made longer still by her humiliation and mounting panic, and the climb was steep. Lachlann was breathing heavily, and she felt the heat of his body through the thin léine he wore.

On the way up, they passed a number of sheilings, low-slung huts made of stacked stone with turf roofs, where more folk stood and stared at them.

Eventually, even Adaira couldn't withstand exhaustion, and she slumped against his shoulder. Her hands ceased beating his back and hung there, although they were still balled into tight fists. He clasped her legs, an arm clamped over them like an iron band, lest she try and knee him.

He carried her through an archway of a high, yet crumbling, double wall, and into a wide, grassy yard.

There, Lachlann set Adaira down.

Panting, Adaira glanced around. Her body trembled, yet she couldn't fail to note how different Talasgair was to Dunvegan. Her father's keep was a huge, solid fortress with deep curtain walls. Yet this place was a blend of ancient and new. The great round tower that rose before them had been built onto on both sides. Another newer watchtower rose on its southern side. Its battlements etched against the sky, where the Fraser pennant fluttered in the wind.

Men, horses, and servants filled the bailey, all going about the last of their morning chores before the nooning meal was upon them.

"Lachlann!"

A man's voice echoed across the yard. Lachlann took hold of Adaira's arm, his grip firm, and they turned to see a huge warrior with wild red hair and a short beard stride toward them.

One look at the man and Adaira knew he was kin to Lachlann, although he was heavier in stature.

"I thought MacLeod would have ye strung up by yer balls by now," the man boomed before he crushed Lachlann in a bear-hug.

Lachlann was forced to release Adaira then as he staggered back. Adaira watched them. The anger had seeped out of her now, replaced by a dread that made her legs tremble under her.

"It's good to see ye too, Lucas." Lachlann drawled, pulling back. "Worried about me were ye?"

The warrior snorted, although his eyes—the same moss-green as Lachlann's—were wary. "I thought ye were dead."

"No, just left to rot in Dunvegan dungeon. Were any of ye planning to come after me?"

Lucas frowned. "Aye ... we were discussing it this morning."

The man didn't even bother to disguise the insincerity in his voice.

Lachlann's gaze narrowed. "Aye ... were ye?"

Lucas pursed his lips as if he found the topic distasteful. Then he glanced over at Adaira. "And who's this?"

Adaira tensed under the man's scrutiny, her body going rigid when Lachlann caught hold of her arm once more and pulled her close. "This is Lady Adaira MacLeod."

The man's brow furrowed. "Ye brought a MacLeod here?"

Lachlann huffed. "She's the reason I'm free." He met Adaira's eye then, for the first time since he'd thrown her over his shoulder on the beach. There was a warning in his gaze as if he dared her to start raging at him again. "Lady Adaira, meet my younger brother ... Lucas."

Chapter Eleven

What a Mess I've Made

"SO YE DRAW breath still."

"Frasers are hard to kill, Da. I see that MacLeod didn't finish ye off either."

Morgan Fraser, propped up by a mountain of pillows in his sickbed, frowned. "Disappointed?"

Adaira, who stood at Lachlann's side, watched him fold his arms across his chest and favor his father with an arrogant smile. "Of course not … it's a great relief to see ye are alive."

Morgan Fraser huffed, before wincing.

Adaira had heard of the wound her own father had inflicted upon him. Malcolm MacLeod had bragged that he'd slit the Fraser chieftain open down one side. She couldn't see his wounds, for he wore a loose léine over his bandages, but she knew her father would be disappointed to know his enemy lived.

They stood in the chieftain's bed-chamber, which sat halfway up the fortress's new tower. The window was open, letting in a brisk sea-breeze.

Lachlann's three younger brothers—Lucas, Niall, and Tearlach—stood to the right of their father's bed. Big, red-haired, and intimidating, all three of them resembled their sire. Watching them, Adaira wondered what their mother had looked like. Una had been Morgan's second wife, and she had not borne him any children.

Morgan Fraser's attention shifted from his first-born then, to Adaira. She'd been waiting for this, yet the force of his stare nearly made her wilt. Even pale-faced and in pain, the Fraser chief's gaze was frightening.

"Lady Adaira MacLeod," he said her name softly. "What an unexpected delight."

He didn't smile as he spoke, so the word 'delight' sounded more of a threat than a welcome. Adaira glanced at Lachlann. She didn't know why she looked his way, for the sight of him made her feel ill, yet he was the only one in this chamber who knew how much she wanted to flee Skye. As much as it galled her, he was the closest thing she had to an ally here.

But Lachlann didn't look her way. He merely watched his father, his expression impassive.

Adaira swallowed and glanced back at the chieftain. Morgan Fraser was still observing her, a speculative look in his green eyes. He was around her father's age, yet whereas her father was corpulent and gouty, Morgan was lean and craggy. She could see that he'd been very handsome in his youth, but something—bitterness perhaps—had given his features a hard edge.

Out of all four sons, Lachlann resembled him physically the most. He had his father's lean ranginess, his watchfulness.

"I'd say I was grateful to ye for saving my son's life," Morgan Fraser continued, his tone still soft, "yet I hear ye didn't do it out of love for the Frasers, but rather a desire to escape yer betrothed."

"Aye, Aonghus Budge," Lucas spoke up, his mouth curving. "Can't say I blame her either."

Morgan ignored his son, instead continuing to observe Adaira.

Swallowing, Adaira dropped her gaze to the floor. His stare was making her sweat; she didn't like the calculating look in his eyes.

"Ye are a bonny wee thing," Morgan continued, "although I've heard yer sisters are true beauties: one as hot as flame, the other as cold as ice." He paused here. "I wonder what that makes ye, Lady Adaira?"

She went still, wishing she was anywhere but here. This man made her feel like she was a cornered deer.

"The earth." Lachlann's answer made Adaira glance up in surprise. "Natural ... and honest."

Morgan grunted in response. "Sounds like ye are half in love with the lass."

Lachlann's brothers sniggered.

"No ... just observant," Lachlann answered coldly.

A smile stretched Morgan Fraser's mouth, but no warmth reached his eyes.

Adaira cleared her throat. This conversation was giving her belly cramps. She longed to be far from all five of these men but needed their help to get away. "Chieftain Fraser," she began softly. "Will ye provide passage for me to travel to the mainland? I still wish to reach my kin in Argyle as planned."

Morgan Fraser's mouth compressed. "Why would I help a MacLeod?"

Adaira glanced at Lachlann, panic rising within her. "But ye said I could—"

"I rule here, lass," Morgan Fraser cut her off. "I don't care what my son told ye."

Adaira went ice-cold at these words. "Please," she whispered. "I have to leave this isle ... I must—"

"Quiet, girl," Morgan snapped, his gaze pinning her to the spot. "Spare me yer pitiful bleating."

Adaira stared back at him, heat rising to her cheeks. Anger, although not the wild fury of earlier, rose within her. She decided then that she hated Morgan Fraser even more than she did his son.

"What does it matter?" Lachlann spoke up, his voice a drawl. "Surely, if ye help the lass escape, ye are hurting MacLeod."

"Perhaps so," Morgan mused. He reached for a cup that sat upon a low table beside the bed and took a sip. Lowering it, he leaned back against the pillows. "But by keeping her here I'd hurt him more."

"No !" Adaira stepped forward, hands clenching by her sides. She turned to Lachlann, meeting his gaze squarely. "Ye swore ye would take care of me. Is this another promise ye are going to break?"

Her comment brought snorts of laughter from his brothers.

"She's got some fire in her belly after all," the one named Niall chortled. "I can see why ye have gone soft on her, brother."

Lachlann ignored the jibe and held her gaze. His expression was hard, although his eyes were shadowed, his jaw tight. His lips parted as he readied himself to respond to her, but his father interrupted. "Never explain yerself to a woman, Lachlann." He snapped his fingers then, the sound cracking like a whip across the bed-chamber. "Look at me, lass."

Reluctantly, Adaira did as bid. However, her heart was now galloping, and her belly roiled. She felt close to being sick. Bile bit the back of her throat when she saw the cold smile on Chieftain Fraser's face.

"I've got many bones to pick with MacLeod," he continued, each word biting. "The bastard stole my wife, nearly gutted me, and would have let my first-born rot in his dungeon. One hundred years wouldn't be long enough for me to take my vengeance upon him." He paused here, letting each bitter word sink in. "But Lachlann has brought me a prize. Ye are now my prisoner, as he was once yer father's."

"Da—" Lachlann interrupted, his gaze narrowed now, but Morgan cut him off with a gesture.

"Our dungeon is a foul pit, no place for a lady, even a *MacLeod*," the chieftain continued, his gaze pinning Adaira to the spot, "so ye will be confined to the top room of this tower until I decide yer fate." Morgan shifted his gaze to Lachlann, who now stood silent and stone-faced next to Adaira. "Take her up and lock her inside."

Lachlann followed Adaira up the tower stairs. Her slender back was ramrod straight, her shoulders rounded. Her hands were hidden from view as she had lifted her skirts to climb the steps.

Neither of them spoke.

Keeping his gaze on her, lest she turn and attack him halfway up the stairs, Lachlann silently cursed.

This wasn't how he'd envisaged his return to Talasgair.

The old bastard was supposed to be either dead or on death's door, not well enough to continue his blood feud against MacLeod.

He hadn't wanted Adaira to be drawn into his father's wrath either. She'd asked him to help her, and he'd gotten her imprisoned.

They entered the tower room. Lachlann hadn't been up here in a while. The room had once been where he and his brothers had taken their lessons with Brother Took, a monk who'd visited from a nearby monastery to teach the Fraser sons their letters.

It was an austere space furnished only with a narrow sleeping pallet, a long table, and four hard wooden chairs. Cold stone pavers covered the floor. There was a tiny hearth in one corner, but it was unlit this afternoon. A narrow window stared out at where the bulk of Preshal More, the tawny mountain to the south, jutted against the sky.

Adaira walked to the center of the room and turned to face him.

He'd expected to see tears in her eyes, yet there were none. She was too angry for that. Just like during their scuffle on the beach, he was struck by how lovely she was when riled. When they'd first met, he'd thought her comely, but when she was angry, Adaira MacLeod was like no other woman. She was magnificent.

Adaira glared at him now as if she'd like to blacken his eye. In fact, her right fist was clenched at her side.

Lachlann stopped before her and dragged in a deep breath. "I shouldn't have brought ye here," he said, his tone terser than he'd intended. It was the closest he could manage to an apology. "I didn't stop to think how Da would react."

"Liar," she hissed out the words between clenched teeth. "Ye have given him exactly what he wanted."

Lachlann frowned. "I'll speak to him. He might soften toward ye in time."

"Aye, and the sun might set in the east. If ye believe ye can change his mind, ye are worse than arrogant—ye are a fool!"

Lachlann's frown deepened. He was getting tired of her insults. Some of the things she'd screamed at him down on the beach would have made a whore blush. Yet underneath it all, she was scared; he could see it in her eyes.

Her small body trembled. He realized then that she was barely clinging to her courage.

Lachlann loosed a sharp breath. "I've made a mess of things," he admitted roughly, "but I promise ye I will try to mend this. Ye will reach Argyle as ye had planned."

Her throat bobbed, and two spots of high color appeared on her pale face. Then she stepped toward him, her hazel eyes glittering. "A promise from Lachlann Fraser is a vain, empty thing." Her voice shook as she forced out the words. "The only person ye care about in this world is yerself."

Chapter Twelve

A Warm Welcome

LACHLANN STRODE INTO the Great Hall to thunderous applause.

His confrontation with Adaira had left a sour taste in his mouth, but the strain of the past few hours dissolved when his father's men slapped him heartily on the back and their wives and children beamed at him.

"It's good to see ye back, lad." Morgan Fraser's right-hand, a grizzled warrior named Thormod, boomed, pushing a tankard of ale into his hands. "Yer brother was getting too comfortable in yer seat!"

"Aye, I'll wager he's been polishing it with his arse morning, noon, and night," Lachlann replied, his gaze swiveling to the long table upon the dais at the far end of the hall. He was pleased to see that Lucas didn't sit in his elder brother's place, to the right of the chieftain's carven chair, but in his usual seat.

He noted too, that Lucas wore a sour look on his face.

Lachlann grinned at him, raising his tankard. He then turned his attention to the crowd of excited retainers that jostled around him. "Open a fresh barrel of ale," he shouted, his voice carrying across the hall. "My return calls for a celebration."

"Aye, and ye brought yer father back a worthy prize too!" Thormod's wife, a rawboned woman named Forbia, cried out. "A MacLeod daughter!"

A roar went up, although this time Lachlann didn't join in the laughter. *The less said about that the better.*

Making his way to the chieftain's table, he stepped up onto the dais.

"Generous of ye, brother," Lucas grumbled as Lachlann approached. "To make free with Da's ale."

"He won't mind," Lachlann replied with a grin, enjoying his brother's irritation. "Make sure ye have a tankard for him."

Then, instead of taking his place next to Lucas, Lachlann deliberately lowered himself into the chieftain's carven chair.

Lucas let out a hiss of outrage, while around them, heads swiveled to stare. "What are ye doing?"

Lachlann stretched back in the chair, placing his arms on the ornate armrests. "Just trying it out ... not as comfortable as I imagined though."

"Ye had better move," Tearlach, the youngest of the four brothers warned him. Unlike Lucas, he wasn't glaring at Lachlann though. Instead, he was grinning and had a wicked gleam in his eye. "Da will have ye flogged for sitting in his chair."

Lachlann cast Tearlach a rueful look. "No, he won't. He's too pleased to have his first-born safely home."

This drew snorts from his brothers. All of them knew the truth of it: Morgan Fraser wasn't a sentimental man. He had four sons and if one died there was always another to take his place. Besides, Lachlann and his father had always butted heads.

Lachlann leaned back in the chair and took a deep draft of ale, sighing at the sweet, sharp taste: the taste of home.

On the floor beneath him, the folk of Talasgair were now taking their seats at the long tables while servants circled with pots of steaming stew. A group of them approached the dais.

Lachlann's belly grumbled in anticipation, reminding him that he'd last eaten at dawn.

"How did ye get out of Dunvegan Castle?" Lucas spoke up, drawing his attention. "It's been puzzling me."

Lachlann studied his brother's face for a moment. Lucas wore an inscrutable expression, although his eyes were hard, suspicious.

"We crept out in the middle of the night," he replied. "Lady Adaira drugged the guards with a sleeping draft."

Lucas inclined his head. "That wee lass ... she freed ye without any help?"

"There was a man who helped her escape. He was big and blond with a scarred face ... one of her father's warriors, I'd wager."

Lucas scratched his short beard as he considered this. "Still ... it's a wonder ye managed to get through the gates unseen ... even at night. Dunvegan's said to be impenetrable."

"Well, we did." Lachlann took another draft of ale, his attention shifting to the huge bowl of venison stew that now sat before him. He reached forward, ripped a chunk off a loaf of bread, and dipped it into the rich stew. He started to eat, aware that his brother's gaze still bored into him.

Lucas didn't believe him, but he had no way of proving him a liar.

Taking another mouthful of stew, Lachlann wondered why he'd withheld the truth of how they'd escaped. Back in Dunvegan dungeon, he'd sworn to Adaira that he'd tell no one about the secret passage—and yet since he hadn't upheld his promise to get her to Argyle, this one shouldn't matter either.

But his knowledge of the hidden passage into the keep was power, and as such was worth keeping to himself.

Adaira managed to hold the tears in until she was alone.

After that, there was no stemming them.

As soon as Lachlann left her, and she heard the grate of a heavy key in the lock, her vision blurred. His footsteps receded down the stairwell before fading into silence.

Adaira sank to the flagstone floor and clapped a hand over her mouth as a sob rose.

She should be on the mainland now, and on her way to her mother's kin. Lachlann's betrayal was a raw, bleeding wound. Did a promise mean so little to him? Anger rose hot and churning within her.

Selfish, lying dog.

But just beneath the anger lay a burning mortification. She'd liked Lachlann Fraser—been drawn in by his good looks, easy manner, and self-confidence. When he'd kissed her, she'd melted in his arms. Despite the awkwardness afterward, that kiss had succeeded in intensifying her growing feelings for him. During the last step of the journey to Talasgair, she'd found her gaze returning to him, an ache of need growing within her.

And all the while he'd been betraying her.

Adaira covered her face with her hands and let out a muffled cry. This was what Rhona had warned her about—predatory men who cared nothing for the wellbeing of foolish lasses. She remembered the worry in her elder sister's eyes as she'd told Adaira to be more careful around men, but Adaira had brushed away her concerns. Even the arranged marriage to Aonghus Budge hadn't made her cautious. From the first moment she'd locked eyes with Lachlann in Dunvegan dungeon, she'd been slowly falling under his spell.

How she must have amused him.

Her father had said never to trust a Fraser, but she'd always believed that was just his bitterness speaking. She now realized MacLeod had spoken true.

Tears burned down Adaira's cheeks, and she pulled herself up off the floor and crawled over to the narrow sleeping pallet. There, she curled up into a ball and wept until her throat was sore, until her eyes burned and her ribcage ached.

At some point servants arrived, two young men. One bore a tray of food, while the other stood in the doorway, eyeing her warily as if he expected her to attack him like a rabid dog.

Lachlann had probably warned them of her terrible temper.

Adaira watched them from the sleeping pallet. She didn't move, didn't speak, just eyed the young man as he placed the tray upon the table, cast her a cool look, turned, and left the room.

Alone once more, Adaira didn't rise from her bed.

The thought of eating made her gorge rise despite that she hadn't eaten properly in days. She was too upset to touch a crumb of it.

What will become of me?

Morgan Fraser terrified her. She'd looked into the chieftain's eyes earlier and felt dread claw its way up her throat.

That man was out for vengeance. She was going nowhere.

Such was his hate for her father he was capable of anything. Would he have her tortured? Would he behead her himself in front of a crowd of his baying kin?

The thoughts made her bowels cramp with terror. She'd been deathly afraid of wedding Aonghus Budge, but she realized now that she hadn't been truly scared, not like now. The thought of what terrible fate might await her made the walls of the chamber close in on her. She shivered as if caught in a fever.

Her father would still be hunting for her. Would he think to look for her at Talasgair? She doubted he would. Suddenly, she missed her father with a force that made her chest ache. He'd be furious with her for running away, yet he'd never let Fraser hold her prisoner. He'd break down the walls of this broch with his bare hands to get her out.

Only, Malcolm MacLeod didn't know she was here—and likely never would.

Lachlann sank into the hot water and released a long sigh.

Finally, he almost felt back to his old self.

He sat in the deep iron tub in his bed-chamber, a medium-sized room with a narrow window looking east over the hills behind Talasgair. Outside, daylight was fading, and the sky was ablaze with red and gold.

It felt good to be back here. It was a drafty, damp space, and cold in winter despite the hearth that burned against one wall—yet this afternoon it felt as spacious and warm as his father's solar.

The servant had added a drop of lavender oil to the water, and the scent wafted through the damp air. Lachlann closed his eyes and inhaled deeply. The smell reminded him of summer, of the courtyard garden on the southern edge of the keep.

Never again would he take the sweet scent of freedom for granted.

Home. His return was bitter-sweet. He was pleased to be here, but circumstances had made things awkward.

On one level he was relieved his father still lived—just because they'd never gotten on didn't mean he wished the old man dead—but on another it complicated life. With Morgan Fraser in charge, he would resume his role as captain of Talasgair Guard, which often took him away from the broch for days at a time. That didn't please Lachlann, for he'd have preferred to stay close to Talasgair. He wanted to keep an eye on his scheming younger brother. Even before Lachlann's capture, Lucas had been forever trying to ingratiate himself with their father.

And then there was Adaira. Lachlann couldn't help her at present, and that frustrated him. He hated having his hands tied like this.

Lachlann let out a long sigh, sinking deeper into the hot water.

The crash of the door flying open and slamming against the wall yanked Lachlann from his reverie. His gaze snapped up to see Lucas striding into his bed-chamber. "What are ye doing in here?" his brother boomed. "The men are still celebrating yer return downstairs. They want stories and boasts of yer escape from Dunvegan."

"They'll have to wait," Lachlann drawled back. He pushed himself up, retrieved a cake of lye soap, and began to scrub under his arms. Despite his sea-water bath, his skin itched with filth. "I'm busy."

Lucas pulled up a stool and lowered his heavily muscled bulk onto it. Lachlann eyed his brother. Lucas seemed to get bigger by the year. Folk here had nicknamed him 'The Giant of Talasgair', such was his height and breadth. He was formidable in a fight although Lachlann was quicker. He'd always been the fastest of the four of them—but that hadn't helped him during the battle against the MacLeods.

"I've just been to see Da," Lucas said after a pause. "If ye take his chair again, he'll have ye flogged."

Lachlann threw back his head and gave a belly laugh. "Bootlicking worm ... I should have known ye would go straight to him."

Lucas's mouth twisted, but he didn't reply to the insult. "Da wants to know if ye have had yer way with the MacLeod lass."

Lachlann stopped soaping himself and favored Lucas with a slow, dark look. However, he didn't answer.

"Well, have ye?"

"What is it to him?"

His brother gave an off-hand shrug. "Who knows ... maybe he's worried she's carrying yer brat. He might have to kill her for that."

A chill feathered across Lachlann's naked skin despite the heat of the bathwater. He thought back to the kiss he'd shared with Adaira and of how he'd wanted to take it further. It was just as well he hadn't.

"I never touched her," he lied. A kiss was a touch. "As far as I know, she's still a maid." That was the truth at least.

Silence fell between them then. Lachlann resumed soaping himself, although the pleasure he'd found in his bath had gone. He wished his brother would take himself off and leave him in peace. Lucas's toadying toward their father irritated him. He'd only been back at Talasgair a few hours and already his brother, the one who'd stood to inherit if Lachlann had never returned home, was seeking to undermine him.

Ye won't get my lands, ye bastard, he thought grimly. *Over my dead body.*

Lucas heaved himself off the stool and rose to his feet, towering over Lachlann. "I'll leave ye to it," he said. His gaze was shuttered.

Lachlann watched his brother leave the chamber, slamming the door behind him with his usual finesse.

Heaving a sigh, Lachlann sank down under the water. The heat enveloped him like a soothing blanket. Resurfacing, he reached for the cake of lye soap once more and started to soap his wet hair.

A frown furrowed his forehead as he did so.

No doubt Lucas would go straight to their father.

Chapter Thirteen

The Happy News

"YE WANTED TO see me?"

Lachlann stepped inside his father's bed-chamber to find the healer tending to Morgan Fraser's wounds.

"Aye," his father rasped. "Come in, and shut the door."

The healer, Domhnall, smeared salve over an ugly scab that stretched down the chieftain's naked flank. Domhnall was a portly man of middling years; his kindly face was tense in concentration as he worked.

One glance at that wound told Lachlann that his father was indeed lucky to still be alive. Though healing, the gash looked angry and sore.

"Had a good look at my war-wound, eh?" His father's voice was sharp. "I can assure ye it looked far worse a few days ago."

"Aye, it did," Domhnall agreed with a grimace. "But it's healing well now … ye shall make a full recovery, milord."

"Good to hear," Lachlann replied, his mouth quirking. He swore his father was indestructible. He'd be well into middle age himself before Morgan Fraser went to his cairn.

"Wrap the wound now, Domhnall," Morgan grunted. He was frowning. Even a moment or two in his presence and Lachlann was already wearing upon him. "I want to speak to my son alone."

"Aye, milord." The healer gave a brisk nod before reaching for a clean linen bandage. "This shouldn't take long."

The healer worked deftly, wrapping the chieftain's torso with practiced ease. While the healer finished tending to his patient, Lachlann took up a place next to the window. It was a grey, windy morning outdoors. Leaden clouds moved sluggishly across the sky, promising stormy weather to come. Despite the chill in the air, his father had insisted Domhnall left the window open.

A short while later, the healer collected his basket of healing powders, tinctures, unguents, and bandages, and hurried from the chamber. After Domhnall had departed, Lachlann remained silent. He watched his father with a hooded gaze, arms folded across his chest. Two days had passed since he'd returned to Talasgair; he'd been awaiting another summons.

"Have ye seen the MacLeod lass since ye locked her up?" Morgan asked finally.

Lachlann shook his head. "No ... why?"

His father's mouth thinned. He didn't appreciate Lachlann answering with another question. "The girl is refusing to eat."

Lachlann nodded. This wasn't news to him. He'd already heard the same. The cook had ranted that they should let the MacLeod scold starve rather than allow good food go to waste. Half the time, Adaira hurled the food back in the faces of the servants. She'd broken over half a dozen clay bowls and cups in the past two days. Nonetheless, the cook dutifully sent up trays at each mealtime as instructed.

"She's unhappy," Lachlann pointed out, "and angry."

"With ye, no doubt."

Lachlann shrugged. "With the world."

"Do ye think MacLeod will come after his daughter?"

Lachlann shook his head. "Only if he knows she's here. Once he exhausts his search on Skye ... he'll think we've crossed to the mainland."

He was aware that his father was observing him keenly then, with a cunning glint in his eye that Lachlann knew well.

"It suits me that Adaira MacLeod doesn't waste away to skin and bone," Morgan said softly. "She must live."

Lachlann's gaze narrowed. He didn't like his father's tone. It made the fine hair on the back of his neck prickle. "Ye have decided what to do with her then?"

Morgan Fraser leaned back against the pillows, wincing as he did so. "Domhnall says I'll be well enough to resume my old duties by Samhuinn. I plan to wed Adaira MacLeod on that date."

For a heartbeat Lachlann merely stared at his father. Had he misheard? "Ye will wed her?"

The Fraser chief's mouth curved into a rare smile. "Aye."

Lachlann didn't move from his position against the window sill. "Why?"

"MacLeod robbed me of a wife," Morgan growled. "And I will rob him of a daughter."

Lachlann drew in a slow, steadying breath. "Malcolm MacLeod will be rabid when he hears ye have wed Adaira," he pointed out. "Do ye want to reignite feuding between ye?"

His father's face tightened into a hard line. "The feud still lives," he spat out the words. "And so does my enemy. This will hurt him in a way no blade could. He'll bleed where no one can see."

Vindictiveness dripped from Morgan's voice. The hatred he bore MacLeod was no natural thing; it had soured into an illness of late.

Morgan Fraser spoke little of Lachlann's mother—the woman who'd borne him four strapping sons—but all at Talasgair knew how he'd loved Una. He'd sworn never to remarry, not while she still lived. But he would break that promise now if it was for vengeance.

Silence fell in the chamber. Lachlann digested this news before realizing that it sat ill with him. His father wore a gloating expression. Adaira was nothing more than a weapon in his hands.

"Can I go now?" Lachlann asked finally. He'd had enough of his father's scheming.

"Not yet," Morgan replied. He'd been observing Lachlann with a hard, predatory gaze, watching his reaction to the news. "I have a task for ye, son."

Lachlann pushed himself off the sill. "Aye, what is it?"

"I want ye to be the one to inform Lady Adaira of the happy news. Go up and tell her now."

Lachlann climbed the stairwell to the tower room, his jaw clenched with anger.

Vicious bastard.

This was punishment, although for what Lachlann wasn't sure. Sometimes when Lachlann looked into his father's eyes, he thought he saw dislike there. Father and son often clashed. Lucas had once told Lachlann it was because they were too alike—but Lachlann hadn't liked that.

I'm nothing like that bitter old curmudgeon.

Reaching the landing before the door, Lachlann halted. He wasn't going to enjoy this, yet it was best to get it over with quickly.

He unlocked the door, pushed it open, and stepped inside.

"Get out!"

A tray flew at his head. Lachlann ducked, and the missile clattered against the pitted stone wall.

He closed the door and backed up against it, ducking again as half a loaf of bread flew at him. He wasn't fast enough this time, and the bread bounced off his temple. Lachlann reeled back. The bread was stale and had a hard crust.

Cursing, Lachlann rubbed his forehead, his gaze settling on the fury who faced him. "Was that necessary?" he growled.

"Aye," she spat. "Leave! I have no wish to see or speak to ye."

Lachlann's gaze traveled over her bedraggled form. Her brown hair was wild and dirty. She'd lost weight, even in the two days she'd been in here. He could see it in the delicate lines of her face. The green kirtle and cream léine she wore were both soiled and in need of laundering. She clenched her fists at her sides, the remnants of her last untouched meal scattered over the floor.

However, it was not her appearance that took Lachlann aback, but her eyes. They were desolate, lost.

Adaira MacLeod was suffering.

Lachlann opened his mouth to speak before hesitating. He knew he could lack charm—but then it didn't matter how he phrased this news, she wasn't going to like it.

"Adaira," he began, gentling his voice as if talking to a nervous horse. "My father has decided yer fate." Their gazes met and held. "Ye will wed him ... at Samhuinn."

His voice died away, leaving a deep silence in its wake.

For a long moment, Adaira merely stared at him. Then he watched as her face drained of color and her eyes rolled back in her head. Lachlann stepped forward to catch Adaira as she collapsed upon the floor.

Chapter Fourteen

Despair

WHEN ADAIRA CAME to, she felt someone stroking her cheek. The touch was soft, although the skin was slightly rough: a man's hand.

Adaira's eyes flickered open, and she looked up into Lachlann Fraser's face.

Like a breaking wave, the memory of his news crashed over her.

I am to be Morgan Fraser's wife.

Tears leaked from Adaira's eyes, trickling down her face.

Lachlann stared down at her. A shadow moved in his eyes. His face was serious, and a nerve flickered in his cheek. He drew his hand back from her face. "Are ye well?"

Hysteria bubbled up within Adaira. "No," she rasped.

She pushed herself up into a sitting position and closed her eyes for a moment. Her head still spun, although she supposed lack of food was partially to blame for her faint. Adaira covered her face with her hands. "Leave me, Lachlann … please," she whispered.

When he didn't move, she tried to stand up. However, her knees buckled under her. Lachlann was there in an instant, supporting her.

"Sit down on the bed, Adaira." He guided her over to the pallet and lowered her down onto it. Then he hunkered down so that their gazes were level. There was concern on his face now. "I'm going to bring ye up another tray of bread and stew," he said, his voice low and firm, "and ye are going to eat it. Ye will make yerself sick if ye continue to refuse food."

Adaira's mouth twisted, even as despair pressed down upon her. "Good."

Lachlann huffed a frustrated breath. "Ye don't mean that."

"I do."

Lachlann frowned. "If ye don't eat, Da will have servants force ye." He gave her a long, steady look. "Ye won't escape him by starving yerself, Adaira. Da's a powerful man. He nearly always gets what he wants."

She stared at him, anger welling like a springtide within her. Adaira welcomed the sensation, for it quelled the urge to start weeping uncontrollably. "This is all yer fault," she rasped the words. "I hate ye, Lachlann Fraser."

His mouth compressed. "And ye are welcome to ... but it changes nothing."

Adaira's right hand balled into a fist. She longed to strike him. He was so hard, so arrogant. The man didn't have an ounce of pity in him.

But Adaira didn't hit him. Instead, she pressed her fist into the straw-stuffed mattress. Her short spell at Talasgair had taught her that the Frasers were ruthless. Morgan Fraser had treated her harshly, and his sons were cut of the same cloth. Lachlann hadn't raised a hand to her when she'd fought him on the shore below the fortress, but he might now.

No wonder Una fled this place.

For the first time, Adaira felt some sympathy for her stepmother. She'd never liked Una much but now realized why she'd left Morgan Fraser. No woman could abide such an arrogant man.

Thinking about Una reminded Adaira of her father, her sisters, and everything she'd left behind at Dunvegan. Fresh tears rolled down her cheeks. She wished now that she'd never run away.

Lachlann rose to his feet before her. Adaira's gaze didn't follow him. She merely stared down at her bare feet and wished him gone.

"Ye need to eat," he said gruffly. "I'll return shortly with something from the kitchen."

"Why the grim face?"

Lachlann glanced up from his half-eaten trencher of stew to find Lucas watching him. They sat at the chieftain's table in the Great Hall with Niall and Tearlach. The high-backed carven chair where the chieftain usually sat was still empty—Lachlann had heeded his father's warning. It would be a few more days yet before Morgan Fraser would be well enough to join his kin and retainers at mealtimes.

"I spoke to Da," Lachlann replied, reaching for a cup of ale.

Understanding lit in his brother's eyes. "So, the lass knows?"

Lachlann nodded. He took a deep draft of wine, draining his cup. It was plum—sour and strong. It suited his mood. He reached for a ewer and refilled the cup to the brim.

"What's wrong?" There was a goading tone to Lucas's voice. "Wanted her for yerself, did ye?"

Lachlann favored him with a dark look and took another gulp of wine. He wouldn't respond to that question, although if Lucas continued to goad him, he'd answer with his fist instead.

Lachlann took another gulp of wine. *Do I want her for myself?* The question arose, unbidden.

He hadn't liked seeing Adaira MacLeod in that state, and he knew he was responsible for it—but that didn't mean he was jealous of his father claiming her. Even so, his mood had been black ever since he'd departed from her chamber. He'd brought a fresh tray of food up to her and stood over her while she slowly ate it. Neither of them had spoken a word.

"It'll seem strange to have Lady Adaira as a stepmother," Niall spoke up, helping himself to another bowl of boar stew. "She's younger than any of us."

"I can't believe he's wedding her," Tearlach grumbled. "She's a MacLeod for God's sake."

"I can see the appeal," Lucas replied, favoring his brothers with a wolfish grin. "MacLeod or not, the lass is a bonny wee thing." He cast Lachlann a look, his grin widening. "The old dog will live forever now."

Niall and Tearlach laughed at that, but Lachlann said nothing. He'd had enough of this topic. He took another gulp of wine, his gaze traveling around the hall. Most of the retainers had finished their nooning meal and were getting up to return to their chores. Some, however, lingered over a cup of wine. Without their chieftain's strict eye upon them, they relaxed more than usual. Since returning, Lachlann had noticed there were a number of faces missing among the men here.

"How many warriors did we lose in the end ... against the MacLeods?" Lachlann asked finally, deliberately changing the subject.

His brothers' expressions sobered.

"Thirty-two," replied Tearlach.

Lachlann tensed. It would take the Frasers of Skye years to recover from such a loss.

"Many of our men are on the mainland still, aiding King David's cause," Lucas added, his face grim, as if reading his elder brother's thoughts. "Warriors are thin on the ground at Talasgair."

Of course. With everything that had happened of late, Lachlann had almost forgotten. The Scottish king was planning a raid across the border. There was currently a truce between the English and the Scottish, but David planned to break it, to push south while the English king's focus was on France.

Lachlann would have joined them if his father hadn't been plotting against the MacLeods. Morgan Fraser had wanted all his sons by his side when he faced his enemy.

"I'll take the Guard out to patrol our borders then," Lachlann replied, his gaze sweeping over his brothers' faces. "MacLeod will know we've been weakened. We don't want the bastard getting any ideas."

Adaira leaned against the stone window ledge and looked out at where the last of the sun's light gilded the huge mountain to the south. Preshal More—that was its name. She'd seen it once from afar when she'd joined her kin on a trip to visit the MacDonalds of Sleat on the southern edge of the isle.

She stared at the bald, rocky outline of the mountain. Its bulk was strangely comforting, a reminder that despite all that had befallen her of late, some things remained constant.

Three days had passed since Lachlann had told her she would wed his father, and in that time an odd calm had descended upon her.

She'd been through such extremes of emotion in the past few days that she now felt drained.

This evening Adaira couldn't summon much feeling at all, save a dull dread that had lodged in the pit of her belly.

On the table a few feet away sat the remains of her supper. Remembering Lachlann's warning, she'd eaten most of it, although every bite had stuck in her throat. Still, her body felt stronger since she'd resumed eating, and her head no longer spun.

A cold breeze fluttered in through the open window. The nights had a bite to them now, and although the servants had lit the hearth in this room, Adaira found herself huddled deep inside a nest of blankets upon her sleeping pallet every morning. The stone she leaned against was as cold as a lump of frozen snow.

Adaira continued to stare out the window, her gaze turning inward now. She thought back to her days at Dunvegan. She'd never fully appreciated how blessed they were, but she did now. Her father's servants loved her, and she'd taken their warmth for granted. Here, the woman who brought up her food and cleared away her chamber pot was stone-faced and cold-eyed.

At Dunvegan, she'd had her own horse and often gone riding with her sisters or her father's men. Her father had even let her keep Dùnglas, her wolf-hound pup, although she wasn't sure Aonghus Budge would have ever let the dog accompany them to Islay.

Adaira swallowed hard, remembering how she used to flit about the keep, carefree and more than a little silly. She'd spent her days learning the pursuits befitting a lady. She could play the harp well enough and was a neat embroiderer.

She'd lived a privileged life, and even seeing her sisters' own struggles—Caitrin's unhappy marriage and Rhona's forced one—hadn't truly touched her. She'd always lived a little apart from it, always believed she'd remain happy.

She didn't believe that now. Her old life seemed as if it had belonged to a princess, and she wasn't that girl anymore. She felt as if she'd aged years in just a few days. That laughing, carefree lass was dead.

The sound of the key grating in the lock drew Adaira from her thoughts. Turning, she watched the door open and Lachlann Fraser step inside.

Adaira went rigid. It was the first time she'd seen him since he'd delivered the news she would wed his father.

Despite that the sight of him made her belly churn, she would have been blind not to notice how attractive he was. His slightly disheveled appearance today only highlighted his arrogant good looks, his swaggering self-confidence.

Lachlann was clad in dusty leathers, a travel-stained cloak hanging from his broad shoulders. His hair was sweaty and plastered against his scalp as if he'd just removed a helmet. He looked as if he'd returned from a patrol.

Shutting the door behind him, Lachlann leaned up against it, surveying her.

Adaira hissed out a breath. "What do ye want?"

His mouth curved. "I've been away ... checking our northern border. Now I'm back I thought I'd check on ye." Lachlann's gaze shifted to the empty tray a few feet away. "I see ye are eating."

Adaira clenched her jaw. "The servants could have told ye that."

"Aye, but I'd prefer to check on ye in person."

Adaira folded her arms across her breasts. The sight of this man was a painful reminder of her own gullibility. Still, the knowledge that he'd been patrolling the border with the MacLeods rattled her.

"There was no sign of yer father or his men," Lachlann said quietly as if sensing the direction of her thoughts. "I'd wager he doesn't suspect ye are here."

Bleak disappointment flooded through Adaira. "Ye can go now," she rasped.

Lachlann pushed himself off the door and crossed to her. Adaira took a rapid step back, cowering against the window frame.

He stopped a few feet short of her, his dark-auburn brows knitting together. "There's no need to shrink from me like I'm Satan himself," he murmured.

Adaira glared at him although underneath her despair she felt a frisson of satisfaction. Finally, a chink in his armor of unshakable self-confidence. He wasn't used to having women revile him. "Ye *are* Satan," she countered. "Ye are arrogant, deceitful, and without a heart."

Chapter Fifteen

Reckless

THE WIND WHISTLED across the hills, bringing with it the scent of autumn. Lachlann urged his horse up to the brow of the hill and reined it in next to his father's. The hawk's claws gripped his left wrist through its leather sleeve, its hooded head moving toward him. Saighead—Arrow—sensed he was about to let her off her leash.

Lachlann cast a glance in his father's direction. This was the first time Morgan Fraser had been out on his horse since the battle. He sat a little stiffly in the saddle, his face tense with discomfort. Yet his gaze was determined as he surveyed the sky. His father's hawk, Stoirm—Storm—shifted upon the chieftain's arm. He too was ready to hunt.

"Shall we let them off?" Lachlann asked. Behind him, he could hear the thunder of hooves as his brothers approached.

"Aye," his father grunted. "I've just spotted a pair of pigeons. They'll do for a start."

The two men removed the hoods from their hawks and unleashed them. Lachlann raised his left hand, letting Saighead launch herself into the sky, her powerful wings causing a draft behind her.

Lachlann watched, momentarily enraptured. There were few things more beautiful to watch than a bird of prey taking flight. Saighead stretched her wings wide and soared high, joining Stoirm as they began their hunt.

Aware that someone was watching him, Lachlann tore his gaze from the sky and met his father's eye.

"Is the MacLeod lass behaving herself?" Morgan asked.

His father rarely referred to Adaira by her given name these days. The chieftain hadn't seen her since her incarceration nearly two months earlier. But with Samhuinn looming, the fire festival that marked the end of the harvest season and the beginning of winter, that soon would change. The nights had started to become long and cold, and the handfasting drew near.

"Aye, well enough," Lachlann replied tersely.

"Is she eating? I've no wish to wed a scarecrow."

"I check on her most days ... and see to it she finishes her meals."

Morgan nodded. "Good."

Lachlann drew in a deep breath then, glancing over his shoulder at where his brothers drew near. He had just a few moments alone with his father. He would have to speak now, or they'd have an audience.

"Are ye really going through with this?" he asked, his voice low.

Morgan huffed. "Aye." He inclined his head, studying Lachlann with a hard, searching look. "Why wouldn't I?"

"Because Adaira doesn't deserve it." The words surprised Lachlann as they left his mouth, yet he didn't stop. This impulse had been growing within him for weeks now. "Da, don't punish her for MacLeod's crimes against ye."

Whenever Lachlann climbed the steps to the tower chamber, he steeled himself to look upon Adaira's pale face, her haunted eyes. Occasionally they exchanged a few awkward words, but for the most part, they remained silent. The first few times he'd visited her, Adaira had raged at him, but after a while, she'd run out of insults and ignored him instead. And with each visit, Lachlann had felt something grow inside him—something that had led to this.

His father stared back at him for a long, drawn-out moment. "MacLeod loves his daughters," he replied softly. "Aye, he's a bully, but there's nothing he wouldn't do for them ... I want him to know what it feels like to lose something he loves."

Lachlann held his gaze. His brothers had reached them and were now reining in their horses.

"God's bones," Lucas panted, his voice rough with irritation. "Ye two ride as if all the demons of hell were behind ye."

Lachlann ignored his brother. His attention remained upon his father. "It won't bring Una back to ye," he said coldly. "Nothing will do that."

Morgan Fraser's gaze narrowed, something dangerous moving in the depths of his eyes. None of his sons ever spoke of Una. She was a forbidden topic at Talasgair. Lachlann had just stepped over an invisible line, but he didn't care. Today, he felt reckless.

"No, it won't," his father replied, his voice developing a lethal edge. "But it'll cut MacLeod deep. That lass will suffer at my hands, and her father will know of it. A man doesn't cross me and get away with it. This is a grudge I'll take to my grave."

Lachlann stared back at him, but in place of his father all he saw was a man—a vengeful and bitter one. Lachlann's younger brothers had always ribbed him over how much he was like his father—how they were destined to forever lock horns, for they knew just how to provoke each other.

If it were true then Lachlann faced a bleak and unhappy future. Was this what he would become?

Adaira watched with suspicion as Lachlann entered the chamber. He carried a large hessian bag, which he set down on the table.

"Good afternoon," he greeted her.

Adaira didn't reply. She noted that he hadn't called her 'aingeal' since their struggle on the beach. There was an odd formality in him these days—very different to the brash individual who'd fled Dunvegan with her. Sometimes he almost seemed subdued in her presence, although today he appeared a little more cheerful.

"What's in the bag?" she asked, deliberately rude. Spending day after day in this tiny chamber was slowly chipping away at her, eroding her naturally optimistic spirit. Apart from Lachlann, the only face she saw was that of the sour-faced maid who delivered her meals, emptied her chamber-pot, and brought her clean clothes.

"A diversion," he replied with a half-smile.

He withdrew a large clay bottle stoppered with a cork and two clay cups. Then he produced a wooden board marked with squares and a small cloth pouch.

"Have ye ever played Ard-ri?"

Adaira frowned. She was a clan-chief's daughter, of course she had. Reluctantly, she nodded.

"Good," he replied. "I'm not the world's most patient teacher." He pulled out two chairs and took a seat on one. "Come on ... let's play a game."

"I'm not playing Ard-ri with ye, Fraser."

He raised an eyebrow. "Why not? Ye must be growing witless with boredom." He reached for the clay bottle and unstoppered it. "I've brought plum wine to make the experience more bearable for ye."

"I don't care. Take yer wine and yer game and leave me be."

Ignoring her, Lachlann poured two cups of wine, before he emptied the cloth pouch and started placing small brown and white counters upon the board before him. One of the counters was twice as high as the others and marked with a crown on top: the king stone.

"Playing Ard-ri with a Fraser doesn't mean ye have to stop hating me," he said as he worked. "I'm not asking for friendship. Just a game."

"I don't understand why ye keep visiting me," Adaira replied. "Haven't I made it clear ye aren't welcome?"

"Ye have, but we Frasers are thick-headed as well as stubborn. I'm the reason ye are here so I like to check ye are well."

Adaira went still. That was the first time he'd even hinted that he felt guilty for what he'd done, and even then the comment was spoken with the flippant edge she'd come to expect from him.

Lachlann fixed her with a level look. "Just one game, Adaira. That's all I ask."

Silence fell between them and then, reluctantly, Adaira rose from the bed, where she'd been perched, and walked to the table. She sat down, pushing her chair back in an attempt to put as much space between them as possible.

Before them, the Ard-ri board sat ready. Ard-ri—or High King—was an old game, and one her father loved. The game simulated a Viking raid: four attacking Viking drakkars were pitted against the Scottish king and his defenders.

Adaira wasn't a strong player; both Rhona and Caitrin had always beaten her at it. She imagined this game would be over with merciful swiftness.

"Do ye want to be the attacker or the defender?" Lachlann asked.

Adaira picked up her cup of wine and took a sip. It was delicious, deep and rich, not like the sour wine that accompanied her meals. "I'll attack," she replied.

Lachlann flashed her a wolfish smile. "Then it's up to me to put up a strong defense." He motioned to the board. "Ye take the first move."

Adaira stared back at him but made no attempt to reach for a counter. "I liked ye once, Lachlann," she said after a pause. "When we fled Dunvegan together, I was in awe of yer courage. I thought ye were a good man, an honorable one."

Lachlann's smile faded. "I'm no saint, Adaira," he replied softly, "but nor am I the worst man ye will ever meet."

"Is that so?"

"Aye ... now go on, make yer move."

Adaira cast Lachlann a look of simmering hate before she dropped her gaze to the board. She focused on it, her lips compressing as she remembered her father's advice on how to play Ard-ri well. He'd told her to attack aggressively, and so she did, moving a counter diagonally across the board so that it sat up against the defending pieces.

Lachlann inclined his head, eyes gleaming. "Interesting move."

Adaira gave him a cool look in reply before she took another sip of wine. "Yer turn."

Hours, and four games of Ard-ri later, Adaira held up her hands in defeat.

"That's it. I'm not playing with ye anymore."

Lachlann leaned back in his chair and crossed one long leg over his knee at the ankle. "Why not?"

"Because I'm tired of losing," Adaira said ungraciously. "Ye crow like a rooster every time ye beat me."

He cast her a look of mock-hurt. "No, I don't."

The clay bottle of wine had long been emptied, and although she felt the most relaxed she had in a long while, she also felt drowsy and hungry. Outside, the light had faded. The maid would arrive with supper shortly.

Realizing their games had indeed ended, Lachlann shrugged and began to put away the counters. Adaira watched him, lazily admiring his profile, before she caught herself.

This afternoon had been a distraction, but he was still the man who'd broken his promise to her. She wouldn't let attraction pull her in, drown her good sense, as it had on the journey here.

"How many days till Samhuinn?" she asked, breaking the silence between them.

Lachlann looked up, his gaze meeting hers. "Five."

Adaira's belly clenched at this news. *So soon.* It felt an eternity since she'd been locked up in here, and yet at the same time, it wasn't long enough. Time marched on. She'd known autumn was slipping toward winter, for the days grew short and the breeze that wafted in through her window had a bite to it in the mornings and evenings. Only, she'd told herself that Samhuinn must be still some way off.

"I tried to talk to Da ... to get him to change his mind," Lachlann said. His face was stern now, his gaze hooded. "But it's impossible. His need for vengeance consumes him—and I'm the last person he'd take counsel from. He'll not be swayed."

Adaira's pulse accelerated. She'd tried not to think of the future, about what it would be like to be Morgan Fraser's wife. Suddenly, Aonghus Budge almost seemed an appealing alternative. He was a boor and a bully, but at least the chieftain of the Budges of Islay wasn't driven by blind hate.

Swallowing hard, Adaira wished she had some more wine to calm her nerves. "What will become of me?" she asked, a tremble in her voice.

Lachlann held her gaze, his jaw tightening. "I don't know."

Adaira leaned forward and grabbed his arm, squeezing tight. "Help me, Lachlann," she gasped. "Ye can't let me wed him."

Lachlann blinked. It was as if a portcullis had just slammed down between them. He took hold of her hand and gently pried her fingers free, then he pushed back his chair, rising to his feet. His face was like hewn stone when he answered her, "I can't."

Chapter Sixteen

A Feast for the Betrothed

"YE WILL JOIN the chieftain and his kin for supper this evening," the maid informed Adaira coldly, setting down the tray of bannocks, butter, honey, and fresh milk.

Despite that she'd been expecting a summons from Fraser, Adaira tensed. Samhuinn was just a day away now. The waiting was finally over.

The maid, a tall, slender young woman with dark-blond hair pulled back in a severe braid, ran a disparaging look over Adaira. "Ye look like a peasant. I will bring ye up a fresh léine and kirtle to wear."

Adaira no longer wore the soiled clothing she'd been captured in. Instead, she was clad in a coarse ankle-length tunic with a tattered plaid shawl around her shoulders. It wasn't what Morgan Fraser would wish to see her in.

The maid's face screwed up then, and she sniffed. "Ye also reek. I'll have a bath prepared."

Adaira sat there numbly, not bothering to answer. Over the past weeks, she'd spoken so seldom she was beginning to wonder if she would lose the use of her tongue. That afternoon a few days earlier playing Ard-ri with Lachlann had contained the longest conversation she'd had with anyone in a long while.

She hadn't seen him since.

Her plea for help had failed, but Adaira wasn't sorry she'd asked him, only that he'd denied her. She knew she'd been trying for the impossible, but she'd had to do it. She'd hoped Lachlann had been nursing a guilty conscience, yet if he had, it wasn't enough to help her.

Seeing that her comments weren't going to be responded to, the maid muttered a curse under her breath and headed toward the door. "Dull wit."

Two burly male servants brought in an iron tub and then filled it with hot water. The maid added scented oils to the bath and left a cake of lye soap, drying cloths, and fresh clothing. Then all of them departed.

Alone in the chamber, Adaira stripped off her scratchy tunic and stepped into the tub. She loosed a deep sigh as she sank into the hot water. Despite the dread that dogged every waking thought, she couldn't deny the bath was a thing of delight.

The scent of rose, a perfume that reminded her of Rhona, wafted up, and she inhaled deeply. She closed her eyes, and for a moment, she was back in Dunvegan in her bower being fussed over by her hand-maid, Liosa.

Adaira's eyes snapped open.

That happy existence belonged to someone else.

Even so, the heat of the water seeped into her chilled bones, and the scent of rose relaxed her. She'd opened the shutters, although she could see little beyond a helmet of grey skies.

In Dunvegan, the locals would be getting ready for Samhuinn, in a yearly ritual that never changed. Groups of men would build bonfires on the hills around the keep. Adaira loved the festival, even if it heralded the arrival of winter. She'd always taken her turn at apple bobbing, although she'd never been good at it. Unlike Rhona, who nearly drowned herself while grabbing hold of the apple with her teeth, Adaira hated getting water up her nose. The taste of roasted hazelnuts and salty oaten bannock were Samhuinn to her.

Although from this year, the festival would take on a different reminder.

Adaira loosed another deep sigh and tried to push thoughts of her impending handfasting from her mind. She glanced down at her nakedness. Her skin had turned pink from the hot water. Her breasts bobbed on the surface, their nipples pebbled from the cold air inside the chamber; the lump of peat burning in the hearth barely took the chill off. She'd regained the weight she'd lost during her first days here.

In a day's time, Morgan Fraser would see her naked, would put his hands on her. Would he hurt her?

Adaira squeezed her eyes shut. She must not think of it. She had to remain strong.

She stayed in the tub until the water cooled, making sure to wash her hair and rinse it thoroughly. Then she climbed out, dried herself off, and dressed. The maid had left her a soft cream-colored léine and a deep blue kirtle. Adaira fingered the fine material before lacing up the front of the kirtle. She wondered if these clothes had once belonged to Una before she ran away. She and Una were of similar stature and build so it was possible.

When the maid re-entered the chamber, flinging open the door without knocking and striding in, she found Adaira seated on her sleeping pallet, combing out her wet hair.

The girl's mouth thinned, and she halted, her gaze sweeping over Adaira from head to foot. Then her lip curled.

Something in that gaze made Adaira's temper flare. She welcomed the heat in her belly, for it consumed the dread. How dare this woman look at her as if she was some lowly wretch.

"Do I pass yer inspection?" she asked coldly

The maid's gaze widened. For a moment, she stared at Adaira, before her cheeks flushed. Adaira's gaze didn't waver. She stared back until the maid looked away. "At least ye are presentable now," the girl muttered.

Lachlann was lowering himself onto the bench at the chieftain's table when an explosion of voices in the hall made him glance up.

His father's retainers, who were also taking their places at the long tables below the dais, were talking excitedly. Their gazes followed the slight figure who entered the hall, flanked by two male servants.

Dressed in flowing blue, her long brown hair curling in heavy waves over her shoulders, Adaira walked proudly into the Great Hall.

Like the lady she was.

Lachlann's gaze devoured her, taking in the slight sway of her hips and the way the kirtle hugged her supple body.

She held her head high, looking straight ahead. Only the tension in her neck, in her unsmiling face, gave her away. Her stoic behavior was impressive, especially after the raw desperation he'd witnessed in her eyes the last time he'd seen her.

Lachlann had deliberately avoided returning to the tower chamber since that day, and yet the look on her face still haunted him, as did her words.

I thought ye were a good man, an honorable one.

He shouldn't have spent so long in her company. The wine and the companionship over games of Ard-ri had lowered both their defenses. Still, her plea for help, which he had so harshly denied, had shadowed him ever since. Seeing her now made his chest ache.

Lachlann tore his gaze from Adaira, to where his father sat next to him. Morgan Fraser also watched his betrothed approach.

With each passing day, the chieftain grew stronger. He still couldn't wield a sword, and the healer warned him that he might never be able to, but outwardly at least he appeared as if he would regain his former strength.

His father tracked Adaira across the floor as if she was a lamb and he was a wolf. It was a cold, predatory look that made Lachlann's hackles rise.

Careful, he cautioned himself. *What do ye care how he looks at her?*

But the truth was he did.

The look on his father's face made Lachlann want to grab him by the neck and slam his face into the table.

Morgan Fraser would ruin Adaira. He would destroy her.

Adaira walked toward the dais, running the gauntlet of hard male stares, and paused before the table. Despite that he sat to his father's right, her gaze never strayed to Lachlann, not once. He was invisible to her. She bowed her head and made a curtsy. It was a brisk, neat gesture.

"Lady Adaira," Morgan Fraser greeted her. "How graceful ye look this eve."

Adaira raised her chin and met his eye briefly before dropping her gaze. She gave the merest nod in response but did not speak.

"What's the matter with her, Da?" Niall spoke up. Lachlann glanced at his brother to see him smirking at Adaira. "Did ye cut out her tongue?"

Morgan cut his son a humorless smile. "Her time in the tower has taught the lass the virtue of silence it seems."

His comment caused laughter to ripple down the table. Lachlann didn't join in.

"Lady Adaira." Morgan Fraser picked up a goblet of wine and turned his attention back to his betrothed. "Come sit next to me. We shall break bread together and speak a little."

Lachlann's mouth thinned. Only his father could make a request sound like a threat.

Adaira tensed but obliged. She walked to the edge of the dais, stepped up, and made her way to the chieftain's side. There she sank gracefully down onto the smaller chair to the chieftain's left.

Around them, the Great Hall was still silent. Every gaze was riveted upon the dais, upon Morgan Fraser and his young wife-to-be. This was the first time many of them had laid eyes upon Adaira. News of her had circulated the fortress for weeks now.

With a click of his fingers, the chieftain motioned to the line of servants that stood, backs ramrod straight, against the wall next to the entrance to the kitchen. "Serve the meal now," he commanded.

Conversation resumed once more: a low rumble, like surf breaking upon a shingle shore. The noise filled the hall, rising up to the blackened rafters above.

This was a special supper indeed, Lachlann noted. The servants brought out swan roasted in butter and herbs, a rich venison stew, tureens of braised leek and kale, wheels of aged cheese, and loaves of fresh bread studded with hazelnuts.

Under other circumstances, Lachlann's mouth would have watered at the sight. But tonight the feast that was set before him didn't appeal. His stomach felt as if a boulder had lodged in the pit of it.

None of his three brothers shared his sentiments though. With grins and laughter, they fell upon the meal as if they hadn't been fed in a week. Wine flowed, and they teased and ribbed each other.

In their midst, Lachlann remained quiet.

Next to him, his father was serving up some swan to his betrothed.

It was a rare thing to see Morgan Fraser wait upon a woman. Even with Una, he hadn't done so. But this was an occasion for ceremony. He was putting on a show for the folk of Talasgair. Tomorrow there would be a handfasting, and they wanted something to celebrate.

Chapter Seventeen

Ill-Tidings

ADAIRA CHOKED DOWN a mouthful of swan.

The meat was rich and smothered in butter. She'd had it once before, at her father and Una's handfasting feast. She'd enjoyed it then, but the taste sickened her now.

Morgan Fraser was not a garrulous man. He said very little as the meal stretched out, yet his silence made the tension within her grow. He watched her with a vulturine look that made her heart race, her palms grow clammy. The last time she'd seen him, he'd been on his sickbed, recovering from a terrible wound. He'd been frightening then, yet the full force of his personality had been checked.

This evening he appeared completely healed. Clad in plaid and leather, his grey streaked red hair pulled back at the nape, he watched her with hard eyes.

"Malcolm MacLeod took a jewel from me," he said after a long while.

The comment was unexpected, and Adaira tensed. She glanced at him, and he snared her gaze, holding it fast. Adaira swallowed. She wanted to look away but found she couldn't.

"My first wife was sweet-tempered but plain-faced," the Fraser chieftain said, his voice barely above a whisper so that none but Adaira could hear him. "She bore me four sons, but I found her company irksome. I was relieved when she died."

Adaira drew in a sharp breath. She didn't want to know all this. She wished he'd cease this tale, but he did not.

"But then Una came into my life. She was Una Campbell then: small, dark-haired, and wild." He paused, his eyes turning a murderous shade of green. "We had barely a year together before yer father stole her from me."

Adaira's pulse fluttered in the base of her throat. He made Una sound like the passive recipient of her father's affections, when in fact it had been her stepmother who'd taken the initiative and fled.

She wasn't about to point this out to Morgan Fraser though. He'd likely draw that dirk at his side and stab her through the throat with it.

She saw the promise of vengeance, of violence, in his eyes, and a shudder went through her. She knew then with certainty that he'd never treat her gently.

He would make her suffer.

Adaira tore her gaze away, breathing quickly, and stared down at the platter of food before her.

"Ye are afraid," Fraser noted. "Good. I want to see fear in yer eyes every time ye look at me."

Heaven knows what would have happened then, what more he might have said. But at that moment, the sound of a commotion from the far end of the hall drew the chieftain's eye.

A tall man clad in leather armor, a travel-stained cloak billowing behind him, strode down the aisle between tables. He wore a weary, hard expression. His dark eyes were riveted upon Morgan Fraser.

"Marcas," Morgan greeted him. Adaira forgotten, he rose to his feet. "What news from the mainland."

The man, who had dark-auburn hair and a chiseled jaw that reminded Adaira of Lachlann's, pursed his lips, his eyes glittering. "Ill-tidings."

A hush settled over the Great Hall.

"Tell it then," Morgan Fraser commanded.

"The battle," the newcomer spoke once more, his gaze never leaving the chieftain's face. "The English crushed us."

The silence grew chill. Adaira glanced across at her betrothed's profile and saw that his face had turned hawkish. "What happened?" he demanded, his voice cracking like a bull-whip across the hall.

"Twelve thousand of us crossed the border," Marcas replied. "We marched south to Durham and faced them there." He broke off, a nerve flickering in his cheek, before pressing on. "And though their army numbered only half the size of ours, they bested us."

The news, humiliating for their people, echoed across the silent hall. However, Marcas wasn't finished.

"We had no choice but to retreat." His face turned stony. Adaira could see that he was a proud man, and each word cost him. "Scotland has lost many men, including a number of clan-chiefs and chieftains. Yer brother Seumas was among them."

Morgan Fraser's face showed no emotion, no reaction to the news. After a heartbeat he leaned forward, his fingers clenching around the handle of a bone-handled knife before him. "And the king?"

The warrior held his gaze. "David was injured in the fighting. He and a few others were taken prisoner. I know not if any of them still live."

Adaira stood within the tower chamber that had been her prison for over the past two moons, and stared at the kirtle the maid had just hung on the wall.

It was exquisite, made of a shimmering lilac material. It glowed in the light of the lantern that burned on the table.

"The handfasting will take place mid-morning tomorrow," the maid told her. She'd brought up jeweled slippers and a gauzy shawl that Adaira would wear for the ceremony.

Adaira tore her gaze from the kirtle, focusing upon the scowling girl.

The maid boldly looked Adaira up and down, her eyes cold. "I will come up shortly after dawn to get ye ready. It's not enough time to make a MacLeod slut presentable though."

"Get out," Adaira said softly.

The maid huffed. "When I'm ready."

Adaira swung around, grabbed a pitcher of water off the table, and threw it at the maid.

The girl squealed and ducked, but it was too late. The earthen jug shattered against the wall, drenching her.

"Get out!" Adaira shouted. "And when I see ye tomorrow, I want to see that sneer wiped off yer face."

The maid backed up, eyes brimming with tears. Adaira advanced toward her, hands balling into fists. The girl gave a squeal of terror, turned, and fled from the room.

Breathing fast, Adaira listened to the key turning in the lock.

It felt a cowardly thing to do, to take the rage she felt toward Morgan Fraser and unleash it upon a servant, yet the maid's rudeness toward her seemed to grow with each passing day.

Her situation here was bad enough without the servants turning on her. She had to start as she meant to go on, or they would think her weak and torment her.

Morgan would bully her, but they wouldn't.

Adaira ran a hand over her face, relieved to finally be alone once more. Ever since Marcas Fraser had delivered the news of Scotland's bitter defeat against the English, the mood at Talasgair had turned grim. The cursing that had followed the initial shock shook the rafters.

Men had leaped to their feet roaring with rage. Morgan Fraser's sons were the loudest of them. All except Lachlann.

He alone had remained silent, hunched over his goblet of wine. His face had been stone-hewn, his gaze shuttered.

Although Adaira had pretended to ignore him throughout the feast, she'd been painfully aware of Lachlann's presence, just a few feet away.

Had he heard the things his father had said to her?

Crossing to her sleeping pallet, Adaira lowered herself down. Her hands were shaking, so she clasped them together and rested them upon her knees.

"Courage, Adaira," she whispered. "What would Rhona do?"

A wry smile twisted her face then. Her sister would have slapped that girl's face weeks ago.

Adaira inhaled a ragged breath as Morgan Fraser's softly spoken threats returned to her. He'd said them to scare her. He wanted her to be a trembling wreck by tomorrow night. He wanted her to weep and cringe before he took her maidenhead.

He's mad, twisted by hate.

Her belly cramped with fear. She just hoped she was strong enough to endure him.

Adaira couldn't sleep that night.

She lay awake in the darkness, staring up at the rafters and listening to the silence. It was quiet up in the tower; the noise in the rest of the fortress didn't reach here.

Adaira's thoughts circled, fear pressing down upon her chest. The wedding loomed like a hangman's noose before her. She didn't want to think of it, yet she couldn't stop herself.

Time stretched out, and she continued to stare into the darkness. It was strange, but she didn't even feel remotely drowsy.

She was still wide awake when she heard the light scrape of footfalls on the stone outside her door—and then a heartbeat later, the clunk of an iron key in the lock.

Adaira sat up, heart pounding.

Who would come to her chamber at this hour? Had Morgan Fraser come to rape her before the handfasting?

Terror exploded in her chest. He'd been angry enough tonight to do it. His rage upon hearing of Scotland's defeat had been a terrible thing to behold. Her own father had a blistering temper when roused, one that could send both his kin and servants running for cover. But she was less afraid of MacLeod than she was of Morgan Fraser. The Fraser chieftain's temper was a cold, vicious thing.

The door opened, and Adaira clutched the blanket to her. "Go away," she hissed, terror pulsing through her. "Or I'll scream these walls down."

Chapter Eighteen

By Moonlight

"QUIET," CAME A harsh male whisper. "Noise travels in this place."

Adaira froze. She recognized Lachlann Fraser's voice instantly.

Fresh panic seized her.

What does he want with me?

Wordlessly, he entered the chamber, crossed to the window, and threw it open. Moonlight filtered in, illuminating his tall form. Adaira's gaze swept over him. He wore a heavy cloak and boots and carried a bundle under his arm.

Lachlann hunkered down so that their gazes were level. His eyes gleamed in the moonlight. "Do ye still want my help?"

Adaira stared at him before silently nodding.

"Good. We're leaving Talasgair ... now."

Adaira stifled a gasp. "Ye will take me to Argyle?" she whispered.

He nodded. "Aye ... if that's where ye wish to go."

Adaira's breathing hitched. She didn't want to hope; this could be some cruel trick. Lachlann could be toying with her.

But before she could question him further, he pushed the bundle he carried into her arms. "Get dressed and put on this cloak and boots," he ordered softly. "We need to go."

He rose to his feet and stepped back, giving her space.

After a moment's hesitation, Adaira pushed aside the blanket and got to her feet. She still wore the fine cream léine of that evening. She pulled on the blue kirtle she'd worn for the feast over the top, her fingers fumbling with the laces. Then she reached down and hauled on the fur-lined boots. Finally, she slung the heavy woolen cloak about her shoulders, fastening it about the throat.

All the while, Lachlann watched and waited. She'd never seen his face so serious. "Ready?"

Adaira nodded once more.

"Follow close behind me ... and don't speak. My father's a light sleeper."

They left the tower chamber, padding softly down the worn stone stairs.

Adaira held her breath as they inched their way across the wide landing, past the door to the chieftain's bed-chamber. Adaira imagined Morgan Fraser slept with one eye open. He didn't seem the kind of man to let his guard down—ever.

It was a long, tense trip to the bottom. At the foot of the stairwell, a single torch burned upon a bracket against the wall. It threw a soft light across a guard, who sat, slumped on the floor.

Adaira drew up sharply, her gaze searching the man's face. For a moment, she thought he was dead, but then she saw the gentle rise and fall of his chest.

Loosing a breath, she cut a glance to Lachlann. Their gazes met and held for a heartbeat.

With a jolt, she realized he really was helping her escape.

Adaira's mind whirled. This didn't make sense. After everything that had happened, she couldn't understand why Lachlann Fraser would help her. What had changed?

There was no time to ask him about it now though; her questions would have to wait.

Lachlann led the way out of the tower, toward the oldest part of the fortress: the ancient stone round tower. Adaira wondered how he planned for them to escape this place. There would be guards everywhere.

But there didn't seem to be, or at least not in the passageways Lachlann was taking. They entered the round tower, where the Great Hall sat in the midst of the old broch, but Lachlann didn't take her into the hall itself. Instead, they skirted a passageway around it.

Halfway along the passage, the scuff of boots against stone alerted them to someone's presence.

Lachlann ducked into the shadows, pulling Adaira with him. Crushed against the long hard length of his body, her heart thundering so loudly she was sure the whole fortress could hear it, Adaira listened to the approaching footsteps.

It was a heavy, unsteady tread. A shadow passed by, a drunken man on his way to the privy.

They waited until all sign of him had passed before Lachlann released Adaira and the pair of them emerged from the shadows. The near-miss had put her on edge; her heart still pounded. However, Lachlann's face, lit by a guttering torch on the wall, was hard and focused.

He then leaned in close to Adaira, his breath tickling her ear. "We're taking the back way out," he whispered. "Keep a few paces behind me until the path is clear. The East Gate will be guarded. Whatever happens, stay silent. Prepare yerself ... things may get bloody."

Adaira nodded, although her belly now pitched and roiled with nerves. She suddenly needed to pee, but there was no time to find a privy.

Lachlann led the way to the back of the broch. As instructed, Adaira followed in his wake, keeping to the shadows a few feet behind him. They passed under a wide stone arch, and Adaira felt crisp air fan her face. The doorway was before them. Lachlann moved out into a moonlit yard and broke into a light-footed sprint. A high stone wall reared up before them, and a narrow wooden gate lay straight ahead.

Silhouetted by burning torches on the walls, Adaira spied two dark outlines of guards on either side of the gate. Adaira covered her mouth with a hand and slowed her pace. Lachlann was running straight for them.

Steel flashed as Lachlann drew his dirk.

A flurry of movement, grunts, thumps, and the scuff of booted feet on dirt followed.

Heart pounding, Adaira crept across the yard. Two prone figures lay on the ground. Lachlann had his back to her as he unbolted the gate.

Adaira stepped over the guards, her legs trembling now. "What did ye do to them?" She'd only whispered the question, but it seemed to echo across the yard.

Lachlann whipped around, gaze narrowed, and grabbed her by the arm, hauling her against him.

"I told ye to keep silent," he hissed in her ear.

"I know, but the guards ... are they—"

"Dead? Aye. Now hold yer tongue. We're not out of danger yet."

Lachlann shoved his shoulder against the gate and, with a creak, it opened. Once again, the noise seemed to reverberate in the night's stillness. There wasn't even the moan of the wind to disguise it.

Tension thrummed through Adaira. Her senses were stretched so taut that she imagined every soul in Talasgair must have heard. She drew in a sharp breath, bracing herself for shouts and the tattoo of running feet.

But no sounds came.

Lachlann took Adaira by the hand and led her through the gate. The land rose steeply on Talasgair's eastern side, and the pair were forced to scramble their way up a rocky slope before they crested the hill.

They'd only traveled a couple of furlongs from the walls when Adaira's lungs started to protest. Her legs felt weak and clumsy under her. After two moons locked away in the tower, her body wasn't used to this sudden exertion. She was relieved that Lachlann held her hand, towing her behind him as he broke into a run.

A short while later, they approached the ruins of another broch, entering it through the remains of an ancient archway. Stacked stone walls, crumbling with age, rose around them. A star-strewn night sky arched above, for the broch's roof had fallen into ruin long ago.

"Where are we?" Adaira gasped, struggling to regain her breath.

"This is Dun Sleadale, an old Pict fort," Lachlann replied. "Come on ... we can't linger here either."

He led her to the far side of the ruins, where a horse awaited them. Relief kicked within Adaira at the sight of it. She watched Lachlann untether the horse and run a hand down the beast's neck.

"Ye planned this?" she breathed.

"Aye," he replied, busying himself with tightening the horse's girth. "We wouldn't get far on foot."

"Why are ye helping me?"

Lachlann stilled before casting a look over his shoulder. "It doesn't matter. Ye asked me to, didn't ye?"

"Aye ... and ye refused."

His expression shuttered, and he turned away. "I ... changed my mind."

Lachlann swung up onto the back of the horse. He then stretched his hand down to her. "Climb up."

Adaira grasped his hand, slipped her foot into the stirrup, and sprang up, settling herself down behind him. She tried to sit back as far as possible, but the shape of the saddle meant that she slid down toward him, her breasts pressed up against his back. Tensing, Adaira loosely wrapped her arms about his waist.

They moved off, leaving the ruin of Dun Sleadale behind. The horse picked its way down the pebble-strewn hillside. The hoary light of the moon lit the path before them.

Adaira tried to guess the time. It was very late, or early depending on how ye looked at it. They would have to ride hard to be far from here by dawn.

The maid would raise the alarm shortly after sunrise if someone didn't discover the dead guards at the East Gate first.

The chill night air stung Adaira's cheeks. It was cold enough tonight for a frost to settle. It didn't take long for her fingers and toes to grow numb.

At the bottom of the hill, they reached an unpaved highway.

"Where does this road lead?" Adaira asked.

"This is the main highway southeast," Lachlann replied, drawing the horse to a halt. "If ye want to take the fastest route to Argyle, this is it."

Adaira caught the edge in his voice and tensed. "What's wrong?"

"My father will be after us at dawn," he said flatly. "He knows yer kin reside at Gylen Castle and that's where we were heading last time. Neither of us will find refuge there."

Anxiety fluttered up under Adaira's ribcage. In their escape from Talasgair, she hadn't even considered that. "So, ye think we *shouldn't* go to Argyle?"

A brief silence stretched out between them. "It would be wiser to find somewhere to wait him out before we cross to the mainland," he replied. "But ye may never be able to go to Gylen Castle as ye had planned ... not now."

Adaira drew in a deep breath. His words were unwelcome, yet she realized he spoke the truth. Once they were far from Talasgair, she'd have to make new plans, but for now, they had other priorities. "Where can we hide in the meantime?"

"My brothers told me that Baltair MacDonald fell in battle. Yer sister is now chatelaine of Duntulm, is she not?"

Adaira went still, caught off-guard by the question. "Aye."

Lachlann turned his profile to her. He was frowning. "Would she shelter us?"

"She would," Adaira replied without hesitation. She trusted Caitrin with her life. "But ye do realize we'll have to ride through my father's lands to reach MacDonald territory?"

"Aye," he growled. "It hadn't escaped me."

"But ye would take the risk?"

Lachlann muttered a curse and raked a hand through his hair. "If Baltair MacDonald was still chieftain of Duntulm, I wouldn't go within ten leagues of the place. The man was loyal to yer father. But if ye think yer sister can be trusted, we can stay with her till the dust settles."

Adaira considered his words. Her first impulse was to insist they rode like the wind south for Kyleakin before taking a boat across the water. She hated the thought of delaying. Every day that she remained on Skye put her at risk of being caught by either Malcolm MacLeod or Morgan Fraser.

And yet, without a destination in mind, they'd be fleeing blind.

She was also wary of Lachlann. He'd risked his neck to free her, but she didn't trust him. The man never did anything unless he stood to gain from it; she'd learned that the hard way.

However, he did have a valid point. His father would follow them to Gylen Castle if he didn't catch them first.

Lachlann's idea to seek refuge at Duntulm was only marginally less dangerous. They risked capture by her father's men, and there was no guarantee Morgan Fraser wouldn't follow them.

"Will yer father hunt us if we cross into MacLeod lands?" she asked, giving her fears voice.

A pause followed, and when Lachlann answered, his voice was bleak. "Aye ... our only advantage is that if we travel northeast, he won't know where we're headed."

Chapter Nineteen

I Did It For Ye

LACHLANN'S GAZE FIXED ahead.

It was fortunate there was a full moon tonight, on the eve of Samhuinn. Without it, they couldn't have traveled in the dark. Even so, Lachlann's attention swept the bare hillsides around them, on the lookout for trouble.

He and Adaira now rode cross country. They'd left the highway behind, and instead of traveling southeast as he'd initially planned, they were riding northeast. Their path would take them through the mountainous heart of the isle, through narrow passes and uninhabited land. He could see the bulk of those mountains in the distance now, their sculpted silhouettes frosted silver.

Adaira pressed up against his back. She'd wrapped her hands around his waist. Despite the layers of clothing they both wore, he could feel the length of her body pressed up against him, and the softness of her breasts, jolting against him with every stride.

The sensation was distracting, although his thoughts were focused on what lay ahead—and on what he'd left behind.

There were some bridges that could only be crossed once—some steps that could never be retraced.

With an ache in his chest, he knew he'd never see the walls of Talasgair again, never catch sight of the Fraser pennants snapping in the wind or hear the wail of a highland pipe calling him home.

The ache increased till it hurt to breathe.

What have I done?

Lachlann's own behavior stunned him. He'd struggled ever since refusing to help Adaira, but when he'd watched his father with her at the feast, something inside him—a cord that had long been fraying—snapped.

The arrival of his cousin Marcas Fraser had thrown the whole evening into an uproar. For a short while, everyone inside the hall had forgotten that there would be a wedding the following day. Instead, they had been outraged to discover Scotland's defeat against the English.

Lachlann too had reeled from the devastating news—but all he'd been able to think about as he sat at the table, listening to Lucas bellow in rage next to him, was getting Adaira out of Talasgair.

It had been the perfect evening to arrange an escape. Everyone was distracted, including his father, who finished the feast early and took Marcas away with him to his solar to discuss the grim details of the battle at length.

Lachlann had taken his horse out for an evening ride and tethered it inside the ruins of Dun Sleadale nearby, before making his way back to the broch on foot. He'd made some excuse to the guards at the West Gate about how the beast had thrown him and galloped off into the gloaming. He'd told them he would go looking for it in the morning.

After that, he'd waited in his bed-chamber, listening as the broch slowly went to sleep. And when the moon had risen high into the sky, he finally made his move.

"I can hear ye thinking," Adaira spoke up, shattering the silence between them. Her voice was soft, yet wary.

"Why? Are ye a sorceress?" he replied. He'd meant to use a teasing tone, but instead, his voice sounded brittle.

Adaira huffed. "I don't need to be a witch to hear the chatter of yer thoughts. Ye are as tense as a board."

Lachlann didn't answer. For once, he had no idea what to say.

Silence fell between them before Adaira eventually broke it. "It was a brave thing ye did ... and I thank ye for it."

Lachlann snorted. He wasn't sure whether it was brave or the act of an idiot.

"I still don't understand why ye did it," Adaira continued.

"Ye don't need to," he replied. "Ye are free, aren't ye?"

"Aye, but—"

"Enough, Adaira," he said, his voice weary. "I'd prefer we traveled in silence."

The rosy blush of dawn stained the eastern sky. Adaira glanced up before bowing her head and splashing water on her face. The water's chill made her suck in a breath.

They had halted in the bottom of a rocky valley. The bulk of huge mountains reared high above them, and a clear burn trickled through the vale. The water was icy and fresh. Filling her cupped hands with it, Adaira drank deep before refilling their water skin. Around her, a glittering frost carpeted the ground.

She glanced behind her, at where Lachlann was in the midst of a long stretch. She heard the muscles and bones in his back and shoulders creak. It'd been a long, tiring night, but they couldn't rest yet.

Adaira's gaze settled upon Lachlann's face. His expression was tense, his features strained. She'd felt the tension growing in him with each furlong they traveled from Talasgair. His mood put her on edge and worried her.

Was he planning something? Would he betray her again?

Adaira drew in a slow, steadying breath. The time had come for them to have a frank conversation. She'd been avoiding this moment, for he'd been evasive every time she'd tried to speak to him—yet a resolve now filled her.

"What's wrong, Lachlann?" Adaira asked, breaking the silence.

Lachlann glanced toward her, his gaze narrowing. "Nothing."

Adaira inhaled sharply. "Ye are lying. Something *is* bothering ye ... and I wish to know what it is."

His brow furrowed. "Adaira." His voice lowered in warning. "Don't—"

"Enough," she cut him off. "Talk to me!"

Lachlann muttered a curse. "What do ye want to know, woman?"

"I want to know why ye helped me ... have ye finally grown a conscience?"

He snorted.

"Do ye regret helping me ... is that it?"

She watched him tense. "Of course not."

"It seems that way to me."

Lachlann stepped back and ran a hand over his face. "Satan's cods," he muttered, frustrated. "I crossed a line last night. I can never go back home."

"It's more than that though, isn't it?" Adaira folded her arms across her chest. "Ye are disappointed because ye wanted to rule."

"I did," he admitted roughly.

Adaira's mouth thinned. "How it must have chafed to see Morgan Fraser still alive when ye returned home."

A muscle ticked in Lachlann's jaw. "I didn't wish him dead."

"Didn't ye?" She noted a faint color now tinged his high cheekbones. She'd succeeded in angering him, but Adaira didn't care. Recklessly, she pressed on. "Ye were so desperate to get home and seize power that ye didn't care about anyone else. Ye didn't care what happened to me."

"I saved ye, didn't I," he growled back. "Ye could show some gratitude."

"It was the least ye could do!" Adaira spat. His arrogance riled her. "All of this mess is yer fault!"

Drawing her cloak around her, Adaira stalked past him.

Lachlann raised an eyebrow as she went. "Where do ye think ye are going?"

"To Duntulm—alone."

"Ye won't get far on foot."

Adaira came to an abrupt halt and spun on her heel, glaring at him. Lachlann had turned and was watching her with a patronizing look that made her want to kick him in the cods. "The Devil take ye, Lachlann Fraser. I couldn't care less where I go, only that I never have to set eyes on ye ever again."

Giving him her back, Adaira strode away, up the rocky incline toward the northeastern edge of the valley.

"Adaira," he called after her. "Come back here."

Adaira ignored him. She was so angry that she felt like picking up stones and pelting him with them.

To think she'd actually thanked him for saving her.

"Adaira!"

He sounded angry now. Good. She hoped he choked on it.

Moments later, she heard footfalls behind her. He was coming after her.

Adaira broke into a run. Her legs were still weak after her incarceration, but she pushed herself on nonetheless. Rage gave her feet wings.

She'd nearly reached the top of the hill when he caught up with her, grabbing her by the arm and pulling her up short.

Adaira swung around, her right fist balling, and punched him in the neck. However, the blow just seemed to glance off him.

"Let me go!" she shouted.

But Lachlann didn't. He held her firm, fending off the blows and kicks she now aimed at his chest and shins.

"Stop it, Adaira," he commanded, his voice tight. She ignored him, writhing in his grip like a landed pike.

"Filthy whoreson," she shrieked. "Get yer hands off me!"

But he didn't.

Instead, Lachlann pulled her roughly against him. His mouth slanted over hers, and he kissed her.

Adaira was so shocked that she momentarily went limp in his arms. She gasped, her lips parting. His tongue slid into her mouth. His kiss was savage, devouring, and hot. It turned the frosty morning into a steam bath. Adaira was helpless under the onslaught.

She'd almost forgotten what Lachlann Fraser's kiss could do to her, that it could literally scatter her wits to the four winds and drain every ounce of will from her body.

The rage drained from her, replaced by a different kind of madness.

His kiss demanded, took, and gave all at the same time. And as it deepened, Adaira melted against him, her fingers splaying across his leather vest. She felt the hammer of his heart against her palm, and a thrill went through her.

When Lachlann ended the kiss and pulled back, he was breathing fast. His skin was pulled tight across his cheekbones. His gaze burned into her. Adaira stared up at him, the spell he'd cast over her slowly drawing back. She started to tremble.

Lord ... no.

"Ye asked me why I did it, and I'll tell ye," he rasped. "I did it for *ye*, Aingeal."

Chapter Twenty

Everything In My Power

LACHLANN CLOSED HIS eyes. He couldn't believe he'd just said that. He wasn't even sure where the words had come from.

He opened his eyes and saw that Adaira was still staring up at him. She'd looked shocked at first, but now her face softened. His chest constricted. The lass had such a pure, good heart. She put him to shame.

"I don't understand," she whispered.

Lachlann drew in a slow, steadying breath. Suddenly, he found it impossible to speak. He released his hold on her shoulder and, reaching up, stroked her face. To his surprise, he noted his hand trembled slightly.

God's bones, what's wrong with me?

Lachlann's fingers trailed down Adaira's cheek, and he felt her quiver under his touch. He watched her lips part, her pupils dilate. He'd wanted her before, on that evening during their journey to Talasgair, but the sensation paled in comparison to how he ached for her now.

He wanted to pull her to the ground, tear off her clothes, and lose himself in her soft, sweet body. The need was so strong it felt like a kind of insanity. But the heavy frost that sparkled around them, and the surety his father would have discovered both their disappearances by now, kept him in check. They couldn't linger here.

Wanting her like this was selfish. She deserved better than the likes of him. Self-loathing welled within Lachlann then, filling his mouth with a bitter taste.

"I couldn't stand by and watch ye wed my father," he finally managed. "I couldn't let him destroy ye."

She gazed up at him, her hazel eyes as wide as moons. "Really?"

Lachlann managed a smile. "Aye," he murmured. "I'm a selfish cur, but not completely without a heart." He paused a moment before he reluctantly released Adaira and stepped back. Frosty morning air filled the gulf between them. "I can't let ye travel alone. It's not safe. Will ye let me escort ye to yer sister's as planned?"

Adaira swallowed before she nodded.

Adaira craned her neck, peering up at the mountains that rose either side. They had become the heavens, with only a thin strip of blue sky between them. The morning sun gilded the peaks, turning some tawny and others red as if they were aflame. Their craggy, carven bulk made Adaira feel small and insignificant—even so, she loved to look upon them.

She would leave these shores soon, but this isle with its great mountains and wild landscape would always have a piece of her heart.

Adaira must have fallen asleep for a while, for she found herself jolted awake against Lachlann's back as the horse stumbled. The stallion had slowed its gait on the uneven footing. However, they had crested the highest point of the pass and were now making their way down the long slope northeast.

As they rode, Adaira found herself reliving their confrontation at dawn and the heated kiss that had followed. It was impossible not to think about it.

I should still be wary of him, she cautioned herself. He'd seemed sincere as he'd gazed into her eyes—but the past two months had taught her that trust had to be earned.

She wasn't sure what to think, what to say, or how to react. Instead, she took refuge in silence.

Even so, Adaira was keenly aware of the heat of his strong back pressed against her breasts, the texture of his fiery hair that kept tickling her nose, and the male musk of his skin that made her breathing quicken.

Desire. He'd given her a heady taste of it.

Adaira closed her eyes and breathed Lachlann in. She shouldn't want him, yet she did.

That afternoon, when they lay deep within MacLeod lands, Lachlann drew the stallion up for a proper rest.

Leaning forward, he patted the horse's slick neck. It had done well, but now the beast needed a breather. They'd stopped on the edge of a stand of pines, where a shallow creek bubbled over grey rocks. The landscape had changed during the day's journey, gradually growing less barren and arid, and more wooded—a sign that they were approaching the northeastern coast. Despite that the sun had shone on them all day, the air was cool.

Lachlann unsaddled his horse, while Adaira sat down on the ground upon a bed of pine needles a few feet away.

"Lachlann," Adaira spoke up, breaking the long silence between them. He could hear the nervousness in her voice. "About what ye said earlier …"

Lachlann tensed. Removing the saddle, he cast a glance over his shoulder. She was sitting, watching him, her brow furrowed.

"Do ye actually care what happens to me?" Her cheeks pinkened as she said these words. It embarrassed her to bring this up, but he could see she was determined.

Lachlann set the saddle down on its pommel and turned back to the stallion, rubbing it down with a twist of grass. "Ye speak as if such a thing is impossible," he replied. "Do ye think it strange that a man would want to protect ye?"

"No ... but it shocks me that *ye* would."

Lachlann huffed. "Ye must think me a cold bastard."

Her answering silence made him grimace. Pausing in his work, he turned to Adaira. Around them, the wind sighed through the pines, yet Lachlann paid it no mind. He couldn't take his gaze off the young woman seated upon a bed of pine needles. She looked like a woodland fairy maid, caught resting in a glade by an unsuspecting traveler.

Lachlann grew still, his gaze feasting upon her.

He could see the signs of fatigue upon Adaira: her face was paler than usual, and there were dark smudges under her eyes. But even so, she was still lovely; her long brown hair spilling over the shoulders of her cloak.

"Have ye ever been completely ignorant of something ... and then wondered how ye could have missed what was right before ye?" he asked softly.

Her head inclined. "No ... I don't think that's ever happened to me."

Lachlann dragged a hand through his hair. "I wasn't brought up to be sentimental," he admitted with a wince. "It took me too long to realize that I'd made a terrible mistake."

To his surprise, Adaira's mouth curved into a faint smile. "Is that the beginnings of an apology I hear?"

Lachlann snorted. "Aye ... Frasers aren't just known for our stubbornness. We also have difficulty admitting to our mistakes."

He broke off there, realizing that he felt on edge, nervous. Pushing the sensation aside, he went to Adaira then and knelt before her, reaching for her hand. Adaira's gaze widened, and he felt her stiffen under his touch—yet she didn't pull away.

"I did ye a great wrong Adaira MacLeod," he said, his voice low and firm, "and I'm truly sorry for it. Now, I will do everything in my power to put things right."

It seemed strange to see Kiltaraglen again.

So much had befallen Adaira since she was last here. She felt like a different person, as if years not months had passed.

Dusk was settling, the last of the sun gilding the world with a beauty that only autumn sun seemed to possess. The loch glittered, and the wind that had chased them north all day died away.

As they rode in, Adaira spied the mounds of unlit bonfires on the hills to the south and north of the village. After dark, those fires would be lit, and the folk of Kiltaraglen would venture outdoors to celebrate Samhuinn.

The road brought them into the port village, in-between twin hills where two more piles of twigs and branches rose against the darkening sky. Men were rolling up barrels for the apple-bobbing.

Adaira gave a wistful smile as she thought of Dunvegan. Would Rhona and Taran be getting ready to enjoy tonight's festivities? She imagined them wandering amongst the crowd, arms linked. They made a striking couple, for, despite their different looks, they were both tall and proud.

Adaira's throat constricted. She missed Rhona. How she wished to see her. Soon though, she'd see Caitrin again. Warmth flowed through Adaira's breast at the thought.

"We'll need to be careful in Kiltaraglen," Lachlann warned her as they rode in. His gaze scanned their surroundings with a warrior's sharpness. "Yer father might have left men here to keep an eye out for us."

Adaira tensed. She hadn't thought of that. She imagined her father might have sent warriors to Argyle, to seek her and Lachlann there, but she hadn't thought he might still be patrolling his lands for them. The thought made a chill prickle her skin.

"We can't stay in the village," Lachlann continued. "News of us will spread fast if we make ourselves visible."

Adaira digested this before sighing. She'd secretly been hoping they'd have a comfortable night in the inn this time at least. "Where do ye suggest we sleep then?"

"We'll make camp in the woods north of the village," Lachlann replied. He then glanced over his shoulder, casting her a smile. "Ye should be able to see the Samhuinn fires from there too."

Chapter Twenty-one

Keeping Warm

THE RHYTHMIC THUD of drums echoed through the night, like the steady beat of a heart.

Adaira sat, back pressed up to the rough bark of a birch, nibbling at a slab of bread and cheese, as she watched the fires of Samhuinn burn.

They lit up the darkness like glowing embers, beacons to call the spirits home.

"A roast hazelnut, milady?"

She started as a tall figure stepped out from the shadow of the trees and knelt next to her.

The aroma of warm roasted nuts wafted over her, and Adaira's mouth watered.

"Lachlann!" She peered down at the tiny basket of nuts he held. "Where did ye get those?"

His face, kissed by the glow of the distant fires, was so handsome it made her belly flutter. His nearness made it difficult to breathe calmly.

"Ye can't have Samhuinn without hazelnuts."

"But ... I thought it wasn't safe for us to wander amongst folk?"

"Together, aye. But a man alone buying a wee basket of nuts doesn't intrigue folk much." He held the basket out to her. "Go on ... I bought them for ye."

Adaira took the basket and helped herself to a handful. They were fresh off the brazier, still hot. Their aroma brought back so many memories that, for a moment, her throat constricted. Then, she popped the nuts into her mouth and sighed. She offered him the basket. "Here ... have some too."

Lachlann took a handful and sat down next to her, stretching his long legs out in front of him. Although they weren't touching, Adaira could feel his nearness. The fine hair on the back of her arms prickled in response.

On the hillside below, laughter rang out. Torches moved, glowing like fireflies in the darkness, traveling up and down from the village.

For a while Adaira and Lachlann merely watched, silence stretching between them. It wasn't a companionable silence but a weighty one. Much had passed between them that day. Adaira felt odd, as if her skin were too tight, too sensitive. She was jittery around Lachlann. To distract herself, she focused on the bonfires in the distance and the showers of red sparks that erupted high into the sky

Finishing off the nuts, Adaira brushed the skins off her hands and met Lachlann's eye briefly. "Thank ye for the hazelnuts. They were delicious."

He smiled back but said nothing.

After a moment Adaira glanced away, her gaze fixing upon the bonfires once more. The tension between them was becoming unbearable. She was so aware of him that, although she was tired from traveling, her body felt restless.

Did it bother him as much as it did her?

It dawned on her then that she ached for him to kiss her again. On a practical level, she was wary of him, but her body told a different story. It obliterated all good sense and filled her with a heady carelessness.

Adaira looked up, to find Lachlann watching her. His face was serious, although his intense gaze ensnared her.

Heart racing, Adaira found herself leaning toward him.

"Adaira." He said her name softly, a hoarse edge to his voice.

Wetting her lips, she swallowed, aware that his attention had shifted to her mouth. Heat rose within her, spreading out from her core.

Lachlann shifted closer to her and reached up, cupping her head with his hands. His fingers tangled in her hair, and then his lips brushed over hers. This kiss wasn't like the one earlier in the day—that embrace had been a claiming. This one was gentler.

Adaira's eyes fluttered closed. Without thinking upon her actions, she parted her lips and allowed her tongue to timidly slide into his mouth.

Lachlann's answering groan emboldened her. She gently bit his lower lip, gasping when he hauled her against him. His kiss changed now, his mouth searing hers. Adaira's head spun, and she clung to him, answering Lachlann's passion with her own. Her tongue explored his mouth, tongue, and lips. His taste made molten heat pool in the cradle of her belly.

A moment later, Lachlann ended the kiss and drew back, breathing hard. Disappointed, Adaira reached for him, but he held her at arm's length. His face was strained, his gaze pleading.

"The Devil roast me alive ... we need to stop ... or I'll forget myself."

Adaira gazed at him, longing for him to do just that. She didn't know what had come over her. The desire he'd sparked that morning had been kindling all day, and now it had burst into flame. She ached for his kiss and felt bereft that he'd deny her.

"Please, Aingeal," he rasped. "Stop looking at me like that."

Confused, Adaira drew back. "Don't ye want to kiss me?" she whispered, hurt.

Lachlann muttered a curse and leaned back against the tree. "Ye have no idea how much."

"Then why won't ye?"

He cast her a look of pure frustration. "Because once I start, I won't want to stop. Ye are a maid ... I don't want to ruin ye."

Adaira tensed. In her haze of lust, she'd forgotten about that. A highborn lass's maidenhead was a valuable thing. It seemed Lachlann understood that better than her.

A wave of recklessness swept over Adaira then. She'd be no chieftain's wife. She had no virtue to cling to. She wanted Lachlann to kiss her again, to discover the magic he'd shown her a glimpse of. A strange thing had happened to them both since leaving Talasgair; it was as if they'd stepped through a door into another world—one she was eager to know more of.

Adaira craved the oblivion of his touch.

Still, wanting Lachlann to pull her into his arms for another fierce kiss was one thing, actually demanding he do it was another.

Shyness overrode recklessness, and Adaira shifted away from him. She now felt embarrassed and a little foolish.

How can ye want someone ye don't even trust? Her conscience needled her then, reminding her just how fragile the bond was between them. It was just as well that Lachlann had pulled away—but all the same, she still ached for his touch.

They sat in silence for a while, and when Lachlann spoke, his voice was subdued. "There's something ye should know, Adaira."

Tensing, Adaira looked over at Lachlann to find him watching her, his gaze shuttered.

"What?" The question came out as a croak. Her nerves were getting the better of her.

His mouth curved. "One promise I did keep. I never told my father or brothers how we escaped from Dunvegan. None of them know of the hidden passage into the dungeon."

Adaira drew in a sharp breath. His admission surprised her, distracting her from her heated, tormented thoughts and disappointment that he'd withdrawn his touch. "Why not?"

He held her gaze. "Some secrets are best kept."

The Samhuinn fires burned, and the laughter and revelry of the folk of Kiltaraglen echoed long into the night.

Adaira and Lachlann eventually turned their backs on the fires and moved away from the edge of the woodland. Moonlight shone through the trees as Lachlann led his horse deep into the woods. Adaira followed. A cold veil settled over the world now, and another night of clear skies promised a frost in the morning. Shivering, Adaira pulled her cloak close.

They made camp for the night in a tiny glade surrounded by ash and oaks. The trees were losing their leaves, and Adaira's feet rustled through them. She stopped, waiting while Lachlann tethered the stallion.

"It's so cold," she breathed. "Can we not light a fire?"

He glanced over at her, his face all sculpted planes in the moonlight. "Not this close to Kiltaraglen ... there will be folk up for a while yet."

Adaira drew her cloak closer. "But we'll freeze."

He cast her another look, one so heated that it made her belly flutter.

Adaira went still. After Lachlann had ended their last kiss abruptly, she'd thought he would avoid looking at her like that. Suddenly, it didn't seem so cold in the glade. Adaira was acutely aware of Lachlann's nearness. Her heart started to hammer. They stared at each other for a long moment. She saw the hunger in his eyes, the way his chest now rose and fell sharply, but he didn't reach for her.

She realized then that he wouldn't.

Lachlann wanted her to make the decision. This needed to be her choice.

Breathing shallowly, Adaira stepped toward him. "Will ye keep me warm?"

She couldn't believe she'd asked him such a thing. Part of her was terrified, and yet another part—one she'd only just discovered—was thrilled by her boldness.

Lachlann wet his lips. "I shouldn't."

Adaira took another tentative step toward him. "What do ye want, Lachlann?"

"Don't make me answer that," he said huskily. "It'll scare ye off."

Adaira held his gaze, her heart hammering so loud she was sure he must have heard it. "I'm not scared," she lied. "And I know what *I* want ... *ye*."

Silence fell between them. Adaira saw a nerve flicker in his cheek and knew he was struggling.

"Come here, Aingeal." The raw edge to his voice made her stomach dive.

Without stopping to think, for she would surely lose her nerve, Adaira stepped forward into the circle of his arms.

Lachlann reached out and cupped her face. The feel of his touch made her stifle a gasp. It had a magical effect, both steadying and exciting her.

Heart pounding, Adaira leaned toward him. Her gaze was on his mouth now. She ached for another taste of him.

With a growl, Lachlann captured her mouth with his.

Adaira couldn't help it; a low groan escaped her. The feel of his lips moving over hers, the glide of his tongue, and the heat of his mouth, unleashed something primal within her. She linked her arms about his neck, pressing herself against him, while she responded to his kiss hungrily.

He was delicious. She could happily drown in the feel of his mouth ravaging hers.

Adaira's hands traveled down, over his broad shoulders to his chest, exploring, before they slid over the hard muscles of his upper arms. Even through the layers of clothing separating them, she could feel his strength, his contained power.

Lachlann gently bit her lower lip, before his mouth trailed down to her neck.

Adaira sighed and sank against him. Her cloak fell away, and his hands explored the curve of her back. Then he cupped her bottom and pulled her hard against him.

Even through the loose material of his braies, Adaira felt Lachlann's arousal—his rigid, hot shaft—pressed up against her belly. A pulse began between her thighs, a deep throbbing ache that made her writhe against him.

Lachlann muttered a curse, grabbed hold of Adaira, and steered her backward.

Two paces brought the pair of them up against the trunk of an oak, a mattress of fallen leaves around their ankles. Pressed against the rough bark, Adaira wound her arms around Lachlann's neck once more, her mouth seeking his.

Their kisses turned wild, wet. Her body pulsed with need, the sensation intensifying when he slid his leg between her thighs. His hands gripped the hem of her léine and kirtle, drawing them up around her hips. The cold night air kissed Adaira's naked skin, but when she shivered, it wasn't from the chill.

Lachlann took hold of her right thigh, lifting it so that she could wrap her leg around his hips. An instant later her core was pressed against the rigid length of his shaft.

Instinctively, Adaira arched up, moving her hips sinuously against him.

Lachlann groaned loudly. He almost sounded as if he was in pain. He clasped his hands around her naked buttocks and ground her against him.

An aching pleasure spread through Adaira's loins. She writhed against him, searching for something nameless, something that teased her, tormented her. Something just out of reach.

Lachlann leaned back from Adaira a moment, tearing his mouth from hers. His chest was heaving, and in the glow of the moonlight, she saw the strain on his face. His eyes were dark and luminous. A light sheen of sweat now covered his skin.

"Ye have no idea," he ground out, his voice ragged, "how much I want ye, Adaira. I could lose control. If ye wish me to stop, it has to be now."

Wild need reared up within her. "Don't stop," she whispered.

He drew in a sharp breath. "I don't want to hurt or scare ye."

"Ye won't." She reached for him, dug her fingers in his hair, and pulled him roughly to her for a bruising kiss.

Lachlann's tongue tangled with hers, all hesitation gone. Then with one hand, he reached down and unlaced his braies.

Breathing hard, Lachlann freed his shaft. Adaira reached down to touch him. Her trembling fingertips traced him. His rod quivered and pulsed under her touch, its tip slick with his need.

Excitement ignited deep in Adaira's belly. She'd never known what sensuality was till that moment, what it meant to want someone with every part of one's body.

Her breathing came in short gasps as he grasped her hips and spread her thighs wide. The slick heat of their bodies connecting caused a whimper to escape her. He held her, pressed at the entrance to her core.

Nervousness fluttered up under her ribcage. This was really happening. Once they did this, there was no going back.

Slowly, taking his time, Lachlann slid into her. The sensation of him filling her, stretching her, made her moan. A deep aching pleasure spread through her lower belly before a sharp pain made her catch her breath.

Lachlann stilled, letting the moment pass and waiting for her to relax against him once more. Then he slid the rest of the way in one smooth movement so that he was buried deep inside her.

Adaira raised her chin and met his gaze. It was almost too much to look at him, too intense, too raw. The pain had been fleeting, and the feeling of exquisite fullness that replaced it made her quiver.

Holding her hips tight, Lachlann began to move inside her in slow, deep thrusts.

Adaira sucked in a breath, and the trembling in her body increased. How good it felt. Her body sang with pleasure.

"Lachlann," she gasped. "I don't ... I can't..." She wasn't even sure what she was trying to articulate. It was just that she could feel a tension building within her, like a rising tide behind a seawall. It scared her just a little.

"Let go, Aingeal," he whispered. "Give yerself up to it."

And she did. Her head fell back as tension rose to its peak within her, and a great wave of pleasure crested the seawall and slammed into her.

Lachlann's body went taut. He threw his head back and gave a deep, raw groan. Then, they collapsed against the oak together, limbs tangled, bodies spent.

Chapter Twenty-two

What will ye do now?

SHIVERING, ADAIRA PRESSED her back up against Lachlann. Once the glow of their lovemaking had faded, the cold started to gnaw into her bones. Yet Lachlann's body burned like a furnace compared to hers, and when he wrapped his heavy mantle about them, a sigh of pleasure gusted out of her.

Adaira felt a rumble in his chest as he laughed. "Better?"

"Aye," she murmured. "Much."

They fell silent then. A sense of well-being, unlike any other Adaira had experienced, settled over her. His warmth cocooned her. She listened to the rhythmic whisper of his breathing, the steady beat of his heart. The scent of leather and warm male skin enveloped her.

She felt Lachlann place a gentle kiss upon the crown of her head. "Are ye comfortable?"

"I think so," Adaira mumbled sleepily. Truthfully, her body had never felt so alive. The dull ache between her legs reminded her of what they'd just shared, of the pleasure he'd given her.

She wanted to ask him if what they'd shared was usual. She had no prior experience, but he would know. Yet she suddenly felt shy in his presence. Her cheeks flushed when she remembered how bold she'd been with him, how lustily she'd responded to his touch.

She'd done it—she'd coupled with Lachlann. There was no undoing it.

She wondered what he thought of her now.

Tomorrow, in the cold light of day, she might end up regretting tonight's abandon, but right at that moment, wrapped in her lover's arms, Adaira could not.

Gradually, fatigue pulled her down into its embrace. Then she felt her eyelids droop and knew she was lost.

Lachlann held Adaira in his arms and listened to her breathing change. It grew deeper, and her body fully relaxed against his.

The feel of her pressed up against him, the tickle of her soft, heather-scented hair against his face, was both a balm *and* a torture.

Despite that exhaustion now dug its claws into him, he still ached for her. He'd wanted to take her again, this time on the leaf-strewn ground, but Adaira looked ready to collapse. He had to show the poor lass some mercy.

Lachlann loosed a deep breath and let his head fall back against the rough bark of the trunk.

This time tomorrow they'd be in Duntulm—and when they reached the fortress, things would change.

Adaira wasn't his wife, or even his betrothed. Indeed, she was promised to *two* other men: Aonghus Budge and his own father. Lachlann had no claim on her.

Once she was safe with her sister, Adaira might change her attitude toward him. She might remember all the reasons she distrusted him—that she'd once hated him.

Lady Caitrin would hear the tale of how he'd made Adaira a promise and then broken it. Adaira's sister wasn't likely to want him to remain at Duntulm once she knew the truth.

Lachlann gently stroked Adaira's hair. She gave a soft sigh and snuggled deeper into his chest.

Swallowing hard, Lachlann stared up at the night sky through the spreading branches of the sheltering oak. There wasn't much he was sure of these days. His decision to help Adaira flee Talasgair had thrown his world into chaos. All the things he'd once set so much store in no longer mattered.

One thing he knew though was that he wanted to protect Adaira, to keep her safe.

He had to find a way to ensure he stayed at her side.

Adaira gazed up at the giant thumb of dark rock, silhouetted against the morning sky. The land rose steeply to the north, and the familiar jagged outline of rocky pinnacles reared overhead. One, in particular, stood out.

She smiled before tapping Lachlann on the shoulder and pointing up to it. "Look ... Bodach an Stòrr."

The Old Man of Storr was one of the isle's most distinctive landmarks, although it had been a few years since Adaira had seen it last.

"Aye, it does indeed look like a giant's thumb buried in the earth," Lachlann replied. "We're headed in the right direction at least."

They had left the woodland north of Kiltaraglen as the first glow of dawn lit the eastern sky, and pushed onward. It was a day's journey north along the coast to Duntulm.

The morning was tranquil, the loch's waters as still as a polished iron disc. However, it was cold enough that their breaths steamed. The frosty morning air bit into Adaira's face, and she found herself huddling against Lachlann's back for warmth.

Despite that they'd slept sitting up on the hard, root-strewn ground, Adaira had rested better than she had in a long while.

She'd slept the whole night through and only woke up when Lachlann stirred.

"Time to go, Aingeal," he'd murmured in her ear.

She'd awoken to find his arms around her, to find her face pressed up against the hard wall of his chest.

Their gazes had met, and he'd given her a lopsided smile that made her breathing catch. "Did ye sleep well?"

"Aye ... thank ye."

He'd bent his head and kissed her then, a soft, lingering touch that still made fire curl in the pit of Adaira's belly. She'd reached up, her fingertips tracing the line of his stubbled jaw.

Last night had seemed like a dream, but this kiss told her it wasn't so.

However, disappointingly, Lachlann had ended the kiss and risen to his feet. Reaching down, he'd helped Adaira up and brushed leaves out of her hair. "We'd better make a start if ye want to reach Duntulm by nightfall."

He'd turned away then, and crossed to the stallion, readying it to ride out. As soon as his back was turned, Adaira had hurriedly smoothed out her kirtle and brushed more oak leaves from her cloak. She'd suddenly felt self-conscious about her appearance and knew she must look disheveled after sleeping rough.

Lachlann, on the other hand, had never looked more attractive to her. She'd longed to step forward and press herself up against him, to tangle her fingers in his hair as she had the night before.

Now, perched behind Lachlann, she was acutely aware of the strength of his back, the breadth of his shoulders, and the play and flex of the muscles in his thighs.

They rode along the narrow road that hugged Skye's northeastern coast. They left MacLeod lands, riding through the smaller territories belonging to the MacNichols and the MacQueens, before entering MacDonald territory. It was a wild, bare coastline battered by prevailing winds. They passed coastal hamlets, where locals fished the cold waters of the Sound of Raasay, and long stretches of stony beaches where puffins nested. And all the while, a chill wind whipped in from the north, bringing with it the promise of winter.

Adaira was glad of the warmth of Lachlann's body against hers, and of the fact that he sheltered her from the wind. The air bit at her exposed flesh this morning.

They stopped at noon, resting the horse and taking a meal of bread and cheese upon the rocks—supplies Lachlann had picked up in Kiltaraglen.

Lachlann's cheeks were flushed with exertion and cold as he handed Adaira her food. "That's the last of it," he announced. "We'll both be hungry by the time we reach Duntulm."

Adaira smiled. She tried to catch his eye, but he looked away. Was she imagining it or did he seem tense, distracted?

"Caitrin will make sure we eat well, don't worry," she assured him.

Lachlann sat down on the sun-warmed rock beside her. "Ye are very close to yer sisters, aren't ye?"

Adaira nodded. "We are friends as much as siblings ... I miss them both."

A shadow passed across his face, and Adaira grew still. "What is it?"

He shrugged. "Ye are fortunate. Ye have seen how things are in my family."

"Aye ... why don't ye get on with yer brothers?"

Lachlann snorted. "Ye have met them. Lucas is a scheming bastard and the other two aren't much better."

Adaira huffed. "Lucas will inherit now."

"Aye," he growled, frowning. "Don't remind me."

Adaira watched him, her own brow furrowing. She knew how ambitious he'd been. It was difficult to let go of such things.

"What will ye do now?" she asked softly. "Now that ye have given all that up." Her pulse raced as she waited for his response. Last night had changed everything between them; suddenly she had to know what his plans were.

Their gazes fused and held, tension rising between them. Adaira's heart started to thunder against her ribs now.

Lachlann tore his gaze away and looked out across the sound. "I don't know," he said roughly. "My focus for the moment is keeping ye safe."

Adaira swallowed. She hadn't taken a bite of her bread and cheese, for her stomach had suddenly closed. "And after that?" she asked, her voice barely above a whisper.

Lachlann's attention swiveled to her once more. "Things will change soon, Adaira ... once we reach Duntulm, we won't be free to act as we please."

Adaira drew in a deep, steadying breath. "What are ye saying?"

He held her eye. "I won't find a warm welcome with yer sister. I'm an outlaw ... she'll want rid of me."

"We won't have to stay with Caitrin long," Adaira countered, her voice rising slightly. "We don't have to wait. We could cross to the mainland immediately."

"And go where? Ye know Gylen Castle isn't a safe choice."

"It doesn't matter. We'll go somewhere else."

Lachlann's mouth thinned. "Ye deserve better than that."

Adaira stared back at him, sickly panic rising within her. "Are ye going to abandon me?"

Lachlann cursed, rising to his feet and scattering the remnants of his bread and cheese. "No, of course I'm not."

"So what are ye saying then?"

He stared down at her, his face suddenly fierce. "I'd bind ye to me, Aingeal," he said, his voice low and firm. "I'd make ye my wife … but I have nothing to offer ye but myself. No fortune, no lands. Only a price on my head that makes yer life forfeit as well."

Adaira stared up at him, her gaze widening. "Are ye proposing to me?"

His throat bobbed. "Aye … and I'm making a mess of it."

Adaira's breathing hitched. "No, ye aren't," she whispered. "Ye have just caught me by surprise. This all seems so sudden."

It was. Just two days earlier she'd hated him, and he'd seemed indifferent to her suffering. It felt like a lifetime ago now though.

Lachlann loosed a deep breath, his gaze never leaving hers. "Time runs against us. I promised to look after ye … but I fear that soon something, or someone, will stop me."

Adaira swallowed. "Lachlann," she said softly, her vision blurring. "Ye don't have to wed me to keep me safe. I'd never let ye do that."

Lachlann shook his head, his expression turning strained. "What if I told ye that I'm in love with ye?" he rasped. "Would that change things?"

Adaira's lips parted in shock.

"I can't give ye a lady's life," he pressed on. "But I will protect ye … I will love ye."

Adaira drew in a shaky breath. Her mind whirled as she struggled to take his words in. His proposal, and his declaration, had completely thrown her—and yet underneath the confusion, a warmth welled within her.

Lachlann watched her for a long moment, a nerve feathering in his jaw. When he spoke, his voice was husky. "Will ye be my wife, Adaira MacLeod?"

Adaira drew in a shaky breath. Tears escaped then, spilling down her cheeks, but she smiled through them, joy flowering in her breast. "Aye," she whispered back, "gladly."

Chapter Twenty-three

The Lady of Duntulm

ADAIRA CRANED HER neck to view Duntulm's proud outline against the darkening sky. Perched high upon a basalt cliff, the fortress overlooked a stretch of water called 'The Minch' and the isles of Tulm and Lewis in the distance.

It was a bleak evening; a wind whipped in from the sea, and the sky had turned leaden with the promise of bad weather. Yet the sight of the MacDonald stronghold filled Adaira with such relief that her vision swam with tears.

Caitrin. She'd see her again.

They approached the castle over a hump-backed stone bridge spanning a river and then through Duntulm hamlet. The village was small, little more than a scattering of stone cottages around a central dirt square. The peaked roof of a kirk rose to the south. There were few folk about, just one or two women bringing in washing before the foul weather hit. Adaira breathed in the pungent odor of peat from cook fires and the aroma of what smelled like mutton stew.

Her belly growled in response.

They rode up the hill toward the keep. Adaira couldn't think of any fortress as well defended as Duntulm. The steep cliffs provided protection on three sides while on the landward side a deep ditch surrounded the high curtain wall. Even Dunvegan, although bigger, wasn't as secure.

Peering around Lachlann, Adaira spied the outlines of men in the gloaming as they readied themselves to raise the drawbridge for the evening.

"Wait!" Adaira called out. "We're here to see Lady Caitrin!"

That got the guards' attention. They halted at the sound of Adaira's voice, and the sight of the huge horse bearing down upon them, before shifting back to let them pass.

A moment later the stallion thundered over the drawbridge and into the fortress.

Lachlann swung down from his horse before helping Adaira to the ground. He craned his neck then, taking in the huge basalt keep and tower that reared overhead. This was his first visit to Duntulm. Perched on a lonely cliff top and commanding a view for many furlongs distant, the castle was an impressive sight.

His attention shifted to the steps that led up to the entrance to the keep, where a tall man with long pale-blond hair tied back at the nape of his neck descended. Clad in leather and plaid, his expression forbidding, the warrior reached the bailey courtyard and strode across to greet the newcomers.

"Good evening." His voice was as unfriendly as his expression. "Who are ye, and what business brings ye to Duntulm?"

Lachlann opened his mouth to reply, for he was used to taking charge in situations like this. However, this time he hesitated. His name wasn't one he should be speaking loudly on this island, if at all.

"My name is Lady Adaira MacLeod, and this is my escort," Adaira replied confidently, meeting the warrior's gaze. "I'm here to see my sister."

The man's eyes widened. His expression softened a little. "Lady Adaira ... does yer father know ye are here?"

Adaira's mouth thinned. "No ... and no one is to tell him."

The warrior nodded slowly, his gaze shifting to Lachlann. His expression hardened.

Tensing under the scrutiny, Lachlann knew this man guessed at his identity. The flame-red hair of the Frasers of Skye was well-known on the isle. One glance at him and folk could guess his parentage.

"Does yer escort have a name?" the guard asked, still staring at Lachlann.

"Aye, but it's best I keep it to myself right now," Lachlann answered.

Adaira broke the tense silence that followed, stepping in front of Lachlann so that she drew the man's gaze. "What is *yer* name?"

"I'm Darron MacNichol," he said after a pause, dragging his attention back to Adaira. "Captain of Duntulm Guard."

Adaira raised her chin. "Captain MacNichol ... please take us to my sister."

MacNichol nodded, his face turning grim once more. "Follow me."

The captain led the way into the keep. They crossed a wide entrance hall and began to climb a narrow stone stairwell. On the way up, Lachlann noted how different Duntulm was to his father's fortress. Talasgair was a blend of the past and the present—an ancient broch attached to a newer tower—but Duntulm was an imposing rectangular-shaped keep. The main tower rose four floors high. It was a solid fortress, with walls over two feet thick, and built of the same basalt as the cliffs on which it perched.

MacNichol led them to a solar on the third level of the keep. It was a large chamber with two windows: one looking south over green hills, the other facing north across the sea. A fire roared in the hearth, casting the chamber in a warm glow.

"Wait here," the captain ordered. "Lady Caitrin will be with ye shortly."

He left them alone then. Lachlann and Adaira shared a look. He could see the excitement in her eyes; she couldn't wait to see her sister. However, Lachlann didn't share the feeling. He knew this meeting wasn't going to go as smoothly as Adaira hoped it would.

Reaching out, he stroked her cheek. However, he jerked his hand away when he heard footsteps rapidly approaching outside the solar.

"Adaira!"

Lady Caitrin MacDonald flew through the door and launched herself at her youngest sister.

Lachlann backed up, giving the pair of them space.

Caitrin was as he'd heard her described: tall and willowy with hair the color of sea-foam. Dressed in mourning black, she was a striking sight. It reminded Lachlann of looking upon a frosty morning. Beautiful, yet cold.

A large set of iron keys hung from a girdle around Caitrin's waist, revealing her status here as chatelaine of Duntulm. The keys rattled as she pulled back from Adaira. Tears streaked her face.

"God's Bones, Adi," she gasped. "When I heard ye had run away, I thought ye lost forever."

Adaira wiped away her own tears. "As ye can see, I'm not lost."

Lachlann moved back farther, edging toward the hearth. He was intruding here.

Eyes glittering, Caitrin reached out and stroked Adaira's cheek. "Da scoured the isle looking for ye. He even sent men to Gylen Castle," she said softly, "and when they said ye weren't there either, I imagined the worst."

Caitrin broke off there, her gaze shifting to Lachlann for the first time. The tenderness on her face disappeared, and her gaze narrowed. Although Lachlann hadn't introduced himself to Darron MacNichol, the man would know who he was—and he would have informed his mistress. A Fraser: her father's escaped prisoner.

Caitrin looked back at Adaira, her frown deepening. "Where have ye been all this time?"

Adaira heaved in a deep breath. "Do ye want to sit down?"

Her sister shook her head, folding her arms across her breasts. "I'd prefer to stand—go on."

Adaira cast a look over her shoulder at Lachlann. He could see the concern in her eyes, but Lachlann merely nodded. They both knew this wouldn't end well. It couldn't be helped or avoided though.

Turning back to her sister, Adaira began to speak. And as she did so, Lachlann stood in silence, watching Caitrin's face.

The woman didn't give much away. Yet when Adaira revealed that Lachlann had betrayed her, taking her back to Talasgair rather than to the mainland as promised, Caitrin's expression altered. Her blue eyes hardened, and her jaw tensed.

Adaira pressed on, explaining how she was locked in the tower and informed by Morgan Fraser that she was to become his wife. She chronicled her time at Talasgair, finishing with how Lachlann had freed her on the eve of Samhuinn.

"We hope Morgan Fraser won't follow us here," Adaira concluded, with another glance at Lachlann. "For he'll have to cross MacLeod lands to do so."

Caitrin didn't answer. Her face, even when she looked upon her sister, had gone stony.

Adaira stepped forward, and took one of her sister's clenched hands, squeezing it. "We won't impose on ye for long," she continued. "As soon as it's safe, Lachlann and I will travel to the mainland."

"Ye can't go to Gylen Castle," Caitrin replied, her voice clipped. "Da has left instructions with our uncle to send word if ye ever turn up there."

"Then we'll go somewhere else," Adaira countered. "Will ye give us shelter in the meantime? Da must never know though."

A ponderous silence fell in the solar, broken only by the crackling of the hearth.

Caitrin drew in a long measured breath before she eventually replied. "Of course I will give ye shelter, my sister," she murmured. "Da has stopped searching for ye, for now, so ye should be safe here."

Caitrin then swung her gaze to Lachlann, favoring him with a baleful look.

Lachlann tensed. He knew what was coming next.

"I thank ye for bringing my sister here," she said coldly. "But at first light tomorrow ye will leave Duntulm."

Lachlann held her eye. He hadn't opened his mouth once during the sisters' reunion and knew that to do so now would only damn him. Even so, Lady Caitrin's imperious attitude was starting to chafe.

Adaira surprised him then.

He'd thought she'd appeal to her sister, plead with her. But instead, she moved back and stood next to Lachlann, her arm curling around his waist. Instinctively, he looped his arm over her shoulder in response.

"No," Adaira said softly. "Lachlann stays here ... with me."

The Lady of Duntulm stared at Adaira, her face paling. Her gaze shifted from Adaira to Lachlann as realization dawned. "This man's a self-serving liar," she finally managed. "Ye shouldn't have anything more to do with him."

Adaira shook her head, and when she answered, there was steel in her voice. "*This* man will be my husband soon. We will not be parted."

Chapter Twenty-four

One Chance

CAITRIN'S SLENDER JAW tightened. Adaira could see anger flickering in her sister's eyes, yet she didn't care. A thrill had gone through her as she'd stood up to Caitrin. Like Rhona, her eldest sister had a habit of thinking she knew what was best for her.

Not anymore.

Caitrin heaved in a deep breath and smoothed her hands upon her skirts. Then, her attention settled upon Lachlann. "Can ye give me a few moments alone with my sister?"

Lachlann inclined his head before nodding. Adaira tensed and looked up at him, but he merely smiled. "I should see to my horse," he murmured. Reaching down, he gave Adaira's hand a gentle squeeze.

With a nod to Caitrin, he left the solar.

Silence followed him.

Caitrin waited a few moments before she pinned Adaira with a hard look. "Please tell me ye haven't lain with him?"

Adaira held her gaze. Her first instinct was to deny the accusation—what business was it of Caitrin's anyway? But then stubbornness intervened. She'd not lie or pretend she was ashamed of what had passed between her and Lachlann.

However, she didn't need to say anything. Her face told the whole story.

Caitrin groaned and ran a hand over her face. "Satan's Cods, no!" Her sister then crossed to the mantelpiece and poured herself a goblet of wine, which she took a large gulp from before turning on Adaira. "Why?"

"Because I wanted to."

"But he *betrayed* ye." Caitrin shook her head as if she couldn't believe her ears. "He gave ye to his father ... a man who would have made ye his whore."

The harshness of her sister's words made Adaira flinch. Caitrin had changed. Time was, she'd never have said such things. "Morgan Fraser never touched me."

Caitrin glared at her. Her face was ashen, with high spots of color upon her cheekbones. "Aye ... but his son has."

"And I welcomed his touch."

"Ye are too trusting. Rhona and I always warned ye that some man would take advantage of it ... and the worst sort has!"

"Enough!" Adaira's temper finally snapped. Caitrin spoke to her as if she was an empty-headed goose. She'd not tolerate it a moment longer. "Ye think ye know me, but ye don't. I have the wits to know a good man from a bad one."

Caitrin's eyes grew huge, and she drew back as if Adaira had just slapped her. "I'm just trying to protect ye," she replied, a rasp to her voice. "I thought ye were dead. And then ye turn up alive and well, with this awful tale. How do ye expect me to react?"

"I expect ye to listen to me. To trust my word."

"But that man's a Fraser! He's—"

"Going to be my husband. He loves me, Caitrin."

Adaira moved over to the hearth and sank down into a chair. Her legs felt weak. Caitrin muttered an oath and took a seat opposite. Her fingers clenched around the stem of the goblet she clutched. Watching her, Adaira noted the lines of tension that bracketed her sister's mouth. Despite that he'd been dead over three months now, her marriage to Baltair MacDonald had taken its toll. Adaira had little idea of what Caitrin had endured during the two years she'd been wedded, for her eldest sister kept her own counsel, yet the change in Caitrin spoke volumes.

"Love is the easy part," Caitrin murmured, staring into the fire. "But what happens when ye are living rough, eight months gone with a bairn? Will love fill yer belly and keep ye warm when ye are both living on gruel in the midst of winter?"

"Lachlann knows how to survive," Adaira replied tightly, "and I'm not completely useless either."

Caitrin favored her with a condescending look that made Adaira's anger rise once more. Caitrin had often resorted to such expressions when Adaira said or did things she thought immature.

Leaning forward, Adaira held her sister's eye boldly. "I'm not who I was, Caitrin. I'll never be a lady now ... not like ye." Her voice was low and steady, even if her heart raced. "For the first time in my life, I can choose my own path. Ye of all people should understand what that means."

Caitrin stared back at her. The scorn drained from her face, replaced by a fragility Adaira had never seen before. Her eyes glistened, and for a moment, it seemed she would weep. Then, Caitrin inhaled deeply, mastering her reaction. "But are ye sure of him?" she asked finally, a husky edge to her voice. "I also know what it means to make the wrong choice."

"Lachlann understands me, and I know he'll keep me safe." Adaira's mouth curved into a soft smile. "I'm happy to be an outlaw's bride."

Lachlann stared at Caitrin, shock filtering through him. "We have yer blessing?"

Caitrin loosed a sigh before nodding. "Adaira and I have spoken … at length … and although I still don't fully understand her choice, I will respect it—for her sake."

The evening was drawing out, and the three of them sat at the table in Caitrin's solar. A simple supper of bread, cheese, salted pork, and apples lay before them. Lachlann had warily taken his seat at the table, expecting another attack from the Lady of Duntulm. But instead, she'd informed him that he could stay on and that she no longer opposed their marriage.

Lachlann cast Adaira a look of disbelief. What magic had she woven here?

In response, Adaira flashed Lachlann a small smile before reaching across and placing her hand over his. Lachlann turned his hand over and laced his fingers through Adaira's. Then he turned his attention back to Caitrin, meeting her eye. "I do love yer sister."

Caitrin pursed her lips. "So she says."

"I *will* make her my wife."

A groove formed between Caitrin's delicately drawn brows. "Aye, on that we are both agreed. The sooner ye wed the better."

Lachlann raised his eyebrows before glancing at Adaira. Seeing her pink cheeks, he realized Caitrin knew what had passed between them. Adaira's sister would be worried he'd planted a bairn in her womb.

The thought had crossed his mind as well.

Lachlann met Caitrin's eye, favoring her with a wry smile. If she wanted them to wed in haste, he wasn't going to discourage her. "Do ye have a date in mind, Lady Caitrin?"

She nodded. "The day after tomorrow. Ye can be wed in Duntulm village kirk. I shall call for the priest."

"That went better than I thought," Lachlann admitted as he escorted Adaira to her chamber later that evening. "I expected Lady Caitrin to have me stoned out of Duntulm."

"I just needed to have a quiet word with her." Adaira glanced up at him, smiling. "Caitrin isn't unreasonable."

Lachlann raised an eyebrow. "She glared at me all through supper. I think she expects I'll abandon ye at the altar."

Adaira huffed. "No, she doesn't … she'll warm to ye eventually."

"Aye, perhaps—but not any day soon."

They reached a wooden door framed by a stone arch, and Adaira halted. She turned to Lachlann, raising her chin so she could meet his eye. He gazed down at her before reaching out and caressing her cheek. His thumb slid along her plump lower lip and desire quickened his breath. Adaira had a lush mouth that was made for kissing.

"Would ye mind if I shared yer bed tonight?" he murmured, his gaze still riveted upon her mouth.

"Best not," Adaira replied, her voice husky. "Caitrin's had a chamber prepared for ye ... downstairs."

"What about a goodnight kiss then?"

"Very well," Adaira breathed, "just one."

Lachlann's mouth curved. Leaning down, he brushed his lips over Adaira's—once, twice—and then he parted her lips with his tongue. Her answering gasp inflamed him. He loved how responsive Adaira was. Her soft moans and gasps excited him beyond measure, as did the way she melted under his touch.

God, how he longed to carry her into that chamber and tear her clothes off. Last night he'd been frustrated by the layers of wool, leather, and linen that separated their bodies. It had been too cold to strip, but he ached to see her naked.

Just two more nights, he reminded himself as he tore his mouth from Adaira's, *and then she's mine*.

"Wicked temptress." Lachlann braced himself against the door and pushed back. Adaira stared up at him from within the cage of his arms. Her hazel eyes were luminous, her lips slightly parted. He stifled a groan. When she looked at him like that it was difficult to keep a leash on his self-control. "I should go then."

"Good night, Lachlann." The hoarse edge to her voice made him ache to take her right there up against the door.

The thought sobered him. Lady Caitrin would definitely cast him out of Duntulm for such an act.

"Sleep well, Aingeal," he replied, stepping away from her. "I shall see ye in the morning."

Chapter Twenty-five

Ill-timing

ADAIRA PICKED UP Eoghan from his crib. "How he's grown," she murmured, holding the bairn against her breast as she turned to Caitrin. "What are ye feeding the lad?"

Caitrin huffed. "Just milk for now, but he's a hungry bairn."

Adaira glanced down at Eoghan's thick thatch of dark hair. Not for the first time, she felt a jolt. Even though he was still a babe, Eoghan MacDonald looked so much like his father it was eerie. Baltair MacDonald had been very handsome to look upon, and Adaira could see that one day his son would rival him in looks. A shadow of misgiving fell over her then, as she stared down at the bairn's chubby face. His sea-blue eyes were his mother's. But would he inherit her or his father's character?

Adaira carried Eoghan over to where a large log burned in the hearth. After the drama of the day before, it now felt peaceful inside the solar. Caitrin was seated at the table, bent over a huge leather-bound ledger as she went through Duntulm's accounts. Alban MacLean, the castle's steward, sat at her side, looking over the chatelaine's shoulder as she copied down the sums he read to her from scrappy leaves of parchment.

"No, milady," he corrected her quietly. "It was thirty sacks of oats we bought from MacLeod this year, not forty."

Muttering an oath under her breath, Caitrin dipped her quill into the pot of ink beside her and corrected the ledger.

Oblivious to Caitrin and Alban's discussion, Lachlann perched on a window seat. It was early afternoon, and although the chill wind had died outside, the sky was grey. Even so, Lachlann seemed content to sit there and gaze upon the view to the south, across the hills that stretched over MacDonald lands. His expression was pensive, his gaze veiled.

Adaira could see he was deep in thought so she didn't disturb him. Instead, she allowed herself to study the man who'd soon become her husband.

Dressed in clean braies and a loose léine belted at the waist, his red hair brushed out over his shoulders, Lachlann entranced her. He'd shaved, and she admired now the clean, strong line of his jaw.

Her belly fluttered as she imagined trailing her lips along it.

This time tomorrow she'd be his wife.

Eoghan squirmed in her arms, his tiny chubby hands reaching up and tangling in her hair. Distracted, Adaira gently pried his fingers free before placing a kiss on the top of his head. His hair was downy and sweet-smelling.

Adaira closed her eyes a moment. Happiness flowed through her, its warmth suffusing her like a hot bath on a cold winter's day. One day, she'd hold her and Lachlann's bairn in her arms. One day, they'd have a family together. She could hardly believe this was real, that soon he'd be her husband.

A tremor of misgiving curled in the base of her belly. After the events of the past months, she wasn't used to things working in her favor. She worried that this happiness would somehow be ripped from her grasp.

At the window, Lachlann shifted.

Adaira yanked her thoughts back to the present and saw that he was frowning. "What is it?"

He tore his gaze from the view, to where Duntulm's chatelaine sat, her brow furrowed as she scratched out sums onto the ledger. "Lady Caitrin, ye have visitors."

"Really?" Caitrin placed the quill in its pot and rose gracefully to her feet. "I'm not expecting anyone." She moved toward the window, Alban and Adaira following her.

Adaira stopped by Lachlann's shoulder, her gaze moving past him to the rumpled blanket of green hills beyond. Sure enough, a large company of riders approached. From this distance, they were tiny, appearing like a column of marching ants. As the four of them watched, Adaira made out the outlines of banners.

Her breathing faltered. What if Morgan Fraser had tracked them north after all?

Beside her, Caitrin drew in a sharp breath. "It's Da."

Cold washed over Adaira, while Lachlann tensed. He tore his gaze from the approaching riders and met Caitrin's eye. "Are ye sure?"

Caitrin nodded, her jaw firming. "The standards bear the MacLeod plaid."

Adaira stared out across the hills, her own gaze narrowing. A moment later she too recognized the gold, grey, and black of her family's plaid.

The warmth of wellbeing that had cocooned her since the day before fell away, and a wave of panic rose. "We can't stay here," she choked. "We have to go ... now."

Caitrin shook her head. "It's too late. They'll see." She reached out and took Eoghan from Adaira. The bairn squawked, sensing the shift in mood. "Ye are going to have to hide while he's here." Caitrin turned her attention briefly to Alban. "Warn Darron and the others not to breathe a word."

"Aye, milady," the steward replied, his heavy featured face creasing with consternation.

Caitrin nodded her thanks and moved away from the window. She then motioned to Adaira and Lachlann. "Follow me."

Caitrin smoothed her damp palms upon the skirts of her black kirtle. She hoped her nervousness didn't show on her face, that her father wouldn't see through her brittle smile of welcome.

Malcolm MacLeod was the last person she wished to see right now.

Standing in the bailey, she watched her father's banner-men ride in through the gate, their horses' hooves thundering over the drawbridge. Suddenly, Duntulm's bailey was filled with them. Alban stood at Caitrin's right shoulder, while Darron flanked her left side. Their silent, stoic presence calmed her, reminded her that she was in charge here.

Her father would not intimidate her.

Clan-chief MacLeod was easy to spot: a broad, thick-legged figure with a wild mane of greying auburn hair and a beard to match. He rode a heavy-set destrier, a beast strong enough to carry his weight.

Caitrin's gaze narrowed. It was nearly two moons since she'd seen her father last, and he'd grown even fatter than she remembered. Una rode into the keep behind him, dark and fey-looking, her blue-eyed gaze sharp.

Caitrin's breath caught when she spotted two familiar faces behind them.

A big man with short blond hair and a scarred face rode through the archway, with a fire-haired beauty at his side: Taran and Rhona.

Joy exploded within Caitrin's breast, and she realized how lonely she'd been of late. Her nervousness forgotten, she hurried forward to greet them.

Rhona reached her first. Her sister swung down off her chestnut mare and rushed at Caitrin. They hugged, and when Rhona pulled away, her grey eyes were shining.

"I've missed ye," she greeted her. "With both ye and Adaira gone, the keep feels so empty."

At the mention of their youngest sister, Rhona's joy dimmed. Caitrin hadn't spoken to Rhona since Adaira's disappearance. But since Adaira had explained everything, Caitrin now knew that Rhona and Taran had helped her escape.

Rhona would be wondering why they'd never arrived in Argyle.

"Ye look well, daughter," Malcolm MacLeod boomed as he lumbered over to them. "Although black washes ye out."

Caitrin's mouth thinned. She would have to wear black for a while yet.

"Good day, Da," she greeted him with a kiss. His whiskers tickled her cheek. "What brings ye all to Duntulm? Had I known, I'd have had a feast prepared for this evening."

"Can't a man pay his daughter a surprise visit?" he rumbled.

"We've all missed ye," Rhona spoke up with a smile.

Taran had stepped up next to her, acknowledging Caitrin with a nod. "We thought a visit north was in order," he added. "Before the bitter weather sets in."

"Ye are all welcome," Caitrin replied, keeping a smile plastered on her face. However, inwardly she cursed their ill-timing. Duntulm wasn't as big as Dunvegan; it wouldn't be easy to keep Adaira and Lachlann hidden. She'd found them lodgings next to the kitchens, in two tiny chambers usually occupied by servants.

It was away from the main keep, and somewhere that Malcolm MacLeod was unlikely to go without good reason.

"Good to hear, lass," MacLeod boomed. "Now, enough chatter. Lead the way to the Great Hall, and open a barrel of yer finest ale. I've got a plague of a thirst."

Chapter Twenty-six

Soft-hearted

"STILL NO WORD of Adaira?" Caitrin took a sip of wine and surveyed her father over the rim of her goblet. She was reluctant to bring her sister up but thought her family might get suspicious if she did not.

"No." Malcolm MacLeod was onto his third cup of ale and was showing no sign of slowing. His face turned thunderous. "I've sent men out far and wide," he growled, "but it's as if she was taken by fairies. The only place we haven't searched is Talasgair itself. If I ever find Lachlann Fraser, I'll rip his head off with my bare hands."

Caitrin nodded, schooling her face into a grave expression. Her father's blustering and threats were commonplace whenever he mentioned his escaped prisoner; only, he had no idea that the man he hunted was hiding in this very keep.

Trying not to think of the chaos that would ensue if her father ever found out, Caitrin glanced across at where Rhona sat. Her sister looked so sad that Caitrin's chest constricted. Rhona needed to know Adaira was safe. Somehow, she had to find a way to tell her.

They sat upon the raised dais at the far end of the Great Hall, a spread of food before them. The servants had pulled what they could from the larder, while cook was furiously preparing some apple and bramble tarts to serve later with thick cream.

"Excellent drop this." Her father wiped his mouth with a meaty hand. "The MacDonalds know how to brew a good ale."

Caitrin frowned. Her father had deliberately changed the subject. He wasn't here to talk about Adaira it seemed. Malcolm MacLeod did nothing by chance. She didn't doubt that Rhona had missed her, but there would be something behind her father's visit.

As if sensing her suspicions, MacLeod fixed her with that level iron-grey stare she knew so well.

"We need to speak of yer future, Caitrin."

Her heart sinking, Caitrin held his eye. "Aye, and what of it?" She knew her tone was surly, yet she didn't care. She was getting used to being the chatelaine of Duntulm and didn't wish for things to change.

"Ye are young and fair, daughter. In time, ye must wed again."

Caitrin drew in a long, steadying breath. Next to Caitrin, Rhona cast her a sympathetic look. They both knew what Malcolm MacLeod was like when it came to finding his daughters husbands. An unwed daughter was a millstone around his neck, a burden he had to rid himself of.

"And in time, I might," she replied. It was a lie. As she felt right now, she never wished to be shackled to another man.

"Have ye heard of our defeat against the English?" MacLeod's face screwed up as he asked this, as if the subject was deeply distasteful—but necessary.

"Aye," Caitrin replied. She doubted there was a soul upon the isle who'd not heard. He must think her a hermit.

"Many Scots died in that battle," her father continued, still scowling. "None of the MacLeods who joined King David have returned yet … few will."

Caitrin frowned. He was leading up to something.

"Baltair's younger brother joined the king, did he not?" Una spoke up. She sat at Malcolm's side, a goblet of wine in hand. She wore a sanguine expression. However, her blue eyes were assessing.

"Alasdair," Caitrin replied. "He joined the army before Baltair and I wed, and hasn't been back to Skye since. I know not where he is."

"I sent word to him after Baltair's death," her father rumbled. He was watching Caitrin with a penetrating look now. "If he lives, he will return to claim his rightful role as chieftain. He will no longer need yer services as chatelaine. Ye will have to return to Dunvegan."

Caitrin swallowed. "And if Alasdair MacDonald never returns? There are no other heirs."

"Then ye remain Lady of Duntulm," Rhona piped up with a grin. She raised her chalice to her sister. "Here's to that, dear sister."

Malcolm MacLeod glowered at them. "No, she won't. One of the MacDonalds of Sleat will step into the breach. Like it or not, Caitrin, ye will still have to wed again."

"Don't worry." Una favored Caitrin with a sweet smile. "We'll begin a search for a suitable husband for ye upon our return to Dunvegan."

Caitrin swallowed a cutting reply. It wouldn't do her any good to start an argument with Una or her father; Malcolm had a fiery temper, and when riled wouldn't let a subject drop. Best to be quietly defiant, as she'd always been.

"Apple and bramble tarts, milady." A servant appeared at Caitrin's elbow, bearing a huge platter of fragrant sweets.

"Thank ye, Galiene," Caitrin responded with a smile. Never had she been so grateful to have a conversation interrupted. "Please, serve them."

Galiene, an older woman who helped Duntulm's cook prepare meals, began to circuit the table, serving Malcolm first.

Seeing her father was distracted, Caitrin leaned toward her sister. "I need to speak to ye," she whispered. "As soon as supper's over, meet me outside the kitchen."

Adaira walked into the kitchen to find Caitrin, Rhona, and Taran waiting. Her step faltered at the sight of them, joy exploding within her.

"Rhona!"

She flew across the kitchen and crushed her elder sister in a fierce hug.

Pulling back from the embrace, Adaira saw that Rhona's eyes glittered with tears. However, her face appeared frozen in surprise. "Adi ... what are ye doing here?" she gasped.

Likewise, Taran appeared floored. His ice-blue gaze searched Adaira's face before it shifted to where Lachlann had stepped up behind her. Taran's expression then hardened.

It was warm in the kitchen, the air fragrant with the aroma of baking. The old cook had stepped outside with her assistants, leaving the party alone. It had been a nervous wait in their chambers. Caitrin had told Adaira and Lachlann she would meet them in the kitchen after supper. They had waited a long while before the cook knocked on the door and whispered that it was safe to come out.

Sensing the shift in mood, the sudden tension in the air, Adaira stepped back so that she and Lachlann stood shoulder to shoulder. She glanced up at him, and their gazes fused for a moment.

Lachlann then swung his attention back to Rhona and Taran. "After Adaira and I left Dunvegan we made our way to Kiltaraglen, where I stole a boat," he began without preamble. "However, instead of taking her to Argyle, I brought her back home with me ... to Talasgair." Lachlann paused here, drew in a deep breath, and plowed on. "I wanted to get home fast, in case my father died and one of my brothers took his place as chieftain. At the time I didn't spare a thought for Adaira. It was only later—when my father announced he planned to wed Adaira at Samhuinn—that I began to realize what a grave mistake I'd made. On the eve of their wedding, I helped her escape ... and here we are."

Silence followed his words. Eventually, Taran finally broke it, his voice wintry. "Ye swore a promise to see Adaira safely to Gylen Castle ... upon yer life. Don't deny it, for I heard ye speak the words."

"I don't deny it," Lachlann replied, "I swore an oath ... and I broke it."

"I told ye what would happen if ye failed to uphold yer end of the bargain, Fraser."

Lachlann frowned. "Aye, and I warned ye not to threaten me."

"Dog!"

In an instant, Taran was on him. A large hand clamped over Lachlann's throat. Taran slammed him backward, and they crashed onto the large scrubbed oaken table that dominated the heart of the kitchen.

"Taran!" Adaira cried out, lunging toward where the two men now wrestled. "Stop it!"

She never reached him, for Rhona grabbed her and hauled her back. "Leave them," she bit out. "That Fraser bastard deserves it."

"No, he doesn't! He—"

The sound of shattering pottery echoed through the kitchen. Lachlann had just grabbed a jug and broken it over Taran's head.

Taran roared and punched Lachlann in the face. An instant later Lachlann arched up under him and drove his knee into Taran's belly. Fists flew as the two men rolled down the table, sending cups and bowls flying.

In the midst of the chaos, Caitrin approached them and threw a pail of water over the brawlers.

"Enough!" she shouted. "Ye will not destroy my kitchen!"

Dripping wet, Taran pushed himself up off the table and wiped the water out of his eyes. Next to him, Lachlann sat up and massaged his jaw, his expression murderous.

Taran cast Adaira a despairing look. "Ye are far too softhearted, lass. Lachlann Fraser can't be trusted."

Adaira glared back at him. She yanked against Rhona's grip, but her sister held her fast. "Lachlann Fraser and I are to be wed tomorrow."

Rhona let go of her so suddenly that Adaira nearly toppled over. She caught herself on the table edge and turned to face her sister. Rhona's face had gone pale, her features taut. "Have ye lost yer wits?"

Adaira clenched her jaw, refusing to answer. However, she could feel anger rising within her like steam off a boiling cauldron of water.

Rhona's attention snapped to her elder sister. "Did ye know about this?"

"Aye," Caitrin replied, her face pained. "I've organized for the priest to wed them in the village kirk tomorrow morning."

Rhona's gaze narrowed. "Ye have been helping them?"

Caitrin nodded.

Rhona cast Caitrin a look of disgust before she rounded on Adaira. "I don't understand."

"Ye don't need to." Lachlann had climbed off the table and now stepped up next to Adaira. He took her hand, his fingers lacing through hers tenderly; yet his face was hard. "This isn't yer life, or yer choice to make. If Adaira doesn't want to wed me then let that be *her* decision."

Silence fell in the kitchen.

Rhona swallowed before shifting her gaze to Adaira. Staring into her elder sister's storm-grey eyes, Adaira glimpsed her hurt, her confusion. Rhona wasn't being malicious. She truly was at a loss. "Is this really what ye want?" Rhona asked finally, her voice catching.

Adaira leaned into Lachlann, finding solace in the warm heat of his body pressed into her side. However, her gaze never left Rhona's. "Aye," she whispered.

Chapter Twenty-seven

Blood of My Blood

"WHAT ARE YE doing today, daughter?"

Caitrin glanced up from buttering a piece of bannock and favored her father with what she hoped was a serene smile. "I always take bread and sweet buns down to the villagers on Wednesdays," she replied.

He huffed. "Can't they make their own bread?"

Caitrin's smile widened. "Aye, Da ... but it's a tradition that Baltair's father began years ago. I like to continue it. It's good for me to talk with the folk here, to learn what they need from me."

Una gave a soft snort. She'd been daintily nibbling a bannock, but now lowered it. She viewed Caitrin with a shrewd look. "Ye think yerself a chieftain now, do ye, Caitrin?"

Malcolm MacLeod chortled at this, although Caitrin stiffened. "No ... I'm chatelaine."

"Aye, that's right," her father rumbled, his grey eyes still shining with mirth. "And soon Duntulm will have a new chieftain, and ye will be wed again."

Caitrin's pulse quickened. She hated her father discussing her future like this. She'd thought once she became Baltair's wife that her father's interference in her affairs was over, but now she was a widow he'd made her his business once more.

Her fingers tightened around the hilt of the knife she was using. She was so tired of men deciding her fate.

Glancing right, she caught Rhona's eye. Her sister watched her with a knowing look. Few understood how she felt, but Rhona and Adaira did, for both their lives had nearly been ruined by Malcolm MacLeod's controlling ways.

"Taran and I are taking a ride along the coast this morning," Rhona announced lightly. "We thought we'd make the most of the sun before it leaves us again."

"Ye are *all* abandoning me," Malcolm MacLeod grumbled. "What am I supposed to do this morning while ye are out?"

It was Caitrin's turn to utter a soft laugh. "Ye will hardly notice our absence, father. Put yer feet up in Baltair's solar and take a well-earned rest. I'm sure Una can entertain ye." She cast her stepmother a look as she spoke, enjoying the way Una's mouth pursed, before continuing. "Later, we'll eat together."

Duntulm village kirk was a stone building with a steep gable roof and a tiny belfry. Constructed of local basalt, the kirk squatted at the southern edge of the village.

Its silhouette, set against a cornflower-blue sky, was a welcoming sight to Adaira. She and Lachlann hurried toward it, cutting through the windswept kirk-yard and the rows of tombstones that surrounded the building.

Lachlann squeezed her hand as they approached the heavy wooden doors. "Nervous?"

"Aye," she admitted, glancing across at his hooded face. He'd pulled the cowl forward so his face was cast completely in shadow; it was impossible to read his expression. "I can't believe this is happening," she murmured. "What about ye?"

He gave her hand another squeeze before reaching out to push open the door. "My guts are in knots."

Adaira smiled. It gave her solace to know he was as nervous as she was.

The awful scene with Rhona and Taran yesterday evening had put her on edge. The conflict had been resolved, but the memory of it had cast a shadow over Adaira's mood. There had been a moment when Adaira had felt despair touch her heart. She didn't want her union with Lachlann to cause a rift between her and her sisters.

And not only that, but her father perched up in Duntulm keep like a giant vulture ready to swoop.

Adaira hadn't been able to sleep for the worry that he'd ruin everything.

But he hadn't. Here they were, entering Dunvegan kirk, and beginning a new life together. The worst was behind them.

Stepping inside the kirk, Lachlann heaved his shoulder against the heavy door and pushed it shut at his back.

A gentle silence greeted the couple, as did the scent of incense and the faint whiff of tallow from the banks of candles lining the walls. Two rows of wooden benches led up to a raised altar. A small party stood beneath it: Caitrin, Rhona, and Taran—and a man Adaira had never seen before. Small and balding, and wearing dark robes, the priest watched them approach.

Adaira's slippered feet whispered on the flagstones. Above her rose a ceiling of wooden beams, and at each end of the kirk, high tear-drop-shaped windows let in the morning sun.

Adaira and Lachlann stopped before the altar and pushed back their hoods. Meeting Caitrin's eye, Adaira flashed her a smile. She had much to thank her eldest sister for. Caitrin was still dressed in mourning black, although her expression was soft this morning; she almost looked like the girl she'd once been. Back before Baltair MacDonald wed her.

Adaira's attention shifted to Rhona. She hadn't been sure her sister—or Taran—would attend the handfasting. Yet they'd both promised, and here they were. And unlike the day before, Adaira could see no anger in their faces or wariness in their eyes.

Dressed in flowing green, her fiery hair pulled back in a long braid, Rhona favored Adaira with a soft smile. Beside her, Taran nodded at Adaira. However, he cast Lachlann a cool, assessing look.

Adaira suppressed a sigh. Lachlann and Taran weren't likely to be fast friends, but at least they were no longer enemies.

Wordlessly, Adaira and Lachlann shrugged off the heavy cloaks they'd worn for the walk down from the castle. The clothing they wore underneath was quite plain for a handfasting. Lachlann wore leather braies and a clean white léine and Adaira a simple green kirtle. However, this morning Caitrin had woven some wildflowers into her hair.

Lachlann looked down at her, favoring her with a soft smile. "Ye look bonny, Adaira."

She smiled back, suddenly shy.

"Are ye ready?" The priest's gentle voice interrupted them.

Adaira shifted her attention to him, studying the man who would wed them. He had a harried yet kind face, and a heavy wooden crucifix hung around his neck.

"Aye, Father," Lachlann spoke up. "Je suis prest." He broke off here and winked at Adaira. "We're *both* ready."

"Please step forward then and join hands."

Adaira and Lachlann did as bid. The feel of Lachlann's fingers entwining through hers, the heat and strength of his touch, caused the thudding of her heart to calm slightly.

The priest stepped close. He held a length of plaid in his hands, MacDonald colors: green and blue threaded with white and red. He began to wind the plaid around their joined hands while he spoke the words that would join them.

Adaira's vision misted as she listened to him. And when it came to the part where they had to recite their vows to each other, she gave up trying to stem her tears. They flowed silently down her cheeks, as Lachlann recited the words, his gaze upon hers.

> "Ye are Blood of my Blood, and Bone of my Bone.
> I give ye my Body, that we Two might be One.
> I give ye my Spirit, 'til our Life shall be Done."

When the vows were completed, the priest unwrapped the plaid that joined them. "Ye are now man and wife," he said with a smile that made the corners of his eyes crinkle. "May yer union be blessed."

Lachlann pulled Adaira into his arms and kissed her soundly. When they drew apart, they were both breathless, and Adaira's pulse beat like a drum in her ears. Still in the cradle of Lachlann's arms, she turned her head back to where her sisters stood. She hadn't looked at them once since the ceremony had begun, for her entire attention had been upon Lachlann.

Rhona was weeping openly, tears streaming down her face. She clutched Taran's arm, as if for support. Caitrin stood quietly next to her. She too wept, but in a gentle, reserved way.

When Adaira and Caitrin's gazes met, her sister's mouth curved in a tremulous smile. "That was beautiful," Caitrin said huskily. "Thank ye for letting me be part—"

Boom.

The kirk doors flew open, crashing against the wall. The entire building shuddered in the impact.

Adaira gasped. She went rigid in Lachlann's arms. His embrace tightened as their gazes swung back to the doors.

A heavy-set figure with wild auburn hair, and an even wilder expression, limped into the kirk, followed by four burly warriors. Una hurried into the kirk behind them.

"Stop this handfasting!" Malcolm MacLeod roared, his voice echoing high into the rafters. "I forbid it!"

Chapter Twenty-eight

The Heart Decides

"YE CAN'T FORBID it," Lachlann replied, his voice ringing out across the kirk. "It's already done. We're now husband and wife."

The sight of Malcolm MacLeod, the man who'd thrown him down into the dungeon to die, and who was now trying to ruin his life once more, made fury rise within Lachlann. How had MacLeod learned of this ceremony?

However, it didn't matter—he was too late.

"Bastard Fraser whelp!" MacLeod limped up to the altar and stopped before them, meaty hands clenched at his side. "How dare ye. No Fraser is wedding one of my daughters—not now, not *ever*."

"I'm sorry ... but they are wed in the sight of God," the priest spoke up timidly. "Ye cannot undo it."

The look the MacLeod clan-chief bestowed upon the priest was so venomous that the small man wilted. His throat bobbed, and he cast Lachlann a pleading look.

Lachlann kept his arm firmly around Adaira as he faced her father. He could feel her fear, the rigidity of her body.

"Da," Rhona spoke up. "Please don't—"

"Silence!" Spittle flew as MacLeod roared. "I'll deal with ye and Taran later. Do ye think the windows of Duntulm keep are blind? Una saw ye two ride off earlier. Only ye didn't take the coast road as ye said. Instead, ye rode directly here." His gaze swiveled to Caitrin, pinning her to the spot. "And ye, lying vixen. Ye carry no basket of bread. Ye hurried straight through the village to the kirk. Una saw it all."

Lachlann drew in a long breath. So, it was his former stepmother who had betrayed them.

Una MacLeod was staring at him, a look of naked victory upon her face. He hadn't seen her in a few years. There were no signs of age upon her; she looked exactly as she had when she'd lived at Talasgair. She was small and dark, with elfin looks. Her eyes were just as sly as he remembered too.

"Stop it, Da," Adaira finally gasped. "None of this matters. Lachlann and I have pledged our lives to each other. Ye can't change it now."

Adaira's words impressed Lachlann. The lass had courage. She was terrified of her father, and yet she faced him.

Malcolm MacLeod hadn't been expecting such a proclamation. He jerked back as if she'd just struck him across the face. Even Una's smirk faded. However, the shock only lasted a moment. MacLeod recovered swiftly.

"Lachlann Fraser is my prisoner," he snarled, his neck stretching out as he glared at her. "And ye are my daughter and will do as ye are bid. Both of ye are coming back to Dunvegan."

Lachlann let go of Adaira and stepped forward, going toe-to-toe with MacLeod. "Yer daughter freed me because she was desperate," he growled. "What kind of father promises a lass like Adaira to the likes of Aonghus Budge?"

MacLeod's heavy-featured face screwed up. "Don't tell me what—"

"I'll tell ye what kind," Lachlann cut in savagely. How he longed to lash out at this man. They were standing so close he could smell the wine on the clan-chief's breath. "A tyrant who thinks nothing of sacrificing his youngest daughter."

The clan-chief roared and lunged for him.

Lachlann had been anticipating the attack. Even so, he hadn't expected such an overweight man to move so fast.

MacLeod's knuckles grazed Lachlann's ear as he ducked.

Lachlann brought up his arm and caught the chieftain's wrist, holding him fast. He barely managed; the man had fearsome strength. He had wrists twice the width of Lachlann's own.

MacLeod snarled a curse and threw his entire weight at Lachlann, slamming into him. They went down on the flagstone floor of the kirk.

Adaira's scream echoed through the building, but neither man paid her any attention. Lachlann was locked in a fight for his life; he didn't dare spare her a glance. Yesterday, when Taran had attacked him, Lachlann had been impressed by the warrior's brute strength. Yet it appeared insignificant to that of Malcolm MacLeod.

Incensed, MacLeod pummeled at him with huge fists, his bulk pinning Lachlann to the floor.

"Stop this," the priest cried, panicked. "This is a house of God. There can be no violence here!"

MacLeod ignored him. Bellowing curses, he slammed his fist into Lachlann's jaw.

Lachlann managed to get his legs free. He drove his knee up into MacLeod's gut. The big man gave a choking gasp and fell sideways. It was an instant's distraction, but all Lachlann needed. He reared up and head-butted the clan-chief in the nose.

MacLeod roared, blood spurting. But instead of quieting him, the blow seemed to drive him to madness. He came at Lachlann, grabbed him around the throat, and threw him backward.

The back of Lachlann's skull hit the flagstones with a crack. His vision darkened for an instant. But when MacLeod's fingers started to tighten around his throat, Lachlann fought him. The madness in the clan-chief's grey eyes, as he loomed above Lachlann, warned him that MacLeod was intent on killing him.

He grappled with the hands around his throat, grabbed hold of the little finger of MacLeod's right hand, and yanked it back.

The crack of breaking bone sliced through the air.

Malcolm MacLeod gave a shout of agony and let go of him. Lachlann rolled away, choking, before bouncing up into a crouching position. The back of his skull ached, as did his throat, but he was ready for the bastard, should he come at him again.

MacLeod glowered at him, tears of pain glittering in his eyes. Then he drew his dirk with his left hand. "I'm going to gut ye, Fraser."

"No!"

A small body hurtled in between them.

"Adaira!"

Lachlann reached for her arm, but she ducked out of his grasp. Instead, she faced her father, stepping forward so that the sharp tip of his dirk nearly touched her breast.

"Get back, Adaira," MacLeod ordered, biting out the words. "Don't interfere."

She shook her head, her gaze never leaving his. "No, Da. Not until ye promise to let Lachlann be."

"Foolish lass." His voice was a low, threatening growl. "Don't ever stand in my way. Once I deal with Fraser, I'll find a suitable punishment for ye."

"No!" Her voice lashed across the kirk. Lachlann saw the high spots of color that had appeared on her cheeks. She wasn't just upset, she was incensed. "I can't live the life ye have chosen for me. Let me be free ... let me be happy with the man I love."

Lachlann's breathing hitched. He stepped forward, reaching for Adaira's arm, but a strong hand clasped around his shoulder and hauled him back. He twisted to see Taran behind him. The warrior's scarred face was grim. "Leave her," he warned, his voice low. "Let Adaira finish this."

Malcolm MacLeod's slate-grey gaze narrowed. "He's a *Fraser*," he spat. "Why did ye have to fall in love with one of them?"

Did Lachlann imagine it, or was there a quaver to the man's voice? The madness was gone from his eyes. They now glittered. From the pain of his broken finger, or something else?

Adaira's throat bobbed. "The heart decides," she whispered. "It doesn't care for feuds or reckoning." She paused here, and father and daughter shared a long silent look.

Malcolm MacLeod's face tensed, still fighting his outrage. "Morgan Fraser will crow over this ... to know his son has wed a MacLeod."

No, he won't, Lachlann thought grimly.

Adaira shook her head. "Lachlann has broken with his father. We will leave Skye and start a new life elsewhere."

MacLeod stared at her. His mouth tightened, a nerve flickering in his cheek.

When the clan-chief spoke, his voice was barely above a whisper, although there was a raw edge to it. "I've failed ye, lass. Ye look at me as if I'm a beast."

Lachlann grew still as he watched. It was painful to see a proud man struggle so. He saw then that despite his foul temper and controlling ways, MacLeod did indeed love his daughters.

"Let us be then," Adaira's voice, although quiet, carried across the silent kirk. "Let me love whomever I choose."

The priest stood a few feet away, his face ashen, while Rhona and Caitrin stood beside him, arms clasped around each other. The sisters' faces were stricken.

A long pause stretched out.

"Da." The pain in Adaira's voice made Lachlann's chest constrict. "Will ye give us yer blessing?"

Another silence fell, this one heavy with tension. Lachlann watched MacLeod's face and witnessed the struggle there. The man was fighting a war within. Pride and anger against a fierce love for his youngest daughter.

The clan-chief closed his eyes and dropped his chin to his chest. His answer came in a whisper. "Aye, lass. I do."

Chapter Twenty-nine

Ten Lifetimes

LACHLANN HELD ADAIRA close and buried his face in her hair. "Promise me that ye will never take such a risk again." His voice held a raw edge. "Ye could have been injured … or worse."

Adaira squeezed her eyes shut. She buried her face in his chest, finding solace in the heat and strength of his body. "I promise," she whispered back.

She hadn't wanted to intervene. But as she'd watched her father draw his dirk, she'd known he meant to slay Lachlann. Initially, he'd wanted to take him prisoner again, which would have been bad enough. But she couldn't bear the thought of seeing her father kill him.

Lachlann could hold his own, she'd seen that. Yet he didn't possess her father's murderous rage. Few withstood it.

She'd acted on instinct then.

Lachlann pulled back and hooked a finger under her chin, raising her face so that their gazes met. His mouth quirked. "So ye love me, Aingeal?"

Adaira huffed. "I was wondering when ye would bring that up."

"So … it isn't true then?"

They stood alone in the kirk. The others, including the priest, had left. Lachlann was watching her with a tender look that made a lump rise in Adaira's throat.

"Of course it's true," she whispered. "Do ye think I'd say such a thing if I didn't mean it?"

Lachlann smiled, his eyes crinkling at the corners. "It was a difficult situation … desperation might have driven ye to it."

Adaira swallowed, suddenly shy. "No," she replied softly. "It just made me brave enough to say what was in my heart."

They left the Duntulm village kirk and walked, hand-in-hand, through the crofters' hamlet beyond. The nooning meal approached. The aroma of baking bread and stew wafted out of the cottages' open doors.

Children, playing outdoors while their mothers readied the meal, called out to the couple.

Adaira raised a hand and waved at them, although she couldn't summon the energy to call out a greeting.

After what she'd just endured, she felt utterly exhausted.

Caitrin was putting on a special nooning meal for their father's visit. They would all be gathering in the Great Hall for it soon. Adaira was tempted to retire to her chamber and hide away, yet she knew she and Lachlann would have to join them for the feast.

Her father had swallowed his pride and given them his blessing. But his acceptance was brittle. She couldn't risk offending him.

Adaira glanced across at Lachlann. "Are ye happy to join the others in the Great Hall now?"

He made a face. "As long as ye are sure yer father won't try to gut me with a carving knife."

Adaira favored him with an arch look. "Not today, he won't."

"Then, aye, I'll join yer kin for the feast, although I can't say I've much appetite."

Adaira linked her arm through his. "Me neither."

He placed a hand over hers and squeezed gently. "I wanted today to be special for ye. I'm sorry it wasn't."

She glanced up at him. "It *was* special."

Lachlann snorted. "Until yer father barged in."

"Thank the Lord, Da didn't interrupt us sooner."

He smiled, and the expression released the last of the lingering tension within Adaira. Lachlann Fraser had a smile that could warm the coldest day of winter.

The smile turned wicked then. "Does this mean ye promise to obey me from now on ... *wife*?"

She jabbed him in the ribs with a sharp elbow. "Not at all ... *husband*."

The aroma of rich boar stew filled the Great Hall. Lachlann dug a spoon into the dumpling that floated in the wooden bowl before him. The meal smelled incredible; a pity then that with Malcolm MacLeod glowering at him at the head of the table, he didn't feel like eating. The healer had splinted MacLeod's broken finger, and his right arm now hung in a sling.

The table before them groaned under the weight of the feast Caitrin had put on for them. There were huge tureens of stew and dumplings, baskets of breads studded with walnuts, wheels of cheese, and a divine-smelling apple pudding. MacLeod had the look of a man who enjoyed such fare regularly. However, he ate soberly, his storm-grey gaze never leaving Lachlann.

A lilting harp melody accompanied the meal. A young woman with dark hair sat by the nearby hearth, a serene expression on her face as she played a soft tune.

It did little to ease the tension in the Great Hall.

Lachlann raised his cup of ale to his lips and glanced at Adaira. She sat beside him, silent and watchful. Like him, she ate slowly.

"A delicious meal, Caitrin." Rhona broke the ponderous silence with a forced smile. "Yer cook could teach Fiona and Greer a trick or two."

"Don't ever mention such to them," Taran replied with an arched eyebrow. "Fiona prides herself as Skye's best cook."

Una huffed at that. Seated at MacLeod's side, the woman wore a petulant expression. "She over-salts her stews, and her bannocks are too heavy," Una said sourly.

The comment earned her a dark look from her husband. "Fiona serves me well, wife," he grumbled. "If ye think ye can do better, maybe I should send *ye* to toil in the kitchen."

Lachlann hid a smile behind his cup. Although he bore his father little goodwill these days, he knew that Una had been the cause of much of Morgan Fraser's bitterness and hate. She sailed through life, taking what she wanted and leaving wrecks behind her. Una had broken off a long-standing betrothal to wed Morgan Fraser. But she'd met her match in Malcolm MacLeod.

The clan-chief shifted his gaze to Lachlann then, pinning him with a hard stare. "How is it ye managed to escape Dunvegan?" His voice was low with a threatening edge. "The guards at the Sea-gate swear they never saw ye."

"Do ye remember how I loved to explore when I was a bairn?" Adaira spoke up before Lachlann had time to ready a suitable reply. "Ye were forever telling me off for wandering through the dungeon?"

Her father nodded, his expression wary.

"Well, one day I discovered a hidden passage there ... it leads out to the woods northeast of Dunvegan."

MacLeod tensed, his gaze narrowing. "What?"

"After I drugged the guards and freed Lachlann, we escaped through it."

A nerve ticked in the clan-chief's cheek. "Why didn't ye ever tell me of this passage?"

Adaira lowered her gaze, chastened. "I liked having a secret ... I'm sorry, Da."

"And ye are the only one who knows of it? No one else was involved in this plan of yours?" MacLeod cut a hard glance toward Rhona. His voice was flinty now.

Adaira shook her head.

Lachlann drew in a slow breath, resisting the urge to look Rhona and Taran's way. Wisely, Adaira had left them out of it.

A brittle silence settled over the table.

Lachlann let his gaze rest fully upon his father-in-law. Feeling the weight of his stare, MacLeod met his eye. He could see the resentment, the simmering anger that needed very little to ignite it.

Although it galled him to do so, Lachlann knew his next words needed to weave peace, not antagonize.

"I love yer daughter," he said, his gaze never wavering. "And I will work for the rest of my life to prove myself worthy of her."

MacLeod's mouth twisted, and he snorted, although the dislike in his eyes dimmed a little. "Ye would need ten lifetimes for that, Fraser."

Lachlann stood by the hearth in the Great Hall, nursing a goblet of wine. MacLeod and Una had retired to their chamber, while Adaira had gone off with her sisters. They would help her prepare for her wedding night.

The emptiness of the hall soothed Lachlann. The crackle of the hearth and the richness of the wine eased the tension in his shoulders.

This was a day he'd never forget. He'd wed the woman he loved, but MacLeod had almost ruined everything. The man was as tenacious as a maddened boar, and just as difficult to fight. He wasn't sure how he'd have handled things if MacLeod had actually come at him with that dirk.

All the same, he hated that Adaira had put herself in danger to save him.

Lachlann ran a hand down his face. He had to do a better job of protecting her in future.

"I misjudged ye, it seems." Lachlann tore himself from his brooding and glanced up to see Taran MacKinnon standing next to him. "Ye aren't the feckless bastard I took ye for."

The warrior wasn't looking at him. Instead, he was staring into the fire, his expression reflective. The firelight played over the two scars that slashed across his features. They were deep and ugly, and Lachlann wondered how he'd gotten them.

Lachlann huffed, his fingers tightening around the goblet. "Ye seem like a good judge of character to me, MacKinnon."

Taran grunted. He glanced over at Lachlann, studying him. "Ye have balls, I'll give ye that ... few men stand up to MacLeod and live."

Lachlann's mouth twisted. "I don't think he appreciated what I had to say."

Taran laughed, a low rumble in his chest. "Maybe not ... but he'll never forget it. Ye didn't just defend Adaira in that kirk, but her sisters as well. Ye told him what he should have heard years ago."

Their gazes met, and for the first time since their meeting in Dunvegan dungeon, the flinty chill in the man's eyes was gone. With a jolt, Lachlann understood that Taran MacKinnon was very different to how he appeared. Beneath that scarred, forbidding appearance lay a kind, big-hearted soul.

He'd helped Adaira escape Dunvegan after all.

Lachlann frowned, recalling the tense discussion during the feast earlier in the day. MacLeod was shrewd; he knew he'd not been told the full story. Lachlann had seen the naked suspicion in his eyes.

"He doesn't know about what happened after Adaira and I left Dunvegan, does he?" Lachlann asked. "About Talasgair ... and my father?"

"No ... ye wouldn't be drawing breath right now if he did." Taran paused here, his gaze shadowing. "MacLeod doesn't know Rhona and I helped Adaira either ... and it's best he never does."

Chapter Thirty

Here We Are

"YE HAVE ALREADY lain with him?" Rhona stared at Adaira, aghast.

Adaira nodded.

"When did this happen?" Rhona demanded. She placed her goblet of wine down on the table beside her with a thud. They sat in Caitrin's solar, in high-backed chairs before the hearth.

"On the journey here," Adaira replied, her mouth quirking. Rhona's shock was almost comical. "In a forest glade on the eve of Samhuinn."

Rhona swung her gaze around to Caitrin. Their eldest sister was looking down at her wine, a smile curving her lips. "Ye knew?"

"Aye." Caitrin glanced up, her smile widening. "Why do ye think I was so keen to see them wed? I had to make sure Fraser made an honest woman of her."

Adaira snorted.

Rhona picked up her goblet once more and took a gulp of wine. She then fixed Adaira with an appraising look. "So ... what was it like?"

Adaira's cheeks warmed. Her mind went blank as she struggled for a response that wouldn't embarrass her or reveal too much. She couldn't think of one.

Rhona was smirking now. Her sister was giving her a knowing look that made her squirm. "I see," she murmured, raising an eyebrow. "Words fail ye, do they?"

Adaira make a small choking sound—rescued when Caitrin cleared her throat and cast Rhona a look of censure. "Stop teasing her."

"I only asked a simple question," Rhona replied, all innocence.

Caitrin then turned her attention back to Adaira. "Was he gentle with ye?" she asked. She wore a tense, pained expression. "A woman's first time can be ... traumatic."

Adaira met her gaze, her chest constricting when she saw that her sister's blue eyes were shadowed. She knew then with certainty that Caitrin had never found any pleasure in Baltair MacDonald's bed.

Adaira's heart ached for her. She wished her sister could know passion, tenderness, and trust in a man's arms. She wished her to experience what she had with Lachlann.

"Aye," she said softly. "He was gentle."

Caitrin smiled, although the expression held a melancholy edge. "I'm glad ... I only want ye to be happy, Adi."

Adaira smiled back, her vision misting. "And I wish the same for ye."

Caitrin glanced away. "I am content now. I like feeling useful, having a purpose that goes beyond being a wife and a mother." Her features tensed then. "I just hope Da doesn't interfere."

"After today he might rethink the way he treats us," Rhona replied.

Caitrin looked up. "I can't believe what Lachlann said to him."

"Or that he's still breathing after saying it," Rhona quipped.

Adaira's mouth curved. "Why do ye think I had to step in?"

Rhona took a sip of wine, her expression turning wistful. "Do ye remember how we three used to sit in Ma's solar and speculate about the men we'd one day marry?"

Caitrin rolled her eyes. "Ye used to scoff at us. Ye were adamant that ye would wed no one."

"I was," Rhona replied with a wry smile. "But fate had other plans for me." Her gaze shifted to Adaira. "Ye were forever going on about how the man who'd one day win yer heart would be strong, valiant, and handsome. Have ye wed the man ye dreamed of?"

Adaira took a measured sip from her own goblet. She knew Rhona was teasing her again, but she didn't mind. The question made her think. "Lachlann is all those things," she said quietly after a long pause. "But he's also real. He can be impatient, arrogant—and infuriatingly stubborn. No one makes me as angry as him."

Caitrin huffed a laugh. "I'm glad to see ye aren't blind to his faults."

Adaira shook her head, smiling. "I'm not perfect either. Lachlann exists in this world, not in my dreams ... I prefer it that way."

"Aye, perfection is boring." Rhona's gaze met hers before a wicked gleam lit in her eyes. "But seducing yer husband isn't. Let's talk about more pressing matters. What are ye going to wear to bed?"

A chill night settled over Duntulm, bringing with it a seeking wind that shrieked across the bare hills outside, rattled the shutters, and moaned against the walls. Despite the keep's thick exterior, the wind still managed to push its way inside. A draft feathered across Lachlann's face as he mounted the stairs to the chamber that he and Adaira would share tonight.

As man and wife.

He opened the heavy wooden door and stepped inside. Adaira was there, awaiting him. She stood before the fire, dressed in a sheer léine that reached her ankles. He could see the outline of her lithe form against the orange glow of the flames behind her. Adaira's long brown hair was unbound and brushed. It fell in heavy waves down her back.

Wordlessly, she turned from the fire, her gaze meeting his.

Lachlann pushed the door closed and leaned against it, drinking her in.

Adaira's loveliness took his breath away. He noticed then the large bed that dominated the chamber; he'd not even seen it when he opened the door, for his attention had been wholly upon Adaira. A bank of candles burned in one corner of the room, bathing the space in golden light.

"The Devil take me ... ye are a bonny sight," Lachlann murmured finally. His gaze left her face, noting the sensual smile that curved her lips, and moved down her body. He could see the outline of her nipples through the léine's thin fabric.

"Come here, Aingeal," he rasped.

Her smile widened, her eyes glowing in the firelight. Still not speaking, Adaira padded barefoot across the flagstones toward him. Lachlann noted then that someone had scattered rose petals over the floor.

When she drew close, Lachlann reached out and hauled her into his arms. His mouth slanted over hers in a deep, possessive kiss. One hand slid up her neck, tangling in her hair, while the other splayed across the small of her back.

Adaira moaned against his mouth. Her fingers dug into his chest through his léine, and she kissed him back with abandon.

Lachlann spun Adaira around and pressed her up against the door. Then he reached down and grabbed the hem of her léine, yanking it up, and stripping it from her. His mouth never leaving hers, he ripped off his own clothing.

Adaira's fingers fumbled as she aided him. And then they were both naked, pressed up against the door, savaging each other's mouths as if they'd been separated for weeks. Need pulsed through Lachlann, made his blood catch fire. His ache for her drove all other thought from his mind.

Their first coupling on the journey here had ignited a hunger within him that he felt would never be sated.

He could never get enough of this woman.

Adaira trailed kisses across his face before gently biting his earlobe. A thrill of pleasure knifed through Lachlann's groin, intensifying the ache there till it was almost unbearable.

Lachlann's hands explored her nakedness: the long length of her back, the plane of her belly, and her lush high breasts that strained toward him.

Slipping his hands under Adaira's buttocks, Lachlann picked her up and stepped away from the door. Then he turned and carried her over to the bed before lowering her down onto it.

Positioning himself between her legs, he parted her trembling thighs and thrust deep, seating himself fully inside her. Adaira gave a hoarse cry, bucking hard against him as she wrapped her legs around his hips and drew him closer still. The sensation, the heat of her, almost undid him; he threw back his head and groaned.

Slow down.

He needed to pace himself or this would be over too quickly. He wanted to savor this moment, their first coupling as man and wife.

Adaira arched back, her lips parting. "This feels too good," she moaned. "My heart could stop from it."

He laughed softly. "I hope not, Aingeal, for I have plans for ye."

He gazed down at Adaira as she lay upon the soft woolen coverlet. Her hair fanned out like a cloud around her, and she stared up at him with such naked want in her eyes that Lachlann almost forgot his resolve to go slowly.

He took hold of both her legs now and raised them so she could hook her knees over his shoulders. Then he rocked against her, taking Adaira in long, slow thrusts, and watching her face as he did so.

Adaira's chest heaved with each movement. Her high pink-tipped breasts, full for such a slender woman, bounced with each thrust, straining toward him. Later, he'd suckle them until she begged for mercy, but right now he just wanted to watch the pleasure that dilated her pupils and made her cheeks flush.

He wanted to make her lose control and cry his name as she did so.

"Lachlann!" Adaira arched up against him and brought him deeper still. Her mouth opened in shock as the angle touched a sensitive place deep inside her. Lachlann watched, drinking her in as her body shook from the force of it. Heat enveloped his shaft, and he felt her contract against him.

Pleasure slammed into him. It was too much. He'd tried to hold back, but he wasn't made of stone. Lachlann gave a hoarse cry and drove into Adaira once more, giving himself up to it.

Adaira sighed and rolled onto her side. She reached out, her hand sliding down Lachlann's sweat-slicked torso. That was the third time they'd made love that night, but it had barely taken the edge off the hunger she felt for him.

She rested her head upon his chest and listened to the thunder of his heart. She stroked the hard planes of his chest and belly, her breath catching as she did so.

Was this what Rhona felt for Taran?

She remembered their kisses, the heated looks she'd seen pass between them when they thought no one was looking, and the expression on Rhona's face the day after their wedding: a blend of serenity and excitement.

Adaira had never known such pleasure could exist; magic lived after all.

"Are ye well, Adaira?" Lachlann asked.

Adaira heard the rasp of exhaustion in his voice and smiled, lifting her head so she could meet his gaze. "Aye, very ... but are ye? I haven't worn ye out already have I?"

He huffed, feigning offense. "*Already*. Just let me have a breather, ye saucy vixen, and we'll see who's worn out."

Adaira laughed. "It was an innocent question." She reached up and stroked his chin. He'd shaved that morning, but she could feel the rasp of new stubble under her fingertips. Continuing her exploration, she traced the sculpted lines of his face: his straight nose, full mouth, and high cheekbones. The first time she'd ever set eyes on him, she'd been struck by Lachlann Fraser's comeliness. Now her attraction to him went far deeper than that.

"I'm so happy," she whispered. "I never thought such happiness was possible."

His green eyes darkened, gleaming as he stared back at her. "I never thought so either ... but here we are." His voice turned husky. "I've never been in love before ... but that all changed with ye, Aingeal."

Adaira smiled. She'd once hated him calling her his 'Aingeal'. She'd found the name mocking. She no longer thought so. The endearment was sweet, heartfelt.

He reached out and cupped her cheek tenderly. "There is nothing I wouldn't do for ye, my darling Adaira."

Tears pricked at Adaira's eyes, and her vision swam. The intensity in his face as he spoke, the way his voice shook slightly, filled her with a surge of love so fierce that she was momentarily struck speechless by it. A surge of protectiveness filled her; the bond they shared went both ways.

When she finally found her voice, it trembled from the force of her feelings. "I know," she whispered.

Chapter Thirty-one

Secrets

LACHLANN WAS SHOEING a horse when he saw Malcolm MacLeod lumber across the bailey toward him.

Letting down the horse's hind leg, Lachlann straightened up. The grim look on the clan-chief's face made him wary. A couple of days had passed since Lachlann and Adaira's handfasting, and although MacLeod had been civil to Lachlann, relations between them were still strained.

"Afternoon, MacLeod," Lachlann greeted him. He kept hold of the iron file he'd been using. Surrounded by MacLeods and MacDonalds at Duntulm, he liked having a weapon in his hand.

Frasers weren't well-liked here.

Malcolm MacLeod stopped, his iron-grey eyes narrowing. "I've just received word from the south. Yer father's men have been searching my lands."

Lachlann tensed. He shouldn't be surprised, for he knew his father wouldn't let things lie, but he still didn't welcome the news. "And?"

MacLeod's frown deepened to a scowl. "We've sent them back across the border with their tails between their legs." He folded his thick arms across his chest. "Now ... why would Frasers be riding across my lands?"

Lachlann shrugged, feigning confusion even as his pulse quickened. "Maybe they've heard I escaped Dunvegan dungeon and have come looking for me."

"And how would they learn that?"

"It's been two months ... folk travel and tongues wag. News could have reached Talasgair."

MacLeod snorted, although the suspicious look in his eyes ebbed.

"Was my father with them?" Lachlann asked, keen to steer MacLeod onto a safer topic.

The clan-chief's heavy-featured face screwed up. "After the wound I dealt him, I'd be surprised if he still breathes, and he certainly won't be traveling far again."

Lachlann swallowed the impulse to tell MacLeod that the last time he'd seen Morgan Fraser the man could ride a horse and was about to wed. He wisely held his tongue. There were some facts it was best Adaira's father remained ignorant of.

Instead, Lachlann frowned. "So ye think he's dead?"

MacLeod's lips compressed. "I hope so. I skewered the bastard like a boar."

Lachlann let out a slow, measured breath, fighting annoyance. Despite that he'd broken with his kin, he didn't appreciate MacLeod's insults. Blood was still blood after all. He wondered if MacLeod was deliberately baiting him.

The cunning light in the clan-chief's eyes confirmed his suspicions. "I don't understand why ye didn't return to Talasgair after ye left Dunvegan," he said after a pause. "My daughter must have wielded quite an influence on ye."

"She did," Lachlann replied. He didn't like the turn the conversation had taken again; they were now skirting the truth MacLeod could never learn.

"I'd heard that Morgan Fraser's eldest was as ambitious as his sire," MacLeod continued. "But ye gave it all up ... for a woman?"

Lachlann could hear the genuine puzzlement in the older man's voice. He resisted the urge to smile. "I did."

"Why?"

Lachlann held Malcolm MacLeod's gaze, his own steady. "Because some things are worth more than land and titles. Yer daughter is more valuable to me than my inheritance."

It had taken Lachlann a while to learn that—so long he'd nearly condemned Adaira to a miserable life—but her father didn't need to know that either.

MacLeod snorted. However, his expression had softened, his gaze gleaming with pride. "Aye, she is."

"The wind is getting up. Shall I take Eoghan indoors, milady?"

"Aye, thank ye, Sorcha. We'll follow shortly."

Adaira watched the dark-haired hand-maid relieve Caitrin of the bairn and carry him away, leaving the three sisters alone on the shore. A fresh wind gusted in off The Minch, foaming the water. Adaira drew her cloak around her, her feet crunching on fine pebbles as she followed Rhona and Caitrin along the strand. The weather was definitely getting cooler; it reminded her that she wouldn't be able to stay at Duntulm much longer.

"When will ye leave for the mainland?" Rhona asked as if reading her thoughts. Her sister's wild auburn hair blew into her eyes, and she pushed it aside impatiently.

"I don't know," Adaira replied. Her belly contracted as she spoke these words. Although she was ready to confront an uncertain future, she was also nervous about it. Where would she and Lachlann end up?

"Ye can go to Argyle as ye had first planned," Caitrin spoke up. Unlike Rhona, who let her long hair fly free in the wind, Caitrin's hair was tightly braided and wound around the crown of her head. She regarded Adaira with a gleam in her eye. "Ye didn't hear it from me, but Da has sent word to our uncle and given his blessing for ye and Lachlann to reside at Gylen Castle."

Adaira halted abruptly, turning to her sister. "Really?"

Caitrin smiled. "Aye ... he's planning to tell ye soon, and ye are to act surprised when he does."

Rhona snorted. "It's not like ye to spill a secret, Caitrin. Remind me never to tell ye any of mine."

"I could see that Adaira was worried about the future," Caitrin replied with an irritated look at Rhona. "I wanted to allay her fears."

Adaira reached out and took Caitrin's hands, squeezing. "And I appreciate it." She frowned then, as something occurred to her. "Morgan Fraser knows I intended to go to Gylen Castle ... what if his men come asking questions?"

"Our uncle won't say anything," Caitrin assured her with a smile. "But if ye are worried, ye can have a quiet word to him after ye arrive."

Adaira nodded, her brow smoothing. Caitrin was right—her uncle had no reason to betray them.

Relief filtered through her. She felt happier knowing they could go to Gylen Castle, and that her uncle would welcome them and keep Lachlann's identity hidden. Life had been so eventful of late, all she wanted now was a little peace.

"Come on, let's turn around," Caitrin replied, pulling the collar of her fur cloak up. "This wind is unpleasant."

"Aye," Rhona agreed. "My hair will look like a rat's nest by the time we reach the keep."

The sisters began to retrace their steps along the beach before they left the shore and took the road through the village. It was late morning and the aroma of baking bread and stewing vegetables greeted them.

Many villagers called out to them, greeting Caitrin, who waved back.

Adaira cut Caitrin a sidelong glance. "Do ye like living here?"

"Aye," her eldest sister replied. "Much more than I did initially."

"I'm glad Baltair's dead," Rhona spoke up. Never one to mince her words, Rhona wore a fierce expression now. "He was a tyrant."

Caitrin loosed a sigh. "I know a wife shouldn't wish her husband dead ... but I did. I felt nothing but relief when I saw him laid out in Dunvegan's chapel. When we buried him in the kirkyard here," Caitrin motioned to the peaked roof of the kirk rising to the south. "I stood there dry-eyed and feared the folk of Duntulm would judge me for not weeping."

"And did they?" Rhona asked.

Caitrin shook her head. "They're good people," she said softly, "and have made me feel very welcome here."

Adaira studied Caitrin's face and saw that her expression was suddenly shuttered. Even with her sisters, she didn't often speak openly. Adaira sensed she was pulling back from them, putting her shields back in place.

Caitrin hadn't always been this way. Before wedding Baltair, she'd been a carefree lass with a sharp wit. But looking at her now, Adaira realized that lass was gone forever.

Perhaps she just grew up, Adaira reflected, *like I had to*. She glanced over at Rhona then and saw that she looked thoughtful. Rhona was easily the most resilient of the three of them. Even as a young lass she'd had a knowing edge to her, an understanding about the ways of the world, that both Adaira and Caitrin had lacked. Yet she'd changed too in the past months. Taran had tempered her wildness.

The three sisters fell silent and made their way up the incline to the keep. The walls of Duntulm rose against the windswept sky, the MacDonald pennant snapping and billowing.

They crossed the drawbridge and entered the bailey to find a large mob of men amassed in the center of it. They were jostling to get a view of something occurring in the heart of the crowd.

Caitrin turned to one of the guards at the gate. "What's going on here?" she demanded, her gaze narrowing.

"Fraser and MacKinnon are going at it, milady," he answered her. "Sounds like a great fight ... I'm sorry to miss it."

A loud grunt echoed across the yard then, followed by a man's curse.

Adaira's breathing hitched. *Lachlann*.

Picking up her skirts, Adaira rushed to the edge of the crowd. She went up on tip-toe, straining to see over the broad shoulders of the men in front of her. Yet it was impossible—they were all much taller than her.

"Let me through!" She elbowed her way through the fray, Rhona and Caitrin close behind her. The men gave way reluctantly, their attention focused on the fight before them.

Adaira reached the edge of the crowd to see Lachlann and Taran, both naked to the waist, battling with blades.

She let out the breath she'd been holding, relief flooding through her. It wasn't a fight to the death—they were sparring with wooden swords.

As the panic drained from Adaira, she found herself studying her husband with frank admiration. He moved with a dancer's grace, easily holding his own against Dunvegan's best swordsman. Adaira had watched Taran fight many times over the years in the practice yard of her father's keep. He was a big man, but he was light on his feet. His scarred face was tense with concentration as he fought.

"Get under his guard, MacKinnon!" Malcolm MacLeod bellowed. The clan-chief stood a few feet away, at the edge of the crowd, his gaze tracking the fight with predatory intensity. "Beat the bastard into the dirt! Wipe that smirk off his face!"

"Da!" Adaira put her hands on her hips, her anger rising. "Don't say such things!"

MacLeod spared his youngest daughter a glance before grinning. "Don't look so fierce, lass. It's just a bit of fun."

Indeed, Lachlann looked like he was enjoying himself. His eyes gleamed and a smile stretched his face. However, his attention didn't shift from his opponent. Sweat poured down his naked chest, the muscles in his shoulders flexing as he lunged for Taran.

His opponent parried, bringing up his blade to block the attack. He then swiftly followed it up with a feint. Lachlann jumped to one side, narrowly avoiding the trap.

The two men moved fast, circling each other as they lunged, attacked, feinted, and parried. Their wooden blades became a blur.

Lachlann managed a circle parry, catching the tip of Taran's sword with his own and deflecting it. He followed up with a swipe at Taran's ribs, slamming into him with the flat of his blade. Taran's hiss echoed across the bailey.

Adaira held her breath. She'd seen few men beat Taran MacKinnon, but Lachlann was close to doing so.

It was then that Lachlann realized Adaira was among the crowd.

His gaze snapped her way, and he grinned.

That was when Taran made his move; one moment of distraction was all he needed.

He lunged and brought his blade down across the hilt of Lachlann's wooden sword, where his fingers grasped. Lachlann reeled back, but Taran was still moving. He ducked past him and slammed his sword into Lachlann's belly.

Lachlann wheezed, as the breath gusted out of him, and sprawled backward onto the dirt.

Adaira gasped, her hand flying to her mouth, while around her the surrounding MacLeod and MacDonald warriors roared with approval.

Standing over Lachlann, breathing hard, Taran grinned. "Novice's mistake that ... letting a woman distract ye."

Lachlann winced, propping himself up onto an elbow. He rubbed the fingers of his right hand. "Aye." His gaze traveled back to Adaira again. Relief flooded through her when his mouth curved into a smile, swiftly followed by frustration. The man was irrepressible.

Lachlann tore his attention from his wife and shot Taran a challenging look. "That's round one to ye, MacKinnon. Best of three?"

Chapter Thirty-two

My North Star

"RAIN'S ON ITS way ... mark my words."

Adaira huffed in frustration and glanced up at the sky. "Nonsense. There's hardly a cloud in the sky."

"Ye obviously haven't looked north then," Lachlann replied with a raised eyebrow, "at the enormous bank of rain clouds rolling toward us." His brow furrowed then. "God's bones, where are ye taking me, woman? We've been walking for hours."

"Oh, do stop complaining," Adaira shot back, striding up the grassy hill. "We're almost there."

The picnic had been her idea. Since their handfasting, they'd hardly had a quiet moment alone together. Her father's presence at Duntulm dominated the whole keep. Their only refuge was their bed-chamber.

Reaching the brow of the hill, Adaira smiled. Ahead, the boughs of tall trees beckoned, but before the woodland ran a glittering burn. Caitrin had told her of this place and had suggested it was the ideal location for a husband and wife to spend a private afternoon together.

"This is the spot!" She glanced over her shoulder at Lachlann. He carried a rolled-up blanket under one arm and a basket in the other hand.

"Thank Christ," he muttered. "What did ye put in this basket—rocks?"

Adaira relieved him of it with a sweet smile. The walk from Duntulm had been longer than she'd realized, and she'd packed rather a lot for their noon meal.

"The effort will be worth it, my love," she told him, stretching up on tip-toe to kiss him. "Ye shall see."

Lachlann smiled, his gaze gleaming as he took in his surroundings. "It's a pretty spot ... I'll give ye that."

"Put down the blanket," Adaira instructed. "I don't know about ye, but I'm starving."

With a grin, Lachlann did as bid. Adaira settled down next to him and produced a large clay bottle from the basket. "Newly pressed cider."

His gaze widened. "No wonder that basket was so heavy … how did ye manage to get yer hands on that?"

Adaira favored him with a conspirator's grin. "I made a plea to Caitrin."

"Generous lass." Lachlann took the bottle from her and poured out two cups of cider. "She comes across a bit stern at times, but it's good to see there's a heart in there."

"Caitrin hasn't had an easy time of it," Adaira murmured, her buoyant mood ebbing as it sometimes did when she thought of what her sister had endured. "Baltair MacDonald was a cruel man," she added with a shudder.

Lachlann's gaze narrowed. "A shadow passed over yer face when ye said his name … did he do something to ye?"

Adaira paused, considering whether to tell him. Lachlann was her husband; there shouldn't be any secrets between them. "He started taking a liking to me during his visits to Dunvegan," she admitted. "I didn't notice at first, but then I caught him staring at me at mealtimes. The day after Caitrin gave birth, he cornered me and tried to kiss me. Rhona interrupted him, thankfully."

Lachlann's expression turned thunderous, and Adaira was glad that Baltair MacDonald was dead. Even so, his protectiveness, his concern, warmed her. "Worry not," she assured him softly. "Baltair never had the opportunity to corner me again." She paused then and took a sip of cider. It was light and fruity. "Before ye met me, I could be a bit silly. Both Rhona and Caitrin warned me that I trusted too readily and always thought the best of folk … even when they'd done nothing to merit it."

Lachlann watched her, his expression softening. "I cured ye of that, didn't I?"

"Ye did."

He glanced away. "I destroyed something in ye, Adaira. I'll always be sorry for that."

"No, ye didn't," she replied, reaching out a hand and placing it on his arm. "Ye forged me."

He looked up, surprised. "What?"

"I was a bit helpless before we met. I'd never have escaped Dunvegan if it weren't for Rhona and Taran. Ye forced me to see the world as it really is. Ye made me strong, like a tempered blade."

His mouth compressed. "Aye, but it was a high price to pay, Aingeal."

"A price we both paid," she said softly, holding his gaze. "We gave up different things, but in the end, it was the making of us."

Lachlann inhaled slowly, his moss-green eyes darkening. "Ye are my north star, Adaira. Every time I look at ye, I'm reminded of what really matters."

Their gazes held for a long moment before Adaira smiled. "Aye, that's why I wanted us to come here today. I never see my husband."

He gave her an arch look. "The Lady of Duntulm likes to keep me busy. I shoed half the horses in her stable yesterday. She wants me to do the other half tomorrow."

Adaira laughed before leaning back and retrieving a cloth-wrapped parcel from the basket. "I think that's why she let me bring these." She pulled back the cloth to reveal a pile of pork and egg pies.

A smile spread over Lachlann's face. "As I said before—she's a generous lass."

Seated on the banks of the burn, they ate their meal and shared the bottle of cider. The day had started unseasonably warm, but it grew chiller as the afternoon wore on. A wind sprang up, driving in from the north, and to Adaira's chagrin, she noted the dark clouds Lachlann had spied on the way here were now looming close.

Presently, fat drops of rain started to patter across the ground.

Adaira, who'd been lying on her side next to her husband, sat up and cursed.

"What did I tell ye?" he said smugly.

"No one likes a 'know-it-all'," she replied tartly. "Come on, help me pack up."

They'd just cleared away the remnants of their meal, and were rolling up the blanket, when the heavens opened. Heavy sheets of rain sluiced across the hillside, battering them.

"We're going to get soaked," Adaira cried, clutching the basket to her.

"Come on." Lachlann took hold of her arm and steered her toward the trees. "Let's see if we can find shelter in the woods."

They dove for the tree line, ducking their heads under the pelting rain. Inside the woods they found a spreading oak to hide under. The tree had lost half its leaves, but it still provided some shelter. Shaking the rain from her hair, Adaira glanced over at Lachlann to find him grinning at her. "Don't say a word," she growled. "Ye insufferable man."

Lachlann's grin turned wicked. "Insufferable, am I?"

"Aye, ye love to be proved right."

He laughed and grabbed hold of Adaira, catching her so suddenly that she squealed and dropped her basket. Then, he pressed her up against the tree trunk and kissed her breathless. Around them, the rain drummed down and thunder rumbled overhead.

Eventually, tearing his mouth from hers, Lachlann trailed a burning line down her neck. "I took ye for the first time against an old oak like this one," he murmured, his voice husky.

Adaira sighed, arching her neck back to encourage his questing lips. She'd never forget that night. It had changed her life forever.

"Shall I take ye again?" Lachlann whispered. He ran his hands down her back and rucked up her damp skirts. "Here in the rain?"

Adaira's breathing hitched, fire surging through her veins. "Aye," she breathed.

Lachlann raised his head from her. "I didn't hear ye, wife." His hand slid up the bare skin of her thigh. "Do ye want me to stop?"

"No," she gasped. She tangled her fingers through his wet hair, pushing his face back down to her exposed neck. "But ye can cease talking now."

Epilogue

Always

ADAIRA HATED GOODBYES.

She knew it was cowardly, but she would have preferred to have stolen away under the cover of darkness than to have to bid her family farewell. Despite her happiness with Lachlann, and her excitement for their future together, she'd been dreading this moment.

Two weeks had passed since their wedding. Malcolm MacLeod had continued to remain at Duntulm, as had Rhona and Taran. Caitrin seemed pleased to have the company and now that she'd made peace with her father, Adaira was relieved too. However, they all knew the moment to say goodbye was looming.

The cool weather was setting in—Lachlann and Adaira needed to travel to the mainland before the first of the winter storms made the crossing treacherous. Adaira had put off naming their departure date, for she'd loved seeing her sisters again, spending long afternoons talking to them as they sewed, spun, or embroidered in Caitrin's solar.

But now, here they all were, standing upon the jetty on the shore to the north of Duntulm village. She couldn't put off the inevitable any longer.

A brisk breeze blew in off the water, bringing with it a chill that drilled into Adaira's bones. They'd delayed longer than they should have. Beside her, Lachlann cast Adaira a smile.

"The boat's ready, Aingeal. It's time to go."

Adaira nodded, turning to the four figures standing behind her: Caitrin, Rhona, Taran, and Malcolm MacLeod. Her stepmother hung back, deliberately keeping her distance. Relations had been cool between Una and her step-daughters during the past two weeks. Adaira would shed no tears over leaving Una behind.

Caitrin was weeping as she stepped forward and threw her arms around Adaira. "I'll miss ye."

Adaira hugged her back, squeezing her eyes shut as tears leaked out. There wasn't any point trying to stem them. It would only make saying goodbye harder. "Once we're settled, come visit us."

"I will," Caitrin replied, her voice husky. "I promise."

Caitrin stepped back, not bothering to wipe her wet cheeks. Even upset, there was a dignity to her sister, a regalness that Adaira knew *she'd* never possess. Caitrin could rule Duntulm as well as any man could.

"Take care, lass." Taran stepped forward and embraced her. The gruffness in his voice belied the warmth in his eyes. His gaze shifted to Lachlann. A look passed between the two men. Adaira had been surprised to discover that they'd become friends of late. They'd taken to sparring every morning in the practice yard and had gone out hunting together two days earlier. "Ye too, Fraser."

Lachlann nodded before smiling. "Keep working on yer feints. Ye often go to the left and give yerself away."

Taran snorted. "And ye are overconfident to a fault. I'd watch that."

Lachlann laughed.

Rhona choked back a sob as she threw her arms around Adaira. "What will I do without ye?" The two of them had spent so much time together over the past fortnight that it had felt as if they'd gone back in time, to the days when neither had been wedded, to when their lives had followed the same path. But those days were gone now; this short period together had been a blessing—one that would always come to an end.

"Ye will be fine," Adaira whispered back. "I'm a nuisance anyway. I prattle too much and get on yer nerves."

"I'll never complain about yer prattling again ... I promise." Rhona pulled away and scrubbed at her tears. Her cheeks had gone blotchy, and her eyes were red-rimmed, yet she was still beautiful.

"Ye will visit me too?" Adaira asked, her gaze flicking between Rhona and Taran.

Taran nodded. "As soon as we can."

Heaving a deep breath, Adaira turned to the last person who waited to say goodbye to her.

Malcolm MacLeod had stood quietly, awaiting his turn. He watched Adaira, his grey eyes gleaming.

"Goodbye, Da," Adaira said softly. "I'll miss ye too."

His throat bobbed. "Will ye, lass?"

"Aye." Adaira stepped close. She meant it too. They'd been through much of late, and there had been times when she'd hated her father. But all that was behind them now. Since their wedding day, MacLeod had slowly thawed toward Lachlann, to the point where he could now look at him without glowering. However, when she looked into her father's eyes now, all Adaira could see was love.

"Thank ye for sending word to Gylen Castle," she whispered. "Yer blessing means a lot to me." She stepped close to her father then and threw her arms about him. His girth made him difficult to embrace, and for a moment, MacLeod just stood there, stone still. Adaira was about to pull back, disappointed that he had not responded, when his arms went about her and squeezed tight.

"Ye are a good girl," he rumbled, his voice thick with emotion. "Ye have yer mother's pure spirit and soft heart. She'd be proud to see ye now."

Adaira swallowed as more tears flowed, burning down her cheeks. Her father had never before said such a thing. He had no idea what his words meant to her.

When she pulled away, she saw that his eyes glittered with tears. However, a moment later, he shifted his gaze to Lachlann and his mouth compressed. "Make sure ye look after my daughter, Fraser."

Lachlann inclined his head. "With my life."

Adaira waved until her arm ached, until the four figures on the jetty were mere specks in the distance. Even then she continued to watch, her gaze upon Duntulm's lonely silhouette, perched upon the cliff edge.

The wind bit and clawed at her, stinging her wet cheeks. She pulled her fur mantle close and tried to ignore the emptiness in her chest. Lachlann sat next to her, but remained silent, giving her the time she needed. Meanwhile, the screech of gulls and the rhythmic splash of the oarsmen were the only sounds. Caitrin had asked four of her men to escort Adaira and Lachlann across the water and ensure they reached Argyle safely.

Eventually, Adaira sniffed and withdrew a scrap of linen. Embroidered and scented with rose, it had been a gift from Caitrin that morning. Adaira dried her face and turned to her husband. "I hated that," she whispered. "It feels as if someone just tore my heart out."

His gaze was soft as it met hers. "That's because ye love more deeply and true than anyone I've ever met," he replied, reaching out and brushing the last teardrops from her eyelashes. "There's no shame in it. It's why we all adore ye. A woman with yer capacity to love will never be alone."

A smile curved her mouth at his words. He spoke them with gruff sincerity.

"Thank ye for understanding," she whispered. "For putting up with my bossy sisters."

He huffed a laugh. "I'm glad ye had the chance to mend things with yer kin before ye went."

Adaira watched him, noting how his eyes shadowed then. Lachlann would not have such an opportunity with his brothers or father. He was dead to them now, or as good as dead if his path should ever cross theirs again.

"I'm sorry yer family is lost to ye," she murmured.

He shook his head, flashed her a smile, and put his arm around Adaira's shoulders, drawing her close. "Ye are my family now, Aingeal," he replied softly. "The only one I'll ever need."

The End.

From the author

I hope you enjoyed the second installment of THE BRIDES OF SKYE.

THE OUTLAW'S BRIDE combines a few of my favorite things. It's an 'on the road story' (I love road trips!) with a bit of adventure thrown in. The story is a twist on the 'savior/protector' theme. Lachlann Fraser was a great character to unravel. Initially, I was going to have him as the 'baby of the family' (like Adaira), but then I decided I'd make him a bit more alpha. At the start of the story, he's driven and ruthless, but I enjoyed the influence that Adaira wielded over him. I liked watching him wrestle with himself and choose love over ambition—and I wanted them both to have a profound influence on each other.

Adaira was quite a change from Rhona. She starts off as an innocent but grows up pretty fast when she realizes that the man she'd trusted has betrayed her. Her peppery temper surprised me (yes, characters do sometimes surprise authors!). Lachlann soon learns that although she's a gentle soul, she's not to be messed with!

I know you all LOVED Taran from Book #1. He was always going to be a hard act to follow for my next two heroes. Lachlann and Taran are nothing alike, but both men had difficult decisions to make. I hope you enjoyed Taran's role in this book—and he'll be appearing in Book #3 too.

Now you'll be wondering what happens to Caitrin. This story is going to be very angsty! There's 'history' between Caitrin and Alasdair so prepare yourself for quite a bit of conflict. Sit tight—Book #3, THE ROGUE'S BRIDE is next up!

Jayne x

THE ROGUE'S BRIDE

BOOK THREE
THE BRIDES OF SKYE

JAYNE CASTEL

Some things cannot be forgotten—or forgiven. The widow trying to forge a new life for herself. The man she once spurned bent on revenge.

Caitrin is a widow left to rule her husband's territory alone. The survivor of a loveless, unhappy marriage, she vows never to let another man control her. Instead, she finds herself in charge of a vast estate.

Alasdair MacDonald returns from war to discover his sister-in-law is chatelaine over his dead brother's lands—territory that now belongs to him.

Caitrin has haunted Alasdair's dreams from the moment she spurned him years earlier. He's never gotten over it, or forgiven her for breaking his heart by choosing his elder brother over him. Now he has a chance for vengeance, to take her young son and her newfound freedom from her. Only he soon discovers that his long-dormant feelings for the beautiful widow can't be so easily set aside.

Map

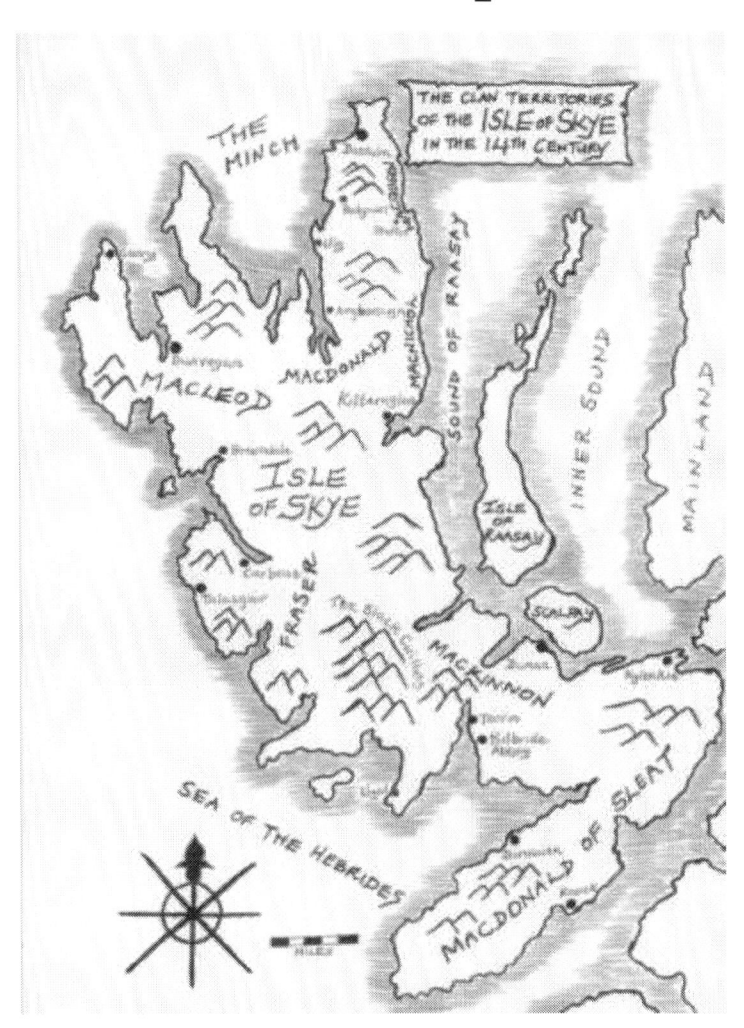

*Memories are dangerous things.
You turn them over and over,
until you know every touch and corner,
but still you'll find an edge to cut you.*
—Mark Lawrence

Chapter One

The Missive

Duntulm Castle, Isle of Skye, Scotland

Winter, 1347 AD

"NOT POTTAGE ... AGAIN?"

Duntulm's cook, an elderly woman with white hair pulled back into a bun and a face as wrinkled as walnut, frowned. "It's a good, wholesome meal, milady."

Caitrin shook her head. "We've had pottage and dumplings thrice over the past week. The men are starting to complain. They want some meat."

Cook's mouth thinned. "We need to watch our stores, milady. Spring is still some way off."

Caitrin suppressed a sigh. "We had the best harvest in years ... and the men brought back many deer and boar from their hunting trips in the autumn. Ye don't need to worry about us running out of food."

Cook wrung her hands, clearly unconvinced. The two women stood in Duntulm's kitchen, a warm space dominated by a long scrubbed oaken table. The sulfurous odor of over-cooked onion, cabbage, and turnip surrounded them.

A huge cauldron of vegetable pottage simmered over the hearth at one end of the kitchen.

Caitrin did sigh then, irritation rising within her. Despite that she and cook planned Duntulm's meals together every week, the woman often took it upon herself to change things. Today was one such occasion.

Caitrin was just about to speak once more when the door to the kitchen opened and a small dark-haired woman entered. Her hand-maid, Sorcha's, cheeks were flushed, as if she'd just come in from the cold.

"Lady Caitrin, a message has arrived for ye." The young woman's eyes were bright; they rarely received missives at Duntulm. The fortress sat upon Skye's isolated northern tip. They had no news of the outside world for weeks on end here. The maid clutched a scroll in her hand, holding it out to Caitrin. "It bears the MacDonald seal," she said, her voice edged in excitement.

Caitrin's belly contracted.

Schooling her features into an expressionless mask, she took the scroll. "Thank ye, Sorcha."

Her hand-maid hovered, her gaze curious. "Do ye need anything, milady?"

"Aye, please check on Eoghan. I'll be up to feed him later."

Sorcha nodded before bobbing into a curtsy. "Aye, milady."

The girl bustled over to the door. Small and curvaceous, Sorcha MacQueen was the bastard daughter of a neighboring chieftain. Unable to keep her under his own roof, MacQueen had given her to the MacDonalds as a hand-maid to the chieftain's wife. Caitrin had expected the young woman to be bitter over it, for her father had essentially washed his hands of her, yet Sorcha seemed resolutely cheerful.

Maybe it was a front. Perhaps, underneath it all, Sorcha harbored sadness and resentment. Caitrin should know—for *she* was adept at holding up a shield to keep others at bay.

She did so even now as she stood with cook, the roll of parchment in her hand. She dared not let her true feelings show.

Instead, she turned to cook.

The elderly woman was watching her intently, a shrewd look in her dark eyes.

"No more pottage for the next week, Briana," Caitrin said, using a sharp tone she knew cook would heed. "And put out salted pork and cheese with the noon meal today."

Not giving cook an opportunity to argue, Caitrin left the kitchen, her ring of iron chatelaine keys rattling at her waist.

Outside, she crossed the snow-covered bailey, her boots sinking into the pristine crust. Then Caitrin navigated the slippery steps and entered the keep. Drawing her fur mantle close, she made her way up to her solar. Even indoors it was freezing today. Her breathing steamed before her. The snow had lain for days now. However, Caitrin's thoughts were not on the weather, but upon the rolled parchment she carried.

She held it gingerly, as if it were a venomous adder, coiled, ready to sink its fangs into her. And when she entered the solar, she had to quash the instinct to throw the missive directly on the fire without reading it.

Sinking down onto a high-backed chair before the hearth, she turned the parchment over, her gaze alighting upon the MacDonald crest. It showed an armored hand clutching a cross.

"Per Mare Per Terras," she whispered the MacDonald clan motto. *By sea and land.* The clan was one of Scotland's largest, stretching its influence down most of the kingdom's western coast.

This message could be from any of them, she told herself as nervousness tightened her throat. *It isn't from him.*

Yet her gut told her differently. None of the other MacDonalds had reason to contact her in the dead of winter. There was only one man who had any business here, and she'd thought him dead.

Had prayed that he'd died in that bloody battle against the English.

It was an uncharitable thought—for she'd never wished him ill previously—but she'd hoped for it nonetheless. She wanted the past buried.

With trembling fingers, Caitrin broke the seal and unfurled the parchment. Then she drew in a deep, steadying breath, and began to read. Like her sisters, she'd learned her letters as a girl. A nun from Kilbride Abbey had traveled to Dunvegan, where Caitrin had grown up, and had patiently taught them. It was something her mother had insisted upon, although after her death the lessons ceased.

Caitrin was grateful that she could read and write. The skills had proved useful for her role as chatelaine. Even so, she'd never been quick at it. She took her time over reading now. The letter was written in a bold, masculine script. It was brief and formal, with a chill undertone.

Dear Lady Caitrin MacDonald, widow of Baltair MacDonald,

News has reached me of my brother's death. I am currently in Inbhir Nis but will travel to the Isle of Skye presently. Upon my return, I will take up my rightful role as chieftain. Please make Duntulm ready for my arrival.

Yer humble servant,
Alasdair MacDonald.

Caitrin stared at the words so hard that her vision blurred.

Alasdair MacDonald was alive; it was there written in ink before her. She knew her father had sent word to the mainland in the hope of tracking down the MacDonald heir—and he'd found him.

Caitrin swallowed, cast the parchment aside, and stood up. Alasdair MacDonald's return put her life at Duntulm at risk.

After Baltair's death, she'd felt adrift, worried for her future. But then she'd returned to Duntulm and assumed the role of chatelaine. She now ran the fortress—and she'd discovered that she was good at it. She liked dealing with the servants, speaking to the villagers, ordering supplies, and making plans for the year ahead.

Would Alasdair allow her and Eoghan to remain living here?

Heart pounding, Caitrin left the fireside, crossed to the south-facing window, and ripped open the shutters. Snow fluttered in, tickling her face. Caitrin leaned on the stone ledge and looked out at the wintry morning. A blanket of white covered the world, making everything look clean and bright. However, dark clouds rolled in from the sea, bringing with them fresh snow. The flakes swirled as they fell upon Duntulm, frosting the battlements beneath her.

Caitrin's solar sat high and gave her a commanding view of the rest of the rectangular-shaped keep. In the bailey below she caught sight of a stocky figure crunching through the snow. Alban MacLean, steward of the castle. He would need to be told that Baltair's brother was alive and returning to take up his role as chieftain.

Over these past months Alban—a gruff but kind-hearted man—had willingly shared rule over Duntulm. Initially, she'd been nervous that he and Darron MacNichol, who captained the Duntulm Guard, might try to overrule her. She was, after all, a woman alone—left in charge of a castle and a great tract of land. But they hadn't.

Caitrin leaned against the ledge and closed her eyes, letting the icy wind and feathery touch of snowflakes caress her face.

These last seven months had been a blessing. She'd had a reprieve from the life her father had set out for her. As the eldest, she'd been the first of her sisters to wed. Two years of misery later, she'd become a widow. But Baltair hadn't even been buried when her father—the MacLeod clan-chief—started talking of the need to find Caitrin a new husband once her mourning period passed.

Caitrin's breathing hitched. She couldn't bear the thought of being shackled to another man, of having to endure his touch, his demands. Being with Baltair had shattered all her illusions about what it meant to be a wife. Both her younger sisters, Rhona and Adaira, were wedded now, and happily so to men who loved them, but that wasn't to be her story.

Not all tales had a happy ending.

An ache grew in Caitrin's chest, and she reached up, rubbing at her breast bone with her knuckles. Opening her eyes, she stepped back from the window. She wished her sisters nothing but happiness, and yet thinking about them made her heart hurt from loneliness.

It was best not to dwell on such things.

"Good morning, Lady Caitrin." A tall warrior with silver-blond hair stepped forward to greet Caitrin as she made her way down the icy steps from the keep into the bailey. "Watch yer step."

Caitrin flashed Darron MacNichol, Captain of the Duntulm Guard, a tight smile. Darron could be a little over-protective at times, although she'd grown fond of him since coming to live here. Baltair had assigned Darron to escort her whenever she left the keep, and initially, Caitrin had worried the man would be as controlling as her husband. However, he wasn't. Darron merely shadowed her, letting her go where she willed.

He followed her now. Reaching the bailey, Caitrin's boots crunched on the fresh crust of snow, and she pulled the hood of her fur mantle up.

"Darron ... I've just received word that Alasdair MacDonald is alive," she said, leading the way toward the gates. "He'll return here soon to take Baltair's place."

Darron didn't reply immediately, and when Caitrin glanced his way, she saw his face was reflective. He was a handsome man, although somber. She rarely saw him smile.

"That is welcome news, milady," he finally replied, although his tone gave no clue as to how he really felt. Darron MacNichol could be infuriatingly inscrutable, like now.

"Aye." Caitrin looked away. "I shall go to the village now and let them know. The folk of Duntulm will be delighted."

She was aware of how flat her voice sounded, but she couldn't force joy into it.

They passed under the portcullis and crossed the drawbridge, taking the narrow road down to Duntulm village. The hamlet was a welcoming sight in the snow, a huddle of stacked-stone cottages with thatched roofs. The village kirk sat behind them, its peaked roof frosted with snow. To the north, the grey waters of The Minch, the stretch of sea that separated Duntulm from the isles beyond, appeared like a sheet of beaten iron against the leaden sky. It had stopped snowing at present, but one look at those ominous clouds warned Caitrin that the break in the weather wouldn't last long.

Caitrin swallowed a lump in her throat. She loved the folk here. She couldn't bear the thought of being sent away.

They were halfway down the hill when Darron spoke, his tone guarded. "Alasdair MacDonald isn't a harsh man, milady. He'll not turf ye out."

Caitrin huffed, keeping her gaze fixed upon the village below. Could the man read minds?

Darron was only trying to reassure her, but he'd just unwittingly made her feel worse. He didn't know of the history between her and the MacDonald heir.

Few besides her sisters did—and even they didn't know everything.

"I'm sure ye are right, Darron," she murmured. "Surely, Alasdair will treat Eoghan and me kindly."

Liar. She wasn't sure of that at all.

She wouldn't be surprised if Alasdair MacDonald now hated her.

Chapter Two

Too Much Ale

Kiltaraglen, Isle of Skye, Scotland

Two weeks later …

"I'LL BET YE three silver pennies that I'll have that wench in my bed by midnight."

Alasdair MacDonald snorted, bringing the tankard to his lips and taking a deep pull of ale. "A bit overconfident, aren't ye? The lass hasn't looked yer way all evening."

Across the table, Boyd raised an eyebrow. "Ye think ye stand a better chance?"

Alasdair smiled back. "Aye."

"We'll see about that." Boyd leaned back in his chair, blue eyes narrowing. "Challenge accepted."

Alasdair huffed, his gaze traveling across the crowded common room. 'The Merchant's Rest', Kiltaraglen's only tavern, was packed tonight. Drunken male voices boomed around them. Situated upon Skye's northeastern coast, the port village was just a day's ride from their destination. Their journey back to Duntulm was almost over.

His attention settled upon a blonde and comely lass, with milky skin and a twinkle in her eye, who was carrying a tray of food over to a table in the far corner. She was the innkeeper's daughter, and Boyd had been leering at her since they'd stepped through the threshold of the inn.

A smile curved Alasdair's lips. Boyd was about to lighten his purse. His second cousin, who hailed from the MacDonalds of Glencoe, got bumptious whenever he was full of drink.

Shifting his gaze back to Boyd, Alasdair saw he was smirking at him. Tall and lanky with a shock of red-gold hair, his cousin had a look in his eye that Alasdair knew well. He liked to turn everything, even wooing women, into a contest.

"Very well," Alasdair drawled. "But ye are not to sulk like a bairn when I win."

Around them, the din increased as two men started having an argument near the fire. The inn had a low ceiling, trapping in the pall of smoke and the odor of roast mutton, unwashed bodies, and damp wool.

Boyd cast him a withering look and raised his hand, catching the serving wench's attention. "Lass!" he called out, beckoning her to their table. "More ale ... can't ye see we're thirsty?"

The young woman retrieved a jug and made her way across the sawdust strewn floor toward them. Reaching the table, she gave both men a bold smile and set the jug down.

"We can't have ye going thirsty, lads," she greeted them. Her gaze then went to the two empty plates that sat between Alasdair and Boyd. "Was the supper to yer liking?"

"Delicious," Boyd replied, his tone so lascivious that Alasdair swallowed a laugh. His cousin was a liar. The mutton had been greasy and tough, and the cabbage overcooked.

The girl eyed Boyd, her smile widening. "Will ye be wanting anything else?"

"Why don't ye pour yerself an ale and take a seat on my lap?" Boyd favored her with a toothy grin. "Take a well-earned rest."

The innkeeper's daughter laughed, not remotely cowed by Boyd's boldness. "Da would beat me for idleness if I did such a thing," she replied with a shake of her head. The girl's attention then shifted to Alasdair, where it halted. "Yer face is familiar ... have I seen ye before?"

Alasdair held her gaze for a heartbeat before he allowed himself a slow smile. "I'm Alasdair MacDonald," he replied.

The young woman's eyes widened, her lips parting slightly. "Ye are Baltair MacDonald's brother?"

Alasdair's smile widened. He could feel Boyd's glare cutting into him. His cousin was a fool if he thought Alasdair wouldn't use his position to his advantage. Baltair had taught him how attractive women found a man with a title.

"Welcome home, milord," the lass said, her eyes gleaming with interest. "When ye didn't return after Baltair's death, we all thought ye lost ... that ye had fallen against the English."

"Well, I'm alive, as ye can see," he replied, saluting her with his tankard.

Her smile widened. "I shall have our best chamber prepared for ye, milord."

"Thank ye," he replied, his gaze holding hers. "And what is *yer* name?"

"Catriona," she said, her voice lowering. "Will *ye* be needing anything else?"

Catriona. The name, so similar to that of the woman he'd once loved, caused Alasdair's breathing to still.

Caitrin. Baltair's widow, and the woman who'd once spurned him. She was only a day's journey away now, currently ruling as chatelaine of Duntulm. He'd sent a letter ahead of him; she would be awaiting his arrival, although he didn't imagine she'd be happy to see him. She probably wished he'd been gutted on an English sword.

Alasdair blinked, shoving thoughts of Caitrin aside. Instead, he leaned forward, his mouth curving. "Aye, bring another jug of ale up to my room, Catriona," he murmured. "And if it pleases ye, join me up there later as well."

The young woman's gaze grew sultry. "Aye, milord," she murmured, inclining her head. "It *would* please me."

She turned then and walked away, her hips swaying tantalizingly. Alasdair watched her go. She was indeed bonny, and not so different in looks from his sister-in-law. An image of Caitrin MacLeod, lithe and blonde, her sea-blue eyes twinkling with laughter, assaulted him then. The wellbeing that the warmth, a full belly, and copious amounts of ale had given him, ebbed.

Irritation surged. Alasdair would have to face Caitrin again soon enough—but he didn't want her ruining this evening for him.

He turned his attention back to Boyd. His cousin sat back in his chair, arms folded across his chest, scowling. "Cheating bastard," he growled. "I should have known ye wouldn't fight fair."

It was Alasdair's turn to smirk now. "Stop whining and hand over those pennies."

Alasdair's eyes flickered open. The light, even dim as it was inside the bedchamber, assaulted him, and he squinted. It was early. The shutters were closed, and a fire still burned in the hearth, casting a golden veil over the inn's best room.

Rolling over, Alasdair stifled a groan. His mouth tasted rank, and his temples throbbed. Too much ale. Last night was little more than a blur of noise and fleeting images.

Alasdair's gaze slid to the back of the naked woman sleeping beside him, and he went still. More details of the night before flooded back. Their coupling had been rough and lusty. His wits addled with ale, Alasdair had almost forgotten to withdraw before the crucial moment, but somehow good sense had prevailed. The lass had seemed disappointed that he didn't spend his seed inside her, but Alasdair was relieved he hadn't.

He didn't want to father a bastard. Truth was, he didn't want to sire any bairns at all.

Catriona shifted, stretching as she awoke. She rolled over to face Alasdair, offering him a sleepy smile when she saw he was watching her. "Good morning, milord."

"Morning," Alasdair rasped. He sat up, wincing as pain thundered through his skull. What did they put in the ale in this place? He'd never awoken with such a sore head after a night of drinking.

Pushing aside the sheet, he rose to his feet and strode naked to where a pitcher of water sat on the sideboard. He picked it up and drank deeply, not even bothering to pour the water into a cup. He was parched and felt more than a little queasy.

As he lowered the pitcher, Alasdair noted that his hands trembled. He frowned. He'd hoped the tremors, which had begun shortly after the battle against the English months earlier, would stop.

It's just the ale, he assured himself. *I'll go easy on it in future.*

"It's still early," the girl crooned behind him. "Ye can have me again before the sun rises."

Her voice, although gentle, made Alasdair stifle a wince. He glanced over his shoulder, meeting her gaze. Sitting there amongst the tangled sheets, her blonde curls tumbling over her naked shoulders, Catriona was a bonny sight. Yet the desire to throw up the contents of his stomach was greater than that to spread her smooth thighs. His temples now throbbed as if someone had taken a hammer to them.

Swallowing down bile, Alasdair turned from her and grabbed hold of the clay washbowl. "Best ye leave me now, lass," he muttered. "I don't feel well."

Caitriona gave a soft huff of annoyance. A moment later he heard the slap of her bare feet on the flagstones. Then the door thudded as she departed the chamber.

The instant he was alone, Alasdair lurched forward and threw up into the bowl.

Chapter Three

Ye Are Looking Well

BOYD LET OUT a low whistle. "What a sight."
Alasdair followed his cousin's gaze west to where a mighty keep rose high against the pale sky. A smile stretched his face—for the first time all day. Last night's excesses had left him feeling wretched for the first half of the journey. Now, with his home in view, his head had finally stopped aching.

"Aye, welcome to Duntulm, cousin."

Boyd cut him a grin. "I used to think ye were exaggerating when ye told me the castle perched like an eagle's eyrie upon the edge of a cliff, but now I see ye weren't."

Alasdair's smile widened. "Aye … no fortress in Skye is as well-defended as Duntulm. All sides of the keep save one are bounded by the cliff-face."

Urging his horse into a brisk canter, Alasdair led the way across a hump-backed stone bridge. He ran a critical eye over the structure as he went, noting the crumbling sides on the western edge. He frowned. Things had been let go in Baltair's absence.

A stretch of tilled fields greeted him on the opposite side of the bridge, followed by a sprawl of cottages. A crowd of eager-faced men, women, and children gathered at the roadside to greet him.

"Alasdair!" An elderly man called out. "The MacDonald heir returns!"

Alasdair slowed his horse to a trot, his gaze sweeping across the villagers' faces. He saw tears on their cheeks and joy in their eyes. His throat constricted. He hadn't expected such a warm welcome. It was humbling to see the folk of Dunvegan had missed him. There had been times over the past months when he'd told himself no one would mourn him if he failed to return. He was glad to see he'd been wrong.

His mood dimmed then, like a shadow passing across the face of the sun.

Caitrin awaited in Duntulm Castle.

He didn't wish to have any contact with his sister-in-law—and yet a part of him, a glimmer of that lovestruck lad he'd once been, longed to see her.

Alasdair frowned, crushing the longing that curled, unbidden, up within him. Such instincts were weakness—they had to be quashed.

Crossing the village, he led the way up the hill toward the castle. Duntulm's high basalt curtain wall loomed before him, the MacDonald pennant fluttering in the sea-breeze. Unslinging his hunting horn, Alasdair raised it to his lips. The sound echoed over the hillside, reverberating off the stone fortress.

Alasdair MacDonald had just announced his arrival home.

Caitrin watched the horses' approach, and a sensation of sick, cold dread seeped over her.

Finally ... he's here.

She supposed that she should be relieved in a way—for the waiting was over at last—but the stone in the pit of her belly weighed her down.

The moment she'd been dreading, ever since the arrival of the letter, had come.

Caitrin picked up her skirts and left the solar. Halfway down the stairs to the bottom level of the keep, she met Sorcha.

"Milady," her hand-maid gasped, out of breath from her hurried climb. "They're here."

"I know," Caitrin replied curtly. "I'm on my way."

Sorcha stepped aside to let her pass, her blue eyes clouded with worry. She was the only one Caitrin had confided in about how she dreaded this moment. Alasdair MacDonald loomed like a specter, about to destroy her peace.

Caitrin continued down the stairwell and hurried out into the bailey to find the newly arrived party there.

A tall, dark-haired man dressed in chain-mail, fur, and leather, stood talking to Darron and Alban.

All three ceased their conversation and looked her way as she approached.

The captain and steward forgotten, Caitrin's gaze remained upon the newcomer.

She barely recognized him.

The Alasdair MacDonald she remembered was tall and lanky with a mop of dark hair and a sallow complexion. Baltair had been favored when it came to looks; his brother had seemed gawky and shy in comparison.

The man before her was lean but strong. Alasdair's shoulders seemed broader, the bony angles and gaunt face had filled out, and his hair had grown long. It now spilled over the shoulders of his fur cloak.

Caitrin's step faltered when his gaze met hers.

Eyes the color of peat—dark-brown, almost black—tracked her path. Predatory. More like Baltair and not like the playful lad who had once brought her a bouquet of meadow flowers.

His features though would never have Baltair's chiseled perfection. They were slightly sharp, hawkish.

He didn't smile as Caitrin approached. Didn't move.

Caitrin forced herself to keep moving, even if her instincts told her to turn and flee.

She kept walking until she was but three yards from him, and there she halted.

"Lady Caitrin." Darron acknowledged her with a respectful nod of his chin. He then stepped aside so that she could welcome the returning MacDonald heir. Alban did the same.

Caitrin swallowed, her mouth suddenly dry. His gaze was so intense that she felt stripped naked under it. She resisted the urge to reach up and check that her hair was tidy; in her rush downstairs she hadn't even thought to take note of her appearance.

Foolish woman, she chided herself. *Alasdair won't care what ye look like.*

It was true. The chill in his eyes spoke volumes. As she'd feared, he wasn't pleased to see her.

"My Lord Alasdair." She dipped into a curtsy and forced a bright smile. "Welcome home. It's good to see ye again. Did ye have a pleasant journey?"

It was cold outdoors, a grey, sunless late afternoon with a damp that made her bones ache—yet suddenly, Caitrin felt flustered. Heat flared in her cheeks, flaming hotter still when Alasdair MacDonald didn't answer.

Caitrin nervously wet her lips. "Milord?"

Alasdair smiled then, although there was still no warmth in his eyes. There was definitely a hard edge to him these days. Two and a half years had changed him. It was like looking into the eyes of a stranger.

"Good morning, Lady Caitrin." When Alasdair spoke, she finally recognized him. He'd always had a different voice to his brother: low and slightly gruff. "Ye are looking well."

Caitrin stared at him, once again resisting the urge to smooth her skirts and touch her hair. She felt unbalanced, strange.

And then Alasdair stepped aside and walked past her without another word. A lanky warrior with long red-gold hair, who'd been standing behind Alasdair, sauntered past her an instant later. The man favored Caitrin with a wink and a roguish grin before he followed Alasdair MacDonald into the keep.

Ye are looking well.

Alasdair ground his teeth together and forced himself not to run up the steps. The huge keep reared up before him.

Dolt. What had possessed him to say something so inane?

Better to say nothing at all than to put himself at a disadvantage with this woman.

Caitrin had always been able to do that—just one look from her and he used to get tongue-tied. It galled him to see that little had changed.

Alasdair walked through the keep's entrance hall and past the wide stone steps leading upstairs. Every nook, every stretch of stone here was as familiar to him as the back of his own hand. Alasdair had expected to be relieved to be home, for he'd missed Duntulm in his time away.

Yet he was distracted.

Even dressed in mourning black, her pale-blonde hair twisted up into a severe style, Caitrin was lovely. He'd been rooted to the spot as she walked toward him.

She'd changed since he'd seen her last. There was a grave dignity to her face, a seriousness in those sea-blue eyes that had been absent in the lass he'd so foolishly courted. Her figure was lusher—motherhood suited her. Baltair had sent word after Eoghan's birth—just a few lines: "I have a son, an heir." The letter hadn't reached Alasdair until after the battle, by which time Baltair was dead.

"Is something amiss?" Boyd asked, appearing at Alasdair's shoulder as he strode toward the doors of the Great Hall. "Ye look grim for a man who's just come home."

"Nothing's wrong." Alasdair cut him an irritated look. "I'm just weary."

Boyd favored him with a sly smile. "Ye never told me that yer brother's widow was so bonny."

"Is she?" Alasdair replied lightly. "I thought she looked like a crow garbed all in black."

Boyd snorted. "That's not what ye told her though, is it? Ye looked like someone had struck ye over the head with a mallet when she walked out into the bailey."

"Enough," Alasdair growled, losing patience. "I tire of yer flapping tongue."

Boyd merely grinned in response, knowing his point had been made.

Seated upon the dais, farther down the table from Alasdair MacDonald, Caitrin took a sip of wine. She barely tasted it, for nerves made her belly clench.

Around them, servants, led by cook and her assistant, Galiene, were bringing out supper: venison stew, oaten bread, and braised kale. A wall of noise surrounded Caitrin, reminding her why she preferred to take most of her meals in her solar.

She found it difficult to relax, to enjoy food, in this cavernous, noisy space.

Five of them sat at the chieftain's table this evening: Alasdair and the warrior with red-gold hair he'd introduced as his kinsman, Boyd MacDonald, along with Caitrin, Darron, and Alban.

Cook favored the chieftain with a wide smile as she placed a bowl of stew before him. "It's good to have ye home, milord," she greeted him. "I've made yer favorite supper."

Alasdair leaned back in his chair, returning her smile. "Thank ye, Briana. It's good to be back."

A few feet away, the steward, Alban, rose to his feet, holding a goblet of wine aloft. Around him, the hall went quiet. The excited chatter of voices settled as all gazes swiveled to the steward.

"Today we've been blessed," Alban announced, his low, gruff voice echoing across the hall. "Today, the MacDonald heir has returned to Duntulm ... raise yer cups. Let us welcome him home."

A chorus of "aye" and "welcome home" followed, thundering high into the rafters. Men and women rose to their feet, raising their cups. Those at the table followed suit, Caitrin included.

Alasdair inclined his head, his smile widening. For a moment, Caitrin glimpsed true warmth in his eyes. He might not be pleased to see her, but he was relieved to be home.

The toast ended, and the folk of Duntulm returned to their meals. Eating slowly, Caitrin found herself sneaking glances at Alasdair. He sat in the chieftain's chair, one arm resting casually upon the carven armrest as he swirled the wine in a goblet. Unlike the other men at the table, who all ate heartily, he'd barely touched his stew. Instead, his gaze had turned unfocused, as if he was suddenly leagues from here.

"Milord?" The steward leaned forward, trying to catch the chieftain's attention. "Alasdair?"

The chieftain blinked, his gaze snapping back to the present. "Aye, Alban?"

"I trust ye had a good trip home?"

"Aye ... the weather was against us ... but that's what happens when ye travel in winter." Alasdair took a sip of wine, fixing Alban with a level look. "How have things been in Duntulm since my brother's death?"

"Quiet, milord," the older man replied with a smile.

"And the harvest ... was it good?"

The steward nodded. "Aye, last summer was the warmest in years. Our stores will see us and the village safely through into spring." Alban glanced at Caitrin then. "Lady Caitrin oversaw the harvest ... she worked tirelessly and made sure every last ear of barley was reaped."

Alasdair's mouth quirked, his attention shifting to Caitrin for the first time since he'd taken his seat at the table. "Is that so?"

"Aye," Alban replied. "Lady Caitrin has managed Duntulm admirably as chatelaine in yer absence."

"That's good to hear."

Caitrin tensed. Was it only her who could hear the mocking edge to Alasdair's voice? She still had difficulty accepting that this swarthy, sharp-featured man was actually Baltair's younger brother. He had a rakish, careless edge that warned her to be wary of him.

Glancing around the table, she saw that Alban and Darron looked unperturbed, while Boyd MacDonald wore a slightly bored expression. Maybe she was imagining things.

"I noticed on the way in that the Cleatburn Bridge is in a poor state, Alban." Alasdair turned his attention back to the steward. "Why is that?"

Alban's brow furrowed. "We had heavy rains in late autumn, milord. It did some damage."

Alasdair met the steward's eye, and Caitrin saw his jaw firm, his dark gaze glint. "Then, we need to repair it."

Chapter Four

Trouble Sleeping

AN ICY WIND gusted in from the northeast, tugging at Alasdair's fur mantle and stinging his exposed cheeks. He hadn't forgotten how cold the wind got up here, on Skye's exposed northern tip. It could cut to the bone. Around him the last of the light was draining from the western sky, deepening the chill. He'd come straight here after supper, even though night had almost fallen.

Pulling up the collar of his mantle, Alasdair stepped forward, his gaze settling upon the headstone in the center of the windswept kirkyard.

All that remained of his elder brother.

Alasdair studied the grave. In the fading light, he could barely make out Baltair's name etched there. The stone had only been in the ground nearly eight moons, and already moss was starting to creep up its sides. After all that had happened, it felt as if his brother had been dead years, not months.

It had taken a while for news of Baltair's death to reach him on the mainland. Alasdair had been in Inbhir Nis when it arrived. He'd felt numb as he'd read the words sent from Malcolm MacLeod. Baltair had fallen in a skirmish against Clan-chief MacLeod's foes, the Frasers of Skye.

Once the shock faded, grief had surfaced. However, it was a sensation mixed with guilt. After his elder brother wed Caitrin, Alasdair had bitterly resented him. Everything fell into Baltair's arms. He'd been good-looking and charismatic—and he ruled northern Skye. Caitrin hadn't been the only woman upon the isle who'd wanted to wed him.

Alasdair's mouth thinned. Women were so predictable. They didn't see past the veneer. Unlike them, he wasn't blind to his brother's faults. Baltair could be insufferably arrogant and had a cruel edge that Alasdair, two years his junior, had often borne the brunt of when they'd been bairns.

But still, he was his brother. The only kin he'd had left.

Alasdair stood there for a while, letting the dark curtain of night settle over the world. He was alone in the kirkyard save a pair of ravens perched on a nearby gravestone. They watched him with cold beady eyes.

He ignored the birds, pulling his cloak tighter as a particularly hefty gust of wind ripped across the hillside.

It was time to go. He'd expected to feel something other than an odd emptiness upon visiting his brother's grave. But he shouldn't have been surprised really, for he wasn't himself these days.

Alasdair sighed, his breath steaming before him in the gelid air, turned from the grave, and strode out of the kirkyard.

At the entrance he found Boyd waiting for him.

His friend had accompanied him here but had then hung back while Alasdair visited his brother's grave.

Boyd nodded as Alasdair approached before falling into step with him. For once, his cousin didn't rib him or offer a flippant comment; something Alasdair felt grateful for. Wordlessly, the two men made their way through the village, down an unpaved street flanked with low stone cottages. The aroma of roasting fowl wafted out from one of the homes, and within another, a woman started singing.

"It's a nice place this," Boyd commented, breaking the silence. "I can see why ye were keen to come home."

Alasdair cast him a sidelong look. "Ye will stay on then?"

Boyd wasn't a close relative, but they'd struck up a friendship over the past few months. Boyd hadn't seemed in a hurry to return to Glencoe after the war, and so Alasdair had invited him back to Duntulm.

Boyd grinned. "Aye, if ye will let me."

"Ye can remain under my roof ... as long as ye earn yer keep."

Boyd rolled his eyes. "Ye are going to put me to work?"

"Aye ... the Duntulm Guard is looking a bit sparse. Talk to Captain MacNichol in the morning, and he'll get ye kitted out."

The two men left the village and took the path that wound up the hill toward the keep. Fires burned upon the walls, staining the pitted rock a deep gold.

"It's good to be here," Boyd said finally, his voice uncharacteristically serious. "Ye could almost think that disaster at Durham never happened ... that the English didn't whip our arses."

Alasdair stifled a wince. "Aye, but they did," he murmured.

Alasdair walked into the chieftain's solar and paused. Burning sconces threw long shadows across the stone walls, welcoming him, and yet he felt like he didn't belong here. It didn't feel right standing in the solar without either his father or brother present.

Shaking his head to rid himself of the sensation, Alasdair pushed the door shut behind him. This solar, and the adjoining bed-chamber, were now his. He'd get used to his new quarters soon enough.

A warm, masculine space surrounded him. Deerskin rugs covered a paved floor, and heavy tapestries depicting scenes of war hung from the walls. A great stag's head sat mounted above a huge hearth, where a lump of peat glowed, throwing out a considerable amount of heat. The stag had been his father's prize. Eoghan MacDonald had been a keen hunter, but, in the end, it was a stag hunt that claimed his life.

Crossing to the large oaken table that dominated the solar, Alasdair poured himself a goblet of wine. He took a sip, the flavor of rich spicy plum sliding down his throat and warming the pit of his belly. He still couldn't stomach the idea of ale, not after the excesses of the night before, but he enjoyed the wine. It took the edge off the tension that had plagued him all day.

This hadn't been an easy homecoming. Baltair was gone, and the woman Alasdair had once ached for was now chatelaine of Duntulm. Despite that he'd thought long and hard about how to deal with her, Caitrin's presence unsettled him.

He hadn't seen her since supper. When he returned from the kirkyard, she'd already retired for the evening. That was good, for even the sight of Caitrin made it difficult to concentrate. Boyd, the shrewd bastard, hadn't missed his reaction to her—which meant Caitrin had probably noticed it too.

Alasdair muttered a curse and downed the rest of his wine in a long gulp.

He needed to harden his heart, to cool his nerves and remind himself that he couldn't stand the woman now.

He had her exactly where he wanted her. Her position as chatelaine was vulnerable. One word from him and she'd have to pack her bags and return to Dunvegan, and her overbearing father. Alasdair remembered Malcolm MacLeod well, and he'd also noted the way Caitrin had stiffened when he'd questioned Alban at supper rather than her. She was proud of her role here. She wanted to stay.

He knew exactly where to start his campaign against her.

Setting the goblet down, Alasdair wandered through into his bed-chamber. Another, smaller, hearth burned there too. A huge four-poster bed dominated the room. Alasdair eyed it warily as he started to undress.

Baltair and Caitrin shared that bed.

The thought made him clench his jaw, a surge of vindictive fury rushing through his veins. The sensation galvanized him. He needed to keep reminding himself of what Caitrin had done to him, of what she'd taken from him.

Mist surrounded Alasdair, closing in on him. He stood ankle-deep in mud, his claidheamh mor impossibly heavy in his hand. Nearby, a man was screaming for mercy. Raw sobs followed, and then the dull, wet sounds of death being dealt.

Alasdair tried to rush to his countryman's side, his sword swinging. And yet he couldn't move. His legs and arms were paralyzed.

Terror pulsed through him. His heart felt as if it would leap from his chest, it was beating so hard.

Figures emerged from the mist. They were coming for him—but he couldn't fight back.

Alasdair sucked in a deep, ragged breath, his eyes flying open.

The mist receded, as did the cries of the dying. He was back in his own bed, in his bed-chamber lit by the fading glow of the hearth.

Chest heaving, Alasdair pushed himself up into a sitting position. It wasn't warm in the chamber, yet he dripped with sweat.

He dragged a shaking hand through his hair and forced himself to take deep, steadying breaths.

Satan's cods. He was sick of these nightmares. They plagued him. Ever since the battle, he'd had trouble sleeping, and whenever he did manage to fall into a deep slumber, his mind transported him back to the battlefield and that cool, misty October morning.

When the whole world had gone to hell.

Caitrin observed Alasdair over the rim of her mug of goat's milk.

He was pale, his eyes hollowed with fatigue.

"Milord," she spoke up, drawing his attention. "Are ye unwell?"

He cast her a look of thinly-veiled irritation. "No."

"It's just ..." Caitrin broke off here, aware that Boyd had glanced up from smearing honey over a wedge of bannock. Likewise, Alban and Darron both looked her way. "... ye look a bit peaky this morning."

"Maybe last night's supper didn't agree with him," Boyd quipped with a wink at Caitrin.

"The supper was fine," Alasdair growled, pouring himself a cup of milk from a pitcher in the center of the table. "I'm just tired."

"Ye have trouble sleeping?" Caitrin knew she shouldn't pry, for Alasdair was now viewing her with a jaundiced eye. Yet she'd fallen into the habit of helping those around her since becoming chatelaine—and she wanted to prove herself useful now.

"Aye ... sometimes," Alasdair replied, his gaze cautious.

"I can ask a servant to brew ye a drink with valerian root before bed," she suggested. "It helps with sleep."

Alasdair nodded, although his frown made it clear he wished her to drop the subject. Caitrin lowered her gaze to the buttered slice of bannock before her. Anxiety churned in her belly as she resumed eating. She'd awoken just before dawn, resolved to prove her worth to Alasdair MacDonald, but instead had succeeded only in annoying him.

"Who has been managing the accounts in my absence?" the chieftain broke the heavy silence that had settled over the table.

Caitrin glanced up to see that Alasdair was looking in Alban's direction. Irritation rose within her, dousing the nerves. Just like the evening before, he was deliberately favoring the steward, as if she had no responsibilities here.

Caitrin cleared her throat. "I have been … although Alban often sits with me to ensure I have the numbers correct."

Alasdair's peat-dark eyes swiveled back to her, his mouth curving. It was his first smile since he'd sat down at the table, and it softened his face considerably. "Of course … I'd forgotten that ye know yer letters."

Caitrin pursed her lips. "Aye, ye once teased me for it … said that lasses were no good at such things."

Surprise flared on his face. Did he think she'd forgotten?

She and Alasdair were almost the same age—born in the same year just a month apart. Before that fateful day in Dunvegan's garden, when she'd rejected him, they'd been friends since childhood. Years earlier, when they were both around nine winters old, she'd told Alasdair that a nun from Kilbride Abbey was teaching Caitrin and her sisters to read and write. Alasdair had roared with laughter.

"Aye … I did." Alasdair watched her for a long moment, his gaze pinning her to the spot. "Shall we see if I was right?"

Caitrin frowned. *Ye weren't.* The words boiled up inside her, but she choked them back. He was deliberately provoking her.

Alasdair smiled. "Meet me in my solar mid-morning," he said smoothly, "and we shall go over the accounts together." He paused here and reached for the last wedge of bannock on the tray before him. "Bring my nephew with ye … I want to meet Eoghan."

Chapter Five

Taken Seriously

CAITRIN OPENED THE ledger and tried to ignore the man who'd just pulled up a seat next to her.

Alasdair was sitting too close—it unnerved her. She was keenly aware of the heat of his body and the scent of his skin mixed with that of leather. In the past, his presence hadn't affected her like this. She didn't understand why it did now.

It was the last thing she needed.

They weren't alone in the solar. Alban wasn't present, but Boyd had joined them instead. Dressed in the leather armor of the Duntulm Guard, the warrior leaned against the window sill, cup of ale in hand. Despite that it was a chill day outdoors, Alasdair had opened the shutters to the small window looking south. However, a few feet away, a fire burned vigorously in the hearth. The warmth enveloped Caitrin in a soft blanket, although it didn't take the edge off her nerves.

She'd never liked the chieftain's solar, and after Baltair's death had rarely set foot inside it, preferring to keep to her own quarters instead. This chamber, with its masculine aggression, reminded her of her husband.

They weren't pleasant memories.

Caitrin cast Alasdair a quick glance and found him watching her, a lazy smile curving his lips.

She wished he wouldn't look at her like that.

"What would ye like to see first?" she asked, all business.

"I'd like to see my nephew," he replied. "Where is he?"

"He'll be here shortly … my hand-maid has just gone to fetch him." Caitrin drew in a deep breath in an attempt to calm her rapidly beating heart. She didn't like that both men were now watching her. Why did Boyd have to be here at all? "In the meantime, let's get started."

"Very well," Alasdair drawled. "Turn to last year's expenses."

Caitrin reached out and leafed back through the pages, smoothing them open at the year's beginning. She then pushed the ledger toward Alasdair so that he wouldn't need to move any closer to her to read it.

She watched his hawkish profile as he leaned forward, his gaze tracking down the page. After a moment he paused. "Ye bought a lot of grain from MacLeod last autumn … oats especially. Why?"

"We didn't have a large harvest of oats," Caitrin replied without hesitation before she met Alasdair's eye. "Baltair had decided to use the lower fields for kale and cabbage instead."

Alasdair raised an eyebrow before shifting his attention back to the ledger. Caitrin watched him continue to read, although with each passing moment she could feel her spine growing more rigid. She hadn't missed the challenge in his voice.

"Ye have made a mistake here," he said after a pause, his finger tracing down one column to the sum at the bottom. "Twelve, eight, thirty-five, and twenty … does not equal seventy-eight."

"It's seventy-five," Boyd piped up with a laugh.

Caitrin's cheeks flamed. Alban had helped her do the calculations. Any errors belonged to them both. However, she wouldn't mention him here—it would only make her look as if she was making excuses for herself. Fury coiled up within her when she saw Alasdair flash Boyd a conspirator's grin. "Aye."

"It was an honest mistake," Caitrin said stiffly, forcing down her ire, "and one that I shall correct."

"See that ye do," Alasdair replied.

A knock at the door interrupted them, bringing Caitrin a reprieve.

"Enter," Alasdair called out, and an instant later Sorcha appeared, carrying Eoghan in her arms. The bairn was awake, clutching to Sorcha, his eyes wide as he surveyed the two strangers in the room.

Next to her, Caitrin sensed Alasdair grow still. She glanced his way to see that his gaze had fixed upon the lad. Eoghan stared back, equally fascinated.

"God's bones," Alasdair murmured. "He looks the image of Baltair."

Caitrin grew even tenser at this comment. She knew it to be the truth, yet hated that Eoghan's similarity to his father was the first thing folk noted when they set eyes on the lad.

"That's not surprising," she replied.

Alasdair cut her a glance, gaze widening at the sharpness of her tone. "Doesn't that please ye?" he asked, his dark brows knitting together. "At least ye have something to remember my brother by."

Caitrin didn't reply. She didn't trust herself to. However, she saw a shadow move in Alasdair MacDonald's eyes and realized that he'd drawn his own conclusions. "The grieving widow, eh?" he murmured.

Caitrin swallowed, dropping her gaze. She'd not engage him on this subject, not now with Boyd and Sorcha present. If he wanted to know about the state of her marriage to Baltair, he could show her some respect by bringing it up in private.

"Would ye like to hold the lad, milord?" Sorcha asked, favoring Alasdair with a warm smile.

Caitrin bit back the urge to say he wouldn't. Her hands clenched on her lap, her fingernails biting into her palms. Yet Alasdair pushed back his chair and rose to his feet. "Very well. Give the lad here."

"He's not used to strangers," Caitrin said tightly. Her body coiled as Sorcha handed Eoghan to Alasdair. Any moment now, Eoghan would start wailing.

"Aye ... but I'm kin," Alasdair replied, not bothering to glance her way.

Swaddled in lambswool, Eoghan stared up at his uncle, chubby fingers reaching forward to explore his leather vest. To Caitrin's surprise, the lad's face didn't crumple. Instead, he favored Alasdair with a beautiful, wide smile.

And in response, Alasdair MacDonald's own face transformed. For a few instants, he wore a soft expression, his dark eyes glowing with tenderness. "It's good to meet ye, Eoghan," he murmured. "Ye never met yer grandsire, but it's a fine name ye have inherited."

"The lad's taken a shine to ye, Alasdair," Boyd noted, grinning.

Alasdair snorted, never taking his gaze off the bairn. "Blood is blood ... the lad knows it too."

"I've never seen Master Eoghan so fascinated with someone, milord," Sorcha said. "Maybe he does sense ye are his uncle."

Alasdair smiled. "Aye ... I'm the closest thing ye have to a father now, wee Eoghan." He tickled the lad under the chin, and the bairn gave a gurgling laugh. "And one day ye will inherit all of this."

Caitrin drew in a deep breath, attempting to quell her irritation and failing. "I'm sure ye will have bairns of yer own, milord," she said, unable to hold her tongue any longer. "Ye won't need Eoghan to carry on the MacDonald line."

Alasdair tore his gaze from his nephew then, his attention fixing upon her. "I don't intend to wed," he said, his voice hardening, "and I won't be siring any bairns. Eoghan is the sole MacDonald heir."

A chill feathered down Caitrin's spine. Why wasn't he planning to take a wife? The proprietary edge to Alasdair's voice made her uneasy.

He handed Eoghan back to Sorcha. Meanwhile, Boyd caught the handmaid's eye and smiled. "We haven't been introduced ... Boyd MacDonald of Glencoe at yer service."

"My name is Sorcha MacQueen," she replied with a shy smile.

"Of the MacQueens of Skye?"

The girl's smile faltered. "Aye ... Chieftain MacQueen is my father."

Boyd inclined his head, his own smile widening "Pleased to make yer acquaintance, lass." His gaze held hers. "Since I'm new to Duntulm ... ye might want to give me a tour of the keep later."

"Captain MacNichol can do that," Caitrin cut in, her voice sharp.

Boyd shrugged, his gaze never leaving the hand-maid. "I'd prefer a prettier guide, milady."

"Thank ye, Sorcha," Alasdair cut in, drumming his fingers on the tabletop. His voice was edged with impatience. "Ye can take Eoghan back to his quarters now. We have work to do."

Sorcha nodded, dropped into a curtsy, and quit the solar. Caitrin noted that her hand-maid now wore a flustered expression, her cheeks pink. After her departure, Alasdair returned to the table and took his seat next to Caitrin once more.

Caitrin met his eye and, seeing the challenge there, tensed. This meeting thus far hadn't been pleasant—and she wagered the mood wasn't about to improve.

Alasdair favored her with a wintry smile. "Shall we return to the accounts?"

"Arrogant cur. He missed no opportunity to make me look small!" Caitrin knuckled away a tear that trickled down her cheek. The stress of the last two days was starting to take its toll.

Sorcha's blue eyes widened. "Milady," she gasped. "I'm sure the chieftain meant no offense."

"Oh, he did."

Caitrin snatched up the woolen tunic she'd been knitting for Eoghan and viciously started to unravel her last session's work. There were imperfections in the knit, a few small holes that annoyed her. She took vindictive pleasure in undoing her hours of labor. *Good*—she preferred anger to tears.

"He went through those accounts, line by line, and picked on the slightest things." She paused in her unraveling and fixed her hand-maid with a look of fury. "He even questioned the amount of produce we've set aside to pay this year's cáin."

Sorcha's brow furrowed, setting down the embroidery she'd just started. "Isn't it enough?"

"Of course it is," Caitrin huffed. "I'm a clan-chief's daughter ... I know exactly how much yearly tribute the king requires of his vassals. The cáin is sufficient."

"But the chieftain doesn't think so?" Sorcha appeared genuinely concerned. Caitrin clenched her jaw. She knew that her handmaid's loyalty would always go first to her master, but even so, it grated upon Caitrin.

A woman was never taken seriously in a man's world, even by other women.

"It doesn't matter what he thinks," Caitrin muttered. Yet as she said those words, a weight settled in the pit of her belly. Unfortunately, Alasdair MacDonald's opinion did matter—and she needed to try harder if she wanted to stay on as chatelaine.

Chapter Six
Too Far

CAITRIN FROWNED, PEERING into the bubbling cauldron of sulfurous, over-cooked vegetables. "I thought we already planned out all the meals for the week?"

"Aye, milady ... we did."

Caitrin glanced over her shoulder, at where cook and her two assistants were busy kneading bread dough on the large table that dominated the kitchen. "Pottage wasn't on the list."

Cook gave her a wary look. "No, but I decided we should have it for today's noon meal. We had old vegetables that needed using up."

Caitrin inhaled deeply. She wasn't in the mood for this. Tired and on edge, Caitrin had gotten up well before dawn over the past week to redouble her efforts as chatelaine. She didn't want to give Alasdair MacDonald any excuse to criticize her.

But now, Briana wanted to cross swords with her—again.

After their last confrontation, she'd thought she and cook had reached an understanding: they made a plan of the week's noon meals and suppers, and then cook followed it. But, clearly, Briana wasn't ready to do as she was told.

"Ye need to start heeding me, Briana," she said finally, careful to keep her tone low, even though she was inwardly seething. "I don't plan the keep's meals with ye because I have nothing better to do with my time. I've made an inventory of the stores and know exactly what needs using up and what doesn't. Those vegetables would have easily kept another few days."

Cook stared back at Caitrin, a mutinous expression settling upon her face. An older woman named Galiene, and a red-headed lass who worked alongside Briana, now exchanged nervous glances. Cook then drew herself up, holding Caitrin's eye boldly. "Ye don't have to plan the meals with me anymore, milady."

Caitrin's gaze narrowed. "Excuse me?"

"I don't need yer help."

Anger curled up like wreathing smoke within Caitrin. Her patience was nearing its limits now. "I care not what ye think ye need," she growled. "As chatelaine, the running of the household is my responsibility ... and that includes this kitchen. Ye take orders from me."

"No, I don't." Cook blurted, the words tumbling out of her now she'd worked up the courage. "The chieftain rules here, milady ... and he says I can prepare whatever meals I choose."

Caitrin went still. "Ye have spoken to Alasdair about this?"

Cook pursed her lips before nodding. "Aye, and he agrees that ye have no need to meddle in my affairs." The victorious gleam in cook's eyes made Caitrin want to slap her face.

Wordlessly, for rage had momentarily rendered her speechless, Caitrin walked to the kitchen door, aware of the three pairs of eyes tracking her path. At the threshold, she halted, swiveled around, and pinned cook under a hard stare. "We'll see about that."

How dare he?

Caitrin stormed across the bailey toward the archway leading out of the castle. It was a chill windy day outdoors, but she was so incensed that she hadn't even gone back inside to fetch her cloak. Instead, she marched over the drawbridge and down the hill toward the village, ignoring the cold that bit into her flesh through her kirtle and léine.

She knew where to find Alasdair MacDonald. He and a group of men had spent the last day beginning work on shoring up the Cleatburn Bridge.

Reaching the bottom of the hill, she strode through the village, attracting curious looks from folk she passed. It was an odd thing to see the Lady of Duntulm out on such a chill day without a winter mantle—or an escort. Darron usually shadowed her whenever she left the keep.

Caitrin, who often liked to wave and stop to chat with the villagers, ignored them this morning. She was too upset to focus on anyone right now—other than the man who'd taken vindictive pleasure in thwarting her ever since his return.

The bridge loomed up ahead, and Caitrin spied the outlines of men working on it. She recognized Darron first, for his pale-blond hair gleamed even in the winter's dull light. He'd just picked up a stone from the back of a wagon, and was about to turn and carry it into the waters of the Cleatburn, when he spied Caitrin approach.

Darron's brow furrowed. "Good morn, Lady Caitrin." His gaze shifted behind her, his eyes narrowing when he realized she was alone. "Ye should have asked one of the guards to escort ye down here."

Irritation surged within Caitrin. She didn't need MacNichol or one of his men following her about.

"Morning, Captain MacNichol," she replied curtly, deliberately ignoring his comment. "Where is the chieftain?"

Darron's frown deepened. "Is something amiss, milady?"

"Just answer me, please."

Darron jerked his head to the left, indicating that the man she wanted was behind him. He then stepped to one side.

Caitrin's gaze shifted to the water, to where Alasdair and Boyd worked, clearing debris from around the bridge's stacked-stone pillars. Both men were shirtless, their braies sodden. Mud splattered their torsos and arms as they wielded heavy shovels.

Without realizing she was doing so, Caitrin found herself inspecting Alasdair's half-naked body. He was lean and strong, the light dusting of hair across his muscular chest tapering down to a hard, flat stomach. Even through her fury, she acknowledged that he was an attractive, virile sight.

Angrily, she shoved the thought aside.

Sensing the weight of her stare, Alasdair looked up, and their gazes fused. An instant later, he smiled. "Lady Caitrin. Have ye come down to oversee the repairs?"

Boyd laughed at this. "Keeping an eye on ye, is she?"

Caitrin clenched her hands by her sides. Their mockery hardened her temper into something dangerous. "I've come from the kitchen." She bit out the words, aware that the surrounding men had all stopped work and were watching her. She didn't care. Let them gawk. "It appears ye have told cook that I have no right to oversee the meals that are prepared for the keep?"

Alasdair's mouth curved. "Aye, and what of it? Briana's been around since my father was a lad. She doesn't take kindly to having another woman oversee her."

"We were getting along fine before ye returned home ... milord."

"Really?" He gave her an arch look. "That's not what she said."

"We'd made a truce," Caitrin snarled. "Briana's a fine cook but manages the supplies poorly. She'd have the keep eating boiled turnip and stale bannocks while she let fresh meat rot in the stores."

This comment brought a scattering of laughter from the surrounding men. Even Darron raised a smile. They all knew it was the truth. Cook was stingy with supplies, as if she'd paid for them out of her own purse.

"My father and Baltair never found fault with her," Alasdair replied. His tone was mild although his gaze had hardened. "Maybe ye are too overbearing."

Overbearing.

Caitrin drew in a shuddering breath. "I'm merely doing my duty as chatelaine," she finally managed, her voice trembling with the force of the rage that caused a red mist to cloud her vision. "Why don't ye let me?"

A heavy silence settled, broken only by the gurgle and chatter of water running over stones and the whistle of the wind. However, Caitrin barely heard those noises, for she could discern little over the thundering of her pulse in her ears. She was so angry that she felt sick.

Alasdair watched her for a long moment before pushing strands of hair from his face with his forearm. "Go back to the keep, Caitrin," he said, his voice low and firm. "We'll discuss this later."

Caitrin swallowed hard. "No, I—"

"Didn't my brother teach ye any manners?" he growled. "Go back ... *now*."

They stared at each other, before fear flickered up within Caitrin, penetrating the anger that had shielded her till now. The mention of his brother turned her blood cold. Baltair wouldn't have stood for such defiance. He'd have waded out of the burn and backhanded her across the face for arguing with him.

Tears of frustration and rage blurred Caitrin's vision. She wondered then how she'd ever once called Alasdair MacDonald a friend. The past years had altered him, turned him callous and cruel.

He'd been wanting to anger her, and in coming down to the bridge, she'd played straight into his hands. She knew though that continuing to rage at him out here would only end badly for her.

Swallowing a sob, Caitrin spun on her heel, picked up her skirts, and fled.

Alasdair watched Caitrin's eyes glisten, her jaw tighten, and wondered if she'd obey him. To his surprise, his breathing quickened. He almost wished she wouldn't. It would give him the excuse to throw her over his shoulder and carry her back up to the keep—an excuse to touch her.

She was beautiful this morning, her sea-blue eyes gleaming with ire, her supple body encased in flowing black. He itched to feel her softness against him.

But a heartbeat later, she turned and hurried away. He could see, from the stiffness of her posture and her uneven gait, that she was upset. Her long blonde hair, braided in a long plait down her back, bounced between her shoulder blades as she walked.

Watching her go, a sensation of loss washed over Alasdair.

He'd enjoyed that altercation—far more than he should have.

"That's quite a temper the lass has on her," Boyd observed.

Alasdair snorted. "Aye ... I'm surprised Baltair didn't whip her for her adder's tongue."

Silence followed this comment.

Alasdair glanced around him to see that only Boyd was grinning. Most of the surrounding men wore hard expressions, while one or two looked horrified. Darron MacNichol was actually glowering at him.

Alasdair went still. Those words had only been said in jest—but he'd misread his audience it seemed.

After a hard morning's work, the men made their way back up to the keep for the noon meal. Captain MacNichol fell in step with Alasdair as they walked up the hill.

Glancing across at him, Alasdair saw that the captain was watching him, his expression shuttered.

Alasdair frowned. "What is it, MacNichol?"

Darron's own gaze narrowed. "Ye should know that Lady Caitrin would never to have spoken to Baltair like that," he said quietly.

"Really?" Alasdair didn't bother to temper the scorn in his voice.

"Aye ... she was afraid of yer brother."

A pause followed. "Did he beat her?"

"If he did, it was behind closed doors."

"But it wasn't a happy union?"

Darron pursed his mouth.

"Answer me, MacNichol."

"They didn't speak much, milord ... it seemed to me that Baltair ignored Lady Caitrin for the most part."

Alasdair digested this news. It didn't overly surprise him. Baltair had never had much use for women beyond swiving them.

Loosing a sigh, Alasdair cast a glance up at where the castle loomed before them. He'd enjoyed putting Caitrin in her place, humiliating her in front of his men, but an uneasiness had settled over him in the aftermath.

Vengeance didn't taste as sweet as he'd expected. He felt strangely empty, disappointed.

Maybe he'd taken things too far.

Chapter Seven
Taking Instruction

ALASDAIR SWALLOWED A mouthful of pottage and stifled a grimace. It was awful: overcooked with a faintly acrid taste as if the bottom of the pot had burned. Alasdair frowned. How was this possible? Cook usually served up delicious meals.

Next to him Boyd also tasted the pottage, his face screwing up. Mumbling a curse, he reached for his goblet of wine to wash it down. "Foul," he muttered. Likewise, the others at the table looked similarly unimpressed with the fare before them.

"I thought cook agreed not to serve up this slop anymore," Alban grumbled. The steward cast Caitrin a questioning look, but she didn't meet his eye. Instead, the chatelaine appeared fascinated with the piece of bread she was buttering.

Caitrin hadn't made eye contact with any of them since taking a seat at the table for the noon meal.

"Lady Caitrin?" Alban, who hadn't been down at the bridge earlier that morning, spoke up once more. "Didn't ye have a word with cook?"

Caitrin did glance up then. "Aye," she replied, her tone clipped, "but it appears I'm to have no say in what meals are prepared in future." Her attention shifted to where Boyd was looking down at his bowl with a look of disgust. "I hope ye like pottage ... because Briana likes to serve it at least four times a week."

Boyd's gaze snapped up, his mouth thinning.

Watching Caitrin, Alasdair noted that her expression was shuttered. He let out a long exhale and pushed his bowl away, reaching instead for some bread. "I don't remember Briana's cooking being this bad," he said mildly. He then pulled a wheel of cheese toward him and cut off a large wedge.

"She's not usually," Darron replied. "Except for when she makes pottage. It's the dish she cooks when she wants to use up old vegetables and grain."

Caitrin glanced Darron's way, gaze narrowed, yet didn't reply.

"Maybe ye should let Lady Caitrin plan the meals, milord?" Alban ventured, frowning. "She knows how to utilize the stores. Cook needs a firm hand."

Irritation flared within Alasdair. He didn't appreciate the steward speaking up on Caitrin's behalf. Of course, the man had no idea what had happened earlier. Alban had served both Alasdair's brother and father. He was a good, solid man who'd always been staunchly loyal to the family he served. Yet it appeared he was also protective of Caitrin.

"Briana knows what she's doing," he growled.

Boyd snorted. "Really?"

Alasdair ignored him, his attention shifting to Caitrin. This time she met his eye. "I shall talk to cook," he said.

Caitrin's mouth thinned. She gave a barely perceptible nod before dropping her gaze.

The noon meal continued, the atmosphere strained. Around them, the rumble of voices in the Great Hall rose and fell along with the clunk of tankards and the clatter of wooden spoons. Servants circled with pots of pottage, offering a second serving.

Alasdair noted that no one partook.

The vegetable stew was barely edible. Cook had chosen a fine time to disgrace herself, especially just after his confrontation with Caitrin.

Alasdair glanced the chatelaine's way once more. At least she wasn't smirking over being proved right. He remembered that Caitrin had never been that kind of lass. Years earlier, when they'd been friends, she'd beaten him once or twice at the board game 'Ard-ri'. His young ego had taken a battering, but she'd been a graceful victor. It was after one such game that he'd realized he was in love with her. It had been a rainy spring afternoon, and they'd been seated near the hearth in her father's Great Hall. He'd visited Dunvegan with his father. Caitrin had taken his king before glancing up at him, a smile of disbelief stretching her face.

The impact of that moment had been like a punch to the guts. Alasdair had been unable to breathe. She'd won more than just a game of Ard-ri that day—she'd won his heart.

Alasdair tore his gaze from Caitrin and took a bite of bread and cheese. What a gullible idiot he'd been.

A short while later, the noon meal ended. Men and women rose to their feet and began filing from the hall, returning to their chores.

"Back to the bridge, milord?" Darron MacNichol asked, getting up.

"Aye," Alasdair replied. "I want to make sure the pillars are shored up by nightfall."

Boyd pulled a face, but Darron slapped him heartily on the back. "Come on, MacDonald. Not afraid of hard graft, are ye?"

Muttering under his breath, Boyd cast Darron a jaundiced look. The men moved off, and Caitrin rose to her feet. She was about to turn from the table when Alasdair spoke.

"Lady Caitrin ... wait a moment."

She paused, although her body had gone rigid. He watched a nerve feather in her cheek; she was uncomfortable in his presence.

"Join me for supper in my solar this eve," he murmured. "I think it's time we spoke privately."

Caitrin's gaze flicked up, her sea-blue eyes alarmed. Her throat bobbed. "My lord," she began, her voice low and hesitant. "I don't think that's necessary."

A lazy smile stretched Alasdair's mouth. "On the contrary, it is," he replied. "If ye are to stay on as chatelaine at Duntulm, ye and I must talk."

Their gazes fused for a long moment, and then, reluctantly, she nodded.

Caitrin stopped before the door to the chieftain's solar and drew in a sharp breath. She'd been dreading this meeting all afternoon. Unable to concentrate on her chores, she'd been unusually snappish with the servants. Even Eoghan's company hadn't relaxed her.

She wished there could be some way to avoid this supper. But there wasn't.

Alasdair MacDonald had been insistent.

Releasing the breath she was holding, Caitrin raised her clenched fist and knocked.

"Enter." Alasdair's voice greeted her.

Tensing her jaw, Caitrin pushed open the door and stepped inside the solar.

Alasdair stood before the fire warming his back. "Good evening, Lady Caitrin," he greeted her with a smile. "Shut the door ... ye are letting a draft in."

Caitrin did as bid, pulling the door closed behind her.

They were now completely alone—for the first time since his arrival at Duntulm.

For the first time since he proposed to her on that balmy summer's day.

Caitrin clenched her jaw. She didn't want to be in this man's presence. Ever since he'd gotten back, he'd taken pains to torment her. He might be smiling at her now, but she didn't trust him. She'd seen the glint in his eyes as he'd humiliated her earlier that day.

And she wasn't about to forgive him for it.

"Don't look so worried, Caitrin," Alasdair said, raising an eyebrow. "I'd just like a word." He motioned to the huge oaken table that dominated the center of the solar, where two places had been set. "Take a seat. The servants will bring the food up shortly."

Caitrin turned, moving woodenly to the table. The sight of it reminded her of how unpleasant he'd been when they'd gone over the accounts together. She wasn't about to forgive him for that either.

Anger coiled within her, overcoming her nervousness. It occurred to her then that she wasn't afraid of Alasdair, not like she had been of Baltair. The few times she'd stood up for herself with her husband, he'd been brutal with her. She'd never have spoken to him as she had to Alasdair today.

But she wasn't going to apologize for it.

Caitrin sat down at the table, and a moment later Alasdair joined her, lowering himself into a seat opposite. He was watching her, an intent expression on his face.

"Ye are annoyed," he noted.

Caitrin started. "No, milord," she said quickly. "I—"

"Yer eyes turn dark blue when ye are riled," he cut her off. "I remember that from when we were bairns."

Caitrin dropped her gaze to the polished wood surface before her. His comment made her feel uncomfortable, exposed.

"Would ye like a cup of wine?" he asked, a smile in his voice.

Caitrin nodded. She glanced up to see Alasdair pour two goblets of bramble wine. He handed one to her.

Their fingers accidentally brushed when she took the goblet, and a shiver went up Caitrin's arm. Unnerved by the reaction, she pulled her hand back and sloshed wine on the table.

"Sorry," she gasped. She went to rise, "I'll find something to wipe that up."

"Please, sit down." Alasdair waved her away. "The servants can clean it when they bring the food."

At that moment there came a knock at the door. "Supper, milord?"

"Bring it in," Alasdair called back.

Fingers still tingling, Caitrin glanced up at the chieftain's face. His smile had gone. His brown eyes were now hooded.

Three servants, led by Galiene, entered the solar. They carried trays of food: a tureen of what smelled like pork and bean soup, fresh bread, and an array of aged cheeses.

Caitrin felt queasy at the sight of it. She hadn't eaten much at the noon meal—for that pottage had been virtually inedible—yet Alasdair's presence robbed her of appetite.

The pair of them sat in silence while the servants placed the platters on the table. Galiene spotted the spilled wine, whipped a cloth from her apron, and mopped it up. She then turned to Alasdair, favoring him with a smile.

"Will ye be needing anything else, milord?"

Alasdair met Galiene's eye, his mouth curving. Galiene, who was nearing her fiftieth winter, had lived at Duntulm all her life. Caitrin sensed the affection between them. "No, that will be all, Galiene ... thank ye."

The servants departed, and Alasdair leaned forward, ladling the thick soup into two bowls. He handed one to Caitrin, and she noted he made sure to keep his fingers far from hers.

Caitrin helped herself to some bread and ripped a piece off it. Despite that she wasn't hungry, eating would keep her busy, give her something to focus on.

Silence stretched between them.

Caitrin feigned a deep fascination for her supper, which she forced down with gulps of strong bramble wine.

She was cutting herself a piece of cheese when Alasdair spoke.

"I've spoken to cook ... she will take instruction from ye in future."

Caitrin glanced up. "She will?"

He shrugged, leaning back in his chair and taking a sip from his goblet. "The men will riot if she serves up any more of that pottage."

Caitrin's gaze narrowed. "Why then, did ye tell her she wasn't to heed me?"

Alasdair stared back at Caitrin, his gaze searing hers. His expression turned serious as a long pause drew out between them. When he answered, his tone was cool. "Because I knew it would hurt ye."

Chapter Eight

Friends Again

CAITRIN STARED BACK at Alasdair. His reply shouldn't have surprised her, and yet it did. When she finally spoke, her voice held a rasp. "So ... this is revenge?"

Alasdair crossed his arms over his chest. "Did ye think I'd forgotten?"

Caitrin swallowed. Her fingers tightened around the stem of her goblet. "Ye are still bitter because I chose yer brother over ye?"

There it was—the unspoken had finally been uttered.

His mouth twisted.

A brittle silence stretched between them, and eventually, it was Caitrin who broke it. "I'm truly sorry for that day, Alasdair ... for hurting ye."

His face hardened. "I don't need yer apology."

"Clearly, ye do," she replied, holding his gaze. "If ye are bent on exacting some kind of petty revenge upon me."

He snorted. "Petty?"

Caitrin drew in a deep breath, forcing down her ire. Even now he was deliberately baiting her. "I thought we were friends," she said after a pause. "When ye proposed, ye took me by surprise."

Heat flooded across her chest at the memory of that afternoon. They'd been walking in the gardens south of Dunvegan, laughing and teasing one another, when Alasdair suddenly halted and turned to her. Then he'd gone down on one knee and proposed—just like that. Caitrin had been so shocked, she'd laughed. Her reaction had been one borne of surprise and nervousness, but the look of hurt on Alasdair's face had haunted her for days afterward.

"Aye," he replied, his voice bitter. "Ye wanted a proposal from my dashing brother instead."

Caitrin swallowed. "I couldn't help how I felt." She paused here, looking into his eyes. "Ye didn't have to run away."

He barked a humorless laugh. "Is that what ye think I did?"

She held his gaze. "Didn't ye? Ye had never shown any interest in joining the king's army before ... and then once my betrothal to Baltair was announced, ye couldn't leave Skye fast enough."

Caitrin finished speaking and dropped her gaze, heart pounding. She hated confrontation—and this one was fast spiraling out of control. Soon one of them would say something there would be no coming back from.

Alasdair didn't reply, and when she looked up, she saw that he was staring into the fire. The ruddy light played across his lean face and the clenched line of his jaw. It reflected off his dark eyes.

Caitrin's belly clenched. He looked furious.

He turned his gaze from the fire then and reached for his goblet of wine.

To her surprise, Caitrin saw that his hand trembled.

"Alasdair ... what's wrong?"

He glanced down at his hand, and his mouth thinned. He then set the goblet down. "Nothing."

"I know I've upset ye but—"

"It's nothing," he snapped.

She frowned. Alasdair met her eye a moment before he muttered a curse and leaned back in his chair, raking a hand through his long dark hair. After a long pause, he finally spoke. "It happens ... sometimes. Ever since the battle, I've been on edge."

Caitrin's frown deepened, and she lowered her gaze to where his hand now rested upon the table. She'd heard of men being scarred by war, not just physically but on the inside, in places where no soul could ever see. "Is that all?" she asked.

He shook his head, his attention shifting back to the fire. "I don't sleep well anymore."

Caitrin nodded, remembering that she'd suggested a brew of valerian root a few days earlier. "It was bad then ... the war?"

Alasdair nodded. He shifted his attention back to Caitrin, pinning her under his stare. "I see I'm not the only one who has changed ... ye have too. Ye are so stern these days, and ye hardly ever smile."

Caitrin tensed. She didn't like how easily he had shifted the focus to her. "It's a while since we saw each other last," she said stiffly. "Of course I'm not the same lass."

"I hear ye weren't happily wed to my brother."

Caitrin sucked in a breath. She should have realized tongues would wag.

"I'm surprised," Alasdair continued. "He was yer choice after all."

Heat rose to Caitrin's cheeks, and she dropped her gaze to the goblet of wine before her. "He was."

"Handsome, charming, and powerful. My brother had women vying for his hand."

Caitrin wet her lips before glancing up. "Ye knew what he was?"

He held her gaze. "Aye ... and I thought ye did too."

She shook her head. "I was infatuated with him."

"And how long did that last?" Alasdair asked, his gaze boring into her.

Heart racing now, Caitrin looked away once more. "Until the wedding night."

Silence fell between them, the hush broken only by the crackle of the hearth. When Alasdair finally shattered it, his voice was tired. "Neither of us is the same person we were, Caitrin. I'll admit that when I arrived home, my first thought was to make ye suffer ... but I see now that it'll only cause disruption in the castle if things continue in this way."

Surprised by his frankness, Caitrin glanced back at Alasdair. His fingers were curled around the stem of his goblet, but he made no move to lift it to his lips.

"Can't we be friends again?" she asked softly. "Like we once were?"

He watched her, his expression softening. Then his mouth curved into a smile. "Aye," he said after a pause. "Perhaps we can."

Caitrin walked back to her quarters with a light step.

She'd never had such a strange conversation. The words that had passed between them had ranged from confrontational and accusing, to conciliatory—and strangely honest.

But in the end, they'd managed to clear the air. They now had a chance to start over. Maybe the atmosphere at Duntulm would finally start to thaw.

On the way to her quarters, she stopped by Eoghan's chamber to check on him. The bairn lay on his side, sleeping peacefully. Caitrin had fed him before joining Alasdair for supper. With any luck, the lad would sleep through into the early hours of the morning.

Leaning on the edge of the cot, Caitrin stared down at Eoghan's face. During her pregnancy, she'd been worried she'd find it hard to love Baltair's child. Yet the moment she'd set eyes on her newborn son, she'd been lost. It was impossible not to love this sweet boy.

She enjoyed her responsibilities as chatelaine here at Duntulm, but she was a mother first. Caitrin's chest constricted as love welled within her. Baltair had given her very little worth keeping—except for this bairn.

Caitrin left her son and slipped silently back into the hallway. Reaching her bed-chamber, she found Sorcha awaiting her. The hand-maid sat by the fire, mending clothing by the light of a cresset that burned on the wall above her. Sorcha glanced up. "Good eve, milady."

"I'm tired, Sorcha," Caitrin informed her with a weary smile. "I think I'll go to bed early tonight."

Her hand-maid nodded, although she looked a little disappointed. It was their nightly routine to sit by the fire and talk awhile before bed.

"Do ye wish me to fetch ye some warmed milk?"

Caitrin shook her head and sank into a chair next to the bed. "No ... not tonight."

Sorcha set her sewing aside and rose to her feet. She crossed to Caitrin and, standing behind her, started to unpin her hair. It was a nightly ritual, one that relaxed Caitrin.

"Is something amiss, milady?" Sorcha asked as she unwound the heavy braid and reached for a hog-bristle brush. "Ye don't usually retire at this hour?"

"I'm just feeling a bit drained."

Sorcha didn't reply immediately. Of course, she knew where Caitrin had been—and would be wondering how the supper had gone. "Are ye still at war with the chieftain, milady?"

Caitrin twisted her head around, smiling as she met Sorcha's eye. "No ... I think we've managed to mend things."

"That's welcome news indeed." Relief flowered across the handmaid's face before her blue eyes narrowed. "Galiene told me about cook. The old woman's a trouble-maker."

"She's never liked having another woman oversee her," Caitrin agreed, turning back so Sorcha could finish unpinning her hair. "Alasdair's return was just the opportunity she needed. Unfortunately, the chieftain was looking for a reason to obstruct me."

"Why would he do that?"

Caitrin hesitated, wondering if she should confide in Sorcha or not. She trusted her hand-maid. Sorcha didn't have a loose tongue. Even so, it was a personal thing to divulge.

"Alasdair proposed to me once," she said finally. "I rejected him in favor of his brother."

Sorcha paused her brushing. "He wanted to wed ye?"

"Aye ... but ye aren't to breathe a word to anyone about this. The chieftain won't want folk knowing."

"I won't tell a soul," Sorcha assured her. She resumed the long slow strokes of the brush. "Why *did* ye choose Baltair over Alasdair, milady?"

Caitrin went still.

"Because Baltair was chieftain?" Sorcha pressed.

Caitrin sucked in a breath. "He was handsome and gallant," she replied after a pause, "the kind of man who dominates any room he walks into. I was mesmerized."

The two women fell silent. Sorcha knew more than anyone in this keep just how unhappy Caitrin had been with Baltair. Sorcha had found her sitting in her solar alone weeping into her hands more than once. He'd treated his wife's hand-maid with thinly-veiled contempt as well. Sorcha liked most folk, but she'd never warmed to Baltair.

"Alasdair MacDonald seems a different man to his brother," Sorcha said finally. "He's proud ... determined ... but I'm glad to see he lacks Baltair's cruel edge." She set the brush aside and went to fetch her mistress's night-rail. "I'm glad he's returned home."

Caitrin smiled. For the first time since seeing Alasdair again, she dared feel the same way.

Chapter Nine

Planting Barley

"WHAT SAY YE, Lady Caitrin?" Alasdair turned, meeting Caitrin's eye. "Shall we plant out the lower fields in oats this year?"

Caitrin hesitated before answering him. She'd been wary when he'd asked her to join him and Alban that morning. They were meeting the villagers to discuss the spring plantings. But, looking into his eyes, he seemed sincere.

"Aye," she replied, casting a look in Alban's direction. She and the steward had already discussed the coming season's plantings at length. Baltair had made a mistake, one that they'd planned to rectify. "We use more oats than any other grain … it makes sense to plant more of it." She paused here, shifting her attention back to Alasdair. "We'll need to set aside at least twenty bags for the cáin."

Alasdair nodded before turning from her. "Go ahead and plant out those fields," he told the men.

"And what of the summer barley," an elderly farmer called out. "It grows badly on the hillside … the land is too dry there. We should move it down to the meadow next to the burn."

"Let's go up to the hill now and take a look at the soil in the barley field," Alasdair replied. "Lead the way."

They followed the knot of farmers down the path amidst rows of kale and cabbages. A light rain fell in a chill mist over the fields. Grey clouds hung low; it was a grim day to be outdoors, yet Caitrin enjoyed the kiss of the misty rain on her face and the fresh air. Winter days inside the keep could start to feel restrictive, the air stale and heavy with the odor of peat smoke.

After a few strides down the path, Alasdair slowed his pace, allowing Alban to draw ahead with the others, and deliberately fell in step with Caitrin.

"Baltair never had much interest in farming," Alasdair said with a rueful smile. "I'm pleased to see that his widow does."

Caitrin compressed her lips. Baltair had been a warrior to the core. He loved hunting and fighting—everything else bored him. "Da always told me that fallow fields and bad harvests are signs of a poor leader," she replied. "Folk are always happier with full bellies."

Alasdair's smile widened. "Wise man, MacLeod." He paused here, his gaze narrowing slightly. "How's he doing these days?"

Caitrin huffed. "Well enough."

"That sounds ominous."

"Da hasn't been that impressed with his daughters of late," she said with a grimace. "Both my younger sisters have had trouble with him over the past year … and I'm likely to soon."

Alasdair inclined his head. "What happened with yer sisters?"

"He tried to force Rhona to choose a husband … and when she refused, he organized games where she was to wed the winner."

Alasdair gave a soft laugh. "That would have been ill news for yer sister. Did she not rebel?"

"She did … Rhona ran away but failed in her attempt to flee the isle. In the end, she wed Taran MacKinnon."

Alasdair's gaze widened. "That scarred brute … yer father's right-hand?"

"Aye, the same. He won the games." Caitrin paused here, her mouth quirking. "She wasn't pleased … but fate turned in her favor. They're now in love."

Alasdair shook his head in disbelief. "And wee Adaira. What happened to her?"

"Da tried to wed her to Aonghus Budge."

"Lord … he didn't?"

Caitrin grimaced. "Luckily, that never came to pass, for Adaira freed a prisoner from Dunvegan dungeon and escaped with him. They're now wed and live in Argyle."

Reaching out, Alasdair placed a hand on her arm, forcing her to stop walking. "God's bones, Caitrin. Ye must be spinning me a tale?"

Caitrin shook her head. Strangely, she was enjoying this conversation. It reminded her of years past when she and Alasdair had swapped stories of the goings-on in their respective castles. It seemed a lifetime ago. "The man she freed was Lachlann Fraser, the Fraser chieftain's eldest," she replied. "Da nearly went mad when he learned of it, but he has given them his blessing now."

Alasdair gave a low whistle, his gaze searching her face. "And what of ye, Caitrin? Surely the old dog has let ye off the leash?"

Caitrin pulled a face. "Ye would think so, yet now I'm a widow, he's already scheming. He wishes to find me another husband."

Alasdair's face tensed. "He does?"

"Aye … I imagine ye will receive a missive from him soon enough, asking ye to send me home."

Alasdair nodded, his gaze shuttering. They resumed walking, following the party up the hillside now to the fallow barley field.

"And what do *ye* wish?" Alasdair asked finally. "Do ye want to wed again?"

Caitrin shook her head. "I'd prefer to remain at Duntulm as chatelaine," she murmured. "I have a son and a life here."

She glanced away then, aware that she'd possibly said too much. It was bold for a woman to make such statements. However, Alasdair had just given her the opportunity to make her wishes for the future clear. He might help her keep her father at bay.

Caitrin met his eye once more and smiled. "I'm glad we are friends again, Alasdair."

He held her gaze for a moment before glancing away. His voice, when he answered, was soft and reflective. "So am I."

They reached the barley field then, a wide gently sloping stretch that crowned the top of a hill behind the lower fields.

The farmers were waiting for them, gathered in a huddle as they bickered together over the best spot to plant the barley.

Caitrin moved past them, walking across the fallow earth a few paces. She then crouched down and scooped up a handful of soil and examined it.

"What say ye, milady?" The elderly farmer approached her, his brow furrowed. "It's too dry, isn't it?"

Caitrin sighed, brushing off her hands and rising to her feet. "Perhaps ... but I'm not sure the meadow next to the burn is the right spot to plant barley either. It gets waterlogged in heavy rain."

"The lady has a point." Alasdair stepped up next to the farmer. "Barley doesn't thrive in wet soil. It needs a well-drained field."

"Aye," Caitrin replied with a smile. "If I may make a suggestion, milord ... I think ye would be best to plant out this year's barley in the field behind the kirk."

The mist had lowered when they made their way back down the hill. The rain shrouded the winter landscape in a heavy veil. Picking her way down the slippery, pebble-strewn path, Caitrin cast Alasdair a quick look. "Ye love this land, don't ye?"

He glanced up, smiling. "Is it so obvious?"

"Aye."

He huffed a breath. "I once found it too small, too isolated ... but after some time away I have a new appreciation of Duntulm."

"I like the folk here," Caitrin replied with a smile of her own. "They've been good to me."

Alasdair met her eye. "I take it, my brother never took ye with him to speak to the cottars?"

Caitrin shook her head, her smile fading. "He sent Alban to do such tasks. I wasn't consulted." She was surprised by the bitter edge she heard in her own voice.

Alasdair raised an eyebrow. He'd noted it too. "Why does it matter that much to ye?"

Caitrin's mouth compressed. "Ye wouldn't understand."

"Wouldn't I?"

Caitrin shook her head, once again taken aback by her own vehemence. "I'm as clever as any man … yet because I'm a woman I've been patronized and dismissed all my life." She couldn't believe she was voicing such thoughts to Alasdair. But as the words poured out, relief settled over her. It felt good to be able to be honest with him. "I only ever once made a suggestion to Baltair about the running of the keep," she said softly, "and he humiliated me in front of his men for it."

Alasdair's gaze clouded. "Like I did by the bridge."

Caitrin looked away. "No … ye didn't go as far as he did."

Silence fell between them as they reached the bottom of the hill and took the muddy path through the fields toward the village. The way was narrow here, forcing them to walk in single file. Caitrin went ahead with Alasdair following a few paces behind. However, when they reached the hamlet, Alasdair increased his pace and fell into step beside her once more.

"Ye *are* a clever woman, Caitrin," he said, favoring her with a boyish smile that reminded her of the old Alasdair. "I can see why ye have been frustrated."

"Aye … better that I was born dull-witted and content with my lot."

He threw back his head and laughed. The sound, warm and rich, filtered through the wet air. "I'd almost forgotten how sharp ye are," he said, grinning. "How I used to enjoy sparring with ye."

Caitrin cast him a sidelong glance. "Ye liked it?"

His mouth lifted at the corners. "Aye … I still do."

Chapter Ten

Deer Stalking

CAITRIN STEPPED OUT into the bailey and raised her face to the sky. The sun had finally appeared after days of grey. It barely warmed her skin but was a welcome sight all the same.

"It's a fine morning to be alive, Lady Caitrin!"

Lowering her face, Caitrin spied Boyd MacDonald emerging from the stables, leading his horse.

"Aye, it is," she replied with a smile. Her gaze drifted over to where Alasdair also appeared, leading his stallion. "Where are ye all off to?"

"To stalk some deer." Boyd flashed her a grin.

Alasdair approached her. Dressed in hunting leathers and a dark-green woolen cloak, he was an attractive, distracting sight. "I remember MacLeod used to take ye and yer sisters deer stalking," he greeted her. "Do ye still hunt?"

Caitrin's mouth curved at the unexpected question. "I haven't been since I wed. Baltair wouldn't let me ride out with him … said a stag hunt was no place for a woman."

Alasdair held her gaze, a smile spreading across his face. The expression made Caitrin's breathing catch.

She shoved the sensation aside. Attraction had no place between a chieftain and his chatelaine. She needed to watch herself around him.

"We're leaving shortly," he said. "Will ye join us?"

Caitrin nodded. Excitement arrowed through her, making her forget her discomfort. "Just give me a few moments," she said, pivoting on her heel. "I need to get changed."

A grin stretched across Caitrin's face. The thunder of hooves crossing soft turf, the sting of the wind on her skin, and the feel of the horse's body under her, made her feel truly alive.

It had been too long since she'd done this.

Alasdair MacDonald rode up ahead, flanked by Boyd and Darron, while a cluster of men from the guard brought up the rear. They'd left Duntulm as soon as Caitrin had gotten ready, and headed south over bare hills. Caitrin rode astride, like the men, having changed into leggings and a plain kirtle that was split at the sides so she didn't need to perch side-saddle.

Up ahead, Caitrin spied the shadowed boughs of woodland approaching. This was where they'd begin the hunt. Reaching the edge of the trees, the party drew up their coursers and swung down from the saddle. Here, they tethered the horses, retrieved their weapons, and continued onward on foot. A small herd of red deer had been spotted in a valley just south of here—they would stalk them.

Alasdair carried a longbow over one shoulder and a quiver of arrows on his back, as did the other men. Only Caitrin didn't bear a weapon. It had been a long while since she'd used a bow, and she feared she'd be a useless shot. Instead, she followed quietly behind Alasdair, Boyd, and Darron.

Caitrin inhaled the damp, pine-scented air, glad of the woolen cloak she wore. Despite that the sun was out today, there was little warmth in it. Winter still held the world in its grip. Pale sunlight filtered in amongst the trees, pooling on the mattress of pine needles below. It allowed the hunting party to move stealthily toward their destination. None of the men spoke, and Caitrin found herself enjoying the peace. Apart from the sanctuary of her solar, the keep was a hive of activity and distraction.

Alasdair led the way through the trees, soft-footed and keen-eyed. He paused now and then, gaze shifting ahead, before he turned, communicating with Boyd and Darron with a nod or hand gesture.

Eventually, they reached the edge of the valley.

Creeping up to the top of the ridge, the hunters fanned out in a line. Caitrin approached Alasdair, crouching down next to him. He was peering through a gap in the foliage. Caitrin craned her neck forward, moving closer to him to get a clear view.

"There they are," Alasdair murmured.

"I can't see anything," she whispered back, her gaze scanning the bottom of the valley. The pines fell back, revealing a swathe of green intersected by a creek.

Alasdair shifted his weight, angling his head toward her. "Shift yer gaze left," he whispered, his breath feathering against her ear.

Caitrin swallowed. His nearness distracted her. She could feel the heat of his body just inches from her. Stiffening, Caitrin forced herself to ignore the sensation.

Tracking her gaze left as he'd suggested, she caught sight of three deer cropping grass at the tree line. They were too far away at present. Alasdair and his men would need to draw closer before any of them would get a clear shot.

Alasdair shifted again, his knee accidentally brushing hers as he twisted right and motioned to Boyd and Darron. He then inclined his head to Caitrin once more.

"The fewer of us who approach them the better," he said softly. "Stay here with the others."

Caitrin nodded. She remained in a crouching position and watched as the three men crept over the edge of the ridge, moving like wraiths through the tall trees. However, her gaze remained upon Alasdair.

He moved with a hunter's grace. Unlike Baltair, who'd looked most at ease when dressed for battle, Alasdair seemed at home here in the midst of the woods. His green cloak made him blend in with his surroundings. His long dark hair was tied back at his nape, accentuating the sharp, lean angles of his face.

He led the way down the hill, winding his way through the trees. The other two men followed him. Up ahead, the deer continued to graze, unaware of the danger that stalked them.

Caitrin watched Alasdair halt between two spruce saplings and motion to his companions. Then he unslung his bow, nocked an arrow, and raised it. Caitrin heaved in a deep breath and went still.

Alasdair sighted one of the deer, a large doe that now cropped grass at the edge of the creek. It was a long shot, one only an experienced bowman would dare make. Nearby, Boyd and Darron had sighted the other two deer. They were all ready.

A heartbeat later, the arrows flew, the whistle of their passage shattering the valley's peace. The doe near the edge of the creek leaped into the air—and then fell, an arrow piercing its neck.

Boyd's curse echoed through the trees as his and Darron's deer bounded away, unhurt.

Alasdair moved, running swiftly through the trees. He emerged at the bottom of the valley and reached his quarry in half a dozen long strides. Steel flashed when he dropped to his knees next to the fallen deer and brought its suffering to an end.

Only then did Caitrin release the breath she'd been holding.

"Good shot!" Boyd slapped Alasdair on the shoulder, "although ye chose the hind closest."

Alasdair grinned back at him. "Ye can never concede defeat gracefully, can ye?"

Boyd snorted. "MacNichol got in the way of my shot, or I'd have brought a deer down too."

A few feet away, Darron looked up from where he had just hog-tied the fallen doe and bound its fetlocks to a pole. "I'm surprised ye didn't scare the hinds off with yer heavy breathing."

"Come on." Alasdair jabbed Boyd in the ribs with his elbow. "Make yerself useful and help MacNichol carry the deer."

Boyd muttered something rude under his breath, but did as bid, stepping forward and taking hold of one end of the pole. He and Darron heaved it into the air, resting it on their shoulders. Then, the party turned and traveled north back through the pine woods, toward where they'd tethered their horses.

Unlike the journey south, the men talked and laughed as they walked, their voices drifting through the trees. The hunting was done. They no longer needed to keep silent.

Alasdair followed at the rear, deliberately slowing his pace so that Caitrin drew up alongside him.

He cast her a smile, admiring her in the pale winter light. She was still clad in black, although he liked her attire, and how she'd donned leather leggings and long hunting boots under her kirtle. He caught a glimpse of her shapely legs with each stride. Her long pale hair hung between her shoulder blades in a thick braid.

"Did ye enjoy that?" he asked.

Caitrin met his gaze, her mouth curving. "Aye … ye look like ye were born knowing how to wield a bow and arrow?"

His smile widened. "Da used to take me out hunting with him before I could walk. I could fire a longbow before my fourth winter."

Caitrin arched her finely drawn eyebrows. "Now ye are exaggerating."

"No … although I'll admit he had a special bow made for me, to fit my size."

Caitrin laughed, a soft melodious sound that made Alasdair's breathing quicken. "I remember seeing ye compete at archery once at the summer games at Dunvegan," she replied. "Ye even bested yer brother."

"Aye." Alasdair's smile turned rueful. "Baltair wasn't pleased about that. He waited till he got me alone before he punched me in the belly."

Chapter Eleven

Before the Beltane Fire

Four months later …

CAITRIN WALKED DOWN the hill, following the line of revelers. Pulling her woolen shawl closer, she glanced up at the sky. It was clear, although the air held a bite as if the ghost of winter still lingered. It had been a cold, wet last few months.

She, like most folk, had been looking forward to Beltane—the night that symbolized the transition from spring to summer. No more huddling around hearths. No more chilled fingers and toes, and having to wear layers of woolen clothing to keep warm.

Halfway down the hill, the Beltane Fire blazed, a beacon that illuminated the night. The heat kissed Caitrin's face as she stopped around ten yards back from it.

"Would ye like me to get ye some ale, milady?"

Caitrin glanced over her shoulder at where Darron stood. She'd almost forgotten he was there, that he'd followed her down from the keep. The man had mastered the art of becoming invisible it seemed.

Caitrin's mouth curved. "Aye, thank ye, Darron."

With a nod, he went off to fetch her a drink. Folk had dragged down barrels of ale and wine from Duntulm's cellar. Cook had spent the last week preparing for this night. Huge rounds of 'Beltane Bannock' sat upon a table and were being sliced up and handed out. Nearby, a row of lamb carcasses finished roasting over a spit.

Boom. Boom. Boom.

Caitrin's attention shifted to where two young men sat beating calf-skin drums. The sound, slow and steady like the beating of a heart, called folk from miles around to join the revelry.

"Here ye are, milady." Darron had returned. He held out a wooden cup of ale to her and a wedge of cake. "I got ye some bannock too."

Caitrin took the bannock in one hand and the cup of ale in the other. Then, with a smile, she bit into the cake. Crumbly and enriched with milk and honey, it was delicious.

Taking a sip of ale to wash down her mouthful of cake, Caitrin's gaze traveled across the milling crowd. She watched as folk from the village approached the fire with unlit torches. They had doused their hearths at home and would light them afresh with the Beltane fire. Folk believed that the fire had protective qualities.

Bleating drifted across the hillside. A woman had brought up two goats to be blessed by the fire. The woman, who wore a harassed expression, led the skittish beasts around the fire, letting the smoke drift over them, before she dragged them off home.

Darron had taken his place next to Caitrin, his fingers curled around a cup of ale. Caitrin studied his profile in the firelight. He wore a pensive expression this evening, and when Caitrin followed the direction of his gaze, she saw it was focused upon Sorcha MacQueen.

Caitrin had given her hand-maid the evening off and left one of the older servants with Eoghan. Sorcha stood at the edge of a group of servants from the keep. She was nibbling at a piece of bannock.

The intensity of Darron's stare took Caitrin aback.

Could it be that the inscrutable Captain MacNichol had gone soft on her hand-maid?

At that moment, as they both watched Sorcha, Boyd MacDonald sauntered up to the lass. The warrior greeted her with a roguish smile. Boyd was a good-looking man and pleasant enough, yet Caitrin found his arrogance grated upon her. However, judging from the blush his greeting brought to Sorcha's cheeks, the lass didn't share her mistress's opinion of him.

Caitrin shifted her attention back to Darron and saw that he'd stiffened, his jaw tightening.

Clearing her throat, Caitrin broke the silence. "There's no need to stay with me," she said with a smile. "I'm happy here watching the fire."

Darron tore his gaze away from where Boyd and Sorcha now laughed together. "I should remain with ye, milady."

Caitrin clicked her tongue, irritated. "I'm perfectly safe, as ye well know, MacNichol. Now stop fussing and go enjoy yerself."

Darron frowned. "Very well, milady. But please, come and find me when ye wish to return to the keep."

"I will."

Caitrin watched Darron wander off, although she noted he didn't head in the direction of Sorcha and Boyd.

Caitrin took another bite of Beltane Bannock and chewed slowly.

In the midst of the crowd, she spotted Alasdair MacDonald.

He was surrounded by a few of his men as they drank and laughed. Alasdair appeared to be telling a story. His hands moved expressively and his dark eyes gleamed. One of his men then said something and Alasdair laughed.

The firelight bathed his face and shone upon his long dark hair, which he wore loose this evening. He'd matured into a striking-looking man, Caitrin had to admit.

She wasn't sure what she thought about the MacDonald chieftain these days.

There were moments when Caitrin could believe they were friends again, as they once had been, while at other times she found herself wary of him. A reserve existed between them now. And yet they'd settled into a comfortable working relationship over the last four months. Caitrin saw Alasdair a few times daily, although never alone. She hadn't joined him for supper in his solar again, and when they did speak, it was usually about factual matters.

Lost in thought, Caitrin continued to observe Alasdair. Another of his men asked him something, and he shook his head. He raised a cup to his lips—and then his gaze lifted, meeting hers.

Caitrin froze.

Mother Mary, he'd caught her staring.

Resisting the urge to tear her gaze away, Caitrin took a deep breath and casually shifted her attention to the fire, as if he was just part of the scene she'd been observing. However, she felt her cheeks warming under the weight of his answering stare.

Raising her cup of ale to her lips, Caitrin took a sip. Nearby, a lass laughed as a young man approached her for a dance.

Seizing the opportunity to look elsewhere, Caitrin focused on the young couple.

The girl was blushing furiously and laughing to cover up her embarrassment. She was small and blonde with a lush figure. The lad who'd approached her stared into her eyes with a look of such naked longing that Caitrin felt heat flush across her chest.

Beltane was a life-affirming evening, a night when the hard-working folk of this isle could cast aside their cares and give themselves up to revelry. Not surprisingly, it was said that many bairns were conceived on this night.

"Enjoying yerself, Lady Caitrin?"

Caitrin yanked her gaze from the couple to see that Alasdair MacDonald now towered over her. She hadn't even seen him leave his place with the other men and approach her.

Caitrin lifted her chin, angling her face up. She wished she was taller; she felt at a disadvantage every time she had to crane her neck to meet a man's eye.

"Aye, thank ye," she murmured. "It's a fair night."

"Ye should have brought Eoghan down here."

Caitrin huffed. "I will when he's a little older. He's getting too big to carry." It was true, the lad was growing like a weed, and now that he could crawl everywhere and had started to pull himself up onto furniture, he was into everything. "Old Lachina is with Eoghan tonight. I hope he behaves himself."

They stood in silence for a few moments, laughter and excited chatter eddying around them. A farmer was ushering his small herd of long-haired cattle past the fire. The beasts were mooing loudly and trying to run back down the hill, much to the entertainment of a cluster of lads nearby, who hooted at the farmer's attempts to herd the cows.

But Alasdair paid none of the chaos any mind. He watched Caitrin steadily. "Do ye remember that one Beltane our clans spent together?" he asked finally.

Caitrin nodded before smiling. "How could I forget? Yer father tanned yer hide after ye tried to set fire to my hair."

Alasdair snorted. "It was windy ... yer hair blew into my torch." He grinned then. "One of yer uncles got caught swiving a woman behind the bonfire ... do ye remember?"

Caitrin looked away, focusing her attention on the dancing flames before her. "Of course," she replied, her mouth curving. "We were the ones who caught him. I had nightmares about Dughall's hairy arse for months afterward."

Alasdair laughed, and Caitrin glanced back at him to see his dark eyes gleamed with mirth. "We used to take delight in observing the goings-on in our households."

Caitrin snorted. "Aye, we were like two gossiping crones, always speculating on which servants would end up wedded ... or bedded."

"And what of those three?" Alasdair jerked his head to the left. Caitrin shifted her attention and saw that Sorcha now had Boyd and Darron standing with her. The captain of the guard was asking Sorcha something. He gazed down at her as he spoke, his gaze intense. Next to him, Boyd wore a slightly irritated expression.

"Which man do ye think yer maid will choose?"

Caitrin raised an eyebrow. "She may pick neither."

Chapter Twelve

Looking for a Wife

"IT LOOKS AS if a storm is brewing."

Caitrin glanced up from where she was picking herbs to find her handmaid looking up at the sky. Following her gaze, Caitrin frowned. The dark grey and purple clouds to the south certainly looked ominous. Four days had passed since Beltane, and the weather had warmed considerably, but it seemed the warmth was about to come to an abrupt end. "Aye, ye could be right," she murmured.

It was a relief to venture outdoors without a cloak or woolen shawl. The afternoon was humid, the air heavy and close. As such the scents of the herbs in the courtyard garden were heady. She breathed in the perfume of the lavender she'd been cutting. This was her favorite place in the keep: a tiny walled courtyard that sat against the western edge of the curtain wall. A riot of flowering and culinary herbs surrounded her.

Both Sorcha and Eoghan had joined Caitrin this afternoon. Her handmaid kept an eye on Eoghan as he crawled over the lichen-encrusted cobbles. The poor lass had been forever wresting objects from Eoghan's fingers and confiscating them before he stuffed them into his mouth.

Caitrin turned to watch her son now. He was sitting up, his pink cheeks flushed, as he examined the sage leaf Sorcha had just given him. Her chest tightened at the sight of him. His dark hair grew thick now, so much like his father's.

Turning back to the lavender she'd been collecting, Caitrin resumed her work, cutting off the tips. She regularly made lavender tonic and lotion. It was good for the hair and skin, and she always made enough to share with other women in the keep.

She'd only been working a few moments when a large splash of water hit her in the face. Another swiftly followed, and then thunder rumbled over them.

Behind her, Eoghan let out a loud squawk.

Caitrin huffed a curse and turned from the lavender bush once more. Thunder boomed again, much louder this time. Eoghan's face crumpled, and he drew in a deep breath before letting out a frightened wail.

"Oh, laddie." Sorcha put down the trowel she'd been using to weed a herb bed. "All will be well ... it's just a wee bit of thunder."

Eoghan ignored her, his crying explosive now. Face bright red, he reached out his hands to Caitrin.

"I'll take him, milady," Sorcha offered, but Caitrin shook her head. She handed her hand-maid the basket of lavender. "Please take this up, I'll carry Eoghan."

Scooping up her son, she murmured soothing words as the bairn hiccoughed against her shoulder.

Meanwhile, the rain was starting in earnest; large wet drops soaked into her charcoal kirtle.

The women made their way out of the courtyard garden into the bailey beyond. Thunder crashed overhead once more and Eoghan's wails turned into panicked screeches. His cries echoed over the bailey, ricocheting off the high surrounding walls.

Men turned their gazes to the hysterical child.

Alasdair MacDonald was one of them. He was leading his horse toward the stables, having just returned from a patrol. Handing the reins to one of his men, he strode toward Caitrin, intercepting her as she headed toward the steps leading up into the keep.

"What's wrong with the lad?" he asked, frowning. "Is he unwell?"

Caitrin shook her head, struggling to keep Eoghan still. He was writhing in her arms. "He's never heard thunder before ... it frightens him."

Their gazes met then, and Caitrin suddenly struggled to draw breath.

Ever since Beltane she'd been aware of Alasdair in a way she hadn't before. She'd found herself stealing glances at him at mealtimes. And just the day before, she'd watched Alasdair from her solar window. He'd been shoeing a horse, and she'd been unable to look away, admiring the play of muscles in his shoulders and upper-arms under the thin material of his léine.

He wore a loose léine this afternoon, stuck to his torso in places from the rain that now swept across the bailey.

Caitrin's breathlessness increased. A strange weakness went through her. She forgot the struggling bairn in her arms, the rumbling thunder, and the rain that was soaking her hair and clothing. Meanwhile, his gaze seared her.

Alasdair broke the spell first, looking away. "Ye had better get the lad inside," he said, a slight rasp to his voice. "Ye don't want him to catch a chill."

Caitrin nodded, gripped Eoghan tightly to her, and was about to flee into the keep when the ground shook beneath her feet. For a moment, she thought it was more thunder, but then movement behind Alasdair caught her eye.

Horses entered the bailey, ridden by men clad in wet leathers and sodden woolen cloaks. The riders out front carried a standard bearing a plaid of red, threaded with green and blue: MacNichol clan colors.

Caitrin's brow furrowed. Such an arrival was unexpected. They weren't due a visit from their neighbors.

The company of riders filled the bailey, and a big man with dark-blond hair swung down from his horse. He strode over to Alasdair, a grin stretching his face. "Good day, MacDonald!"

"MacNichol!" Alasdair greeted him with an equally wide smile. "What are ye doing here?"

The two men embraced before the MacNichol chieftain slapped Alasdair hard on the back. "I thought it time I paid the new MacDonald chieftain a long overdue visit." He pushed wet hair out his face, his gaze sweeping over the bailey courtyard.

"Uncle!" Darron MacNichol strode out of the stables, grinning.

Oblivious to the rain that now hammered down, the two men hugged.

Chieftain MacNichol's eyes were gleaming when he pulled back. "It's been too long." He saw Caitrin then, and he inclined his head, smiling. "Lady Caitrin."

"Good day, milord," she greeted him. The rain had drenched her and Eoghan now. The bairn still squawked loud enough to bring down the heavens. She then favored Gavin with an apologetic smile. "Excuse me, but I must get my son inside."

"Aye," Alasdair replied with a grimace, just as more thunder boomed overhead. An instant later, lightning lit up the sky. "None of us should linger out here."

"How long has it been since we saw each other last?" Gavin MacNichol regarded Alasdair over the rim of his goblet.

"A while," Alasdair replied with a wry smile. "At least four years, I'd wager."

The MacNichol chieftain snorted. "I remember now." He cut a glance to where Darron sat a few yards away. "It was when I accompanied my nephew here. The pair of ye could barely grow half a beard between ye ... and now look at ye both. One's a guard captain and the other is a chieftain." He shook his head. "Makes me feel old."

Darron laughed. "That's because ye *are*, uncle."

"Not too old to whip yer arse," the chieftain rumbled.

Observing the MacNichol chieftain, Caitrin noted that his face bore lines that hadn't been there the last time she'd seen him. During her marriage to Baltair, he'd visited Duntulm twice—the first time with his wife, the second alone, for his wife had been ill. Gavin MacNichol now neared his fortieth winter, but he was still an attractive man: blond and broad-shouldered with warm blue eyes. Yet recent events had left their mark upon his face. He looked tired.

"Milord," Caitrin spoke up, meeting his eye. "I was so sorry to hear about Lady Innis."

The MacNichol chieftain's gaze shadowed, and the light went out of his usually affable face. "Aye ... thank ye, Lady Caitrin. I can't believe it has been nearly a year since she died." He raised his goblet to his lips and drank deeply. "With her gone, and losing many of my men to the war, my broch feels empty these days."

"I'm sorry, Gavin," Alasdair spoke up, frowning. "I didn't know about yer wife."

MacNichol waved him away. "No offense taken. Ye were off fighting for Scottish freedom. Ye weren't to know."

An awkward silence fell across the table then. They were seated in the Great Hall. Outside, the storm still raged, battering the thick stone walls, while indoors the air was humid and heavy with the odor of wet wool and leather.

Gavin MacNichol reached for more wine. "In the meantime, life goes on ... as it must," he said quietly. His attention returned to Caitrin. "I received word from yer father two days ago, milady."

"Ye did?" Something in the man's tone made Caitrin tense, as did his change of expression.

"Aye ... he tells me that ye are in search of a new husband?"

Caitrin's fingers tightened around the stem of her goblet. She'd known her father would start meddling sooner or later. He'd gone suspiciously quiet of late, which could only mean he was planning something.

"*He* is in search of a husband for me, milord," she said after a pause. "However, I am content to remain as chatelaine here."

"So ye don't wish to remarry?"

Caitrin swallowed, suddenly uncomfortable. She was aware that all the men at the table—Alasdair, Darron, Boyd, and Alban—were watching her.

"No," she murmured. "I don't."

The chieftain held her eye for a long moment before his mouth curved. He shifted his attention to Alasdair then, his expression curious. "I take it that Lady Caitrin has proved herself invaluable to Duntulm?"

"Aye," Alasdair replied. His expression had turned serious, his gaze shuttered. "She ran things well after Baltair's death ... and continues to do so."

"So ye will let her remain here? A good chatelaine is hard to find."

Alasdair nodded, although his face had tensed, warning Gavin MacNichol to cease his line of questioning.

Heeding him, his guest took a sip from his goblet and glanced back at Caitrin. "It's a pity ye aren't interested in wedding again, milady," MacNichol said, favoring her with a warm smile. "For I am looking for a wife."

Chapter Thirteen

A Waste of a Good Woman

EOGHAN'S WAILS ECHOED down the hallway.

Caitrin picked up her skirts and hurried toward his bed-chamber. She'd just left her solar, and was about to descend the stairs, when she heard his cries. Eoghan usually had a nap mid-morning, but it appeared he'd awoken early.

Inside the warm, dimly-lit chamber, she found Eoghan red-faced and gripping the sides of his cot.

"What is it, my wee laddie?" She scooped him into her arms. "Worry not … Ma's here."

Caitrin carried Eoghan across to a chair and sat down. Her son was growing heavy to hold now. She'd recently weaned him, and he'd taken to solid food with relish. As she settled Eoghan on her knee, her hand brushed his face.

Caitrin frowned. It was warm in the chamber, as Sorcha made sure the hearth was well stoked, but Eoghan's brow was hot to touch. His cheeks were flushed, not from crying, but fever. He hadn't been outdoors long in the rain the afternoon before—but he appeared to have caught a chill.

The bairn wriggled on her knee, his flushed face scrunched up as he cried. Murmuring to him, Caitrin cradled him against her breast. After a few moments, Eoghan quieted. Caitrin closed her eyes, enjoying the peace. Gavin MacNichol's visit had thrown the keep into chaos. They hadn't been expecting him, so there had been chambers to ready for him and his men, and extra food to be prepared.

Caitrin had just come up from the kitchens, where cook had been in a temper about having no time to plan for the visitors. Caitrin had left her with instructions to put out an extra haunch of mutton with the noon meal. Briana had muttered under her breath about this but had acquiesced in the end.

She'd been much more compliant of late since Alasdair had spoken with her.

Once Eoghan had calmed, Caitrin lay him back into his cot. She needed to find Sorcha. Slipping out of the bed-chamber, she had almost reached the stairs when she met her hand-maid.

"I was coming up to fetch ye, milady," Sorcha greeted her with a smile. "The supplies have just arrived."

This was good news, for Caitrin had been waiting for a delivery of goods from the mainland for days now: cloth, spices, and other items that were difficult to buy on the isle. She wanted to make an inventory of the items before they were put away.

"Thank ye, Sorcha," Caitrin replied. "I've just seen Eoghan. He has the beginnings of a fever. Can ye please stay with him while I see to the supplies? I hate to leave him when he's upset."

Sorcha's brow furrowed, worry lighting in her blue eyes. "Of course."

Leaving her hand-maid to look after Eoghan, Caitrin fetched her wooden board and a stub of charcoal from her solar. She then continued down to the bailey. Picking her way across the muddy ground, doing her best to avoid the puddles left by yesterday's storm, she approached a large wagon. A young man had just pulled back the hide tarpaulin, revealing tightly stacked wooden barrels and crates.

"Good day, Tory," she greeted the servant.

"Good morning, milady," Tory returned the greeting with a grin. "Shall we take these into the stores?"

"Open them up first, please," Caitrin instructed. "I want to make sure we've gotten what we ordered."

He obeyed, using a knife to pry the lid off a small barrel. A sweet, woody scent drifted into the damp air, and Caitrin peered inside, a smile curving her lips. "Cinnamon," she breathed. She'd forgotten that she'd ordered some all those months ago—the scent reminded her of mulled wine at Yuletide.

Scratching a note on her board, Caitrin nodded to Tory.

"Open that one next to it."

The young man pried the lid off another small barrel, which was filled with black peppercorns. Another costly spice, and one which would hopefully last them a while.

"Make sure ye close those barrels well," Caitrin ordered, "and put them on the top shelf in the stores."

"Aye, milady." Tory carried the barrels of precious spice away, leaving Caitrin alone. She was just scratching another note when a male voice behind her made her start. "Good day, Lady Caitrin."

She glanced over her shoulder to see that Gavin MacNichol had approached. Her heart sank at the sight of him. After the words they'd shared the day before, she felt a little uncomfortable around the chieftain. She'd always liked Gavin, but during that meal, she'd seen the glint of interest in his eyes. Her father hadn't helped matters either, but she didn't want to encourage him further. She also didn't want to linger out here in the bailey any longer than necessary. With Eoghan so restless, she needed to return to her son as soon as possible.

"Good day, Chieftain MacNichol."

"Busy, I see," he observed. The corners of his eyes crinkled as he smiled. "Alasdair is lucky to have yer help here."

"These are long-awaited supplies," she replied, favoring him with a smile of her own. "The first since the war."

He gave her a long, searching look. "It's good to see ye happy again, lass." Caitrin tensed, and when she didn't answer, he continued. "Innis told me how unhappy ye were ... but the last time I visited, I didn't need anyone to point it out to me. I've never seen a woman with such sad eyes."

Caitrin dropped her gaze to the muddy ground, aware that Tory would return soon. MacNichol had been so direct she didn't know how to respond.

"Baltair could be a brute, and he wasn't easy to like," the chieftain said after a pause. "I'm just sorry he put ye off wedding again."

Caitrin glanced up, meeting his gaze. Gavin MacNichol was watching her with a soft look that made her feel wretched.

"Not every woman is meant to be a wife," she replied, her tone brittle.

He inclined his head. "No ... but it's a waste of a good woman such as yerself."

"How is he?" Caitrin let herself into her son's bed-chamber to find Sorcha seated by the fire, sewing in hand. Eoghan lay asleep in his crib.

As soon as the supplies had been dealt with, she'd made her way back upstairs.

Sorcha cast aside her sewing and rose to her feet, her face tense with concern. "His cheeks are very red ... but he has been sleeping since ye left."

Caitrin crossed to the crib and gazed down at her son's sleeping face. Sorcha was right. His cheeks were deeply flushed now, and when she pressed a hand to his forehead, she drew in a sharp breath. He was burning up. "Go and fetch a healer, Sorcha," she ordered. "Quickly, please."

Sorcha nodded. Without another word, she left the chamber.

Alone, Caitrin let out a deep sigh. Massaging a tense muscle in her shoulder, she continued to watch Eoghan, calmed by the steady rise and fall of his chest.

It's only a fever, she reassured herself.

Why then did cold dread curl in the pit of her belly?

"Where are ye off to in such a hurry?"

Sorcha was looping a woolen shawl over her shoulders as she crossed the keep's entrance hall, when a familiar voice hailed her. She glanced over her shoulder to see Darron MacNichol approach.

"Wee Master Eoghan has a fever," she replied briskly, "I'm off to the village to fetch the healer."

Darron stepped close to her. "I'll come with ye."

Sorcha clicked her tongue. "There's no need for that, MacNichol. Ye don't have to escort a hand-maid."

He favored her with a stubborn look. "Ye serve Lady Caitrin, Sorcha. That makes ye my responsibility as well."

Sorcha huffed. "Suit yerself."

They made their way outside and crossed the bailey under an overcast sky, their boots splashing through the mud. Crossing the drawbridge, Sorcha avoided looking down at the deep ditch that surrounded the curtain wall on three sides. If she ever slipped and fell into it, she'd break her neck for sure.

Striding down the hill toward the village, Sorcha stole a glance at Darron. The captain of the guard was an enigma. Upon her arrival at Duntulm, she'd suffered something of an infatuation for him. But after realizing he barely noticed her existence, she'd promptly put him out of her head.

These days though, he'd altered in his manner toward her. It seemed that everywhere she went, Darron MacNichol appeared. He wasn't a garrulous man, yet he'd approached her at Beltane—much to Boyd's irritation.

Boyd MacDonald. She wasn't sure she trusted him. He often went out of his way to speak to her—and when he did his charm was breathtaking—but just yesterday she'd heard two of the scullery maids gossiping about how he'd stolen a kiss from one of them. Sorcha had gone cold. Suddenly, his compliments and melting looks took on a different meaning.

Pushing thoughts of Boyd aside, Sorcha broke the silence between her and Darron. "Is yer uncle still at Duntulm?"

Darron glanced her way. "Aye ... Gavin leaves tomorrow. Why?"

"I heard he's looking for a wife."

Darron raised an eyebrow. "Are ye interested?"

"Of course not." Sorcha cast Darron an irritated look. As the bastard daughter of the MacQueen chieftain, men like Gavin MacNichol were far beyond her reach. "Galiene told me that he was showing an interest in Lady Caitrin."

Darron snorted. "Galiene has the loosest tongue in the keep."

"Is she wrong?"

"Ye shouldn't gossip, Sorcha. It's unbecoming."

"Oh, stop being such an old woman, MacNichol, and answer me."

He cast her a censorious look. "My uncle is a widower. If he's considering taking another wife, there's nothing strange in that."

"He's wasting his time on Lady Caitrin ... she doesn't wish to wed again."

"I know," he replied with a shake of his head. "And she's not the only one. Alasdair MacDonald doesn't want to wed either it seems."

Sorcha nodded, remembering the chieftain's words that day in his solar months earlier when she'd brought Eoghan in to see him.

When Darron spoke once more, his tone was introspective. "Ye didn't meet Alasdair before he went away, did ye?"

"No ... I arrived at Duntulm the same time as Lady Caitrin. He'd already joined the king's cause."

"The war changed him," Darron said, glancing her way once more. They'd almost reached the bottom of the hill now. "There's an edge to Alasdair that wasn't there before ... like he's expecting someone to sneak up behind him and sink a knife into his back."

Sorcha nodded. "I've seen him staring off into the distance sometimes," she murmured. "He's tries to hide it ... but he's troubled."

Silence stretched out between them for a few moments before Darron broke it. "Do ye ever give some thought to yer own future, Sorcha?"

Surprised, Sorcha cut him a sharp glance. "Not really ... why?"

His gaze met hers. "Do ye wish to one day wed?"

Embarrassment flushed through Sorcha at the direct question. "I ... don't know," she stammered, trying to tamp down the heat that was now rising up her neck. "I've not thought about it."

Chapter Fourteen
A Trifling Thing

"DARRON ... WHERE'S LADY Caitrin this evening?" Alasdair put down his goblet, his gaze settling upon Captain MacNichol. "She usually takes her supper with us."

Darron glanced up from his bowl of stew. "Hasn't Lady Caitrin spoken to ye, milord?"

"Not since this morning ... why?"

Darron frowned. "I thought she would have told ye."

Alasdair went still. "Told me what?"

"Her son's ill ... she'll be upstairs with him."

Silence fell at the table. After a long moment, Gavin MacNichol broke it. "Poor lad. Is he—"

"What's wrong with him?" Alasdair cut in.

"A fever."

Alasdair tensed. Why hadn't Caitrin sent word? If his heir was ill, he had the right to know. Pushing down his irritation, he met Darron's eye once more. "Has the healer been fetched?"

"Aye."

Alasdair pushed himself back from the table and rose to his feet. "I'd better check on the lad."

"Can't it wait till after supper?" Boyd spoke up. He'd just finished setting up a board with stone markers. "I thought we were going to have a game of Ard-ri?"

"Later," Alasdair snapped.

Without another word, he turned on his heel and left the Great Hall.

"Lady Caitrin," Sorcha slipped into the bed-chamber closing the door behind her, "the chieftain is here ... he wants to see Master Eoghan."

Caitrin, who'd been rocking Eoghan in her arms, tensed. "Let him in," she murmured.

Sorcha nodded before disappearing into the hallway beyond.

A moment later a tall figure stepped into the dimly-lit room. Dressed in plaid braies, a léine, and a leather vest, Alasdair wore an unusually severe expression.

"Good eve, milord," she greeted him.

"How is my nephew?" he asked. "I hear he has a fever?"

His brusque manner made Caitrin frown. "He does, milord."

"Where's the healer?"

"I sent him away. He's visiting again in the morning." Caitrin rose to her feet, cradling the hot body against her. Her arms ached from holding him, yet she didn't want to put him back in his crib, not yet.

Alasdair walked forward so that he loomed over her. However, it wasn't Caitrin he was focused on at that moment, but the bairn. His brow furrowed further when he reached down and touched the lad's flushed face. "He's on fire."

"Aye ... he must have caught a chill yesterday."

Alasdair glanced up, his gaze spearing hers. "Why didn't ye call for me?" he asked softly.

Guilt wreathed up within Caitrin. "I didn't want to bother ye," she murmured. "I thought it was a trifling thing."

It was a lie. She'd deliberately kept Eoghan's fever from Alasdair. A fierce protective instinct had come over her when she'd realized Eoghan was unwell. She'd hoped that it would break during the night, and Alasdair wouldn't have been any wiser.

His expression hardened. "He's the MacDonald heir. I have the right to know if he's ill."

Annoyance surged within her, pushing aside the guilt. This was why she'd not told him. She didn't like how Alasdair claimed ownership over Eoghan. He was her son, not his property.

Alasdair straightened up, his dark brows knitting together. "The healer is to stay with him until the fever abates," he announced, stepping back from her. "I don't want him leaving Eoghan's side."

Caitrin's lips compressed. "But he has other patients to attend."

"None more important than Eoghan MacDonald. Send a servant to fetch him back. Tell him I shall pay him for his time."

With that Alasdair turned and strode from the bed-chamber.

Alasdair stepped into the hallway to find the hand-maid Sorcha waiting there.

His sudden appearance made her start. "Milord?"

He nodded curtly before stepping past her to the stairwell. Behind him, he heard the hand-maid re-enter the bed-chamber. Frowning, he climbed the stairs to the next level of the keep, to his solar.

He'd almost reached the door when a voice hailed him. "Milord!"

Alasdair turned to see Alban hurry up the last of the steps behind him, puffing like an old plow horse. The steward grasped something in his right hand, which he thrust at Alasdair when he reached the landing.

"A rider just arrived from Dunvegan," he announced, red in the face from his climb. "He brought this for ye."

Alasdair looked down at the rolled parchment, sealed with wax. It bore a stamp he recognized instantly: a bull's head between two flags. *The MacLeod crest.*

The steward hovered, his face expectant, but Alasdair turned from him. "Thank ye, Alban. I'll read it in my solar."

Letting himself into his quarters, Alasdair carried the message over to the fire. With an irritated sigh, he broke the seal and unfurled the parchment. Then he read it.

Dear Chieftain Alasdair MacDonald,

It is now nearly a year since my daughter was widowed. I understand Caitrin has proved herself useful as chatelaine at Duntulm, but I feel the time has come for her to wed once more.

I have made inquiries and have three suitors who wish to meet with her. Please make arrangements for her to return to Dunvegan at yer earliest convenience.

Yer humble servant,
Clan-chief Malcolm MacLeod.

Alasdair lowered the parchment, a frown creasing his brow. He'd expected such a letter to arrive sooner or later. Gavin MacNichol had warned them that MacLeod was growing restless.

Caitrin had no wish to wed, or to leave Duntulm, but her father had other ideas.

Malcolm MacLeod wasn't a man to be crossed.

Alasdair's already sour mood darkened further as he realized he didn't want Caitrin to leave.

He'd returned home intent on making her suffer for the hurt she'd caused him—but after a while, his quest for revenge had felt childish, pointless. Instead, they'd slowly built up a companionship that he'd grown to enjoy.

Certainly, he was annoyed that she'd deliberately tried to hide Eoghan's fever from him—it really was unacceptable behavior—but such things could be overcome.

Alasdair loosed a breath and placed MacLeod's letter on the mantelpiece. He wouldn't think about Caitrin's fate tonight, not with Eoghan burning with fever. He'd discuss this with her once her son had recovered.

Caitrin gently lay the back of her hand on Eoghan's brow—and let out a sigh of relief.

His skin was warm, not burning hot as it had been. After two long days and nights, the fever had broken.

The healer had informed her that her son was over the worst, before he departed the keep, face gaunt with fatigue, his purse heavy with silver pennies.

Leaning against the edge of the cot, Caitrin closed her eyes. That was the second fever that Eoghan had suffered since his birth, although it was much worse than the first. Even the healer had started to look worried as the second night wore on.

But now the worst was over.

Caitrin felt wrung out. Her eyes were gritty from lack of sleep, her head heavy. She needed to rest.

As if reading her mistress's thoughts, Sorcha spoke up. "I'll watch over the lad, Lady Caitrin. Why don't ye go and lie down awhile?"

Opening her eyes, Caitrin cast a grateful smile over her shoulder at her hand-maid. "I don't know what I'd do without ye, Sorcha."

The young woman smiled back, her cheeks dimpling. She looked tired in the grey light that filtered in from the open window. It was a sunless day outdoors. Sorcha's face was strained, her eyes hollowed.

Caitrin was sure *she* looked far worse.

"Ye are a good mother, milady," Sorcha replied. "Ye couldn't have done more for Eoghan."

Caitrin heaved a sigh. "I keep blaming myself. I shouldn't have had him outdoors ... if he caught a chill because—"

"Ye don't know that, milady," Sorcha cut her off, her voice firm. "Ye aren't to blame."

Caitrin pushed herself away from the edge of the crib. "I just thank the Lord it's over," she murmured.

Eoghan was all she had. She couldn't bear to lose him.

Leaving Sorcha with her son, Caitrin made her way back to her own quarters. She entered her solar: a small, yet comfortable space, warmed by a glowing hearth. A servant had been in here, she noted. They'd left a tray of food—bannocks with butter and honey—for her.

Caitrin had thought she'd be too exhausted to eat, but the sight of the food made her belly growl, reminding her that she'd missed supper the night before. Seating herself at the table, she poured out a cup of milk and started to butter a wedge of bannock.

She was halfway through her meal when a knock sounded at the door. "Come in," she called, expecting to see a servant.

Instead, Alasdair MacDonald appeared. Leaning against the doorframe, he folded his arms across his chest and favored her with a tired smile. "I saw the healer leave earlier. He tells me Eoghan is on the mend?"

Caitrin put down the bannock she'd been about to bite into. She had not spoken to Alasdair since their brief conversation two days earlier. "Aye," she replied, her manner guarded. "His fever broke just before dawn."

"I'm relieved to hear that."

Not knowing what to say to him, Caitrin fell silent.

"Are ye angry with me?" he asked after a moment.

"No," Caitrin replied warily.

Pushing himself off the doorframe, Alasdair took a step into the solar. "I haven't been inside this chamber for years," he said, his gaze shifting around the solar. "Not since my mother was alive. It was Ma's favorite spot ... but I see ye have made it yer own."

His words eased the tension between them, and Caitrin nodded. Indeed, since her arrival at Duntulm, she'd imbued the solar with her own character. There were baskets of dried herbs and flowers dotted around the space. Colorful hangings, which she and Sorcha had spent the last three winters laboring over, covered the damp stone walls.

Alasdair met her eye then. "I'm sorry about how I spoke to ye last. I was worried about Eoghan ... it made me harsher than I intended."

"I was worried about him too," she reminded him quietly, "but I also owe ye an apology ... I should have told ye he was unwell."

Alasdair's gaze clouded. "Why didn't ye?"

Caitrin looked away. "I don't know."

He'd take offense if she told him the truth. Despite that they'd gotten along well over the past few months, when it came to Eoghan, she still didn't trust him.

She glanced back to see Alasdair watching her. "Are we still friends, Caitrin?" he asked softly. The way he said her name made a shiver of pleasure run down her spine.

Doing her best to ignore the distracting sensation, Caitrin frowned. "Of course."

He gave her a lopsided smile. "Then would ye have supper with me this evening in my solar?"

Caitrin heaved in a deep breath. The air between them was suddenly charged. She wasn't sure she wanted to spend an evening alone with him. It was best they kept their relationship well-defined. He was the chieftain, and she was his chatelaine. They spoke daily about what needed to be done to keep Duntulm running, but they didn't need to take things further than that.

Yet she couldn't refuse without giving offense. The boyish smile he gave her then, unraveled the last of her reserve toward him. He looked so hopeful she couldn't deny him.

"Very well," she huffed before favoring him with a smile. "Now, please go away and let me finish my bannocks in peace."

Chapter Fifteen

I Don't Want This

CAITRIN TOOK A sip of wine. The deep, spicy flavor exploded on her tongue, and she glanced up, eyes widening. "This is delicious ... what is it?"

"Spiced black plum," Alasdair replied with a smile. "The last of the wine laid down by my father."

Caitrin lowered her gaze to the deep red wine in her goblet, before she took another sip. "I thought we didn't have any of that left?"

His smile widened. "Aye ... that's because ye don't know of Da's secret store."

Caitrin inclined her head. "Clearly not."

The evening was drawing out. They had long since finished their supper of pork and kale pie. The servants had cleared away the dishes before Alasdair suggested they shared a goblet of wine together. Caitrin had now taken a seat before the window while Alasdair leaned up against the stone ledge opposite.

Alasdair drank from his goblet, his expression turning wistful. "No one could make wine like my father. We haven't had a decent drop here since he died."

Caitrin watched him, noting Alasdair's relaxed posture as he leaned against the sill, legs crossed at the ankles before him. She'd been tense upon first entering the solar—for she couldn't set foot in this chamber without remembering Baltair—but after a good meal, she was starting to unwind.

The tension and worry of the past days slowly unraveled, and she found that she was enjoying the evening. The shutters were open, giving her a view of the deep indigo sky, where the stars were just twinkling into existence. The air filtering in was cool and laced with the scent of the sea.

"The seeds are sown for the summer now," she said finally. "All we need is a few months of sunshine."

He huffed a laugh. "Ye are never guaranteed that on this isle."

"I saw the new grain store yesterday."

"Aye." He met her eye, his mouth curving. "What do ye think of it?"

"It's a very clever design ... I never thought of raising it so high off the ground."

Alasdair smiled. "It keeps rodents out. I saw one similar in Inbhir Nis ... ye needed a ladder to get up to it. We're going to build three more before summer ends."

Caitrin inclined her head, studying him. "Ye make a fine chieftain, Alasdair MacDonald. The folk of this land are fortunate to have ye."

Alasdair held her gaze. "Are they?"

The atmosphere suddenly altered between them, a tension rising that had been absent earlier. Suddenly, Caitrin felt nervous. She looked away and took a large gulp of wine to fortify herself.

"I know Eoghan is important to ye," she said finally, "but why not find yerself a wife and father children of yer own?" She raised her chin, forcing herself to meet his eye once more. "The MacDonalds of Duntulm risk dying out."

His gaze guttered, and yet he didn't reply. Instead, he looked away, focusing upon the dark sky outdoors.

Caitrin's breathing quickened. She probably shouldn't have spoken of something so personal, and yet this issue had been bothering her. "Alasdair?"

He shifted his gaze back to her, and the look on his face made Caitrin swallow hard. She curled both hands around the goblet as if anchoring herself to it.

"After ye wed Baltair, I made a decision." His voice held a rasp. "If I couldn't have ye, I would have no one."

The words fell heavily in the solar.

For a long moment, Caitrin merely stared at Alasdair, and then her chest constricted as guilt tore into her. She knew she'd hurt him—but the wounds went deeper than she'd thought. "Ye shouldn't throw yer life away like that," she whispered. "It's a waste. Ye would make a fine husband and father."

He set his goblet down on the window ledge with a thump. "I'm not sure I would."

Caitrin heaved in a deep breath. Suddenly, it felt airless inside the solar, even though she sat next to the open window. Caitrin put down her goblet and rose from the seat, taking a step away from him. "I should go," she said quietly, her heart racing now. "It's late."

Alasdair moved.

One moment, he'd been standing there, watching her with eyes aflame, the next he stepped forward, covering the distance between them. He reached out, grasped Caitrin's shoulders, and pulled her toward him.

Then he bent his head and kissed her.

It was a searing, hard kiss—and it scattered Caitrin's thoughts like autumn leaves caught by the wind.

At first, she was shocked and stood there rigid as his mouth slanted over hers. And then the feel of his lips on hers ignited something deep in Caitrin's belly. His touch made her body quiver.

Still gripping her shoulders, Alasdair pushed Caitrin back against the wall. His lips parted hers, his tongue sliding into her mouth as he deepened the kiss. The hard length of his body pressed up against hers. The spicy male scent of him filled her senses. He kissed her as if he was starved.

Caitrin gave in to the heat of Alasdair's embrace for a moment, before a chill washed over her.

What am I doing?

If she submitted to this, she'd risk losing everything she'd worked so hard to achieve here at Duntulm. Independence. Respect. She wouldn't let another man control her. Caitrin's hands went up to Alasdair's chest.

Never again.

She braced herself against him, pushing hard.

Alasdair pulled back, surprise filtering over his face. "Caitrin?"

"I can't," Caitrin gasped. She slid along the wall, away from him. "We can't."

Alasdair frowned, his eyes shadowing with concern. "What's wrong?"

He took a step toward her, but Caitrin held out a hand, warning him not to come any closer. "No ... Alasdair. Please don't."

He stopped short, his face going taut. "I'd never hurt ye."

Caitrin shook her head. She should have seen this moment coming. Tension had been building between them for a while now; it had only been a matter of time.

"This was a mistake," she whispered.

His features hardened. "We haven't done anything wrong, Caitrin. All I did was kiss ye."

"No." The word ripped from her. "I don't want this."

She backed up from him, knocking into the edge of the oaken table that dominated the center of the solar. Then she turned and fled from the chamber.

Alasdair watched Caitrin run from him.

He took two swift steps to follow her and then brought himself up short.

No.

His heart slammed painfully against his ribs as the door to the solar thudded shut, and he heard her footfalls receding quickly down the hallway beyond.

I don't want this.

The words had struck him like physical blows. They still stung in the aftermath.

Alasdair dragged a hand through his hair and spat out a curse.

He hadn't meant to kiss her. The conversation had spiraled out of control, and then he'd forgotten himself. Alasdair hadn't thought about the consequences of his actions. He'd reached for her on instinct, and when she was in his arms, her mouth under his, he'd been unable to stop kissing her.

Caitrin had tasted even better than in his dreams.

But then she'd pushed him away. She didn't want him.

Alasdair strode back to the window and threw himself down on the window seat, where Caitrin had been sitting until a few moments earlier. He reached for his goblet of wine and stopped. His hand trembled badly as if he were an old man struck by palsy.

Jaw clenched, Alasdair fisted his hand and lowered it to the window-sill.

He couldn't believe he'd made an utter fool of himself for the second time—kicked in the guts twice by the same woman.

It had taken everything he had to reach for Caitrin. And she'd rejected him—again. Only this time it felt worse. This time he'd been kissing her, and she'd recoiled from him.

There was no coming back from such an act. Caitrin had made her feelings clear.

Alasdair squeezed his eyes closed. The pain that constricted his chest made it hard to breathe. Disappointment and hurt churned within him, making his bile rise.

Enough.

Alasdair opened his eyes, his gaze shifting to the mantelpiece, where the rolled missive from Malcolm MacLeod still sat. He'd been meaning to discuss it with Caitrin during supper but had forgotten.

Truthfully, he'd been reluctant to, for he'd wanted her to remain in Duntulm.

But that was before he'd kissed her, before she'd shoved him away from her as if his very touch made her skin crawl.

I don't want this.

No—she couldn't stay here. Caitrin needed to go home.

Chapter Sixteen

He Will Want for Nothing

CAITRIN STABBED HER finger with the needle before letting out a curse.

Shocked, Sorcha glanced up from her own sewing. "Milady?"

Caitrin cast the hand-maid a baleful look but didn't reply. Instead, she sucked on her injured finger, which now throbbed. She wasn't in the best frame of mind for embroidery. Her nerves felt stretched tight as a drawn bow-string this morning.

"Is something amiss, Lady Caitrin?" Sorcha asked gently.

Caitrin shook her head. "I'm just tired," she replied. "After so much worry over Eoghan." She cast a glance left at where the lad sat upon a rug, playing with blocks of wood. He was building a tower, which he then knocked over with a squeal of laughter. Caitrin's expression softened as she watched him. The sight of her son was like a balm, soothing her anxiety.

As long as she had Eoghan, life was manageable.

"I'm so relieved he's better," Caitrin murmured.

"Aye, milady. We've all been worried about him."

Caitrin glanced up, smiling. Sorcha's words soothed her. "I'm sorry I've been snappish this morning."

The hand-maid held her gaze. "Ye are more than just tired, milady," she observed. "Ye have been jumping at shadows since dawn."

Caitrin sighed, considering whether to confide in Sorcha about what had happened between her and Alasdair the evening before. She sometimes felt so alone, and at moments like this missed her sisters terribly. Rhona and Adaira had always been there for her, but they couldn't listen to her now.

"I—" she began, but a knock on the door to the solar prevented her from continuing.

"Come in," she called, irritation rising. No doubt one of the servants wanted her help with something, only this morning she didn't have the patience it. She just wanted to be left in peace for a while.

The door opened and a tall, dark-haired figure stepped inside.

Caitrin went cold, dread curling in the pit of her belly. Alasdair was the last person she wanted to see this morning. She'd deliberately broken her fast in here, avoiding the chaos of the Great Hall—and hiding from this man.

Sorcha hurriedly put aside her sewing and rose to her feet, smoothing her skirts. "Milord," she greeted him with a curtsy.

"Morning, Sorcha." Alasdair favored the hand-maid with a smooth smile. "Could ye give Lady Caitrin and me a few moments alone, please?"

"Of course." Sorcha stepped away from the fireside, scooped up Eoghan, and left the chamber.

Silence followed her departure.

Caitrin had thought that Alasdair's smile might fade once Sorcha was no longer present, yet it did not. He sauntered over to the hearth and took the seat that the hand-maid had just vacated, crossing one ankle at the knee with loose-limbed grace. Then he leaned back and viewed Caitrin with a shuttered gaze.

"Good morning, Caitrin."

Swallowing, in an attempt to ease the tightness in her throat, Caitrin met his eye. "Milord."

"I hope ye are no longer upset?" he drawled. "I assure ye I won't touch ye again."

Caitrin stared back at Alasdair. She couldn't believe the change in him. Last night he'd been vulnerable before her. The naked want on his face, the hunger in his eyes had haunted her later as she'd lain in bed, trying in vain to fall asleep. Yet now, he was utterly composed and wore a lazy half-smile as if she amused him.

He was treating her like he had upon his arrival at Duntulm months ago—and she knew why.

He was trying to cover up the fact she'd offended him, wounded his pride.

Caitrin's breathing quickened as panic curled up within her. She'd pushed him away to preserve her status here, to protect herself and Eoghan—and yet angering him wouldn't help them either.

Afterward, when she'd been safely back in her bed-chamber, Caitrin had felt wretched over how violently she'd pushed him away. He hadn't hurt her—in fact, the brief kiss had consumed her—yet she'd shrunk from him. She didn't blame him for taking offense. She felt the need to explain.

"Alasdair," she said hoarsely. "About last night ... I must—"

"Please, Caitrin," he cut her off with a lazy wave of the hand. "We don't need to ever mention it again. Ye made yer feelings clear, and I'll respect them ... I'm not here to talk about that." He reached under the neckline of the leather vest he wore and withdrew a rolled parchment. "This came from yer father two days ago. I was waiting till Eoghan was better before giving it to ye."

Caitrin took the letter from him and unfurled it. Then she silently read the missive, going cold as she did so.

Finally, her father had run out of patience.

"I imagine ye knew this day would come," he observed. The dry tone to his voice made Caitrin glance up, her gaze spearing his. He was still smiling, and it was starting to make her angry. "Ye had better start packing yer bags."

Caitrin drew herself up, her fingers clenching around the letter. "What if I wish to remain here?"

He arched a dark eyebrow. "Yer father wishes otherwise."

"And ye?"

The easy smile faltered then and his gaze hooded. "I think it's best if ye leave Duntulm."

There it was, the anger that simmered just beneath the surface, hidden by an urbane smile and a devil-may-care veneer.

Caitrin quelled the urge to cry, blinking furiously. She loved living at Duntulm. She hated the thought of returning to Dunvegan, of being paraded in front of suitors—of being put back inside a cage.

"When?" she finally managed, the question coming out in a croak.

"Tomorrow. We'll set off just after dawn." Alasdair paused here, his gaze boring into her. "But Eoghan will be remaining here."

Caitrin jerked as if he'd just struck her. Then she lurched to her feet, her embroidery falling to the floor. "No!"

Alasdair slowly pushed himself up off the chair, as if he had all the time in the world, and rose to his full height. He towered over her, but Caitrin lifted her chin, fists clenching at her sides. "Ye will not take my son!"

His mouth quirked. "Eoghan is my heir."

"So ye keep saying. But he's not yer property. He's half MacLeod, and he's not staying here."

"Aye ... he is. Eoghan is weaned now. He doesn't need ye anymore. I will teach him everything he needs to know—so that one day he can take over from me ... he will want for nothing."

"I'm his mother," Caitrin countered, "and I'll go nowhere without him."

Alasdair snorted. "Ye will ... even if I have to throw ye over the back of yer horse and tie ye down."

Caitrin stared up at him, trembling now. "This is monstrous," she rasped, heart pounding. "What kind of man would separate a mother from her bairn?"

"One who wishes to ensure the MacDonald bloodline endures."

"That's all ye care about, isn't it?" Caitrin snarled. "Having an heir. Ye are a cold-blooded, heartless rogue, Alasdair MacDonald!"

Alasdair stepped closer to her, his gaze never leaving hers. The smile had faded, and a nerve flickered in his cheek, revealing that her words had managed to wound him. "Aye, I am," he murmured. "But very soon I will be the least of yer concerns."

"I can't believe it, milady," Sorcha whispered, aghast. "The chieftain wouldn't do such a thing."

Caitrin straightened up from where she'd been laying out her clothes on the bed ready for packing. The look of abject horror on her handmaid's face, the disbelief in her eyes, made Caitrin's anger bubble to the surface once more. "Well, ye should believe it," she snapped. "For it's true."

Sorcha's dark-blue eyes now glittered with tears. "But why?"

"Because he's been looking for a way to hurt me … and he's found it."

"But ye seemed to get on well of late." The lass knuckled away a tear that now trickled down her cheek. "I thought ye might—"

"Well ye thought wrong," Caitrin cut her off. "Now stop looking at me with cow eyes and help me pack my things."

Sorcha heaved in a deep, shuddering breath and nodded. A large wicker chest sat on the floor at the foot of the bed ready to be filled with Caitrin's belongings.

Caitrin got to work, rolling, folding, and packing with ruthless efficiency. Her movements were jerky as anger roiled within her. She'd been harsh with Sorcha, and didn't mean to be—but when the lass had tried to tell her that Alasdair MacDonald wasn't capable of such cruelty, something within her had snapped.

I should never have let my guard down with him.

It was too late now for such regrets, too late to change things. She'd almost begged him earlier—only pride had prevented her—but she knew that wouldn't help her. He'd only despise her all the more.

"I'm sorry, milady." Sorcha's broken whisper pulled her out of her seething thoughts. Caitrin glanced up from her packing to see that her hand-maid now stood, head buried in her hands. Her shoulders were shaking. "I can't bear the thought of ye going away," she gasped, "of ye leaving Eoghan behind."

Grief bubbled up within Caitrin. She hated to see Sorcha so upset; she could deal with her own suffering, yet she hated to see it in others.

Wordlessly, she pulled Sorcha into her arms. However, this only made the girl start to sob. Tears stung Caitrin's eyelids then, scalding her cheeks. She'd told herself she wouldn't weep until she was alone, but it was impossible not to, not with Sorcha inconsolable. They clung together for a few moments before Sorcha drew back, her face distraught.

"Surely yer father will oppose this?" she choked out. "He won't let MacDonald keep ye from yer son."

Caitrin loosed a heavy sigh and shook her head, wiping at her wet cheeks with the back of her hand. "My father is a calculating man … political alliances have always meant more to him than the happiness of his daughters. Why do ye think he's so keen to see me wed again?"

"But surely he wouldn't want ye separated from yer bairn?"

Caitrin favored Sorcha with a sad, watery smile. "No … but if it keeps his neighbor appeased, I doubt he'll oppose it."

Chapter Seventeen

Out for Vengeance

A COOL WIND fanned Caitrin's face.

Her throat was raw from weeping, her eyes swollen. She was barely aware of those who escorted her: Alasdair up front and Darron behind, with a handful of the Duntulm Guard bringing up the rear.

All she could think about was Eoghan, and how it had ripped out her heart to leave him.

Sorcha had been heartbroken that morning. She'd helped her mistress finish packing, all the while weeping. Now that Eoghan was weaned, Sorcha would bring the lad up within the walls of Duntulm. Caitrin trusted Sorcha and knew Eoghan was in good hands. Yet that didn't make her feel any better. *She* was the lad's mother. She needed to be with him.

Tears flowed silently down Caitrin's cheeks. She didn't bother to wipe them away. Casting a glance over her shoulder, she looked upon the high basalt curtain wall of the fortress. Sorcha would be watching from her solar window, Eoghan in her arms.

Pain gripped Caitrin's ribs in a vise, and she turned away from Duntulm.

Instead, her gaze settled upon the man who rode ahead of her, leading the way out of Duntulm village. Alasdair sat tall and proud in the saddle, his long dark hair tied back. He appeared completely unmoved by what he was doing to her.

She'd grown to hate her husband during their marriage and to fear him. But the loathing she now felt for his younger brother made those emotions seem gentle.

If she had a dirk, she'd throw it at him, and enjoy seeing the blade sink between his shoulder blades.

Since their confrontation in her solar, she hadn't seen him—not until this morning when she'd been escorted downstairs to the bailey, where her saddled horse awaited.

Even then, he'd barely acknowledged her. Impatience bristled off his body while she mounted and servants loaded her belongings onto a cart that would accompany them south.

He was out for vengeance; she'd seen it in his eyes the day before.

She didn't think anyone could be so cruel. It shocked her to the core—but at the same time, a defiance rose within her.

He won't win. Caitrin clenched her jaw, pushing against the despair that threatened to smother her. *I'll get my son back. I'll fight this ....*

Night settled over the world, and the last of the rosy sunset faded from the western sky.

Caitrin sat upon a boulder, staring sightlessly at the hearth the men had just lit. It wasn't a cold evening, yet the fire provided a focal point for the small camp. They'd erected a tent a few yards back, where Caitrin would rest tonight. The men, Alasdair included, would sleep around the fire and take turns keeping watch.

"Here's yer supper, milady." Darron hunkered down before Caitrin and handed her a wooden platter with bread, cheese, and salted pork upon it. Caitrin took it without a word. "There's a skin of ale as well," he added, placing the leather bladder at her feet.

Caitrin nodded. She wouldn't touch the food; her stomach was clenched in a tight knot. She was too angry to eat.

Darron went to rise to his feet but hesitated. She saw the sympathy in his eyes. "I wish things were different, milady," he murmured, keeping his voice low so that none of the others heard him. "Ye shouldn't be separated from yer son."

Caitrin swallowed a sudden lump in her throat. She'd spent the day in brooding silence, rage seething inside her. Anger made her feel better as it forced down the grief and despair of losing Eoghan. But with just a few kind words Captain MacNichol threatened her composure. Her vision now blurred. "Thank ye, Darron," she said softly. "Ye have been a good friend to me over the last few years ... I'll not forget it."

Darron's mouth curved into a rare smile although his gaze remained solemn. "If there's anything I can do, milady ... just ask."

Caitrin blinked rapidly and heaved in a deep breath. She needed to save her tears till later, for when she was alone. "Just keep an eye out for Eoghan, will ye?" She favored him with a brittle smile.

"Of course," he promised. "Ye have my word."

Darron moved away, returning to the fireside, where one of the men had started singing a bawdy drinking song about a lonely traveler, lusty wenches, and a tavern in the midst of winter. Boyd was grinning at the singer, raising his cup of ale at the end of each lewd verse.

Alasdair sat amongst his men, eating his salted pork and bread. He raised his gaze and smiled when the warrior finished his song and the others cheered. Boyd slapped the singer hard on the back and demanded another.

Not once did Alasdair look her way.

Caitrin set the tray aside and reached for the skin of ale instead. She took a large gulp of the sweet, warm liquid. She wasn't the least bit hungry, but the ale would blunt the world's sharp edges, for a short while at least.

The last of the light faded and night cloaked the campsite. There was no moon so Caitrin found herself watching the stars instead. They were particularly bright tonight. The sight steadied her, as did the knowledge she'd soon see her sister Rhona.

They would reach Dunvegan tomorrow morning, and she would be in a familiar place at least. Once she'd been delivered, Alasdair would leave, and she would be spared having to look upon him.

Caitrin took another deep pull of ale. The drink relaxed her, although her fury continued to simmer. He'd had his vengeance on her—how she wished she could revenge herself upon him.

Around the fire, the singing eventually ceased. The men spoke now in low voices punctuated by the odd burst of laughter. After a while, the world around their campsite grew quiet. They'd made camp at the edge of woodland, and the wind that had buffeted them on the journey south had died.

Weary, Caitrin rose to her feet and, without a word to any of the men, retired to her tent. Inside she found a small brazier burning and a thick fur spread out upon the ground, where she would sleep.

Stretching out, Caitrin rolled onto her back and listened to the rumble of the men's voices beyond.

Eoghan.

Caitrin wrapped her arms around her torso, squeezing her eyes shut as a wave of loss crashed into her.

Her son would be wondering where she was, why she never came into his bed-chamber to tuck him in and sing him a lullaby.

I'll find my way back to ye, my darling.

Tears leaked from her eyes, trickling down her cheeks, where they soaked into her hair. Despair pressed down upon her like a great boulder upon her chest, but she wouldn't give into it.

She wouldn't give up. She owed it to Eoghan to be strong.

I promise.

Alasdair leaned forward and poked the glowing embers with a stick, ignoring Darron. He'd deliberately sat apart from the others, while Boyd took the first shift of the night watch.

But the captain had sought him out.

Darron lowered himself onto the edge of the large flat stone where Alasdair sat. Neither man spoke, yet Alasdair could feel the weight of the captain's stare.

Moments passed, and eventually, Alasdair turned to him with a scowl. "For God's sake, MacNichol ... out with it."

Darron's mouth thinned. "Taking Lady Caitrin's bairn from her seems ... harsh."

Alasdair snorted, although his ire rose at Darron's impertinence. "It *is* harsh—but necessary. Eoghan is the last of my family's bloodline. He must stay at Duntulm."

Darron fell silent, his attention shifting to the glowing embers of the fire pit before them. "Lady Caitrin did a fine job as chatelaine," he said finally. "I don't understand why ye would send her away."

Alasdair frowned. "Ye know why ... her father wants her to remarry."

Darron glanced his way. "But *ye* could wed her?"

Alasdair threw back his head and laughed. "I'd be the last man in Scotland that Lady Caitrin would deign to wed."

"Why?" Darron looked confused now, and Alasdair wished the man would cease his incessant questioning. "Ye seem well suited."

"Appearances deceive, MacNichol," Alasdair replied, his tone making it clear that the conversation was over.

The night was still, the darkness smothering. Alasdair found he couldn't settle.

Rising from the fireside, he walked to the edge of the camp, stepping up next to where Boyd stood watch.

"I'll take over," he said quietly. "Ye get some rest."

Boyd glanced over at him. "Are ye sure? I can keep watch for a while yet."

"I can't sleep anyway. There's no point in both of us being awake."

Boyd nodded, although his face, illuminated by the faint glow of the torch behind him, was thoughtful. "Still not sleeping?"

Alasdair shrugged. "Some nights are better than others." He cast an eye over Boyd. Unlike him, his cousin appeared to have emerged from the war unscathed. "Ye sleep easy these days then?"

Boyd gave a jaw-cracking yawn and stretched. "Aye ... like a bairn." He clapped Alasdair on the back and stepped away from him. "My bedroll beckons. I'll leave ye to it."

His cousin walked off, returning to the camp and leaving Alasdair alone.

Somewhere in the undergrowth, an animal rustled, and then an owl softly hooted. Alasdair drew in a deep breath, listening to the slumbering land around him. The night sounds were gentle, calming, yet they did little to relax him.

He felt as if he stood upon a knife's edge. Every nerve in his body was taut, ready to fight. It was as if danger lurked behind each surrounding shadow. He'd get little rest tonight.

His encounter with Caitrin in the solar had thrown his world back into chaos. It had been a slap in the face, a brutal reminder of why he should have never let his guard down with her.

He had no one to blame but himself.

He'd been a gullible fool twice now. The first time he could have claimed ignorance, but this time he'd known full well the risk he'd been taking.

Alasdair stared out at the darkness, his gaze unfocused. He'd hurt Caitrin deeply by taking Eoghan. There was no worse revenge he could have exacted upon her. MacLeod's demand had been the perfect excuse to send her away while keeping his nephew.

Vengeance.

It had once been his constant companion, especially after he learned of Baltair's death. Yet, for a brief few months, it had released him from its claws, allowing him to hope that one day he might know happiness again. That was—until two days ago.

Now the beast had seized him once more. It perched upon his shoulder and whispered to him. It told him that Caitrin deserved his wrath—that she deserved to suffer as he had. As he did now.

Alasdair drew in a deep breath. Aye, this was what he'd wanted, what he'd planned for on the journey back to Duntulm all those months ago. He should feel jubilant, vindicated that he'd finally achieved his goal.

Why then did he simply feel hollow?

Chapter Eighteen

Return to Dunvegan

"LORD, HOW I'VE missed ye!" Rhona MacKinnon flew across the bailey and threw her arms around Caitrin. She drew back from her sister, storm-grey eyes gleaming. Tall and statuesque with a mane of auburn hair, Rhona looked as vibrant as ever. "Ye don't write often enough!"

Caitrin swallowed a lump in her throat and forced a smile. She was aware that she and Rhona had an audience. Alasdair MacDonald and the rest of her escort were approaching the keep just a few strides behind her. The dove-grey bulk of Dunvegan keep towered above them. Much bigger than Duntulm, Malcolm MacLeod's fortress faced west. It perched on the edge of a loch surrounded by lush green, with rugged hills at its back.

Usually, Caitrin was happy to come home, but this morning the sight of Dunvegan brought her no solace. It was just a reminder of what lay in store: a forced marriage.

"I'm sorry I'm so terrible at keeping in touch," she replied. "The days pass and then, before I know it, a month has gone by and the letter I promised to send ye is still sitting on my desk half-written."

Rhona gave an unladylike snort. "It sounds as if ye are much busier than me." Her gaze shifted from Caitrin then, moving past her to the rest of the company. "Where's Eoghan?"

Caitrin stiffened, struggling to keep the smile plastered to her face. She didn't want to tell Rhona about Eoghan now, not with Alasdair MacDonald just a few feet behind her. "He's remained in Duntulm."

Rhona frowned. "But ye usually travel with him?"

"Not this time ... he's in good hands. Sorcha is minding him while I get this over with."

Rhona nodded, her gaze shadowing. "That makes sense I suppose. Da's got the bit between his teeth. He has three suitors lined up already ... they'll keep ye busy enough. Ye will be able to send for Eoghan once all this is done." She looped her arm through Caitrin's, and together they walked toward the set of steps leading up to the keep. "I bet the lad has grown."

"Aye." Caitrin's face was starting to ache from the effort it was taking her to keep the smile frozen to her face. "He'll be walking soon." Caitrin paused here, desperate to change the subject. "Have ye heard from Adaira? The last letter I had was two moons ago."

"I heard from her last around then too," Rhona replied. "It sounds as if Gylen Castle suits her and Lachlann very well. Ma's family welcomed them without hesitation. The descriptions of her new life there made me quite jealous."

Caitrin huffed a laugh. "Then we shall have to organize a visit to see her ... I have to admit I'm curious about Ma's kin. I'd love to visit Gylen." Even to her own ears Caitrin's voice sounded forced. Of course she wanted to visit Adaira, but right now her priority was Eoghan.

They entered the keep and made their way through a wide entrance hall with stairs leading off it to the left and right. Straight ahead were the heavy oaken doors leading to the Great Hall.

"The noon meal is still being prepared," Rhona said, steering her toward the left stairwell. "Come on, let's go to the women's solar. There's so much I've got to tell ye."

Caitrin set down the goblet of wine she'd just taken a sip from and tried to focus on her sister's happy news. "Congratulations ... I'm so pleased for ye both."

Rhona beamed back at her. "I've been throwing up my bannocks in the mornings for over a week now ... the healer confirmed it this morning. I'm with child."

Caitrin smiled. "Taran must be overjoyed."

"That's an understatement. He hasn't stopped grinning since I told him." Rhona paused here, her gaze searching. She set aside her own goblet of wine. "There is something up with ye, Caitrin. I sensed it from the moment I set eyes on ye downstairs."

Caitrin swallowed. She'd always been adept at masking her feelings from others—even her sisters—but not today it seemed. Her vision misted then; she was so tired of being strong, of having to keep up a wall. Now that she was alone with Rhona her defenses crumbled.

Bowing her head, she covered her face with her hands and began to weep.

Rhona was at her side in an instant, her arm circling Caitrin's shoulders. "Caitrin ... what's wrong?"

"It wasn't my choice to leave Eoghan behind," Caitrin finally gasped. "Alasdair MacDonald is keeping him ... as his heir."

She raised her face, turning to her sister. Rhona's face had gone ashen. "But he can't keep ye from yer son," she whispered.

Tears streamed down Caitrin's face. "He can ... and he has."

Rhona's features tightened. "Only the worst kind of rogue would do such a thing!"

"Aye ... I didn't think him capable of such an act, but I was wrong."

"Why would he be so cruel?"

Caitrin loosed a breath. "He's never forgiven me for spurning him."

She deliberately didn't mention the incident of a few days prior. She wasn't sure how to articulate it. Rhona knew about the proposal Alasdair had once made though.

Rhona stared at her for a moment, before her expression hardened. It was a look Caitrin knew well—the look of a woman steeling herself for a fight. "MacDonald will not get his way. Da will learn about this. He'll put things right."

"No, Rhona," Caitrin replied firmly. She sniffed, wiping her wet cheeks with her sleeve. "Da will only make things worse ... if he helps at all."

"How can ye say that?" Rhona scowled. "Eoghan is a MacLeod as much as he's a MacDonald. Da will tell that bastard to send yer son to ye."

Caitrin shook her head. She'd already had this discussion with Sorcha; it wearied her to have to explain it to her sister as well. "Ye have a short memory, Rhona. Da's alliances mean more to him than we do. Ye would be wasting yer breath."

"But after what happened with Adaira he might—"

"That was different," Caitrin cut her off. "Adaira forced Da's hand that day. If I want Eoghan back, I need to be the one to fight for him."

Rhona's gaze narrowed, and she folded her arms across her breasts. "But how will ye do that. We live in a man's world."

Caitrin's expression hardened. "And that's why we must fight using our own weapons."

"Ye should have brought Eoghan with ye," MacLeod grumbled. "I haven't glimpsed my grandson in months."

"Ye shall see him on my next visit to Dunvegan," Alasdair assured MacLeod with a smile. "I thought it best Lady Caitrin wasn't distracted ... ye want her to focus on finding a husband, do ye not?"

Across the table, Caitrin tensed. She glared at Alasdair, but he ignored her. Instead, he sipped from his goblet with a nonchalance that made her temper flare.

The MacLeod clan-chief's brow smoothed. Tall, broad, and heavy-set with greying auburn hair, he had eyes the color of a stormy sky. He was a portly man and had gotten so fat of late that it was difficult to see where his chin ended and his neck began. "Aye ... maybe ye are right."

"We can travel to Duntulm together, Da," Caitrin spoke up, forcing a lightness of tone she didn't feel. "Once I've chosen a suitor."

"There will be no time for that," Alasdair replied before MacLeod had a chance to answer. "I imagine ye will be wed as soon as ye choose a suitor. Yer new husband won't want ye disappearing to Duntulm."

"Aye," MacLeod said, eyeing the MacDonald chieftain in surprise. He then shifted his attention to Caitrin. "He's right again, lass. I've sent word. Yer suitors are due to arrive tomorrow. One of them is traveling from the mainland."

Caitrin clenched her jaw, dropping her gaze to the plate of boiled mutton, turnips, and oaten bread before her. Around her, the table went quiet. They sat in Dunvegan's Great Hall, a massive space dominated by two hearths. The noon meal had just been served, and the greasy odor of mutton hung in the air.

Steeling herself, Caitrin glanced up, her gaze traveling to where Rhona and her husband, Taran, sat watching her. Rhona wore a pinched expression, while Taran, whose scarred face gave him a frightening look at the best of times, was scowling. Rhona must have told him about Eoghan, for her brother-in-law then favored Alasdair MacDonald with a dark look.

"Ye are fortunate indeed, Caitrin," Una, her stepmother, spoke up. Small and dark, Una favored Caitrin with a smug smile. "One of yer suitors is my brother, Ross. A fine warrior he is too—any woman would be lucky to have him."

MacLeod huffed, holding his goblet up for a passing servant to fill. "Gavin MacNichol and Fergus MacKay are both worthy too. We'll see whom Caitrin prefers."

Caitrin went still. Chieftain MacNichol was one of her suitors? She remembered then her brief conversations with him during his visit to Duntulm—and the interest she'd glimpsed in his eyes.

Across the table, Caitrin saw Alasdair MacDonald stiffen. While Gavin had indicated an interest in Caitrin during his visit to Duntulm, Alasdair obviously hadn't imagined he'd take it further.

"What if she doesn't like any of them?" Caitrin's younger brother, Iain, asked. A sallow-faced lad with sharp features and a mop of auburn hair, he was watching his father, a gleam in his grey eyes.

Caitrin frowned. She didn't like the evident pleasure Iain took in asking this. She'd had little to do with the lad over the past few years, but Rhona had warned her about his vindictive streak.

"My daughter will do her duty." MacLeod rumbled before turning his attention to Caitrin. She stiffened at the hard look in his grey eyes. The events of the past year hadn't softened him it seemed; he still saw his daughters as his pawns. "If she refuses to make a choice, I shall do it for her."

MacLeod raised his goblet to his lips and took a large gulp. He then shifted his attention to Alasdair, his expression lightening. "Will ye stay on in Dunvegan awhile, MacDonald?"

Caitrin froze. *No ... Da. Please don't.*

Alasdair inclined his head. "I should really return to Duntulm."

MacLeod snorted. "What's the hurry? Stay on for a few days and enjoy some fine MacLeod hospitality. I've got a boar hunt organized for tomorrow."

Silence fell at the table. Caitrin held her breath. She stared down at her meal, willing Alasdair to refuse. However, when the hush drew out, she raised her gaze and looked at Alasdair. He met her eye briefly before he shifted his attention to MacLeod and smiled, raising his goblet to the clan-chief. "Why not? I like a good hunt."

Caitrin caught up with Alasdair in the entranceway outside the Great Hall once the noon meal had ended. Hurrying ahead of him she stepped into his path, forcing him to stop.

Alasdair halted, while Darron and Boyd continued on.

"Why are ye staying?" she demanded, rounding on him.

He cast her an infuriating smile. "Yer father insisted."

"Ye could have refused."

"It seemed rude."

Caitrin drew in a sharp breath, fighting the anger that made her want to slap his face. "Twisted bastard—ye are remaining here to spite me," she accused. "To gloat when I am forced to wed."

He barked out a laugh. "Ye give yerself too high an importance, Caitrin. I'm staying to appease yer father, and for no other reason."

She stepped close to him, drawing herself up as tall as she could. Even then, she still had to angle her head back to meet his gaze. Alasdair stared back at her, a challenge in his eyes. He was goading her, and she hated him for it.

"Ye are an unwelcome guest, MacDonald," she snarled. "Ye might fool my father with yer smiles and flattery, but I know what ye are. Keep out of my way."

Chapter Nineteen

First Impressions

CAITRIN STOOD IN her bed-chamber, nervously smoothing the skirts of her sky-blue kirtle. It was the first time since Baltair's death that she'd worn any color besides black. She felt naked without her somber clothes.

Heaving in a deep breath, she glanced over her shoulder at her sister's hand-maid, Liosa. "So, they're all waiting for me in the Great Hall, are they?"

The maid paused in brushing Caitrin's hair. "They are, milady."

Caitrin swallowed, nervousness rising in her breast. She wasn't ready for this. "Have ye seen them?" Although Caitrin had already met Gavin MacNichol, she had no idea what her other two suitors looked like.

"Aye ... I was in the bailey when they rode in."

"And?"

Liosa's green eyes grew round. "Ye are fortunate, milady. They're three fine warriors." She sighed then. "I can't decide which of them is the most handsome."

Caitrin cast a look over her shoulder at where Rhona perched upon a seat near the window.

Her sister met her eye with a wry look. "At least Da isn't trying to wed ye off to the likes of Aonghus Budge."

Caitrin pulled a face. "I'd rather he wasn't trying to wed me off at all."

Rhona studied her a moment, her expression turning thoughtful. "Ye are taking all of this better than I would," she murmured. "I take it ye have a plan of some kind?"

"Perhaps." Caitrin looked away, allowing Liosa to finish brushing her hair. She had piled half of it on the top of Caitrin's head while allowing the rest to tumble free down her back. It was the first time she'd worn her hair loose in a long while.

"That sounds mysterious," Rhona replied. "Are ye going to keep it to yerself?"

Caitrin glanced back at her. "For the moment."

Rhona's gaze narrowed. "Ye didn't use to be this secretive."

Caitrin didn't reply, despite that she could sense her sister's frustration.

"Well?" Rhona pressed.

Caitrin sighed. "All I care about is getting Eoghan back," she admitted. "There's no point appealing to MacDonald, or Da ... but if I choose a husband wisely, he might be able to help me."

When Rhona didn't answer, Caitrin turned to face her. Liosa gave a huff of frustration and stepped back, giving up on her finishing touches to Caitrin's hair. "Do ye think that's calculating of me?"

Their gazes met before Rhona's full-mouth curved. "No ... I think it's clever."

The soaring strains of a harp greeted Caitrin when she stepped inside the Great Hall, Rhona following close behind her. It was early evening, and supper would be served soon. Her father's retainers hadn't yet entered the hall. However, a small group sat upon the raised dais at the far end.

Caitrin's heart raced, and she surreptitiously wiped her damp palms upon the skirt of her kirtle. She hadn't been looking forward to this—but now the moment had come to greet her suitors, she wished she could turn and flee back to her bower.

She had no wish to sit and simper before these men, not when her son was in her enemy's keeping. And yet, if she wanted Eoghan back, she had no choice.

Her father and Una sat at the head of the table, with the three suitors flanking them. They weren't alone though. Taran, Alasdair, Boyd, and Darron sat at the opposite end of the table.

Caitrin stiffened at the sight of Alasdair. She'd hoped he wouldn't be present for this meeting. Yet she should have known he'd make a point of attending—if only to watch her suffer.

The moment she stepped inside the hall, she felt Alasdair's attention swivel to her. The weight of his gaze unsettled her, but she ignored him. Instead, Caitrin shifted her attention to the three men who had come to woo her.

Breathe, she counseled herself. *Don't let any of them see ye are nervous.*

Gavin MacNichol met her eye, a warm smile stretching his ruggedly handsome features. Next to him was a dark-haired warrior with swarthy good looks and bright blue eyes. Instinctively, Caitrin knew this must be Ross Campbell. The family resemblance to Una was striking. The third suitor, Fergus MacKay, was a broad-shouldered man with a mane of thick brown hair and green eyes. An appreciative smile stretched his comely face as he watched Caitrin approach.

Drawing in a deep, steadying breath, Caitrin favored them with a warm smile and stepped up onto the dais. "Good eve, milords ... thank ye all for coming."

Alasdair's fingers tightened around the stem of his goblet.

All conversation had ceased when Caitrin entered the hall. Alasdair's gaze hadn't been the only one to track her path toward them.

It was a surprise to see her not wearing black. The sky-blue kirtle clung to her lithe form, accentuating the high curve of her bust, the womanly flare of her hips. It brought out the color of her eyes, the creamy texture of her skin. Her hair, which she usually wore up in prim braids, tumbled down her back.

Alasdair had forgotten to breathe as she'd walked toward the dais—forgotten about anything except the beauty gliding toward him.

And then, he'd watched her attention focus upon the three men seated near MacLeod.

When she'd smiled, his gut had twisted.

That smile wasn't for him—it would never be for him. Especially now.

The three suitors rose to their feet. MacNichol, the oldest of them, stepped forward first to greet Caitrin. "It's a pleasure to see ye again, milady," he said with a smile. He took her hand and raised it to his lips for a brief kiss.

Jealousy knifed through Alasdair, causing him to suck in his breath.

His reaction caught him off guard. When MacLeod had invited him and his men to join them for a goblet of wine and a light supper, he'd been happy to accept. He was curious to see Caitrin's suitors and her reaction to them. He wanted to see her struggle, possibly even disgrace herself.

But he hadn't expected this—this stomach-wrenching surge of possessiveness.

As if Caitrin belonged to him. As if he had any claim on her.

Alasdair stared down at his wine and struggled to master his reaction. When he glanced up, the tall, raven-haired man with midnight blue eyes had stepped forward to greet Caitrin. He too took her hand and kissed the back of it. "Ross Campbell at yer service, milady."

The third suitor approached her then, dropping to one knee before Caitrin. "Such a vision of loveliness," he boomed in a deep baritone. "A fairy queen stands before me."

"Daughter, meet Fergus MacKay, son to the chieftain of Strathnaver," MacLeod spoke up with a grin. "He has traveled a long way to meet ye."

Caitrin inclined her head, favoring MacKay with a gentle smile. "I am honored, milord."

Alasdair raised his goblet to his lips and took a deep draft.

Jealousy writhed in his gut like an eel. He tried to quell it, but the beast would not be calmed. It had been a mistake to accept this eve's invitation. But now it was too late. He would have to sit through torture.

Caitrin took a seat at the long table. Gavin MacNichol sat to her left while Ross Campbell and Fergus MacKay faced her.

When Liosa had claimed her suitors were all fine-looking men, she'd thought her to be exaggerating. The hand-maid tended to go a bit silly over such things and couldn't be trusted to give an accurate view. However, this time, the lass was right.

It didn't help ease Caitrin's nervousness though. It had been a while since she'd been the center of attention like this.

Courage. Ye need to do this ... for Eoghan.

Squaring her shoulders, Caitrin's gaze swept over the faces of her three suitors. "I'm flattered ye have come all this way," she addressed them with another smile. "I look forward to getting to know each of ye a little better."

She glanced over then, at the man seated next to her. Gavin MacNichol smiled back. Despite that he was around eighteen years her elder, the MacNichol chieftain was still a virile man. He wore his long blond hair unbound this eve. He looked less weary than the last time she'd seen him. His blue eyes were warm as he poured her a goblet of wine.

Opposite her, Ross Campbell was dangerously attractive. The warrior, who appeared to be in his late twenties, had a magnetic gaze and chiseled features. The sensual edge to his gaze as he briefly met her eye made Caitrin uneasy. She imagined he was used to women fawning over him.

Fergus MacKay was of a similar age to Campbell, although his looks were less brooding. He was built like an ox; his leather jerkin strained against his muscles. MacKay stared at her, his fern-green eyes gleaming with frank admiration.

Caitrin surveyed her suitors under lowered lashes. She needed to think. Which one would get her closer to Eoghan? Which one might even defy MacDonald for her?

She decided then that she would make her position clear.

"I should start this eve by telling ye what I'm looking for in a husband," she declared, her voice carrying across the table.

Silence fell. No one here—visitors or kin alike—had expected Caitrin to be so direct. A lady didn't speak so. But Caitrin didn't care. Her time as chatelaine had taught her the value of taking control of situations before others did.

"My future husband will be honest and loyal," she continued. "A fair-minded man who would never seek to undermine or mistreat me in any way."

She shifted her attention down the table then, past Rhona and Taran's shocked faces, to where Alasdair MacDonald sat. His face was pale and strained, his gaze hooded. He didn't look happy at all, and Caitrin felt a surge of vindictive pleasure.

Good.

Caitrin looked back at her father to see that Malcolm MacDonald was frowning, his gaze perplexed. He was probably wondering what had come over her. Caitrin had never spoken out of turn like this.

An awkward pause followed while Caitrin waited for her suitors' responses.

Ross Campbell met her eye and inclined his head slightly, his expression amused. Next to him, Fergus MacKay favored her with a wide grin, whereas Gavin MacNichol merely smiled, his blue eyes twinkling.

Then, unexpectedly, MacNichol raised his goblet into the air. "Shall we toast to that then?"

At the head of the table, MacLeod struggled to his feet. "Aye ... a toast." He too held his goblet high, although he now wore a slightly stunned expression.

The suitors raised their goblets, smiles stretching their faces.

"To the lovely Lady Caitrin," Fergus MacKay boomed, with a wink to his two competitors. "May she find a man among us worthy of her beauty ... and failing that ... may the best man win!"

MacNichol threw his head back and laughed at this, while Campbell smirked.

Raising the goblet to her lips, Caitrin took a sip of sloe wine. The liquid warmed her belly, soothing the last of her nerves. The courtship she was about to endure was a game, she might as well try to enjoy it.

"I'm taking MacDonald out boar hunting tomorrow." Her father's hearty voice jerked Caitrin's attention back to the head of the table. "Ye three must join us." He then picked up the MacLeod drinking horn—taken from a massive ox. "When we return, there will be feasting and dancing ... and the mightiest hunter among ye will have to drain this."

"There will also be wooing," Una reminded her husband, casting him an exasperated look. "Maybe ye shouldn't encourage heavy drinking, my love. Caitrin's suitors must keep their wits about them."

"Of course, wife." MacLeod dismissed Una's comment with a wave of his hand. "Although a real man should be able to hold his drink *and* win my daughter's heart."

Chapter Twenty

Competition

ALASDAIR THRUST THE spear deep into the boar's chest.

Man and beast were so close that he could smell its pungent odor: oily and slightly sweet. Staring into the beast's eyes, Alisdair watched them glaze over. Then it fell to its knees and collapsed with an agonized wheeze.

A cheer went up in the clearing.

"Well met, MacDonald!" Malcolm MacLeod limped toward him, a grin splitting his face. "I've never seen anyone bring down a boar with such style."

Breathing hard, Alasdair straightened up and pulled his spear free of the boar's chest. It had been a clean kill. He'd rammed the spear into its heart.

MacLeod slapped him on the back. "Nothing like a good boar hunt, eh?"

Alasdair nodded, still out of breath from the dance the boar had led him on. In the end, he'd closed in on it, flanked by Taran MacKinnon on one side and Gavin MacNichol on the other. All three men wielded boar spears, but it was only Alasdair who'd managed to get close enough to strike.

"Impressive," MacNichol congratulated him with a wide smile, while MacKinnon merely gave a reluctant nod. Ever since his arrival at Dunvegan, Caitrin's brother-in-law had viewed Alasdair with a jaundiced eye.

"I thought ye were about to get yerself gored," Fergus MacKay called out. He still sat astride his courser.

Ross Campbell had pulled his horse up next to MacKay's, his dark-blue eyes narrowing as he viewed the massive dead boar at Alasdair's feet. Campbell then cast Alasdair an incredulous look. "Ye are either lucky or extremely skilled."

Alasdair tossed both men a careless smile. "I knew what I was doing ... ye need to get close enough to look yer opponent in the eye before ye end him."

"Aye," Clan-chief MacLeod agreed with a snort. "Yer Da always did that ... every time we went out hunting I expected him to be speared in the guts by an enraged boar."

He didn't add that Eoghan MacDonald had actually died while out hunting, although it had been during a stag hunt. He'd fallen from his horse and snapped his neck.

Nearby, a whimper punctuated the clearing. One of the dogs that accompanied them was bleeding, caught by the boar's sharp tusk on its shoulder. Turning his attention from MacLeod, Alasdair crossed to the hound, hunkering down before it. The dog whined again and tried to lick his hand. It was a young, rangy beast with a wiry grey coat and soulful dark eyes.

"How deep is it?"

Alasdair glanced up to see Taran MacKinnon looming over him. He'd forgotten that the scar-faced warrior was master of MacLeod's hounds.

"Deep enough to need some stitching," Alasdair replied, stroking the dog's ears.

MacKinnon knelt next to him, and the dog nuzzled his arm, delighted to be the center of attention. "Does it need binding for the trip back?"

Alasdair shook his head. "The tip of the tusk sliced across the bone, but not deep. It should stop bleeding shortly."

"Good." MacKinnon gave a tight smile. "Lady Adaira would never forgive me for letting her hound bleed to death out on a hunt."

Alasdair glanced up at him. "This is her dog?"

"Aye. His name's Dùnglas. He's barely a year old. She picked him out of a litter when he was a pup."

Alasdair smiled. Grey Fort: a noble name for a wolfhound.

The dog gave another whine before nudging Alasdair's arm once more.

"Go on," Alasdair murmured, giving his ears another rub. "Ye will live, lad."

He rose to his feet, leaving MacKinnon with Dùnglas, and turned back to where the other men had dismounted from their horses and gone to inspect the boar he'd taken down.

It really was a prize. The beast had been in its prime. It had a coarse ebony coat, long deadly tusks, and a mane of spiky bristles that stretched from the crown of its head to the end of its spine.

Alasdair was still gazing at it when raindrops, cool and wet, splashed onto his face. He glanced up to see that the sky had gone a deep, ominous grey.

Nearby, MacLeod also looked up, his heavy brow furrowing. "That's us done for the morning," he announced. "Let's get this beast over the back of one of the horses and make for home."

The rain swept over the woodland northeast of Dunvegan in blinding sheets. The hunting party had turned back, but the decision had come too late—the rain had arrived, soaking them all within moments.

Initially, Alasdair resisted, bowing his head and pulling up the hood of his woolen cloak. But after a while, there didn't seem any point. The rain kept coming, even heavier than before.

Finally, he just surrendered to it, pushing down his hood and letting the rain run down his neck in a river. The rain was cool, but not cold. This storm brought the smell of warm earth and lush vegetation: the scents of summer.

At some point on the journey back to Dunvegan, Alasdair found himself riding next to Gavin MacNichol. The chieftain had been traveling alongside his nephew, but then Darron moved ahead to join Taran MacKinnon, leaving Alasdair and Gavin alone.

Like Alasdair, Gavin hadn't bothered resisting the rain. He hadn't even pulled his hood up, and his dark blond hair was slicked back from his wet face. He cast Alasdair a wry smile. "Looks like I won't need to bathe before this afternoon's feast."

Alasdair huffed in response. He'd intended to avoid the feast, but since he'd brought that boar down, the clan-chief intended to make a fuss of him. MacNichol, Campbell, and MacKay would compete for Caitrin's attention like stags during rutting season. He didn't want to see Caitrin smile at them and flirt with them.

His belly twisted. One of them would become her husband. *One of them will bed her.*

Alasdair hadn't considered this outcome when he'd decided to heed MacLeod's letter. He'd thought only about distancing himself from Caitrin, about making her suffer. Maybe this was his punishment for keeping Caitrin's son from her?

Perhaps he deserved it.

Silence stretched between them before Gavin spoke once more. He had to raise his voice to be heard over the thrumming of the rain.

"How are things in Duntulm these days?"

Alasdair glanced over at him. "Well enough ... I'm kept busy."

"The life of a chieftain isn't as exciting as some think, is it?" MacNichol replied. "There are walls to be built, crops to be planted, and an estate to be managed ... not to mention all the petty disputes ye have to deal with."

Alasdair's mouth curved. "Aye ... I had two farmers visit me last week. They were bickering over a goat."

MacNichol laughed. "Have ye missed the warrior's life ... fighting for king and country?"

Alasdair's expression sobered. "No, I haven't."

Gavin MacNichol studied him for a long moment before he spoke once more. "Three of my men returned home from the mainland a few days ago. They tell me the battle near Durham is to be named after the English commander."

Alasdair raised an eyebrow. "Lord Neville?"

"Aye, they're calling it the Battle of Neville's Cross."

Alasdair snorted. "The victor always gets to write history."

Gavin's brow furrowed then. "Ye would have seen a lot of yer countrymen die. That never leaves ye."

Alasdair drew in a deep breath. He wasn't about to admit to MacNichol that it hadn't. "We should have won that day," he growled. "Our force was much bigger than theirs."

"So, what happened?"

"We were poorly positioned," Alasdair replied looking away, his gaze focusing on the rain-swept woodland path before him. "The mist lay heavily as we readied ourselves for battle, and when it lifted, we saw that we stood upon rough ground. Our movement was made difficult by ditches and walls. We started the battle on the defensive ... and it only got worse from there."

MacNichol's frown deepened. Alasdair didn't blame him; the whole thing was a sorry, humiliating affair.

"I hear they've taken King David prisoner," Gavin said finally.

"Aye, he was badly injured, but I think he still lives. They took him back to England with them. I doubt he'll ever set foot on Scottish soil again."

The two men fell silent then, each brooding over the loss that had cost all of them dearly. After a lengthy pause, Alasdair spoke, deliberately changing the subject. "I was surprised to see ye here," he said casually. "I didn't realize ye wanted to pursue Lady Caitrin?"

MacNichol's mouth quirked. "Who wouldn't? She's a lovely lass ... and she's proven that she can run a castle too."

Alasdair forced down a surge of irritational jealousy. He liked Gavin MacNichol, but at that moment he wanted to choke the life out of him. "And what say ye to yer competition? Both Campbell and MacKay are younger than ye."

Gavin laughed, not remotely offended by this observation. When he'd sobered, he winked at Alasdair. "Many women appreciate an older man. We make better lovers."

Chapter Twenty-one

Ye Want to Choose Wisely

CAITRIN CLOSED THE shutters against the rain and began to pace the solar. The chamber—filled with embroidered cushions, dried flowers, and pieces of weaving and sewing in progress—was a warm, comfortable space that would forever remind Caitrin of her mother. She'd always liked this room, but this morning she couldn't relax here.

Just two days back in Dunvegan, and she already felt bored and restless. She was used to moving about Duntulm, her chatelaine's keys rattling at her waist, overseeing servants and making decisions about the running of the keep.

Here, she felt useless.

"For the love of God, sit down," Rhona chided her. "My belly's already churning. Watching ye circle this chamber is making it worse."

Caitrin huffed, stopping and turning to face her sister.

Rhona's face was pale this morning, her expression strained. She sat rubbing her lower sternum. "How long will this go on?" she muttered.

"I felt ill most mornings until I was around three months in with Eoghan," Caitrin replied with a sympathetic smile. "But I hear it differs with each woman."

Rhona sighed, her hand shifting to her belly. She wasn't showing signs of carrying a bairn yet as it was still early. "I wish Taran could share some of this," she grumbled. "Men have the easy part."

Caitrin gave a soft, humorless laugh. "They do indeed."

Rhona's grey eyes clouded. "I'm sorry, Caitrin. That was insensitive of me … ye must be missing Eoghan terribly."

Caitrin swallowed, her hands clenching by her sides. "I can't bear the thought of never seeing him again … it feels as if there's a gaping hole in my chest where my heart should be."

Rhona put aside the embroidery she'd been working on. "Ye will see him again." Her jaw firmed then. "Have ye got any further with that plan of yers?"

Caitrin nodded, taking a seat opposite her. A large loom sat to her left, with a half-finished tapestry on it. Caitrin had been trying to work on it, but then restlessness had overtaken her. She picked up the tapestry beater, a wooden comb she used to push the strands of yarn into place, but didn't resume work. Instead, she traced her fingertips along the teeth of the beater.

"I've met all three of them now," she replied softly, staring down at the comb, "and later I'll decide who can best help me get Eoghan back."

"Any early thoughts?"

Caitrin glanced up. "Gavin MacNichol is a neighbor, and he makes regular trips to Duntulm ... he might be a good choice."

Rhona frowned. "He's on good terms with MacDonald though, and might not want to fall out with him."

"Ye think I should choose someone more aggressive?"

Rhona shrugged. "Perhaps. MacKay looks like he has some fire in his belly."

"What about Ross Campbell? Would he help me?"

Rhona went still, her expression turning thoughtful. "I'm not sure what to think of him. Maybe it's just because I don't like Una. He's difficult to read." She grinned then. "Although Campbell's certainly the best-looking of the three. Liosa can't stop sighing over him."

Caitrin snorted. "I care not about looks." It was true. She wasn't searching for a man who'd make her knees go weak or one to fall in love with. Finding a husband wasn't her choice, but if she had to wed, it would be to a man who'd treat her well, who valued her happiness—and who realized how important it was for her to be with her child.

Rhona smiled. "Ye had better think on what to ask them later then," she said, rising to her feet. "Ye want to choose wisely."

Rhona then reached for a woolen shawl, wrapping it around her shoulders.

"Where are ye going?" Caitrin asked with a frown.

"It's nearing noon," her sister replied. "The men will be back at any moment. I'm going down to the stables to wait for Taran." She cast Caitrin an appraising look. "I'll find Liosa on my way and send her up ... ye had better start getting ready for the feast."

Caitrin watched Rhona leave the solar, the door thudding shut behind her.

Loosing a sigh, Caitrin leaned back in her chair. She still toyed with the beater, turning it over and over in her hands, but made no move to resume her weaving. In truth, although she knew what she must do, she dreaded the coming feast and the hours of music and dancing that would inevitably follow.

She wasn't looking forward to making idle chatter and smiling till her face ached. She wasn't looking forward to pretending that she wanted a husband at all.

Alasdair swung down from the saddle, landing lightly on the cobblestones. The rain beat down on his head, and he blinked water out of his eyes. He'd thought the storm might abate during the journey back to Dunvegan, but if anything, the rain was even heavier than earlier. The roar of it filled his ears as it thundered down into the bailey.

Leading his horse into the stables, his boots squelching with every stride, Alasdair breathed in the odor of wet horse, dog, leather, and wool. Around him, men grumbled as they tied their horses up inside the stalls and began unsaddling them.

"Come on lads, finish up here and get inside." Malcolm MacLeod's voice boomed through the stables. "Soon ye shall be feasting and making merry."

Behind Alasdair, Boyd paused while unsaddling his horse and glanced over his shoulder at him. "Does MacLeod ever let anything dampen his spirits?"

Alasdair pulled a face. "Don't let his ready smile fool ye ... Malcolm MacLeod's not someone ye want to get off-side with."

"His daughter's imminent remarriage has clearly put him in a jovial mood."

"Aye ... MacLeod loves an opportunity to break out the ale."

Boyd pushed his wet hair out of his eyes before grinning at Alasdair. "I'm enjoying Dunvegan."

"Don't get too comfortable. We're leaving tomorrow."

Boyd's face fell. "So soon?"

"Aye." Alasdair turned from him and started rubbing down his horse. "Tell the others we'll be riding out shortly after dawn."

The events of the last day had made Alasdair realize that it had been a mistake to agree to stay on in Dunvegan. The sooner he returned to Duntulm and put Caitrin out of his mind, the better.

He'd just removed his stallion's saddle and bridle when a firm nudge to his left leg drew his attention. A wet, bloodied wolf-hound sat at his feet, gazing up at him with soft eyes.

Dùnglas.

Alasdair let out an amused snort. "What are ye doing here, lad?"

"Shouldn't that dog be in its kennel?" Boyd muttered. "It risks getting trampled on in the stables."

"Aye ... I'll take him back when I finish here." Alasdair would also see to the beast's shoulder while he was at it. Growing up, he'd helped look after his father's dogs. As a keen hunter, Eoghan MacDonald had taken much pride in his kennel of wolfhounds.

Alasdair finished seeing to his horse and then made his way out of the stables, Dùnglas limping along at his heel. His wet clothing was starting to itch. After he saw to the dog, he would stop by his quarters and get changed before joining the others in the Great Hall.

As he approached the stable entrance, Alasdair spotted a tall woman with fiery auburn hair. Rhona MacKinnon was standing just inside the doorway, a damp shawl wrapped around her shoulders, awaiting her husband.

Rhona's gaze seized upon Alasdair as he neared. Her attention shifted from him to the dog following him before she frowned.

Alasdair favored her with a nod.

"Finally found a friend have ye, MacDonald?" she sneered.

Alasdair cast Rhona an answering smile. "At least the dog knows its place ... milady."

Chapter Twenty-two

Dancing and Feasting

THE STRAINS OF a lute and a harp echoed through Dunvegan's Great Hall, rising above the rumble of voices.

Caitrin took a sip of wine, her gaze traveling down the rows of tables that filled the wide space beneath the dais.

She'd rarely seen the Great Hall so crammed. Her father's retainers and their families packed the long tables, as did his warriors. There were also a number of faces she hadn't seen in years, clansmen who lived throughout MacLeod lands.

They'd all come to witness Caitrin choose her next husband.

Inhaling deeply, Caitrin shifted her attention to the huge array of food that covered the table before her: platters of roast venison, a rich goat stew, and a selection of breads and braised vegetables. A great roast goose stuffed with apples and nuts dominated the table.

Caitrin helped herself to a morsel of goose. The meat was rich and delicious, although her nervous stomach took the edge off her enjoyment. She doubted she'd be able to eat much of the spread. Despite that she'd vowed to try and enjoy herself, anxiety now bubbled up within her.

So much depended on tonight.

Her three suitors sat opposite her this eve, all of them dressed in their best léines and braies. Each wore a diagonal sash of their clan-plaid across his chest.

To Caitrin's chagrin, her father had seated Alasdair MacDonald next to her this afternoon, to MacLeod's right. Apparently, his guest had brought down a huge boar during the hunt. Her father wouldn't stop talking about it.

"Such a fine pair of tusks shouldn't go to waste. I shall have the boar's head preserved and mounted for ye," MacLeod announced, raising his goblet to Alasdair in yet another toast.

Alasdair smiled, raising his own goblet. "Thank ye, Malcolm."

MacLeod grinned at him and turned to a passing servant. "Fill my horn with mead and bring it here." He then turned his attention back to Alasdair, his expression turning sly. "Let's see if ye can drain it in one go. Few men can."

Despite her nerves, Caitrin fought the sudden urge to smile. To her knowledge, only her father had ever managed to drain the horn in one go. He loved to challenge men to drinking contests. She doubted Alasdair would manage it.

Alasdair seemed unmoved by the challenge. He merely smiled and waited for the horn. Moments later, it arrived: the great curved ox's horn, tipped in silver. Years earlier, MacLeod had faced the rampant ox armed only with his dirk and slayed it before cutting off one of its horns as a trophy.

"Ye won't be able to drain that, MacDonald," Fergus MacKay called out. "Hand it to me, and I'll show ye how a real man drinks."

Alasdair ignored him. Then, raising the horn to his lips, he tipped back his head and began to drink.

The other men at the table called out, some cheering him on while others heckled. Impressively, Alasdair paid none of them any mind. Caitrin watched his throat bob as he swallowed the mead in steady gulps.

"Drink, drink, drink!" Boyd bellowed from the far end of the table. The feasting had barely started, and the warrior was already well into his cups. At the tables below the dais, men had risen to their feet, necks craning to catch a glimpse of the commotion going on above.

Caitrin's gaze widened as she watched Alasdair continue to drink. The horn was nearly three times the size of a normal tankard. He should have drained most of it by now?

Even her father was starting to look impressed.

Alasdair reared back then, yanking the horn away from his mouth. His gaze had gone glassy, and his face was paling. For a moment, Caitrin was sure he would be sick.

Her father grabbed the horn off him and peered inside. "Ye did it!" he said, his voice incredulous. "I don't believe it."

A roar thundered down the table as Alasdair's men shouted their approval. However, their chieftain looked unwell. He gripped the edge of the table, squeezing his eyes shut a moment. His throat bobbed as he forced down the last gulp of mead. Caitrin noted the sheen of sweat on his face.

"He hasn't won yet," MacKay boomed, a delighted grin spreading across his face as he eyed Alasdair. "He's about to puke his guts out … look!" MacKay winked at Caitrin. "I'd move aside, milady. Ye don't want that pretty gown ruined."

Alasdair opened his eyes, his jaw tightening. To Caitrin's surprise, and disappointment, he appeared to recover. Inhaling deeply, he relaxed his grip on the table edge. He then straightened up and cast Fergus MacKay a sickly smile, his gaze glinting. "Yer turn?"

The feasting lasted a long while. After the meat dishes had been enjoyed, servants brought out wheels of aged cheese, platters of fruits, and raspberry tartlets. Mead, ale, and wine flowed—and the noise of conversation gradually grew more raucous.

Caitrin both ate and drank sparingly.

She wanted her wits about her for the dancing, when she would have the opportunity to speak to each of her suitors in turn.

At the table, those surrounding Caitrin all paced themselves differently. Her father downed food and wine with abandon, while Una picked at her meal like a sparrow. MacNichol and Campbell ate and drank moderately, while MacKay drained tankard after tankard of ale. Next to Caitrin, Alasdair ate slowly and barely touched the goblet of wine before him. After downing that horn of mead so quickly, Caitrin wasn't surprised. His face remained pale for some time afterward.

She and Alasdair didn't speak during the feast, choosing instead to ignore each other. Yet she was aware of his presence next to her, even when she was talking to one of her suitors. All three of them worked hard for her attention during the feasting. They teased each other, flattered her, and plied Caitrin with questions.

When the last of the food was cleared away, Caitrin was exhausted. She could easily have slunk away to her bower, but there was the dancing still to come. She wouldn't be able to leave for a long while yet.

The lutist and harpist changed their tune, instead shifting to a playful jig, while the tables were pushed back and the hall cleared.

A line of men and women then took to the floor.

"Lady Caitrin." Fergus MacKay rose to his feet, swaying slightly. "I'd like to have the first dance with ye, if I may?"

Caitrin nodded. She got up and stepped down from the dais, joining the others at the end of the line. Fergus followed, taking her hand, and then they began. Two steps forward, two steps back, and then a twirl. Caitrin knew all the steps, for she and her sisters had done this one many times over the years. This was a dance that all high-born lasses knew, for it was popular at handfastings and other celebrations.

After the twirl, Caitrin picked up her skirts and followed the other dancers around in a circle. She moved in short, gliding strides while keeping her back ramrod straight.

The music grew more strident. Caitrin twirled, stepped, and dipped, while the onlooking crowd started to clap. She loved to dance, and it felt good to move after the long feast. The music caught alight in her veins, and she let it carry her away.

Alasdair watched Caitrin move.

He was unable to take his gaze off her, tracking her across the dance floor as she glided backward and forward. She circled Fergus MacKay, the pair of them edging around each other, drawing together and then apart. He watched MacKay say something to her before Caitrin smiled back at him.

Alasdair sucked in a sharp breath.

Caitrin had never looked so lovely. She'd left her long pale-blonde hair completely unbound, although someone had threaded daisies through it. Rather than the sky-blue kirtle of the day before, she wore a gown of shimmering pale green.

It hurt Alasdair to look upon her. Each moment was torture, and yet he couldn't tear his gaze away.

"Tell me of yer home in Strathnaver," Caitrin asked as she circled her dance partner. "I have yet to visit the mainland."

Fergus MacKay flashed her a wide smile. Despite that he'd looked unsteady on his feet when he'd risen from the table, he danced with surprising grace. "My father resides at Castle Varrich, where I grew up," he replied. "But these days, I rule the lands around Borve Castle."

The dance brought them close, and MacKay's smile faded, his gaze growing intense. "It's a wild, beautiful coast, milady. I look forward to showing it to ye."

They circled around each other, back to back now.

"Do ye visit Skye often?" Caitrin asked.

"Every year or so," he replied. "Why?"

Caitrin twisted her head right, meeting Fergus MacKay's eye. "My son resides at Duntulm ... I don't wish to be parted from him."

"I'm afraid ye will be," he said softly, regret in his green eyes. "Ye shall bear my sons ... that will make it easier to forget the one ye left behind."

Caitrin dropped her gaze. Indignation pulsed through her. Did MacKay really think a woman could just forget such things?

The dance ended then, and MacKay led Caitrin back to her seat. Another dance started up, a lively jig that had most of the onlookers clapping their hands and stamping their feet as the dancers whirled.

Caitrin was glad she was waiting this one out. It gave her time to think.

Fergus MacKay had just made her decision easier. If she wed him, she'd never see Eoghan again. Sipping her wine, she deliberately swiveled around on the bench, facing the dancers, so that her back was to Alasdair MacDonald. It was easier to pretend he wasn't sitting next to her if she kept her back to him.

Once the dance ended, another gentler one commenced. And this time, Ross Campbell led Caitrin out onto the floor.

Una's brother was an excellent dancer. He moved with fluid grace, his midnight-blue eyes tracking Caitrin with a near predatory intensity.

"Milord," she admonished him softly as they drew close and she twirled around him. "Don't stare so ... it makes me uneasy."

Campbell laughed, and immediately Caitrin relaxed. The expression softened his face and eyes. "I apologize ... but it's because ye are a bonny sight, milady," he replied. "There are many men in this hall who are unable to take their eyes off ye."

Caitrin inclined her head, acknowledging the compliment. "Da tells me that ye serve the MacKinnon clan-chief at Dunan," she said lightly. "How long have ye been there?"

"I fostered at Dunan as a lad." They shifted apart for a spell then, as Caitrin and Ross danced to opposite sides of the floor. When they neared each other once more, he caught her eye. "Duncan MacKinnon is more of a father to me than my own."

Caitrin suppressed the urge to frown. She'd heard tales of Duncan MacKinnon—and none of them good. He was said to be a harsh man, one who made Malcolm MacLeod look soft-hearted in comparison. Rhona had told Caitrin that Taran had been pleased to leave Dunan and serve MacLeod instead. However, Campbell clearly held him in high regard.

"How exactly do ye serve him?" she asked.

"I'm Captain of the Dunan guard and the clan-chief's right hand."

Caitrin heard the pride in Campbell's voice, but also the edge. He wasn't used to being questioned by a woman, to having to explain himself to one. Ross Campbell was charming when he wanted to be, and yet Caitrin wondered if he wished for a demure wife who'd have little to say for herself. She sensed his loyalty would always lie with Clan-chief MacKinnon.

Such a man wouldn't help her get Eoghan back.

Chapter Twenty-three

The Bonniest Lass on Skye

"YE MUST BE tired, milady?" Gavin MacNichol asked with a smile. "Ye have only missed one dance so far."

Caitrin sighed, taking the chieftain's hand as they moved forward with the other dancers in a line. "Aye," she admitted. "My feet are aching."

"That's the problem with having three suitors all vying for yer attention."

Caitrin cut him a swift look and saw that he wore a wry expression. "Da thought it would be a good idea," she murmured. "To have all three of ye meet me over a short period … as ye might have guessed, he's eager to see me wed again."

They left the line and circled their way, back to back, across the floor.

"He certainly is," MacNichol answered when they passed each other once more. "Although I remember ye telling me back in Duntulm that ye didn't want another husband?"

Caitrin met his eye. "I don't," she admitted. "But have ye tried refusing Malcolm MacLeod anything?"

MacNichol huffed a laugh. "He's informed us that we will hear of yer decision at noon tomorrow."

Caitrin tensed, irritation surging within her. She cut a glance across the hall at where her father sat, drinking horn in hand. Typical of him not to share that decision with her.

"Ye didn't know," MacNichol observed.

Caitrin shook her head. She moved away and twirled. When she returned to his side, Gavin MacNichol was frowning. "Ye have had a difficult time, lass. I'm sorry for that … I'd like to see ye happy."

Caitrin swallowed. His kindness unbalanced her. "It's difficult for me to be," she murmured. "When MacDonald has my son."

MacNichol's blue eyes clouded. "I heard about that," he admitted. "But I'd make sure ye saw him often … he'd grow up knowing ye were nearby."

Caitrin held his gaze, a lump rising in her throat. It was a kind offer, but it wasn't enough. She wanted Eoghan by her side. And yet, she was beginning to realize that Gavin MacNichol was indeed the only one of the three suitors she could consider—the only one she'd feel even comfortable with.

Drawing in a deep breath, Caitrin was about to speak when movement out of the corner of her eye drew her attention.

Alasdair MacDonald approached. He wore a determined expression.

Stopping before them, Alasdair met Gavin's eye. "May I interrupt, MacNichol?"

The two men's gazes fused for a moment, and the MacNichol chieftain frowned. Caitrin thought, hoped, that he might refuse. But then he gave a swift, curt nod. Gavin glanced over at Caitrin. "Till the next dance, milady."

Caitrin swallowed, casting him a pleading look.

MacNichol didn't heed it. Instead, he walked away, leaving Alasdair and Caitrin facing each other in the center of the dance floor, men and women circling around them.

Heat rose to Caitrin's cheeks. "What are ye doing?" she demanded between gritted teeth.

Alasdair flashed her a hard smile. "Dancing with the bonniest lass on Skye of course." He took her hand then and pulled her after him so that they fell in line with the other dancers. The feel of his fingers clasped through hers was a brand against her skin. She'd held the hands of all three of her suitors, but none had affected her like this. Alasdair's touch, the firmness of his grip as they halted, turned, and began to dance, made her pulse race like a bolting horse.

Caitrin knew that everyone upon the dais, her father included, would be watching them. They'd be wondering why MacDonald had interrupted one of her suitors—why he was dancing with Caitrin at all.

"What's the point of this?" Caitrin growled.

He gave a soft laugh. "I already told ye."

Alasdair let go of her hand then, his fingers trailing across her palm. Heat shivered up her arm, and Caitrin clenched her jaw. Picking up her skirts, she took mincing steps forward with the other women, bobbing with each stride.

When she completed the steps and made her way back to her partner, Caitrin was fuming. Her feet and back ached, and her heart was sore. She didn't have the patience for whatever game MacDonald was playing.

"Ye will anger my father," she hissed. "None but my suitors should be dancing with me."

Alasdair smirked. "Ye aren't wed yet, milady."

"They might object to yer insolence."

He laughed. "Which one? MacNichol has just bowed out, Campbell couldn't care less who ye dance with, and MacKay has drunk so much he can barely stand."

"Swine." Caitrin circled around him, doing slow turns as the music changed tempo. "All ye have done of late is torment me ... I shall be glad to see the back of ye."

"Aye, I can see ye are eager to find yerself a husband now we are in Dunvegan. All yer talk of remaining a widow was empty, wasn't it?"

Caitrin sucked in a breath. "I don't *want* to wed again."

He barked a laugh, moving around her as the music changed once again. "Liar. I've seen yer smiles, the looks ye give them. Which one will it be?"

Incensed, Caitrin rounded on him. "Bastard! How dare ye?"

Alasdair turned to face her. His mouth curved. His dark eyes blazed. "Don't be coy, Caitrin. We all know ye are no longer the blushing maid. The truth is ye can't wait to warm another man's bed."

The crack of Caitrin's hand colliding with Alasdair's cheek echoed across the hall.

The music stopped, and the dancers halted, swiveling to where Caitrin and Alasdair faced each other in the center of the floor.

Breathing hard and not caring that every eye in the Great Hall was now riveted upon her, Caitrin glared up at Alasdair. "Ye have a forked tongue, MacDonald," she snarled. "If it were up to me, I'd have it ripped out."

Alasdair took his seat once more upon the dais, aware that the atmosphere there had changed. The expressions around him weren't friendly.

MacLeod was glowering, and Caitrin's three suitors stared him down. MacNichol's usually affable face was hard, Campbell's eyes had narrowed, and the furrows on MacKay's brow looked deep enough to split open his forehead. Farther down the table, Rhona and Taran MacKinnon were glaring at him.

Alasdair ignored them all, although it was harder to ignore his stinging cheek.

Caitrin had struck him hard.

Her act had brought the festivities to an abrupt halt. However, as Alasdair picked up his goblet of wine and raised it to his lips, the music restarted. He glanced over his shoulder to see that the dancing had resumed as if nothing had happened.

Caitrin had returned to her seat next to him. She'd turned her back to him again, cradling a goblet of wine in her hands as she watched the dancing. Her shoulders were tense, her spine rigid.

The dancing continued for a short while longer before MacNichol rose to his feet and approached Caitrin. He favored her with a smile, ignoring Alasdair. "Shall we finish that dance?"

Caitrin nodded, rising to her feet and following him onto the floor.

Alasdair took another gulp of wine. A squeal of laughter reached him from the far end of the table. Boyd had just pulled a serving maid onto his lap, but the lass didn't seem to mind the attention. Her giggle rang out across the dais once more while Boyd nuzzled her neck, his hands reaching up to grope her breasts.

Alasdair shifted his gaze from his cousin, back to the dance floor, to where Caitrin and MacNichol circled each other.

He wasn't sure what had been going through his mind when he'd left the dais and strode onto the floor to interrupt their dance earlier. All he knew was that he'd been sitting there watching her with each of her suitors, laughing and smiling as they'd spoken to her—and, finally, he'd been unable to bear it. The beast within—a seething jealous animal that had tormented him all day—had driven him to his feet and across the floor toward them.

Alasdair looked away from the dancers and stared down at the dark wine in his goblet.

Idiot.

It was just as well he was leaving at first light tomorrow.

Chapter Twenty-four

Before It's Too Late

FINALLY, ALASDAIR TOOK his leave of the Great Hall. The dancing had ended, and the only folk still present were men drinking or playing at knucklebones or dice. Caitrin had left with her sister as soon as the last dance finished.

No one said anything as Alasdair rose to his feet.

MacLeod was deep into a game of Ard-ri with Campbell, while MacNichol looked on. The clan-chief's wife, Una, had retired with the other women. A few feet away from the game, MacKay had slumped face-first onto the table and was starting to snore loudly. Farther down the table, Taran MacKinnon was playing knucklebones with Darron—and Boyd was nowhere to be seen.

Alasdair's mouth thinned. No prizes for guessing where his cousin was. At least he'd enjoyed his evening.

Alasdair bid none of those upon the dais good-night, although Gavin MacNichol glanced up as he left the table.

Ignoring him, Alasdair walked out of the hall and into the cool entrance-way beyond. Cressets burned on the pitted stone walls, throwing out long shadows. The air there felt light and fresh after the muggy, smoky interior of the hall.

Taking the stairs up to the second level, Alasdair made his way along a narrow corridor toward his chamber. His limbs dragged, and his head hurt; he couldn't wait to close the door on the world for a few hours. He'd nearly reached his chamber when a voice at his back hailed him.

"MacDonald."

Swiveling around, Alasdair's hand immediately when to his side, where he usually carried his dirk. However, he hadn't worn it tonight and so his hand clutched at nothing.

Gavin MacNichol stood behind him. The chieftain's brow furrowed. "Apologies ... I didn't mean to startle ye."

"Ye didn't," Alasdair replied tersely, cursing how edgy he'd become, another lingering effect of that bloody battle. MacNichol was the last man he wished to see right now. "What do ye want?"

"A few moments of yer time."

Alasdair frowned. "Now?"

"Aye." MacNichol motioned to the doorway a few yards behind him. "Step into my chamber … we can talk there."

Alasdair hesitated. He wasn't in the mood for a chat. However, Gavin MacNichol wore an unusually stubborn look on his face, and Alasdair sensed that the man wasn't about to walk away.

With a huff of irritation, Alasdair followed him into his chamber.

Rectangular-shaped with a tiny shuttered window on the far wall, the bed-chamber was an almost exact replica of the one Alasdair was staying in. A large bed took up one corner and two high-backed chairs faced a small hearth, where a lump of peat burned. Outside, the rain pattered on the wooden shutters.

MacNichol lowered himself into a chair and stretched out his long legs before him, crossing them at the ankle. "Take a seat."

Alasdair approached the fireside and stopped before it. "I'd prefer to stand. Say yer piece, and let's be done with this."

Gavin MacNichol eyed him before giving a weary shake of his head. "I'm not blind, MacDonald."

Alasdair's gaze narrowed, although he didn't respond.

"I should have seen it earlier," MacNichol continued. "I don't know why I didn't. Ye are in love with Lady Caitrin."

Alasdair stiffened. To mask his discomfort, he scowled. "No, I'm not."

MacNichol gave a soft laugh. "Aye, ye are. I know the look. I've been there myself."

"Well, ye are mistaken," Alasdair drawled, stepping back from the fire. "Is that all ye have to say?"

"No." MacNichol's tone hardened. "Why are ye letting the lass go?"

Alasdair folded his arms across his chest. "MacLeod wants Lady Caitrin to wed again. It has nothing to do with me."

"Then why the Devil didn't ye take her for yerself? Ye could have saved us all a trip."

Alasdair drew in a deep breath, his anger rising. However, he deliberately left the question unanswered.

MacNichol's gaze narrowed. "Ye are stubborn and proud, MacDonald. Careful, or it'll be yer downfall."

Alasdair went still. "What's any of this to ye?" he growled. "Lady Caitrin is likely to choose ye … isn't that what ye want?"

MacNichol snorted. "I don't want another man's leavings. Caitrin will choose me because of what I offer, not for love. I've already wed once for duty. I'll not do it again."

The frank admission made Alasdair pause. "I thought ye were happily wed?"

Gavin MacNichol held his gaze for a long moment. "Eventually ... aye. But Innis wasn't my choice. I loved her younger sister, but that wasn't who our families wanted me to wed."

"And where's her sister now?"

MacNichol's gaze clouded. "She took the veil at Kilbride."

Silence fell in the chamber. Alasdair shifted uncomfortably. He wasn't sure how to respond, or what the man wanted from him exactly. He wished only to leave.

"I don't tell ye this for sympathy," MacNichol continued, his tone sharpening, "but as a warning. Ye stand upon a crossroads. If ye don't decide which road to take, fate will do it for ye ... and ye will have to live with the consequences for the rest of yer life."

Alasdair snorted. "Ye forget that the lady in question hates me."

Gavin MacNichol raised a dark-blond eyebrow. "Does she?"

"Aye, ye saw for yerself tonight."

MacNichol gave a dry laugh. "I might not be blind, but *ye* are. The moment ye took her hand tonight, Caitrin's cheeks flushed. We all saw the way she looked at ye."

"In loathing?"

The chieftain shook his head, his mouth curving. "Love and hate are close cousins, lad. Talk to her ... before it's too late."

Caitrin was sitting by the fire, staring at the dying embers, when someone knocked on the door to her bed-chamber.

She frowned. It was late. After returning from the Great Hall, she'd thought that she'd fall into bed exhausted. However, she'd been unable to relax.

The day's events had left her drained yet restless. Fury still churned in her belly at what Alasdair had done, how he'd treated her. She'd hoped he'd leave the hall after she slapped him—but he hadn't. Instead, she'd been forced to ignore him for the rest of the evening, all the time painfully aware of his presence.

She hated how responsive she was to him, how the touch of his skin against hers had set her blood aflame. She hated him, and yet her body betrayed her.

Caitrin's throat constricted then. Tomorrow Alasdair MacDonald would be the least of her concerns—for then she'd have to choose a husband.

Thud. Thud.

Again, someone knocked. Rising to her feet, Caitrin padded barefoot across to the door. Dressed in her night-rail and robe, she wasn't in a state to welcome visitors. However, she guessed it would be Liosa or Rhona coming to check on her. She wished they wouldn't fuss.

Caitrin opened the door and froze.

Alasdair MacDonald stood there. Hair tousled, he wore a slightly wild expression.

Time paused for a moment as their gazes locked, and then Caitrin reacted. She stepped back and moved to slam the door in his face.

Alasdair shifted forward, jamming his body against the door and preventing her from closing it on him.

"Get out," Caitrin growled. Rage slammed into her, and she shook from the force of it. She couldn't believe the man had the nerve to try and barge his way into her bower. "I'll count to three, and if ye aren't gone by then, I'll scream this keep down."

"Caitrin," he rasped, his dark eyes searing hers. "I need to speak to ye. Just let me say my piece, and I'll go … I give ye my word."

"What? Here, in my bed-chamber? Have ye lost yer wits?"

"Aye." The pain in that one word made her pause. "And that's why I implore ye to hear me out. *Please*, Caitrin."

Chapter Twenty-five

Make Ye Mine

A LONG MOMENT passed. Caitrin stared into Alasdair's eyes, witnessing naked desperation. What was wrong with the man?

"Make it quick then," she growled, "and then go."

He nodded.

Slowly, she released the door and stepped aside, allowing him to enter her bed-chamber. His presence dominated the small space, and Caitrin immediately regretted letting him in.

Alasdair moved over to the fireplace before turning to face her. His eyes were haunted pools in the fire's soft glow. "I've been cruel to ye," he said finally. "And I'm sorry for it."

Caitrin pulled her night-rail close and frowned. "Ye came here to apologize?"

Alasdair's features tightened. "I know this won't be easily put right."

She drew herself up, her temper simmering. "Ye are right ... it won't. Ye have taken my son from me. I'll *never* forgive ye for that."

His throat bobbed. "Ye are angry with me."

"I don't need ye to state the obvious, MacDonald." Fury pulsed through Caitrin. "And if that's all ye have come to say, ye can get out now."

His face went taut. He stared down at her, his eyes suddenly bright. "I shouldn't have separated ye from Eoghan."

"So ye realize that now, do ye?"

A shadow moved in his eyes. "No, I knew before ... I just didn't care."

Caitrin's temper flared hot. "Because I wouldn't kiss ye?"

He ran a hand down his face before he muttered a low oath. "Ye make me sound contemptible."

"That's because ye are." Caitrin stepped back. Her heart now thundered against her breast bone. "Leave now, Alasdair. We're finished here."

But he didn't move. He merely stared at her, his face so bereft that an arrow of compassion speared Caitrin's chest. She couldn't stand the man, yet the pain in his eyes made her catch her breath.

"Leave," she repeated, her voice rising as panic seized her.

Alasdair moved then, but not toward the door. Instead, he stepped closer to her and, unexpectedly, went down on one knee.

Caitrin sucked in a breath. "What the Devil are ye doing?"

"I'm sorry, Caitrin." His voice was raw. The words sounded like they'd been ripped from him. His eyes glittered with tears. "If I could, I'd go back in time and undo it—all of it. Give me a chance, and I'll prove to ye that I'm not the rogue ye think I am. I'll spend the rest of our lives proving it to ye."

Caitrin's lips parted in shock. "What are ye saying?"

A beat of silence followed.

"I love ye, Caitrin … I always have," he rasped. "I thought I'd mastered it … but the moment I returned to Duntulm and saw ye, I knew I'd been lying to myself."

Shock rendered Caitrin momentarily speechless. When she finally found her tongue, she realized she was trembling. "Ye truly are a hateful man, Alasdair MacDonald," she whispered.

He gazed up at her, naked pain upon his face. "I know."

"Love is an act, not just a word." Her voice shook as she spoke. "If ye love me, why have ye put me through so much misery?"

"I have no excuse … only cowardice." A nerve flickered in his cheek. Tears glittered on his long dark eyelashes.

Caitrin swallowed as her own vision misted. "Why didn't ye say something months ago?"

He drew in a shuddering breath. "I was about to … on the night I kissed ye in my solar."

"So, this is *my* doing?"

He shook his head. "No … it's entirely mine." His gaze ensnared hers then. "Do I repulse ye, Caitrin?"

The question caught her off-guard. She stared down at him, her lips parting. When she managed a response, her voice was barely above a whisper. "No. Why would ye think that?"

"Ye shrank from me that night."

Caitrin swallowed. "I panicked," she replied huskily. "I was determined never to let another man control me." She broke off here, brushing away a tear that now trickled down her cheek. With everything that had happened since, her decision seemed pointless now. Soon she'd be a wife again, and her life as chatelaine of Duntulm would be nothing but a memory.

Alasdair's gaze guttered. "I thought ye couldn't stand to touch me."

Caitrin wrapped her arms around her torso, hugging herself tight. It wasn't cold inside her bower, but suddenly she shivered. "I tried to explain myself the following day," she said. "But ye never gave me the chance."

A deathly hush followed her words. Despair welled up within Caitrin. What an awful mess all of this was. "Please get up, Alasdair," she whispered.

Seeing him on one knee before her reminded Caitrin of that fateful day, nearly three years earlier—and of the proposal that she'd spurned.

He didn't move. "Will ye wed me, Caitrin?"

Caitrin stopped breathing.

"I'll love ye and cherish ye ... for as long as I have the breath to cool my porridge. And I will never try to separate ye from Eoghan again."

Silence drew out between them. When Caitrin replied, her voice was brittle, pleading. "Please, Alasdair ... get up."

He complied this time, rising to his feet before her. However, the desolation she now saw in his eyes suddenly made it difficult to breathe. With a jolt, she realized that she cared whether Alasdair suffered or not.

Despite everything—she cared.

"Ye will not wed me?" he asked softly.

She met his eye. "If I refuse, will ye still deny me Eoghan?"

They stared at each other for a long moment, before Alasdair answered. "No ... as soon as I return to Duntulm, I will send him to ye." He paused then. "I see it's too late now ... ye hate me."

Caitrin swallowed. She'd told herself many times over the past days that she detested him. She wanted to rail at him, to tell him that she wished him dead, yet the words wouldn't come.

"I don't hate ye," she whispered brokenly. She squeezed her eyes shut as more tears welled. How she wished she did hate him. "I too have done things I'm sorry for."

"Ye have nothing to apologize for," he rasped.

Caitrin opened her eyes, not bothering to wipe away the tears that now trickled down her cheeks. "We were good friends once, but I destroyed our friendship," she whispered. "I laughed in yer face when ye proposed to me ... it was a cruel, thoughtless thing to do. Ye deserved better."

Their gazes fused. Alasdair didn't answer, and so she continued.

"When ye returned to Duntulm it didn't take me long to realize ye are ten times the man yer brother was. Had I seen that years ago, I could have spared us both a lot of pain."

Alasdair's mouth twisted. "As could I ... if I hadn't been so bitter."

"Ye have been through a lot in the past years," she said softly. "I admire yer strength."

Alasdair shook his head. His gaze dropped to the flagstone floor between them, and a tear trickled down his cheek. Watching him, Caitrin's throat constricted.

Long moments passed, and then, wordlessly, he moved toward her, bridging the gulf between them. Reaching out, he gently took hold of her wrist.

The feel of his fingers, warm and strong, against her skin made Caitrin draw in a sharp breath. Gaze still averted, he drew her hand toward him, before turning it over and placing his lips upon the fluttering pulse inside her wrist.

Caitrin stopped breathing.

His lips seared her skin. She felt naked standing before him.

Alasdair gently trailed his lips down from her wrist to the palm of her hand. He kissed her gently there, holding her hand against his face. Instinctively, Caitrin spread her fingers against his cheek. It was wet. She curved her fingertips under the lean line of his jaw and felt his pulse, pounding as fast as hers.

Caitrin closed her eyes as her own tears slid silently down her face.

She'd been resisting this for months now. She couldn't deny it any longer. She couldn't keep lying to herself, telling herself that it was better to remain alone. Like the waxing moon and the turning of the seasons, this thing between them couldn't be stopped. While they both drew breath, it would torment them.

Caitrin's lips parted, but the sigh that escaped her quickly turned into a gasp when Alasdair pulled her into his arms. Yet, instead of kissing her, his lips trailed over her face, brushing away her tears. The touch, feather-light, yet overwhelmingly sensual, made her limbs tremble.

"Ye are everything to me," he whispered as his lips trailed down her jaw. "I can't pretend anymore."

And then his mouth captured Caitrin's, his lips slanting hungrily over hers.

The kiss was wild, devouring. Caitrin let out a soft moan. She reached out with her free hand—for he still gripped the wrist he'd kissed—her fingers splaying out over his heart.

Alasdair ended the kiss then, his breathing ragged. He stared down at her. "The thought of ye wedding another tears me up inside."

Caitrin stifled a gasp. His voice sent shivers of need across her skin.

He pulled her hard against him this time, cupping the back of her head with his hands while he kissed her again. Caitrin leaned into him, her body turning molten as his tongue parted her lips. She'd never known a kiss like this, had no idea a kiss could make her pulse with raw need.

When Alasdair drew back once more, she struggled to draw breath.

"Tell me to stop, and I will," he said, his voice ragged, his eyes aflame. "Otherwise I'm going to make ye mine."

Chapter Twenty-six

Mo Leannan

CAITRIN GAZED UP at Alasdair. His words had rendered her speechless.

"Do ye wish me to leave ye be?" A nerve flickered in Alasdair's jaw. He held her in the cage of his arms, and she felt tension ripple through him. He thought she would push him away, send him from her.

Caitrin drew in a trembling breath. "No," she whispered. "Stay."

That was all he needed.

Alasdair lowered his head and claimed her mouth once more, pulling her against him. The heat of his body hard against hers was searing. Caitrin reached up, her arms entwining around his neck as she sought to pull him closer still.

His hands slid down her back as he kissed her, his touch firm and sensual. The feel of his hands exploring her body pushed all thoughts, all cares from her mind. The world shrank to the feel of his tongue, his lips, to his hands that now shifted to her breasts, opening her robe and untying the laces of her night-rail. Moments later, the garments fell to the floor.

Caitrin stood naked before him.

Breathing hard, she watched his gaze devour her.

Motherhood had changed her figure, made her breasts fuller, her hips a little broader. Small puckered stretch marks marked her belly, and she forced herself not to cover them with her hands. There wasn't any point in hiding from him.

She glanced down at her body to see her breasts strained toward him, her swollen pink nipples aching for his touch.

When she looked back at Alasdair, she watched him wet his lips, his high cheekbones flushing. He heeled off his boots and shrugged off his léine. Then he unlaced his braies and let them drop to the floor.

His body, long and lean, made her suck in a breath—as did the sight of his shaft. Fully erect, it strained up against his belly. Her knees trembled as a shiver of fear went through her. The only man she'd ever lain with was Baltair. Before now she'd only ever known roughness and brutality at a man's touch. However, when Alasdair reached for her, pulling her gently into his arms, the fear dissipated.

The feel of their naked flesh touching caused her to whimper. His skin was so hot, she wanted to taste it. She bowed her head to his neck and gently bit the tender skin there.

Alasdair growled, his chest rising and falling sharply while she continued her exploration, her tongue tracing the whorls of hair on his chest before she discovered that his nipples pebbled under her touch. She nibbled one, and he gasped. The male musk of his skin was intoxicating. She suddenly felt dizzy with want.

Alasdair's hands went to her hair, and his fingers tangled in the soft curls. Then he pulled her up and kissed her again. This time, it was slow and sensual—a kiss that made Caitrin melt into his arms. The feel of his arousal pressed up against her belly made shivering excitement pool in the cradle of her hips. Restlessness rose within her. She needed more.

Alasdair picked her up, his hands sliding under her buttocks, and carried Caitrin to the narrow bed. Together, they collapsed onto the mattress. Tearing his mouth from hers, he bent his head to her breasts and suckled them, drawing each nipple deep into his mouth. He sucked hard until she groaned under him, before continuing his leisurely progress down her body. Then he spread her legs and knelt down between them.

Caitrin groaned, arching back against the cool coverlet. Her body thrummed with pleasure now, radiating out from a hot pulse at her core. His tongue, his fingers, made her forget her own name. She felt boneless, just a molten pool of want. Her body began to quiver.

Softly, she moaned his name.

He rose up between them, spread her legs wider still, and positioned himself at the entrance to her womb. Caitrin glanced down between them, her breath catching at the sight of his shaft pressing against her damp nest of blonde curls.

"I'm going to take ye slowly, mo leannan," Alasdair breathed. Sweat coated his body. His hair fell like black silk over his broad shoulders. "I want to make this last."

Caitrin could only groan in response. *My lover*. She didn't care what he did, as long as he was inside her.

He entered Caitrin then, inching into her, stretching and filling her. And then he began to move in long, easy strokes.

Throwing her head back, Caitrin gave a long shuddering moan and embraced the waves of pleasure that now pulsated out from where their bodies joined. Alasdair changed position, hooking her legs over his shoulders before he continued his deep, slow, and deliberate thrusts.

The look on his face, the strain as he struggled to keep a leash on his control, excited her beyond measure. She wanted to see him unravel, just as she was.

Caitrin let go of any lingering inhibitions and angled her hips up to meet each thrust, bringing him deeper still. She arched back and let her groans fill the bower, writhing against him.

It had never felt like this before—she now understood what all the fuss was about. Why her sisters had gotten coy, secretive expressions on their faces when they'd spoken of lying with their men.

It was magic, an enchantment she gave herself up to willingly.

"Caitrin," Alasdair gasped, his voice raw with need. His hands cupped her buttocks as he thrust hard into her now, his self-control slipping. Caitrin cried out, pleasure radiating out in deep, throbbing waves from the cradle of her lower belly.

Then Alasdair drove into her once more, and a rush of heat exploded inside her as he gave a throaty cry.

Trembling on the bed, Caitrin looked up to see that Alasdair was bent over her. His sweat-slick body quivered. He was struggling to catch his breath. Reaching out, Caitrin brushed the hair out of his eyes. Panting, Alasdair raised his chin, and their gazes fused.

It was a long, hot look, infused with more meaning than either of them could articulate.

Caitrin awoke to the sound of anguished groaning.

Pushing herself up onto one elbow, her gaze fell upon Alasdair. The last of the glowing embers in the hearth softly illuminated the narrow bed where they lay. Alasdair was asleep next to her on his back, but he was not at peace. He writhed and twitched, his skin gleaming with sweat. His features were twisted into a grimace, and his hands clenched and unclenched by his sides. He appeared to be in the grip of a violent dream.

As Caitrin observed him, he flinched before crying out.

"Alasdair."

He paid her no mind, his body going rigid, and then his head jerked from side to side. "No ... no."

"Alasdair!" She reached out, gripped his shoulder, and shook him.

His eyes snapped open. He stared up at Caitrin, but it was as if he wasn't even seeing her.

"Alasdair?" Her voice rose in concern. "What is it? What's wrong?"

Gradually, the wildness faded from his eyes. A moment later he focused upon her, and his face relaxed. "Did I wake ye?"

Caitrin's mouth quirked. "Aye ... and likely half the keep."

He muttered a curse and closed his eyes, running a hand over his face. "Sorry ... I have bad dreams sometimes."

Caitrin watched him, her brow furrowing. "Since the battle?"

"Aye."

Caitrin's frown deepened. "Tell me of them."

His eyes flickered open, and he cast her a pained look. "Ye don't want to hear of such things."

She huffed. "Let me be the judge of that."

Alasdair heaved a deep breath and rolled over onto his side, facing her. "They're always the same," he began hesitantly. "I'm right back there in the mist and the mud. The English are running at me ... like ghosts through the fog. All I can hear is the screams of men as they die ... and I know I'll fall soon, skewered on an English blade."

Caitrin watched him steadily. "But ye didn't."

His mouth twisted. "Maybe I should have. I've not been right since, Caitrin. I jump at shadows, I can't sleep, and sometimes my hands shake like I'm an old man. I might not look it, but I'm broken ... on the inside where no one but ye can see."

Caitrin's breathing constricted at these words. She reached out, her hand clasping his. "I can't imagine how ye must have felt," she murmured. "How it must feel to see all those men fall around ye ... but I don't think ye are broken. Just like a wound to the body, this too will heal."

He huffed, although his eyes glittered. "Will it?"

"Aye." She squeezed his hand. "Ye won't have to face it alone now."

Their gazes met and held. His throat bobbed. "Are ye saying that ye—"

"Aye," she cut him off with a wobbly smile. "I will wed ye, Alasdair MacDonald."

He stared at her for a moment, before joy spread across his face, chasing away the lingering horror of his nightmare.

Alasdair reached for Caitrin. When their faces were just inches apart, he gave her a tender smile. His eyes shone with tears. "I meant what I said earlier," he said softly, "about loving and cherishing ye to my dying breath. All I've ever wanted is ye, Caitrin, and yet all I've done of late is make ye suffer. I want to make it up to ye ... but I don't know where to begin."

Caitrin stared back at him before a slow answering smile curved her lips. Reaching up she traced his lower lip with her fingertip. "Ye can start by making love to me again," she whispered. Her cheeks flushed at her own boldness, but she didn't stop.

Instead, she let her hand travel down his jawline and neck to his chest. Her fingers then slid down the taut plane of his stomach, before they wrapped around his shaft. It pulsed in her hand, hot and hard, straining toward her. "After that, we shall see."

Chapter Twenty-seven

Forgiveness

"THIS IS UNEXPECTED." Malcolm MacLeod viewed Alasdair and Caitrin with a jaundiced eye before his gaze shifted to the three men who also stood in his solar: Gavin MacNichol, Ross Campbell, and Fergus MacKay. "Do any of ye have anything to say about this?"

A heavy silence filled the solar, broken only by the patter of rain against the shutters. The bad weather had settled in, turning the world grey and misty. The huge hearth to Alasdair's left roared this morning, throwing out much-needed heat. A great stag's head mounted above the fire glared down at the chamber's occupants.

MacNichol broke the silence first. "I have no objection," he said, his mouth quirking into a rueful smile. "Who am I to stand between two lovers?"

Alasdair met his eye, and a look passed between the two men.

Next to MacNichol, Campbell wore an inscrutable expression, although his gaze was hard. "I've nothing to say," he said tersely, casting MacLeod an irritated look. "Other than ye have wasted my time."

MacLeod's heavy brow furrowed. "I didn't know MacDonald had an interest." He cast Alasdair an accusing look then. "Why didn't ye tell me ye wanted to wed my daughter?"

"I was under the impression she didn't want me," Alasdair replied, holding his eye. "I was wrong." He glanced over at Caitrin then. Her face was tense, her blue eyes wary. She'd been nervous about this meeting. He didn't blame her, for their future rested on what was decided here.

The pair of them stood shoulder to shoulder as they faced her father. Wordlessly, Alasdair reached out and took her hand, interlacing her fingers with his. Caitrin's answering squeeze reassured him.

"Campbell's right," MacKay growled. "Ye have wasted all our time. I didn't travel here to be made a fool of."

Alasdair cut MacKay a sharp look. "No one's made a fool out of ye, Fergus. Lady Caitrin was free to choose between us ... and she has."

"Aye ... but I wager the lass always knew she'd choose ye."

"No, I didn't," Caitrin replied. Her voice was soft, although with a steely edge just beneath. "I met with all of ye in good faith."

MacKay glared back at her. "Ye have made a mistake choosing him. I could have given ye Strathnaver ... a vast tract of land, far superior to any on this barren rock."

His comment made MacLeod stiffen. Alasdair too tensed at MacKay's insult but held his tongue. He was too happy this morning to let anything ruin it. He understood MacKay's bitterness. The man was disappointed—he was lashing out.

"Let them be," MacNichol cut in, his voice weary. "Lady Caitrin has made her choice, and we must accept it."

Fergus MacKay spat out a curse. "Ye may, but I don't. The Devil take the lot of ye ... this is the last time I have anything to do with the MacLeods of Skye."

With that, MacKay strode from the solar, slamming the door behind him with a force that made the chamber shudder.

"Well ... that's an important relationship ye have just cost me, daughter," Malcolm MacLeod said sourly. "It's just as well ye are wedding a MacDonald and strengthening the link between our clans ... or I would be very displeased with ye right now."

"Ye do realize that MacKay was always going to be a poor loser?" MacNichol pointed out. "He was sure Lady Caitrin would select him."

Campbell snorted at this, raising a dark eyebrow as he cast the MacNichol chieftain a disbelieving look. "That oaf? He never stood a chance."

Alasdair smiled, while MacLeod's glower eased. Campbell's comment had succeeded in easing the tension in the solar. Alasdair gently squeezed Caitrin's hand and glanced at her. He was glad to see that much of the tension had ebbed from her face. She looked up, meeting his eye, and smiled.

MacLeod huffed out a breath before crossing to the sideboard, where he reached for a jug of wine and set out five goblets. "A toast is in order then," he rumbled, pouring out the wine.

He handed out the goblets, pausing once he'd passed Caitrin hers. He fixed his daughter in a level stare. "Is this truly yer wish, lass?"

Caitrin nodded. She smiled once more, a soft expression that made her eyes darken. The sight made Alasdair's breathing quicken. "Aye, Da. It is."

"Very well." MacLeod held up his goblet. "Let us toast to yer handfasting." He paused then, his gaze narrowing as it pinned them both to the spot. "There will be no time for second thoughts, mind. If ye wish to wed, then there will be no delay. Ye shall be handfasted in Dunvegan chapel tomorrow at noon."

Rhona had gone very quiet.

She and Caitrin were sitting in the women's solar. Rhona was working upon her tapestry, while Caitrin wound wool onto a spindle. It was late afternoon, and usually, at this hour they would have taken a walk together in the gardens. However, rain still fell outdoors, so they were forced to remain inside the cool, damp stone walls of Dunvegan Castle.

When the silence finally got too much, Caitrin put down her spindle, fixing her sister with a level stare. "Out with it."

Rhona glanced up from her weaving. "What?"

"Ye have something to say to me. I am waiting."

Rhona huffed, favoring her with a rueful look. "Words fail me, sister ... I'm struck dumb."

"That's a rarity," Caitrin replied with a snort. "I should annoy ye more often."

"Cheeky wench," Rhona growled. Their gazes met, and her features tightened. "Of late, ye keep yer own counsel. Sometimes I think I hardly know ye."

Caitrin inclined her head. "Because I didn't say anything about Alasdair?"

"Aye. Ye had plenty of opportunities to tell me how ye truly felt about him ... but ye didn't. Don't ye trust me?"

Caitrin loosed a sigh. She heard the hurt in her sister's voice and was sorry for it. "It's hard to speak of something ye haven't even admitted to yerself," she said after a pause.

Rhona's gaze narrowed. "Ye didn't know how ye felt?"

Caitrin shook her head, dropping her gaze. "When I knew Alasdair before, we were friends. I didn't see him in any other way. But when he returned to Duntulm, something changed between us. We both fought it initially. Alasdair still resented me, and I was determined to continue as chatelaine ... after Baltair I promised myself I'd let no man rule my life again."

"But what Alasdair did to ye." Rhona was scowling now. "It was unforgivable."

A wry smile tugged at Caitrin's mouth. Her sister could be dogmatic at times. She was like their father: certain lines could never be crossed, and once they were, there was no going back.

"I thought so too," Caitrin admitted softly. "There have been times over the past few days, if ye had given me a dirk, I'd have happily stabbed him through the heart with it."

Rhona's grey eyes grew wide. "And ye are going to wed this man?"

Caitrin sighed. "Aye ... I can't describe it, Rhona. I started the day hating him ... but after he came to my chamber and told me how he felt ... and explained himself ... my feelings changed."

"So ye aren't doing this just to get Eoghan back?"

Caitrin shook her head. "Alasdair agreed to return Eoghan to me, whether or not I decided to wed him." She paused here, meeting her sister's gaze. "I'm doing this because I want to."

Rhona exhaled sharply. "I just hope ye are seeing things clearly."

"Surely ye understand, Rhona?" Caitrin replied with a shake of her head. "On yer wedding night with Taran, ye were set to hate him forever ... and yet by the next morning yer feelings toward him had completely changed."

Rhona's brow furrowed. "That was different."

"How? He entered those games without telling ye, knowing that ye would feel betrayed. Ye were then forced to wed a man ye didn't want." Caitrin paused here. "Yet one night alone together made all the difference."

Rhona actually blushed then, dropping her gaze. When she looked up, there was understanding in her eyes. "It did," she said softly.

Silence stretched between the sisters then, as each retreated into their own thoughts. Finally, Caitrin picked up her spindle once more and resumed winding wool. "Forgiving Alasdair was much harder than hating him," she admitted softly. "But I realized I would know no peace until I did."

Alasdair pulled up the hood of his cloak and exited the keep, making his way down the slippery steps to the bailey below. The rain fell in heavy sheets, sweeping across the courtyard in waves. It didn't seem to have let up since it had begun the previous day.

Crossing the cobbled bailey, Alasdair made his way toward the stables. However, instead of taking the left door into where the horses were kept, he ducked through a low doorway into the lean-to where MacLeod housed his hounds.

The smell of wet dog assaulted his nostrils as he entered. The lean-to was open on two sides, letting in light and a little rain. The dogs didn't seem to mind though. Most of them were asleep, curled up together at the back of the space, although they stirred when Alasdair appeared.

Tails wagging, many lurched to their feet. The first to reach the edge of the enclosure was a young, leggy wolf-hound with a wiry grey coat.

Dùnglas jumped up against the wooden boarding lining the enclosure, whining with delight at the sight of Alasdair.

"Easy lad." Alasdair smiled as he tried to fend off the dog's clumsy feet and wet tongue. He leaned down and examined the injury to the wolf hound's shoulder, pleased to see the stitched cut had started to scab over now.

Gently, he pushed Dùnglas back into the enclosure. However, the hound tried to get back up again. Its tail was wagging so hard now that its whole body moved from the force of it.

"Looks like ye have found yerself a new friend."

Alasdair glanced over his shoulder to see Taran MacKinnon standing behind him. Wearing a rain-splattered leather cape, his short hair slicked back against his scalp, the warrior was an intimidating presence.

Alasdair huffed a laugh. "Aye ... yer wife thinks the dog is the *only* friend I'll make here at Dunvegan."

MacKinnon's mouth curved. "Ye would be right there. Rhona would like to see ye gelded."

He moved closer, his gaze shifting to where Dùnglas had climbed up onto his hind legs again so that he could get to Alasdair. "Are ye looking for a new hound?"

Alasdair shook his head. "I've already got plenty of them back in Duntulm."

"One more won't make a difference," MacKinnon replied with a shrug. "Dùnglas is a funny one ... since Adaira left, he's never bonded with anyone else, and he keeps apart from the other dogs. I think he'd be happier elsewhere."

Alasdair absently stroked the hound's head. "I suppose I could take the dog back with me ... if ye don't want him?"

MacKinnon nodded, as if the matter was settled, before he crossed his arms and turned to face Alasdair. "I hear there's to be a wedding here tomorrow."

Alasdair's mouth quirked. "Aye ... I'm sure ye are invited."

"I don't care if I am or not," MacKinnon replied with a snort. His gaze narrowed then. "I take it the lady is willing?"

Alasdair raised an eyebrow. "Of course ... I'd not force Caitrin to wed me."

"Good to hear," MacKinnon grunted.

Chapter Twenty-eight

Vows

"YE ARE BLOOD of my Blood, and Bone of my Bone." Alasdair MacDonald's voice echoed through the silent chapel. "I give ye my Body, that we Two might be One. I give ye my Spirit, 'til our Life shall be Done."

Caitrin held his gaze as he spoke. Her skin prickled at the words; they were the same ones she'd heard Lachlann Fraser say to her sister in Duntulm kirk barely ten months earlier.

Adaira had wept as Lachlann made his vows—but Caitrin was dry-eyed. She'd never wept easily in front of others. She was too private, too proud. A small group had gathered behind them in Dunvegan's chapel: her father and Una, her brother, Iain, Rhona and Taran, and Alasdair's men.

Caitrin had been aware of their gazes upon her as the ceremony had started, but as Alasdair finished his vows, and she began hers, she forgot they had an audience.

She couldn't tear her gaze away from Alasdair's; the intensity in his peat-brown eyes made the rest of the world fade. The sincerity in his voice made her throat tighten.

"Ye are now man and wife," the priest announced when Caitrin had completed her vows. He was smiling as he unwrapped the length of plaid that bound their hands. The priest met Alasdair's eye briefly. "Ye may kiss yer bride now."

Caitrin's breath stilled when Alasdair stepped close, gently cupped her chin, and raised her face to his. He then gave her a soft, slow, lingering kiss that made the small party watching the ceremony cheer.

Alasdair pulled away, favoring Caitrin with a sensual smile that made her pulse quicken.

"Come, wife," he murmured. "Take my arm."

Alasdair held out his elbow to her, and she took it. Together they walked down the aisle and out of the chapel.

The wail of a highland pipe echoed through the Great Hall of Dunvegan, accompanying the handfasting feast. The noise inside the hall was so great that Caitrin could barely hear herself think. In truth, she preferred the lilting music of a harp to the screech of the highland pipe, yet with the feasters making such a noise, the gentler sound of the harp would have been drowned out anyway.

Before her lay a great spread of pies, cheeses, fruit, and oatcakes dripping in butter and honey. The large pies were filled with left-over meat, vegetables, and boiled eggs, and topped with a thick suet and oaten crust. The cooks, Fiona and her daughter Greer, had done well at such short notice, especially since they'd had to prepare another feast just two days earlier.

The aroma filling the hall was divine, and unlike at the last feast, Caitrin actually had an appetite for the fare before her. It was hard to believe only two days had passed since she'd sat here, her stomach in knots, dreading having to choose a suitor.

None of the three men were at the feast. MacKay had left in a rage shortly after he'd stormed from MacLeod's solar. MacNichol and Campbell had both left at dawn the morning after.

"Wine, Caitrin?" Alasdair leaned forward, raising his voice to be heard over the din. He held up a ewer of spiced bramble wine.

Caitrin nodded, smiling. "Thank ye."

They sat together at the center of the table upon the dais. Alasdair's elbow brushed against hers as he bent forward to refill her goblet. Before them sat a platter of two different pies; it was tradition for husband and wife to dine off the same platter at their wedding feast.

Caitrin was reminded then of her handfasting feast to Baltair. They too had been wed in the chapel at Dunvegan, as her father had wished, and the feasting had gone on late into the night. She'd been happy that day, glowing with hope and pride at her handsome husband. Yet that glow had only lasted a short while. Later, when Baltair took her maidenhead, her happiness shattered. Even then, knowing it was her first time, he'd been brutal.

"Ye seem pensive, Caitrin," Alasdair observed. The din in the hall was such that he had to lean close to speak to her. The scent of leather and clean male skin enveloped her, and she breathed it in. "Is something amiss?"

Caitrin shook her head, pushing aside her memories of the past. Baltair was dead; she would keep him that way. He had no place at this table.

"Just reflecting a little," she replied, taking a sip of wine, "and getting used to the idea of being a wife again."

Alasdair's gaze fused with hers then, and just like during the wedding ceremony, their surroundings disappeared—even the wail of the highland pipe and her father's booming voice.

"Baltair was a fool," Alasdair said, his expression turning fierce. "He didn't know how lucky he was."

Alasdair reached out, entwining his fingers with hers. His touch made Caitrin's breathing quicken. She felt as if she'd only just had a taste of him the night before last. It wasn't enough. They had not lain together since and already it seemed like an eternity. She ached for him. Caitrin watched Alasdair's pupils dilate and knew that he'd been affected by the touch the same way.

"I have my faults, Caitrin," he continued, before his mouth twisted into a self-recriminating smile. "More than I'd like to admit ... but I'll never ignore ye ... never frighten ye. I'd do anything in my power to make ye happy."

Caitrin held his gaze, a lump rising in her throat. Something deep inside her breast—something that had been tightly knotted ever since she'd wedded Baltair—unraveled.

"Ye already have," she whispered.

Caitrin collapsed upon the bed with Alasdair. There, they lay spooned together, panting and sweat-slicked, his arms fast around her. A soft sigh escaped Caitrin. Her body felt weak and boneless, her senses completely scattered. She enjoyed the sensation and the abandon that had caused it.

They'd been hungry for each other.

The handfasting feast had seemed to go on for an age, after which there had been dancing. Eventually, they'd been able to take their leave, although not without fanfare.

Much to the delight of onlookers, Alasdair had scooped Caitrin into his arms and carried her from the Great Hall. Face flaming from the men's bawdy comments and laughter, Caitrin had huddled against Alasdair's chest.

However, once they'd reached the chamber where they would spend their first night as man and wife, her embarrassment faded.

They'd come together like beasts, tearing off each other's clothes, before Alasdair pushed her down on all fours on the bed and took her.

"I liked that," she murmured when her breathing had slowed.

"Me too," he replied sleepily, placing a kiss on her shoulder.

"The effect ye have on me, Alasdair ... ye only have to touch my hand, and my whole body answers."

He kissed her shoulder once more, trailing his lips up to her earlobe. Caitrin's eyelids fluttered with pleasure as his tongue explored the shell of her ear. "It's the same for me," he whispered back.

Alasdair's arms tightened around her. Caitrin felt his body relax against hers, his leg slung over her hips protectively. She closed her eyes, enjoying the warmth of his body curled against hers. Alasdair's breathing grew slow and even, and she realized that he'd fallen asleep. A heavy languor pressed down upon her too.

Outside, she could still hear the hiss of the rain. She didn't care about the gloomy weather though, or that they would have to set off for Duntulm in it the following morning. Soon she would be reunited with Eoghan, but right now she was wrapped in her husband's arms.

A soft smile curved Caitrin's lips. At this moment, she was exactly where she wanted to be.

Rhona watched her sister ride out of the bailey. Caitrin sat astride a grey palfrey, a delicate mare with a mincing gait. She rode alongside her husband, Alasdair MacDonald. He towered above her upon a bay courser. A grey wolfhound loped along beside his horse, its gaze keen.

"Isn't that Adaira's dog ... Dùnglas?" Rhona asked, glancing at where Taran stood beside her.

"Aye," he replied with a smile.

"Why is he leaving with MacDonald?"

"Dùnglas took a shine to Alasdair ... I thought the hound would be happier elsewhere."

Rhona favored her husband with an incredulous look before she shifted her attention back to the departing riders. A light rain fell this morning, and the clouds hung low over Dunvegan. All of the MacDonald party wore woolen traveling cloaks and had pulled up their hoods.

As she descended the incline toward the Sea-gate, Caitrin turned, her gaze catching Rhona's. She then smiled and raised her hand in farewell. Rhona waved back, her vision misting.

Caitrin turned away, and a moment later, she disappeared through the gate. Shortly after, the rest of the party from Duntulm followed, the clip-clop of their horses' hooves ringing against the wet stone.

"Don't look so worried, love. She will be fine."

Rhona swallowed before glancing up at Taran. He was watching her, a soft look in his eyes. "Really," she said huskily. "Can ye be sure of that?"

"No ... but ye can't be certain she'll be miserable either."

Rhona huffed. "I thought ye didn't like him?"

"I hardly know the man," Taran replied evenly, "but now that he has done right by yer sister, I'm prepared to revise my opinion of him."

Rhona's mouth thinned, before her gaze shifted back to the Sea-gate, almost as if she expected Caitrin to reappear at any moment. "If I ever find out he's mistreated her, I'll ride to Duntulm and sink a dirk into his guts," she growled.

"There will be no need for that, mo ghràdh," Taran replied, amusement lacing his voice. "Ye can see MacDonald adores her."

Rhona drew back, favoring Taran with an arch look. "What's wrong with ye this morning?"

Taran smiled, his eyes crinkling at the corners. To most folk, he had a frightening face, made even more so by a formidable expression. But to Rhona, he was the most handsome man she'd ever seen. It was nearly a year since they'd been wed, and with each passing day, she grew to love Taran MacKinnon more.

"Nothing," he replied. "Only that I know what it's like to lose yer heart to a woman ... long before she knows ye exist."

Rhona felt chastened by that, remembering how she had seen Taran before they'd been wed. He'd been her father's faithful warrior, her servant, and a friend of sorts. But she hadn't seen him as a man. "Ye think it's a good match then?" she asked, still unconvinced.

Taran nodded before he slung an arm around her shoulders and turned her back toward the keep. The others, who'd come out to see the MacDonald party off, had all dispersed, including MacLeod and his wife—driven indoors by the wet weather. "Perhaps. But only time will tell," he replied before he leaned in and kissed her. "Come on ... let's get out of this rain."

Chapter Twenty-nine

Sing for Us

ALASDAIR STOLE A glance at the woman who was now his wife

It didn't seem real.

He had much to thank Gavin MacNichol for—the man had made him see sense, had made him look truth squarely in the eye. He'd taken a risk. His visit to Caitrin could have gone terribly wrong. She could have rejected him and thrown him out of her bower. She could have called for her father's guards and caused an ugly scene.

But she hadn't.

Something had shifted within him since that night. It was as if a bitter thorn that had been festering within his flesh had finally been lanced. He felt lighter, freer. He hadn't realized just how big a burden he'd been carrying. Ever since making the decision to take Caitrin back to her father, he'd struggled with it. What a relief it was to cast the weight aside.

They were riding east, across a stretch of bare hills. The rain clouds hung over them in an oppressive grey curtain. Shortly after leaving Dunvegan, they'd been soaked through. Strangely, Alasdair didn't mind. He felt as if he'd been reborn; all the things that used to matter didn't.

Glancing right, he saw that Dùnglas was managing to keep up with him. The wound to its shoulder was healing well. The wolfhound trotted along, tongue lolling. It had shadowed him ever since leaving Dunvegan. Alasdair smiled. He'd almost forgotten about taking the dog with him, but when he'd led his horse out of the stables that morning, Dùnglas had been there, sitting upon the cobbles in the rain, waiting for him.

It was as if the hound knew he was leaving and was determined not to be left behind.

Alasdair glanced up, his gaze sweeping the road ahead. To the southeast, he spied great brooding peaks just visible through the shroud of rain and mist, but they weren't heading that way. By the end of the day, they'd cross into MacDonald lands and then turn north for Duntulm.

For home.

Alasdair cut Caitrin another glance, his gaze lingering on her profile as she looked ahead. Sensing his gaze upon her, his wife shifted her attention to Alasdair.

"What is it?" she asked, her lips curving in a way that made him wish they were alone. During the two nights they'd spent together, Caitrin had surprised him; she was lustier and more sensual than he could have ever hoped or dreamed. She had given herself to him wholeheartedly.

Alasdair smiled back. "Just gazing upon my wife's beauty."

Caitrin huffed although her eyes gleamed. "Ye have a honeyed tongue, Alasdair. I'm wet, bedraggled, and smell of wet wool and horse."

"Aye ... but ye are still the bonniest lass I've ever set eyes on." He gave her a long look then that made her cheeks pinken. "Or ever will."

She cleared her throat, embarrassed by his declaration. Yet he saw from the twinkle in her sea-blue eyes that she'd responded favorably to it. "Ye are a rogue, husband. The world is filled with fair-faced women. How do ye know ye won't meet one prettier?"

"None lovelier than ye, Caitrin," he replied. "That I promise ye."

As dusk neared, they made camp at the bottom of a shallow valley. The rain continued falling in a steady patter upon the already soaked earth. Caitrin dismounted from her palfrey, her already soaked boots squelching on the wet grass. They stood in a grove of beech trees, where the men started to erect an awning between three trees for the party to shelter under, and another a few yards away for the horses.

The bedraggled wolfhound they'd brought from Duntulm shook out its wet coat and sat down under a tree, watching the men work.

"If this continues, we'll have to build ourselves an arc and row the rest of the way to Duntulm," Boyd MacDonald grumbled as he removed a roll of hide from behind his saddle. "We'll be lucky if we find any dry wood for a fire."

Darron MacNichol snorted, relieving him of his roll. "Well, I'm sure if anyone can, it is ye. Off ye go and find us some then."

Boyd's lip curled. As a member of the Duntulm Guard, he now took orders from Captain MacNichol and had no choice but to do as bid.

Watching the brief interaction between the men, Caitrin noted that there was little in the way of friendship between them. She remembered the scene back at Beltane and wondered if their rivalry over Sorcha MacQueen's affections had anything to do with it.

At the thought of Sorcha, warmth filtered over Caitrin. This time tomorrow she'd be warm and dry and back in Duntulm—with Eoghan in her arms. They'd been apart for only a few days, but it felt like months to her. She was impatient to see him again.

Once the awning had been erected, Caitrin helped the others roll out dry sheets of hide around a small hearth area. Grateful to be out of the rain, Caitrin removed her sodden cloak and hung it up on a branch. It was sheltered here, although with the air so damp, she doubted her cloak would dry much overnight.

Boyd and a couple of other men returned presently with armloads of firewood, although some of it was damp. While the others settled themselves on the hide, Darron crouched down next to the hearth and got a fire going. He used a flint and steel to light a pile of tinder that he'd carried with him wrapped in an oiled cloth. It took a few tries, and a bit of ribbing from the likes of Boyd, but he eventually managed to light a fire.

Caitrin watched the bright gold tongues of flame licking at the damp wood and released a sigh. It wasn't a cold evening, but the air was heavy with moisture. The fire was a beacon of color and warmth, a ward against the encircling grey.

They ate a simple meal of oaten bread, butter, and boiled eggs washed down with ale. Caitrin sat shoulder-to-shoulder with Alasdair, listening to the rumble of conversation around the fireside. Despite that her clothing felt damp and itchy against her skin, and that an uncomfortable night awaited her, a warm sensation of well-being settled over her.

With a jolt, she realized that the feeling was happiness.

She'd not felt like this in a long while. After Baltair's death, once she'd taken up the role of chatelaine, Caitrin had thought she'd been content in her new life. In reality though, she'd been living in dread, for she'd known that at some point a man—be it her father or Baltair's brother—would shatter her peace.

Now, there was no dread. She was the Lady of Duntulm once more, but this time she'd not cower before her husband. The bond between her and Alasdair was still new, yet she had a knowing deep in her bones that he'd be good to her.

Once the supper had ended, the men started passing around skins of ale. Caitrin took a delicate sip from one before casting a look at her husband. The hound he'd brought with him had somehow sidled up to the fire and now sat pressed up against Alasdair's right side. The dog appeared so content it almost looked as if it were smiling.

"Should I be jealous?" she asked, stifling a laugh.

Alasdair met her eye, his mouth curving. "Don't mind Dùnglas ... he seems to think I'm some long-lost relative."

"Just as long as he doesn't want to share yer bed when we get home."

Alasdair snorted. "No chance of that."

"Curse this rain." Boyd's voice interrupted them from across the fire. "We need some cheer to chase away the gloom." He turned his attention to the young warrior who'd sung the bawdy songs on their journey to Dunvegan. "Come, Finlay, give us another one of yer tunes."

"Those aren't songs fit for a lady's ears, Boyd," Alasdair pointed out.

His cousin snorted. "Lady Caitrin won't mind."

Darron cleared his throat. "I remember ye having a good voice, Alasdair. Why don't ye sing for us?"

Boyd's eyes widened, and he cut Alasdair a reproachful look. "All those months together and ye never let on ye could sing."

Alasdair shrugged. "There wasn't much cause for it, was there?"

Caitrin inclined her head, focusing on Alasdair. He actually looked a little embarrassed. "Go on," she murmured with a smile. "I'd like ye to sing for us."

He met her eye and gave her a pained look. "Ye would?"

"Aye ... if it means I don't have to hear of swiving lusty tavern wenches."

Her comment brought bursts of surprised laughter from the surrounding men. Alasdair raised an eyebrow, and Finlay's cheeks glowed red.

Caitrin said nothing more though, and finally, Alasdair loosed a defeated breath. "Very well, wife ... here is a song more suitable for yer ears."

A pause followed, and then Alasdair began to sing. He had a low, slightly husky voice, and sang a slow ballad, one that Caitrin had never heard before.

> "Oh the summer time has come
> And the trees are sweetly blooming
> And wild mountain thyme
> Grows around the purple heather.
> Will ye go, lassie, go?
>
> And we'll all go together,
> To pull wild mountain thyme,
> All around the purple heather.
> Will ye go, lassie, go?
>
> I will build my love a tower,
> By yon clear crystal fountain,
> And on it I will pile,
> All the flowers of the mountain.
> Will ye go, lassie, go?"

Alasdair finished his song, his voice fading into silence. The fine hair on the back of Caitrin's forearms prickled, and she let out a slow breath, realizing that she'd forgotten to breathe while he sang.

"That was beautiful," she whispered.

He ducked his head, smiling. "Ye enjoyed it then?"

"Aye."

Across the fire, Boyd snorted. "Ye have a fine voice, I'll give ye that cousin ... but did ye have to choose something so ... feeble?"

Alasdair threw back his head and laughed. "I know plenty of other songs."

"Why don't ye sing us one?" Boyd grinned at Caitrin then. "None that'll offend yer lady's ears, mind."

They rode into Duntulm under the drumming rain, approaching the fortress from the south. However, when he crested the top of the last hill, Alasdair pulled his courser to an abrupt halt.

"What is it?" Caitrin pulled up her palfrey next to her husband, her gaze following the direction of his.

She didn't need him to answer, for an instant later, she saw for herself what the problem was.

When they'd left Duntulm, the Cleatburn had been a meandering stream that cut east of the village, spanned by an old humpbacked stone bridge.

It was now a turbid torrent, covering the meadows and the outlying cottages. Sod roofed dwellings peeked out of the rushing water, and the bridge was completely gone. Villagers were wading through the water, trying to salvage what they could and rescue livestock from the flooded meadow.

Alasdair cursed, gathered his reins, and urged his horse down the hill. Dùnglas bounded along behind him, and Caitrin followed. The mare broke into a brisk canter, her hooves cutting into the wet turf. Caitrin pulled her up at the bottom of the hill, just in time to see Alasdair leap down from his horse, tear off his cloak, heel off his boots, and stride toward the water.

"Alasdair!" Caitrin called after him, wondering where on earth he was going.

And then she saw her.

The young woman was drifting downriver toward the sea, clinging to a tree trunk. Her cries floated across the hillside, barely audible over the roaring of the water.

Darron rushed past Caitrin, hot on Alasdair's heels, the others close behind him. However, by the time they reached the water's edge, the chieftain had already plunged in and was swimming in long strokes toward the lass.

"Get some rope," Darron shouted.

Caitrin sprang down from her horse and rushed to one of the horses the men had abandoned, retrieving a heavy coil of hemp rope. She then picked up her skirts and hurried to the water's edge, where Dùnglas sat whining, staring after Alasdair.

Darron took the rope from Caitrin and handed one end to Boyd, who was looking on, bemused by both men's actions. "Keep ahold of the end," Darron ordered. "I'm going to see if I can get the rope out to Alasdair."

With that, Captain MacNichol waded into the water after his chieftain.

Chapter Thirty

Irreplaceable

CAITRIN STOOD ON the water's edge, her heart in her throat. The Cleatburn raged like a beast. No one should be swimming in the torrent, least of all her husband.

"Alasdair!" Darron had waded in to waist height. "Catch the rope!"

The chieftain twisted, attempting to tread water as the rope sailed toward him. It hit the churning water with a slap, and Alasdair lunged for it.

Panic surged through Caitrin when he went under, disappearing from view. "Alasdair!"

Dùnglas stood up and started barking, his hackles rising.

For a sickening heartbeat or two, there was no sign of Alasdair, and then he appeared, surfacing like a seal just yards from where the woman still floated downstream, the rope clutched in his hand.

He reached the young woman—who was now sobbing in fear, for she clearly couldn't swim—and wound the rope around the tree trunk.

"Ready!" he called to Darron.

The other men in the party had taken hold of the rope behind Captain MacNichol, and together they all heaved the log, with its two passengers, into shore. A crowd had now gathered at the water's edge. An elderly woman stepped up beside Caitrin, sobbing. "That's my Hilda. Ye found her … I thought her lost!"

Alasdair helped the young woman up onto the shore. She was shivering and weeping, but when she spied the old woman, she left Alasdair's side and ran to her. "Ma!"

Alasdair rejoined the others then, still out of breath from his swim. Water ran in rivulets down his body. His sodden clothing clung to him. His hair was slicked back, accentuating the lean angles of his face.

Dùnglas approached the chieftain, tail wagging, and nuzzled against his leg. Alasdair glanced down at the wolfhound before giving an exasperated snort. "Bloody useless dog." However, he still reached down and stroked its wiry coat.

Caitrin stepped forward. "I thought I'd lost ye," she gasped, unable to keep the anxiety out of her voice. "When ye went under ... I ..."

Alasdair held her gaze before a smile curved his lips. "I'm a strong swimmer, Caitrin. I'd never have gone out there otherwise."

Caitrin punched his arm. "I didn't know that, did I?"

His gaze clouded. "Did I worry ye?"

"Aye." She was close to tears now. "Don't scare me like that again."

Wordlessly, Alasdair pulled her into his arms. It didn't matter that he was soaking wet; after the morning's travel so was she. The drum-beat of his heart against her ear calmed her.

After a moment she pulled back, pressing into his side, as Alasdair looped a protective arm around her shoulders. He then turned his attention to his men. "Get the villagers up to the keep. We'll house them there until the water recedes."

"Aye, milord," Darron replied with a nod. He then moved away, marshaling his men to do the chieftain's bidding.

Together, Alasdair and Caitrin turned to face the swollen Cleatburn.

"It's stopped raining," Caitrin noted, raising her gaze to the sky. "For the first time in days."

"Just as well," Alasdair murmured. "Or there would soon be nothing left of the village."

Caitrin's gaze swept across the churning water, to where the bridge had once stood.

"All that work ye did on the bridge over the winter," she said with a sigh, "and the river has destroyed it."

Alasdair huffed a laugh, his grip around her shoulders tightening. "Bridges can be rebuilt, love," he murmured. "But some things are irreplaceable."

Sorcha hurried out into the bailey, Eoghan balanced on her hip. She was pleased to see the rain had finally stopped although the sky was still the color of lead.

Picking her way around the large puddles, Sorcha approached the bedraggled crowd that had just entered the muddy courtyard. Caitrin was among them, her blonde hair curling in wet tendrils around her face. She walked, hand in hand, with Alasdair MacDonald, leading their horses behind them. A lanky grey wolfhound trotted along at the chieftain's heels.

Sorcha halted, gaze widening. The chieftain and Lady Caitrin holding hands—this was a sight she'd never thought to see.

When she spied her hand-maid, Caitrin cried out, leaving Alasdair's side.

"Ye are back!" Sorcha greeted her. "I can't believe it."

"Aye." Caitrin threw her arms around Sorcha and Eoghan and hugged them both tight. Drawing back, she smiled, her eyes gleaming. "What a sight ye both are. Let me have a look at my wee laddie."

Sorcha handed Eoghan to her. Caitrin spun the lad around, laughing as he squealed in delight. Sorcha saw then that her mistress's cheeks were wet with tears. Eoghan wrapped his soft arms around his mother's neck as she hugged him once more. Caitrin buried her face in his soft dark hair and inhaled deeply.

"How I've missed ye, Eoghan," she said softly, her voice choked with emotion. "Yer smell, the chirping laugh ye make when ye are happy … how ye say my name."

"Ma," Eoghan gurgled happily, not understanding what his mother had just said.

"I know sweetheart," she whispered, and Sorcha started to weep at the love she saw shining in her mistress's eyes. "I'm home."

Caitrin carried Eoghan away, heading back toward the steps leading into the keep, while Sorcha attempted to compose herself. She didn't want the chieftain's men gawking at her or making fun. The others were approaching now, and she suddenly felt self-conscious for weeping.

Captain MacNichol was heading her way.

"Welcome home, MacNichol." Sorcha scrubbed at her wet cheeks with the back of her hand and favored him with a watery smile.

"Good day, Sorcha." He stopped before her, and although he was rain-soaked and mud-splattered, she realized with a jolt just how handsome he was. His leather braies and léine were plastered against his hard, muscular body, and his wet blond hair was pulled back at the nape of his neck. "We return with happy news, as ye can see."

Her gaze searched his face. "What happened?"

He stepped close, glancing over his shoulder to make sure they weren't being overheard. "I'm not really sure," he murmured. "One moment we're watching Clan-chief MacLeod parade suitors before his daughter, the next we're standing in Dunvegan chapel watching MacDonald and Lady Caitrin wed."

Sorcha's eyes widened. "They're married?"

"Aye, the day before last."

Sorcha gasped. "But I thought they hated each other?"

Darron's mouth lifted at the corners. "Clearly, they didn't."

Sorcha was about to reply when a loud voice boomed across the bailey. "Good day, bonny Sorcha."

She glanced right to see Boyd MacDonald striding toward her. Like Darron, he was wet and dirty from his journey. However, he wore his usual irrepressible smile.

"Greetings, Boyd," she replied warmly. "It's good to see ye back too."

Boyd grinned. "How about a kiss then … to show me how pleased ye are to see me?" He stepped close, and Sorcha immediately shrank back.

"What's this?" Boyd's grin turned mischievous, and he reached for her.

Sorcha ducked out of reach, stepping back into a muddy puddle in her haste to avoid his grasping hands. She didn't enjoy being grabbed at like she was a spring lamb he was trying to catch.

"Coy, are we?" Boyd's grin turned into a leer.

"Leave the lass be, MacDonald," Darron rumbled, a warning note to his voice. "Clearly, she doesn't want to kiss ye."

Boyd snorted, drawing back. His gaze narrowed as it settled upon Sorcha. "That's not very friendly, lass."

Sorcha swallowed and took another step back, not caring that she now stood ankle-deep in cold water. Her pulse raced. She'd been happy to see both Darron and Boyd—but the latter's behavior had put her on edge. Boyd had never taken such liberties before.

"I'd better get back inside," she murmured, picking up her skirts so that they didn't drag in the muddy water. "Lady Caitrin will need my help."

With that, she turned and hurried away.

It was loud inside the Great Hall of Duntulm. The roar of voices echoed through the space like storm-driven waves pounding a rocky shore. Extra tables had been carried in, for all those villagers who'd been temporarily rendered homeless by the flood. Servants carried out tureens of thick salted pork and cabbage stew, served with large loaves of coarse bread.

Caitrin took a sip of wine and let out a long sigh, glancing across at her husband. Alasdair sat upon his carven chieftain's chair, goblet of warmed wine in hand, surveying the sea of hungry village folk beneath him. The air was heavy with the smells of food, wet wool, and peat smoke. It wasn't a pleasant odor, but no one seemed to mind. They were all just happy to be somewhere warm and dry, and to fill their bellies.

The rain had stopped now at least, and with any luck, the Cleatburn would quickly recede. Then work could start on repairing the damage the flood had caused.

When the last of the food and drink had been served, Alasdair rose to his feet.

"People of Duntulm." His voice echoed through the Great Hall, quietening the din. "Today might not seem like a cause for celebration, but I have news to share with ye." Alasdair glanced down at Caitrin then, his eyes shining. He then shifted his attention back to the sea of faces beneath the dais. "Three years ago ye welcomed Lady Caitrin to these lands. Ye have seen her strength, her justness, and her capability. I inform ye now that this woman, whom I know ye all love and respect, is now my wife. She will rule Duntulm at my side."

Shock rippled across the hall. Nervousness tightened Caitrin's belly as she looked on. Alasdair's words had filled her with joy, yet what if the people here didn't love her as much as he believed?

An instant later she realized her fear was unfounded.

A roar went up, as men and women rose to their feet and raised their cups in the air.

"To the chieftain and his lady!" Alban MacLean shouted, his leathery face creased with joy.

Raucous cheering followed, shaking the hall to its foundations. Smiling, Alasdair reached down, pulling Caitrin to her feet so that she stood next to him. Then, he placed an arm around her shoulders, drawing her close.

Caitrin's vision misted. She'd never expected such a response. Meeting Alasdair's eye she grinned. "Ye are well-liked here," she said, raising her voice so he could hear her over the din.

His smile widened. "Aye … and so are ye."

The cheering settled and the feasting began. Caitrin and Alasdair took their seats once more. Helping herself to some stew, Caitrin felt warmth seep through her. The atmosphere in the hall was more joyous than Yuletide. A simple meal sat before them, but it didn't matter. It was moments like these that made life worth living.

The stew was delicious and the bread fresh and nutty. Wine flowed, and laughter echoed high into the rafters.

Eventually, her belly full, Caitrin leaned back in her chair. She wrapped her fingers around the goblet of wine she held. Like Alasdair, she'd changed into dry clothes upon arriving home, but there had been no time to relax in their quarters together. They'd both come straight back downstairs as there had been much to organize before supper.

"I feel as if the damp has drilled into my bones," Caitrin said with a sigh.

"Aye," Alasdair replied, massaging a stiff muscle in his shoulder. "I'm looking forward to a hot bath later."

Caitrin shot him a smile. "I'll ask Sorcha to have one brought up to yer bed-chamber."

"*Our* bed-chamber," he corrected Caitrin, before leaning in and kissing her. "I was hoping ye would join me."

Chapter Thirty-one

All We Need Is Time

THE SIGHT OF the huge iron bathtub, filled with steaming water, made Caitrin release a sigh of pleasure. She sniffed then, catching the scent of rose and lavender. Sorcha had added oils to the water.

The tub sat in the midst of Alasdair's bed-chamber—or what was now their marital bed-chamber. It was the same one she'd shared with Baltair, and Caitrin had been worried that setting foot inside the chamber again would raise unpleasant memories. Yet, this eve, it didn't.

Finally, it seemed as if Baltair's ghost had stopped haunting her steps. For the first time since his death, Caitrin's body didn't tense when she thought of him.

It was cozy and warm inside the chamber. The shutters to the single window had been closed tightly, and a fire burned in the hearth. A few feet from where Caitrin stood, she watched her husband disrobe.

Alasdair undressed with the unconscious self-confidence that only men seemed to possess. Most women were prone to cower, to try and cover their breasts with their hands, but a man merely tossed his clothing aside and stood there in his naked glory, without a care.

Caitrin was glad of it, for her gaze feasted upon Alasdair, taking in the long, hard planes of his body and the way the firelight danced across his skin.

Throwing aside his braies, Alasdair turned to her. "Are ye going to join me in the tub?"

Caitrin's mouth quirked. "Are ye sure there's room in there for the both of us?"

A slow smile spread across his face. "Aye."

Without shifting her gaze from his, Caitrin started to unlace the front of her kirtle. It had been a long, tiring day. They'd just retired to their bedchamber. Once supper had ended, Caitrin had tucked Eoghan into bed, and Alasdair had made sure all the villagers whose homes had been flooded had bedded down in the Great Hall. However, as Caitrin undressed, the day's fatigue lifted from her.

She'd been looking forward to this moment, to finally being alone with Alasdair.

The rest of the evening belonged to them.

Alasdair stepped into the iron tub and lowered himself into the hot, fragrant water. "I'll smell like a lass after this," he complained, wrinkling his nose.

Caitrin laughed. "Apologies ... Sorcha is used to preparing a bath for me. I'll tell her to be less generous with her scented oils in future."

Naked, her slender limbs and gentle curves glowing in the gilded light of the hearth and the candles that burned around them, Caitrin walked toward the bathtub. Alasdair watched her, transfixed, his mind suddenly going blank.

Every time he saw Caitrin naked he felt like a gauche youth, a simpleton who didn't know what to do with such a sight except gape.

"God's bones," he breathed finally. "Ye are so beautiful it hurts to look upon ye."

Caitrin's mouth curved. She then stepped into the bath and sank down into the water opposite him.

They stared at each other for a long moment, a veil of steam encircling them. Alasdair shifted so that his legs encircled Caitrin, and she was able to stretch out her legs before her. "See," he said with a grin. "I told ye we'd both fit."

Caitrin arched an eyebrow before reaching for a soft cloth and cake of lye and holding them out to him. "Come on then, let's bathe before the water cools."

Alasdair inclined his head, smiling. "I'd like ye to wash me."

She huffed a laugh. "I'm sure ye don't need my assistance."

He gave her a sultry look. "What I need and what I want aren't the same thing, my love ... will ye?"

She appeared almost shy then, dipping her head so that her hair fell in loose pale waves around her face. Of course, despite that she'd been wedded before, Caitrin was new to love play. He sensed her sudden nervousness. Even so, she obliged, moving onto her knees so that she could reach him properly.

Dipping the cloth into the water, she soaped it before beginning to wash his shoulders and chest.

The feel of her touch sliding across his skin made Alasdair let out a long sigh. He leaned back, resting the back of his head against the rim of the tub, and gave himself up to the sensation.

Caitrin seemed to be taking her task seriously. She lifted up his arms, washing under them, before soaping his arms and hands. Then she returned to his chest and began a leisurely path down to his stomach. Then she stopped.

Alasdair's eyes flickered open to see that she was staring down at his groin. His gaze shifted to where his shaft strained up out of the soapy water.

Caitrin glanced up at him. "Can I?"

"Ye don't even have to ask," he replied, his breathing quickening. "I'm all yers."

Caitrin smiled, her gaze dropping once more to his arousal. Then she wet the cloth, soaped it once more, and began to slide it up and down his shaft.

Alasdair groaned. His head fell back as he gave himself up to the sensation. Then, moments later, the cloth disappeared, and he felt her fingers encircle him. He reopened his eyes to see her attention fixed wholly upon his rod, her lips parted as she pleasured him.

Lust slammed into Alasdair like a charging bull. The blend of innocence and desire in this woman undid him.

With a growl, he pulled her up so that she was above him, her legs spread over his erection. Then, guiding her hips, he lowered Caitrin onto him. He inched into her, watching her face as he did so. He loved how a flush appeared on her cheeks, how her eyes widened, the deeper he penetrated.

When he pulled her down so that he was fully seated within her, she gave a soft cry, her chest now rising and falling sharply.

Alasdair drew in a slow, deep breath, shifting his attention down to her breasts. They were delicious: small and pert but with large pink nipples that were as firm and sweet as ripe strawberries. He angled his hips so she leaned toward him, allowing him to feast on her breasts. He drew a nipple deep into his mouth and sucked till she moaned. Suckling her, he reached down and gripped her hips, gyrating them so that they began to gently move together.

Caitrin gasped, her lithe body trembling in his grip.

Alasdair groaned against the breast he suckled. He loved how quickly she responded to him, how little it took for him to bring her to the edge.

It excited him beyond measure.

They were so aware of each other that even a heated glance across a crowded room was enough to arouse him. The feel of being buried deep inside her was enough to bring him to the brink of madness.

Tearing his mouth from her swollen nipple, he gazed up at Caitrin. She was lost in a haze of pleasure, neck arched back, eyes closed, and an expression of rapture upon her face.

"Caitrin," he rasped. "My love."

She opened her eyes and gazed down at him. "Alasdair," she whispered, her breath hitching. "Mo chridhe."

My heart.

Alasdair sucked in a breath. This was the first time she'd uttered such an endearment to him, the first time she'd openly acknowledged that she felt as he did.

He reached up, pulling her down for a kiss. Their mouths collided, hungry and devouring. Alasdair gripped her hips, lifting her. He then slid her up and down the length of his shaft with relentless determination. He wanted to take her over the brink, to see her shatter.

Caitrin cried out into his mouth, her body shuddering now. But still she rode him, the bathwater splashing over the sides of the tub onto the floor. Neither of them paid it any mind, and when Caitrin finally sobbed his name, Alasdair's cries joined hers.

Caitrin stretched out on the bed, smiling. She felt as if she was floating, untethered from the earth.

"What are ye looking so pleased about?"

Her eyes flickered open to see that Alasdair had propped himself up on an elbow and was staring down at her.

Caitrin's smile widened. "If I say, ye will be insufferable."

His mouth twitched. "How so?"

She reached out, her fingertips tracing the whorls of dark hair on his chest. "Ye are a wonderful lover."

He did smile then, as she'd known he would, delight twinkling in his eyes. "Why, thank ye, milady."

"I mean it."

He captured her hand in his and brought it to his lips, kissing her fingers gently. "I know ye do. Although I don't think I can take all the credit ... ye play yer part."

Silence stretched between them. Caitrin stared up at him, her smile fading. "Do I? Sometimes I worry that ye must think me cold ... emotionally that is ..."

He inclined his head. "Why would I think that?"

"Because I hold back my feelings ... I know I do." She swallowed. "I don't think I've ever trusted a man ... any man."

His gaze widened. "Even yer father?"

Caitrin huffed. "Especially him. He's behaved better of late, but any woman who puts her faith in Malcolm MacLeod's loyalty is a fool. Ye know what he did to my sisters."

Alasdair nodded. Releasing her hand, he reached out and stroked her cheek with the back of his hand. "I want ye to trust me," he said softly, "and I will work to earn it. Even if it takes me the rest of my life."

Chapter Thirty-two

Duntulm Fair

One month later ...

CAITRIN WALKED AMONGST the crowds in Duntulm village. A sense of contentment settled over her like a warm cloak. Of all the festivals that marked the year, this one was her favorite: Duntulm Fair. Her home of Dunvegan held a similar festival a little later in the summer, yet she preferred this one.

Folk from miles around came for the festival, swelling Duntulm's population to nearly five times its usual size. The screech of a highland pipe echoed through the streets, although the sound was almost drowned out by the excited chatter of conversation.

Caitrin walked slowly, aware that she had a footpad. Instead of Darron shadowing her—for Alasdair had relieved him of that duty as soon as they'd returned to Duntulm—a leggy wolfhound loped along at her heels. Dùnglas had become a constant presence in their lives of late. Eoghan loved him, and the hound now lived indoors, sleeping in a basket in the chieftain's solar at night, and following his master and mistress around during the day as they went about their duties.

Caitrin had thought the dog might get underfoot and annoy her, but it hadn't. She enjoyed going out for walks with Dùnglas at her side. The hound was also a constant reminder of Adaira.

Surveying her surroundings, Caitrin noted how tidy and prosperous the village looked. Greenery, boughs of pine and hawthorn, decorated the humble cottages, and the streets were filled with stalls boasting the best of the summer produce. She was pleased to see that there remained no sign of the devastating flood of a month earlier. The Cleatburn had now returned to its usual flow, and Alasdair and his men had built a make-shift wooden bridge over it, while they started work on a new stone bridge. One that would hopefully withstand the test of time.

Eoghan perched in a sling on Caitrin's back, chubby arms waving at passersby. It was a joy to wander here, enjoying the kiss of the sun on her face. The weather leading up to the fair had been grey and wet, but this morning the day had dawned bright.

Caitrin stopped to buy herself a square of rich cake dripping in butter and honey. She had to eat it quickly, lest the honey dripped over her clothing. Dùnglas sat gazing up at her wistfully as she finished the cake and licked honey off her fingers.

"Don't look at me like that," she admonished the dog. "There will be plenty of scraps for ye later."

Caitrin moved on down the crowded street. She walked by men having arm-wrestling contests. An excited crowd swirled around them, shouting encouragement. Not far from the waterfront, a pretty lass with a crown of daisies in her hair danced with other maids before a clapping crowd. Caitrin stopped to watch the dancing, as did many young men. Most of the lads were gawking at the lass with the crown of flowers—this year's Summer Queen.

Amongst the crowd, Caitrin spotted many of those who worked within Dunvegan keep. Galiene had even managed to drag cook out from her lair. Briana watched the dancing with a grin on her face, her hands full of sticky cake. Sorcha was there too. Caitrin's hand-maid had joined the dancers. She laughed with the other lasses as she spun and dipped, her hair flying behind her.

Spotting Caitrin, Sorcha broke away from the dancers and joined her. She linked her arm through Caitrin's, and they moved on, toward the shore. "Will ye watch the men race, milady?" she asked.

"Of course," Caitrin replied with a smile.

She hadn't always felt this way. Baltair used to take part in the race, and she'd made a point of staying away, browsing the stalls while he competed. It was tradition that the MacDonald chieftain took part.

But this year was different. This year Alasdair was competing.

Caitrin caught the gleam in her handmaid's eye. "I imagine ye won't bother attending?" she asked, feigning innocence.

Sorcha favored Caitrin with a coy smile. "I wouldn't want to miss watching a dozen handsome men strip down to their braies, would I?"

Caitrin laughed. Her hand-maid could be almost prudish at times, but then surprise her with a bawdy comment like this.

The two women made their way down to the shore, Dùnglas padding along behind them. Garlands and bright buntings of meadow flowers and heather decorated the streets, leading down to the wooden jetty where small boats bobbed in the tide.

Caitrin stopped, her gaze shifting out across the sparkling water. "How far will they swim?"

Sorcha pointed to where a small blue boat bobbed with the incoming tide. "Out to that dinghy and back."

They stopped talking then, realizing that the race was about to start: a row of men were undressing ready for it.

Caitrin's attention immediately strayed to Alasdair. He had his back to her as he pulled his léine over his head, revealing his long, finely muscled back, narrow waist, and broad shoulders. He turned then, tossing his léine aside, and her attention traveled to the dark hair covering his chest, tapering down to his belly.

Despite that she'd seen him naked countless times now, the sight made heat pool in Caitrin's lower belly.

Shifting her focus to Sorcha, Caitrin saw her hand-maid was watching Darron MacNichol. The warrior had also stripped down for the race as he chatted to Alasdair. Farther down the line, Boyd MacDonald readied himself to race. Tall and lean, his blond hair tied back, Boyd glanced over his shoulder. His gaze rested upon Sorcha until he caught her eye, forcing her to shift her attention from Darron. Then he winked.

The men moved down to the waterline, their bare feet slipping on the loose shingle, and then in a flurry, they dove into the water.

Caitrin stifled a gasp. Despite that it was summer, the water would still be freezing.

The swimmers struck out toward the boat. It was hard to tell who was in front. The water foamed around them. However, as they circled the boat, the swimmers drew apart.

Sorcha gripped Caitrin's arm. "Look, the chieftain and Boyd MacDonald are in the lead."

Caitrin raised her hand to shield her eyes from the sun, squinting. "Aye … it'll be a close race too."

Cheering echoed out across the water. Most of them were calling Alasdair's name.

As if hearing them, Alasdair inched forward. He swam in long confident strokes, moving ahead of Boyd.

Caitrin clapped her hands, her voice joining the rest of the watching crowd. Likewise, Eoghan started to squeal with excitement, his chubby arms and legs waving in the sling. Dùnglas started to bark then, adding to the chaos.

Caitrin clasped her hands together as the swimmers drew close. She was sure Alasdair would win, but then, just yards from shore, Boyd put on a spurt of speed and reached the beach just before him.

Cries of disappointment echoed over the shore, Caitrin's among them.

Boyd staggered up onto the beach, wiping water from his eyes. Oblivious to the fact that everyone had been cheering on the chieftain, he wore a wide, victorious smile.

Alasdair followed him out of the sea. Spying Caitrin among the spectators, he made his way toward her. "I'm slowing down," he gasped as he reached the women. "Time was, no one could beat me."

Boyd stepped up beside him. "That's only because ye had never raced me." He then grinned at Sorcha. "I'm half-selkie, didn't ye know?"

Caitrin frowned. She wondered, if that was the case, why Boyd hadn't dived in to help that woman on the day they'd arrived home from Dunvegan. If her memory served her correctly, Boyd had remained on the shore holding the end of a rope while Alasdair risked his life.

Alasdair snorted before waving to the men who were pouring out cups of ale from barrels on the jetty. "Get Boyd a drink, he's earned it." He then turned his attention back to his wife. "I'm glad ye came to watch the race," he said, before giving a sheepish smile. "Even if I didn't win."

"I don't care about that." Caitrin stepped close, pushing Dùnglas out of the way. The hound had a habit of wrapping himself around Alasdair's legs whenever it got the chance. She stretched up and kissed his wet lips. "Ye were still magnificent."

Sorcha took a bite of pie, savoring the rich flavor of venison. It was a treat she only got to enjoy a few times a year. This midsummer's fair was the best she could remember. The good weather had brought in huge crowds.

The pie was hot, and Sorcha ate it gingerly, careful not to spill the filling down the front of her kirtle. Pale blue, the color of a summer's sky, it was the prettiest one she owned; she didn't want to ruin it. She stood in the shade between two cottages at the edge of the festivities. As she ate, Sorcha's gaze skirted the crowd.

The chieftain and his lady were enjoying the fair together. Lady Caitrin still carried Eoghan on her back, although the lad had now fallen asleep. She and Alasdair watched the dancing. Heads bent close, they laughed over something.

It warmed Sorcha's heart to see them so happy. One day, she too hoped to find such contentment.

Finishing her meal, Sorcha brushed pastry crumbs off her fingers. Her gaze shifted away from the chieftain and his wife, continuing through the crowd. She realized then that she was looking for Darron. Ever since his return from Dunvegan, they'd been spending more time together. He often sought her out when she'd finished her chores, and over the last week, they'd shared an ale in the Great Hall before retiring for the night.

Sorcha had found herself starting to think about him—a lot.

Instead of spying Darron in the crowd though, her gaze alighted upon Boyd. He was approaching her.

When he'd first arrived in Duntulm, Boyd MacDonald had drawn her eye, with his arrogant swagger and boyish smile. But these days Sorcha wasn't so sure of him. His manner, once charming, had developed an aggressive edge to it. Discomfort settled over her when he stopped before her.

"I was wondering where ye had got to," he greeted her.

"Why?" she asked innocently. "Were ye looking for me?"

He grinned. "Aye ... thought ye might like to congratulate me properly for my win."

"I already have."

He laughed. "I'd like more than a few words, lass. How about that kiss ye keep promising me?"

Sorcha stiffened. "I have promised ye no such thing."

Boyd moved closer, and Sorcha instinctively shifted back into the space between the two cottages. That was a mistake because it took her out of view of the crowd of folk filling the market square.

"Ye don't need to tell me," he said, lowering his voice intimately. "I can see ye want it."

"Nonsense." Sorcha kept her voice light although inside she felt a frisson of alarm. "Ye are quite mistaken, MacDonald."

"I don't think so."

Sorcha tried to edge around him. She'd had enough of such talk. He was making her uncomfortable, and she wished she hadn't let him take her out of view of the crowd. "I think I'll return to the dancing."

"I'll still have that kiss though." He grabbed her arm. His fingers bit into Sorcha's flesh, and he shoved her back against the white-washed wall. "Ye have been tempting me for months now."

His mouth came down on hers roughly, cutting off the scream that rose in Sorcha's throat. Without thinking, she brought her knee up, jabbing him in the cods.

Boyd ripped his mouth from hers and let out a hiss of pain.

She thought it would be enough to make him let go, but it just seemed to enrage him. His grip tightened, and he dragged her down the alley between the two dwellings.

Fear slammed into Sorcha, and she began to struggle. "Let go of me!"

His hand slammed over her mouth to stifle her protests. He threw her up against the wall, his free hand fumbling with her skirts. "Keep yer mouth shut," he growled, "and spread yer legs for me."

Sorcha didn't obey him. She couldn't shout for help, for his hand prevented her, but she started to struggle wildly, clawing at him. Boyd MacDonald wasn't a big man, but he was lean and wiry, and much stronger than her.

Terror pulsed in her breath as she felt his hand on her thighs, raking her skin. He was trying to wedge his thigh in between her legs. He was going to rape her, right there, just yards away from where folk were enjoying the fair. Sorcha wasn't strong enough to fight him off.

And then, as suddenly as he'd grabbed her, Boyd jerked away.

Sorcha sagged against the wall to see Darron drag Boyd backward by his hair. Then he spun him around and punched him hard in the face. Boyd staggered, blood pouring from his nose.

Cursing loudly, Boyd righted himself. "Keep out of this, MacNichol," he rasped, wiping away the blood with the back of his hand. "It's my turn now to have some fun with the wee whore."

Darron growled before his fist shot out once more. He hit Boyd in the eye, and the man went down like a lump of peat, where he lay groaning.

Captain MacNichol then crossed to Sorcha. His face was pale and taut as he stared down at her. "Did he hurt ye?"

Chapter Thirty-three

Willing

ALASDAIR SURVEYED BOYD under hooded lids.

"Do ye have anything to say in defense of yerself?"

Boyd stared back at him before folding his arms across his chest. Darron had made a mess of his face. His nose had been flattened, his nostrils were encrusted with blood, and his left eye was purpled and had already swollen shut.

Boyd's response, when it came, was spoken in a growl. "I thought the lass was willing."

"Willing?" Darron growled from behind them. "Ye were trying to rape her."

Alasdair's gaze remained focused upon Boyd. "Were ye?"

A chill silence settled over the market square. They stood in the midst of the wide space, a large crowd of village folk looking on. The merriment and dancing had ceased the moment Darron had dragged Boyd out by the hair into the center of the square.

Boyd's mouth thinned. "No."

The hiss of an enraged intake of breath interrupted them. Sorcha stood next to Caitrin. The handmaid's face was ashen although her eyes were ablaze. "He dragged me out of the square, threw me up against a wall, and tried to force himself on me," she said, her voice shaking with the force of her rage. "I was *not* willing."

Boyd shrugged. "And ye would trust the word of that MacQueen bastard over mine?"

Alasdair drew in a long, measured breath. Boyd was starting to sorely test his patience. He wasn't sure how much longer he'd be able to keep a leash on his temper. "And what of Darron. Are ye calling him a liar too?"

A nerve flickered in Boyd's cheek. "MacNichol has had his eye on the lass for months … he's just jealous I got in first."

"Dog," Darron snarled. "I'll blacken yer other eye." He stepped forward, hands clenched by his sides, but Alasdair halted him with a hand to the arm.

Turning back to Boyd, Alasdair fixed him with a hard stare. "I brought ye into my home and gave ye a place in my guard. Is this how ye repay me?"

Boyd's lip curled. "There's no need to be over-dramatic, cousin. Don't work yerself up over some goose-brained slut."

Alasdair went still, his fists clenching at his sides. The anger inside him coiled like a serpent readying itself to strike. "That's it, Boyd," he growled. "Ye are out of chances."

His cousin shrugged, his battered face creasing into an expression of scorn. "If ye say so, *milord*."

"I do. Ye are to leave Duntulm. Today."

Shock turned Boyd's face slack. "Ye are sending me away?"

Alasdair nodded. "I'll send word to yer kin in Glencoe. They shall know what ye have done, and that ye are on yer way home."

Boyd stared at him—and a moment later something ugly moved in his blue eyes.

Without warning, he lunged for Alasdair, his right fist swinging for his face.

Alasdair was ready for him, for he'd been waiting for Boyd to turn nasty when he realized the game was up. Alasdair grabbed Boyd's wrist, moving back with the blow. Then he brought his knee up sharply and drove it into his assailant's gut.

Boyd collapsed onto the ground, where he coughed and wheezed as he struggled to regain his breath.

Alasdair turned his attention to Darron. "Escort Boyd south, out of sight of the keep," he rasped, "and make sure he doesn't come back. He's a disgrace to the clan."

Darron's mouth thinned, his gaze glinting. "With pleasure." The captain and another warrior heaved Boyd to his feet and dragged him from the square.

Alasdair watched as they led him away, rage pulsing through him like a Beltane drum.

Caitrin didn't take her gaze from her husband's face.

Alasdair was staring after Boyd, his face hard, gaze burning. His skin had pulled tight over his cheekbones. Caitrin had never seen him look so angry.

Heart pounding, she released Eoghan from the death-grip she'd been holding him in. The lad was uncharacteristically subdued, as if picking up on the surrounding tension.

"Alasdair?"

Tearing his gaze from where Boyd had just disappeared, dragged away by the guards, Alasdair met her eye. Around them, the people of Duntulm started to talk amongst themselves in low, excited voices.

"Sorry ye had to see that," he murmured, his gaze softening.

Caitrin raised an eyebrow. "I've seen worse."

Alasdair's gaze widened before his mouth curved. "Of course ye have ... ye are MacLeod's daughter after all."

"Aye ... I've witnessed my father beat men half to death for crossing him."

Alasdair huffed. "And there was me holding myself back on yer account."

Caitrin held his gaze. "I'm glad ye did. Ye have seen enough blood and violence, Alasdair." She paused then, her mouth curving. "Don't worry ... Darron's likely to give him a parting gift before he sends him south."

Her husband smiled then, the expression chasing away the lingering anger in his eyes. "Aye."

Caitrin turned her gaze then to the young woman who stood silently beside her. Sorcha's usually sunny face was pale, her eyes bloodshot and swollen from crying. She stared down at her clasped hands, her expression haunted.

"I did nothing to encourage him," she whispered. "I promise, milady."

Caitrin's chest constricted at the pain in the girl's voice. Reaching out, she pulled Sorcha into a hug, difficult since Eoghan now wriggled in her arms. "I know ye didn't," she murmured. "He didn't need an excuse. Don't blame yerself."

"But I shouldn't have let him corner me."

"Ye weren't to know he'd behave so. Don't worry ... ye are safe now."

Alasdair stepped close to the hand-maid, his brow furrowing with concern. "Do ye need to see a healer, lass?"

Sorcha shook her head. She drew back from Caitrin, extracting Eoghan's fingers from her hair. The lad had grabbed a handful of the handmaid's dark tresses. Meeting Alasdair's eye, she offered him a wan smile. "I'm well, milord," she replied. "Just shaken."

Caitrin had worried that the incident with Boyd would cast a shadow over the day. Yet not long after Boyd was dragged away, the fair continued as if nothing had happened. Laughter and singing drifted across the market square once more.

However, there were a few folk who were subdued in the aftermath.

Sorcha returned to the keep early, while Alasdair and Caitrin left the crowds, making their way east of the village to where the stone bridge over the Cleatburn was taking shape.

Alasdair carried Eoghan now, for Caitrin's arms and back had started to ache. Pride shone in Alasdair's eyes, and the lad was delighted to have his uncle carry him. He squealed and burbled gibberish, pointing at things as they walked. Dùnglas padded after them, although the dog was distracted by clumps of heather and rocks he felt compelled to lift his leg at.

Caitrin stopped on the western bank of the Cleatburn and surveyed the bridge. The half-built structure was twice the size of the old bridge. It was made of basalt blocks of stone and thus much sturdier than its predecessor, spanning the water in a graceful curve.

"Alasdair ... did ye design this yerself?" she asked.

"There's a beautiful bridge in Inbhir Nis," he replied. "It's much bigger than this one, but I studied it while I was there."

Caitrin tore her gaze from the structure and glanced over at him, smiling. "Just as well ye did. It's remarkable."

Alasdair smiled back. "Like that bridge, we built this one with a pointed arch. It makes it less likely to sag at the crown ... it'll also put less strain on the supports."

Caitrin nodded. She was impressed by his knowledge. "When will it be finished?"

"In a month, I'd guess ... if the fine weather holds, we'll be able to work faster." Alasdair grimaced then, grabbing Eoghan's hand as the lad grabbed hold of his hair and yanked.

Watching them, Caitrin smiled once more. She liked seeing Alasdair and Eoghan together. The family resemblance was there, although Alasdair's features were more hawkish than his nephew's.

I wonder when we shall have our first bairn.

The thought made warmth spread across her chest. She looked forward to giving him children: sons or daughters, she didn't mind which.

She thought then of her sisters. Rhona's belly would have become noticeable by now. When would Adaira and Lachlann start a family?

A tiny kernel of sadness lodged in Caitrin's breast then, as she thought about her sisters. She loved her life here at Duntulm, her marriage, and her son. Yet Rhona and Adaira were a part of her. She suddenly missed them with a force that made her chest ache.

"What is it, love?" Alasdair's voice brought Caitrin out of her reverie. She glanced up to see he was watching her. "Ye look leagues away."

She smiled. "I was just thinking about my sisters ... I miss them."

Alasdair's mouth curved. "Well then ... we should organize another visit to Dunvegan ... and perhaps a trip to Argyle."

"Really?"

"I'll see what I can do. We should cross to the mainland before the cold weather sets in."

A smile spread across Caitrin's face. The past month since their wedding had been an exciting, wondrous time. It was as if she'd been reborn; all the hurts of the past slowly faded into the mist. She woke up every morning, curled up in her husband's arms and wondering how it was possible to feel so happy.

She'd told Alasdair that she found it difficult to trust, but as the days passed, she found herself opening up to him more and more. With him she didn't need to be wary, to keep an eye out for dark moods or a vicious temper.

Alasdair still suffered nightmares—even if they had started to become less frequent and intense. The tremors in his hands had ceased of late, but sometimes she still caught him staring off into the distance—caught up in unpleasant memories. The wounds he'd brought home with him from war were gradually starting to heal.

Caitrin's vision misted. Alasdair wasn't like the other men she'd known. As much as she loved her father, Malcolm MacLeod was not a man who treated any woman, even his wife, as an equal. He had no use for conversation with them, preferring the company of his men and a horn of mead. Baltair had been much harsher than her father though. MacLeod at least suffered the opinions of his daughters, even with bad grace at times. Baltair had forbidden her from expressing her views entirely. She'd learned that lesson quickly upon coming to live at Duntulm.

But with Alasdair, there were no rules she had to follow, no subjects she had to avoid. She could be herself completely, and he loved her for it.

The friendship they'd once shared as bairns, the ease in each other's company, had been reforged—and with it a deeper bond. Something that had taken root inside Caitrin's breast and grew stronger with each passing day.

Caitrin stepped close to her husband. Then, going up on tip-toe, she leaned in and kissed him. "I love ye, Alasdair MacDonald," she murmured. "Sometimes the force of it overwhelms me."

He stared down at her, his dark eyes gleaming. "Ye don't know how I've longed to hear those words," he murmured, his voice catching. "I was beginning to think I never would."

Caitrin cupped his face with one hand while taking hold of one of Eoghan's grappling fingers with the other. "I've known for a while now ... I've just been waiting for the right time to say it." Her mouth curved then. "Ironic really ... for I once thought I loathed ye."

He huffed. "Gavin MacNichol told me that love and hate are close cousins."

"They are." Caitrin then inclined her head. "What passed between the two of ye?"

"What do ye mean?"

"I saw the look he gave ye that morning in Da's solar. He said something to ye."

Alasdair favored her with an enigmatic smile. "Nothing of importance."

Caitrin drew back. "Very well ... keep yer secrets then."

His smile widened. "There aren't any. We just had words that's all." His expression turned rueful then. "I was jealous of MacNichol, ye know? I thought ye would choose him."

"I would have," she admitted. "If ye hadn't made yer feelings known."

Their gazes fused. "It took everything I had to go down on one knee before ye again," he murmured. "I'm not sure what I'd have done if ye had sent me away."

"Ye were brave to say what ye did," Caitrin replied softly. "I'm so glad ye took the risk."

He smiled. "Ye have a tender heart, wife."

Caitrin stared up into his eyes, her fingers stroking the line of his jaw. "Aye, and it belongs to ye."

JAYNE CASTEL

Chapter Thirty-four

A Man of My Word

CAITRIN TOOK A seat at the table, next to her husband.

The noon sun warmed her face, and a sea breeze tickled her scalp. Three weeks had passed since Duntulm Fair, and the Cleatburn Bridge was now complete. To celebrate, Alasdair MacDonald had put on a feast. All the folk of Duntulm—from the high to the low—had been invited.

Alasdair rose to his feet, raising the tankard he held into the air. Caitrin glanced over at him, admiring his strong profile, lean features, and flowing raven hair. Alasdair looked every inch a chieftain today, especially since he wore the MacDonald sash over his léine.

They sat at the center of a long table that had been erected in the center of Duntulm village's market square. Locals, both from the village and the keep, packed its length on both sides.

Once Alasdair stood up, the chatter of excited conversation died down, and all eyes settled upon their chieftain. Caitrin saw the respect in the men's eyes and the appreciation on the women's faces. Alasdair had won their hearts, as he had hers.

"People of Duntulm." Alasdair's deep voice traveled across the square. "Thank ye all for joining us here. Today we celebrate our new bridge, but also much more. I want to thank ye all for the support ye have given me and my kin over the years. We've had difficult times—famines, wars, and sickness—but ye have stayed here, farmed this land, fished these seas, and kept our people strong. I will not forget it. By sea and land, the MacDonalds stick together."

"By sea and land!" A roar went up. Men and women raised their tankards.

When Alasdair sat back down, Caitrin flashed him a smile. "Well spoken."

An excited chatter rose around them as the feasting began.

His mouth curved. "We MacDonalds have a way with words."

Caitrin snorted. "And a self-confidence that knows no bounds."

He laughed. "Admit it ... it's just one of the many things ye love about me."

"Conceited cockerel," she muttered, smiling. Of course, he knew she did.

"Ye look radiant today," Alasdair said as he handed her a goblet of sloe wine. "I don't think I've seen the smile leave yer face since dawn."

Caitrin laughed and took a sip of wine. "On a day like this, I have much to be happy about."

"And what's that?" he asked, a teasing edge to his voice.

"A sunny sky, fine food and wine, and a handsome man by my side," she replied. "What more could a lass ask for?"

Alasdair grinned. "The lady is easy to please it seems."

Caitrin didn't reply, instead merely favoring him with an enigmatic smile. She wondered then if she should ask him about the trip he'd promised they'd take to Argyle. He hadn't said anything since the day of the fair, and as summer crept on, she wondered if he'd forgotten.

Her gaze shifted down the table then, taking in the faces of the servants, retainers, farmers, and artisans who made up their community. A sense of belonging settled over her. She wasn't born here, on Skye's isolated northern tip, and yet this place was her home much more than Dunvegan ever had been.

Under the table, something nudged her knee. Caitrin glanced down to see that Dùnglas sat at her feet. She glimpsed his dark eyes and whiskery muzzle and smiled. The dog was hoping someone would drop a tasty morsel down to him. With a sigh, Caitrin picked up a piece of pork from the platter before her and dropped it under the table.

"Ye will encourage the hound to beg," Alasdair warned.

Caitrin glanced up guiltily. "I can't stand it," she replied with a contrite smile. "When he looks at me with those soulful eyes, I can deny him nothing."

Alasdair huffed. "I shall have to try that with ye in future ... and see how far it gets me."

Caitrin shook her head in mock chagrin before her gaze returned to farther down the table, where Darron MacNichol and Sorcha MacQueen sat together. The pair were deep in conversation, oblivious to the feasting and drinking going on around them. It was a heart-warming sight. For days after Boyd's attack, Sorcha had been out of sorts: pale and tense. But from the looks of things, she'd now put the ordeal behind her.

Caitrin nudged Alasdair with her elbow. "It looks like we might have a handfasting in Duntulm before long."

His gaze followed Caitrin's down the table before he glanced back at her. "Are ye match-making, wife?"

"No," Caitrin said innocently, spearing a piece of pork with a knife. "Just making an observation. Look at them, Alasdair ... and tell me they won't be wed by the spring."

The cèilidh started mid-afternoon. Once the long tables and scraps of food had been cleared away, a man pulled out a fiddle and began to play, while his wife sang a bawdy song about a farmer's wife, her foolish husband, and her two lovers. The song had folk laughing and clapping along by the second verse.

Caitrin watched Darron and Sorcha run into the midst of the dancers. Their faces were flushed from wine and the sun. Darron twirled Sorcha around, while she laughed.

Caitrin observed them wistfully, tapping her foot to the music.

"We never finished that dance," Alasdair's voice intruded. "Ye slapped my face and sent me on my way instead."

Caitrin turned to him, her mouth curving. "What a shrew ye have wed."

He smiled, holding out his hand to her. "May I have *this* dance, milady?"

Caitrin inclined her head. "Of course, milord."

He led her out into the dancing, and a moment later they were caught up in it, whirling, stepping, and turning in time to the music. Caitrin danced until her feet ached and she felt light-headed. After that, she returned to the table and took a restorative sip of wine.

Galiene arrived then with Eoghan. Caitrin took the lad from the woman and bid her go and find some food and drink, and enjoy herself. Eoghan looked around, his chubby face eager, his blue eyes bright with curiosity. Caitrin gave him a chunk of bread, and he began to chew at it. Eoghan then looked up at Alasdair before grinning.

"Dair."

Alasdair smiled at the lad's attempt at his name. He couldn't yet manage long words, but he'd become quite talkative of late. "Dair!"

Caitrin's throat constricted when Alasdair reached out and ruffled Eoghan's thick black hair. There was genuine affection in his peat-brown eyes when he looked upon his nephew. "Ye are a good-natured lad, aren't ye?"

Eoghan dropped the chunk of bread he'd been mauling and held out his hands to Alasdair. "Dair!"

Alasdair laughed and took him from Caitrin. The lad clutched at Alasdair's léine and sash, squealing with delight when his uncle rose to his feet and bounced him in his arms. Alasdair then glanced down at Caitrin with a grin. "I think someone else wants a dance. We'll be back soon."

Caitrin watched Alasdair and Eoghan make their way into the dancing, her gaze misting with love as she watched them.

Alasdair was a good father to the lad. She hadn't expected him to treat Eoghan like a son, yet he had. Eoghan would grow up loved at Duntulm.

The celebrations stretched out and would continue long into the night. However, Alasdair, Caitrin, and Eoghan left when the bairn started to get tired. Leaving the laughter and music ringing out across the hillside behind them, they climbed the hill back to the castle. Eoghan was asleep, slumped against Alasdair's chest. Dùnglas trotted along, trailing the couple like a shadow.

A cool wind skirted across the hill and mist had crept in from the sea. Although this day had been a fine one, Caitrin imagined that they'd awaken to a foggy morning the following day. That was how it was upon Skye. No two days of weather were alike.

They'd nearly reached the brow of the hill, and the drawbridge that spanned the deep ditch encircling Duntulm's curtain wall, when the bellow of a hunting horn reached them.

Caitrin stifled a gasp. She knew that horn. It was one she'd grown up with, had heard every time her father took his men and dogs out on a hunt.

Turning south, her gaze alighted upon a company of riders approaching over the brow of the nearest hill. Pennants of gold, grey, and black, threaded with red, fluttered in the breeze.

Caitrin's heart soared at the sight.

She swiveled on her heel, her gaze meeting Alasdair's, and saw that he wore a knowing smile.

"Ye invited Da?"

"Aye, as well as Rhona and Taran MacKinnon. They were supposed to arrive yesterday, in time for the feast, but it looks like they were delayed. It matters not, for the boat doesn't leave for two days."

Caitrin stilled. "The boat?"

Alasdair stepped close, reaching up with his free hand to cup her cheek. "Ye didn't think I'd forgotten, did ye? We're taking a trip to Argyle to see yer sister, and I've invited Rhona and Taran to join us."

Caitrin stared at him a moment before joy exploded in her breast. She threw herself into his arms, accidentally waking Eoghan who gave a low whimper and snuggled back into Alasdair's chest.

Kissing Alasdair hard on the lips, Caitrin beamed up at him. "Ye remembered!"

He smiled down at her, his gaze filled with tenderness. "Aye ... and I'm a man of my word."

Epilogue
I Made Ye a Promise

CAITRIN'S FIRST GLIMPSE of Gylen Castle was of a stone tower etched against a grey sky, surrounded by an emerald blanket of green.

Clutching at Rhona's sleeve, Caitrin pointed east. "Look … there it is!"

The sisters stood at the bow of the large boat that sailed across the choppy waters of the Firth of Lorne. A brisk breeze had whipped up the surface of the water, making the boat roll. Rhona and Caitrin clung together for stability, clutching the railing.

The castle perched upon a rocky outcrop, commanding a view for miles around. Although it formed part of Argyle, Gylen didn't actually sit upon the mainland. It sat instead upon the rocky Isle of Kerrera, just off the coast.

Caitrin's mother's people resided here—Clan MacDougall. Adaira had assured Caitrin in her letters that their uncle had given her and Lachlann a warm welcome, and that they enjoyed their life at Gylen. But even so, Caitrin felt nerves flutter in the pit of her belly.

She hoped that Adaira and Lachlann truly were happy here and that no unpleasant surprises awaited them.

"It's impressive," Rhona said, pushing her unruly auburn hair out of her eyes. "I'd thought Adaira must be exaggerating."

Caitrin smiled. She'd imagined the same, for their sister could be prone to over-enthusiasm. The tower that rose from the grey-stone keep had graceful lines. It was very different to the more bulky and squat silhouettes of Dunvegan and Duntulm.

"Adaira has no idea we're coming." Caitrin's gaze dropped to the approaching rocky shore. A long wooden jetty jutted out to meet them. "I can't wait to see her face."

"Hopefully, she's at home," Rhona replied. One hand rested on her belly as she spoke; it had started to swell now under her kirtle, visible when the wind pushed her clothing against her form.

"I hadn't thought of that," Caitrin said with a frown. "But I'm sure our uncle will entertain us until she returns."

Rhona huffed. "I'll be glad to get off this boat. It's rolling makes me queasy."

Caitrin nodded, casting her sister a sympathetic smile. It had been a rough ride across from Skye. They'd had to weather two rain squalls and a constant wind that had quickened the journey but made it more uncomfortable.

Rhona held her gaze, her storm-grey eyes piercing. "I haven't had the chance to say much to ye, Caitrin. We never seemed to have a moment alone once we arrived at Duntulm, but I'm truly happy for ye. I look at yer face now, and I see my sister again."

Caitrin's mouth quirked. "I feel a different woman," she admitted. "But I haven't gone back to who I was before I wed Baltair. That girl is gone forever."

Rhona's eyes clouded. "I must admit that I had my doubts. I thought ye mad for wedding MacDonald. I'm happy to see I was wrong."

"So am I," Caitrin replied.

Rhona favored her with an arch look. "Taran did tell me all would be well between ye. He's been insufferably smug to be proved right."

"He's a wise man yer husband," Caitrin said with a teasing smile. "Taran says little but notices much."

"Ready to disembark?"

Caitrin glanced over her shoulder to find Alasdair standing behind them, a coil of oiled rope in hand. Dùnglas sat at his side, tail wagging. Since the hound had once belonged to Adaira, they'd decided to bring him with them to Gylen Castle. Behind Alasdair, Taran and two others were readying the boat to dock, trimming the sail and maneuvering it toward the jetty with long oars.

"Aye," Caitrin replied before grinning. "I don't think Rhona or I have a love for the water."

A short while later, Caitrin MacDonald stepped onto Argyle soil for the first time. Her legs wobbled under her as she made her way up the wooden jetty. They took a few moments to adjust to a solid surface, and she was glad of her husband's steadying arm.

Alasdair carried Eoghan strapped to his back. The lad was restless, hands waving as he wriggled against the restraints. Now that he could stand, pulling himself up on any solid object he could find, Eoghan no longer liked being carried.

Dùnglas ran ahead, eager as them to be on land again.

The small party made their way up the path from the jetty, carrying leather bags and satchels with them. The road up to the castle wound over rocky headland, although beyond Caitrin spied grassy hills dotted with cottars' huts and grazing sheep. It was a peaceful spot, if a little windswept.

They'd almost reached the gates, which were open this afternoon, the jagged teeth of the iron portcullis raised, when a small figure appeared. She was a comely young woman with long walnut-colored hair, dressed in flowing green. Picking up her skirts, she broke into a sprint, her slippered feet flying over the stony path.

Caitrin's breath caught. *Adaira.*

Her youngest sister collided with Rhona first and threw her arms around her. Adaira's face was wet, her hazel eyes gleaming, as she pulled back. "I can't believe it! Ye came!"

Rhona laughed, knuckling away a tear of her own. "Of course we did. I made ye a promise, didn't I?"

A lean grey wolfhound bounded up to Adaira then, nearly knocking her off her feet.

"God's bones," Adaira gasped, averting her face from its eager tongue. "Who's this?"

"Don't ye recognize wee Dùnglas?" Rhona asked, laughing. "He's a bit bigger than when ye saw him last."

"Dùnglas?" Adaira pushed the hound off her before reaching down to pat him. The dog's tail whacked against her skirts as he pressed against her. "Ye have grown into a beast!"

"He lives at Duntulm now," Caitrin said, "but I thought ye would like to see him again."

"Aye." Adaira's gaze shone as she shifted her attention to Caitrin.

Stepping around Dùnglas, she crushed her sister in a tight hug. For a small woman, Adaira's grip was fearsomely strong. Drawing back from the embrace, Adaira's gaze searched Caitrin's face, curiosity lighting in her eyes. Although Caitrin had sent no word of her marriage—or had yet said anything about her change in circumstance—Adaira knew. Caitrin saw it in her expression.

Adaira's attention shifted to Caitrin's left, where Alasdair stood with a now grizzling Eoghan on his back. "Alasdair MacDonald?"

Caitrin glanced back to see Alasdair smile at Adaira. "Aye, greetings Lady Adaira. It has been a while."

Of course, the pair had met briefly when Alasdair had visited Dunvegan intent on wooing Caitrin. It seemed like a lifetime ago now.

"Alasdair is now chieftain of the MacDonalds of Duntulm," Caitrin said gently, turning her attention back to her sister.

Adaira dropped into a neat curtsy. "Milord."

"He and I are wed," Caitrin added.

Adaira's eyes grew huge. Her gaze flicked between them both. "Ye wed and didn't invite me?"

Caitrin favored her with an apologetic smile. "The circumstances of our marriage were ... unusual, Adi." She looped her arm through her sister's and steered her toward the gates. "Come ... my belly needs settling after that rough crossing, and if Eoghan doesn't get out of that sling soon, he'll turn Alasdair deaf."

Up ahead, another figure appeared: a tall man dressed in leather braies and a crisp linen léine. He walked with a loose-limbed, confident stride, a smile creasing his handsome face. Fiery auburn hair, of an even brighter shade than Rhona's, blew around his face.

Lachlann Fraser.

Caitrin cut a glance back to Adaira. "Ye are happy, Adi?"

Her sister nodded, her expression glowing when she too glanced up to see her husband approach. "Very," she replied softly.

They continued up the path toward where Lachlann had stopped and waited for them. Adaira now clung to Caitrin's arm as if she feared her sister would run off. "I want to hear the whole story about ye and Alasdair," she insisted in a low voice. "Ye are to leave nothing out."

Caitrin laughed and shared a grin with Rhona, who'd fallen into step next to her. Alasdair walked behind them with Taran as they approached the gates.

"I'd forgotten how bossy ye can be," Rhona chastised Adaira, still grinning.

Caitrin met Adaira's eye and smiled. "I'll definitely need to take a seat and have a good platter of food and drink before me. This tale is a long one."

The End

From the author

I hope you enjoyed the conclusion to THE BRIDES OF SKYE. This has been my first 'quick-release' series. I actually managed to release all three books a month apart in April, May, and June 2019! Whew!

Writing a revenge story is much more complex than I thought it would be! It's not a theme I embark on that often, but I'd been waiting for the opportunity to get my teeth into such a tale. Caitrin and Alasdair gave me the chance! Often seething resentment is built on misunderstandings, and so I gave our lovers plenty. A young man's ego is a fragile thing, having Caitrin laugh at him when he proposed would have been hard to take, and then when she marries his brother shortly after the damage is complete. Likewise, when Alasdair separates Caitrin from her son, he does something that's very hard to forgive.

THE ROGUE'S BRIDE is a highly character-driven story. I enjoyed exploring how far we'll let our past dictate our future, and delving into the nature of forgiveness. Caitrin and Alasdair were both unhappy at beginning of the story, and I really wanted to give them a HEA. Of course, you met Caitrin back in Book #1, when she was married to Baltair, so I hope her story was worth waiting for!

I had to do a bit of research into PTSD for this story. Such things hadn't been diagnosed back in medieval times, but PTSD existed all the same. As those of you who've read other novels by me will know, I like to write about flawed heroes. Alasdair had a lot to contend with, not just the bitterness of losing the woman he loves to his brother, but the trauma of war as well.

The Battle of Neville's Cross was a real battle. It took place on 17 October 1346, just half a mile from Durham, England. As explained in the novel, the battle was a crushing defeat for the Scottish. The invading Scottish army of 12,000 led by King David II was defeated with heavy losses by an English army of approximately 6,000–7,000 men led by Lord Ralph Neville. King David survived the battle and was taken prisoner by the English. For those Scots who did survive and manage to flee with their lives, the memories of that fight would have been harrowing.

The novel's main setting, Duntulm, is an actual castle set high upon a cliff on The Isle of Skye's windswept northern coast. It was the MacDonald stronghold for many years. These days it's nothing more than a ruin, but enough remains that I was able to get a clear picture of what the keep would have looked like.

Jayne x

About the Author

Award-winning author Jayne Castel writes epic Historical and Fantasy Romance. Her vibrant characters, richly researched historical settings, and action-packed adventure romance transport readers to forgotten times and imaginary worlds.

Jayne has published a number of bestselling series. In love with all things Scottish, Jayne also writes romances set in Dark Ages Scotland ... sexy Pict warriors anyone?

When she's not writing, Jayne is reading (and re-reading) her favorite authors, cooking Italian feasts, and going for long walks with her husband. She lives in New Zealand's beautiful South Island.

Connect with Jayne online:
www.jaynecastel.com
www.facebook.com/JayneCastelRomance/
https://www.instagram.com/jaynecastelauthor/
Email: **contact@jaynecastel.com**

THE BRIDES OF SKYE: THE COMPLETE SERIES

Printed in Great Britain
by Amazon